MIDNIGHT

MAO TUN

FOREIGN LANGUAGES PRESS
PEKING

First edition 1957
Second edition 1979

Jacket Design and Illustrations

by Yeh Chien-yu

Printed in the People's Republic of China

Publisher's Note

This translation has been made from the Chinese edition brought out in May 1955 by the People's Literature Publishing House, Peking. Our sincere thanks are due to Mr. A. C. Barnes who took much trouble in polishing the draft translation made by Hsu Meng-hsiung.

ABOUT "MIDNIGHT"*

In 1928, finding my freedom of movement restricted in Shanghai, I left quietly for Japan. After more than a year in Japan I returned to Shanghai in the spring of 1930. It was just about this time that the Kuomintang politician Wang Ching-wei and the various warlords who were opposing Chiang Kai-shek held their Enlarged Conference in Peking to challenge the Chiang Kai-shek régime in Nanking. At that time the civil war between the North and the South was in progress and the labour movement in Shanghai and other cities was at its peak.

During this period I was suffering from severe eye-trouble, and my doctor had ordered me a rest from reading for eight months or even a year. Apart from the eye-trouble I was suffering from neurasthenia, and so decided on a complete rest. Among my friends in Shanghai at that time were active revolutionaries and liberals, while old acquaintances from my home town included industrialists, civil servants, businessmen and bankers. Having little else to do then, I passed much of my time among them and learned from them much that had been unknown to me before and began to understand a little of what went on "behind the scenes." It struck me that all this new information might be put into a novel. When my eyes were better, and I could read once more, I went through some of the articles and essays which were being written then on the nature of Chinese society. When I compared my own observations with the theories put forward in these articles, I became even more attracted to the idea of writing my novel.

The active revolutionaries of Shanghai were at this time busily engaged in launching a full-scale revolutionary movement, and

---

* This is an excerpt from a talk given by the author in 1939 to a group of students at a school in Sinkiang.

fierce struggles were being waged on all fronts. I did not actively participate in all this work for the revolution at that time, but I had had some experience of similar work before 1927. Although the situation in 1930 was quite different from that in 1927, I was still able to appreciate most of the problems and difficulties with which the revolutionaries were faced.

In the spring of 1930 Shanghai began to feel the repercussions of the world depression. China's own capitalists, bowed under the yoke of imperialist economic aggression, their growth hindered by the existence of the feudal forces, now tried to escape the crisis which confronted them by intensifying their exploitation of the working class: hours of work were increased, wages were cut, and workers were dismissed wholesale. This evoked fierce resistance from the workers, and an economic struggle broke out, in which every economic battle soon turned into a political battle, so that conditions at the time were favourable to the progress of the mass movement.

I decided that my novel should deal with three aspects of the current situation: (1) how Chinese industrialists, groaning under foreign economic aggression, were hindered on the one hand by the feudal forces and threatened on the other by the control of the money-market by compradore-capitalists, and how they tried to save themselves by employing even more brutal methods and intensifying their exploitation of the working class; (2) how, as a result, the working class was obliged to put up a fierce resistance; and (3) how the national capitalists, at enmity alike with the Communist Party and the people as a whole, were finally reduced to the only alternative of capitulating to the compradores (the tools of the imperialists), or becoming compradores themselves.

A novel of such content, of course, would offer scope for dealing with quite a number of problems, but I decided to restrict myself to a refutation of the Trotskyite fallacy. I would use my facts to prove that China, far from becoming a capitalist country, was being reduced to the status of a colony under the pressure of imperialism. There were a number of people among China's bourgeoisie, it is true, who had much in common with the old

French bourgeoisie; nevertheless the China of 1930, unlike eighteenth-century France, was a semi-colony, which meant that the outlook for China's bourgeoisie was particularly bleak — it was, in fact, utterly hopeless. Such were the circumstances which gave rise to the attitude of vacillation in the national bourgeoisie. I intended also to refute some of the fanciful theories advanced by bourgeois scholars in those days. Typical of these theories was the following: China's bourgeoisie could save itself — by which they meant developing industry and setting up a bourgeois régime — by opposing the national, democratic revolutionary movement led by the Communist Party and at the same time opposing feudalism and compradore-capitalism. As it turned out, Chinese capitalists like Wu Sun-fu, who opposed both the working class and the national, democratic revolution led by the working-class party, were left with no alternative but to become compradores themselves.

I set to work on the novel before the summer of 1931 had really begun. I was rather ambitious then, and planned to cover both town and country at the same time. I had only completed the first few chapters when summer came — an exceptionally hot summer, with the temperature in the nineties every day for more than a month. The attic which served me for a study became unbearably hot, and there was nothing for it but to stop writing for the time being. Later, I was taken ill again and the book had to be put aside until the summer of 1932, when I came back to it. It was not until that December that I finally had the manuscript completed. During the break in writing my interest had waned and with it my courage. When I came back to it and ran my eye over what I had written I felt dissatisfied, for I realized that my original plan had been too ambitious and that I was attempting something beyond my abilities. Accordingly, I decided to abandon half my original plan — the part dealing with the country — and restrict myself to the city. To do this, I attempted to interweave three strands, represented by compradore-capitalists, reactionary industrial capitalists, and the revolutionaries and the working masses. The reactionary government of the time subjected all publications to an extremely severe censorship, and if I had given a full, frank account of the activities of the revolutionaries I would never have got the book published; so, to ensure that it would see the light, I had to be satisfied in places with slipping in hints and indirect allusions. Among the book's many shortcomings one of the more regrettable is that it was not possible to portray the revolutionaries as the principal characters.

Mao Tun

May 1939

PRINCIPAL CHARACTERS

Wu Sun-fu	*industrial capitalist, owner of the Yu Hua Silk Factory*
Lin Pei-yao	*Wu Sun-fu's wife*
Wu Huei-fang	*Wu Sun-fu's younger sister*
Wu Ah-hsuan	*Wu Sun-fu's younger brother*
Wu Fu-fang	*Wu Sun-fu's elder sister*
Tu Chu-chai	*Wu Fu-fang's husband, a banker*
Tu Hsin-to	*Tu Chu-chai's son, who has studied in France*
Tu Hsueh-shih	*Tu Chu-chai's younger brother, an engineering student*
Fan Po-wen	*Wu Sun-fu's cousin, a poet*
Lin Pei-shan	*Lin Pei-yao's younger sister*
Chang Su-su	*Wu Sun-fu's cousin, a girl student*
Li Yu-ting	*a professor of economics*
Wu Chih-sheng	*Wu Sun-fu's cousin, a sociology student*
Chiu Chun	*a lawyer, Wu Sun-fu's legal adviser*
Lei Ming	*a staff officer in Chiang Kai-shek's army, Lin Pei-yao's former suitor*
Huang Fen	*a petty politician in the Wang Ching-wei clique*
Sun Chi-jen	*owner of a shipping company, Wu Sun-fu's partner*
Tang Yun-shan	*general manager of the Yi Chung Trust Company, a politician in the Wang Ching-wei clique, Wu Sun-fu's partner*
Wang Ho-fu	*owner of a coal-mining company and acting general manager of the Yi Chung Trust Company, Wu Sun-fu's partner*
Chou Chung-wei	*owner of a match factory*
Chu Yin-chiu	*owner of a silk factory*
Chen Chun-yi	*owner of a silk goods factory*
Hsu Man-li	*a society girl*
Han Meng-hsiang	*a stockbroker*
Chao Po-tao	*a powerful speculator in government bonds, a compradore-capitalist*
Shang Chung-li	*Chao Po-tao's confidant*
Lu Kuang-shih	*a stockbroker*
Liu Yu-ying	*Chao Po-tao's mistress, Lu Kuang-shih's daughter-in-law*
Feng Yun-ching	*a speculator in government bonds*

Feng Mei-ching	*Chao Po-tao's mistress, Feng Yun-ching's daughter*
Fei Hsiao-sheng	*Wu Sun-fu's bailiff in his home town*
Tseng Tsang-hai	*Wu Sun-fu's uncle, a despotic landlord*
Tseng Chia-chu	*Tseng Tsang-hai's son*
Tu Wei-yueh	*manager of Wu Sun-fu's silk factory*
Mo Kan-cheng	*chief clerk in the same factory*
Kuei Chang-lin	*a trade union official of the Wang Ching-wei clique, blackleg in the pay of the management*
Pockmarked Li	*an overseer, blackleg in the pay of the management*
Wang Chin-chen	*a forewoman, blackleg in the pay of the management*
Yao Chin-feng	*a factory girl, blackleg in the pay of the management*
Chien Pao-sheng	*a Kuomintang trade union official in Wu Sun-fu's factory*
Chien Chiao-lin	*a factory girl, Chien Pao-sheng's underling*
Chou Erh-chieh	*a factory girl, Chien Pao-sheng's underling*
Hsueh Pao-chu	*a forewoman, Chien Pao-sheng's underling*
Ho Hsiu-mei	
Chang Ah-hsin	*factory girls who led a strike organized by the Communist Party*
Chen Yueh-ngo	
Chu Kuei-ying	
Tsai Chen	*labour-movement workers*
Ma Chin	
Ke Tso-fu	*a Communist, a leader in the labour movement*
Su Lun	*a Trotskyite*

I

THE sun had just sunk below the horizon and a gentle breeze caressed one's face. The muddy water of Soochow Creek, transformed to a golden green, flowed quietly westward. The evening tide from the Whangpoo had turned imperceptibly, and now the assortment of boats along both sides of the creek were riding high, their decks some six inches above the landing-stages. Faint strains of music were borne on the wind from the riverside park, punctuated by the sharp, cheerful patter of kettledrums. Under a sunset-mottled sky, the towering framework of Garden Bridge was mantled in a gathering mist. Whenever a tram passed over the bridge, the overhead cable suspended below the top of the steel frame threw off bright, greenish sparks. Looking east, one could see the warehouses of foreign firms on the waterfront of Pootung like huge monsters crouching in the gloom, their lights twinkling like countless tiny eyes. To the west, one saw with a shock of wonder on the roof of a building a gigantic neon sign in flaming red and phosphorescent green: LIGHT, HEAT, POWER!

It was a perfect May evening. Three 1930-model Citroëns flashed over the bridge, turned westward, and headed straight along the North Soochow Road. Passing a block west of the Shanghai Chamber of Commerce Building on the corner of North Honan Road, where the creek below was usually thronged with steam-launches plying upriver, the three cars slowed down. The driver of the first car said in a low voice to the hulking fellow sitting beside him in black silk:

"The Tai Sheng Chang Company, isn't it, Kuan?"

"Of course it is," replied his companion, also in a low voice.

"Surely you haven't forgotten already? That bitch must be making you soft in the head."

As the bodyguard, for such he was, spoke, he showed large, strong teeth. The car jarred to a stop and Kuan quickly scrambled out, placing his hand on the Browning at his side as he did so and glancing all round. Then he went round and opened the other door and stood holding it, looking stern and forbidding. A head stuck out cautiously — a square, pimply, purplish face with thick eyebrows and round eyes. Spotting the signboard over the gate with the name "The Tai Sheng Chang Shipping Company," the man emerged completely and quickly made for the building with his bodyguard close behind him.

"Is the *Flying Cloud* arriving soon?" the purplish-faced man asked in a loud and arrogant voice. About forty, powerfully built and imposing, he struck you at once as a solid and prosperous businessman, accustomed to giving orders. Before the words were out of his mouth, the clerks sitting there in the office jumped up as one man, and a tall, thin young man, smiling broadly, stepped forward.

"Yes, Mr. Wu, very soon," he answered respectfully. "Please take a seat." He turned to a boy, "Go and get some tea."

While he was speaking he drew up a chair and placed it behind the visitor, whose fleshy face twitched in what could have been a smile as he glanced at the young man, and then looked out towards the street. By now the visitor's car had moved on to make room for the second, out of which a man and a woman appeared and came into the hall. The man was short and stoutish with a bland and pallid face, while the woman was much taller, and bore a certain resemblance to the other man with her square face, although her skin was smooth and fair. Both she and her husband were in their forties, but in her fashionable dress she did not look more than thirty. The husband greeted the first arrival:

"Why, hello, Sun-fu! Are we all waiting here?"

Before the purplish-faced man could answer, the spindly youth quickly chimed in with a broad smile:

"Yes, here, Mr. Tu. I've just heard her hooter and sent someone to keep a look-out at the landing-stage. He'll run back as soon as the boat arrives. I don't think we'll have to wait more than five minutes. Only five more minutes."

"Ah, Fu-sheng! I'm very glad to see you're still here. Yes, the best way to learn a trade is to stick to it. Father has often said you're very keen. How long is it since you saw the old man last?"

"I paid a visit to Old Mr. Wu only a month ago while I was home on leave," babbled the spindly youth Fu-sheng in reply, dazzled by Mrs. Tu's compliments; then, placing a chair behind her and another behind her husband, he begged her to take a seat.

Then he bustled about serving tea and offering cigarettes round. This young man was the son of an old servant of the Wu family. He had always been a nimble-witted lad, so Old Mr. Wu had asked his son Sun-fu to put him in this shipping office as an employee. The two men and the woman remained standing, looking every now and then towards the entrance. There at the gate another hefty fellow was standing with his back to the door, looking vigilantly right and left — Mr. Tu's bodyguard.

Mrs. Tu sat down first with a sigh of relief. She dabbed her lips with a print silk handkerchief, then said over her shoulder to Mr. Wu:

"When I went home with Chu-chai last year to visit the ancestral graves, we travelled on this same *Flying Cloud*. It's a fast boat and didn't stop on the way, and we did the journey in half a day, but it did roll terribly, and made my joints ache. I'm sure father must be having an awful time of it today. Of course, being paralysed like that, he can hardly move a muscle." She turned to her husband: "Chu-chai, do you remember how father complained of feeling giddy last year when he had been sitting down too long . . . ?"

Mrs. Tu paused and sighed slightly, her eyes reddening at the edges. She was going to say something more when a steam-whistle screeched, and a boy dashed in announcing excitedly:

"The boat's drawing level with the landing-stage!"

Mrs. Tu instantly rose, laying a hand on Mr. Tu's shoulder. Fu-sheng dashed out, at the same time looking back to say:

"Mr. Wu, Mr. Tu, Mrs. Tu, there's no need to hurry. Wait till I've seen to things before you come out."

All the clerks in the office began to bustle about. Somebody summoned two stout porters who had been standing by, and who immediately ran in, took up a cane-chair, and carried it off. Wu Sun-fu, looking out on the street, said to Mrs. Tu:

"On our way home you'll sit with father in the first car — No. 1889. I'll keep Huei-fang company in the second, and Chu-chai'll have Ah-hsuan in the third."

Mrs. Tu nodded and looked towards the entrance, moving her lips as she silently recited Buddhist sutras. A cigar in his mouth and a smile on his lips, Tu Chu-chai glanced at Wu Sun-fu as much as to say: Let's go now. Just then Fu-sheng came back frowning with annoyance.

"What a nuisance!" he said. "There is a Soochow Line tug occupying the landing-stage."

"That doesn't matter: let's go and see," Wu Sun-fu interrupted and made off with his bodyguard. Tu Chu-chai and his wife followed; Fu-sheng and the other bodyguard, who had been standing at the door, brought up the rear.

The *Flying Cloud* was moored alongside a tug, commonly known as a "company boat." The large cane-chair was placed in readiness on the forcdeck, the two bearers waiting on either side. Along the wharf there was not the usual bustle and din. On the landing-stage several men from the shipping company were shouting and trying to shoo off the rickshawmen and hawkers, who kept pushing forward. While Wu Sun-fu and the Tu couple were picking their way across the deck of the tug, a cabin boy helped Old Mr. Wu out on deck and sat him down in the cane-chair. Fu-sheng ran up and made signs to the bearers to hoist up the old man and carry him carefully on to the "company boat." The old man was met by his son, daughter, and son-in-law, who were relieved to find him none the worse for the voyage, except for red blotches on his temples. But he did not speak; he merely glanced at them, nodded his head slightly, and closed his eyes.

Huei-fang, the old man's fourth daughter, and Ah-hsuan, his seventh son, also came aboard the tug from the *Flying Cloud*.

4

"How did father feel on the journey, Huei-fang?" Mrs. Tu asked her younger sister in a whisper.

"Pretty well, though he kept saying that he felt giddy."

"Let's hurry up and get to the cars," said Wu Sun-fu impatiently. "Fu-sheng, go and tell the chauffeur to bring the new car round first."

Leaving the old gentleman in the care of the ladies, Wu Sun-fu, Tu Chu-chai, and the lad Ah-hsuan went ashore first. The new car drove up, while the bearers landed the cane-chair with its occupant. They got the old man settled in the car, and Mrs. Tu took her place beside him. Her perfume seemed to wake him, and he opened his eyes to see who it was and said in a slow and quavering voice:

"Is that you, Fu-fang? I want Huei-fang to come with me — and Ah-hsuan as well."

Wu Sun-fu, who was in the second car, heard this and frowned slightly, but said nothing. He knew how eccentric and obstinate his father was — so did Chu-chai. So Huei-fang and Ah-hsuan squeezed into the car beside their father. Fu-fang, who couldn't bear to leave her father, remained where she was, so that the old man was now sandwiched between his two daughters. The engine started up but as the car moved forward the old man suddenly cried in a shrill voice:

"*The Supreme Scriptures of Rewards and Punishments!*"*

It was a strange, strident cry — a flare of light in an old flickering life. His old eyes gleamed, the faint reddish patches on his temples turned a deep red, and his lips trembled.

The driver immediately braked and cast a startled glance over his shoulder. The other two cars also stopped. Nobody knew what had happened. Only Huei-fang understood what it was her father wanted. Fu-sheng had come up, and she told him:

"Fu-sheng, run back to the boat and look in the dining-room for a book in a yellow damask-covered case."

Twenty-five years before Old Mr. Wu had had a fall from a horse, and an injury to his leg had led to partial paralysis. He

---

* An ancient book based on the belief in divine retribution.

had since developed a strong faith in the religious book on virtue rewarded and vice punished. Every year he had given free copies of the book to fellow-believers as a practice of virtue. He had also copied the whole book in his own neat and pious hand, and this transcript had become for him a talisman against vice, with which he could never part for a moment.

Very soon Fu-sheng was back, holding the book with both hands. Old Mr. Wu took it and laid it reverently on his lap. He closed his eyes again, a faint smile of peace on his shrivelled lips.

"Carry on now, driver," Mrs. Tu ordered quietly. With a sigh of relief, she sank back into her seat and rested her head against the cushioned back, smiling with satisfaction. The cars were gathering speed, turning east along the North Soochow Road, crossing Garden Bridge, turning south, then racing along at half a mile a minute, the record speed for the 1930 model.

*

It is one of life's little ironies that someone should be driving through the wide streets of Shanghai — that great city of the East with a population of three million — in such a modern conveyance as a motorcar, yet holding *The Supreme Scriptures* in his hands, his mind intent upon one text: "Of all the vices sexual indulgence is the cardinal; of all the virtues filial piety is the supreme." In the case of Old Mr. Wu, the irony was all the more remarkable because he genuinely believed in *The Supreme Scriptures*, unlike those racketeers of Shanghai who swindle money out of the public under the cloak of philanthropy. Thirty years back, Old Mr. Wu had been a "reformist" of the first water. In spite of the fact that his father and grandfather had been vice-ministers enjoying the Emperor's generosity in no small degree, he was full of the "revolutionary" ideas of the time, and as a young man had been a leading light in the universal conflict between fathers and sons of those days. He would probably not now be buried all day in his *Supreme Scriptures* but for the fact that he had fallen from his horse in a cavalry exercise and received an injury to his leg which had since brought on paralysis. Soon afterwards he suffered a further blow in the death of his wife. He lost all his youthful vigour, which seemed to have run out of him when he fell off his horse. For twenty-five years he had not set foot outside his study, had not read anything except *The Supreme Scriptures of Rewards and Punishments*, nor had anything to do with the world outside. The conflict between father and son had now become an irretrievable reality for him and his son Sun-fu, and he now seemed as cantankerous and eccentric to his son as his father had once seemed to him. His study had been his castle; his scriptures his coat of mail. For ten years he had stubbornly refused to make peace with his son.

Now, although he was riding in a motorcar of the latest design, it did not mean that he was relenting towards his son. On the contrary, he had repeatedly declared that he would rather die than see his son living a life completely deviating from the path of righteousness. He had never really wanted to come to Shanghai, nor had his son tried to insist that he should. Lately, however, local bandits had been very active and in the neighbouring province the Reds had been gaining ground like a prairie fire. Wu Sun-fu had thought it no longer safe for his father to remain in his country home. It was, in fact, an expression of filial piety. It had never occurred to the old man that bandits or Reds would harm a pious, virtuous old man like him, but invalid as he was, unable to move and unable to sit up or lie down without help, what else could he do but let them haul him out of his castle, load him on board a boat, and finally thrust him into this monster of a motorcar. Just as, twenty-five years ago, his paralysis had ended his career as a reformist and forced him to surrender to his vice-minister father, so now this same accursed infirmity was threatening to cut short his "virtuous" cause and force him to stoop to his modern industrialist son. Could there be no end to his tragedy?

Nevertheless, he still had his *Supreme Scriptures of Rewards and Punishments* to afford him its precious protection. He had also his two precious children, his son Ah-hsuan and his daughter Huei-fang, to be at his side, so that although he was now plunging into the "sinners' paradise" of Shanghai, he was strong in the belief that he could keep himself morally intact. He had closed his eyes long enough to regain his mental composure and now he opened them calmly and confidently to look once more at the world.

The car was racing along like mad. He peered through the wind-screen. Good Heavens! the towering skyscrapers, their countless lighted windows gleaming like the eyes of devils, seemed to be rushing down on him like an avalanche at one moment and vanishing at the next. The smooth road stretched before him, and street-lamps flashed past on either side, springing up and vanishing in endless succession. A snake-like stream of black monsters, each with a pair of blinding lights for eyes, their horns blaring, bore down upon him, nearer and nearer! He closed his eyes tight in terror, trembling all over. He felt as if his head were spinning and his eyes swam before a kaleidoscope of red, yellow, green, black, shiny, square, cylindrical, leaping, dancing shapes, while his ears rang in a pandemonium of honking, hooting and jarring, till his heart was in his mouth.

When some time had passed without mishap, the old man slowly recovered his breath and became conscious of voices humming about his ears:

"Shanghai is not so peaceful nowadays either, Huei-fang. Last month the buses went on strike, and now the trams are out. Not long ago there was a big Communist demonstration in Peking Road. Hundreds of them were arrested, and one of them was shot dead on the spot. Some of the Communists were armed, too! Sun-fu says the factory workers are restless and might make trouble or riot at any moment. And the walls of his factory and house have often had Communist slogans chalked all over them."

"Haven't the police ever caught them?"

"They have caught some, but they cannot catch all of them. Oh, dear! I really don't know where all these desperate characters come from. . . . But my dear, you do make me laugh with your get-up. Your dress might have been in fashion ten years ago but now you're in Shanghai you must follow the fashion. You must get yourself a new outfit first thing tomorrow morning."

Old Mr. Wu opened his eyes again and saw that he was surrounded by a sea of little box-like motorcars like the one he was sitting in, all standing quiet and motionless, while not far ahead a stream of cars and vehicles of all kinds was rushing higgledy-piggledy in one direction and another stream the other way. Among the cars men and women of all sorts and conditions were dashing along as if the devil was on their tail. From somewhere above a shaft of crimson light fell upon him.

Here, at the crossing of Nanking Road and Honan Road, the cars going across were being held up by the traffic lights.

"I haven't met Sun-fu's wife yet, Fu-fang," whispered Huei-fang. "I'm afraid she'll die laughing when she sees what a countrified girl I am."

She cast a furtive glance at her father, then gazed out at all the fashionable women sitting in the cars all round them. Fu-fang giggled, and took out her handkerchief to dab her lips. A whiff of perfume assailed the old fellow's nostrils, and it seemed to upset him.

"I really can't get over you, Huei-fang. When I went home to the country last year, I didn't see any of the country girls wearing such old-fashioned clothes as yours."

"That's true. Even country girls like to look pretty and smart nowadays. But father won't let me. . . ."

All this talk about fashion acted like a needle on the atrophied nerves of the old man. His heart fluttered, and his eyes fell instinctively upon Fu-fang and he saw now for the first time how she was decked out. Though it was still only May, the weather was unusually warm and she was already in the lightest of summer clothing. Her vital young body was sheathed in close-fitting light-blue chiffon, her full, firm breasts jutting out prominently, her snowy forearms bared. Old Mr. Wu felt his heart constricting with disgust and quickly averted his eyes, which, however, fell straight away upon a half-naked young woman sitting up in a rickshaw, fashionably dressed in a transparent, sleeveless voile blouse, displaying her bare legs and thighs. The old man thought for one horrible moment that she had nothing else on. The text "Of all the vices sexual indulgence is the cardinal" drummed on his mind, and he shuddered. But the worst was yet to come, for he quickly withdrew his gaze, only to find his youngest son Ah-hsuan gaping with avid admiration at the same half-naked young woman. The old man felt his heart pounding wildly as if it would burst, and his throat burning as if choked with chillies.

The lights changed to green, and the car moved forward in a motley sea of traffic and humanity. On and on they went, while the din of the traffic, the stench of petrol-fumes, the women's perfume and the glare of neon signs pressed down like a nightmare on his frail spirit until his eyes blurred, his ears sang and his head swam; until his over-wrought nerves ached as if they would snap and his pounding heart could beat no faster.

His breathing became wheezy, but amid the roar of the metropolis neither Fu-fang nor Huei-fang nor Ah-hsuan could hear it. His face turned ashen, but in the red and green glare nobody noticed the difference.

The car raced on at top speed. Their lighted windows gleaming through the trees, the flats at the roadside rushed up one after another and were gone in a flash. The cool evening breeze set the wind-screen rattling. Huei-fang drew a sigh of relief as if a great weight had been lifted from her mind and said to Ah-hsuan:

"This time we've really come to stay in Shanghai, I suppose. But what is it that's so attractive about Shanghai that people keep pouring in? If you ask me, I rather hate the bustle and noise. It gives me such a headache."

"You'll like it when you get used to it," said Fu-fang. "Everybody's running away from the countryside now that the bandits are on the increase, and settling in Shanghai. Look at these new houses on either side of the road; they've sprung up during the last two years. No matter how many new houses are built, there are always people waiting to move in."

She opened her red handbag, took out a powder-puff, and began making up her face in the little mirror fixed inside the bag.

"I think it's quite peaceful in the country. Seems there are less rumours of trouble there. Isn't that so, Ah-hsuan?"

"Peaceful? I can't agree. Why, only two weeks ago a company of troops arrived in our town and demanded that the Chamber of Commerce should supply them with fifty young women — to darn and wash for them, they said. When the Chamber of Commerce said that they couldn't help them, the soldiers set out themselves to find them. The fruiterer's wife next door was grabbed, don't you remember? And our maid didn't dare set foot outside the house for several days."

"But that's outrageous! Of course, here in Shanghai we never know what's actually happening down in the country. We have heard that the Communists kidnap women and communize them."

"But I've never seen a Communist in our parts. Anyway, that company of soldiers made enough trouble as it is."

"Oh, Ah-hsuan, what a fool you are!" said Fu-fang with a sigh. "Of course you've never seen a Communist! If you had done, you wouldn't be here now! Chu-chai says they're up to all sorts of tricks now. They're everywhere. You'll find them in all walks of life, and there's no stopping them. And you don't even know they're there until they strike like a bolt from the blue."

Huei-fang shivered inwardly at this, but Ah-hsuan, who did not quite understand what it was all about, just threw back his head and laughed. He was immensely tickled by Fu-fang's account of the elusive, will-o'-the-wisp Communists. He thought to himself: So the Communists pounce on you like a bolt from the blue, do they? Why, that's magic. He was the baby of the family and, although now a good-looking lad of nineteen, he was still rather naive, having always been his father's favourite.

The chauffeur sounded the horn and the car turned into a quiet, shady side-street, where the lamplight filtered through a dense screen of leaves and splashed Fu-fang and the others with flecks of light. The car began to slow down as it approached the house. Gathering up her things, Fu-fang turned to her father and said quietly:

"Father, we're there."

"He's asleep."

"Don't shout so, Ah-hsuan. You know, Fu-fang, while father's resting with his eyes closed, he allows no one to disturb him."

The chauffeur gave three blasts on the horn, holding on to toots, trailing the last one to announce their presence. The black iron gate in front of the big foreign-style building immediately swung open, and the car glided into the drive. Ah-hsuan jumped up from his seat and, looking round, saw that the other two cars were following behind and that several servants and an armed policeman were standing by the entrance. Then the iron gate clanged shut and the cars swished on up the asphalt drive, through a tunnel of dark, overhanging trees through which occasional lights twinkled. The car swung sharply and there in front of them was a large, brightly-lit, three-storeyed building. The car lurched to a stop amid radio music which floated through an open window.

A maid's clear voice announced:

"Madame! Mr. Wu and his father and the others are here."

Old Mr. Wu, who had only just recovered from his attack of dizziness, opened his eyes with a start of surprise. The first things that his returning consciousness seized upon were the ravenous way his son Ah-hsuan had gazed at the half-naked woman in the street and his daughter Huei-fang's voice as she had complained: "Even country girls like to look pretty and smart nowadays, but father won't let me. . . ."

So his precious children had undergone a change the moment they had entered the "sinners' paradise"!

*

The radio was switched off, and the sound of women's laughter carried through the windows. Then a bustling clickety-clack of high-heeled shoes was heard as three dark figures loomed up. One of them proved to be a tallish, svelte young woman in a pink dress. She hurried up to the first car, her hips swaying as she walked, pulled open the door and greeted them gaily:

"How did you enjoy your journey, father? Fu-fang, is this Huei-fang? And Ah-hsuan?"

Old Mr. Wu was immediately enveloped in an overpowering gust of rich, heady perfume, and through the fragrant haze saw a round, clear-skinned face beneath an unruly mop of wavy hair, with bright, sparkling eyes, and startlingly red lips parted in a ready smile. She tilted her curly head slightly and said in a tinkling, silvery voice:

"Sun-fu, you and the others go in first. Fu-fang and I'll help father out of the car. Huei-fang, will you get out first?"

Old Mr. Wu summoned up his last ounce of strength to shake his head, but nobody noticed it. Huei-fang stepped out brushing against the wavy hair of the young lady. Fu-fang put her right arm under the old man's left arm to support him while Ah-hsuan also lent a hand. Thus he was propelled out of the car willy-nilly and passed to the wavy-haired lady, whose smooth arm immediately encircled his waist. In a swirl of enticing laughter and overwhelmingly fragrant scent, Old Mr. Wu could only shudder and clutch against his breast *The Supreme Scriptures of Rewards and Punishments*. A thought flashed through his tortured mind: "They must be demons or evil spirits, these people!"

Extreme disgust and anger seemed to infuse the old man with unwonted strength, which enabled him to mount the stone steps quite easily on the arms of his daughter and daughter-in-law. The big drawing-room was flooded with light and filled with people. When Old Mr. Wu stepped into the room, he was met by his son and son-in-law. Then two wavy-haired young girls rushed up to him. They asked him how he was and, laughing and chattering, hustled him into a high-backed armchair.

The old man looked around him, his wide eyes burning with disgust, anger and excitement, and his face purpling. He saw the room whirling with lights and colours, whirling more and more swiftly. Near by him a queer-looking, round and shiny thing stood on a small table whirring and turning from side to side, making a wind which took his breath away, like a golden-faced witch swaying her head and casting a spell over him. And the more this golden, flashing disc swayed, the bigger it became, until it filled the whole room, until it filled all space. All the red and green lights, all the geometrical shapes of the furniture and all the men and women were dancing and spinning together, bathed in the golden light. Mrs. Wu Sun-fu in pink, a girl in apple-green, and another in light yellow were frantically leaping and whirling around him. Their light silk dresses barely concealed their curves, their full, pink-tipped breasts and the shadow under their arms. The room was filled with countless swelling bosoms, bosoms that bobbed and quivered and danced around him. Wu Sun-fu's pimply face grinned and Ah-hsuan's lustful eyes shone among the dancing breasts. Suddenly, all these quivering, dancing breasts swept at Old Mr. Wu like a hail of arrows, piling up on his chest and smothering him, piling up on *The Supreme Scriptures of Rewards and Punishments* on his lap. He heard wild, seductive laughter and the room rocked and swayed as if it would collapse.

"Devils," cried Old Mr. Wu, as golden sparks showered before his eyes. He felt his chest crushed under an enormous weight, and something seemed to explode inside his head. Suddenly there sprang out of the ground before him two women, Mrs. Wu Sun-fu and the girl in apple-green, both laughing with wide-open, blood-red mouths as though they wanted to swallow him. Something seemed to snap in his head. He turned up his eyes, and knew no more.

"Uncle, don't you recognize me? I'm Su-su, Chang Su-su," the girl in apple-green Grafton silk asked him and giggled, while Mrs. Wu Sun-fu let out a startled scream and dropped the cup of tea which she was holding out for the old man. All the other people in the room started up in surprise. For a brief moment you could have heard a pin drop; then there was a rush of feet, and they thronged round Old Mr. Wu, all shouting and asking questions at once. He looked deathly pale, his head drooping to the side and his mouth frothing. *The Supreme Scriptures of Rewards and Punishments* fell to the floor with a heavy thud.

"Father! What's the matter with you? Wake up! Wake up!" cried Mrs. Tu in a trembling voice, holding her father's head in her hands, while Tu Chu-chai, her husband, peered round her shoulder, frightened out of his wits.

Wu Sun-fu was gripping his father's hand. When he saw many servants pressing round, he flared up:

"Get out of the way, all of you. Hurry up and fetch an ice-bag."

"An ice-bag! Get an ice-bag!" the servants shouted as they scrambled out of the room to find one. "Old Mr. Wu's having a stroke!" The girl in light yellow who was standing a little way apart grasped Chang Su-su's hand and asked:

Something seemed to snap in his head. He turned up his eyes, and knew no more.

"Su-su, what happened? You saw the old man faint away, didn't you?"

Chang Su-su stood speechless, her eyes staring and her chest rising and falling. Mrs. Wu Sun-fu gasped:

"I was holding out a cup of tea for father . . . I saw, I saw him . . . saw his head drooping . . . his eyes closing . . . his mouth foaming . . . his face turning pale. Is it a stroke? Or an attack of phlegm? Huei-fang, has father ever had attacks like this before?"

Fu-fang was pinching her father's upper lip. Huei-fang was standing in a daze with tears trickling down her cheeks. Fu-fang repeated Mrs. Wu Sun-fu's question:

"Huei-fang, has father ever had attacks like this before? Has he? Come on, you must tell me."

"If it's an attack of phlegm, it isn't serious if only he can cough. After a cough or two, he'll come to."

This diagnosis came from Tu Chu-chai. He glanced at Wu Sun-fu, fumbled nervously for his snuff-box and gave it to him. Wu Sun-fu took it, then turned on the servants furiously: "There are too many people crowding round. The heat of your bodies alone's enough to suffocate the old man. . . . Where's that ice-bag got to? . . . Pei-yao, we don't need you here for the time being: go and ring up Dr. Ting . . . Wang Mah, you run and get an ice-bag." He turned to Fu-fang: "Don't worry, Fu-fang. Father's heart is still beating. But we shouldn't leave him sitting in this chair. Let's carry him over to the couch." He immediately put his arms round the old man to pick him up, and then the others came and lent him a hand. By the time Old Mr. Wu was lying on the velvet-cushioned couch, Mrs. Wu Sun-fu came back from the telephone to tell them that the doctor would be over in ten minutes and that in the meantime he should lie undisturbed in a quiet room. The maid brought in an ice-bag, and Wu Sun-fu quickly laid it on the old man's forehead. He shouted to another servant, Kao Sheng, who was standing in the doorway:

"Go and call two or three men to carry Old Mr. Wu into the small drawing-room. The doctor will be here any moment, so tell the porter to look out for him."

Suddenly the old man's hand twitched. He made a noise in his throat and a frothy mucus oozed out of his mouth. "Oh, good!" several voices exclaimed with some relief. Young Mrs. Wu pulled a white handkerchief from Chang Su-su's lapel and wiped the old man's lips with it. She cast a worried glance at her husband, who frowned. Fu-fang and Tu Chu-chai also looked worried. The blue veins on the old man's forehead now stood out like worms, the rasping in his throat became louder and quicker and the froth still oozed from his lips. Suddenly, his hand twitched again, and his eyelids fluttered a moment and then remained half closed.

"Oh! what's keeping Dr. Ting? Let's carry father into the other room now," muttered Wu Sun-fu, wringing his hands with impatience. He motioned to the four servants standing by to lift the couch on which the old man was lying and carry it into the small drawing-room. He followed behind with his wife, Tu Chu-chai, Fu-fang, and Huei-fang. Ah-hsuan, who had been standing by gaping, came to, looked round in alarm, scampered into the parlour, and slammed the door behind him.

*

An uneasy silence fell upon the people left in the large drawing-room. Chang Su-su, leaning against a big, luxurious radio-cabinet, was gazing pensively at *The Supreme Scriptures of Rewards and Punishments* lying on the floor. Two young men were sitting on a sofa, resting their heads on their hands, drawing slowly at cigarettes and from time to time glancing nervously towards the door of the other room.

The room was still softly lit and the golden disc of the electric fan continued to whir and turn slowly from side to side, sending a cool breeze over everybody and ruffling their clothes. These people, who had hitherto been used to comfort and pleasure, now felt a vague uneasiness.

The girl in light-yellow silk was sitting by the piano, idly turning the pages of a score. She bore a striking resemblance to Mrs. Wu Sun-fu and was, in fact, her younger sister, Lin Pei-shan.

Chang Su-su, who had been lost in thought, suddenly came to as if she had an idea. She looked up sharply and glanced round for somebody to speak to. Catching the eye of Lin Pei-shan, she ran over to her, struck her palms together, and whispered earnestly in an undertone:

"Pei-shan, I'm afraid it's all over with Old Mr. Wu! I've seen people —"

Hearing this, the two young men on the sofa jumped to their feet in surprise and looked at Chang Su-su with questioning eyes.

"How can you be so sure about it?" asked Lin Pei-shan hesitantly, standing up.

"How can I be sure? Well, this is not the first time I've seen somebody die!"

Several servants had gathered around Chang Su-su and when they heard her say this, they could not help bursting out laughing; but Chang Su-su kept a straight face. She lowered her voice and went on mysteriously:

"Do you think it was phlegm he was oozing out? Oh no! Not at all! He was foaming at the mouth. When people die in hot weather, they usually foam at the mouth just as he did. I know: I've seen it. And wouldn't you call today hot? Eighty degrees, although it's only the sixteenth of May. Am I right, Yu-ting? Go on!"

Chang Su-su turned and looked at one of the two men as much as to say that he should nod his head to bear her out. The man, Li Yu-ting, was of medium height, had a sharply pointed face and wore thick-lensed glasses. He neither agreed nor disagreed with her, but merely smiled cryptically, which did not please her at all. She glanced at him resentfully, pursed her little scarlet lips and muttered crossly:

"I shan't forget this in a hurry! Teachers usually are pretty spineless, but you university professors are even worse. Your students don't hesitate to speak their mind, but you professors dare not turn to the left or to the right. Then you have to take all the knocks and grin sheepishly. But we aren't in class now, Professor Li: we are in Mr. Wu's!"

Li Yu-ting stopped smiling and looked considerably chastened. The other man, Fan Po-wen, who was standing behind Lin Pei-shan, whispered something to her which made her snigger and flash an amused glance at Chang Su-su. The latter crim-

17

soned, swung round, bore down on Lin Pei-shan, and said with mock annoyance: "What mischief are you two up to? Saying things behind my back, are you? Come on, say you're sorry."

Lin Pei-shan edged away, giggling and protecting herself with her hands in case Chang Su-su should tickle her, and appealed to the young man:

"Po-wen, you started the trouble; how can you just stand there and watch?"

Just then they heard the sound of a horn and a car drew up outside. A tall middle-aged man in foreign dress hurried in, followed by two nurses in white uniforms, one of them carrying a bulging Gladstone bag. Chang Su-su let go of Lin Pei-shan and rose to greet the man:

"How do you do, Dr. Ting? The patient's in the small drawing-room."

So saying, she tripped across to the door of the other room and opened it noiselessly for the doctor and nurses, then slipped in herself, closing it behind her.

Smoothing her tousled hair, Lin Pei-shan said to her cousin:

"Did you see how the doctor's car raced up to the door? Just like a fire-engine."

"Ah, but his job is to kindle a spark of life in the old man, not to put it out!"

"There you go again: poetry! Huh!"

Lin Pei-shan cast a saucy glance at Fan Po-wen and moved towards the door of the other room. The door opened and Chang Su-su tiptoed out. Then a nurse appeared in the doorway, motioned a servant to come over, and handed him an enamel basin for some water. She withdrew behind the door and closed it.

Everybody looked at Chang Su-su inquiringly. She gave a slight shake of her head and without a word walked glumly round a rosewood table. She stopped in front of Lin Pei-shan and the others and said quietly:

"Dr. Ting says it's cerebral haemorrhage and puts it down to over-excitement. He can't say yet whether he's going to live or not. Fancy it being over-excitement, though!"

They exchanged glances in silence. "Fancy that!" echoed Li

Yu-ting lamely after a moment, as if trying to make up for upsetting Chang Su-su.

"Yet to my mind it doesn't really seem as strange as all that. It would be quite natural for Old Mr. Wu to become over-excited. Just think what it's been like for him living quietly down in the country. He hasn't set foot outside the house for the last twenty years or so. It's been nothing short of a living grave, that study of his that he's been cooped up in all this time. And now today he's suddenly been rushed off to Shanghai, where he sees and hears and smells so many strange, new things which cannot but over-excite him. He's getting on in years and his health isn't all that good; it would be strange if he *didn't* have an attack of cerebral haemorrhage."

Fan Po-wen spoke slowly with a feminine lilt in his voice, and his face beamed smugly. He sought Lin Pei-shan's eye, and she returned him a wry smile. Chang Su-su saw this. She deliberately kept a straight face and snorted:

"Poet laureate! You're even poetizing on someone's death now!"

"I may have chosen an unfortunate subject, Miss Chang, but I don't think I deserve such a dressing down."

"All right, then: would you rather it was your Miss Lin telling you off?"

This time it was Lin Pei-shan's turn to blush. She snorted and walked off in a huff, followed by Fan Po-wen. Chang Su-su knitted her brows in a worried frown and paced round the rosewood table once more, while Li Yu-ting just stood there rubbing his chin. An oppressive silence fell on the room, broken only by the monotonous whir of the electric fan and the occasional hoot of a car in the street, though even these sounded dull and drowsy. A few servants stood motionless in the doorway, and Wang Mah and another maid were whispering with their heads together, their lips moving silently.

The door of the small drawing-room opened and the tall figure of Dr. Ting emerged. He took a cigar from a silver case on an oval brass table, lit up, and sank into an armchair.

"How is he?" asked Chang Su-su softly, going across to him.

"He's in a pretty bad way. I've just given him another injection."

"Don't you think he'll last the night?"

"I doubt it!"

*

Dr. Ting discarded his cigar and went back into the other room. Chang Su-su went softly across to the door and pulled it up behind him. She wheeled round, ran back to Lin Pei-shan, threw her arms around her waist, and pressed her face against hers. Stamping her feet, she whimpered:

"Oh, Pei-shan! I do feel upset! I can't bear to think about people dying, and dying so suddenly. I don't want to die — I *won't* die!"

"But we all have to go one day."

"No, not me! Pei-shan, I won't die!"

"Perhaps you're different from everyone else: when you get old, you can slough your skin like a snake and be young again! . . . Anyway, don't keep pawing me so. Look what a mess you're making of my hair! Oh, leave go of me, do!"

"Never mind. You can go to the beauty parlour again tomorrow. Listen, Pei-shan: if I must die, I'd rather die of over-excitement."

Lin Pei-shan started in surprise and looked into Chang Su-su's eyes, which were shining with an unusual excitement which she had never seen there before.

"To die of excitement! Yes, I think that would perhaps be the nicest way to die. But the sort of excitement I want is not the sort the old man had today. No, what I want is the excitement of some great upheaval like a storm, a volcanic eruption, an earthquake, or to see the whole universe in chaos. Ah . . . that would be wonderful, magnificent!"

After this outburst, Chang Su-su let go of Lin Pei-shan, stepped back, sank into a rocking-chair, and buried her face in her hands.

Li Yu-ting and Fan Po-wen, who had been standing by listening, broke into a laugh. It seemed that the way Chang Su-su had struck out and then retreated amused them greatly. Seeing that Lin Pei-shan was still standing there absorbed in her own thoughts, Fan Po-wen went over and took her hand. She started at the touch but, when she saw it was Fan Po-wen, gave him an arch look. He jerked his thumb in the direction of Chang Su-su and whispered:

"Now you can see what's wrong with Su-su. She is very much in need of excitement, but that dreary professor has none to offer. Anyway, what she just said shows she's got some poetic talent, I think."

Lin Pei-shan smiled at first, but, when she heard his last remark, she gave him an icy glare, snorted, and moved languidly away. Realizing that she had misunderstood him, he ran after her and caught her by the shoulder, but she angrily shrugged his hand off, ran through the back door, and slammed it in his face. He hesitated for a second, then dashed over, flung open the door and shouted, "Pei-shan!"

The slam startled Chang Su-su out of her reverie. She looked up, then dropped her eyes again. Her gaze fell on *The Supreme Scriptures of Rewards and Punishments* in its yellow damask case lying on a low rectangular table before her, picked it up, and began turning over the pages of neat characters written on high-grade Chinese paper. She paused at an epilogue written by Old Mr. Wu in mid-spring, 1924, which read:

> I have had a hundred thousand copies of *The Supreme Scriptures of Rewards and Punishments* reprinted for distribution among my fellow-believers, and also transcribed the whole text with my own hand. . . .

Chang Su-su burst out laughing and was about to read on when somebody spoke to her from behind:

"Now *there* was a man who may truly be said to have had a faith and to have been loyal to it all his life."

It was Li Yu-ting, leaning over the back of the chair, a cigarette between his fingers. Chang Su-su glanced at him over her shoulder, then looked down again at the book. After a while, she laid the book on her lap and asked abruptly:

"Tell me, Yu-ting: what sort of a society are we living in?"

Li Yu-ting was taken aback by this unexpected question, but, being a professor of economics, he did not find it difficult to say something:

"It's a tall order, your question. But you can find an answer in the next room. There you have a successful financier and a captain of industry. That little drawing-room is Chinese society in miniature."

"But there's also a pious old man — a believer in *The Supreme Scriptures of Rewards and Punishments*."

"Yes, but the old man is — he's dying fast."

"But in our country there are heaven knows how many more like him."

"Never mind. They'll die directly they arrive in Shanghai. Shanghai is. . . ."

Li Yu-ting broke off when the door from the next room opened and Mrs. Wu Sun-fu came out. Except for a slight frown this beautiful young woman was as lively as ever. When she saw that Li Yu-ting and Chang Su-su were alone together here, she shot them a surprised glance, but immediately changed it to a hospitable smile. She called for the butler Kao Sheng and the maid Wang Mah. When they came in, she said:

"It seems the old master cannot be expected to last the night out. Kao Sheng, you telephone to the factory for Mr. Mo Kan-cheng to come round at once. Then draw up a list of relatives and friends of the family to be notified when he passes away. And have your men tidy up the garden and everywhere and get the spare chairs and tables out of the attic. If you're shorthanded, go and get some helpers from Mr. Tu Chu-chai's place. Now, Wang Mah, you take some maids to tidy up the guest-rooms on the second floor and change all the net curtains, table-cloths and loose covers."

"What about a shroud for the old master? And what kind of wood —?"

"You needn't bother about that. Anyway, it hasn't been decided yet. We shall probably call in the International Undertakers. You just tell Mr. Mo Kan-cheng to bring with him as many men from the factory as he can spare."

"By the way, the Tai Sheng Chang Shipping Company's just sent over the old master's luggage, twenty-eight pieces all told."

"All right, Wang Mah, you go and check them, and anything that isn't needed for the time being you can put in the attic."

Hearing someone in the next room call her name, Mrs. Wu Sun-fu hurried back to the small drawing-room. Before closing the door behind her, she stuck out her head and asked:

"Su-su, do you know where Pei-shan and Po-wen have vanished to? Will you fetch them for me, please?"

Chang Su-su nodded but did not move. She was still reflecting on her discussion with Li Yu-ting and was thinking of picking up the thread where they had left off. Li Yu-ting was pacing up and down and drawing on his cigarette in silence. By now it was nine o'clock, and out in the garden people were coming and going and bustling about. The lights among the trees, in the summerhouses and on the rockeries were switched on. Wang Mah led several stout women servants into the large drawing-room, where they began changing the crimson net curtains for white ones. There was a large bundle of loose covers on the floor, and even the carpets were taken out to be beaten.

There was a scuffle from the next room, and suddenly there came the sound of sobbing voices and cries of "Father!" Chang Su-su and Li Yu-ting looked tense. She rose and walked nervously up and down, then ran across the room and pushed open the door. As the door opened, the big room was filled with the sound of sobbing. Dr. Ting came out, rubbing his hands together, and said to Li Yu-ting, "It's all over."

Wu Sun-fu followed him out, his face gloomy. He told the servants to ring up Mr. Chiu Chun, a lawyer, and ask him to come round. He turned to Li Yu-ting:

"Yu-ting, I hope you can stay with us tonight and give us a hand. It's now gone nine and the newspapers may not be willing to accept our obituary notice as late as this, but it must appear tomorrow morning without fail, so I wonder if you'd be good enough to go and arrange it? Chu-chai is wording it now. It's to go to all the five leading papers, of course." He turned to the butler: "Kao Sheng! Why isn't Mr. Mo Kan-cheng here yet?"

The servant, who was standing on the steps outside, was just going to answer, when Fu-fang ran out and seized Wu Sun-fu by the arm and said:

"I've just talked things over with Pei-yao about the shrouding and we think we'd best put it off until the day after tomorrow in the morning. We need a little time for the preparation and, besides, we'd better wait until Uncle Tseng Tsang-hai has arrived. We can't afford to slight him: you know what a fuss he makes."

Wu Sun-fu paused for a moment and then said firmly:

"We'll send him a telegram tonight. He may or may not arrive in time for the shrouding, but we can't put it off simply because of him. If he complains of anything, I'll answer for it. The shrouding takes place at two o'clock tomorrow afternoon, come what may."

Fu-fang would have liked to say something more, but he had already rushed back to the next room. Fu-fang eventually followed him in.

Just then, Lin Pei-shan and Fan Po-wen, hand in hand, came out of the dining-room into the right-hand corner of the big room. They were taken aback at the din and bustle. Lin Pei-shan said softly:

"It looks as if the old man's gone."

"If so, I'm not in the least surprised. When he lived in the country he existed like a mummy. The country was his grave, in which he couldn't decompose easily. In this modern city of Shanghai he has done. He's gone, and good riddance. One mummy of old China the less. Old China herself is a mummy five thousand years old, and she's decomposing fast. She can't weather the storm of this new age much longer."

Lin Pei-shan smiled wryly, and threw Fan Po-wen a sly glance of pretended vexation.

II

ABOUT five o'clock next morning there were a few drops of rain in the wind. It was much cooler than the evening before — a drop of nearly ten degrees — but by nine o'clock the sun, now blazing high in the sky, had dispersed the lowering clouds and the temperature was up again to eighty degrees. One felt the menace of an even severer heat-wave.

The ushers at the Wus' residence, holding aloft white cardboard signs indicating their function and wearing coarse black gowns tied at the waist with long, wide strips of thick white cloth for belts, scurried to and fro in the scorching sun, from the main gate to the large drawing-room which was being used as a "ceremonial hall," and then back again to the main gate to escort in more newly-arrived mourners. Every one of them was tired and perspiring freely. Until half past ten, the eight of them now and then managed to snatch a moment's rest on the wooden benches beside the funeral musicians at the main gate, where they would mop their brows with the loose ends of their white belts and fan themselves with the cardboard signs while they regained their breath, grumbling because Mr. Wu Sun-fu had not employed more men to do this job. By midday, however, when the sun was beating down mercilessly on their heads, the visitors had begun to arrive in an endless stream, and the two bands, one at the main gate and one before the hall, were both playing non-stop. The ushers rushed back and forth like robots, too busy now even to think of grumbling about Mr. Wu. They could at most cast envious glances at the six masters of ceremonies who were standing idly before the funeral hall.

The hooting of cars . . . the funeral din of flutes, trumpets and gongs . . . the bawling of waiters as they elbowed their way back and forth with shouts of "Tea here!" and "Lemonade for this gentleman!" . . . the noise of chauffeurs and rickshaw boys clamouring for tips . . . the raised voices of policemen and plain-clothes men shooing idle onlookers away from the main gate . . . the acrid smell of cigarette smoke and the odour of human bodies — all mingled together and penetrated every corner of the Wu mansion and its acre and a half of garden.

The dining-room next to the funeral hall was packed with people. A huge mahogany sideboard stood across it like a bridge, partitioning it into two sections. In the right-hand wall of the interior section were windows looking out on to the garden; close to the windows stood a tall trellis covered with banksia roses, which afforded fragrance and shade to the whole room. In the left wall there were two doors, one of which opened on to a veranda on which guests were sitting clustered around tea-tables, holding forth noisily on "gold bullion," "silver bars," "cotton yarn," and "taels and cents," their talk punctuated by the pfft! of lemonade-bottles being opened. Close by a door at the extreme end of the veranda sat a man of about thirty in a khaki uniform and long riding-boots, with three or four enamel badges on his chest. He was sitting alone in a rocking-chair, slowly sipping lemonade and glancing every so often at the door beside him. It was closed, but whenever it opened an inch or two an intoxicating perfume and silvery laughter escaped through the crack.

Suddenly the man in uniform put down his glass and stood up, his spurs jingling, and sprang to attention, then made a low bow to a woman appearing in the doorway.

Mrs. Wu Sun-fu was rather taken aback by this unexpected show of courtesy, but by the time he had straightened up she had recovered her composure and nodded with a smile.

"Ah, Colonel Lei! You here? . . . Nice of you to come."

"Oh, don't mention it. I was planning to come tomorrow to say goodbye, but when I heard that this had happened, I felt I had to come to pay my last respects. They tell me Old Mr. Wu passed away yesterday evening. If so, Madame, you must have had quite a time of it!" replied Col. Lei, smiling respectfully, at the same time glancing over Mrs. Wu Sun-fu's mourning dress:

an ankle-length black gauze dress with tight-fitting three-quarter length sleeves discreetly flattering her tall, elegant figure. She wore no make-up. Beneath her fine arched brows, her eyes, though just a little red from crying, were still as bright as they always had been, dancing and shining with infinite wisdom and boundless charm. The colonel's heart fluttered. This was the first time he had seen this lovely creature as "Madame Wu." Deep in his heart lingered the memory of another lovely creature of five years ago, when she was not yet "Madame Wu" but just "Miss Lin Pei-yao" and her image suddenly rose before his eyes again and tugged mercilessly at his heartstrings. The reappearance of this ghost from the past — and at such a moment as this — seemed so cruel. Without waiting for her reply, he compressed his lips, made another bow, and left hurriedly. He made his way through the babel of voices holding forth on "gold" and "cotton yarn," and into the inner half of the dining-room.

*

As soon as he stepped into the room, he was hailed by two voices simultaneously:

"Look, here's Colonel Lei! You're just in time to help us out."

This simultaneous appeal to a third party worked like a charm and the voices which had been raised in argument suddenly subsided. All eyes turned to Col. Lei as he stood in the doorway, causing the vision of Mrs. Wu Sun-fu's simple beauty to vanish from his mind. He smiled and let his eyes travel over the faces turned towards him, then swung his right hand up in a salute and cut it sharply away. He walked over to the group, clapped a short, fat man on the shoulder and grasped a hand held out to him, and said heartily:

"Not talking about gold and cotton yarn and the prices again, are you? Quite beyond me, all that sort of thing." The short, fat man raised his eyebrows in mock incredulity and laughed, but before he had a chance to say anything, the youngster who had shaken hands with the colonel broke in with:

"Gold and cotton yarn? No, nothing like that — and not the subjects you *are* an expert in, either, like the foxtrot or the tango or the 'Rio Rita' songs. No, we're discussing the military situation. Come on and sit down with us."

"I know you, Huang Fen: you've never got a good word to say for it," said Col. Lei frowning in feigned protest and squeezed in on the sofa beside Huang Fen, who was in European dress. The two had been fellow-cadets at the Whampoa Military Academy and after graduation had been in action together. They were on fairly good terms, but the things in which Col. Lei was interested and at which he excelled were a closed book to Huang Fen; conversely, whenever the conversation came round to Huang Fen's "work," on which he was so keen, Col. Lei, although he could be trusted to respect the other's confidences, always shook his head. Just lately the two of them had seen each other almost every day, but every time they met they quarrelled. Seeing that Huang Fen was in one of his provocative moods again with all these people present, Col. Lei felt ill at ease. He would have liked to escape but he could not just walk out on him.

There was a brief spell of modest silence as if, before the newcomer, nobody was in a hurry to express his opinion now. Meanwhile, the gathering in the other half of the dining-room broke into peals of laughter and someone shouted: "Serve him right! . . . Give him what for!" The voice sounded rather familiar to Col. Lei. He looked to see who it was, but his view was blocked by the short, fat man and another man with a small head perched on a slender neck, sitting with their backs to the huge sideboard at a square table cluttered up with lemonade bottles and fruit-dishes. When the short, fat man saw that the colonel was looking at his companion, he thought that the colonel probably wanted to get to know him, so he quickly rose and said:

"Let me introduce my friend to you, Colonel Lei: Mr. Sun Chi-jen, manager of the Pacific Steamship Company."

The colonel smiled and nodded to Sun Chi-jen, who produced a card. Col. Lei gave it a cursory glance and said:

"Oh, I see, Mr. Sun, you're also running a long-distance bus service in northern Anhwei. Congratulations on your possessing the means of both land and water transportation!"

"Quite so," chimed in the short, fat man, before Sun Chi-jen could reply. "Mr. Sun's a man of energy and vision. Unfortunately, that part of Anhwei is at present involved in the war, and consequently Mr. Sun's business has had to be temporarily suspended. . . . But tell us, Colonel Lei, how is the war really going just lately?"

He had a reputation for engineering friendships between strangers and was a skilful flatterer. He was nicknamed "Red-tipped Match" — not only because he owned the Kwang Tah Match Factory, but also because he had the knack of kindling the flame of friendship. His real name — Chou Chung-wei — was therefore eclipsed in a way by this nickname.

No sooner were the words out of his mouth than several other voices chorused:

"Yes, tell us what really is going on."

Col. Lei smiled slightly and answered vaguely:

"More or less what you read in the papers."

"The papers keep telling us the Central Army is winning, but according to the rumours going round the town things aren't going so well. And if the papers don't give reliable information, their readers get all the more panicky," a man in his forties with a drooping moustache observed in a ringing voice. Col. Lei recognized him as Wang Ho-fu, general manager of the Ta Hsing Coal-mining Company. They had met once in a county in Honan, where the colonel was commanding a regiment.

Everybody nodded agreement with Wang Ho-fu's observation. Sun Chi-jen spoke next, wagging his head on his long neck:

"Perhaps the rumours are exaggerated, but there's no end of wounded coming in just now. One of our boats called at Pukow the day before yesterday and was immediately commandeered to move over a thousand wounded to Changchow, Wusih, and some other places along the railway. According to some of the wounded, things are in a pretty bad way."

"And the Japanese papers say that a certain important man from the South has reached an understanding with a certain important man from the North and that he'll soon stage a *coup d'état*," put in a man named Chu Yin-chiu, the owner of a silk factory, sitting opposite Sun Chi-jen. As he said this, he cast a malicious glance at Col. Lei and at the same time nudged his neighbour, a thin man of about forty named Chen Chun-yi, the owner of the Wu Yun Silk Goods Factory, but the latter just smiled.

Col. Lei was not conscious of the malicious look in Chu Yin-chiu's eyes, nor did he notice the quick exchange of knowing glances between Chu and Chen; nevertheless he felt rather uneasy. As an officer on the active list, he was naturally embarrassed at such a conversation, especially with the indiscreet Huang Fen at his side. After a moment's hesitation he said to Sun Chi-jen:

"I see, one of your boats was used to move more than a thousand wounded, eh? Yes, well, there have been quite a lot of casualties just lately. Sacrifices are inevitable when there's any serious fighting. But don't forget the enemy is being hit even harder. Huang Fen, don't you remember when we were fighting along the Peking-Hankow Railway in '27? The casualties among our 4th and 11th Armies were well over twenty thousand and you saw nothing but wounded men in Hankow and Wuchang. But we won in the end, didn't we?"

By this time he was slightly flushed, and he glanced round at his listeners to see what effect his words had produced. He was now eager to change the subject but Huang Fen jumped in with a sarcastic smile and asked pointedly:

"Did you mention the battle of '27 along the Peking-Hankow Railway? That was altogether different from what's happening now. The casualties were heavy then because our men fought and died with a will. But, today, I'm sure it's quite a different story, eh?"

The colonel's face suddenly blanched, as if a shell had fallen beside him. He stood up, looked all round, sat down again, and managed to cover his nervousness with a smile:

"My dear fellow, don't talk such nonsense!"

"Nonsense, is it? It's the truth, and you know it is. Otherwise, why are you still back here, and not at the front?"

"I'm leaving for the front the day after tomorrow," Col. Lei answered loudly with a triumphant smile. This heroic declaration of his greatly moved his listeners, and was even heard by people in the front half of the room. There was a sudden silence, and several people came round from the other side. They hadn't quite heard what it was all about; they only saw Chou Chung-wei, the "Red-tipped Match," his face wreathed in smiles and his hand on the colonel's shoulder, saying to Sun Chi-jen:

"Mr. Sun, I suggest that we give Col. Lei a send-off tomorrow evening. Do you agree?"

Before Sun Chi-jen could answer, Wang Ho-fu chimed in:

"Col. Lei's an old friend of mine, so let it be on me . . . or, if you insist, we can split it three ways."

Then the group split up. Chou Chung-wei, Sun Chi-jen, Wang Ho-fu and three other men sat at a square table, centred round Col. Lei and exchanging compliments and commonplace politenesses. The other group, consisting of Chu Yin-chiu, Chen Chun-yi and several others with Huang Fen in their centre, were clustered under the windows on the right-hand side of the room, most of them standing, still discussing the military situation. The few people who had come across from the front half of the room joined this group. Huang Fen spoke loudly and unreservedly to one of the newcomers, a man by the name of Tang Yun-shan:

"Yun-shan, do you know what? Col. Lei is going to the front! That proves that they're hard pressed there; otherwise they wouldn't have posted him."

"You're telling me! A few days ago the New First Division, a crack division, was practically wiped out in a battle at Yehchikang. Trained by German officers, and with the most up-to-date German equipment, they still didn't have a chance against the daredevils of Feng Yu-hsiang's Northwestern Army. . . . But what's the colonel going to do at the front? Just be a staff officer?"

"They'll probably give him a brigade, as so many brigade commanders and regiment commanders have been killed in action — at least half a dozen of them so far."

"They say," broke in Chu Yin-chiu, "that an army commander has been killed and another high-ranking officer wounded. Is that true, do you know?" Tang Yun-shan laughed, glancing at

Huang Fen as much as to say: You see how news gets around! Before his chuckle had died away somebody added:

"No, the army commander hasn't been killed. He's seriously wounded. Someone has seen him in the French Hospital on Route Père Robert."

Chen Chun-yi, as if afraid that his listeners might not readily credit his statement, said this in a categorical tone of voice and also appealed to a tall, hefty man, Dr. Ting, to bear him out:

"Dr. Ting, I'm sure you can confirm that what I just said is not just a rumour. I understand Dr. Po of the French Hospital was a fellow-student of yours. You must have heard about it from him?"

All eyes now turned to Dr. Ting. At first he seemed not to understand what it was all about and why Chen Chun-yi was bringing him into it. Then he smiled as if he had just understood and said with deliberation:

"You're right, lots of officers have been wounded. In my profession I have to know the difference between different kinds of wounds — bullet wounds, bayonet wounds, shrapnel wounds, and so forth. But when it comes to commanders of armies or brigades or regiments I don't know one from the other. In the eyes of the surgeon, there's no difference between the wounds of army commanders and the wounds of common soldiers: I just deal with them as they come, and I've no idea who is an army commander or even if there are any."

His attentive audience laughed and then fell silent, as if not satisfied with this answer and Chen Chun-yi shook his head in disappointment. Then a babel of argument broke out again. Suddenly, someone dashed over from the other side — a young man wearing a flannel suit and with his hair sleeked back. He hurriedly squeezed into the doctor's group, where his keen eyes singled out a middle-aged man in a pale-blue silk gown and with a toothbrush moustache. He clapped him on the shoulder and cried excitedly:

"Hey! Chuang-fei, government bonds are dropping again! What are you going to do with your hundred thousand Army Disbandments? There are rumours flying about and everybody's expecting prices to drop even further."

This was even more alarming than the news from the front. Li Chuang-fei, the man with the toothbrush moustache, turned deathly pale. Chou Chung-wei, Col. Lei and the rest of their group hurried over to find out just what was happening. This was an age of speculation. How could anybody with any sum of money resist dabbling in government bonds? People reacted differently to the news of slump. The bears were jubilant and grinned from ear to ear, while the bulls tried hard to swallow their disappointment.

"Government bonds down again! Limit reached and trading closed!" somebody shouted through the door to the people on the veranda, and immediately there was a rush into the dining-room of those who had been expatiating on "gold" and "cotton yarn." With staring eyes and craning their necks, they peered and jostled back and forth, all shouting at once and demanding:

"Is it Tariff going down?"

"Army Reorganization, did you say?"

"Army Disbandment?"

The five or six people who had remained in the front section of the dining-room were also attracted by this sudden turmoil over government bonds, but kept their distance and just looked on. Among them were Fan Po-wen and Wu Chih-sheng, a sociology student and a distant relative of Wu Sun-fu. Fan Po-wen narrowed one eye and muttered:

"Oh, speculation fever, speculation fever! And you, deluge of gold, may you overflow, overflow and smash through your dikes! . . ."

He gave Wu Chih-sheng a hearty slap on the back and boomed:

"Chih-sheng, do you know that smart young fellow in the white flannels that dashed in a moment ago? He's a queer fish. Han Meng-hsiang is his name; stockbroker by profession, but writes poetry as well — quite good poetry, too. Funny combination, that — poetry and lucre! But that's enough about him: let's go and look for Tu Hsueh-shih and Pei-shan. We may find them in the small drawing-room, and the air there may be cleaner and not reek of money-grubbing as it does here."

Without waiting for his agreement, Fan Po-wen dragged Wu

Chih-sheng away with him. By now the dining-room had thinned out, and only a handful of businessmen who were not greatly concerned about the vicissitudes of government bonds and a few people who were more concerned with politics, such as Col. Lei, Huang Fen and Tang Yun-shan, still lingered there, helping themselves to more lemonade and chattering away. But their conversation had now turned from war and politics to amusements — roulette, bordellos, greyhound racing, romantic Turkish baths, dancing girls, film stars. Col. Lei felt more at home on these subjects and threw his reserve to the winds.

*

As midday approached the mourners decreased in numbers and the two bands took turns to play, occasionally stopping altogether. When they did so, the unusual quiet made the people in the dining-room feel as if their ears had been suddenly unstopped and their talk about Turkish baths, dancing girls and film stars sounded unusually loud.

Suddenly, they all fell silent as if ashamed to hear their own smutty talk in the sudden quiet.

Tang Yun-shan involuntarily raised his hand to scratch his bald head, glanced round, and burst out laughing; then all the others quickly took their cue from him and laughed in unison to cover the embarrassing situation.

When the laughter had subsided, Col. Lei turned to Chou Chung-wei and said seriously:

"Everybody is saying that while gold is dear and silver is cheap Chinese industrialists have an excellent opportunity to develop their enterprises and sell their products. How far is that true?"

Chou Chung-wei closed his eyes and shook his head, then opened them again and replied with some bitterness:

"I for one am the victim of dear gold and cheap silver. The raw materials needed for making matches, such as chemicals, timber and boxes, are all imported. The price of gold rises and with it the prices of raw materials: does that do me any good? Shall I use Chinese materials, then? If I do, I am confronted with a whole string of taxes — raw material tax, transit duty, *likin* levy — which make our own raw materials dearer than imported ones. On top of that, Japanese and Swedish matches offer serious competition to Chinese matches, and our people don't know what patriotism is and won't buy Chinese-made goods. . . ."

Chou Chung-wei broke off in the middle of his patriotic speech when his eyes chanced upon a box of "Phoenix" brand matches, made in Sweden, lying beside a silver-plated ashtray. He coughed with embarrassment, pulled out a handkerchief, and wiped his plump face vigorously. Tang Yun-shan sniggered, purposely reached out for the Swedish matches, and lit a Garrick. Blowing out a cloud of smoke, he slapped Chou Chung-wei heavily on the shoulder and said:

"I beg your pardon, Mr. Chou, but to tell the truth, your own products could bear improvement. Leaving out your safety matches for the moment, people say that your red-tipped matches don't strike easily. They won't stand comparison with your esteemed name."

Chou Chung-wei's face reddened like one of his own red-tipped matches, but Sun Chi-jen came to his rescue:

"Mr. Chou's hardly to blame for that. His workers are pretty tough and not easy to manage. Since trade unions have come into being, a lot of factories have been suffering from idleness and have been turning out poor-quality products. Isn't that so, Mr. Chu?"

"That's it, but that isn't all. Take our silk industry, which is in a pitiful state. It's being attacked from four sides: workers demand higher wages; we're up against competition from Japanese silk in foreign markets; taxes at home are crushing; and the bankers are stingy with their loans. I ask you, what hope is there for us, what with high production-costs, dwindling markets, and a shortage of capital? It breaks my heart just to think about it all."

This sad tale came from Chu Yin-chiu. As he told it, the vision of his four enemies hovered before his eyes, with the bankers in the lead trying to strangle him. The Dragon-boat

Festival* would be upon him soon and all the banks and money-lenders that had had dealings with him had warned him that they would make no more advances and that he would have to settle up promptly what was outstanding. But how could he settle up with them? The price of silk was dropping, and his exports were falling off. He drew a deep sigh and went on resentfully:

"Since last year there's been plenty of cash about in Shanghai. Nobody can say money's tight. But our bankers only invest in government bonds and land, ten or twenty million dollars at a time — simply throwing money about. When we industrialists get a bit short and try to get a loan of a paltry hundred thousand or eighty thousand dollars on some securities, they fight shy of us as if we were murderers after their blood. . . . And their terms are so extortionate that — well, they make me see red!"

They all thought Chu Yin-chiu was being rather too outspoken and nobody seemed willing to make any comment. Though Huang Fen seemed sympathetic, he could not help saying:

"I don't see why you have to depend entirely on foreign markets to sell your products. If you do, where do our own silk goods manufacturers get their silk?"

"Yes, I don't see that, either. Mr. Chen, you're the man to explain that to us," Col. Lei interposed, appealing to Chen Chun-yi, the owner of the Wu Yun Silk Goods Factory.

But the manufacturer merely smiled, and Chu Yin-chiu, the silk producer, supplied the answer:

"The silk goods manufacturers used to buy only our second-grade silk, and now they buy very little even of that; they prefer to buy Japanese silk and rayon. For our top-grade silk, we have always had to rely on the French and American markets, but for the last couple of years the Japanese Government has gone all out to encourage the Japanese silk producers to export their silk and cocoons by making such exports duty-free. As a result, Japanese silk has crowded out Chinese silk in Lyons and New York."

---

* The Dragon-boat Festival falls on the fifth day of the fifth lunar month. Chinese merchants used to settle accounts on this day and also on the Mid-Autumn Festival.

Col. Lei and Huang Fen sprang up with exclamations of amazement and looked one by one at the circle of faces around them, hoping to discover in them some sign of agreement, but, to their even greater astonishment, there was not the slightest expression of surprise on any of these faces, as if it were quite natural for Chinese silk goods manufacturers not to use Chinese silk. Chen Chun-yi said with deliberation:

"We've no other way out than to use some Japanese silk or even rayon. Take Mr. Chu's silk, for example. Production-costs are high, which means a high price. If we buy his silk, we pay the high price and 65 dollars and 60 cents purchase-tax per picul into the bargain. As for silk produced in the provinces, the prices have recently gone up as those of local silk have, and we have to pay 111 dollars and 69 cents purchase-tax per picul as well. And all that is just paying for the raw material. When it's been made into silk goods, we have to pay a whole string of taxes in addition — production duty, transit duty, market duty, and what have you. Every move the goods make, there's another tax to pay. Of course, all these taxes are paid eventually by the consumers. But it means our sales are reduced. Now, if we are to keep up our sales, we must find a way of reducing costs, and the only way we can do that is to put in some cheaper raw materials. . . . The consumers complain of high prices, but it doesn't mean that the producers are making anything out of it."

For a while no one spoke. The sound of the trumpets and flutes of the band outside drifted in on the wind, so melancholy that it might have been a dirge for the Chinese silk industry. Wang Ho-fu, who had been silent all the while, suddenly stood up, clapped his hands together, and said jokingly:

"Let's leave it at that, then! Mr. Chen goes on using his Japanese silk and rayon, while Mr. Sun and I, as long as the war lasts, hang on in Shanghai and have a good time going around the dog-tracks and brothels! To hell with industry! Let's enjoy ourselves while we can."

As he was saying this a sudden breath of perfume heralded a young woman in a sleeveless, black silk summer dress in the latest Paris style, which set off her smooth, white skin and her fresh red lips. She did not speak at once, but just stood smiling in the doorway and sweeping her eyes over the gathering.

The first to realize that she was there was the short, fat man, Chou Chung-wei. He sprang up with a cry of delight, waved his arms excitedly, and cried:

"Everybody stand up and welcome Miss Hsu Man-li, the Flower of Society!"

All the men turned round. Before they could assume the special smile which they reserved for greeting attractive women, Miss Hsu was already giggling uncontrollably, her hips swaying and her mouth hidden behind a handkerchief. Col. Lei rose and stepped forward, holding out his hand, and said:

"Miss Hsu, you're late. We'll have to punish you!"

"And how are you going to do that?" asked Hsu Man-li with mock seriousness, swaying her hips once more and tilting her head on one side. She went up to Col. Lei, squeezed his hand, held it a few seconds, then dropped it and turned to greet the others.

The conversation revived magically. Chu Yin-chiu and Chen Chun-yi, who had a moment ago been grumbling, were now beaming. While Hsu Man-li was busy chatting with the others, Chu Yin-chiu leant across and whispered something to Tang Yun-shan, who burst out laughing and looked at her intently. Chu Yin-chiu turned to Chen Chun-yi, deliberately raising his voice:

"I remember now, Mr. Chen. The woman who booked in at the Cathay Hotel with Chao Po-tao yesterday was. . . ."

Hsu Man-li turned her head sharply, riveted her eyes for a fleeting moment on Chu Yin-chiu and immediately looked away again. Without interrupting the smooth flow of her small-talk, she strained her ears to catch every word Chu Yin-chiu might be saying for her benefit.

But it was Chen Chun-yi's voice that she heard next:

"Chao Po-tao? The one who goes in for government bonds? He's a big bull — grabs anything that's going in the way of government stock."

"And anything going in the way of women, too. Only yesterday I met him with a certain widow."

Chu Yin-chiu pretended to lower his voice, but he knew very well that Hsu Man-li could still hear it. He noticed that she seemed to be trembling all over and that even her laugh was rather forced and shaky.

By now Col. Lei was completely engrossed in the "Flower of Society" and their conversation became more and more lively and intimate, until he said something which set her blushing; she tilted her head coquettishly and giggled. Wang Ho-fu, who was sitting nearby, stuck up his thumb in admiration and was going to applaud, when Tang Yun-shan brushed past, grasped Col. Lei by the shoulder and cried:

"I say, old chap! What are you trying to do — kill a bull?"

"Why? I never go in for government bonds," replied the colonel blankly.

"Well, then, when somebody else has already cornered something, why do you try so hard to get her away from him?"

As he said this, Tang Yun-shan burst out laughing himself. Chu Yin-chiu and Chen Chun-yi applauded gleefully and roared with laughter. Hsu Man-li blushed furiously though she pretended not to notice the taunt, and tried to pass it off by calling for lemonade. But everybody guessed what it was all about and the big dining-room rang with peals of laughter.

The ragging might have gone on if Tu Chu-chai had not suddenly appeared.

As if suddenly realizing that they had come to mourn the death of Old Mr. Wu, who was at this moment lying in the next room, and that Tu Chu-chai was the dead man's son-in-law, they all instantly checked their levity and tried to look serious, and some of them yawned.

As usual Tu Chu-chai was all smiles and greeted everybody courteously, at the same time mumbling as if to himself:

"Where's Wu Sun-fu gone? He isn't here either!"

"He hasn't been here," said one of them. Tu Chu-chai frowned in perplexity, excused himself politely, and hurried out again. Then Hsu Man-li slipped out, closely followed by Col. Lei. By now everyone was tired of sitting about, and some of them went out on to the veranda to look for friends. Only Huang Fen, Tang Yun-shan, Sun Chi-jen remained, still huddled on a sofa, talking quietly and seriously about the "Enlarged Conference of the North"* and the strategy of General Yen Hsi-shan and General Feng Yu-hsiang.

*

Failing to find Wu Sun-fu anywhere, Tu Chu-chai went out into the garden, cut across the asphalt drive and clambered up a big artificial hill. In a hexagonal pavilion at the top of the hill two gentlemen were waiting for him rather impatiently. One of them was in his forties, of medium height, with a pointed face and black, piercing eyes. He was Chao Po-tao, the wizard of the stock market, the man Chu Yin-chiu and the rest of them had just been talking about. Seeing Tu Chu-chai panting up the steps, he said to his companion:

"Mr. Shang, look, Tu Chu-chai's on his own. It looks as if Wu Sun-fu won't bite."

"Mr. Shang" slowly fingered his three-inch bushy beard, but made no reply. Sixty if a day, he had a square face, large ears and small eyes, and bore himself with dignity. If the Hung Hsien dynasty of Yuan Shih-kai had not collapsed, he, Shang Chung-li, might have qualified for the honour of "Literary Attendant" in the imperial court. As it was, he had abandoned an official career and gone into business and become chairman of the board of directors of a trust company, which he regarded as quite a come-down.

Tu Chu-chai sat down and mopped his brow with a handkerchief, then looked up and said to Chao Po-tao and Shang Chung-li:

"I couldn't find Sun-fu anywhere about the house. He wasn't

---

* In May 1930 Yen Hsi-shan and Feng Yu-hsiang, then warlords in the North, joined with Li Tsung-jen, a warlord in Kwangsi Province, and certain other warlords in the South in the formation of a military alliance aimed against Chiang Kai-shek and launched a full-scale war against him in Honan Province and other places. In July of the same year the Kuomintang politician Wang Ching-wei, in conjunction with Yen Hsi-shan, Feng Yu-hsiang, and the various other warlords who were opposing Chiang Kai-shek, held their Enlarged Conference in Peking, at which they decided to set up a government in opposition to the Chiang Kai-shek régime in Nanking. This military alliance was smashed by Chiang Kai-shek's forces soon after it was formed.

in the ceremony hall nor in his room, nor in the dining-hall. His wife and sisters couldn't tell me where he'd gone. And I couldn't very well go around asking everybody I met, as you'd told me to be careful not to attract too much attention. . . . Well, you might as well tell me all about your plan so that I can talk it over with Sun-fu later on."

"Well, as I told you just now, the idea is that the four of us club together on the quiet to buy long in the government bonds;* but first we must raise four million dollars in ready cash within two days. Mr. Shang and I haven't the necessary capital, but if you and Sun-fu are willing to come in on it, we'll go right ahead with it. If you're not, we'll say no more about it," said Chao Po-tao, talking quickly in Pekinese with a Cantonese accent, while his deep-set eyes flashed a keen glance at Tu Chu-chai to observe his reaction.

"I don't see why you should want to buy long, though. For the past few days, government bonds have been dropping as a result of the war, and although they may come up again some time in the future, you surely don't think the war's going to be over straight away? Anyway, it's an open secret that the government troops are very hard pressed just now along the Lunghai

---

* In those days government bonds were the chief object of speculation on the Shanghai Stock and Bond Exchange. Independent of their face value, their market quotation constantly fluctuated as a result of the ceaseless civil strife. Quotations were also greatly influenced by the manipulation of speculators. Those who expected a change in the political situation in favour of the government would "bull" the market, i.e. buy long, in the belief that prices of the bonds would rise, while those who thought prices would weaken would "bear" the market, i.e. sell short. In addition there were the small speculators who gambled on skilfully-spread rumours or "inside information" — all the tricks and ruses of the big "bulls" and "bears" to influence the market in their favour. So the prices of the bonds went up or down at each session of the Exchange, depending on the buying or selling pressure. Thus, even though political conditions might actually remain unchanged, the cut-throat fight between the "bulls" and the "bears" went on in the Exchange. In these speculative transactions no delivery of the bonds themselves or the total amount of cash involved was looked for. All the money the "bear" or the "bull" needed to have was the amount he thought would be sufficient to cover his net loss by the settlement date. This made it possible for speculators to gamble in bonds involving many times the money they possessed. Such general practice, however, did not exclude the employment by the more powerful speculators like Chao Po-tao, as described in the latter part of the book, of all sorts of political tricks to bring their opponents to ruin.

and Peking-Hankow railways. Small holders are selling out in a rush. Even if you buy in heavily, you won't be able to hold up the prices. Besides, the settlement's only ten days away. Does it mean that you want to do the buying beyond that date? If so, four million won't be enough . . . !"

"That's the way everybody looks at it, but there's more to this than meets the eye: we have a secret!" interrupted Chao Po-tao, cutting Tu Chu-chai short and smiling mysteriously. Tu Chu-chai tilted his head back and closed his eyes as if he were thinking hard. He knew that Chao Po-tao was infinitely resourceful, knew how to bluff his way, and had contacts in the army and in political circles, so perhaps he had got hold of secret information about the military situation. But on second thoughts that didn't seem likely. Tu Chu-chai opened his eyes again only to meet Chao Po-tao's, sharp and cunning. It suddenly occurred to Tu Chu-chai that Chao Po-tao, a bull, confronted with the coming settlement at the Dragon-boat Festival, was probably in a panic about his financial affairs and that his "secret bull company" idea was merely a scheme to save himself. . . . But why was Shang Chung-li going in with Chao Po-tao? The old rogue was not buying long! With these thoughts racing through his mind, Tu Chu-chai looked into Shang Chung-li's face for his answer.

But the old man looked perfectly at ease and raised three fingers to stroke his beard.

"What's the secret?" Tu Chu-chai asked offhandedly, at the same time weighing all the possibilities in his mind. He had almost made up his mind to put them off and make good his escape before he was persuaded to have a hand in their "plot." But Chao Po-tao's answer came as a shock:

"Mr. Shang guarantees that the Northwestern Army will call a halt to their advance. Before the settlement for this month is due government bonds will certainly rise again."

Although Chao Po-tao said this in a very low voice, the news struck Tu Chu-chai like a bolt from the blue, blotting out the din in the garden and the efforts of the two bands. He looked at Shang Chung-li in amazement and asked doubtfully:

"Are you so sure about it, then, Mr. Shang?"

"It isn't a matter of *being* sure: it's a matter of *making* sure," replied Shang Chung-li quietly, stroking his beard and smiling at Chao Po-tao. Tu Chu-chai was still in the dark: the words "making sure" puzzled him. In the ordinary way he had enough confidence in Shang Chung-li when he acted as a guarantor for some business transaction or other, but this case was out of the ordinary and so much would be at stake that he felt he had to make sure of everything. Hesitation and uncertainty were written all over his goat-like face.

Chao Po-tao slapped his thigh and laughed, then leant across and said quietly and seriously to Tu Chu-chai:

"As I was saying, we have a secret. Everybody knows that an army can be bribed to win, but nobody seems to have thought of bribing it to *lose* a battle. What's one defeat more or less if you're getting paid for it?"

Tu Chu-chai could scarcely believe his own ears. He racked his brains, stood up, stretched out his right hand to give Shang Chung-li the "thumbs up" sign, and burst into compliments:

"Mr. Shang, my congratulations on your rare wisdom and acumen! This is really wonderful!"

"So you've made up your mind to go along with us, then. How about Wu Sun-fu? Will you speak to him as soon as possible?" Chao Po-tao immediately urged, wanting to clinch the matter there and then.

But Shang Chung-li saw that Tu Chu-chai was still wavering slightly. He knew that the latter, although he always had an eye for the main chance, was extremely wary, unlike Wu Sun-fu who was fearless and energetic, so he qualified his remarks:

"Although the person who deputizes for us in negotiations with the authorities on the other side has reached agreement on the terms, we wouldn't say that it's irrevocably fixed. Any deal with military men, you know, is necessarily touch-and-go, as they may change their minds at the last minute. My idea is, you'd better talk it over with Wu Sun-fu and get in touch with us later in the day."

"So you've agreed on terms?"

"Yes: three hundred thousand dollars," Chao Po-tao answered with an air of impatience.

Tu Chu-chai stuck out his tongue, withdrew it, and grinned.

"No more, no less. We can't afford more, and they won't do it for less. Thirty thousand dollars a mile. If they retreat ten miles, they'll get three hundred thousand dollars," said Shang Chung-li deliberately, fixing his cunning little eyes on Tu Chu-chai's goat-like face.

For a moment no one spoke; then Tu Chu-chai, the light of determination in his eyes, looked first at Shang Chung-li and then at Chao Po-tao. Simultaneously, the three of them burst out laughing, then put their heads together in an animated conversation.

Meanwhile, on the other side of a pond in front of the pavilion, three young men and two girls were sitting on a lawn in the shade of some willows, debating hotly among themselves. The girls were not taking a very active part in the debate, but their giggles were enough to disturb the geese who were enjoying a siesta on the waters of the pond.

"Let's leave it at that," said a lively cat-faced youngster. "Be quiet, everybody, and I'll run and fetch them." He was Tu Chu-chai's brother Hsueh-shih, an engineering college student.

"Do you agree, Miss Lin?" Wu Chih-sheng asked Lin Pei-shan, who pretended not to hear, but continued to hold Chang Su-su's hands and seesaw backwards and forwards.

Fan Po-wen, standing next to Lin Pei-shan, smiled non-committally.

"No objections? Passed unanimously!" cried Tu Hsueh-shih as he ran off towards the house. Wu Chih-sheng walked up and down with bent head for a while, stopped before Fan Po-wen and challenged him excitedly:

"There's another point. Will you take a bet on it?"

"Let's hear it. It may not be worth betting on."

"My point is: can Huei-fang and Ah-hsuan change their temperaments?"

"I won't take a bet on that."

"I will, Chih-sheng, but tell me first what *you* think. Will they change or *won't* they?" interrupted Chang Su-su, letting go of Lin Pei-shan's hand and coming over to Wu Chih-sheng.

"What's the bet — a kiss?"

"If I win, I certainly don't want to kiss *your* ugly mug!"

Fan Po-wen and the others roared with laughter, except for Chang Su-su herself, who just stood there hopping on one foot. She was thinking about Huei-fang's reserve and her staid expression. It was enough to exasperate you and make you feel sorry for her just to look at her. As for Ah-hsuan, although he was fairly good-looking, he was rather scatter-brained — sometimes he seemed bright enough, but at other times he was terribly muddle-headed. Huei-fang and Ah-hsuan were two monuments to the educative influence of the late Old Mr. Wu and his *Supreme Scriptures of Rewards and Punishments*. It made her feel uncomfortable to think about them and she forgot all about the bet. Just then Tu Hsueh-shih ran back with two men in tow: Prof. Li Yu-ting and Mr. Chiu Chun, Wu Sun-fu's legal adviser.

From the hexagonal pavilion on the artificial hill opposite, the laughter of Chao Po-tao, Shang Chung-li and Tu Chu-chai carried down to the lawn. Li Yu-ting looked up at them, then tugged at Chiu Chun's arm and whispered:

"Look! The Big Three of the financial world. What do you think they are up to now?"

Chiu Chun smiled and was going to answer, when Wu Chih-sheng's voice broke in:

"Mr. Chiu Chun and Prof. Li, we want your opinion. . . . Speak frankly, as I've got a bet on with Fan Po-wen: Can a man protect his national interests and his class interests at the same time? Is there a conflict between the two?"

"Mr. Chiu and Prof. Li, don't be afraid to state your views squarely. This is very important, as Wu Chih-sheng and Fan Po-wen have a bet on it," Tu Hsueh-shih put in emphatically, glancing at Lin Pei-shan, who tried to look indifferent. Squatting down, she began picking up fallen rose petals and arranging them in the character *wen*.

Chiu Chun shook his head modestly, so Li Yu-ting spoke up first:

"That all depends on the social status of the man concerned."

"Yes, we've had examples of that. Suppose, in view of the depression in the silk industry, Wu Sun-fu said to his workers: 'Our production-costs are so high that we can't compete with

Japanese silk producers and our silk industry'll be ruined. To cut the cost of production we must cut your wages. For the sake of our national interests, you'll have to bear up and be content with lower wages.' The workers would reply: 'The cost of living's so high that we don't get enough to eat as it is. If you cut our wages any more, we're done for. You mill-owners have plenty of money and never know what starvation is. If you want to look after our national interests, you'll have to put up with a cut in your profits.' So you see that there is something to be said for both sides, but on both sides there is a clash between national and class interests."

"Of course, starvation is no joke . . ." began Li Yu-ting, then hesitated and raised a hand to scratch his head. Chang Su-su looked hard at him, but he was not conscious of it. There was silence as everybody waited for him to finish the sentence. Across the pond, the pavilion echoed with another gust of laughter. Li Yu-ting looked up with a start and then went on to finish what he was saying:

"On the other hand, capitalists must make a profit. No profit, no business!"

Wu Chih-sheng laughed exultantly and turned to Fan Po-wen:

"There now! What did I say? This is just what I expected from Prof. Li. My dear poet, you've lost one bet already. Now for the other one. If you'll just state your side of the case. . . . Su-su, see that Pei-shan doesn't run away."

Fan Po-wen smiled icily but remained silent, so Tu Hsueh-shih jumped in and spoke for him:

"The workers put in a demand for higher wages. The boss says: 'If you want higher wages, you'd better go and work somewhere else. I can easily get someone to replace you.' But the workers refuse to go and insist on their demand for higher wages. . . . There's a problem for our legal adviser."

"Both capital and labour are under contract. Neither can force the other to do anything against their will."

Wu Chih-sheng and the others laughed and even Fan Po-wen joined in. Lin Pei-shan, who had been squatting on the ground and pretending not to take any notice, sprang up and was about to make her escape, when Wu Chih-sheng and Chang Su-su blocked her way, crying:

"Now, now. Don't run away! The poet's absolutely defeated and you must settle his account for him, otherwise we'll take our case to the lawyer here. Tu Hsueh-shih, you're our guarantor and you must fulfil your obligations."

Lin Pei-shan giggled but refused to speak. At the first opportunity, she slipped under Chang Su-su's arm and raced away along a parti-coloured cobbled path, skirting the pond and turning right. With a surprised "oh!" Chang Su-su followed in pursuit. Fan Po-wen, holding Wu Chih-sheng by the shoulder, said:

"Don't get excited. Just wait. Tu Hsueh-shih's going to pass judgement."

"What? A guarantor be a judge? Simply isn't done. Besides, we didn't agree on this beforehand."

"It was agreed: 'If the lawyer's or the professor's views prove inconclusive, Tu Hsueh-shih shall arbitrate.' Now I consider both their views ambiguous. It isn't fair just to say that I'm the loser."

"Both views are irresponsible and superficial, since they didn't give any reasoning," broke in Tu Hsueh-shih, his cat-like face suddenly very stern.

Not only was Wu Chih-sheng surprised at this, but the lawyer and the professor were also puzzled. Everybody clustered round Tu Hsueh-shih, waiting for him to go on.

"All this talk about national interests, class interests and capital-and-labour contracts is a lot of nonsense — mere words. I recognize only the state. And the helm of the state must be in the firm grip of an iron hand. What's important is to get things done, not to theorize about them. No one should be permitted to oppose these men who rule the state with an iron hand. For instance, if Chinese silk can't compete with Japanese silk, then it's the duty of the rulers to cut the workers' wages on the one hand and on the other to compel the Chinese capitalists to sell at the lowest possible prices, so that Chinese silk can hold its own against Japanese silk in the European and American markets. If the capitalists refuse to obey, then the state should confiscate their factories."

Tu Hsueh-shih concluded his speech abruptly, glaring around and swaggering as if he were the "iron hand."

His listeners smiled, but no one spoke. They heard Chang Su-su and Lin Pei-shan giggling as they approached from the clump of trees at the other end of the pond. Fan Po-wen looked round at the sound of the voices, then clapped Tu Hsueh-shih on the shoulder and jeered:

"Jolly good! But unfortunately, you're neither a capitalist nor a worker, still less a 'man of iron hand.' And what's more, your little speech was just as 'superficial and without any reasoning' as anything else. Please remember, my bet with Wu Chih-sheng wasn't about what should be done, but who could guess what the lawyer and the professor were going to say. . . . But let's say no more about this betting business — let's call it a day."

With this Fan Po-wen ran off to meet the girls.

"Oh, no, my dear poet, you don't get away with it as easily as that," shouted Wu Chih-sheng, running after Fan Po-wen, while the lawyer and the professor stood there and laughed.

Just as Fan Po-wen and Wu Chih-sheng got up to Chang Su-su and Lin Pei-shan, they saw three men coming towards them: Chao Po-tao, Shang Chung-li and Tu Chu-chai. They were talking in an undertone as they walked along, but, at the sight of the youngsters, they fell silent and turned aside without a word along the cobbled path towards the willow grove, at the same time making a detour on their way back to the house to avoid being seen by Chiu Chun and Li Yu-ting. But Li Yu-ting's sharp eyes had spotted them and, tugging at the corner of Chiu Chun's jacket, he said quietly:

"Look, the Big Three of the financial world! See them? Something big in the air, by the look on their faces."

"Perhaps they're worried about the 'man of iron hand' who's just been born in our midst!" replied Chiu Chun with a smile, and Li Yu-ting laughed. Absorbed in his own thoughts, Tu Hsueh-shih did not hear the quip meant for him.

*

On the stone steps in front of the ceremonial hall Tu Chu-chai ran into a new arrival, a distant relative of the Wu family, Lu Kuang-shih by name, a stockbroker and assistant manager of the Great Asia Trust Company. The moment he saw Tu Chu-chai he buttonholed him and whispered in his ear:

"I've got a tip for you. The Central Army's fighting better now, and government bonds will soon be up again. Strictly confidential! But most people are still expecting a fall, and small holders are anxious to sell out while they can. Why not make the most of this opportunity and buy up several hundred thousand? I know you've only been going in for gold bars, but now you must try government bonds as well just this once. Go on, do yourself a bit of good while you've got the chance."

Lu Kuang-shih may have given this tip with the best of intentions, but it only scared Tu Chu-chai, who was contemplating having a hand in the secret bull-company. As he listened, he paled and began to have misgivings: surely the news of Shang Chung-li's plan hadn't leaked out already? Or was the Central Army in fact getting the upper hand now? Were Chao Po-tao and Shang Chung-li playing a shabby trick on him? Or was this man Lu Kuang-shih just rumour-mongering for his own ends? Tu Chu-chai was in a quandary and did not know what to say. He tipped Chao Po-tao a wink — he had in fact only meant to look and see what his reactions were, but somehow the look turned into a wink. Even an old hand like him had made a blunder this time.

Fortunately, he was rescued from his embarrassment by the arrival of the butler Kao Sheng, who hurried over to him and said:

"Mr. Tu, the master would like to see you. He's in the library."

Relieved, Tu Chu-chai answered "Thank you" and turned to Lu Kuang-shih:

"Excuse me a moment. I'll be seeing you later. Please make yourself at home in the dining-room. — Kao Sheng, get Mr. Lu some tea."

Having got rid of Lu Kuang-shih, he and the other two went out into the garden again and found a quiet corner, where they held another whispered conference, their faces lighting up with pleasure.

"Well, I'm off to see Sun-fu. Po-tao, you'll deal with Lu Kuang-shih; you can find him in the dining-room. Mr. Shang, you'll get things straightened out with the man from the North," said Tu Chu-chai finally, and the three men went their different ways.

When he reached the library Tu Chu-chai was surprised to find Wu Sun-fu sitting there with his brows knitted in a deep frown. He had not looked so upset as this even when Old Mr. Wu had died the night before. Directly Tu Chu-chai sat down, and before he could say a word, Wu Sun-fu tossed over a sheet of paper. It was a telegram, and it read: "Unrest among peasants, troops inadequate, situation critical, advise measures, urgent, Fei, 7th."

Tu Chu-chai paled. Though he had not so much property at stake in their home town as Wu Sun-fu had, it was inevitable that he should feel upset to hear that the place where he had his ancestral home and graveyard was now in danger. Laying down the telegram, he glanced at Wu Sun-fu and said briefly:

"What do you propose to do, then?"

"I'll do what's humanly possible. It's lucky the old man and Huei-fang and Ah-hsuan got out two days ago, otherwise I shouldn't know what to do with them. At the moment I've only a pawnshop, a local bank and a rice-mill marooned there, and although they're worth more than a little, they're not a matter of life or death. . . . You ask what I propose to do. Well, I've wired my agent Fei Little Beard to put my ready cash in a safe place and move out what goods he can from the business premises. Of course, it may be that it's only a false alarm and that things will settle down again soon. That garrison is under strength and something ought to be done about it; we should send a joint telegram to the provincial government to send down the security troops immediately to restore order."

Wu Sun-fu did not look quite like his usual self. He had been rambling on before he came to the point — the wire to the provincial government. He handed Tu Chu-chai the draft which he had made and pressed the bell on the wall behind him.

The door opened softly and two men entered, the butler Kao Sheng and Mo Kan-cheng, the chief clerk in the factory.

Wu Sun-fu frowned even more when he saw that Mo Kan-cheng had come without being sent for and snapped sternly:

"I didn't send for you. I told you that you needn't come here today, but stay and look after the factory. It's more important for you to remain there."

The old clerk was frightened out of his wits by this reproof. He simply answered "Yes, yes" and stood rooted to the ground.

"Has anything gone wrong in the factory?" asked Wu Sun-fu offhandedly, relaxing his features. He was not thinking of the factory, but of his home town and the threat of a riot among the peasants. Mo Kan-cheng's tremulous reply came as a surprise:

"Things in the factory are none too pleasant, sir. . . ."

"What? Out with it! What's the matter?"

"Perhaps it isn't all that important, but . . . but I don't like the way things are shaping. We haven't yet announced the wage-cut, but the women have somehow found out about it. Since this morning they've been . . . well, they've been going slow. So I came to ask you, sir . . . what should we do about it?"

Wu Sun-fu's face suddenly darkened and he sat speechless, the purplish pimples on his face turning livid with rage. All of a sudden he sprang up and bellowed like a madman, cursing the women workers and cursing Mo Kan-cheng and his subordinates:

"So they're going slow now, are they, the bitches? I'll show them a thing or two! And what have you lot in the office been doing about it all this time? Huh! all you're fit for is loafing about and skylarking and flirting with the girls! Perhaps it was one of your fools who let on about the wage-cut."

Mo Kan-cheng just stood there hanging his head and hardly daring to breathe. His helpless manner served only to fan the flames of Wu Sun-fu's rage: his right hand on his hip and his left clenched and poised on the edge of the steel desk, he glared round the room with eyes ablaze as if looking for something to fix his teeth into. He suddenly discovered the butler Kao Sheng standing stiffly in the corner, and immediately turned on him furiously:

"What are *you* doing here?"

"I just came in when you rang, sir."

Wu Sun-fu remembered the telegram and realized that Tu Chu-chai was still there, sitting on the other side of the table. By now he had glanced through the draft and was engrossed in his own thoughts, his eyes closed and a cigar jutting from the corner of his mouth.

Wu Sun-fu picked up the telegram and handed it to Kao Sheng, waved him away and said:

"Send this off at once — the quicker the better."

He sat down on the chromium-plated swivel-chair, scribbled a few words on a slip of paper, then crumpled it up and threw it into the waste-paper basket. He hesitated, his pen poised.

Tu Chu-chai opened his eyes, and when he saw Wu Sun-fu's perplexity he said softly:

"Sun-fu, I think the smooth way is better than the rough."

"That's what I was thinking . . ." replied Wu Sun-fu, a little calmer now. Rolling his pen between his fingers, he turned to Mo Kan-cheng:

"Kan-cheng, sit down and tell me all about what happened this morning."

The old clerk, who was quite used to Wu Sun-fu's moods, realized that he could now speak up boldly and that there was no longer any need to keep up the pretence of terrified helplessness, so he sat down at once in an easy-chair beside the desk and began slowly:

"This morning at about nine o'clock, forewoman No. 2, Wang Chin-chen, ran into my office to report that Yao Chin-feng in Row No. 12 had made a mistake and was being insubordinate about it. Then forewoman No. 9 Hsueh Pao-chu asked Yao Chin-feng to come along to my office. Then what should happen but that all the women in Row No. 12 switched off their machines and were backing up Yao Chin-feng by making a disturbance. . . . I was just going along to see what I could do to stop it, when I heard a lot of shouting and screaming, and up came Hsueh

"So they're going slow now, are they, the bitches? I'll show them a thing or two!"

Pao-chu dragging Yao Chin-feng along with her. By this time all the women had switched off their machines. . . ."

Wu Sun-fu frowned, looked sharply at Mo Kan-cheng, and cut him short impatiently:

"Make it brief. Just tell me how things stand now."

"At the moment only a small proportion of the five hundred and twenty filatures are running . . . and the women who *are* still working are only spoiling the cocoons."

At this Wu Sun-fu growled angrily, sprang up, dropped back into his chair, and asked quickly:

"What's the reason for this go-slow?"

"They're demanding that we sack Hsueh Pao-chu."

"Why's that?"

"They say she hit Yao Chin-feng. . . . And they are demanding a cost-of-living allowance, too. They made the same demand once before when the price of rice went up to twenty dollars per picul and now they're bringing it up again."

Wu Sun-fu snorted and turned to Tu Chu-chai. "Chu-chai, I can tell you it's no fun running a silk factory. When rice goes up, the workers demand a cost-of-living allowance; but when the price of silk drops, we make a loss — but no one makes us a silk allowance! Right: go back, Kan-cheng, and tell them this: if they want a cost-of-living allowance, I will close down my factory."

Mo Kan-cheng said "yes" but his little rat's eyes stared at Wu Sun-fu with great embarrassment.

"What now?"

"Yes, sir . . . er . . . excuse me, but I'm afraid that if you tell them you're going to close down the factory just at this moment, it might cause trouble. . . ."

"What do you mean?"

"This time, the women seem to be more united, as if it's all been arranged beforehand."

"Pooh! What are you — a lot of zombies? You haven't a clue what's going on until something happens, and then you come crying to me. Forewoman No. 2, Wang Chin-chen, and the overseer Pockmarked Li both get my special bonus, don't they? Yet they don't seem to be doing much in the way of keeping an eye on the women. You'd think I had too much money and nothing to spend it on, the way I keep feeding those dogs for nothing."

By now Mo Kan-cheng had plucked up courage again and spoke up. "They do do their best, both of them. They're continually watching and listening to see what the women are up to, but you'd think they had the word 'informer' written all over them: everywhere they turn they come up against a brick wall and they find it difficult to ferret out any information at all. I'm telling you, sir: you'd think the women were possessed, the way they go on. Yao Chin-feng used to be quite obedient, but now she's one of the ringleaders. All you hear in the workshop now is: 'The last time we demanded a cost-of-living allowance, you soft-soaped us with false promises, but this time we really mean business! Don't you dare tell us you're going to cut our wages. We want a cost-of-living allowance. D'you hear? A cost-of-living allowance!' I hear they're having trouble in other factories, too. You'd think the workers were all possessed by devils."

"Possessed by devils, eh? Ha, ha! I can tell you what sort of devils, too: high cost of living and hunger. But there's another devil, a much more terrible one than that: world depression and slump. . . ."

Wu Sun-fu broke into loud, cynical laughter, pain and despair written all over his purplish face; but he quickly recovered his customary firmness and determination. Gesticulating excitedly, he went on, his lips twisted in a savage smile.

"Very well, you devils — we'll see! Think I'm done for, eh? Oh, no! We'll have a go first! — Now, Kan-cheng, how did the women come to know about the wage-cut? One of your people in the office must have let on about it!"

Mo Kan-cheng was taken aback by this question, and cold shivers ran down his spine. He hesitated, then a sudden idea struck him, and he said furtively:

"I suspect Tu Wei-yueh. That young man has gone daft just lately. All he thinks about all day is Chu Kuei-ying, one of the girls in Row 19. People are always seeing him going in and out of her house. . . ."

The door suddenly opened, and the voice of Fu-fang interrupted Mo Kan-cheng in the middle of what he was saying.

"Sun-fu, the men from the International Undertakers have arrived with the funeral things, but I don't think the coffin is quite good enough," said Fu-fang, pausing in the doorway and looking in at her husband sitting opposite to her brother.

"Hold on; I'll be with you in a minute. Chu-chai, could you just go and have a look at it?"

Tu Chu-chai, waving a hand, spoke to his wife through the cloud of cigar-smoke:

"We shan't be long. It's early yet. If the coffin's no good, we can change it in plenty of time."

"Early? It's a quarter past twelve already and the visitors are having lunch."

So saying, Fu-fang went away again. Wu Sun-fu turned to Mo Kan-cheng and snapped out his orders:

"Now, go straight back to the factory and put up a notice announcing a paid half-holiday this afternoon in memory of the late Old Mr. Wu. See to it that the women go home — we don't want them staying in the factory and making trouble. But you and your men will have some special work to do this afternoon: you will go about among the women, work on them separately and break their unity. You've got until this evening to get the job done. Meanwhile, you can call in policemen from the Bureau of Public Safety to guard the factory, and send a report to the Bureau of Social Affairs about the trouble. As for that fellow Tu Wei-yueh, send him round to me this evening. Got that? All right, then, make yourself scarce."

Having got rid of Mo Kan-cheng, Wu Sun-fu stood up, drew a deep sigh, and muttered to himself:

"Damn this factory business! I should have had a bank instead of a factory right from the start. If I had, I could have had something by now to show for it, with my ability and capital. The Shanghai Commercial and Savings Bank only had a hundred thousand dollars when they started up, and look at them now. . . ."

He paused and stroked his chin, then pulled himself together and smacked his right fist into his left hand.

"No! I must carry on! There are not many of China's national industries left: you can count them on the fingers of one hand. And the silk industry is especially important to the future of the nation. . . . If only the country were something like a country and the government were something like a government, Chinese industry could really do well in the future. . . . Chu-chai, I've got an idea, but there's no time to tell you about it just now. Let's go and see the coffin they've sent first."

"Just a minute. I've got something important to tell you, too."

Tu Chu-chai took the cigar-stub out of his mouth and stood up. He moved closer to Wu Sun-fu and told him the whole story of the "plot" devised by Chao Po-tao and Shang Chung-li. When he came to the end, he asked, "Now, Sun-fu, do you think there's a catch in it? If you won't go in, I won't either."

"A million each? Half the sum cash down today?" Wu Sun-fu asked rather non-committally and with a straight face.

"Yes, that's their idea. Chao Po-tao's plan is this: this afternoon, he'll sell out three million short to bring the price down even more. . . ."

"Yes, that would certainly do the trick. There may be a drop of two or three dollars. Then we cover, I suppose?"

"No, not yet. In tomorrow's first session, we'll sell another — five million short, in Chao Po-tao's name."

"Oh! Then the slump will set in. If Chao Po-tao, the famous bull, sells, the small-fry holders will panic and rush to sell out. Then, of course, when people see the market is falling, a lot of new bears will be coming on the scene."

"Exactly. So we'll wait until tomorrow's afternoon session before we begin covering. We'll cover slowly and in small lots, here and there, so as not to attract attention. When we get to within a few days of the settlement, we should have collected at least fifty million. . . ."

"And then the news of the Northwestern Army's retreat will suddenly break and there'll be an uproar!"

"Exactly. Then all the small-fry will rush to buy and turn bulls. With the settlement and the Dragon-boat Festival only a few days off, the bears will also be anxious to cover, faced as they will be with a rapid rise."

"Then we'll unload our fifty million, and they'll look on us as their saviours!"

At this the two of them roared with laughter together, their eyes gleaming with delight and excitement.

Wu Sun-fu stopped and said briskly, "Done! Let's go in and win! But we are making it so easy for the big bull Chao Po-tao to take advantage of this deal, and make a packet out of it for himself. We must put forward our own terms, in addition to what we shall gain on the bonds. Let's go and find him and talk it over."

With these words they left the library. The "great scheme" which Wu Sun-fu had been turning over in his mind for some time had now flooded his entire consciousness.

III

IT was two o'clock in the afternoon. The sky was cloudy and the heat oppressive. The International Undertakers had not yet delivered the coffin ordered by Fu-fang — one with a thick pane of glass let into the lid so that Old Mr. Wu's remains could be seen. The two sisters, Fu-fang and Huei-fang, had rejected the first coffin delivered as unsatisfactory and ordered another, so the shrouding ceremony had to be put back one hour. Meanwhile they kept hurrying the undertakers up both by telephone and by special messengers. The Wus were all ready and were only waiting for the arrival of the coffin from the undertakers to complete the ceremony.

Many of the mourners had already gone and there remained only a few relatives and close friends and a number of people who had no other calls on their time. They were chatting in scattered groups in the cool of the garden and waiting patiently for the shrouding.

The dining-room was now deserted except for a handful of servants clearing away the beer and lemonade bottles and sweeping up the litter of fruit peel on the floor. As they worked, they grumbled among themselves:

"Our master's a hasty one and no mistake! He even tries to rush an important thing like his father's funeral in one day. You just can't do things like that!"

"Ah, that's his quick temper makes him like that. Kao Sheng says he was in a filthy temper in the library this morning — frightened Mr. Mo from the factory out of his wits, he did! Old Mr. Wu was lucky to get out when he did: another couple of days and it would have been too late. I hear a telegram came this morning saying that the peasants are up in arms down there in the country. That's why he's in such a state, I suppose."

This remark was made by Li Kuei. He had originally been a footman to Mrs. Wu Sun-fu's parents and, after their death, had come over to the Wu household. If the thirty-odd servants in the household could be said to have party affiliations, then Li Kuei was on the side of his mistress.

"They've spent more than five hundred and sixty dollars today on cars and tips alone. And the guests got through thirty dozen bottles of beer and lemonade," said another servant, changing the subject.

"I expect the tip for us will be at least a thousand dollars," said Li Kuei. At the words "a thousand dollars" everyone cheered up, but in a moment their despondency returned, for they knew from experience that the tip would be divided up among the servants according to their grades and that even if it were divided up equally, it would have to go round among more than a hundred when you include the ushers, musicians, masters of ceremonies and all the others hired for the occasion, so that in the end each one would get only a miserable little sum. At this prospect they all became half-hearted in their efforts and were even more lethargic than before the tip was mentioned. They were just about to give vent to their resentment again when someone came in.

It was Fan Po-wen, looking no more cheerful than the despondent servants. He stopped in the middle of the room, wheeled round, and muttered to himself:

"Why, there isn't a soul here! I say, Li Kuei, have you seen Miss Pei-shan anywhere?"

But he was off without waiting for a reply. He went through the other section of the dining-room, out on to the veranda, then into the drawing-room looking round with wide eyes. The room was rather quiet just now, and he found none of the ladies there. Several women servants were keeping vigil, sitting on a bench against the wall and looking like a row of black clay figures. The body of Old Mr. Wu was lying on its bier in the centre of the room, heaped about with mounds of flowers among which large blocks of ice glittered coldly.

Fan Po-wen shivered in spite of himself, quickly pushed through the white curtains out on to the stone steps in front of the house. He drew a deep breath and looked up at the sky, a cold feeling of loneliness and desolation flooding his poetic soul.

By the archway over the stone steps the funeral musicians were dozing and hugging their instruments. After hours of hard work they were now snatching forty winks while they could and saving their energy for a final effort at the shrouding ceremony.

Fan Po-wen found everything an eyesore: it was all so conventional, vulgar and disgusting that he could hardly contain himself. Just then, Wu Chih-sheng came running up the asphalt drive full of excitement, as if he had made a discovery. Seeing Fan Po-wen standing there alone, he grasped him by the arm and dragged him off with him. Following him absently, Fan Po-wen asked, "Have you seen Pei-shan anywhere?"

"I'll tell you about it later. Just now I want you to come along and see something — quite an eye-opener, I assure you!"

Wu Chih-sheng led Fan Po-wen through a lilac grove to a quiet corner on the east side of the garden, where there was a greenhouse, covered over now with a mat awning. To the left of the greenhouse were three foreign-style rooms with open windows hung on the outside with patterned Japanese screens of fine bamboo. From behind the screens came gusts of laughter.

"Why, this is a billiard-room. I don't play billiards, you know," said Fan Po-wen, shaking his head, but Wu Chih-sheng immediately put his hand over Fan Po-wen's mouth and whispered in his ear, "Be quiet. Just have a look, and you'll see what kind of billiards they're playing!"

The two of them tiptoed up to one of the windows and peeped in. A scene of revelry met their eyes. The society girl Hsu Man-li, her feet bare, was dancing gracefully on a billiard-table. Her arms outstretched and one leg held high in the air, so that her whole weight was supported on the point of the other foot, she pirouetted rapidly on the smooth, soft baize, the hem of her dress flaring out like a parasol and revealing her soft white thighs and her round hips sheathed in pink silk underwear. Chu Yin-chiu, Sun Chi-jen, Wang Ho-fu and Chen Chun-yi were sitting on high stools by the billiard-table, clapping their hands and laughing hilariously, while Chou Chung-wei brandished a billiard cue as if he were conducting an orchestra. Suddenly, Hsu Man-li leapt lightly on to the next billiard-table. This feat brought a roar of applause from the onlookers, but just then she seemed to slip. She twisted and swayed as if she was going to fall, but Col. Lei dashed forward and caught her in time, hugging her to his chest.

"No cheating! You shouldn't take advantage of her like that!" protested Tang Yun-shan, balancing Hsu Man-li's high-heeled black satin shoes on his bald head.

Then a riot ensued. The men and the girl struggled together, laughing and shouting hysterically. The four onlookers jumped down from their stools and joined in.

Outside the window Fan Po-wen pulled Wu Chih-sheng aside, frowned and said scornfully, "What's so unusual about that? Is that all you dragged me over here to see? I've seen worse than that!"

"But aren't these people the 'pillars of society' who are always holding forth on propriety between the sexes?"

"Huh! Don't be so naive. They may *talk* about morals, but they still have to dance their death dance. Do you know what's meant by the death dance? Well, as the villages become more and more bankrupt, the abnormal development of the cities becomes faster, the price of rice and gold soars, the civil war becomes fiercer, the unrest among the peasantry more widespread — and the death dance of the rich becomes wilder. There's nothing new about it. Why should we be watching it? We'd be better employed looking for Pei-shan and the others."

Fan Po-wen turned to go, but Wu Chih-sheng pulled him back.

Meanwhile, the billiard-room had become the scene of another performance. Somebody was croaking a song. Wu Chih-sheng hauled Fan Po-wen back to the window. Hsu Man-li was still dancing on the table, this time not so fast. The short, fat man Chou Chung-wei was squatting on the floor and hopping about like a frog, clicking his tongue and balancing Hsu Man-li's shoes on his head. The singer turned out to be Col. Lei; with his chest sticking out and his head thrown back, he could not have looked more earnest and serious if he had been singing a marching-song.

With a glance over his shoulder at Fan Po-wen, Wu Chih-sheng darted to the door of the billiard-room, jerked aside the bamboo screen, burst into the room and shouted:

"Bravo! The latest amusement — the death dance!"

The dancing, singing and hopping stopped dead, and the revellers stood transfixed with surprise. Just at that moment the silence was shattered by the mingled sounds of *sonas*, flutes and trumpets as the funeral music struck up: the shrouding had at last begun. Chu Yin-chiu jumped up and led the way out, shouting as he ran:

"Come on, everybody! They've started."

They all rushed out behind him, including Chou Chung-wei, who had forgotten that he still had the lady's shoes on his head, while Hsu Man-li stamped her bare feet on the billiard-table and shouted for help. The colonel, seeing an opportunity of displaying his gallantry, snatched her up in his arms and followed the crowd as far as the greenhouse, where he retrieved her dainty little shoes for her.

*

When the party from the billiard-room reached the house they found the front steps packed with people. The trees were hung with white paper lanterns which shed a mournful yellowish light amid the greenery and the sky was so overcast that it seemed like evening.

The trumpets were hooting and screeching away so weirdly that they set one's teeth on edge. An attendant with a large bundle of burning incense in his hand, seeing Chu Yin-chiu's party crowding up, began distributing a stick to each of them.

Fan Po-wen took one and immediately let it drop to the ground, then, seeing a gap in the crowd, he pushed his way in. Wu Chih-sheng followed him, brandishing his incense-stick to clear a way.

Tang Yun-shan craned his neck to look round, then winked at Sun Chi-jen over his shoulder and said, "What are we waiting here for?"

"What about going back to the other place?"

"No, but we can cut through the asphalt path round the back way to the dining-room," suggested Chou Chung-wei, looking to Wang Ho-fu and Chen Chun-yi for support.

"Have you noticed? Someone's missing: the colonel and the young lady!" said Chu Yin-chiu with a wink, but his voice was drowned by an even louder blast of funeral music. Chen Chun-yi pulled him along as he followed Chou Chung-wei and the others when they cut through the veranda in front of the dining-room. As they passed the trellis with the banksia roses they spotted Col. Lei and Hsu Man-li emerging from a grove and hurrying towards the funeral hall.

They found the dining-room empty, as they had expected, and the door leading to the funeral hall was closed. The moment Chou Chung-wei opened it a little he was greeted by a combined blast of trumpets, *sonas* and flutes, reinforced by the weeping and wailing of the mourners. He was surprised to find right under his nose a coffin and a heap of funeral paraphernalia. He quickly closed the door again and turned and shook his head.

"I think we'd better stay where we are. What does it matter if there's a wall in between?"

As he said this, he collected all the incense-sticks and without ceremony stuck them into a decorative Foochow lacquered vase on the table, then sank his bulky frame into a sofa. For a while everybody was silent.

Chu Yin-chiu, sitting opposite Chou Chung-wei, puffed away furiously at a Garrick, his eyes closed as if he were thinking hard. Then he suddenly opened them at Chen Chun-yi and said, "If people can't collect their accounts by the end of the quarter, it's all because of the war. Everybody's in the same boat. Surely the local banks you deal with can help you out a bit?"

"As a matter of fact, I've been to see them about it time and again. They only say money is tight and so on and so forth. It's infuriating. . . . I think I might approach Tu Chu-chai later on; perhaps he'll help me out," answered Chen Chun-yi with a sigh. He saw in his mind's eye the ugly, half-dead faces of the bank managers who had refused him loans, and beside them the bland goat-like face of Tu Chu-chai; he felt the latter held a ray of hope for him. But Chu Yin-chiu said coldly and sceptically, with a shake of his head:

"Tu Chu-chai? — Oh!"

"Yes, and what of it? Don't you think there's any hope there? I only need a small sum — even a hundred and twenty or thirty thousand dollars would do," said Chen Chun-yi hastily, watching Chu Yin-chiu's face. Before the latter could answer, Chou Chung-wei chimed in:

"A hundred and twenty or thirty thousand? You call that a small sum? I need only fifty or sixty thousand, and I can't even get that. Whenever we factory owners call on the bankers, all we get is scowls. But that's not surprising, really, when you come to think about it: they naturally prefer to use their capital to buy government securities. One day's work on the Exchange and they've made a hundred thousand dollars. And that's mere chicken-feed to them."

"That's perfectly true," said Tang Yun-shan. "You couldn't say fairer than that. And that's why I always say that the root of the trouble is that the government's off the rails. Once it gets on the right track, all government bonds will go to developing industry. Then finance and industry will really co-operate, which is more than they do now, when all the financiers are interested in is profits. But to bring stability into politics you can't merely depend upon military men. The men who run the industries, the industrial capitalists, should bring their influence to bear upon politics."

Tang Yun-shan was never slow in seizing an opportunity of making propaganda for the party he supported. He had always shown solicitude about industrialists, big or small, and known how to deal with them. Even though his arguments had been heard again and again, he never tired of harping upon them once more whenever the opportunity presented itself. And his invariable conclusion was: "Our Mr. Wang Ching-wei* is strongly advocating democracy and genuinely wants to develop China's industries. China has plenty of money for industry, but

---

* Wang Ching-wei, see footnote, p. 40.

military expenses eat it up." As Wu Sun-fu shared this point of view, a close friendship had lately sprung up between him and Tang Yun-shan.

They had to cut short their conversation when from the funeral hall there came an ear-splitting din of funeral music and wailing, punctuated by a loud hammering on some wooden object. The noise continued, but gradually they got used to it and picked up the thread of their conversation again.

Distracted by worries about the financial settlement coming with the Dragon-boat Festival, Chu Yin-chiu regarded Tang Yun-shan's ideas as sound, but they did not really have any bearing on his own personal problem, which was simply how to carry over his security loans so that he would not have to sell his silk at a painfully cheap price, and so that he would be able to keep his factory running at the same time. In a word, his problem was to obtain ready cash. Though his debts amounted to over a hundred thousand dollars, he had in hand two hundred bales of fine and coarse silk and a large stock of cocoons. On balance, he was not in debt. His creditors had no need to be worried about their money, but you'd think he hadn't a penny to his name the way they kept pressing for repayment.

Chu Yin-chiu felt irked as he thought about all this. He was sure the bankers had a particular aversion to him, and Tang Yun-shan's ideas didn't help him solve his problems. He snorted and said icily:

"Mr. Tang, whatever you may say, I'm sure the people who go in for gold and government bonds have a special sort of conscience. Even if the government issues bonds earmarked for industry, do you think they'll be enthusiastic about buying them? No, of course they won't. The main part of a bank's business is investment. Subscriptions to bonds are investments of one kind. If they give us a loan, we offer them a security and pay them interest, don't we? But they still won't raise a finger to help. So I say they've a queer sort of conscience. . . ."

"Ha, ha, ha, ha! . . ."

Chou Chung-wei's laughter broke in upon Chu Yin-chiu's grumbling. The short, fat fellow sprang up and placed himself between Tang Yun-shan and Chu Yin-chiu with arms outspread as if trying to separate two brawlers.

"Now, now! Stop bickering," he boomed. "No businessman will ever miss an opportunity to make money — the more, the better. Mr. Chu has his difficulties and the bankers have theirs. . . ."

"I agree with you there," broke in Tang Yun-shan, seeing a chance to back up his argument. "The greater part of the bankers' capital is locked up in government bonds. Whenever the bonds fall, the bankers get a nasty jolt, find themselves in urgent need of cash. . . . For instance, Mr. Chu's creditors are now calling their loans. That's why I say all the trouble's caused by the unstable political situation."

"Mr. Sun Chi-jen's just suggested something," continued Chou Chung-wei. "It's a wonderful idea, a very sound idea, indeed. And he isn't joking, either."

As he said this, his face became red with excitement and his voice rose and made everyone look round. Tang Yun-shan and Chu Yin-chiu turned to Sun Chi-jen expectantly.

"Come on, Mr. Sun," urged Chen Chun-yi, "tell us all about it. What do you propose?"

Sun Chi-jen did not reply immediately, but just smiled and drew slowly at his cigar. Wang Ho-fu, who knew what it was all about, could hardly wait any longer. Glancing at Sun Chi-jen for approval, he cleared his throat and outlined the latter's "excellent idea":

"Mr. Sun and I have talked it over several times already. It's quite simple, really. It's like this. We industrialists will club together to set up a bank of our own in order to finance our own enterprises. At the moment cash is pouring into Shanghai from further inland; it's easy enough to sell shares, and we should have no trouble getting deposits. With a million dollars capital and a million or two in deposits, we could easily make a go of it. If we get permission to issue banknotes later on, so much the better. . . . Well, that's the gist of it. We've only talked about it so far: we haven't actually done anything about putting the idea into operation yet. Now that Mr. Chou's let the cat out of the bag, I suppose we'd better talk it over."

Wang Ho-fu, though he had a naturally loud voice, purposely kept it down. What with this and the terrible din from the next room, everybody had to strain their ears to hear what he was saying. Actually, the idea was "quite simple." It was not that the idea itself was new: some industrialists had done it before. What was new was that Sun Chi-jen was advocating the collaboration of men of different trades, not just of one trade — these men, his listeners, for instance, represented widely divergent interests conditioned by their different trades. As they listened in silence to Wang Ho-fu's unhurried exposition, their keen minds quickly grasped this fact and each immediately began to conjure up visions of his own personal schemes being realized by such an arrangement. After Wang Ho-fu had finished, they all sat brooding over his suggestions in silence for a while.

Then Tang Yun-shan, who was not an industrialist, spoke up: "Mr. Sun's plan can't go wrong so long as it is endorsed by powerful men and organized on a large scale, I suggest we approach Wu Sun-fu about it. I don't think we can do it without him. Don't you think that's about the size of it, gentlemen?"

"Yes, that's it! That's just what Mr. Sun and I have said all along," said Wang Ho-fu in his usual loud voice.

They continued their discussion and gradually got round to concrete plans. Chen Chun-yi and Chou Chung-wei, who were not very strong financially themselves, hoped that Sun Chi-jen, as a shipping manager, and Wang Ho-fu, as a mine owner, had plenty of capital which they could easily divert to the proposed enterprise. On the other hand, Sun Chi-jen and Wang Ho-fu thought that the other two, being ex-compradores, must have a decent sum available. But they all pinned their hopes on Wu Sun-fu, who had long been known for his capital, resourcefulness and drive. Chu Yin-chiu, though he talked enthusiastically, had his doubts whether Wu Sun-fu would be willing to come in on it. He knew that Wu Sun-fu was free from pressure from the bankers and that he was comfortably off when everyone else in the silk industry was feeling the pinch. Four or five months ago, before prices had plunged, hadn't he managed to clear a thousand bales in the export market? This had enabled him to speed up production to meet delivery, while everyone else in the industry was thinking of closing down for the time being. But even this happy man had one sorrow: he was short of dry cocoons. As for new cocoons, it had been a bad season and quotations were high. Of course, he could use Japanese dry cocoons, but the Japanese foreign exchange was going up, even though Japanese cocoons were free from import duty, so that, on balance, Japanese cocoons were just as dear.... Absorbed in such calculations as these, Chu Yin-chiu sat pensive and silent.

Suddenly a new idea struck him. He looked at Tang Yun-shan and caught his eye.

"Mr. Tang," he said, "to set up a bank would be our salvation, no doubt; but the government shouldn't just stand by and watch industry go downhill when it is on industry that national prosperity and the people's livelihood depend. You've just said that the government should use all money from bonds for the development of industry.... Of course, this wouldn't be practicable at the moment, but the government could at least issue special bonds to save a particular branch of industry which happens to be in distress. What do you think?"

Chu Yin-chiu said this for reasons of his own. He was of course quite clear about it in his own mind, as he had just spent quite a while working it all out. But Tang Yun-shan did not seem to catch on, and before he could answer, the door of the funeral hall opened and in came Dr. Ting. Rubbing his hands as usual, the doctor said with a sigh of relief:

"It's finished now. The International Undertakers have done a good job. Now that they've done the colouring, Old Mr. Wu lies in his coffin as if he were asleep. His face looks flushed.... Why, it's half past three already!"

Just then two servants came in with platefuls of refreshments: lemonade, ice-cream, iced almond-jelly, fruit consommé, cream layer-cakes, and all sorts of foreign-style delicacies. The table was laden with eatables, and all conversation was suspended while the guests attacked them.

Dr. Ting ran his eyes over the table but shook his head and refused to touch anything. He was quite well-known as a stickler for wholesome food. Tang Yun-shan was about to tease him, when the other door of the dining-room opened and a maid looked in and said, "Could you spare a moment, Doctor?" Mrs. Wu Sun-fu was not feeling well. As Dr. Ting hurried off, Wu Sun-fu came in from the drawing-room to thank the mourners for coming. Seeing him come in, Tang Yun-shan quickly put down his half-eaten cake and cried excitedly, "Ah, you've come just right, Sun-fu! We want your opinion about an important scheme. It was suggested by Mr. Sun Chi-jen and Mr. Wang Ho-fu here."

The two men smiled modestly and outlined their plan. Jerking his thumb towards Tang Yun-shan, Wang Ho-fu laughed and added, "We have only been toying with the idea. We hardly expected that Mr. Tang would bother you with it. You've had a tiring day, but if you're interested, we can talk about it some other time."

"Now's the time!" protested Tang Yun-shan. "Sun-fu is never tired when he is keen on something."

It seemed that he was more enthusiastic about it than anyone else. As he ushered people into the other section of the dining-room he rubbed in once more his theory on industrialists' unity as a condition of political stability. He maintained that if the industrialists had their own bank, that constituted an important step towards their unity.

Withholding his opinion for the moment, Wu Sun-fu listened to Tang Yun-shan holding forth. He knew only too well about the financial standing and abilities of these industrialists before him. There was not much they could do on their own. As for himself, he was not one to underestimate himself. If he went in with them, things would take on a new look, for he had the knack of making ordinary men into men of ability. Only he was not sure at the moment whether these men would unanimously proclaim him their leader. As he pondered, he ran his keen gaze over them to observe the expression on their faces. Seeing that only Chu Yin-chiu was comparatively indifferent and reserved, he took advantage of a lull in the general conversation to ask him:

"What do you think of the plan, Mr. Chu? At the present moment, we silk manufacturers are having difficulties all round.

It has always been my hope that one day just such a bank should be organized to help keep industry on a more even keel."

"Mr. Wu, you're being too modest in asking for my opinion. We're all old friends here and know all about each other. At the moment only you have the necessary resources to get things going, so we naturally look to you to help us out."

Chu Yin-chiu sounded sincere enough, and Chen Chun-yi and Chou Chung-wei were the first to clap their hands in approval. But Wu Sun-fu frowned as it dawned upon him that these three men's idea was not to subscribe for shares in the projected bank, but to get someone else to finance it and supply them with generous loans. Wu Sun-fu was about to reply, when Sun Chi-jen interjected:

"Let's be quite frank about it. My idea is essentially to set up a bank to finance a few specific industries. The usual run of bankers absorbs deposits and speculates in land, gold and government bonds. The most they do for industrialists is to make them occasional loans on securities. But if we set up this bank, we'll go all out to support a few of the more hopeful industries, such as the long-distance coach services in North Kiangsu and the mines in Honan. As for helping out those industries which are stranded at the moment, that'll only be one of our minor functions. . . . I am all for the scheme myself; the only trouble is that I haven't the resources."

Chen Chun-yi and Chou Chung-wei looked at each other in consternation: they never thought Sun Chi-jen would keep a scheme like this up his sleeve all this time before mentioning it. Since they did not feel that any good could ever come of it for them, their enthusiasm began to cool off. Chu Yin-chiu smiled grimly, knowing only too well that Sun Chi-jen's proposal for a bank to finance buses and mines was just "a lot of eyewash." Chu Yin-chiu was very good at guessing other people's thoughts by his own.

However, Wu Sun-fu's eyes gleamed with excitement, for Sun Chi-jen was a comparatively new acquaintance, and Wu Sun-fu had hardly expected that this man with his small head and long neck would turn out to be so far-sighted and unconventional. He felt that he had at last found a fine man after his own heart.

Wu Sun-fu himself was ambitious, adventurous and plucky, and he naturally preferred to work with men of his own calibre. He hated to see good industries go to rack and ruin in the hands of inexperienced, inefficient, timorous or mediocre men, and whenever he came across such bunglers, he wanted to cut them down without mercy and take their enterprises into his own iron hand.

His keen gaze searching Sun Chi-jen's face, Wu Sun-fu nodded thoughtfully. Now he wanted to see whether Wang Ho-fu was equally go-ahead. He turned to Wang Ho-fu on his left and asked deliberately, "What's your opinion, Mr. Wang?"

"On the whole I agree with Mr. Sun; but whatever we aim at eventually, we should keep our plans fairly flexible at first. With things as they are at the moment, I don't think we can expect people to subscribe for shares in a bank set up for the express purpose of financing new enterprises. I think we should run it as an ordinary bank in the beginning."

Wang Ho-fu spoke with his usual bantering smile, which contrasted strongly with Sun Chi-jen's reticence and taciturnity. Northerner as he was, Wang Ho-fu combined a humorous disposition with a great tenacity of purpose.

Wu Sun-fu smiled and struck the arm of his chair with two fingers.

"Done!" he said resolutely. "When you two gentlemen lead the way, I'll follow."

"You're joking, Mr. Wu. It's for us two to follow *your* lead."

"Ah! You three make a good trio!" interrupted Tang Yun-shan, slapping his thigh and laughing noisily, "you see eye to eye and you're evenly matched in strength and skill. Here's an eternal triangle which will succeed!"

He quickly suppressed his mirth and suggested seriously, "As far as I can see, you three should start organizing a consortium. . . ."

As he said this, he turned to Chu Yin-chiu and the other two in case they should feel out of it. "Do you agree with me, gentlemen? And all those who are here now will be the promoters."

These three men, who had been listening in silence, had expected that Wu Sun-fu would reject Sun Chi-jen's wild scheme. Now things had turned out just to the contrary. On top of that

Tang Yun-shan was pressing them to come in. For the moment they did not know what to say, for, apart from the fact that they had no capital to spare at the moment, even if they could obtain some, they would prefer to wait and see before plunging into such an ambitious scheme.

The conversation had taken a slightly embarrassing turn, but they were saved by the arrival of the butler Kao Sheng.

"Mr. Tu would like to see you, sir," he said to Wu Sun-fu. "He's waiting in the small drawing-room."

Wu Sun-fu, apparently guessing what it was about, excused himself and went out, but Chu Yin-chiu caught up with him in the doorway and blurted out:

"You know I've a security loan from Mr. Tu Chu-chai, which is due very soon. I wonder if you'd be good enough to put in a word for me?"

Wu Sun-fu avoided his eye but, before he could answer, Chu Yin-chiu went on, "Just three months' grace. That will do."

"But you know I spoke to him about it only the day before yesterday. We're all good friends and ought to help each other out when we can. But so far as I can see, he's in a tight spot himself at the moment. Money is tight, and he's afraid that things may turn for the worse, so he's calling all loans as they fall due. You aren't the only one involved. . . ."

"In that case there's only one way open to me: I'll have to go bankrupt!"

Chu Yin-chiu said this in such an earnest tone that Wu Sun-fu almost believed him. But a sharp glance at his face told Wu Sun-fu that this was only Chu Yin-chiu's diplomacy. Rather than call his bluff, he said coldly, "It would hardly come to that. Your assets exceed your liabilities, so how can you talk about going bankrupt?"

"Then the only alternative is that I close down for three months."

At this Wu Sun-fu could scarcely conceal his annoyance, for he knew very well that just now every silk factory was like a powder-magazine: it needed only a single spark to set the place ablaze and lead to a general strike throughout the industry. The last thing he wanted was a strike on his hands just when he was speeding up production to meet a contract. Chu Yin-chiu, of course, was aware of all this, and his talk of "closing down for three months" was nothing but a threat. After a moment's hesitation, Wu Sun-fu adopted a different tone.

"I'll do my best for you, anyway. I'll let you know the result later on."

Then, before Chu Yin-chiu could involve him any deeper, Wu Sun-fu made good his escape, a malicious smile on his lips.

*

Tu Chu-chai was waiting impatiently in the drawing-room. He had been taking a large quantity of snuff and sneezed twice. He wandered absent-mindedly over to the door and glanced out just in time to see Wu Sun-fu escape from Chu Yin-chiu. The mixture of anger and misery in his face surprised Tu Chu-chai, who supposed that there had been trouble in Wu Sun-fu's factory or that another telegram had come from the country.

"What's the matter?" he inquired hurriedly, stepping forward. "More trouble?"

Wu Sun-fu smiled bitterly but did not reply. He closed the door and threw himself down wearily on to a sofa.

"Life's just one long battle," he said. "We're walking over a mine field. At any moment you may be blown to pieces!"

Tu Chu-chai paled at what seemed to be a confirmation of his fears. But Wu Sun-fu's manner suddenly changed and he smiled bitterly.

"So that so-and-so Chu Yin-chiu thinks he can play tricks on me, too, eh?" he said with assumed unconcern. "Ha!"

"Oh, Chu Yin-chiu, is it?"

Tu Chu-chai felt relieved and sneezed violently.

"Yes, him. The one you saw just now. He wants you to extend your loan for another three months . . . or rather, at least three months, by the tone of his voice. Apart from that, he thinks he can play a mean trick on me — says he'll go bankrupt or close down his factory. He's trying to intimidate me. He takes us for a pack of fools that he can monkey about with as he likes."

"I see . . . and what did you say to him?"

"I said I would see him later. . . . But, Chu-chai, are you going to give him a further extension?"

"If he absolutely refuses to settle up, there's nothing I can do about it. It isn't much, though — only eighty thousand dollars, and I hold his pledge: a hundred and fifty bales of medium-grade dry silk. . . ."

Before he could finish, Wu Sun-fu jumped up and paced up and down like a hungry caged lion, then sat down again and settled himself lower into the sofa.

"Why bother with him?" he asked sardonically, shaking his head. "You aren't a charitable institution, and you shouldn't let him take advantage of you. — You don't really believe he's short of money, do you? Well, he's not. He's just mean, mean and stupid, and if there's one thing I can't stand, it's a man who's mean and stupid at the same time. I remember some time ago he refused to sell his B-grade silk when the price was nine hundred taels and good enough to cover the cost. Pure meanness! Later on, the price dropped to eight hundred and fifty taels. He imagined it would go up again, and, instead of selling, bought in fifty bales of Szechuan silk. That will show you how stupid he is, though he wouldn't have done such a stupid thing if he hadn't been so mean. He's just not fit to be in business! And he can't manage his factory properly, either. The silk from his factory is very poor — full of hairs. He is ruining the reputation of the whole silk industry. It's a crying shame that a man like that should have all those first-class new Italian machines! . . ."

"What are we to do, then?" interrupted Tu Chu-chai, who was totally ignorant of factory management and was getting impatient.

"What are we to do? Let him have another seventy thousand to make it up to a hundred and fifty thousand."

"What? Another seventy thousand?"

Tu Chu-chai was so startled that he spilt a pinch of snuff all over his lap.

"Yes, I said seventy thousand dollars," said Wu Sun-fu, smiling. "But I don't mean you should extend the old loan of eighty thousand and give him a new loan of seventy thousand on top of that. He must still pay off the old loan when it falls due. What we shall do is to give him a new security loan of a hundred and fifty thousand dollars and deduct the old loan of eighty thousand plus an interest. . . ."

"I really don't understand why we have to go about it in such a round-about way. All Chu Yin-chiu wants is that the old loan should be extended, isn't it?"

"Look here, old man! It's like this. The new loan of a hundred and fifty thousand dollars would be for one month only. As for the pledge, we won't accept any kind of silk, finished, raw, or mixed. We'll accept only dry cocoons. And the agreement will be that in case of default the creditor shall have the right to foreclose. . . . And, besides, you will act only as a middleman and nothing more. We'll say that the new loan's to be negotiated with a certain consortium and that you'll be glad to recommend him."

Wu Sun-fu stopped and fixed his sharp eyes unwaveringly on Tu Chu-chai's goat-like face. He knew that this elder brother-in-law of his was at once suspicious and avaricious and that he could never be straightforward and commit himself to anything. Wu Sun-fu was now quietly waiting for Tu Chu-chai to work things out. Meanwhile, he fell to imagining Chu Yin-chiu's cocoons tumbling into his lap in a month's time. And perhaps in due course of time — say, three or four months' time — even those new Italian machines might come under his own efficient and careful management.

Just then the door of the small drawing-room opened and in came Mrs. Wu Sun-fu, looking rather out of sorts. She sat down quietly in a chair opposite Wu Sun-fu and looked at him as if she had something to say. He remembered that a short while before she had complained of a pain in the chest and had sent for the doctor. Just as he was going to ask her how she was, Tu Chu-chai stood up, sneezed and said:

"All right, I'll do as you say. . . . But, Sun-fu, are you sure his cocoons will make a good enough pledge? What if they don't come to the hundred and fifty thousand dollars?"

Wu Sun-fu burst out laughing.

"Chu-chai," he said, "are you really afraid the pledge's not worth that much? I'm only afraid Chu Yin-chiu won't want to part with his cocoons. I expect they will cease to be his in a month's time, unless he acquires the touch of Midas by then, and then we'll see once more what a fool the man is. Anyway, why is he hoarding nearly two hundred thousand dollars' worth of cocoons in that little factory of his? He bought up so many last year that the prices soared and the rest of us were the losers. It's high time someone relieved him of his cocoons."

"Oh, what a snake you are!" exclaimed his wife, her haggard face lighting up with a dazzling smile.

The two men looked at each other and burst out laughing.

"That's settled, then. . . . There was something else I wanted to see you about — oh, yes: Chao Po-tao rang me up to tell me he'd taken the first step. About the second step, there's apparently been an unexpected change in the market, so we'll have to work out a different approach. He's waiting for us in the Cathay Hotel. . . ."

"Then let's go," said Wu Sun-fu briskly. "We can discuss the consortium idea in the car."

The two of them went out of the drawing-room and after a moment the car could be heard starting up outside of the window.

Left alone, Mrs. Wu Sun-fu gave herself up to day-dreaming and let her thoughts wander. The sound of the car took her back seven or eight years to when she was still Miss Lin Pei-yao, a student at the missionary school, to the time when, for the first time in her young life, she had gone for an outing in a car with some of her school friends — girls in their teens who never dreamed that the wine of youth would one day be drained dry. Their heads were full of visions of valiant knights and handsome princes from *Ivanhoe* and *The Tempest* and of the realm of poesy with its islands, its ancient castles, its great forests and its moonlit balconies. Their school, hidden away as it was on the edge of a spacious park outside the city, seemed to them just such an enchanted land, and there they used to dream their rosy dreams of the future. She herself, Miss Lin Pei-yao, endowed with her scholarly father's idealistic temperament, was especially fond of building castles in the air, and on many a balmy, moonlit night she would lie awake with starry eyes, enjoying the beautiful dreams her imagination conjured up.

But these "midsummer night's dreams" of hers were destined, as such dreams always are, to be short-lived. Her father died after a short illness, and her mother did not long survive him. The realities of life were beginning to invade her virgin heart. Then, just when her whole world had crumbled about her ears, another kind of "tempest," as heroic and tragic as the other, claimed her attention: the stirring movement against the Thirtieth of May Massacre.* There suddenly came into her life a young man who to her eyes seemed like a knight from the Age of Chivalry. She was frightened and delighted. Then this young man, who had flashed through her life like a comet, suddenly disappeared and left her heart-broken.

And after that she had —

At this point in her reverie she shivered and came to with a start. She jerked up her head as if startled and looked all round. The entire room was as luxuriously and fashionably furnished as any woman could wish: large oil paintings on the walls, curios on the sideboard, vases of flowers, expensive furniture and, in addition to all this, a parrot in a cage. Nevertheless, Mrs. Wu Sun-fu felt something was missing. Ever since she had become mistress of this house, this feeling that there was "something missing" had been preying on her mind on and off.

In her student days she had filled her mind with idealistic images from the English classics which she had never since been able to forget. During these past few years she had come to know something of the realities of life, but they had not yet made her realize that her husky, strong-willed husband, with his purplish, pimply face, was one of the knights or princes of the twentieth-century industrial world. These industrial knights and princes might not be able to fence and ride like the knights and

---

* On May 30, 1925, the students and workers of Shanghai held a demonstration in the International Settlement to protest against the killing of a Chinese worker Ku Cheng-hung by the management of a Japanese cotton mill in Shanghai for his part in organizing a strike. The British police in the Settlement opened fire on the demonstrators, inflicting heavy casualties. This atrocity gave rise to a country-wide anti-imperialist movement.

princes of the olden days, but they could do wonderful calculations on the abacus and drive motorcars. But Mrs. Wu Sun-fu could not appreciate this, nor could she come to realize that she herself was far from being a mediaeval "lady fayre."

"Visitor!" croaked the parrot, startling Mrs. Wu Sun-fu out of her day-dream. Standing in the doorway was an upstanding young man in uniform, a suspicion of a smile on his handsome, dignified face and a twinkle in his eye — Col. Lei!

Mrs. Wu Sun-fu looked up with a start: for a split second dream and reality had merged into one in her mind. She could hardly believe her eyes. Col. Lei bowed and came over to her, the sound of his measured tread finally bringing her back to earth. At the same time, her innate sense of duty and politeness immediately took possession of her again and she put on a smile and rose to greet him.

"Why, it's Col. Lei! Do take a seat. . . . You wanted to see Sun-fu? He's just gone out."

"Yes, I saw him go, madame," he replied in a soft, courteous voice. "He asked me to stay to dinner."

Instead of sitting down, he remained standing about a yard away from her, his bright eyes searching her rather bewildered face.

She instinctively smiled and stepped backwards to sit down again on the sofa.

For a moment neither of them spoke, and there was an awkward silence.

Col. Lei dropped his eyes from Mrs. Wu Sun-fu's face to stare at the floor, trembling slightly. Suddenly he thrust his right hand into his pocket, stepped forward, his head still bowed, and blurted out:

"Madame Wu, I'm leaving for the front tomorrow morning. There's hardly any chance of my coming out of it alive. So this is the last time I shall see you, the last time I shall be able to speak to you. Madame Wu, I have something here I'd like to give you."

He lifted his head again and drew his hand out of his pocket. It was a book. He flicked it open in the middle and offered it to her with both hands.

It was a tattered old copy of *The Sorrows of Young Werther* in Chinese, and between the pages was a faded white rose.

Memories of the stormy "Thirtieth of May Movement" launched by the students of Shanghai came flooding back when she saw this tattered book and its faded rose, making her tremble from head to foot. She snatched the book from his hands and stared at him, speechless with emotion.

Col. Lei forced a smile and seemed to sigh. "Madame Wu," he went on, "you may regard the book and the rose as a gift from me, or, if you like, as something you are looking after for me. You see, my parents are dead and I have no brothers or sisters, and practically no close friends. There is only one thing I've treasured all my life: this book with its faded rose. Before I go to the front I want to give these treasures to the person I trust most. . . ."

Mrs. Wu Sun-fu let out a sudden cry and her face flushed.

Col. Lei paused a second, then went on urgently and insistently:

"Madame Wu, I've chosen you to look after them, and I hope you won't refuse them. I can never for one moment forget how I came by the book and the rose. One evening five years ago, an evening just like this, a close, muggy evening, I received this flower from the hand of a most dignified, noble, and lovely lady — my reward for my adoration of her. This book *The Sorrows of Young Werther* has witnessed our — Madame Wu, I hope you won't mind if I say — our love? But, poor student that I was, I dared not hope . . . circumstances would not permit it. Madame Wu, you must have seen that. And then . . . you must see now why I suddenly ran away from the angel I worshipped. I went to Canton and entered the Whampoa Military Academy. Later, I followed the colours from Kwangtung to Peking and rose from company commander to regimental commander. I crawled in and out of piles of corpses, was nearly killed several times and I lost everything except this book and this rose, which I never parted with for one moment. But after I'd escaped from the jaws of death, what did I find when I got back! I searched Shanghai for six months and more before I found my luck was out. Now my hopes are dead and my courage is gone. Madame

Wu, I'm going to battle again — this time to die. But I can't let this book and this rose be shattered to pieces on the battlefield. Now I've found the right person to look after this tattered book and this faded rose for me. . . ."

Col. Lei's voice shook, and beads of perspiration broke out on his forehead. He took a deep breath and sank on to a nearby chair. Mrs. Wu Sun-fu's face had turned pale from red and she gazed at him dumbfounded.

Col. Lei smiled bitterly and suddenly straightened up as if torn by some inner conflict. He stood up abruptly and went up to her again.

"Madame Wu," he said slowly and hoarsely, "I'm glad I've had the opportunity of telling you all this. Now I can die content."

He raised his hand in a salute and turned to go.

"Lei Ming! Oh, Lei Ming!"

Mrs. Wu Sun-fu had sprung up and called after him in a quavering voice.

Col. Lei stopped in his tracks and wheeled round. But she had nothing to say to him. Her face crimsoned, her eyes swam and her chest heaved violently. Suddenly she stretched out her arms; Col. Lei ran to her and she threw herself into his arms and buried her face in his shoulder. Col. Lei bent his head and their lips came together.

"My dear!" squawked the parrot, startling them out of their embrace. Mrs. Wu Sun-fu started as if woken from a dream and pushed Col. Lei away; then, clutching the book to her breast, she ran out and upstairs to her room, where she flung herself on the bed. Soon the white embroidered pillowcase was wet with her hot tears.

"Now I've found the right person to look after this tattered book and this faded rose for me...."

IV

ON the afternoon of Old Mr. Wu's funeral, in the town of Shuangchiao, about seventy miles from Shanghai, Tseng Tsang-hai, Wu Sun-fu's uncle on his mother's side, was reclining on an opium-couch in his large, gloomy house, having one of his habitual fits of temper.

Now in his fifties, this senior member of the landed gentry was known in those parts as the "Local King." Since at the age of forty, he had had his first and only son, whom he doted on, his greed, avarice and meanness had become worse than ever. Unfortunately, the boy was a good-for-nothing, with the result that his father, who should have been enjoying his retirement by now, had to continue to manage the household affairs on his own and even bother himself with such trivialities as getting in provisions.

Besides, for the last two or three years he had had a run of bad luck. When for the first time the Kuomintang flag had flown over the town of Shuangchiao, there had been a great deal of noisy but serious shouting of such slogans as "Down with the despotic landlords and gentry!" Greatly alarmed, Tseng Tsang-hai had fled from the town and gone to stay in Shanghai for a while. Later, the youngsters who had been responsible for the disturbance either escaped or were arrested, and Shuangchiao returned to normal again. But from then on Tseng Tsang-hai's régime did not continue to go unchallenged, for another group of youngsters far from shouting "Down with the landlords!" installed themselves in the town as "New Nobility" and began to usurp many of the privileges which Tseng Tsang-hai had enjoyed exclusively until then. He found it hard to believe that his own status had been so undermined and reduced. The "New Nobility" not only had as much say in the running of the town as he did, but even seemed quite anxious to oust him completely. Whenever he was thwarted by them he would grumble, "When you're old you're treated as a back number." His only consolation was a rather forlorn hope about his son's future.

This afternoon, Tseng Tsang-hai was fuming on his opium-couch, not because he was being hounded by the "New Nobility" again, but because the telegram from Wu Sun-fu announcing the death of his father had arrived much too late. When the telegram was put into his hand, he had been overjoyed to see that it was from his nephew, a famous man in Shanghai who was always getting his name in the papers. He had thought the telegram must be some urgent message from his nephew seeking his advice. The fact that even his important nephew looked to him for advice put him in a different category altogether from the "New Nobility" who only yesterday had been a pack of snivelling young puppies. But when the telegram turned out to be an obituary notice, his spirits sank. He was furious. What annoyed him was that this was nothing more than a commonplace notice of death, instead of some important matter requiring his advice — it was not the sort of thing he could carry around in his pocket to show to people and brag about. And then the telegram had been delivered appallingly late. On top of that, his nephew had failed to show him the courtesy due to an uncle: he had sent only an ordinary telegram — and even that only as a matter of form — instead of a specially chartered boat to fetch him to Shanghai. In his bygone days of power and prestige he would, under similar circumstances, have given the telegraph office hell for the delay, but, as it was, he was now an old man who did not count for much and there was nothing he could do except fume and rage in silence.

Suddenly he scrambled off his opium-couch and paced up and down. He took the telegram to the window where the light was better and perused it carefully once more. His anger flared up again and he felt an overwhelming urge to go and storm at the "muddlers" at the telegraph office, when his labourer Ah Erh came in perspiring and spattered with mud. Finding his master in an ugly mood, Ah Erh just stood back panting noisily.

"Ah, you're back, eh? I was thinking that Chilichiao Village had been shifted during the night so that you couldn't find it! I was just going to report you missing to the police. . . . You'd better watch your step! If you carry on the way you're going, you'll find yourself in prison one of these days!"

As Tseng Tsang-hai pronounced this threat, he tilted his head on one side and glared at Ah Erh. He always launched into a tirade like this whenever Ah Erh came home late from an errand, though he would never have done anything about it. But, this time, Ah Erh had the bad luck to walk in just when his master was boiling with rage. Then Tseng Tsang-hai really lost his temper at the sight of Ah Erh standing there just panting and mopping his face instead of reporting the result of his errand at once as he usually did.

"You scoundrel, you!" shouted Tseng Tsang-hai hoarsely, stamping his foot. "Speak up, can't you? How much did you collect?"

"Not a penny. — They're having a meeting in the village today and they were banging gongs everywhere to let people know about it —"

Ah Erh stopped short and lifted the hem of his blue jacket to wipe his face once more. As he closed his eyes he could see several thousand villagers at a meeting with countless red banners fluttering on their hoes, and several thousand terrible eyes blazing. His ears instantly rang once more with the crashing of gongs and the angry roar of the crowd. He felt his heart pounding as if it would burst and he went hot and cold all over.

Tseng Tsang-hai had no idea what was going on in Ah Erh's mind and Ah Erh's unusual reticence made him see red.

"To hell with their bloody meeting! Your business was to collect debts for me. Didn't you tell them: 'If you don't settle up today, Mr. Tseng'll send the police round tomorrow and put you under arrest'? Didn't you tell the bastards that? — Meeting be damned!"

"All right, then: you carry on and send the police! But you won't see me going there again — not even if you cut off my head. All the villagers have joined some association. . . . The moment they see me they know what I am there for. They swear at me and try to keep me there and want me to. . . ."

There was a note of suppressed defiance in Ah Erh's voice and he did not even say "sir." This was no small offence, but fortunately Tseng Tsang-hai was too busy worrying about his uncollected debts to notice it. He cut Ah Erh short with a thump on the table.

"Blast their association!" he roared. "Chen Lao-pa — I know he's a committee member of that confounded peasants' association. He's a money-lender himself, and he allows them to get away with their debts to me! I'll call him to account! I've never heard of such nonsense! Perhaps you're lying to me, you scoundrel — I don't suppose you went near the place! Mark my words: I'll find out if you didn't, and you won't get away with it. . . ."

"It isn't Chen Lao-pa's association. It's a new one. Nobody knows about it except the people in the village. People here in the town haven't heard about it yet. They had their first meeting this morning — they were beating gongs to call the people up. There were thousands there — all barefoot and wearing short jackets; there wasn't a single gown among them. They're all genuine poor villagers. . . ."

Ah Erh had begun his tale gleefully, unabashed by Tseng Tsang-hai's threats; but he broke off suddenly when he saw that his master had gone deathly pale, and that his hands were trembling as he collapsed on to the opium-couch and closed his eyes. During the ten years that Ah Erh had worked for him, Tseng Tsang-hai had always seemed a formidable figure, so it came as a revelation to see him shaken and unnerved like a defeated fighting-cock.

Ah Erh suddenly wavered. A good-natured fellow at heart, he could not bear to see his master in such a bad way. If he were to cause this old opium-smoker to drop dead from fright, it would be a terrible crime! The gods would surely punish him by cutting short his life! However, he need not have worried, for Tseng Tsang-hai suddenly opened his bloodshot eyes and glared fiercely, and his face became livid. He sprang up, seized the opium-pipe, sprang forward in a rage, and aimed a blow at Ah Erh's head.

"You scum, you!" he screamed. "You're as bad as they are! How dare you lot start a rebellion!"

Crack! . . . the long ivory opium-pipe broke in two. It had missed the labourer's head altogether, for Ah Erh had warded it off with his brawny, sun-tanned arm, but this attack made his blood boil and he stood his ground with glaring eyes. Still brandishing the broken half of the pipe and thundering away, Tseng Tsang-hai snatched up a pewter candlestick and hurled it at Ah Erh's face. This, too, went wide of the mark; but when it hit the ground the sharp spike at the top pierced Ah Erh's shin and made it bleed. Ah Erh's eyes blazed with anger. "Kill the bloody old fleecer!" the villagers at Chilichiao had shouted, and this phrase now came back to him with particular vividness, and made him clench his fists. If Tseng Tsang-hai tried to come one step nearer, he was more than ready to fight!

Suddenly a pandemonium of cursing and screaming broke out in another room and the next moment an attractive young woman burst in upon them, weeping and wailing, and threw herself on Tseng Tsang-hai, so that the old man was nearly thrown off balance.

"What's the matter, Ah-chin?" asked Tseng Tsang-hai dejectedly, leaning on the table. Hard on the first woman's heels came another, tall and sturdy, and immediately the room rang with their shouting and cursing. Shaking his head and sighing, Tseng Tsang-hai took refuge on his opium-couch, where he lay with closed eyes. Although he was known far and wide as an old hand at manipulating lawsuits, he was utterly helpless when it came to sorting out the quarrels between these two women — his daughter-in-law and his unofficial concubine. He had no alternative but to leave them to it and take no notice.

Ah Erh had slipped out of the room, leaving the two women screaming abuse at one another while a wet-nurse with Tseng Tsang-hai's grandson in her arms and a scullery-maid stood under the eaves outside, listening and watching. Tseng Tsang-hai was taking comfort in a sizzling opium-pipe, regretting the broken ivory pipe and wondering what this new association in

Chilichiao Village was all about. He now felt rather sorry that he had let himself go like that in front of Ah Erh just now. His scheming mind was soon busy on another train of thought: So the Communists are egging the villagers to join an association and to hold meetings, are they? That means they must have something big up their sleeve! But there's nothing to be afraid of, really: there's the battalion of regulars in the town, besides the local security corps. This would be a good opportunity to get the Bureau of Public Safety to round up some of the Communists and deal with them — and how about calling my debtors who won't pay up Communists. . . . Then another thing: nobody in the whole town has heard about what's going on in Chilichiao Village! These "New Nobility" here who are always trying so hard to squeeze me out are just asleep! At the thought of the ignorance of the "New Nobility" Tseng Tsanghai's haggard face lit up with a smile of complacency. He knew now how he could recover all the debts owing him, principal and interest, and also how he could expose the incompetence and weakness of the "New Nobility." If they had not even heard of the existence of Communists in the village, what business had they to be where they were?

"Very well, I'll do it," he suddenly said aloud. "I'll teach the 'New Nobility' a lesson! Ha, ha!"

Well pleased with himself, Tseng Tsang-hai cackled triumphantly and laid down the opium-pipe. His hoarse voice filled the room, and not until he heard it himself did he realize that the women's brawl had somehow stopped completely. He looked round in surprise and discovered his concubine sitting at a table opposite the opium-couch, her face buried in a handkerchief as if she were crying.

"Ah-chin!" Tseng Tsang-hai called softly. No answer. He did not know what to do. He hoisted himself up on the couch and was intending to go across and say something to soothe her, when she uncovered her face and glared disdainfully at him. She had not been weeping at all, though her eyes were red.

"I'm going back home to the country tomorrow," she shrilled. "I'm not going to stay here to be insulted and ill-treated. What do you take me for?"

Suddenly she started crying — or rather sobbing, for she shed no real tears.

"Oh, what do you keep quarrelling with that woman for? I've no time to deal with her. Just wait until Chia-chu comes home, and then I'll tell him to take his wife in hand. And I'll tell him to give her a good hiding, and then you'll be even with her. Come now, it's nothing much, really. Don't take that sort of woman seriously. . . . Now, you go and see if my bird's-nest porridge is ready. I want to have it straight away, because I'm going out on urgent business."

While he was saying this, he walked over and wiped her face with his loose, opium-stained sleeve, as if to dry her tears, but she shook her head, looked askance at him and snorted:

"Hm! Do you mean all that?"

"Of course I mean it! When I say someone must be punished, you can be sure that they will be. I'm master here; I don't have to lift a finger — somebody else'll do it for me. Remember when your husband came here to make trouble not long ago? I promised to punish him for you, didn't I? And didn't I get the police to deal with him? This time, it's a bit different, though: you can't very well hand your own daughter-in-law over to the police. I'll have to get my son to deal with her. He'll be home any moment now, and then I'll tell him to give the bitch a good hiding. And what I say goes."

"Huh! So what you say goes, does it? What about that gold ring you promised me last month? You still haven't —"

"Ah, that's a different matter, though: that costs money. — Anyway, what's the use of a gold ring? You can only wear it on your finger, but it won't do you any good there. Wouldn't it be much better if I put the money in the bank to earn some interest for you? Now, run along and see to my porridge, and when I come home, I'll give you a passbook for a hundred dollars. Satisfied?"

She apparently was, for she went out looking rather pleased with herself. He chuckled, gratified by his diplomatic coup. He returned to his couch and began cheerfully roasting a large bead of opium.

Hardly had he put the pellet into the bowl of the pipe and

begun drawing at it, when pandemonium broke out again in the back of the house, this time with a man's voice adding to the din: his son Chia-chu had come on the scene. Tseng Tsang-hai gripped the pipe harder and sucked away at it as if nothing had happened, when a shrill accusation caught his ear above the hubbub of cursing and shouting:

"You shameless hussy! The old man can't satisfy you, so you go and set your cap at the young one! You don't imagine I'm going to let you get away with that, do you?"

The voice was his daughter-in-law's and was answered by a laugh from the concubine Ah-chin. Suddenly, the son's voice broke in with an angry roar, while his wife sobbed and swore, and soon the sounds of weeping, cursing and fighting had blurred into a chaos of noise.

Tseng Tsang-hai stopped smoking. He must try to understand what she had meant by: "The old man can't satisfy you!" Although all this was not so important to him as his financial affairs and he could afford to disregard it, nevertheless he felt rather upset and ill at ease. What perturbed him more was the idea that his son was quite willing to beat his wife not out of filial duty and obedience to his father, but for another reason altogether! Tseng Tsang-hai became quite miserable at his loss of authority over his son.

Suddenly, heavy footsteps roused him from his reverie. His son Chia-chu stood before him: an ugly, wild-looking youth of nineteen. Throwing a book he was holding on to a chair with a thud and sitting down on a square stool by the couch, he looked towards his father.

"Chia-chu," said Tseng Tsang-hai, before his son could open his mouth, "Old Mr. Wu has died. I had a telegram from your cousin Sun-fu. You're free at the moment, so you can go to Shanghai tomorrow to offer our condolences. — And you can get your cousin to find you a job while you're about it."

He spoke slowly as he put forward the idea he had just worked out, while his heart contracted at those phrases "the old man . . . the young one . . . satisfy you!"

"I don't want to go to Shanghai. I've some urgent business on my hands. Give me fifty dollars."

"What! Money again?" exclaimed Tseng Tsang-hai, rolling over and sitting up. "Ah, you don't realize how difficult it is to make money. 'Urgent business,' eh? You'd better tell me all about it first."

Instead of answering his father at once, Chia-chu fumbled in his pocket and pulled out a black card, which he thrust under his father's nose.

"What do I want money for? I'm throwing a party!" he swaggered. "Look at this: see what it is?"

Tseng Tsang-hai's sharp eye and alert mind told him at once that it was nothing less than a Kuomintang party card! He was rapturous. He snatched it, rubbed his eyes, and examined it closely in the light of the opium lamp: yes, it was a party card, right enough. It had on it his son's photograph and the inscription: "Party Membership Card No. 23, so-and-so District. . . ." — "So you rank as high as twenty-third, eh?" the old man muttered gleefully to himself. He picked up his spectacles from the opium-plate, settled them on his nose, and carefully examined the party seal stamped on the card. When he was satisfied, he went over respectfully to his son and urged him solemnly:

"Look after it, son, and don't lose it."

He broke into a happy laugh and patted his son on the shoulder.

"So you're emerging from obscurity at last!" he went on. "I've always said you won't find a puppy in a tiger's den! — Give a party by all means. Have all your friends in this evening to celebrate. Will fifty dollars be enough? No, I'll give you a hundred. And then tomorrow night I'll invite my old friends in as well. Oh, yes, I've got something else to tell you. Just a minute, till I've finished this pipe."

The old man felt triumphant. He lay down on the couch again and began drawing hard at his pipe. His son was smirking with satisfaction, but as he couldn't find anything more to brag about, he joined his father on the couch and carefully tucked his party card away in an inside pocket. Both of them treasured this card, but for quite different reasons. To Chia-chu it was as good as a passbook with which he could always get plenty of money to splash around out of the old fool.

When Tseng Tsang-hai had finished his pipe, he picked up the teapot, put the spout to his lips and gulped down several mouthfuls of tea.

"Chia-chu," he said in a low voice, "I've got some important information for the police. I was planning to go and tell them myself, but now I think you ought to go instead. Now that you're a brand-new party member, you ought to assert your authority and try your hand at something important and distinguish yourself! Yes, this is a rare opportunity for you. That's two strokes of luck we've had today!"

Chia-chu was rather taken aback by the idea of having to go and see the police, and could only gape and stare foolishly. He was obviously not at all keen on the idea, and in any case he would not know how to go about discussing things with the police.

"Ah, I can well imagine you've got stage-fright!" said Tseng Tsang-hai half reprovingly and half affectionately. He shook his head, then suddenly changed the subject:

"Chia-chu, have you any idea how many secret opium-dens there are in the town? Do you know how many men go to see Mademoiselle San — the girl who lives behind the grocer's shop in Chien Street? And do you know how much is smuggled through the customs barrier every month?"

Tseng Chia-chu just stared, not knowing what to say. As a matter of fact, he was a regular customer of ladies of the town like Mademoiselle San, but it was none of his business how many men they might be entertaining besides himself. As for opium-dens and smuggled goods, he had never given them a thought.

Tseng Tsang-hai slapped his thigh and laughed happily.

"You don't know? Naturally a young man doesn't bother his head about such things. But, now you're a party man — one of the élite! If you're going to do your job properly, you must get to know about local conditions. You should go around and try to find out about this and that. Information won't come and knock at your door. . . . However, don't worry: your old man knows all the ropes and he'll soon show you your way around!"

Tseng Chia-chu had turned red in the face, perhaps because

he was ashamed of having his ignorance shown up by his father; or it may have been that he was becoming impatient because the hundred dollars had not yet materialized. He pursed his lips and remained silent. Just then, his wife came in in high dudgeon. She sat her child on a chair and put one arm round it, then turned to her husband as if she were going to say something, but before she could open her mouth the child started crying. At the same time it wet itself: the chair was soaked and some dripped on to the floor.

Chia-chu scowled and screwed up his face with exasperation. He sat up abruptly on the couch and was just going to rave at his wife, when he saw that the child was scrabbling his feet on the book he had just brought in.

"Hey, you little beast!" he roared as he sprang forward and snatched the book from under the child's feet. He looked at it: it was dripping wet and torn beyond recognition. As he pulled it out the child lost its balance and almost fell off the chair. Terrified by the realization that it had done something wrong, it stopped crying and took refuge in its mother's bosom with its little mouth wide open.

Tseng Tsang-hai's expression changed abruptly when he saw that the soiled book in his son's hand was no other than *The Three Principles*, a theoretical treatise of the Kuomintang. He sprang off the couch and stamped his foot.

"God Almighty!" he wailed. "Fancy letting the child wet all over this of all books! If people get to hear about this, there'll be hell to pay! Oh, God! What a thing to happen!"

The child, terrified, began howling again. Tseng Chia-chu did not really understand why his father should be making such a fuss over a book; nevertheless, having a vague idea that something terrible had happened, he flew into a rage, and suddenly caught hold of his wife and began thrashing her. As the din of howling from mother and child and shouting and cursing from Chia-chu rose about his ears, Tseng Tsang-hai shook his head and sighed; there was nothing he could do but lie down and smoke again. After a while he remembered that he had to go to the police station on important business, so he got up, shook down his long gown, and departed, leaving the pandemonium behind him.

*

The streets were crowded as usual. Shuangchiao Town had a population of nearly a hundred thousand and boasted a few local banks, pawnshops, silverware shops, as well as a power-house, a rice-mill and an oil-refinery owned by Wu Sun-fu. Most of these establishments had sprung up during the past four or five years.

Tseng Tsang-hai walked with leisurely strides through the streets, looking at the shops and the modern places of amusement, thinking that there were now many more opportunities of making money than in days gone by when he had been the "Local King." If he had not had a run of bad luck for the last two or three years, he would doubtless have made a cool hundred thousand dollars out of the boom. Although he had a chance of making a come-back any day now, just the same, he couldn't help feeling regretful about what he had missed. He slowed down and had to stop in front of the Tai Pai Restaurant, so dense were the crowds.

Suddenly a voice hailed him from behind: "Where are you off to at such a moment?"

Tseng Tsang-hai glanced over his shoulder, to see Li Sze, the opium-seller. In a way he and the opium-seller were intimate friends and did not stand on ceremony, but before so many people in the street Tseng Tsang-hai was embarrassed by the familiar manner of this fellow who tugged at his sleeve and called him just plain "you." Anybody would think an opium-seller was the social equal of a man who had always prided himself on his family and position. It irked Tseng Tsang-hai, but he could not very well say anything, as he had to reckon with the fact that Li Sze's underworld influence was growing daily with the mounting prosperity of the town. Restrained by this consideration, he had to stifle his displeasure, and, in spite of himself, greeted Li Sze with a nod.

"I'm going to the police station," he replied with a smile, "on some official business."

"You'd better turn back," Li Sze advised him pretentiously. "Whatever your business, there's nothing doing today."

He spoke with a note of arrogance in his voice, as if he were the superintendent himself.

"Why? Have they got a new superintendent?" asked Tseng Tsang-hai sarcastically, annoyed at the other's tone of voice. Hardly were the words out of his mouth when he regretted it: he could not afford to offend an influential man like Li Sze.

Luckily, Li Sze did not notice the implication. He led Tseng Tsang-hai over to a quiet spot across the street, where he put his mouth to the old man's ear and whispered:

"Haven't you heard the news?"

"What news?"

"A Communist detachment's arrived at Chilichiao Village. They're coming to raid the town tonight!"

At this Tseng Tsang-hai's heart missed a beat and he paled. He did not mind about there being Communists in Chilichiao and the news that they were coming to raid the town. What upset him was that Li Sze had stolen a march on him and that his secret was a secret no longer! The opportunity of gaining some kudos for himself or his son had slipped through his fingers. Yet, old stager that he was, after the initial shock he immediately gathered his wits about him and shook his head in feigned disbelief.

"You don't believe it?" Li Sze went on in a confidential whisper. "Listen, I'll tell you something; there's hardly anybody knows about it yet. I heard it from somebody at Colonel Ho's place. The colonel's concubine's cleared out already. She went on Pockmarked Wang's boat. True as I stand here!"

Tseng Tsang-hai's face was now quite ashen, for he had begun to realize that the situation was really serious. When earlier in the day he had heard from his labourer Ah Erh about the mass meeting in Chilichiao Village and the beating of gongs and so on, he had dismissed it as something staged by a lot of helpless, unarmed peasants; but now it looked as if the Communists were armed and meant business. His fear was now not of someone stealing his son's thunder, but of losing his life and property.

"How many rifles have the Communists got?" he asked anxiously.

"About a hundred, so I've heard."

Tseng Tsang-hai felt somewhat relieved. Although his plan for making a name for his son had fallen through, he was comforted by the thought that there was no real danger. He smiled and glanced at Li Sze's cunning face.

"Only a hundred?" he said calmly and unconcernedly. "Nothing to be afraid of. We've got a whole battalion of troops stationed here."

"Huh! We may have, but they haven't been paid for three months."

"And then there's the local security force."

"Eleven out of ten of them opium-addicts! — I should advise you to be careful, though, and hide up for a while. It's no joke, this time. There have been rumours flying about for the past two days, but of course, you've been too busy cuddling your concubine on the couch all day to notice what's going on outside. — But it may not be as bad as all that. Though you'd better be careful and watch out. I don't mind telling you I've given orders for my men all over the town to load their guns in case. No sleep for them tonight!"

With this Li Sze hurried off.

Tseng Tsang-hai stood cogitating a while but could not make up his mind what to do. If he moved out, it would cost him a lot of money. Better sit tight for the time being and risk it. If anything really *did* happen, and his life and property were threatened, he could always take his cue from the battalion commander's concubine and slip away to the county town. Now that he had no secret to win himself some glory with, there was no point in going to see the police superintendent, so he decided to go home.

There was someone waiting for him in the hall when he arrived home. The moment Tseng Tsang-hai saw that the man had a little tuft of beard under his chin, he recognized him as Fei Hsiao-sheng, better known as Fei Little Beard, Wu Sunfu's agent in the town.

"Ah, you're back, Mr. Tseng. I just came to tell you that

Mr. Wu Sun-fu has sent me a wire asking for a hundred thousand dollars to be remitted to him within three days. I should like your advice."

That Fei Little Beard should come straight to the question of money was a shock to Tseng Tsang-hai.

"I've been looking through the books," Fei Little Beard went on with a smile, "and I find that you owe Mr. Sun-fu's local bank here some twelve thousand dollars, and that the loan has long been overdue. I didn't really want to mention it, but Mr. Wu sounded very strict in his letter and I haven't managed to collect the whole amount, so I have to come and ask you to help me out. I shall be very grateful for anything you can do to help."

Tseng Tsang-hai's face fell. There was no love lost between him and the agent. Tseng Tsang-hai had often told people right and left that Fei Little Beard, during the several years he had been Wu Sun-fu's caretaker, had lined his pocket at Wu Sun-fu's expense, at the same time doing everything possible to prejudice his nephew Wu Sun-fu against him, with the result that all he could get in the way of a loan was a miserable twelve thousand dollars. Now Fei Little Beard was coming round dunning him and giving himself airs as his master's agent. Tseng Tsang-hai, deciding that he ought to be taken down a peg, answered sarcastically:

"You are a good and loyal servant to my nephew, Mr. Fei! I'll surely recommend you for promotion. — Now I have some news that will surprise you: my brother-in-law died soon after he arrived in Shanghai. I've had a telegram from my nephew asking me to go to Shanghai and supervise the funeral. I'm leaving tonight. As for the money, I'll see him about it myself, so you needn't bother about it now."

"I see," said Fei Little Beard, with a faint smile which hinted that he had seen through Tseng Tsang-hai's bluff. "I've also received a telegram from Mr. Wu Sun-fu about his father's death. But, of course, I didn't know he'd asked you to go and supervise the funeral."

He made no further mention of the money, but rose to go. He was just about to take his leave when Tseng Tsang-hai stopped him.

"What's the hurry?" he said. "I've got something else to tell you. — Now, if Sun-fu wants as much as a hundred thousand dollars, it must be for an emergency. Tell me how much you've collected so far."

"Only half the required amount, fifty thousand dollars."

Fei Little Beard sat down again, still wearing a smile, but implying by his tone of voice that he was not altogether pleased at Tseng Tsang-hai's prying. Old fox as he was, Fei Little Beard knew that Wu Sun-fu had not much respect for his uncle, but he was still his master's uncle, and he didn't dare be too rude to him. But Tseng Tsang-hai's high-handed manner was getting too much for him to stomach. The old man was definitely over-reaching himself this time, putting on airs as if he were somebody of importance.

But, far from toning down his insolent manner, Tseng Tsang-hai pursued:

"Only fifty thousand? You haven't sent it yet, I suppose? Well, then, give it to me and I'll take it to Sun-fu myself when I go."

Fei's eyebrows shot up: he could hardly believe his ears. He tugged at his little beard and stared at Tseng Tsang-hai's thin face.

"Go and fetch the money at once," the latter continued firmly. "You may hold me responsible for it. Don't you know about the Communists in Chilichiao Village? They're coming to raid the town this very night. We can't leave all that money lying around here tonight; I must take it with me to Shanghai. Sun-fu's interests are as important to me as my own. In this emergency I can't just stand by and see him lose money like that."

"Oh . . . that! Early this morning I heard the rumour and sent Mr. Sun-fu a telegram asking for his instructions. If there should be any trouble tonight, I've made arrangements for looking after the money all right. After all, it's my job and I shouldn't like to bother you about it."

"But could you really bear such a heavy responsibility in an emergency such as this?"

"Yes, I shall be all right, Mr. Tseng," Fei Little Beard said firmly. "Thank you for your kind offer all the same."

He rose to go, but suddenly sat down again and turned to look into Tseng Tsang-hai's face, which betrayed his rage and mortification.

"Mr. Tseng," he inquired, "where did you get the news that there's going to be trouble tonight?"

"Colonel Ho told me so himself, just after he'd received a secret report, and . . . er . . . it seemed as if Colonel Ho was a bit scared himself. Do you know who went to the county town on Pockmarked Wang's boat this morning?"

"Yes. Colonel Ho's concubine, going to return a call from the Magistrate's wife. — Ah, I see! . . . But I don't suppose you've heard the news, Mr. Tseng: at two o'clock this afternoon the colonel told the Chamber of Commerce that he accepted full responsibility for the defence of the town. But he also said, 'We haven't been paid for three months. What about making up the men's pay to raise their morale?' Then he asked them for a loan of thirty thousand dollars."

"Did the Chamber of Commerce let him have it?"

"Of course it did — cash down. . . . Ah, it's getting dark! I must hurry off. . . . What time do you leave, Mr. Tseng? I'm afraid I shan't be able to see you off on the boat. Please forgive me."

Fei Little Beard made a low bow, then made off in great haste.

Tseng Tsang-hai hypocritically bowed Fei Little Beard out of the hall, then came back fuming with rage. He paced round the hall grinding his teeth and groaning. During the past three hours he had thought up many wonderful plans, but now they had all fizzled out. He had even failed to get that fifty thousand dollars out of Fei Little Beard. He could not have hated him more if he had murdered his father.

While searching in his mind for some means of revenge, Tseng Tsang-hai walked absently along a veranda to the door of the lounge. Inside, on the opium-couch, a tiny yellow flame was dancing in the opium-lamp. As he blundered in, there was a sudden scuffle and two dark figures sprang up on the couch. Even in the dim light of the lamp he recognized one of them as his son and the other as his concubine.

"You swine!" he screamed.

Then suddenly there was a mist before his eyes and he felt a burning sensation around his heart. As his legs gave way beneath him, he instinctively felt for a chair and collapsed weakly on to it, his few straggling wisps of beard twitching with emotion.

When the mist cleared, Ah-chin was gone and Tseng Chia-chu was crouching on the couch like a frightened dog, gazing apprehensively at his father.

His son's incest, Ah chin's brazenness, Fei Little Beard's villainy, the Communist threat from Chilichiao Village — all these were seething and churning together in his mind. He wanted to roar his resentment and reassert himself, but he did not know quite where to begin. Finally his jealousy got the upper hand, and he turned on his son.

"You swine!" he raved hoarsely. "If you're such a glutton, you might at least go and pick up your women outside: I wouldn't mind that. But you'd rather stay at home and have it on tap, wouldn't you, you scum? If you put her in the family way, what are you going to call it — brother or son? That bitch Ah-chin —"

He was cut short by the crackle of rifle-fire in the distance. This was the signal for an immediate outburst of prolonged firing. It was like a firework display on New Year's Eve. Tseng Tsang-hai jumped and cried frantically:

"Oh, God! We're done for! — Come on, you young swine, get outside and see what's happening, and quick about it! See which direction they're coming from and how far away they are!"

But Tseng Chia-chu did not budge; he just cowered down even lower. Suddenly Ah-chin rushed in sobbing and wailing, her dishevelled hair hanging over her face. She clutched hold of Tseng Tsang-hai and wrapped herself round him like a snake.

"It was your son made me do it!" she sobbed. "I tried to stop him, but he, he —"

Tseng Tsang-hai knocked her away with a vicious slap in the face; he was too enraged to say anything. Meanwhile, the sound of firing was coming nearer, and angry shouts could be heard in the street. Chia-chu's wife ran in crying with her baby in her arms, followed by a whole troop of women nurses, kitchen-maids and chamber-maids, in a terrified, hysterical flock.

Suddenly the firing became louder than before and the stutter of a machine-gun was added to the noise. The old man was rushing in mortal terror into the back of the house when his servant Ah Erh dashed in, running into him full tilt and throwing him to the floor.

"Quick!" gasped Ah Erh, with not even a glance at his master. "Hide in the back, in the kitchen-garden! And keep your heads down! There's bullets flying about everywhere and soldiers all over the place — all round the house!"

"So the Communists are on the run, are they?" asked Tseng Tsang-hai gleefully, scrambling to his feet with a sudden spurt of energy and clutching at Ah Erh's sleeve.

"It's the soldiers fighting the security force . . . the soldiers are fighting among themselves!"

"Tcha! Get out with your blasted drivel!" snarled Tseng Tsang-hai, the master again, when he heard Ah Erh's reply. Looking round sharply, he saw a red glow reflected on the walls round the yard — somewhere down the street a fire was blazing away. The staccato chatter of a machine-gun was heard again. Supposing that the worst was over, Tseng Tsang-hai ordered the women to collect up all the valuables and some clothes, while he himself took the opium-lamp and went over to a desk in the corner of the room, where he opened a deed-box and took out a large sheaf of land-deeds, IOUs and passbooks and stuffed them into his pockets. His son suddenly sprang off the opium-couch, where he had been crouching motionless all the while, and joined his father in the rummage. Suddenly there was a noise of shouting which seemed to come from just behind them. Tseng Tsang-hai dropped the papers in terror and ran towards the backroom; but in the dark doorway he bumped into someone and a hand clutched at his sleeve.

"Oh, save me from them, sir!" wailed a woman's voice.

It was Ah-chin again. Just at that moment a flaring light lit up the room from outside and in the glare Tseng Tsang-hai saw several men, each with a torch in his hand. When Ah-chin recognized one of them as her husband, she was terrified. Her knees gave way beneath her and she sank to the floor, where she buried her face in her hands and collapsed in a heap. Tseng Tsang-hai took advantage of the confusion to make his escape. He fled blindly and in a twinkling he had vanished.

"Now, you shameless hussy!" thundered Ah-chin's husband. "Where is the old swine?" But Ah-chin just sobbed. Two of the men had caught hold of Chia-chu and were hustling him over to a young man who was standing there.

"The old perisher's bolted out the back way!"

"No need to go after him, Chin-pao," cried several voices together. "The lads out the back'll spot him all right."

Just then, Chia-chu's wife burst into the room, her hair all over her face. Seeing her husband held by two men, she hurled herself upon them; but someone seized her by the hair from behind and pulled her sharply off.

"What do you think you're on?" he roared.

"What am I on? What have you got hold of my husband for?"

She threw herself to the floor and began screaming hysterically. Seeing Ah-chin squatting nearby, she rolled over, seized hold of her with both hands, and bit her shoulder savagely. In a moment the two women were fighting in a heap on the floor.

"You are the cause of all the trouble, you bitch! . . . You don't care whether they're old or young — you'll have them all. . . . I'll kill you! I'll kill you!"

Shouts were heard and torches flashed in the back of the house, and soon three men, one of whom was Ah Erh, dragged Tseng Tsang-hai into the room. The old man was smothered in dirt from head to foot, and was desperately imploring them to spare his life. Ah-chin's husband darted forward and crashed his fist into his face.

"You old swine!" he rasped through clenched teeth. "Don't want to die, eh?"

"Kill him! Lynch him, the bloody old shark!"

A sudden roar of anger swept through the room, but the young man wearing a pistol came across and restrained them.

"You old swine!" he rasped through clenched teeth. "Don't want to die, eh?"

"Shut up, all of you!" he rapped out sternly. "He'll be tried first!"

"Come on, then: let's try him! He's a money-lender, a bloodsucker! He took my farm, the old shark! . . ."

"The old swine took my wife and had me beaten up by the police!"

"He's always setting the police on us! He ought to be lynched!"

"Ah! and I suppose you're in the Kuomintang as well, aren't you?" cried the young man with a pistol, raising his voice above the din.

Tseng Tsang-hai's heart missed a beat at this question. For some inexplicable reason he decided that there was hope for him yet. He pulled himself together and looked the young man straight in the eye in the glare of the torchlight.

"No, not at all," he assured him vehemently. "No one hates the Kuomintang more than I do. I've had quite a number of them arrested and shot in my time. If you don't believe me, you can make an investigation. — Oh, yes, Ah Erh here can tell you about it. Ah Erh. . . ."

"If you were not in the Kuomintang before, I am sure you are now!"

The young man cut him short. With a glance at Chia-chu, who was gazing at him with startled eyes, he continued, "And what's your son?"

"I'm not one! I'm not in the Kuomintang!" Tseng Chia-chu protested desperately. But hardly were the words out of his mouth when Ah-chin, who had stopped fighting for the moment, sprang up and shrieked:

"Oh yes you are! Just now you showed me that black card and threatened me with it and made me. . . . Oh, forgive me, Chin-pao! They forced me to do it. I couldn't stop them."

Then the machine-gun fire started up again. The young man glanced outside, then pulled out his pistol and shouted:

"Two of you stay here on guard. The rest of you come with me and bring the old shark and his son with you."

As they clattered out with their flaring torches, Tseng Chia-chu's wife, who had been sitting on the floor gaping blankly, now sprang up and ran weeping after them. Just as she got outside, she tripped over something and fell flat on her face. Ah Erh, who had been left behind on guard with another man, helped her to her feet.

"Have you gone off your head?" he cried roughly. Then, as if to console her, "It's nothing to do with you. They're the ones who've done wrong and they'll have to suffer for it, not you. Now get in the back, and don't go rushing about."

*

Meanwhile, Tseng Tsang-hai and his son were being hustled through the streets, where they saw peasants in red scarves and armed with a varied assortment of weapons, running here and there in twos and threes. They brushed past Li Sze, the opium-seller, who was being walked away by a group of unarmed peasants. Tseng Tsang-hai tried to catch his eye, but he was hurried by so quickly that even this was not possible. They were now heading west, in the direction of the firing. Every two or three minutes came the angry chatter of a machine-gun. All the shops and houses were shuttered and barred, with an occasional ray of light escaping through the crack of a door.

Gusts of wind carried smoke and smuts and a smell of burning — somewhere another fire was blazing away.

After turning a corner they found their way blocked by a milling crowd. Not far ahead was the high front wall of the Hung Chang Pawnshop. The two Tsengs and their captors were soon swallowed up in the motley, jostling crowd of variously armed peasants and soldiers in red scarves. Suddenly, from the top of the pawnshop wall, there was a flash and a burst of machine-gun fire raked the street below. The Tsengs, at the corner of the street, suddenly found themselves in the line of fire.

"Scatter! Quick!" thundered a voice from the middle of the crowd. Tseng Tsang-hai and Chia-chu were bundled across the street by their captors and they all lay flat under the eaves of a shop while rifles cracked all round them. Tseng Tsang-hai looked like a corpse, except that his staring eyes still rolled in terror. Chia-chu's terrified gaze was riveted on the flashes from the muzzle of the machine-gun ahead of him. There was a sudden crackle of rifle-fire from behind the pawnshop and a plume of smoke curled up against the sky. As it thickened, a red glow appeared and tongues of flame shot upwards: the pawnshop was on fire. The machine-gun fire died down a little, and at the same time a deafening roar rose around them.

"Charge! Charge!"

Innumerable figures sprang up from the ground and from their hiding-places round corners and under the eaves of the shops, then charged forward like a whirlwind.

The men guarding the Tsengs joined in the charge, but two of them immediately turned back and withdrew with their prisoners down the street. Before the four of them had gone more than a few steps, the machine-gun on the pawnshop wall raked the street with a final burst, and they threw themselves to the ground. Another wave of peasants and red-scarfed soldiers came rushing up the street towards the pawnshop and swept over them as they lay there.

The chatter of the machine-gun gradually petered out.

Tseng Chia-chu, hugging the ground, at first thought it was all up with him. Then he tentatively moved his limbs and found, to his surprise, that he was intact and unhurt. He sat up and looked at his father: he was doubled up on his side, with blood oozing from his gaping mouth. The two peasants were also dead. Tseng Chia-chu gazed in stunned silence for a moment, then sprang up and ran for his life.

Panic-stricken, he ran into a deserted lane. He tripped over something and fell, but bounced up again immediately. He instinctively looked over his shoulder in the direction of the pawnshop and saw the flames leaping up against the sky and shedding a red glow all round. Shouts and cries could still be heard against the background of intermittent rifle-fire. While his attention was distracted, he again stumbled against the object on the ground. He automatically looked down: it was a dead man with a red scarf around his neck and a pistol still in his hand. An idea suddenly took shape in Chia-chu's mind: he unwound the red scarf from the dead man's neck and wound it around his own, then snatched the pistol from his hand and ran on.

The firing had now almost ceased, and all that could be heard were the crackle of the fire and the confused clamour of voices in the distance. The lane was as quiet as the grave: every door was shut fast, and there was not a glimmer of light to be seen. Chia-chu continued on his way, peering right and left as he went like a hungry stray dog on the prowl. As he neared the end of the lane he suddenly stopped. In front of him stood a two-storeyed house with a light in the window. He hesitated a moment, then went up and knocked at the gate, a savage gleam in his eye.

"Thank God, you're back!" came a young woman's voice as the gate opened, but when she saw it was a stranger standing there pointing a pistol at her with murder in his eyes, she let out a scream and ran back into the house. Chia-chu ran after her without a word. They ran across the yard and as she reached the door of the room with a light in the window, the woman tripped over. Disregarding her, Chia-chu burst into the room, where he was met by the terrified face of a wrinkled old woman and vaguely heard her shriek.

He bounded up the stairs and into a bedroom. A lamp was burning and the bed was hung round with a white curtain. He ripped the curtains aside and saw a child's rosy little face above a green silk quilt. He quickly raised the quilt and let it fall back, then whirled round and made for a wardrobe. He flung open the door and began rummaging around inside.

"Mummy! Mummy!" the child began crying. Chia-chu started at the noise and in a panic he fired at the bed. The deafening report sounded even louder and more appalling in the stillness of the little room. Startled, Chia-chu let the pistol drop to the ground. The child cried louder still, and footsteps pounded up the stairs. The next moment the young woman burst screaming into the room and flung herself at the bed. She picked up the child and, hugging it to her, she leant motionless as a statue against a table by the bed and stared dumbly at the intruder.

More out of instinct than anything, Chia-chu picked up the pistol and aimed it at the mother and her child, his face as black as thunder and his heart thumping wildly. As he stood there, the old woman tottered in and fell trembling on her knees in front of him.

"Don't kill us, kind sir! Please don't kill us! Take our jewellery and money, but don't —"

"Give 'em here, then! And quick about it!" Chia-chu rapped out, feeling calmer and dropping the muzzle of the pistol towards the floor.

The child began whimpering again, murmuring "mummy" and burying its face against the young woman's breast. She smiled a little to know that her baby was still alive.

Chia-chu's heart beat faster, for he suddenly recognized her now that she had smiled: she was the wife of a haberdasher in the main street, a woman he had often gazed at with lustful eyes. He glanced from her to his pistol, then stepped forward. He suddenly seized hold of her, flung her on to the bed, and tried to strip her. She was so stunned by this sudden assault that for a moment she seemed paralysed but she soon gathered her wits about her and began resisting frantically, her blazing eyes riveted on Chia-chu's savage face.

"Please spare us, your honour! Have mercy on us! Please leave her alone!" shrieked the old woman desperately, her voice quavering with emotion. She tottered over, grasped his legs, and tried to pull him off. The trinkets and silver coins she had brought for him spilled out jingling on to the floor.

"Keep off!" Chia-chu roared, and viciously kicked the old woman away. As he did so, the young woman wrenched herself away from him, rolled out of his reach and sprang to her feet.

"Now I know who you are!" she shrilled hysterically. "I know you! you're that old shark Tseng Tsang-hai's son! That's who you are!"

Chia-chu's face became suffused with rage. In a panic he picked up the pistol from the edge of the bed and fired point-blank at the young woman.

V

TWO days later, the Shanghai newspapers reported the peasant rising in Shuangchiao Town in a few lines in obscure corners. Such occurrences had, of late, become so frequent that they had lost their news-value, and in any case they only upset the readers, so the papers kept such news-items down to a minimum. Besides, the readers had got so used to news of this kind that they treated them just as they did the frequent cases of kidnapping in the city. They just glanced over such items and thought to themselves: "What, again?" at the same time congratulating themselves that the place in question did not happen to be their own home town.

The long years of increasingly violent civil war and peasant unrest had, in a way, trained the rich in the virtue of keeping calm — although their fear of finding themselves involved in a sudden upheaval also grew with each passing day.

It was with mixed feelings that Wu Sun-fu read the news about his home town in the morning paper. He had just finished breakfast and was sprawled on the sofa with his paper, while his wife sat opposite him on a chair, puckering her brows slightly and looking cross and depressed. Suddenly Wu Sun-fu threw the newspaper aside and laughed ironically.

Mrs. Wu Sun-fu's heart missed a beat. She nerved herself to look at her husband, though her face had paled slightly. Sensitive as she was, she thought he was sneering at her. He must have found out her secret! Her pallor suddenly turned to a flush of shame.

"What's the matter, Pei-yao?" asked Wu Sun-fu tautly, as if making an effort to control himself. "Humph! It had to be, I suppose, and now it's happened!"

She felt his dreadful, piercing eyes searching her face.

Her face paled again, and her heart began thumping with fear. Then something seemed to snap inside her head and she suddenly decided to make a clean breast of everything. The thought of her husband making a scene gave an ugly look to her face.

But Wu Sun-fu was too engrossed in his worries about Shuangchiao to notice her unusual mood. He swung himself off the sofa and paced up and down, shaking his fists angrily. He stopped and looked down at his wife's bent head.

"So it's happened at last," he muttered to himself. "Oh! Shuangchiao Town! Three years ago, my ideal —"

"Shuangchiao Town?" she interrupted, looking up sharply. She suddenly realized that his ironical laugh and "it's happened" referred to something else. She felt slightly relieved but rather ashamed of herself. She could not suppress a blush, and the expression in her eyes was one of mortification and guilt. She felt sorry for her husband, and if at this moment he had shown her a little love, she would willingly have buried her head in his shoulder and told him everything. She would have told him she was sorry and would have sworn to be a good and faithful wife to him.

But Wu Sun-fu merely laid his hand lightly on her shoulder and said dully:

"Yes. A mob of rebellious peasants has broken into our home town. For three years I've spared no effort to try and build it up into a model town, and now it's all finished! Oh, Pei-yao, Pei-yao!"

This *cri du coeur* acted electrically on her and she immediately warmed to him. But when she looked up at his face, she sensed straight away that this cry was not for her but for his Shuangchiao Town, his "ideal of a model town." She went cold again and felt like bursting into tears.

"Two or three months ago I began to fear that trouble of this kind was brewing," he continued, quite unaware of the conflicting emotions in his wife's mind. "And now the inevitable's happened!"

He narrowed his eyes and looked past her, then suddenly exploded furiously.

"How I hate them — those idiots in charge of the town! What the hell were they doing? They've got a whole battalion there and two machine-guns! Are they afraid of hurting somebody, or what? Pah! — And what the devil's that idiot Fei Little Beard up to? I suppose he's dead! He hasn't even answered my telegram. A whole day's gone by, and still not a word from him! If I hadn't happened to see the news in the paper, I'd never have known! We might as well be waiting in the dark to have our throats cut, for all we know about what's going on!"

He stamped his foot, then threw himself fuming on to the sofa. He picked up the paper, glanced at it with a frown, and threw it aside. He switched his narrowed eyes to his wife. Her silence exasperated him.

"Pei-yao," he demanded as calmly as he could, "why don't you say something? What are you thinking about?"

"Well, er, I should say . . . well, one's ideals are bound to fall to the ground sooner or later."

"What on earth do you mean?" he bellowed angrily, his eyes bulging with indignation. Then suddenly he fell silent, picked up the paper again, and held it up in front of his face. He was not really reading it but just fuming inwardly behind it. He was firmly convinced that his anger was "justifiable" in the circumstances. Normally, he was calm, firm and full of self-confidence; for he knew how to fight his opponents. He could be cruel, but he could also be smooth and sly. He might sometimes storm and rage, but that did not necessarily mean he was really angry. What made him really angry was when he found his own men muddling and bungling, as he had the day before yesterday with Mo Kan-cheng; and at times like that he became so angry that his health was threatened. But now he was more furious than ever, now that Shuangchiao Town had fallen to the rebels, because his arm, long as it was, could not reach those responsible for the fiasco.

His thoughts travelled from those responsible for keeping the peace in Shuangchiao to their superiors in the county, in the province, and even to the supreme authorities responsible for the whole country. The more he thought about it, the more muddled and upset he became. He threw down his paper and stared down absently at the carpet with its modern designs and the parquet floor around it, as he sat there as motionless as a statue.

The exquisitely furnished room was silent except for the rustle of the parrot in its cage as it preened its feathers.

The butler Kao Sheng opened the door quietly and peered round it. Sensing the tense atmosphere, he suddenly hesitated as if he had been struck dumb and stood transfixed in the doorway, not knowing whether to come in or not, his eyes appealing mutely to his mistress.

"What is it?" asked Mrs. Wu Sun-fu irritably, glancing at her husband as she spoke. Wu Sun-fu looked up sharply to see Kao Sheng with a couple of visiting cards in his hand.

"All right," he said gruffly, with a gesture of impatience. "Show them into the drawing-room."

He stood up and paced to and fro for a moment, then looked at himself in the mirror to make sure that his expression was back to normal. Satisfied, he went across to his wife and patted her gently on the shoulder.

"Pei-yao," he said, "for two days now you've looked worried and rather depressed. Don't fret so much about things: I'll think of something! You've always been delicate."

He took her hand and gave it a gentle squeeze, as if to transfuse some of his own courage and optimism into her. Without waiting to see what effect his words had had, he let go of her hand and strode out of the room.

Mrs. Wu Sun-fu leaned back in her chair, her head resting on the top of the back and her eyes brimming with tears. She understood what her husband had said, every word of it, but she knew, too, that she would never be able to make him understand her own thoughts and feelings: he was too engrossed in his "business" for that. A strange sensation welled up inside her, but whether it was one of bitterness or pleasure she could not tell.

*

Wu Sun-fu was smiling as he stepped into the drawing-room. The first to rise and greet him was Tang Yun-shan.

"Sun-fu!" he cried, and began sympathetically: "I hear your

home town has been captured by the rebels. It just proves how incompetent the provincial authorities are!"

"We've only just seen the news in the morning papers," broke in Wang Ho-fu, gripping Wu Sun-fu's hand and sighing sympathetically. "But I suppose you've had a detailed report from your people in the town. Is it really as bad as the papers say, after all? They say there were quite a lot of troops stationed there — a whole battalion, wasn't it? How on earth did they let it happen?"

Wu Sun-fu smiled and asked his visitors to sit down.

"It's only in China," he began calmly, "that you find this strange phenomenon: our bandits are quite extraordinary in their violence. I've only just read about it myself in the morning papers. No other news has come through yet. I've no idea how bad the situation really is, and I don't know what to do about it. — But where's Mr. Sun Chi-jen got to?"

"He's been detained on business," muttered Tang Yun-shan in reply, lighting a cigarette. "He asked me to stand in for him."

While he was trying to speak and draw on his cigarette at the same time, the smoke caught in his throat and made him cough.

"We didn't choose a very fortunate moment for our meeting," said Wang Ho-fu tactfully, with a smile at Wu Sun-fu, "just when there's been trouble in your home town. As you've only just heard the news yourself, I've no doubt you'll be busy enough today making arrangements, so I suggest we put off our meeting to another day."

Before Wu Sun-fu could reply, Tang Yun-shan jumped in first.

"Out of the question!" he cried. "I don't imagine for one moment that Sun-fu will agree to that. Sun-fu's no milksop: he's a man of action and initiative. I've yet to see him dithering and dawdling over anything! And when it comes to a piddling little problem like this, he just slaps on his thinking-cap and there you are — it's solved! Well, don't let's waste any more time! Let's get down to business!"

Wang Ho-fu and Wu Sun-fu could not help smiling at the tone of voice in which he said this: it was the one he always used when handling political and party affairs.

"Well, so far as Tu Chu-chai's concerned," began Wu Sun-fu, getting down to the matter in hand, "I've discussed it with him twice already, and he'll probably come in with us, I think. But he won't be able to make up his mind for sure until after the Dragon-boat Festival. He always takes his time, you know, and that's his strong point. I should say there is a four-to-one chance of his coming in on it. If you remember, gentlemen, we decided the night before last to work on the principle of keeping our numbers down when necessary. In view of this I don't think we should co-opt Chu Yin-chiu, Chen Chun-yi and Chou Chung-wei. Though, of course, the decision on that rests with you two gentlemen."

"Will there be enough of us without them, then?" interjected Tang Yun-shan anxiously, then cackled inanely.

Wu Sun-fu smiled without answering, knowing well that all Tang Yun-shan wanted was to rope in a whole group of industrialists, regardless of whether they had any capital or not, and organize them into a body which would engage in political activities. And when it came to the tortuous mazes behind the scenes of the business world, Tang Yun-shan was a complete novice. Wu Sun-fu, who had been to Europe and America, was not an old-fashioned merchant, but a modern industrialist, and although he always kept one eye on politics, his main attention was firmly on the profit-and-loss aspect of his business, and from this aspect it never for one moment wavered.

Wang Ho-fu had just been sitting there with a smile on his lips, stroking his moustache and nodding; when he saw that Wu Sun-fu just smiled faintly in reply to Tang Yun-shan's question, he intervened himself.

"What do you mean, Yun-shan?" he asked. "Are you afraid of someone else snapping them up? You needn't worry about that! I used to think Chou Chung-wei and Chen Chun-yi had pots of money, seeing that they started off as compradores, and that's why I had ideas of including them. But now I understand from Sun-fu they've got nothing left but their signboards. In business, whether you're setting up a bank or anything else, you must be realistic. You can't afford to run a business as a sweepstake. Don't you agree, Sun-fu?"

"All right, all right!" interjected Tang Yun-shan hastily. "I'll accept the decision of the majority." Then, with a rapid glance at his companions' faces, he opened his briefcase and took out a large folder.

"Now, I have here," he went on, "Sun Chi-jen's draft plan for the project. Shall we look at it now?"

The "draft plan" turned out to be a brief note containing a few lines on three points: firstly, a capital of five million dollars, one-third of which to be collected first; secondly, a few new enterprises — textiles, buses, mines, chemicals; and thirdly, financial aid for several enterprises already in existence — certain silk factories, silk goods manufactories and steamship companies. As a matter of fact, it was no more than a summary of various points which had been brought up on a previous occasion.

As Wu Sun-fu glanced over the "plan," the words conjured up in his mind visions of a forest of tall chimneys belching black smoke, a fleet of merchantmen breasting the waves and a column of buses speeding through the countryside. He smiled with satisfaction. These were no castles in the air. An experienced industrialist like him did not mind a humble beginning so long as he had a large-scale plan to work to. This optimism was confirmed by the experience which he had accumulated in building up his home town from scratch. His first step had been to set up a small power-house in Shuangchiao Town as the starting-point for building up his "Shuangchiao kingdom." There, his achievements had not been insignificant; but his scope had been limited by the small population — barely a hundred thousand. His activities in Shuangchiao Town had been mere child's play compared with this present scheme.

As he reflected along these lines, Wu Sun-fu felt that the fall of Shuangchiao Town was not such a terrible blow after all. His pimply face shone with excitement as he laid Sun Chi-jen's "draft plan" on the table. He looked at Wang Ho-fu and was going to say something to him, when Tang Yun-shan unexpectedly interjected:

"Since we're not going to ask Chu Yin-chiu and the rest of them to come in with us, why should their factories be included for financial assistance? Isn't that being rather inconsistent? Of course," he added hastily, with a self-conscious laugh, "I don't really understand all the ins and outs of the business — I just wondered, that's all."

There was a note of suspicion in Tang Yun-shan's voice: although he didn't quite understand what it was all about, he seemed nevertheless to have a shrewd idea that there was a catch in it somewhere.

Wu Sun-fu and Wang Ho-fu exchanged amused glances and burst out laughing. They turned to look at Tang Yun-shan's face with its mixture of cunning and naivety, then he, too, burst out laughing. Not expecting to get an answer from either of them, he picked up the plan and looked through it for something else to talk about, but Wu Sun-fu snatched it from him and said:

"There's something in what you say, Yun-shan. Anyway, since you're one of us now and are going to be manager of our bank or whatever it is, we ought to let you in on what's going to happen. Well, now, the reason we want to keep Chu Yin-chiu and the others out of it is because they have no capital and if they come in they'll be partners in name only and won't be any earthly use to the business. On the other hand, their factories are a part, however small, of Chinese-owned industry. They are now going downhill and it looks as if they'll soon have to close down. If they do, it'll be a loss to our national industry. If they are eventually bought out by foreign interests in Shanghai, it'll mean an increase in foreign influence in China and an even greater loss to Chinese industry. So it's up to us to assist them for the good of Chinese industry. It's in pursuance of this aim that all the enterprises earmarked for aid in the plan have been included."

Wu Sun-fu stopped abruptly, bringing his forefinger down with a crack on the table to emphasize his point, his face beaming self-righteously. He spoke with such earnestness and lucidity that he made Tang Yun-shan feel rather small and regret his suspicions. Even Wang Ho-fu, his customary smile replaced by an air of seriousness, was deeply impressed by Wu Sun-fu's arguments.

"You're quite right, Sun-fu," he agreed solemnly. "I can see you have the country's best interests at heart. Chinese industries have been going for about fifty or sixty years now, and, even if we don't count the government enterprises run by such men as Li Hung-chang in the Ching dynasty, there have still been scores of privately run industries; but what success have they had? It's always been the same old story: through mismanagement, most of them have gone broke and fallen into the hands of foreign businessmen. — I tell you, Yun-shan, it's a crying shame when an enterprise is left in the hands of incompetent fools. They do neither themselves nor their country any good, and in the end they play into the hands of the foreigners. So we must be careful not to bungle things in the same way in our own enterprise, and if necessary we must advise even our closest relatives and friends to stop playing the fool, and make way for somebody who can do the job properly."

Tang Yun-shan burst out laughing again. Now he understood what it was all about. He was not so stupid, after all.

The three of them then got down to discussing some of the new enterprises included in the plan. No longer an "outsider," Tang Yun-shan began to feel almost like an expert. He quoted freely from the section on "Industrial Construction" in Dr. Sun Yat-sen's book *Plan for China's Construction*. He held that, as soon as the civil war was over, genuine democracy would be put into practice, and Sun Yat-sen's projects, the "Great Eastern Harbour" and the "Four Big Trunk Railways," would be built in a very short space of time. In view of this, he suggested that they should invest now in sites close to the projected great harbour and the railway lines for their future enterprises. As he put this to them, he opened his briefcase and fished out a map. He then marked certain spots on it with a pencil, giving an enthusiastic commentary as he did so. When he had finished, he drew a sigh of relief, as if he had just completed a monumental task, and turned to his two industrialist friends.

"Well, gentlemen, what do you think of my idea?" he beamed. "Sun Chi-jen thinks quite highly of it. Later on I'll draw up a more detailed plan in writing so that we can publish it when we get going and advertise for shares in the bank."

Wang Ho-fu had nothing against it, but he hesitated to commit himself. Instead, he turned and looked expectantly at Wu

Sun-fu, waiting for him to give his opinion first, for he considered Wu Sun-fu wiser, more resourceful and more decisive than himself.

But, strange to say, Wu Sun-fu, who was known for his drive and ability to make snap decisions, now hesitated and looked worried, for in his opinion the "Great Eastern Harbour" and the railways were so many castles in the air. It is true he was imaginative, but he was also a realist. He always believed in incorporating a high ideal in a plan at the very outset and keeping it in view as one's ultimate objective, but he would not accept a mere castle in the air. After a moment's hesitation he said with a reluctant smile:

"Yes, I suppose that's not a bad idea. We need something in the way of an attractive signboard. Actually, our plan could consist of two parts: Yun-shan's idea for the first part, and Sun Chi-jen's draft for the second; we could call the first part the external aspect and the second the internal aspect, the first being for public consumption as our ultimate objective and the second constituting our immediate objective. In this way, we'll have something solid to get on with, and then one day, when the 'Great Eastern Harbour' and so on have been completed, we'll be able to expand even more. How does that sound to you, Hofu?"

"A capital idea!" Wang Ho-fu cried gleefully, completely won over. "It can't go wrong!"

His jubilation was interrupted by the arrival of the butler Kao Sheng, who hurried in and whispered something in Wu Sun-fu's ear. The other two noticed that Wu Sun-fu winced momentarily. He sprang up, excused himself hastily, and hurried out of the room.

Wang Ho-fu and Tang Yun-shan remained still for a moment, and the only movement was of the latter's shiny bald head, and of the smoke of his cigarette, which spiralled upwards from his lips like bubbles rising to the surface of a pond. Suddenly, he stubbed out his cigarette and dropped it into the ashtray.

"Capital five million dollars, one-third of which cash down," he muttered to himself. "That's a little over one and a half million. Hm, you can't do much with that!"

He glanced at Wang Ho-fu, who appeared not to have heard him, but was quietly relaxing with closed eyes, or perhaps he was busy with some plan of his own. Tang Yun-shan looked at the plan once more and counted the new projects listed there. There were at least five of them, including even some heavy industries. Now, even he, layman as he was, could not believe that five million dollars was enough to go round, let alone a mere million and a half. An exclamation suddenly burst from his lips:

"Ah! there's a great flaw in this! A very great flaw! We must definitely go into it with Sun-fu!"

Startled, Wang Ho-fu opened his eyes wide, but when he saw Yun-shan's serious expression, he burst out laughing. Tang Yun-shan, however, who ordinarily roared with laughter on the slightest pretext was in no laughing mood now.

"B — but, Ho-fu!" he spluttered. "Five million won't be enough, will it?"

Wu Sun-fu came back into the room just in time to see Tang Yun-shan agitatedly pointing at the draft, and to hear him say, "Five million won't be enough, will it?" He understood in a flash, but for the moment he was too preoccupied with what Tu Chu-chai had just told him on the telephone about an unfavourable development in the stock market to make any comment, so he just let him rave on.

Wang Ho-fu, realizing what was the matter, began to explain it to Tang Yun-shan in simple terms:

"It's like this, Yun-shan: we intend to do things step by step, not start all the enterprises at once —"

"Then why should we be applying for a government licence for everything in the plan?" protested Tang Yun-shan with a glance at Wu Sun-fu.

"Yes, but taking out a licence first," explained Wang Ho-fu testily, becoming impatient of Tang Yun-shan's naivety, "is just like making advance bookings at a theatre."

"To tell the truth," joined in Wu Sun-fu, dropping into a chair, "the first thing we'll do once the business gets going won't be to set up *new* enterprises, but to help out those of the *old* ones which are a bit shaky. But, all the same, we have to make advance bookings, so to speak, for new enterprises."

"That's all very well," retorted Tang Yun-shan, "but what happens if they don't *want* us to help them out? Your million and a half capital will be standing idle!"

"Ah, but we'll have a way of *making* them want to!" Wu Sun-fu assured him with a sardonic smile.

"Yun-shan, money need never stand still. And how far do you think a mere million and a half would go if you put it into government bonds?"

"Ho-fu's right," corroborated Wu Sun-fu. "Since our company is to be essentially a financial scheme, it'll be one of the main lines of our business to speculate in government bonds."

All this only made Tang Yun-shan all the more confused. He scratched his bald head and stared at the other two as if he were apologizing for being such a "greenhorn," though deep down he had more than a suspicion that they were deliberately avoiding the point at issue.

The door opened, and the butler Kao Sheng could be seen outside standing politely aside to allow a visitor to pass into the room. It was Sun Chi-jen, beaming all over his face. It was obvious at a glance that he was the bearer of good news. Tang Yun-shan was the first to notice him.

"Ah, Chi-jen!" he cried, jumping up. "You're just in time! I was just getting out of my depth. I herewith relinquish my office as your locum tenens!"

Sun Chi-jen gave a start, thinking that something must have gone wrong, but he was reassured when Wu Sun-fu and Wang Ho-fu burst out laughing and hurried forward to greet him. They assured him that they had discussed his plan and passed it unanimously, and that they would get going as soon as a date had been fixed.

"Chi-jen, I understood you were otherwise engaged," Wu Sun-fu said. "I'm glad you managed to get here after all."

"I had an appointment with a friend of mine," replied Sun Chi-jen, sinking into a rocking-chair. "Nothing important, really, but in the course of our discussion I stumbled on just the sort of thing we want —" His long neck swung round towards Wu Sun-fu.

"Guess what it is, Sun-fu!" he beamed. "Well, in three days we can set up our company!"

This was news indeed! Everyone looked overjoyed but no one spoke. They just turned and looked expectantly at Sun Chi-jen.

"Now you know it takes a long time to get a licence from the Ministry of Finance for a banking company, but we can't really afford to wait. If we called ourselves a consortium, we could take out a licence more easily, but our activities would be rather limited, and we don't want that. But now I have a solution. There's a certain trust company which is willing to co-operate with us — I say 'co-operate,' but actually, of course, we'll control the concern. The reason I dashed over was to break the news, so that we could discuss it and decide what to do. If you all think it would be a good idea, we can work out the terms we shall offer them."

Sun Chi-jen spoke slowly and deliberately, but his little head wagged with excitement.

An animated discussion ensued: questions, replies, pondering, and planning. The atmosphere was suddenly charged with excitement and tension. They expected Wu Sun-fu to subscribe two hundred thousand dollars within a week, but he felt rather hard put to it to do it, for just lately he had borrowed close on a million dollars — from various banks and money-lenders to pay his share in Chao Po-tao's "bull company" and on top of that he still had no idea how much he had lost in the incident in his home town. Consequently, his financial "manoeuvring power" had been much reduced. Nevertheless, he made up his mind on it and agreed to Sun Chi-jen's proposal, which was that within a week of the trust company accepting their terms, the three of them should each pay in two hundred thousand dollars as his share of the initial capital, so that they could begin operations without more ado.

They also decided that their first move would be to make a loan to help out the two industrialists Chu Yin-chiu and Chen Chun-yi.

"You'll arrange things with the trust company, then, Chi-jen," said Wu Sun-fu with enthusiasm. "I think we'd best leave that side of it entirely to you." He was quite confident of success, like a general on the eve of a decisive battle.

"Shan't we try to get any more subscriptions of shares, then?" Tang Yun-shan asked hopefully.

"No!" chorused the others firmly.

Tang Yun-shan forced a smile, though he was inwardly rather disappointed. It was now quite clear that he would never have the opportunity of seeing his masterpiece, his great industrial scheme, in the papers. But he quickly swallowed his disappointment and soon he was talking and laughing again.

*

After seeing his visitors off at the gate, Wu Sun-fu returned to the drawing-room and paced confidently up and down for a while. By now it was ten o'clock and time for him to go to the factory. He went into his study and wrote out two telegrams, one to the county government and one to Fei Little Beard, care of the county government. Then he rang for Kao Sheng and gave him his orders:

"Mr. Tu Chu-chai'll be ringing up later on. Ask him to get in touch with me at the factory. Two telegrams for Li Kuei to send off at once. And now the car!"

"Very good, sir. Are you going to the factory now, sir? There's a Mr. Tu from the factory to see you — he's been waiting some time at the lodge. Will you see him now, sir?"

Wu Sun-fu had forgotten that he had sent for Tu Wei-yueh, and this was the second time he had come. The first time he had waited a whole evening without seeing a sign of Wu Sun-fu, and now he'd come just when he was busy. After a moment's hesitation, Wu Sun-fu said rather impatiently, "Oh, all right; show him in."

Wu Sun-fu sat down at his desk. He glanced over the staff list, trying to remember what Tu Wei-yueh looked like, but without much success. There were so many petty clerks in the factory that even he, shrewd as he was, could not be expected to remember them all individually. His thoughts wandered to the "pep-talk" he had given the women the day before, and the various reports submitted by Mo Kan-cheng. Yes, everything seemed to be going smoothly. All he had to do was to use a little more tact, and the storm would probably blow over.

He felt so relieved at the thought that when Tu Wei-yueh came into the room, his purplish face, usually so stern, was brightened by a ghost of a smile.

"So you're Tu Wei-yueh, are you?" said Wu Sun-fu, leaning forward slightly and darting his keen eyes over the young man. Tu Wei-yueh bowed but made no reply. He showed no signs of nervousness, but returned Wu Sun-fu's glance frankly. As he stood there, erect and dignified, his clear, healthy face was completely expressionless and his bright eyes were alert and composed.

"How long have you been at the factory?"

"Two years and ten days," Tu Wei-yueh answered briefly and quietly. His exactness pleased Wu Sun-fu.

"Where do you come from?"

"I've the honour to be a fellow-townsman of yours."

"Oh . . . from Shuangchiao Town, eh? Who vouches for your good conduct?"

"Nobody."

Wu Sun-fu was amazed. He reached out for the staff list for more information about this young man, when the latter himself explained:

"As you may remember, I came with a letter of recommendation from Old Mr. Wu, your father. You put me in the General Office as a junior clerk. Since then I've never been told that I need someone to vouch for me."

Wu Sun-fu's face twitched in what could have been a smile. He remembered now: two years ago, his late father had recommended this young man as the son of an old friend of his, who also happened to be a pupil of Wu Sun-fu's grandfather. Wu Sun-fu, who had never liked his father's way of life and his old-fashioned outlook, now suddenly looked at Tu Wei-yueh with transferred disfavour. He scowled and came straight to the point.

"It's been reported to me that it was you who let on about the wage-cut and so caused the sit-down strike the other day."

"That's right: I told some of the women that a wage-cut was coming soon."

"You did, did you? Quite the little talebearer, aren't you? You know damn well it's against the regulations!"

"I don't remember seeing anything of the kind in your *Factory Regulations,* Mr. Wu," Tu Wei-yueh replied calmly, gazing composedly at Wu Sun-fu's angry face.

Wu Sun-fu narrowed his eyes and looked at Tu Wei-yueh, who just stood there with a quiet dignity, his features betraying not the slightest sign of uneasiness. He was the first employee who had not quailed before Wu Sun-fu's basilisk eye. Wu Sun-fu could not help secretly admiring this cool and courageous young fellow. His face relaxed a little as he said in a milder tone of voice:

"In any case, you shouldn't have told them. Can't you see what a lot of trouble it's caused?"

"I'm afraid I can't agree with you there. Since there's going to be a wage-cut, what difference does it make whether the women know about it now or later on? Besides, even if you hadn't decided to cut their wages, they'd have gone on strike just the same. It was bound to happen sooner or later."

"What the devil do you mean by that?"

"Just this: the women already know that you've got a contract for a large quantity of silk and that you're speeding up the work to meet the order on time. Naturally enough, this is an opportunity for them and they don't want to miss it."

At this, Wu Sun-fu's face became convulsed with rage.

"What!" he rasped through clenched teeth. "They know about my contract? They know even this? I suppose you told them that, too, did you?"

"In a way, yes. They'd heard about it from some other source, and when they came and asked me, I just confirmed it. I couldn't have told them a lie. I'm sure you'll agree, Mr. Wu, that a man who tells lies is the last man to rely upon."

With a bellow of rage, Wu Sun-fu banged on the table and sprang to his feet.

"You scoundrel!" he roared. "You're just toadying to the women!"

To this Tu Wei-yueh did not reply, except to bow slightly and smile his calm smile.

"I know you carry on with some girl named Chu. You're just trying to get round her!"

"Mr. Wu, please don't drag my private affairs into it!" said Tu Wei-yueh calmly and defiantly, a glint of resentment in his keen eyes as he stared at Wu Sun-fu.

Wu Sun-fu's expression had also changed. He now looked firm and cold-blooded, and much more formidable than when he was ranting and raving. Tu Wei-yueh could see from all this what was coming to him, yet he was not in the least perturbed. He was intelligent, resourceful and courageous, but he was also stubborn. He was not without a certain affection for his job too, but he would never stoop to fawning on his employer in the way Mo Kan-cheng did. He stood there with a faint smile, calmly awaiting Wu Sun-fu's final disposal of him.

An oppressive silence fell upon the room. Wu Sun-fu stretched out his hand to press the bell on the wall. At a touch of his finger, Tu Wei-yueh's fate would be sealed. However, he suddenly changed his mind, took his hand away, and turned to scan Tu Wei-yueh's face once more. Alertness, calmness, courage: he could see them all in the youngster's face. A young man like this, if properly handled, could be very useful, he mused. There was no one to touch him on the whole of his staff. But was he reliable? These days, the more ability, drive and initiative a young man had, the more likely he was to have wild ideas. But that was something he could not tell at first sight. Wu Sun-fu thought hard and long, and when he finally sat down his expression was not so fearsome as it had been a few moments ago, though his voice was still harsh when he spoke again:

"The way you behave is nothing short of egging the women on to make trouble."

"You ought to realize, Mr. Wu, that that is something nobody could do!"

"You're just an agitator!" Wu Sun-fu raved angrily.

No answer. Tu Wei-yueh merely drew himself up and smiled sardonically.

"What are you sneering at?"

"Am I sneering? If I sneer, Mr. Wu, it's because I should have thought you would at least have realized that everyone must live and that everyone wants a decent standard of living. That fact alone is the most powerful incentive to agitation."

"Tst! Nonsense! The women have more sense than you. They realize that there are other points of view to be considered besides their own. They realize that capital and labour must work together. Didn't you see the way they quietened down when I explained things to them yesterday? And don't the trade union people support me, and aren't they doing their best to find a solution? Oh, yes, I know there are some dangerous elements among the women, inciting them to make trouble. They pretend to have the women's interests at heart, but all the time they're trying to take the bread out of their mouths by losing them their jobs. I'm in possession of detailed information about them and I know these dangerous elements are just the dupes of someone outside who's just leading them up the garden path. I'm for peace, myself, and I don't like the idea of enforcing high-handed measures; but as the owner of the factory I'm like the head of a family, and as such I can't allow any black sheep among my employees. I'll have to expose the evil intentions of the trouble-makers, so that the women may know them for what they are, and fight them themselves from within!"

"Mr. Wu, was it just to tell me all this that you summoned me here twice?" Tu Wei-yueh asked disdainfully, his face still not betraying a flicker of emotion, as soon as Wu Sun-fu paused for breath.

"Eh? What else were you expecting?"

"Nothing. But I should have thought that you might have had something else to say."

Wu Sun-fu stared at the young man in astonishment and was beginning to wonder whether he had not a madman to deal with.

"Get out!" he suddenly stormed. "And leave your badge here!"

Slowly and calmly, Tu Wei-yueh took out his employee's badge and laid it on the table. He smiled, bowed slightly, and turned to go, when Wu Sun-fu suddenly called him back.

"Just a minute! If you'll just come down to the factory with me, you'll be able to see for yourself how quiet everything is now and how game the women are to consider the interests of the factory as a whole!"

Tu Wei-yueh turned and looked Wu Sun-fu in the eye. The smile had never left his face, and Wu Sun-fu could see now that it was not the smile of a madman at all.

"What are you smiling at?"

"I'm smiling . . . at the thought that it's usually calm before a storm — so calm that there isn't even a breath of wind!"

Wu Sun-fu's face suddenly purpled, but he immediately pulled himself together. His experienced eye had at last discovered something unique in Tu Wei-yueh's attitude, something which told him that this young fellow was decidedly not mad, but something quite out of the ordinary. Wu Sun-fu asked as politely as he could:

"Do you mean to say the information I've had from Mo Kan-cheng is incorrect? Do you mean to say that the trade union people will side with the women to fight against me?"

"I've no idea what Mo Kan-cheng's told you. No, I don't think the trade union people would turn against you. But surely you must know how little use they really are to you?"

"Eh? Do you mean —?"

"These union people may be rather important in your eyes, but the women don't care a damn for them."

"You mean they're useless?"

"It's not quite as simple as that. If the women had confidence in them, they'd naturally be very useful; but as they seem to be on your side, the women don't trust them. This so-called trade union's nothing more than a figure-head — no, I don't think you could even call it that any longer, for even a mere figure-head, as you're probably well aware, has its uses as a stimulant, and our trade union hasn't even that much usefulness. Now that the unrest among the women is getting really serious, the union has been shown up for the empty bubble that it is. They want to do as you tell them and at the same time keep up the pretence of representing the interests of the women. I suppose I'd better be frank with you. The union leaders want to come to a secret understanding with you, while at the same time they still put on an act with the women of protecting their interests."

"What do you mean, 'understanding'?"

"They want a five per cent rise in the monthly bonus and a special two-dollar bonus for the Dragon-boat Festival."

"What! A bigger bonus and one at the festival as well?"

"Yes, that's the idea they're putting into the women's heads. They hope such a concession will stave off the women's demand for a cost-of-living allowance. If they can't even do this for them, their bubble will be pricked. Since they run the union, it's inevitable that they should try to play this sort of trick."

Wu Sun-fu's face became distorted with rage.

"So that's their game, is it?" he snarled. "How is it that Mo Kan-cheng hasn't told me anything about it? Has he fallen asleep on the job?"

Tu Wei-yueh smiled cynically.

After a moment Wu Sun-fu calmed down and eyed Tu Wei-yueh narrowly.

"Why didn't you come and tell me all this earlier?" he demanded abruptly.

"You didn't ask me earlier, Mr. Wu," replied Tu Wei-yueh dryly, a self-satisfied glint in his eye. "Anyway, I shouldn't have thought a mere clerk doing odd jobs in the office and earning twenty dollars a month would be expected to send in reports of this kind. But things are different now that you've taken back my employee's badge. Now I am just the son of your father's friend. We're just two friends chatting about this and that — the union, conditions in the factory, and so on. I don't mind discussing these things now that there's no danger of arousing jealousy or being accused of crawling or stabbing anyone in the back."

Feeling the sting in Tu Wei-yueh's remarks, Wu Sun-fu forced a smile; he couldn't help admiring this formidable young man. He couldn't understand how it was that he had failed to notice him before when he had been at the factory for two years.

"You appear to be a young man of strong will," he said tentatively.

"Yes, Mr. Wu," smiled Tu Wei-yueh. "Except for my will-power, there's nothing else I've got that I can take a pride in."

The insinuation in his reply seemed quite lost on Wu Sun-fu, who bent his head in thought for a moment, then suddenly burst out:

"So they want an increased bonus and a special bonus into the bargain, do they? I just can't agree to that. Can you see any way of putting an end to the trouble without giving in to them?"

"You can refuse if you like, but if you do the trouble will end in quite another way."

"You think the women would dare to riot?"

"That depends on how you go about it, Mr. Wu."

"The way you look at it, I must give them something, then — isn't that so? All right, then: I may as well help the union people to play their trick."

"You can do it that way if you like."

Wu Sun-fu was none too pleased at this reply. He glanced quickly at the smiling face of Tu Wei-yueh.

"What else can you suggest?"

"Just work it out, Mr. Wu: How much would it cost you, if you did what the union people want you to do?"

"About five thousand dollars, I suppose."

"Right," continued Tu Wei-yueh calmly. "Five thousand dollars is not what you'd call a large sum of money. But perhaps a smaller sum than five thousand could produce even greater results, if only you can find someone who knows how to make good use of it."

Wu Sun-fu's thick eyebrows seemed to twitch, but his face betrayed not a flicker of emotion. His keen eyes gradually fastened themselves upon Tu Wei-yueh's face in a penetrating gaze that seemed to go right through him, so that even Tu Wei-yueh, for all his coolness, felt rather ill at ease. He dropped his head and bit his lip.

Wu Sun-fu suddenly stood up and boomed, "Do you know what the women are up to now?"

"No, I don't. I expect you'll find out when you get to the factory," countered Tu Wei-yueh, looking the other in the face and drawing himself up to his full height. Wu Sun-fu could not help laughing good-humouredly. He realized that once this young man had made up his mind not to give anything away, there was nothing he could do to make him. His obstinacy annoyed him rather, but he admired his firmness, and had now made up his mind to enlist the young man as an ally. He picked up a pen and, without sitting down, scribbled a few lines on a sheet of note paper and gave it to Tu Wei-yueh.

"I took your badge away just now," he said with a gracious smile, "and now I'm giving you this in exchange."

The note said briefly, "To Mr. Mo Kan-cheng. This is to inform you that as from this month Mr. Tu Wei-yueh's salary will be increased by fifty dollars. Sun-fu, May 19."

Tu Wei-yueh glanced over the note and laid it on the table. He said nothing, and his face was as expressionless as before.

"What!" gasped Wu Sun-fu, staring at Tu Wei-yueh in amazement. "Don't you want to work for me?"

"Thank you very much for your kindness, Mr. Wu, but I couldn't accept it. This piece of paper won't enable me to do anything worth while."

For the first time Tu Wei-yueh betrayed some emotion in his voice, as he frankly returned Wu Sun-fu's gaze.

Wu Sun-fu did not say anything, but quietly pressed the bell on the wall; then, picking up his pen again, he added a few words to the note: "All inspectors and forewomen below Mo Kan-cheng will take orders from Tu Wei-yueh as from today. Disobedience will not be tolerated." He threw down the pen and turned to the butler who had just come into the room. "Send the car round to take Mr. Tu here to the factory."

Tu Wei-yueh read the postscript, looked at Wu Sun-fu intently for a moment, then bowed: "As from today, I have the privilege of serving you, Mr. Wu."

"If a man's got ability, I'll always give him a fair chance. I'm well aware that there are a lot of very able young men about these days, but unfortunately I'm always too busy to be able to spend much time getting around among the younger people. — And now you can go back to the factory and tell the women that I'll do my best to give them satisfaction. — And if you want to see me about anything, just drop in any time."

Wu Sun-fu's face beamed with satisfaction, for his keen powers of observation and appraisal told him that the trouble in the factory would soon be over.

*

However, a man like Wu Sun-fu could not be content with a single achievement. He began pacing the floor, sunk in thought. Suddenly a doubt began to trouble him: Was he such a good judge of men after all? Though he had always kept his eyes open for capable men, he had overlooked this Tu Wei-yueh until this moment. Another thing: he had not been able to anticipate this trouble in the factory, and right up till yesterday he still had no accurate idea of how strong the women really were. As a matter of fact, he had been blinded and deceived by his own underlings, and even found himself under the menace of his unruly workers. Now, even though he had high hopes of finding a solution to the immediate problem — and a solution which was to his advantage — nevertheless, it had cost him a pretty penny. Taking things all in all, it had been a serious setback for him.

It was not that he grudged spending an extra two or three thousand dollars — he sometimes lost more than that in a few games of mahjong, and gladly — but to have to pay out because of his subordinates' inefficiency was a different matter and he would have to put a stop to it. Foreign businessmen, he mused, were naturally more far-sighted and they knew how to manage things with a rod of iron, but then they had loyal and competent staff. It was this last that lay behind their ability to deal with difficult situations easily and make a success of everything they did. In industrially backward China, on the other hand, there was no such force of trained staff available. The office staff he had in his factory were no better than a lot of hangers-on sponging on a local squire. All they were fit for was dodging their work, fawning on him, and making a mess of everything. As these thoughts passed through his mind, Wu Sun-fu suddenly lost hope in the future of China's youthful industry. There was not even a reserve of staff to fill the lower administrative grades, to say nothing of the higher grades.

People like Mo Kan-cheng, for instance, were not fit to be anything more than rent and debt collectors in a country town.

"As from today, I have the privilege of serving you, Mr. Wu."

The forewoman Wang Chin-chen and the overseer Li the Pockmarked were a couple of scoundrels whose only abilities were bluffing, bickering, beating the women, and taking his bribes. For all that, he had not got rid of them because it was so difficult to find competent, reliable staff. Besides, with his own eagle eye watching over things all the time, there should never have been any trouble. How was he to know that he was on the verge of disaster? It must be that the workers were not so tractable as they used to be!

The more Wu Sun-fu pondered as he paced to and fro, the more depressed he became. He had always believed in hiding his fits of depression from other people, even from his wife. It was this custom that had enabled him to win the trust and respect of other people, and he also regarded it as the best method of self-discipline. But there was one disadvantage. Whenever he locked himself up and fretted and brooded alone, he was always acutely aware of his loneliness. He felt like a commander-in-chief racking his brains without a trusted aide-de-camp to confide in or an able staff-officer to advise him. Just a short while ago he had taken a liking to Tu Wei-yueh and promoted him on the spot to a position of great responsibility; but he was suddenly assailed by doubts — not about the young man's talents, about which he had no qualms, but about his ideas. Nowadays, he believed, the more intelligent, capable and spirited a young man was, the more dangerous were his ideas, and the more likely he was to be possessed by the "evil creed" of communism.

This worry nagged at Wu Sun-fu until he was on the verge of despair. Middle-aged men like Mo Kan-cheng were useless and young men like Tu Wei-yueh were dangerous. Yet how could he keep the wheels of industry turning on his own? He scowled with frustration and clenched his teeth, then picked up the telephone and barked into it. He had decided to tell Mo Kan-cheng to keep an unobtrusive eye on Tu Wei-yueh.

But when he heard Mo Kan-cheng humming and hawing like an imbecile at the other end of the line, Wu Sun-fu suddenly changed his mind and rasped sternly at him instead:

"Have you received my note? . . . Right! All the staff will

obey Mr. Tu's orders — and no shirking! . . . Money? Well, he'll want some for — um, 'expenses'. . . . Let him have what he wants, and he can account to me personally. Understand?"

Wu Sun-fu put down the receiver and smiled grimly. Now that he had taken the plunge and put Tu Wei-yueh on trial, he would have to keep an eye on this likable yet alarming young man himself. And he had to show himself consistent and firm of purpose and not let his employees know that he could sometimes waver — that he had put a man in a job and yet hesitated to trust him.

He left the library in a hurry and walked along the veranda to the drawing-room.

His bulletproof motorcar was waiting for him in front of the steps outside the drawing-room, and his chauffeur and Old Kuan, his bodyguard, were chatting idly.

The door of the small drawing-room was ajar and Wu Sun-fu heard sounds of gay youthful laughter coming from inside. He frowned and automatically glanced to see his wife, Lin Pei-shan, and Fan Po-wen with their heads together. He had seldom paid attention to them, but this time he felt suddenly annoyed. Coughing tactfully, he stepped into the room with an expression of displeasure on his face.

Surprised, the three of them started apart to reveal a fourth, Ah-hsuan, who had been hidden between Mrs. Wu Sun-fu and Fan Po-wen. The boy was still engrossed in some book or other quite unaware of Wu Sun-fu's presence. The latter walked up to them, glaring round the room and finally stopping to fix his gaze on Ah-hsuan.

Ah-hsuan suddenly came to and looked quickly up and, seeing who it was, self-consciously put the book down. Lin Pei-shan had gone over and sat down by the window and was tittering behind her hand. Wu Sun-fu had only intended to assert his authority, but he was becoming really annoyed. He restrained himself, however, and casually picked up the book and glanced at it. It was a collection of Fan Po-wen's verses.

"Modern poetry, eh? You youngsters are very fond of that sort of thing, aren't you!"

His tone and smile conveyed a hint of sarcasm. He glanced

at Fan Po-wen, and began idly turning the pages. Then a poem caught his eye:

> Gone are the lovely banks of the Su
> Whose winding way was edged with tender green,
> Usurped by motorcars like beetles black
> Enveloped in a swirl of yellow dust;
> And the vulgar villas of the idle rich
> Have sullied the quiet grace of West Lake.

Wu Sun-fu broke into a contemptuous laugh. He suddenly remembered that Fan Po-wen had often accused the "vulgar bourgeoisie" of not understanding that sublime and sacred subject — Art. This view of Fan Po-wen, which he had thought merely ridiculous before, was now offensive to him. Modern youth were just like that: either romantic and decadent, or radical and perverted. As he looked at the poet Fan Po-wen standing before him, his mind flashed to Tu Wei-yueh who had just left him. Since he could not very well give the poet a lecture he turned to take it out on his younger brother.

"Well, well, Ah-hsuan! You've only been in Shanghai a few days, and you've already become a man of culture! Unfortunately, only a talented man can be a poet, and one could hardly call you talented!"

"But there's a famous saying that a poet can be either a genius or an idiot," put in Fan Po-wen sarcastically, with a knowing wink at Lin Pei-shan. "In Ah-hsuan one can catch a glimpse of the poet. Anyway, he's much more hopeful than Mammon sitting in his golden palace." This witticism made Lin Pei-shan giggle uncontrollably and even Mrs. Wu Sun-fu couldn't help smiling. Wu Sun-fu and Ah-hsuan, however, remained serious; then Ah-hsuan looked up quickly in bewilderment to see that Wu Sun-fu was frowning. Though not a "poet" himself, Wu Sun-fu understood quite well what Fan Po-wen meant. He detested people who showed off their cleverness in glib phrases, and believed that only a nincompoop could indulge in such petty tricks of speech just to get a laugh from the ladies. He glared briefly at Fan Po-wen and turned to go, when the latter said:

"I say, Sun-fu, I really don't understand why you have to stay in the silk business. There are lots of other ways of making money, you know."

"Silk's the only Chinese industry that can win back some of the money that's going out of the country," replied Wu Sun-fu, as if he grudged an answer; his dislike of the poet was more intense than ever.

"Oh, is it? Chinese silk goes abroad, is made into silk goods, and then sold back to China. Look at Pei-yao and Pei-shan — they're wearing Chinese silk from abroad! Last month I happened to be in Hangchow and I noticed that on nine looms out of ten they were using Japanese rayon. This year alone Shanghai merchants have imported over eighteen thousand bales of Japanese rayon at a cost of some nine million eight hundred thousand dollars! At present the export of Chinese silk to Europe is at a standstill, and the New York market is flooded with Japanese silk, while Chinese silk is just piling up in the manufacturers' warehouses. And while you are bemoaning the fact that there is no market for your silk, Chinese silk goods manufacturers are importing Japanese rayon. Isn't that a curious phenomenon and a handicap to Chinese industry?"

Fan Po-wen delivered himself of this oration as if he was anxious to free himself of the stigma of "romantic poet," but for all that, Wu Sun-fu's dislike of the poet was in no way lessened; in fact, it made him dislike him all the more. As an industrialist, he was not interested in such superficial views on the bad luck of Chinese silk. The chief mission of an industrialist, as he saw it, was to develop industry, to increase the number of factory chimneys, and to expand the market. If his silk went through a factory in a foreign country and came back to China in modified form, that was not his concern. It was the job of the government to take care of that. An industrialist could not cut off his nose to spite his face!

"Ha! the same old platitudes!" snorted Wu Sun-fu cynically, as he shrugged his shoulders and walked off. In the doorway he turned his head to call his wife into the dining-room, where he warned her sternly:

"Pei-yao, I think you should keep an eye on your sister, and not let her fritter away her time as if she were still a child."

Mrs. Wu Sun-fu stared at her husband, not knowing what to make of it.

"Po-wen," he went on, "may be intelligent and witty, but he's got no 'go' in him. I don't like to see Pei-shan going round with him all the time. Fu-fang's told me that she would like to make a match between her and Tu Hsueh-shih. So far as I can see, Hsueh-shih's the more promising of the two."

"Oh . . . I see," his wife answered hesitatingly after a long pause, still staring at him. "Don't you think we'd better leave her to make her own choice?"

She did not like Fan Po-wen particularly — she had lately changed her mind about him — nor did she think highly of Tu Hsueh-shih. She had a plan of her own for her sister.

Wu Sun-fu frowned irritatedly, but said no more. With a glance at his wife, who stood there deep in thought, he slipped out into the garden, got into his car, and snapped at his chauffeur:

"The club!"

VI

FAN Po-wen and Lin Pei-shan were sitting together on a red bench in a shady, secluded corner of Jessfield Park. They had been there for half an hour.

Fan Po-wen had Lin Pei-shan's handbag in his hands and was toying with it, with that debonair and carefree expression on his face which a poet must have. His head on one side, he was listening with rapt attention while she murmured softly and desultorily, her voice rising and falling. Though they were sheltered by a clump of cypresses from the gaze of passers-by and from the slanting rays of the setting sun, Fan Po-wen felt tiny beads of perspiration breaking out on his temples — but whether it was because there was no breeze or for some other reason it was hard to tell.

Lin Pei-shan was wearing a thin, light-blue frock, low-cut and sleeveless. She was sixteen and just at the age when her developing figure had reached a plump perfection. Her rounded breasts seemed to be bursting out of the close confines of her lace-edged white silk slip. As she talked she traced lines on the grass with the point of her shoe. She was lively yet dispassionate, as if she was not telling him about herself at all, but about someone else who did not concern her.

Her voice gradually tailed off and soon she stopped altogether; then, with a sparkling smile, she tilted back her head to gaze at the reddening clouds overhead.

"Go on, Pei-shan!" urged Fan Po-wen, turning suddenly towards her after sharing her contemplation of the sky for a while. "You're keeping me in suspense, you know." Once more he wiped his perspiring brow, then fixed his eyes a little nervously on her pretty face.

Lin Pei-shan returned his look, but without the least sign of nervousness or excitement — just a languid smile. Then, suddenly, she giggled and made a gesture as much as to say "That's all."

"There's nothing more to tell," she said in her clear, tinkling voice. "I've told you everything. Aren't you satisfied?"

"I've heard enough, but not understood enough," Fan Po-wen flashed back glibly. Lin Pei-shan giggled and stretched herself, letting one arm flash past Fan Po-wen's face as she did so. The breath of fragrance from her arm so unnerved him that he completely forgot what he had been going to say. He could only gaze, infatuated, at her round bright eyes beneath slender eyebrows, her gleaming white teeth between scarlet, slightly parted lips, her smooth white neck and her swelling breast; and as he gazed, all sorts of vague, confused thoughts chased each other through his brain. When his eyes went up again to her face, he found her as calm, dispassionate and impersonal as she always was. Her smile was tender, but apparently without any special significance. Fan Po-wen felt something nagging at his mind and suddenly remembered what it was he was going to say:

"I really can't understand why Sun-fu doesn't agree that you and I —"

"That's Sun-fu's affair," she broke in before he could finish. "There's no point in going over it again!" Neither her face nor her voice betrayed any unusual excitement or annoyance.

Fan Po-wen was taken aback at her reply: her indifference puzzled him. He waited a moment, then, as she seemed to consider the subject closed, he tried another approach:

"And there's something else which I don't understand — why is it that your sister disagrees, too?"

"I've no idea. I just told you what she told me. What's the point of bothering our heads about it?"

She sounded so detached and impersonal that he began to feel exasperated. With an effort, he resisted the temptation to scintillate, and said simply:

"Don't be so silly, Pei-shan! Surely you don't just go around repeating like a parrot what your sister says? Why don't you try to think for yourself? You speak as if your own feelings weren't involved. It is as if you had become completely detached from yourself and were looking at yourself from a distance. Pei-shan, you ought to be yourself. Haven't you any ideas of your own? Do try to find yourself!"

"But I'm here, sitting beside you. It's me that's been talking with you all this time! If there *is* another me, I've never known it, and I don't want to know, either. My sister told me certain things in confidence and asked me to keep them to myself, but since you kept asking me and since some of the things she said concern you, I just repeated what she said to me. But now you want to know what my own ideas about it are — well, as a matter of fact, I never have any definite ideas about anything. I always feel there's good and bad to everything, and I've never really worried what anyone thinks of anything. Well, are you still not satisfied? Oh, it's really difficult to know what else to say!"

Her voice was soft and tender and she smiled as she spoke, which made Fan Po-wen feel a little better, in a way. But he was conscious that she had said a great deal without touching the crucial point — her real attitude towards him.

He drew a sigh and rested his chin dejectedly on his upturned palm, while his eyes strayed from the grass beneath his feet to her shapely calves. On a sudden impulse, he snapped open her handbag and looked in the little oval mirror inside the flap. He saw a face which was neither too round nor too pointed, a fine-looking intellectual face, rather triangular. It was a little pale at the moment, but the pallor was tinged with a sadness that would appeal to any sensitive young girl. The mirror trembled, and the reflection suddenly disintegrated and became all eyebrows and eyes — long thick eyebrows matched by long, intelligent eyes. When the eyes and the eyebrows were viewed as a whole, however, a restless melancholy could be discerned behind the expression of intelligent awareness. In short, it was a face to win the love and sympathy of a sentimental girl of, say, twenty. If it chanced to attract a girl of sixteen like Lin Pei-shan — lively, innocent, and free from worldly cares — it was simply because of its well-shaped lips, always parted in a mysterious smile and always ready with an amusing quip. After gazing in the mirror awhile, he sighed and snapped the handbag shut. When he looked up at her again, he found a tender smile still playing round her lips, and when he looked into her limpid eyes, he seemed to see all the little confidences and intimacies he had ever shared with her reflected there. Could all this be swept away by Wu Sun-fu's or his wife's "disapproval," then? Never! He was suddenly filled with an excitement and a boldness such as he had never known before.

"Pei-shan! Oh, oh, Pei-shan!" he cried, suddenly grasping her hand.

Interpreting this *cri du coeur* as just another of his customary endearments, she neither moved nor spoke, but merely glanced at him in reply. She had a far-away look in her eyes, and was clearly thinking of something else, something far removed from the present scene. But Fan Po-wen had no inkling of this. Her hand seemed warmer and softer than ever before, and the mere touch of it set him a-tingle. Although it was quite commonplace for them to hold hands, at this moment it held a strange attraction for him. He moved his head closer, intending to steal a kiss, but as he was almost touching her cheek, his courage suddenly failed him: he was afraid of being snubbed. He covered his embarrassment by repeating lamely:

"But why should Pei-yao now object to it?"

"Oh, dear! Didn't I just tell you I don't know?"

Her reply came quickly, as if she was surprised at the question. Then she smiled again. Her reply was tempered with a certain warmth, which he took to imply: "It's entirely up to you. To me, it's all the same." His heart gave a leap and his face flushed hotly. He looked at her with desire in his eyes, from her face down to her breasts and from her breasts back up to her face. Everything radiated a youthful charm and an irresistible warmth and softness. A sudden idea flashed into his bewildered mind: just a little firmness on his part, and she would yield, wouldn't she? He was about to put his idea into action, when he was startled by a rustle in the clump of cypresses behind them. He started nervously, and his boldness suddenly evaporated.

A cool breeze sprang up, and birds were twittering in the trees opposite. A flock of pigeons fluttered down on to the grass in front of them and began strutting about, stopping now and then to cock their heads on one side and look at the young couple. Fan Po-wen shifted his attention to the pigeons. There was something of the poet about their deportment, and he was tempted to write a short poem about it.

Lin Pei-shan, who seemed to be deep in thought all this time, suddenly gave a strange little laugh, as if to herself, and gently withdrew her hand from his. "I want to go back now," she suggested as she stood up. "I've been sitting on this hard bench so long that I'm stiff all over."

His poetic mood was immediately extinguished. He stood up and looked at her in bewilderment, wondering why she was in such a hurry. Though sitting in the park had not contributed materially to the solution of his problem — twice he had made up his mind to take the plunge and each time his courage had failed him — yet how poetic it had been, just the two of them quietly sitting there alone! He would have preferred to stay there, but he did not want to disagree with her (he had always done as she suggested), so he just heaved a disgruntled sigh.

In the ordinary way, his gentle passive resistance would have made her say something which he could have used to bring about a favourable turn in the situation. But today she was not her usual self. She just took her handbag from him and declared icily:

"I really do want to go home! I'm just fed up with everything here!" Without waiting for his reply, or even asking him to accompany her, she turned on her heel and walked briskly towards the park gate. In a few seconds she was out of sight among the trees. He went after her a short way and looked all round, but there was no sign of her.

*

He stood in frustration for a few moments, not knowing what to do for the best. At first he thought of running straight to the park gate and waiting for her there. But his masculine pride — the wounded pride of a young man when snubbed by a girl with whom he had been on good terms — stopped him.

Fan Po-wen walked disconsolately on through the park, looking as if he had lost something. The sun was sinking fast and couples began streaming into the park. They brushed past him, chattering and laughing, and seemed to be sneering at him and giving him suspicious glances. He envied and hated them at the same time, especially the men, who looked just like the rich, potbellied businessmen that he so despised. He felt quite out of place in such self-confident, arrogant company.

Now, should he go back to Wu Sun-fu's place and dally with her again? No, he thought, no self-respecting man would do that! What about going back to his room in the Tai Lai Hotel, then? No, that was the last thing he wanted to do. Suddenly this carefree poet wished he had a home to go to — a home with parents and brothers and sisters; but he had none. He felt he must be the loneliest man in the world. Then, true to the time-honoured tradition among depressed poets, an idea began to form in his mind: death. He paced along with bent head, his fertile imagination toying with the idea of dying. To think of him, a young poet with a carefree air which would make any girl's heart flutter, suddenly dying in front of all the members of the fair sex who were gracing the park on this lovely May evening! What a shock that would be for them! Would it not bring every female in the park, all the shy, soulful, sentimental young girls, to weep tears of sympathy over his handsome dead body — or, at least, make their dear hearts beat faster? Would that not be the most fitting, the most poetic death a poet could die? He could imagine no better way of turning his sorrow into happiness and his defeat into victory!

As luck would have it, a conveniently placed pond lay just ahead. This was as good a place as any, for all the young couples would stop when they reached this point, to sit on the benches round the pond. "I'll do what the great poet Chu Yuan* did!" he thought, as he made quickly for the pond; but, to his disappointment, there were hardly any suitable girls on the benches to witness the tragedy. Several foreign children were sailing a toy boat on the pond. A girl in white and a boy in grey were

---

* A great Chinese poet (340-278 B.C.). Exiled because of his patriotism and fearless criticism of the collaborationists, he finally drowned himself.

launching a handsome two-foot yacht. Its three red silk sails bellied out in the wind as the yacht sailed majestically away, leaving a faint trail of white in its wake, while the children ran along the bank beside it, whooping and laughing.

Fan Po-wen's poetic mood suddenly returned, and he soon had a couple of decent lines of poetry. All thought of suicide vanished from his mind as he decided that the poem was well worth finishing, but before he could work out the third line, the wind veered and a sudden gust made the little yacht heel over and capsize.

To tell the truth, Fan Po-wen was even more dismayed and upset at this unexpected disaster than the children themselves. On the voyage of life, he thought, one is often caught in such squalls, squalls which can capsize one's little boat. Man, poor creature, is nothing more than the sport of the inscrutable wind of fortune. Again he steeled himself, stepped back with a flourish, and tensed himself for a plunge into the pond. But just then he was seized by a sudden doubt, a doubt miraculously reinforced by the sound of a voice calling him from behind.

He straightened up and looked round to find Wu Chih-sheng standing just behind him and smiling at him.

Hardly knowing why, Fan Po-wen blushed, and stole a glance at Wu Chih-sheng's face and was relieved to see that his friend had apparently not realized his intention. He smiled as naturally as he could as he went across to greet him.

"On your own?" said Wu Chih-sheng. "Just watching children playing, eh?"

Was there just a hint of suspicion in his voice? Whatever it was, there was something odd in the way he said this.

Fan Po-wen gave a silent and evasive nod, but Wu Chih-sheng pressed him further, "Really alone?"

Fan Po-wen again nodded and forced an uneasy smile. He wanted to escape, but decided after all that Wu Chih-sheng's company was perhaps preferable to roaming up and down alone. He only hoped his friend would talk about something else. As if in answer to his prayer, Wu Chih-sheng immediately changed the subject.

"Have you heard about Chang Su-su? I thought you told me

He felt he must be the loneliest man in the world.

the other day that she was often brimming over with poetic sentiments —"

"Why? what's the matter with her now? Down with the plague?"

"No, she's not the type to be infected so easily! No, the trouble is, she can't get on with Li Yu-ting. The professor doesn't measure up to her expectations and she's quite down in the mouth about it."

At this news Fan Po-wen laughed gleefully. He felt grateful to Wu Chih-sheng for telling him, and became his usual facetious self again.

"But of course!" he said. "It was as inevitable as one and one making two! How could a girl like Su-su, who craves for 'strong stimulation,' ever be satisfied with a dry-as-dust professor? But I'm surprised at her, of all people, letting it get her down! It isn't worthy of her poetic spirit!"

"But Professor Li's just as disappointed in Chang Su-su, you know!"

"What! That dull schoolmaster so good that he —?"

"He's certainly very good at some things — money matters, for instance."

"Oh! . . . So it's a question of money, is it?"

"Of course! He's heard that her father's practically broke now, so he's every reason to be disappointed in her."

When he heard this, Fan Po-wen stared in open-mouthed amazement for a moment, then suddenly burst out laughing.

"Humph!" he shrugged. "These bourgeois make me sick with their 'money'!"

"That's because you make them sick with your modern poetry!" said Wu Chih-sheng sardonically, but with assumed seriousness. Fan Po-wen flushed, then immediately paled. He glared resentfully at Wu Chih-sheng and turned to walk away. He seemed genuinely upset, but he had gone only a couple of yards when he turned and came back. He laid his hand on Wu Chih-sheng's shoulder, and said in a low, serious voice:

"I hear they're going to make a match between you and Lin Pei-shan."

Wu Chih-sheng's face registered nothing. He glanced unconcernedly at Fan Po-wen, and replied unhurriedly, "Oh, but I've heard a different story."

"What's that? Come on, out with it!"

"In this modern age men choose their women, but women also choose their men. Men toy with women, but women also toy with men!"

Fan Po-wen's face fell and he was tempted to walk away. He decided this was his unlucky day. Everywhere he turned, he ran up against a brick wall. It was exasperating. Even his sense of humour seemed to have deserted him, leaving him in an irritable mood. But Wu Chih-sheng pretended not to notice.

"To tell you the truth," he said solemnly, looking Fan Po-wen straight in the eye, "Lin Pei-shan's waiting for you."

Fan Po-wen started violently, supposing that she hadn't gone home after all, but was still in the park waiting for him.

"Where's she waiting for me?" he asked agitatedly.

"In her heart, of course. She's waiting for you to get the Nobel Prize for Literature!"

As he said this, Wu Chih-sheng burst out laughing. Without a word, Fan Po-wen turned on his heel and stalked away, this time in earnest, and disappeared into the trees. Wu Chih-sheng gazed after him with a smile, but he couldn't help feeling a little amazed that the poet should stalk off in a rage like this, without even a glance over his shoulder. He waited a minute or two until he was sure that the poet was gone for good, then ran up on to a mound hidden in a clump of trees lying back from the pond.

"Huei-fang!" he called. "It's getting late. We'll have to get a move on if you want to see the zoo."

Huei-fang was leaning against a willow, dabbing her eyes with a handkerchief. Without a word, and with only a glance at Wu Chih-sheng, she followed him out of the trees. Her eyes were red from crying. When they had gone a short way, she caught up with him and asked him faintly, "Chih-sheng, was he going to throw himself into the pond? He looked as if he was."

"I didn't ask him."

"Why not? Well, you should have done, then. — When we were following him just now, he kept behaving strangely, all the way here. I thought then that there was something wrong. And when we met Lin Pei-shan on the way in, she looked a bit out of sorts, too...."

Wu Chih-sheng burst out laughing. He gazed at his cousin a moment before he went on:

"Fan Po-wen will never commit suicide, though he's threatened to do so over and over again. When you thought he was contemplating suicide, he was actually composing a poem — *Ode to a Pond*, perhaps. No, a poet like him would never really take his own life. You needn't worry about him!"

"Humph! I should worry! It's no concern of mine! Though —"

She blushed as she stopped short and walked on with bent head. Deep down in her heart she held a picture of Fan Po-wen as a gentle creature deserving of sympathy. She fell back behind Wu Chih-sheng again. When they had gone a little farther, she sighed softly, and, a tear trickled down her cheek.

*

An indefinable sadness had come over Huei-fang these last few days. Her heart seemed as taut as a drum, and the slightest stimulus from others' joy or sorrow set it vibrating in sympathy. When she was alone in her room, she felt numbed by an icy despair. In company, she felt out of place and nervous, as if everyone was brow-beating her. She felt quite alone in the world, and wanted more than anything a sympathetic friend, so that she could fling her arms round his neck and cry her eyes out, and pour out all her troubles to him. These few days in Shanghai had seemed an eternity. Her heart was full, but there was no one to tell.

Perhaps it was her loneliness, and this alone, that made her sympathize so easily with the love-lorn Fan Po-wen. However, as she walked along with Wu Chih-sheng, her own troubles and the changing scenes and faces about her gradually drove the poet's dear, sad face from her mind. At the zoo, she was attracted by a bear in a cage — a huge, black thing pacing to and fro like a philosopher, then rearing up on its hind legs and shaking its big clumsy head like an idiot. This made her smile, and for a moment she forgot even her own unhappiness.

Wu Chih-sheng ran across a fellow-student and fell into conversation with him. His friend, a brilliant-looking youngster despite his tousled head of hair, kept glancing at Huei-fang as they talked together. Their voices gradually dropped to a whisper, but she caught occasional snatches without really paying much attention to what they were saying.

"Your fiancée?"

"No — my cousin!"

Huei-fang blushed. Though she did not understand the foreign word "fiancée" she guessed what it meant from Wu Chih-sheng's answer. She turned away embarrassed and walked over to a cage in which she saw a family of monkeys leaping and gambolling about. They reminded her of a troupe of performing monkeys she had seen several years before at a temple fair at home. She could still remember one of them — it kept grinning and showing a mouthful of gleaming white teeth. That was her last, happy memory of the temple, for when she was fourteen and already looked a well-developed young lady, her father, the late Old Mr. Wu, would not let her go to the temple fairs any more because he thought the sexes mingled too freely there. Now, at the sight of all these monkeys, memories of her childhood days came flooding back, and she just stood there dreamily in front of the cage, looking to see whether one of the monkeys would grin at her.

But of all these monkeys not one grinned. They seemed to have acquired something of a townsman's nervousness, for all they seemed to be doing was scuttling and leaping all over the place and chattering hysterically. Huei-fang was rather disappointed, and she was just going to turn away and look for Wu Chih-sheng, when something unusual caught her eye. On a wooden box in the corner of the cage were two monkeys, one lounging lazily on its back and the other hunting for lice in the first one's fur, a serious expression on its face. You could tell from their intimate manner that there was some close link between them, she thought — yes, that was it! They were husband and wife! Huei-fang just stood there and gazed at them, while an indescribable mixture of feelings tumbled through her mind: something akin to gladness — or was it desolation? It was both of these and a sort of empty yearning besides. She did not dare look, yet she could not bear to tear her eyes away. She just stood there in a trance, until roused by Wu Chih-sheng's voice.

"Come on, they're closing in a minute."

Startled, she turned her head and gazed blankly at Wu Chih-sheng, not really taking in what he said. Then a sudden blush spread from her tender dimpled cheeks over her whole face.

She felt ashamed and flustered, as if he had read her secret thoughts. She was on the verge of crying, but managed to blink the tears away. Without a word she turned and walked blindly on. The zoo had become almost deserted, but she was quite unaware of the fact. She had only gone a few steps, when she came to a seat. She sat down dazedly and buried her face in her handkerchief.

"Huei-fang, are you feeling all right?" asked Wu Chih-sheng softly, obviously blind to what was going on inside her. "The zoo is closing at five, and the keepers are coming round to turn us out."

This blindness of his was hardly to be wondered at, for he had only mixed with modern city girls like Lin Pei-shan and Chang Su-sụ and so, of course, was a complete stranger to the secret sorrows and emotions of old-fashioned "boudoir maidens" like Huei-fang. What was surprising, however, was that his very ignorance gave Huei-fang a sense of relief, and she gathered some comfort from his gentle, sympathetic voice. She uncovered her face and smiled bravely up at him with tear-bright eyes, then stood up and replied with a trace of shyness:

"I'm all right now — let's go home, then."

The sun was already disappearing below the horizon, the evening breeze was cool and exhilarating, and every moment brought a fresh wave of visitors into the park. Wu Chih-sheng would have preferred to stroll about a little longer, or go and have a drink at the soda-fountain which had been set up under a mat awning, but Huei-fang was shy of the large crowds, especially those young couples who always seemed to be looking at her so suspiciously. She insisted on going home, though she knew she would not be any happier when she got there.

They were walking back past the pond, where all the benches

were now fully occupied, when they noticed a young man sitting on the grass against a tree not far from the pond, his head bent as if he was having a nap. Even from a distance, Huei-fang's sharp eyes told her that it was Fan Po-wen. She glanced at Wu Chih-sheng inquiringly. Wu Chih-sheng, who had also spotted him, smiled at her and nodded, then crept up behind Fan Po-wen and clapped his hands over his eyes from behind.

"Take your hands away! Who is it? Stop messing about!"

Fan Po-wen's protests were half-hearted and he made no attempt to move. Huei-fang came up behind Wu Chih-sheng and stood watching for a moment, then stepped lightly round the tree and stood beside Fan Po-wen. Wu Chih-sheng only held his hands tighter over Fan Po-wen's eyes, though he could not help laughing.

"Wu Chih-sheng, is it? I'd know that laugh anywhere. If I've guessed wrong, you can cut my head off!"

"You didn't have to guess. I gave myself away. Now, guess who's here with me."

This time, Fan Po-wen refused to guess. He just struggled to shake himself free, while his face became quite red from his exertions.

"Let go of him, Chih-sheng!" pleaded Huei-fang, feeling sorry for Fan Po-wen. But as she spoke, Fan Po-wen finally managed to break Wu Chih-sheng's hold, and sprang to his feet rubbing his eyes. When he turned round, he saw Huei-fang; he grasped her hand and said with a polite bow:

"You've saved my life, Miss Wu! I'm deeply grateful to you!"

She hurriedly snatched her hand away and turned her back on him, while a sudden blush spread over her cheeks. However, she could not help asking timidly:

"So you haven't gone back after all, Mr. Fan. What have you been doing here all alone?"

"Er — composing poems," he answered, tilting his head on one side and looking up at the sky, as if, oblivious of everything else, he was absorbed in reciting his poems mutely to himself. Wu Chih-sheng was greatly amused at this, but managed to keep a straight face as he threw Huei-fang a meaningful look. Fan Po-wen sighed and stamped his foot, then went up to Huei-fang and began:

"Whenever I'm in low spirits I take comfort in poetry. My poems are my tears. And the worse I feel, the better are my poems. — And now, just as I was putting the finishing touch to a wonderful poem, this lout Chih-sheng had to come along and break the spell. Now I've forgotten every word of it!"

As she hung upon his every word, Huei-fang gazed at his pale but stirring face, while her heart fluttered with a strange sensation which she never before experienced.

"All right, then," Wu Chih-sheng broke in indifferently: "I'll leave you to your versifying. Good-bye!"

He turned and walked away, swinging his arms. After a moment's hesitation, Huei-fang gave Fan Po-wen a lingering glance and reluctantly followed Wu Chih-sheng. Fan Po-wen gazed after them until they had almost disappeared into the crowd, then, with a sudden laugh, he ran after them and caught up with them.

"I don't feel like composing now," he said, with a suggestion of pleading in his voice, as he caught Wu Chih-sheng by the arm. "Mind if I tag along?"

"But we're going home now," said Huei-fang, who usually waited for Wu Chih-sheng to speak first. She smiled shyly at Fan Po-wen, then hurriedly dropped her eyes.

"Then I'll . . . I'll come along to your place, too," Fan Po-wen decided after a moment's hesitation.

They did not talk much on the way. When they reached Wu Sun-fu's house, the porter was just closing the black iron gate, but, when he saw who it was approaching, he pulled it open again.

"There's some people here from Shuangchiao Town, Miss," he said with a grin. "They said they got out by the skin of their teeth."

This news immediately roused Huei-fang from her day-dreaming. With a little cry of surprise she darted into the house. Three days before she had overheard Wu Sun-fu telling somebody the bad news about her home town, but it had been so unexpected that she had not thought it could be at all serious, and had dismissed it from her mind. Now she seemed to realize suddenly that something terrible had actually happened, and her face paled at the thought.

*

She found a crowd of people gathered in the large drawing-room, standing about and talking excitedly. Her eyes first fell on Fei Little Beard. The old man was standing there in a grey gown, doing his best to answer a barrage of questions from Mrs. Wu Sun-fu and Ah-hsuan at the same time. Huei-fang went over to them and stood watching Fei Little Beard gasping and gesticulating.

"It was at eight o'clock, er, no, nine — that's it, nine o'clock, Madame, that the Hung Chang Pawnshop went up in flames. If Colonel Ho's two machine-guns hadn't been there, the rioters and the soldiers who'd mutinied wouldn't have set fire to the shop — don't you think so, Madame? The machine-guns were up on the turret blazing away like anything but it wasn't any use! —"

"I say, Fei Little Beard!" interrupted Ah-hsuan, tugging at his arm. "What happened to my picture-books? I had them in a box. You haven't told me yet what happened to them."

Fei Little Beard could only stare at Ah-hsuan blankly, since he had not the slightest idea what "picture-books" he meant. Mrs. Wu Sun-fu laughed, while Huei-fang took the opportunity to get a word in: "Is it true that the whole town's been ransacked? I wouldn't believe it — a town as big as that! Was it just the pawnshop that was burned down? What about our house?"

"Our house wasn't touched, Huei-fang," Mrs. Wu Sun-fu assured her. "But now we'd better let Mr. Fei have a rest — he must be very tired after all he's gone through. We can talk about it later when Sun-fu comes home. But really, a mutiny!"

Mrs. Wu Sun-fu looked suddenly worried, as if she was wrestling with some knotty problem. She stood staring blankly into space for a moment, then pulled herself together and forced an unnatural smile. She waved Fei Little Beard to a seat, and then slipped out.

Ah-hsuan started pestering Fei Little Beard about his box of picture-books again, while Huei-fang turned her attention to a group of young men by the window — Fan Po-wen, Wu Chih-sheng, Tu Hsueh-shih, and a stranger in a foreign suit — all listening to a man who was telling them how the rioters and mutineers had attacked the pawnshop. Huei-fang thought his voice sounded familiar but she could not place him just from the view she had of his back. Suddenly he turned and she could see his profile: a long horse-like face with a snub-nose, stand-out ears and bristly shock of hair. She saw at once that it was Tseng Chia-chu, and it was as much as she could do to suppress a startled cry at the sight of him, for she had always loathed him. Despite the fact that he was posing as a refugee and was being regarded with sympathy, Huei-fang still had no wish to see him, and she wished even less to be drawn into conversation with him. After some hesitation, she went through into the dining-room and sat down near the open door with her back to the young men and strained her ears to catch their conversation.

"So you snatched a pistol from a mutineer," came Fan Po-wen's sarcastic voice, "and had to shoot a few peasants before you could make your way out of the town, eh? Whew! What a hero!"

"Yes, I know how to look after myself all right!"

"But what about your father?" asked Tu Hsueh-shih in a voice even more caustic than Fan Po-wen's had been, his cat-eyes glaring indignantly as he spoke. "With your immense courage you should have had no trouble at all in getting him out of danger. But you only managed to save your own skin. And you didn't worry about your wife and child, either!"

Tseng Chia-chu had not expected a rebuff like this, and for all his boasting he was now beginning to feel that the situation was becoming embarrassing. Yet, being a born liar, he was unruffled and ready with a brazen reply:

"Oh, that. . . . They're quite safe where they are. Not many people know them, and anyway, they can always go and hide with some good friends of ours if things get worse. Not like me: I'm well known all over the town. Wherever I go, there's somebody who knows me. Who doesn't know me, Mr. Tseng, Junior?"

"Would you please tell us your official position in Shuangchiao Town, Mr. Tseng, Junior? You must be the mayor. I'm sure you wouldn't accept anything less, would you?"

This was another cut from Fan Po-wen. As he spoke, he nudged Wu Chih-sheng and winked at Tu Hsueh-shih.

The young man in the foreign suit just stood looking on, a cold smile on his lips and an expression of general discontent on his face. He was Tu Hsin-to, Tu Chu-chai's eldest son and Tu Hsueh-shih's nephew, a student just back from Paris.

Tseng Chia-chu's embarrassment was increasing with every minute. Ignoramus though he was, he knew there was no such official as mayor in his town, so he was rather surprised at Fan Po-wen's compliments. But when he looked closely at Fan Po-wen, he changed his mind and told himself that this imposing, well-dressed man must have had some reason for his remarks and that he himself, ignorant as he was of such matters, must be mistaken. He smiled uneasily and tried to look important. Little caring whether he was overstepping the mark with his boasting, he replied without batting an eyelid:

"Yes, of course I'm the — er — the mayor of the town. You're quite right I wouldn't be satisfied with anything less than that. Stands to reason. What's more, I'm number twenty-three, look at this!"

He laid special stress on the word "this," but nobody appeared to understand what he meant. He quickly fished out of his pocket two cards: his visiting card and his party card. He laid these cards on the upturned palms of his grubby paws and held them out for inspection. His party card was soiled and crumpled, but his visiting card was brand-new as he had had it printed overnight during the three days he had spent in the county town after his flight from Shuangchiao Town. Tu Hsueh-shih snatched the cards and was just going to look at them more closely, when Fan Po-wen burst out laughing, for his sharp eyes had not only spotted the party card but also the small characters on the visiting card identifying its owner as party member No. 23 of such and such district branch in such and such a county.

When Tu Hsueh-shih also saw these details, he flung the cards angrily on the floor.

"Rubbish!" he snapped. "It's people like you that have ruined the country!"

"Don't be so rude, Hsueh-shih!" broke in Wu Chih-sheng, who had remained silent till now. "Don't you realize that these cards are more precious than one's father, wife, and child put together?"

Then, with a contemptuous glance at Tseng Chia-chu, he grasped Fan Po-wen by the arm and pulled him into the dining-room. Tu Hsueh-shih and Tu Hsin-to followed them, the former kicking the door shut behind him with a bang.

The four of them made a beeline for a sofa under the window, and sat down without noticing Huei-fang sitting quietly by the door. They just sat and roared with laughter, while Tu Hsueh-shih continued his imprecations against Tseng Chia-chu. Fan Po-wen happened to be sitting directly opposite Huei-fang, so he was the first to notice her. He hurriedly stood up and planted himself in front of the other three.

"Guess who else is in the room besides us!" he said.

"Nobody," came Wu Chih-sheng's swift reply. "Unless it's your love-lorn muse who's never absent from your mind for a single moment."

But Fan Po-wen, refusing to be drawn, just stepped aside to reveal a blushing Huei-fang. Wu Chih-sheng stood up and said the first thing that came into his head to cover up his embarrassment:

"Huei-fang, meet Tu Hsin-to, Brother-in-law Chu-chai's son."

"He's a student just back from France, Doctor of God-knows-what, versed in sericulture and apiculture, artist, Bakuninist, and —" Fan Po-wen had intervened to enumerate Tu Hsin-to's titles, but broke off in the middle and burst out laughing.

Tu Hsin-to neither laughed nor showed any embarrassment. Instead, he bowed gravely to Huei-fang and held out his hand. When he saw that she was keeping her hands at her side, and that she returned his bow rather awkwardly, he smiled pleasantly and let his hand drop. He had only been back in the country three days, but he knew how complicated Chinese society was.

It was, perhaps, for this very reason that he had been in a dozen or so schools during his four years in France and had tried his hand at a variety of subjects: horticulture, poultry-farming, apiculture, mining, water conservancy, textile manufacture, shipbuilding, war chemistry, politics, economics, literature, philosophy, the fine arts, medicine, applied chemistry and so on and so forth. To each subject he had devoted a few days or even a few weeks, and so had earned the title of "Doctor of God-knows-what." If he had acquired anything in particular in France, it was his own version of Bakuninism — a philosophy of life which amounted to "I don't like anything and I don't care about anything." And this, of course, was just another aspect of his "wide learning."

Had he any ideals? Yes, plenty. To be more accurate, when he was lying in bed, his head swarmed with ideals; but the moment he left his bed, all that was left was his attitude of "I don't like anything and I don't care about anything." He was not a great talker, but he was quite a mild, affable sort of man.

Fan Po-wen, Wu Chih-sheng, and Tu Hsueh-shih fell silent, not knowing how to carry on the conversation before the young lady. Although Tu Hsin-to did not like to push himself forward and hold forth in company, when he saw that no one seemed willing to say anything he thought there would be no harm in saying something to liven up the atmosphere.

"Anyone who's new to Shanghai," he began lightly, and with a smile, "must find it rather incredible. It's a hotbed of all sorts of ideologies. . . . Look at Monsieur Tseng, for instance. You all think him disgusting, but, actually, a man like that is to be pitied, too. — Aunt Huei-fang, you must know what he's like: am I right about him?"

Huei-fang was surprised at being called "aunt" by a man several years older than herself, and found herself giggling with embarrassment. Fan Po-wen also laughed and clapped Tu Hsin-to on the shoulder.

"Now don't you start calling me 'uncle'!" he warned him. "I was afraid you might any moment!"

"There you go again, Po-wen!" cried Tu Hsueh-shih. "It's people like you who do nothing but joke that are ruining the country! And as for that fellow Tseng, he's really shocking. It makes me furious just to think about him. Didn't I tell you when we saw him arrive that he was a rotter? Well, now we've proved it! I'd like to give him what for. If it had been anywhere but here, I'd have given him a good hiding."

As he spoke, he glared round and puffed out his cheeks, so that he looked perfectly ridiculous, as he always did when he was angry. It was now Fan Po-wen's turn for another quip.

"That's right! Give him what for! You're just the right man for the job. You can hit him with the 'iron hand' you're always talking about, but he can take it, because he's so thick-skinned!"

"I quite agree with you, Mr. Tu," broke in Huei-fang. "Mr. Tseng is really horrible. He has such shifty eyes. — Oh, I wish I knew how things really are at home!"

She had thrown off her shyness to say this because she was afraid that Tu Hsueh-shih and Fan Po-wen were going to start quarrelling. Her interruption had diverted the conversation to Shuangchiao Town for a while. Tu Hsin-to remained reticent and looked on with an indifferent smile, though he nodded his appreciation of Fan Po-wen's witticism. They were, in a way, the best of friends. Tu Hsueh-shih disliked his nephew just as much as he did Fan Po-wen. He said harshly to the latter:

"You just keep your mouth shut, Po-wen! Freedom of speech is China's curse. Too many cooks spoil the broth, you know. Our only hope is to put the reins of government into iron hands, and put a stop to all this idle chatter. The reason why bandits are always on the rampage is because our military commanders are not doing their job properly. As likely as not some of them are even giving the bandits a free hand so that they'll have a chance of distinguishing themselves —"

"Yes, but everyone's got to live — even a bandit," interposed Wu Chih-sheng. "There's no two ways about it. The reason why there are so many bandits about isn't as simple as you might think."

Wu Chih-sheng firmly believed that, as long as the problem of distribution of wealth remained unsolved, China — and, indeed the whole world — would remain in chaos.

"Yes, everyone's got to live," agreed Fan Po-wen. "But I think the root of all the trouble is money. It's because of money that Shuangchiao Town's been attacked and looted. It's because of money that capitalists are building factories where there used to be paddy fields. The smoke from factory chimneys blots out the sky and pollutes the beauties of nature. And it's because of money that peasants leave their lovely villages and crowd into the city to live in grimy rabbit-warrens and submerge their humanity!"

As Fan Po-wen once more gave vent to his poet's longing for unspoiled natural beauty, he glanced at Huei-fang. She did not understand much of what he was saying, but, when she saw the look of utter sadness on his face, she warmed to him and a spontaneous smile of sympathy came to her lips.

Tu Hsueh-shih's mouth was working with impatience and he was just going to cut Fan Po-wen short, when Lin Pei-shan burst into the room, bag in hand, apparently just back from a stroll. Her first words were: "Have you seen the wild horse and the clay idol in the other room? I thought I'd come to the wrong house!"

Everyone roared with laughter. Lin Pei-shan twirled round to see Fan Po-wen and Tu Hsueh-shih. Her gaiety suddenly vanished. Pressing her lips together in a wry smile, she swept across the room and out through the back door.

She ran upstairs and burst into her sister's room. The light-blue satin curtains were drawn and the room was in darkness. She touched the switch and the sudden blaze of light roused her sister, who was lying back on a sofa in a reverie.

The sisters looked at each other in silence, then Lin Pei-shan ran across and crouched down beside her sister. She flung her arms round her neck and whispered anxiously, "Oh, Pei-yao! He — he said it to me today. What shall I do!"

Mrs. Wu Sun-fu, not understanding who had said what, turned to look her sister in the face and saw that she looked both anxious and miserable.

"I mean Fan Po-wen — he said he loves me!"

"Well, are you in love with him?"

"Me? I don't know."

Mrs. Wu could not help laughing. She shook her head, and extricated herself from Lin Pei-shan's embrace. She was going to say something when her sister went on, "I feel I love everybody and yet nobody."

"Oh, don't be silly!"

"Shouldn't I say that?"

"It may be true, but you shouldn't think things like that, because one day you'll have to get married — you'll have to make up your mind about someone — someone to be your life companion."

Lin Pei-shan inclined her head in thought for a moment, then rose to her feet and said dejectedly, "To be all the time with one and the same man? How monotonous! Look at you and Sun-fu!"

At this Mrs. Wu started with surprise, and a couple of things she had in her lap tumbled on to the floor: a tattered copy of *The Sorrows of Young Werther* and a faded white rose. As Mrs. Wu gazed down abstractedly at them, her heartache which had been temporarily interrupted by the arrival of her sister, now came back with renewed vigour.

"Would you say that Sun-fu isn't terribly keen on Fan Po-wen, then?" asked Lin Pei-shan at last, though her voice betrayed no interest. With an effort, Mrs. Wu repressed her own turbulent feelings and looked up at her sister. After a moment's silence she answered, "Yes, he has in mind another man who, he thinks, is even more eligible than Fan Po-wen."

"Is it Tu Hsueh-shih, the one you were telling me about?"

"What do you think of him?"

"I'm sure I don't know."

This "don't know" business perplexed Mrs. Wu until she noticed an unusual glint in Pei-shan's eye which made her decide that her sister was just being shy. She laughed and asked softly, "Won't you even take your own sister into your confidence? Just say one word and I'll understand."

"I think . . . if I marry Tu Hsueh-shih, I'll always be thinking of somebody else —"

Lin Pei-shan broke off, and a faint flush crept into her cheeks. Mrs. Wu felt her own heart beating faster at these words. Lin Pei-shan tittered nervously, then averted her face, and muttered as if to herself:

"To marry one man and always be thinking of someone else — wouldn't that be horrid, Pei-yao!"

As she said this, she flung herself upon Mrs. Wu, put her hands on her shoulders, and buried her face in hers like a child. Mrs. Wu's face was burning hot, and Lin Pei-shan started back in surprise when she felt it. When she looked and saw that her sister's face was flushed and that there were tears glistening between her lashes, she could only stare in amazement. Mrs. Wu's face slowly paled as she saw through her tears the image of herself before her marriage in her sister standing before her: the same looks, the same figure, and the same innocence and vivacity tinged with fantasy as she had had. And like herself her sister was now at the crossroads, and in danger of being drawn into a life which did not make sense. Surely her sister was not destined to share her own fate? She felt sick at heart as these thoughts went through her mind.

"Pei-shan," she blurted out tremulously, "who is it you're always thinking about? Po-wen?"

"No, it's not him — oh, I don't know! Oh, Pei-yao, I want to cry — I just want to cry!"

Lin Pei-shan flung her arms round Mrs. Wu and hugged her close as she said this. Her voice trembled but she did not burst into tears. All at once, she let go of Mrs. Wu with a nervous giggle and skipped out of the room again.

Mrs. Wu stared at the waving blue curtain over the door, then parted her lips to call her sister back, but changed her mind. Two large tears welled up in her eyes and fell on to her hand. As she bent her head to look at the book and the faded white rose lying on the carpet at her feet, a wave of overwhelming sorrow swept over her. She threw herself face downwards on the sofa in a daze and moaned miserably.

"How about Pei-shan? Can she be taking my place? . . . No, surely not! Who is it she's got in mind, then? Oh, my foolish heart! They say the fighting's getting worse at the front. . . . If he's killed, it's finished, finished! — But didn't he say he'd come back? Oh, I'll be afraid to see him again. . . . Oh forgive me, let me go! Let me go and hide myself somewhere!"

VII

THREE days later. All the morning not a breath of wind had stirred. The sky was heavy with becalmed banks of grey cloud, behind which sidled a watery sun. Dragonflies zigzagged among the trees, bumping from time to time against the greyish-green wire-netting screens over the windows and startling the flies which had settled there, so that they flew up with a buzz and circled aimlessly around in front of the windows awhile, before settling again to crawl on the screens, where they would stretch out their hind legs and rub them slowly together as if they were deep in thought.

Inside the wire-screened windows was the Wus' luxuriously furnished drawing-room, with Wu Sun-fu pacing up and down, his face as clouded as the sky. Suddenly he stopped and looked up at the clock on the wall.

"Eleven already," he muttered, "and still no ring!"

He had been waiting anxiously for a telephone call from Chao Po-tao and Tu Chu-chai, for it was today that the fate of their joint speculation in government bonds would be decided. For the last few days the market had been buzzing with the news that the Central Army was beginning to win its battles. But speculators in general preferred to bide their time; only small buyers were active, but they could not push up the prices to any appreciable extent. The day before, the victories of the Central Army had been splashed across the front page of every newspaper. This morning, the early session of the Exchange had opened with a two-to-three-dollar rise on all government bonds. On the floor a sea of heads pushed and jostled, and the shouting of buyers and sellers made the place sound like a field of battle, so that it was impossible to make oneself heard above the din. The raised hands were all palm-upwards. But Chao Po-tao needed only to unload about two million to make the prices drop again to only fifty cents above the quotation of two days before. People said that the big bears had decided to hold out until today and see which way the wind was blowing before buying in. The fate of Wu Sun-fu and his fellow-speculators would be decided within the next twelve hours, for the settlement was due the following day.

Wu Sun-fu frowned as he looked out through the window at the sullen sky, then smiled with an air of resignation and strode into the library to ring up Tu Wei-yueh at the factory. On this front he was rather more confident of victory, but here, too, today was the day which would decide the outcome. This morning was the deadline for Tu Wei-yueh and Mo Kan-cheng to put an end to the week-old go-slow strike.

He was just picking up the telephone, when the door opened and a squarish face with a tuft of beard on its chin peered round the door as if wondering whether to come in or wait outside. Wu Sun-fu put down the receiver and called out, "Come on in, Fei. Any reliable news?"

Fei Little Beard squeezed in crabwise, closed the door quietly and tiptoed across to the desk where Wu Sun-fu was sitting.

"Yes, there's some," he muttered timidly, looking down at the floor. "But it's not too good. The bandits have withdrawn from the town and spread out into the surrounding villages. All the shops in the town are still closed. The troops sent out by provincial authorities are still stationed in the county town, and are afraid to come anywhere near —"

"Troops be damned!" Wu Sun-fu interrupted impatiently. "Just tell me about my losses." In his agitated state of mind, he found the cheerless gloom of the room depressing, so he reached across the desk and flicked on the table-lamp. The light which filtered through the yellow silk shade picked out his gloomy, purplish face and his thick eyebrows twitching with anxiety above his ruthless eyes.

"Oh, yes, the losses . . . er, it hasn't been possible to make a clear estimate yet. I'm afraid the losses are considerable — the

Hung Chang Pawnshop, the Tung Yuan local bank, the oil mill, the power-house —"

"I know they've been ransacked. You needn't tell me about that again! What I want is a detailed list of definite losses, not a rough estimate! You stayed in the town three days just to tell me all this, eh! Three days, and you still haven't made a clear estimate? Pah!"

Wu Sun-fu became angrier with each word and pounded on the desk. What made him angry was not so much the losses he had sustained — he could well afford to dismiss a loss of a hundred or two hundred thousand dollars with a mere frown — no; it was Fei Little Beard's dithering and incompetence that made him so furious. Moreover, he was on tenterhooks to know how much money was left over after the losses, so that he could plan ahead how to tide over his present financial difficulties on the eve of the Dragon-boat Festival.

Seeing that Fei Little Beard was tongue-tied, Wu Sun-fu went on, "Now, how much do you think we can get back on our loans?"

"Let me see . . . sixty per cent, I should think, seeing that most of the shops in the town haven't suffered much loss. Only the rice-shops, the piece-goods shops were cleaned out. Yes, I think there's a good chance of getting back sixty per cent. Besides, the county town is still intact —"

"You should have told me all this sooner!" Wu Sun-fu cut Fei Little Beard short once more, but he sounded more peaceable now, and a ghost of a smile passed across his lips. He was confronted with three major problems: the go-slow strike at the factory, the Stock Exchange battle, and the rebellion in his home town. He now had a clue to the third problem, for sixty per cent of his loans meant about sixty or seventy thousand dollars in cash at his disposal. It was not a big sum, but, like a commander-in-chief in planning an offensive, now that he knew what forces he had in hand, he knew how best to deploy them for the attack.

"One of the motors in the power-house is damaged —" Fei Little Beard stammered, hanging his head. However, before he finished his sentence, there was a sudden flash of lightning, followed by a deafening clap of thunder which seemed to rock the room; and on top of the thunder came a torrential downpour, and Fei Little Beard's feeble voice was swallowed up by the angry roar of the elements. Just then Tu Chu-chai burst into the room, his goat-like face glistening with beads of sweat.

"Whew, what a thunderstorm!" he exclaimed. "No wonder the phones are out of order. Your phone's out, isn't it, Sun-fu?"

He sat down on a sofa opposite Wu Sun-fu and pulled out a large handkerchief. He spread it over his face and began wiping vigorously. This was not just to wipe away the perspiration: it was something he always did whenever he was in a quandary.

Wu Sun-fu knew at once that something had gone wrong on the Exchange. He smiled slightly and, strangely enough, he now felt more at peace in his mind. In another minute or two he would know whether they had won or whether they had lost. Though, of course, it was quite natural for a man as far-sighted and broad-minded as he was to be as cool and calm as usual. He turned to Fei Little Beard and waved him away.

"Fei, you'd better leave for Shuangchiao Town at once. Collect as much of the money as you can and bring it back to me without delay. Don't worry about the damaged motor in the power-house. I'll send someone down to see to it tomorrow. You must try and get to the town before nightfall. You can hire a motor-boat, and you leave before one o'clock. That's all. Off you go!"

"Very good —" Fei Little Beard assented dismally. He had come ashore from a steam-launch less than an hour back, and had scarcely had time yet to stretch his legs. Now he was told to embark again — to crouch in a little boat and to be swayed and jolted about! To go back to a town surrounded and watched by armed peasants! This was certainly an unpalatable proposition. But he knew his hasty-tempered master would brook no disobedience, so he swallowed his disappointment, and shook down his gown and left without another word. Wu Sun-fu and Tu Chu-chai began talking about the day's events on the Exchange.

Their conversation was hardly audible against the crash of the thunder, and the roar of the rain, but by watching Tu Chu-chai's lip movements, Wu Sun-fu managed to get the gist of what he was saying. When the lips stopped for a moment, Wu Sun-fu laughed bitterly and shouted, "You say there are still new bears turning up? They must be mad!"

"That's what's so queer about it all. I've never seen such a crazy market. Wait and see what happens in the afternoon session, though."

"What have we got left in hand?"

"Four or five million. If we unload them, we can stop the rise and turn it into a drop. If we don't, we're sunk."

"Unload the lot, then. Anyway, we shan't be losing on it."

"Oh, no? Have you forgotten that we've paid out three hundred thousand dollars?"

"No, I haven't forgotten," said Wu Sun-fu gloomily, "but the loss won't work out at more than eighty thousand dollars apiece, and we can write that off as 'military expenses.'"

He stood up and began pacing up and down. The thunder had stopped by now, but the rain was coming down in torrents and a wind had sprung up; and to the noise of the storm was added the howling of the wind in the trees outside. Tu Chu-chai sat in silence, imagining he was back on the floor of the Exchange in the seething, bawling crowd with its tense, sweating faces and its foul, stifling atmosphere. And all this confusion was caused mainly by Chao Po-tao and himself and the other two plotting behind the scenes and now they were hoist with their own petard! It was terrible! Tu Chu-chai shook his head and sighed.

"I just can't understand why so many big bears are still holding out and refusing to cover. Tomorrow's settlement day, and yet this morning new bears were still cropping up!"

"But is it that new bears are cropping up? Or is it just Chao Po-tao playing a shabby trick?"

As he said this, Wu Sun-fu suddenly turned to look Tu Chu-chai in the face and thumped the table with his hand. The other sprang to his feet in dismay. Why had he not thought of this before? He must have been dazed by the noise and stuffiness on the floor of the Exchange! His voice was excited and angry as he replied:

"Oho! So that's it, is it? Yes, I wouldn't be at all surprised. But what an infernal cheek!"

"Yes, we've been taken in nicely!"

Wu Sun-fu threw back his head and laughed bitterly, but his voice was drowned by a sudden clap of thunder. Tu Chu-chai lit a cigar and puffed vigorously at it before observing slowly:

"If it's true, then Chao Po-tao's no friend of ours. Anyway, we won't let him get away with it. But we'd better wait and see what happens in the afternoon session, Sun-fu. It's too early yet to know for certain how things will turn out."

"Let's hope so!"

"It's not merely a hope — we've a good chance of snatching a victory at the last minute. I'm going to see Shang Chung-li right away, and then, after lunch, I'll go along to the Exchange and see what's happening."

Tu Chu-chai rose to go, and Wu Sun-fu followed him out to the front steps. Just as he was getting into the car, Tu Chu-chai suddenly stopped, turned round, and pulled Wu Sun-fu back indoors, where he asked him gravely:

"What news has Fei Little Beard brought back from the town? What are the losses?"

"He didn't give me a clear picture — no details."

"What did you send him straight back for just now?"

"To collect what's left over," smiled Wu Sun-fu, his look of despondency vanishing abruptly. "You see, I'm going to concentrate all my financial strength on that trust company and turn it into a base for big operations."

Tu Chu-chai hesitated a moment, and then asked, "Are you really set on going through with this business of Chu Yin-chiu? Are you sure it isn't a bit touch-and-go?"

Wu Sun-fu made no reply to this question, and only glanced at Tu Chu-chai.

"I admit I don't know much about industry and so on," Tu Chu-chai went on, "but as far as I can see its future isn't going to be all roses. Besides, Chu Yin-chiu's no fool and he knows quite well his machines and factory buildings are worth more than five hundred thousand dollars. You don't imagine he'd let us take over for only three hundred thousand? Besides, he's a bit of a backbiter, and he'd give us a bad name and make things awkward for us if we tried to force something out of him. I hear he's already putting it about that we're trying to twist him foul and so on. I met Chao Po-tao just a short while ago, and he gave me to understand that Chu Yin-chiu was already negotiating with him for a loan of a hundred and fifty thousand dollars or so on his machinery so that he can pay back the loan we made him on his cocoons when it falls due in a month's time —"

Tu Chu-chai broke off inconclusively and flicked the ash off his cigar. Then he turned to gaze out of the window at the rain which was coming down in sheets, although the sky seemed to be clearing slightly. When he turned round again, it was to see Wu Sun-fu smiling mirthlessly.

"And did Chao Po-tao promise him a loan?" Wu Sun-fu asked.

"He's probably still thinking it over. Since he's going in with us in our company, he's being very courteous and considerate on the surface. He said that if a loan to Chu Yin-chiu is harmful to our interests, he'll have to refuse it —"

"You must definitely tell him to refuse it, then, Chu-chai."

"That's just what I wanted to discuss with you. So far as I can see, the silk industry's in a bad way just now, so I think we'd better go carefully. If Chu Yin-chiu can get the money from Chao Po-tao to pay back his loan, we can let it go at that."

"No, Chu-chai!" protested Wu Sun-fu, jumping up. "We can't just sit back and let things slide!"

A shaft of sunlight escaped through a rift in the clouds behind the curtain of rain and bathed his face in a yellowish glow. Wu Sun-fu's voice rose above the drumming of the rain. "We've been doing our damnedest to relieve Chu Yin-chiu of his cocoons. We can't give up now, just when we've almost got our hands on them! No, Chu-chai, we can't just let things slide! Tell Chao Po-tao to refuse him the loan. Our trust company has the priority of making him loans: we made a special stipulation to that effect in the contract of the old loan. In fact, as you may remember, we let him off with a favourable rate of interest — a mere *five* and a half per cent a month — in exchange for that stipulation. Chu-chai, you must tell Chao Po-tao that he must respect our contract rights."

Tu Chu-chai stared at Wu Sun-fu for a moment, then took the cigar out of his mouth, and said with a sigh, "Well, we shall see what we can do after we're through with the most urgent business. At the moment our stock business is quite a handful. I'm off to see Shang Chung-li now."

*

The rain was easing up and turning to a thick, misty drizzle, while the sky was more leaden and overcast than ever. And Wu Sun-fu's heart felt as leaden as the sky. There was still a ray of hope, though, since there were so many unpredictable fluctuations on the Stock Exchange; but the signs of the last two days, however, seemed to indicate that somebody was out to kill the bulls — which was really rather odd. There could be only one explanation: their secret must have leaked out already! Wu Sun-fu had never trusted Chao Po-tao and now he could not help suspecting that he was stabbing him in the back. He paced up and down, his hands clasped behind his back, thinking to himself: A gamble on the stock market isn't much of a risk — unless you go in with Chao Po-tao, and then you're taking a very great risk indeed!

It was now already half past eleven, but Tu Wei-yueh at the factory had not yet telephoned the expected news of victory. Since there was no point in worrying about Chao Po-tao and the stock speculations for the moment, Wu Sun-fu mustered up his energies to deal with the situation in the factory. He told Kao Sheng to ring through, but it turned out that the telephone was in fact out of order, and it was impossible to get through. Exasperated, he jumped into his car and left for the factory to investigate in person.

In the streets, everything beyond a radius of fifteen yards or so was shrouded by the drizzle and appeared as a misty blur. The top floors of several tall buildings were visible through the mist, their windows shimmering with a pale, yellowish light like rows of great eyes. From a distance they seemed to be floating in mid-air, like buildings seen in a mirage, instead of being their usual solid and imposing selves. There seemed to be no end to this thick mist, and as the car ploughed on through its clinging dampness the wind-screen became like frosted glass, so that even the nearest passers-by seemed to be so many grotesque phantoms; everything had undergone a misty sea-change and every outline had become blurred.

Wu Sun-fu was slumped back in the right-hand corner of the car, his left leg sprawled along the seat beside him as he glanced out of the windows, breathing heavily. Suddenly an unusual sensation came over him: he was one of the captains of industry, ruthless and go-ahead — yet were his prospects really anything more than a mirage — just castles in the air? And what were the people around him but so many blurred, misshapen figures? His progress in industry was just like his present journey — an aimless rush through a blinding mist!

A chilly sensation crept up his spine and spread out until his face paled and his eyes lost the sheen of courage and keenness.

The car turned in through the factory gates and past the workshops with their windows dismally lit up by the yellowish glare from inside. The damp air vibrated with the smooth hum of machinery. In the ordinary way, this hum would have made him feel elated and his experienced ear would immediately have told him the tempo of work, but just now, although his senses were as alert as ever, his mind was clouded and his heart heavy.

He waited until Kuan, his bodyguard, had opened the car door for him before he slowly got out. Mo Kan-cheng and Tu Wei-yueh had already come out to meet him, and when Mo saw how ashen and grim his face was, his heart sank. Wu Sun-fu glanced coldly at Mo Kan-cheng and then at Tu Wei-yueh and made straight for his office.

He called Tu Wei-yueh in first. The young man seemed quite calm and at his ease as he said, without waiting until he was spoken to, "Your telephone at home was out of order, sir, and I couldn't get through until ten minutes ago, and by that time you were already on your way. They got the line back into service just a bit too late to catch you, unfortunately."

Wu Sun-fu could not help a slight frown, but he nevertheless forced a smile. He sensed the implication behind Tu Wei-yueh's words: that it was really not necessary for him to come to the factory at this moment. The arrogant, cocksure young man obviously thought that by dashing over to the factory in such a fluster, instead of waiting at home for the news of victory (as they had arranged beforehand), Wu Sun-fu was not showing absolute confidence in his trusted lieutenant, which was not in keeping with the time-honoured principle of "If you use a man, don't suspect him; if you suspect a man, don't use him," and was not at all the way a really great man went about things. As he looked into Tu Wei-yueh's face, Wu Sun-fu secretly applauded his firmness and astuteness, though he dared not admit to the young man that the reason he had hurried over so soon was that he had had qualms about his ability to carry out his task. He smiled faintly and said reassuringly:

"Well, it's nearly twelve o'clock, isn't it? I expected to find that my commander at the front had been completely victorious. I've come, rather unexpectedly perhaps, to speak to the prisoners, as it were."

"Even so, you've come just a bit too early, Mr. Wu," said Tu Wei-yueh bluntly, his face as calm and impassive as ever.

"What! But didn't I just hear the machines — do you mean to tell me they're just letting the machines run on as usual, and going slow the way they've been doing the last few days?"

"Please go in and you can see for yourself, sir," Tu Wei-yueh said unhurriedly, as cool and dignified as ever.

Wu Sun-fu snorted and glared at Tu Wei-yueh, his piercing eyes filled with a mounting rage. But the young man was unabashed. He just drew himself up and met the glare with a smile.

"I should like your instructions, sir," he asked abruptly. "Are you still set on a 'peaceful settlement'?"

"Of course I am, but there's a limit to my patience!"

"I see! . . . and you set the deadline for today — you said that the day before yesterday. But, after all, the workwomen are human beings — they've got their own ideas and feelings. But what makes things worse is that their ideas are complicated and their feelings are easily roused. For example, three days ago they were all for Yao Chin-feng, the girl in Row 12, but today they've turned on her; they're calling her a stooge and accusing her of betraying their interests. The situation's taken a turn for the worse just now. You probably remember Yao Chin-feng: tall and thin, little round face, slightly pockmarked, thirtyish, been here three years and six months? Well, as a matter of fact it was she who started the strike —"

"Yes, I remember her: the one you were working on to bring her round."

"I did bring her round, but now all the other women are calling her a stooge in our service, and of course a known stooge is no earthly use to us. All the work I've put in on her for the past few days has just been wasted."

Wu Sun-fu snorted, but said nothing.

"We've been very careful about the whole thing," went on Tu Wei-yueh, "and only a very few of our people were in the know; and anyway, Yao Chin-feng still kept up a pretence of being on the side of the women. I don't suppose for a minute the women had the slightest suspicion that their leader had been bought over, so it's quite clear that it's one of our people who has let on about it."

"Oh! So that's it, is it? Have you found out who it was?"

"Yes, Hsueh Pao-chu, one of the forewomen. By splitting on us like that, she's sabotaged the whole plan."

"What! One of the forewomen do a thing like that — try to curry favour with the women? She must be mad!"

"It's all because of jealousy. Those two women are deadly enemies — Hsueh Pao-chu is envious of Yao Chin-feng's merit."

"Call them in to see me!" snapped Wu Sun-fu, springing to his feet. But Tu Wei-yueh remained still, waiting for Wu Sun-fu to cool down and countermand this futile order of his. Wu Sun-fu stared at Tu Wei-yueh for a while, then slowly recovered his composure and sat down again.

"The interfering bitch!" he muttered to himself through clenched teeth. "She's making more trouble than all the women put together! So she's fed up with working for me, eh? — Right: Wei-yueh, tell Mo Kan-cheng to give this Hsueh woman the sack!"

"Don't you think there's an even better way out than that, Mr. Wu?"

"Eh? What do you think we ought to do, then?" Wu Sun-fu's tone of voice was sharp, as if his patience was finally exhausted.

"I would suggest, Mr. Wu, that you put up a notice announcing three things: double pay for the day of the Dragon-boat Festival; the discharge of Yao Chin-feng and the promotion of Hsueh Pao-chu to the rank of supervisor," Tu Wei-yueh spoke with deliberation, drawing himself up boldly as he did so. Wu Sun-fu listened in silence, gazing meditatively into space with narrowed eyes for a short while. Suddenly he laughed and said:

"A counterplot, eh? Are you sure it'll work?"

"Yes, I think so. Since eight o'clock this morning I've been doing my best to patch up the awkward situation created by Hsueh Pao-chu, and I think I'm getting somewhere at last. I've just remembered: you've already approved the double pay. I hope you'll also agree to the discharge of Yao Chin-feng and the promotion of Hsueh Pao-chu. Later on we can countermand these orders; then it'll be regarded by the women as a concession to them and be the means of clearing up the trouble. After all the trouble we've been to to get Yao Chin-feng as our contact among the women, we can't discard her just like that."

A sudden blast from the hooter resounded through the factory making Wu Sun-fu start violently and pale slightly. Didn't factory workers always sound the hooter as signal for a riot? The next instant he realized it was the signal for lunch-break, and his smile of relief also gave his tacit consent to Tu Wei-yueh's proposal.

"The trouble will be over by this afternoon, I can assure you, Mr. Wu. After that there'll be nothing more to do but give rewards to a number of people for the help they've given us. May I have your instructions in this connection?"

Tu Wei-yueh laid before Wu Sun-fu a list of recommendations which he had prepared. The latter ran his eyes over it and then asked with a frown, "These two fellows Chien Pao-sheng and Kuei Chang-lin are members of the trade union. Must we give them rewards as well?"

"Yes, I think we must. They have different backgrounds and

belong to different factions, but this time they've managed to come to an agreement on the question of working for your interests."

"Agreement? Yes, they're sure to be in agreement about tapping me for money; but they're far from being in agreement when it comes to fighting for power in the union or taking advantage of trouble among the women to score off one another. As a matter of fact, the main reason why this go-slow trouble has dragged on for nearly a week is that these two scoundrels have been at loggerheads. They couldn't agree on working for me and dealing with the women!"

"But they haven't quarrelled for the last two or three days. Chien Pao-sheng's even taken my advice to yield a bit to Kuei Chang-lin."

"That doesn't mean that they're really out to work for me. They're just trimming their sails to the wind, for their own ends. I could well afford it, but I just won't give a penny to people like that."

With this firm rebuff, Wu Sun-fu snatched up a pen and crossed the two names off the list, then initialled it and handed it back to Tu Wei-yueh. He stood up and looked out of the window at the women passing by. He frowned as a disagreeable memory came back to him, but almost immediately his expression returned to normal. As he left the office, he enjoined Tu Wei-yueh once more:

"It's imperative that the whole thing be settled by tomorrow. My patience ends today."

His loud voice and stern expression as he said this made the clerks gathered in the outer office start with alarm, but by the time they had weighed the significance of his words, his car was already purring majestically out through the main gate to a chorus of derisive jeers from a knot of women standing just outside.

Tu Wei-yueh immediately called a meeting of Mo Kan-cheng and three or four of his immediate subordinates, including Kuei Chang-lin. The news that Wu Sun-fu's patience was at an end, and that he had made the next day the deadline for a settlement, soon spread through the whole factory. The supervisors and forewomen took this to mean that Wu Sun-fu was intending to resort to more forceful methods. This was a matter of great excitement for them, for they knew very well that if he abandoned his policy of "peaceful settlement" for one of compulsion, it would mean the end, or at least the decline, of the Tu Wei-yueh régime. Although they did not dare protest openly against Tu Wei-yueh's rule, they were not at all happy about it.

Knowing perfectly well what was going on in their minds, Tu Wei-yueh made a point of telling them first of all that Wu Sun-fu was not at all satisfied with Chien Pao-sheng and Kuei Chang-lin. Then he broached the main subject of the meeting:

"Now, Mr. Wu has ordered three things: double pay on the day of the festival, the dismissal of Yao Chin-feng, and the promotion of Hsueh Pao-chu to the rank of supervisor."

This announcement was met with incredulous stares from everyone and a passionate protest from Kuei Chang-lin. "Why, that's kicking a man when he's down! It's not fair! And what's Hsueh Pao-chu done that she should be promoted?"

"It's not fair on Yao Chin-feng!" broke in Wang Chin-chen, one of the forewomen. "You ought to have stuck up for her, Mr. Tu, instead of letting her down like this. You told me to make up to her, and now she's got the sack and Hsueh Pao-chu, the one who's been asking for trouble, has been promoted. What sense is there in that?"

Indignant as she was at the apparent injustice of it all, she hardly dared blame it on to Wu Sun-fu, on whose favours she battened, but had to restrict herself to taking it out on Tu Wei-yueh.

The latter, however, declined to answer. He just squared his shoulders and smiled calmly.

"Mr. Wu accuses me of not being able to get on with Chien Pao-sheng. All right: I admit it. We are enemies. We're both in the union for a living, but he wants to hog the lot, so of course I have to fight against him. If Mr. Wu doesn't care who's fighting who in the union, and if he's only interested in clearing up the trouble with the women, then why does he have to go and promote Hsueh Pao-chu? She's trying to throw a spanner in the works and it's Chien Pao-sheng who's behind her egging her on. He's jealous of me, and he's always having a go at me. Everybody knows that."

As he delivered himself of this long tirade against his rival, Kuei Chang-lin's eyes flashed and he almost foamed at the mouth with excitement, though he adopted a more moderate tone in his references to Wu Sun-fu, because, of all those present, he himself was the only one from the union and was dependent only on the union for a living, whereas all the others depended on their employer for their livelihood and naturally did not dare criticize Wu Sun-fu's way of doing things in front of Tu Wei-yueh.

Again Tu Wei-yueh smiled nonchalantly and remained silent. Mo Kan-cheng said, "Of course, if that's the way Mr. Wu Sun-fu wants it, we'll just have to do it that way. But, Mr. Tu, if we've got to clear up the trouble today, what are we going to do about it?"

"That's what we're going to discuss now," replied Tu Wei-yueh. He flashed a glance at one of the supervisors, Pockmarked Li, and one of the forewomen, just as they were smiling at him. They had been Tu Wei-yueh's new favourites ever since he "came to power." He squared his shoulders, glanced rapidly round the circle of faces, and began in a loud voice:

"Let's leave the question of Yao Chin-feng and Hsueh Pao-chu out of it for the moment. Mr. Wu has always been a very fair man, and I can give you my word for it that he won't let anyone down who's really put their back into it and has his interests at heart. He says that this trouble must definitely be cleared up by today, and he's promised double pay over the festival. The only thing that worries me now is that some of the hard cases like Ho Hsiu-mei might kick up rough and spoil the whole show. We must be tough with them and stand no nonsense. Li, I'll leave that to you. Just put the wind up them; that'll be enough —"

"Just leave it to me!" said Pockmarked Li eagerly, his bushy eyebrows twitching with glee. He was a member of the underworld, and at any time he could call up a dozen of "the boys" for a fight.

"Put the wind up them?" cried one of the forewomen, Wang

Chin-chen, scornfully. "That's not going to be as easy as you think! You'll find you've got a job on scaring Ho Hsiu-mei and her lot — you'll find them tougher than you bargained for!"

Pockmarked Li glared indignantly and was just going to argue about it when Tu Wei-yueh restrained him.

"Wang Chin-chen's right, you know, Li. The best thing you can do is to get hold of Ho Hsiu-mei when you get the chance, and cart her off to the theatre. She's out at lunch just now, so you'd better get a move on and get the job done — and mind you don't make a hash of it. If you haven't had your lunch yet, you'd better get ten dollars from the cashier so that you can treat your mates to a meal when they've finished the job. — And remember: all this has got to be kept quiet!"

"Kept quiet?" muttered Kuei Chang-lin sarcastically. "You can't trust those two so-and-sos Chien Pao-sheng and Hsueh Pao-chu to keep it quiet — but then sometimes it pays not to keep things quiet!"

Mo Kan-cheng gave Pockmarked Li his ten dollars, and the latter departed well pleased with himself. Tu Wei-yueh gave Kuei Chang-lin a hard look, but did not say anything, then turned and asked one of the forewomen, "How did you get on, Ah-chen?"

"Well, about half of the women think that Yao Chin-feng's in the right. They say Hsueh Pao-chu's a capitalist stooge and that she's been spreading rumours just to get Yao Chin-feng into trouble. And they say that Ho Hsiu-mei is jealous of Yao Chin-feng and wants to push herself forward."

"Well done! Now, Ho Hsiu-mei won't be coming in to work this afternoon, so I want you to put it round that Mr. Mo's taken her to the theatre —"

"What, me?" protested Mo Kan-cheng hastily. "Now, look here, old man, don't go dragging me into all this!"

Kuei Chang-lin, Wang Chin-chen and Ah-chen laughed, but Tu Wei-yueh kept a straight face and patted Mo Kan-cheng reassuringly on the shoulder.

"Of course it's you who'll have to take her to the theatre," he assured him. "And now you must go and find Pockmarked Li — you'll find him somewhere around Ho Hsiu-mei's place —

and arrange to come on the scene and rescue her when Li's boys have lured her away to some out-of-the-way spot. Then all you have to do is to invite her to the theatre."

"And what if she refuses?"

"Then you'll have to use your head. Tell her you're just taking her into the theatre to hide until the wolves have cleared off. You're an old man, so she won't suspect you, and she's sure to do as you suggest."

"And what if Mr. Wu gets to hear of it? There'll be hell to pay!"

"Don't you worry about that. I'll do any explaining that needs to be done. Off you go, then! And now, Ah-chen, you run along and do your bit — and mind you don't let the cat out of the bag!"

After they had gone, there were only three people left in the room: Tu Wei-yueh, Kuei Chang-lin and Wang Chin-chen. With a wry smile, Tu Wei-yueh fixed his keen gaze on Kuei Chang-lin's face: the face of a man nearing forty, square, with small eyes that did not quite match, and with a rather villainous cast to its features, which showed increasing signs of uneasiness beneath Tu Wei-yueh's piercing gaze.

Suddenly Tu Wei-yueh laughed, then asked coldly, "Chang-lin, do you really mean to go on being at daggers drawn with Chien Pao-sheng?"

Instead of answering, Kuei Chang-lin shook himself, put his hands on his hips, and glared at Tu Wei-yueh.

"Come now, what chance have you got against a man with his pull?"

"Huh! Pull? He's got damn-all pull! He's nothing more than a high official's lap-dog."

"Exactly, but that's just where you lose. Your Mr. Wang Ching-wei's away in Hongkong."

Kuei Chang-lin's face fell, and the aggressive glint in his eye gave way to a look of fear and uncertainty.

"You needn't worry, though. There's only Wang Chin-chen here, and she's a good friend of yours. I can tell you quite frankly that Mr. Wu Sun-fu keeps in touch with friends of Mr. Wang Ching-wei, so, when you come to think of it, you and

Mr. Wu Sun-fu are in the swim together, as it were. So you ought to be willing to do your best for Mr. Wu Sun-fu in factory affairs. Am I right?"

"If Mr. Wu Sun-fu knows everything about me, then why should he have given Yao Chin-feng the sack and promoted Hsueh Pao-chu? And besides, I've done my best for him all through this trouble, haven't I? I'd like to ask him that to his face and see what he says!"

"Mr. Wu isn't playing the game," interposed Wang Chin-chen. "Mr. Tu, why don't you have a word with Mr. Wu about it before you put up the notice?"

She thought she was being very tactful in supporting Kuei Chang-lin and at the same time hinting at Tu Wei-yueh's influential position, but, to her surprise, Tu Wei-yueh frowned and snapped at her:

"You can leave Mr. Wu out of it! He's too busy to bother himself about such trifles. I, Tu Wei-yueh, am responsible here. When I say to him that Yao Chin-feng should be fired and Hsueh Pao-chu promoted, he just nods his head, and what I say goes."

"Then you've done Yao Chin-feng an injustice on your own responsibility!" cried Kuei Chang-lin, springing up and shaking his fist. Wang Chin-chen pulled him back by the hem of his coat. Tu Wei-yueh threw back his head and laughed as if he had not seen the ham-like fist being brandished under his nose. The fist was withdrawn automatically when it came within a few inches of his face, and a venomous humph was heard. Tu Wei-yueh had stopped laughing and his face was as calm and expressionless as ever.

"Pah!" he suddenly spat out. "You fool! It's all too complicated for your thick head! Can't you imagine how the women will react when they hear that Hsueh Pao-chu's been promoted and Yao Chin-feng discharged? They'll suspect Hsueh Pao-chu and support Yao Chin-feng again —"

"But how can they support her when she's been sacked?"

"Chang-lin, please . . . why can't you stop and think before you speak? Haven't I told you Mr. Wu Sun-fu'll play fair with everybody in the long run? It won't do any good standing here grumbling. You'd be better employed working on the women. As for Chien Pao-sheng, I'll teach him a lesson yet, and in public too, one of these days. And remember, both of you, that I'm on your side. I give you my word for it. Understand? Off you go, then."

Having dismissed them, Tu Wei-yueh took a piece of paper and began wording the notice.

The hooter blared its summons from one end of the factory to the other, and the women streamed into the workshops. The buzz of voices began to swell in to a tide, but this time the tide was to flow through a channel which had been engineered by Tu Wei-yueh.

*

When he left the factory Wu Sun-fu had gone straight to the Bankers' Club. Except for Sundays, he usually lunched here, for here he could meet his friends in a cheerful atmosphere, and sit around chatting for an hour or so. But today, as he stepped into the well-appointed dining-room, he was struck by the absence of the usual warm and cheerful atmosphere. He was not met by the smiles and jovial greetings of his cronies. The few people there were all strangers, and their talk, mingled with the clatter of knives and forks, was either about the war or about dancing girls and dog racing. They seemed to have nothing better to talk about; they were just trying to kill time while they ate. At a table under the windows sat three middle-aged men whose chubby faces, beaming with complacency, suggested that they had lived a comfortable and idle life in the country as rich landlords and usurers. They sat with their heads together conferring in whispers. Wu Sun-fu chose a place facing them, two or three tables away.

Outside the windows everything was still obscured by the thick, misty drizzle, so that one might have imagined that the prosperous industrial city of Shanghai had disappeared from the face of the earth, leaving only this dining-room with its half-a-dozen young bloods talking listlessly about dancing girls and greyhound racing, its three feudal landlords, and its industrialist, Wu Sun-fu, worrying about his battles on the three fronts.

Wu Sun-fu sighed dejectedly and ordered a brandy. When it

came, he sipped at it nervously.

There was no denying it: he was between three fires; and there was no denying that he had been fighting back as hard as he could. At a moment like this, when his fate was still in the balance, it was futile for him to start thinking about how he should advance if he won, and he was too distraught to plan a withdrawal or counter-attack in case he was defeated. In any case, he did not know where to start in his planning for the future, since he had no idea what the extent of his losses would be. All he could do for the moment was to drown his sorrows in his brandy. He felt rather like a prisoner waiting in the condemned cell.

The brandy picked him up somewhat — or at least, it restored his usual quickness of hearing. One of the three whisperers spoke a little more distinctly than the other two, and Wu Sun-fu clearly overheard a snatch of conversation which made him sit up.

"Now that we've gone as far as this, we must either go the whole hog or else drop it altogether. I'm in favour of putting up a fight, myself. All this talk about a victory by the Central Army is just a rumour put about by the bulls. You know that fellow Chao? Well, he's one of the big bulls and he's rigging the market. Though I don't believe he's so keen on pushing up the prices just now that we need worry about him."

Wu Sun-fu could see the speaker in profile — a long, narrow face with a wispy, drooping moustache. His companions were listening in silence, one of them resting his chin on his upturned palm and holding a coffee-cup in the other hand as he gazed thoughtfully into space. After a brief pause they both began speaking at the same time, but their voices were so low and indistinct that it was only from their expressions that one could tell that they were arguing with the man with the moustache. They were obviously speculators in government bonds, and bears at that.

Wu Sun-fu glanced at his watch and saw that it was already ten minutes to one. Newcomers arrived from time to time, but curiously enough there was not a single familiar face among them. He fiddled abstractedly with his knife and fork as he turned over in his mind the remarks the man with the moustache had just made. Could it be that they represented the trend of thought among the bears as a whole? It was hard for him to say. But obviously the market was still in a state of flux, and a life-and-death struggle was going on there. Perhaps this was the reason why he had not met a single acquaintance here today. Anyway, there was no point in hanging about here. He pushed aside his plate and was just going to get up, when he saw two familiar faces: Han Meng-hsiang and Li Yu-ting, the former being a stockbroker and a close friend of Chao Po-tao.

Seeing Wu Sun-fu there, Han Meng-hsiang smiled to him and came across.

"Both sides are holding out as long as they can," he whispered. "Chao Po-tao's furious."

"What! — Furious, is he?"

Wu Sun-fu was taken off his guard for a moment, but quickly recovered his composure, so that his question sounded off-handed enough not to rouse the other's suspicions.

"Chao Po-tao doesn't go for small fry," said Han Meng-hsiang quietly, smiling and glancing round at Li Yu-ting. "He goes whaling. It's all or nothing with him! Wait until the afternoon session opens at two, and then you'll see!"

Just then, one of the three men at the other table, a pale, corpulent little man, bobbed up and called across, "Mr. Han Meng-hsiang!" His two companions were still engrossed in their tête-á-tête. Han Meng-hsiang nodded to Wu Sun-fu and went across to join the others. An animated conversation ensued — doubtless about the day's events on the Stock Exchange.

Wu Sun-fu now invited Li Yu-ting to join him for lunch, and they chatted for a while about this and that. Wu Sun-fu, his face flushed with the wine, suddenly brought up the subject of Chang Su-su.

"My wife was telling me the other day that you and Su-su have had a bit of a tiff."

"Oh, we've never been serious about it — not enough to have a tiff, anyway!"

Li Yu-ting sounded rather embarrassed as he replied. Remembering the way Fan Po-wen and Wu Chih-sheng had ragged him, he felt more uncomfortable still. But Wu Sun-fu did not seem to notice his embarrassment. Gulping down a large mouthful of lemonade, he continued cheerfully:

"You know, Su-su's lively and independent like her father and clever and sharp like her mother. I think she'd be too much of a handful for you, Yu-ting!"

Li Yu-ting's only reply was a wry smile as he bent his head to tackle the leg of chicken before him.

A boisterous laugh came from Han Meng-hsiang at the other table, followed by a noisy, heated argument between the four of them. A deep voice boomed above the babel: "All you've got to do, Yun-ching, is to chase up your tenants for a bit more rent, and there you are!"

The man with the moustache shook his long head and said mournfully, "No, that's no good. It's been a bad year, and everywhere the peasants are rioting and refusing to pay their rents." At this the babel of voices broke loose again.

Wu Sun-fu knit his brows in a frown, covered his wineglass with his hand, and asked, "What's the news? Anything special?"

"I hear there's a big scheme afoot," Li Yu-ting replied casually, laying down his knife and fork and wiping his mouth with his napkin. "And it happens to concern you, too."

"A big scheme that concerns me?" returned Wu Sun-fu in an equally casual tone, putting on a light-hearted smile. "Well, I haven't heard anything about it!"

He assumed Li Yu-ting was referring to the trust company. After all, it was no secret, really, though he was a little irked at the speed with which the news had spread. As it turned out, however, he was in for a shock.

"It's not what you're thinking, though," Li Yu-ting went on. "You're not one of those who are launching the scheme. You're one of the people it's aimed at. That's what I meant when I said it concerns you. I should have thought you would have heard about it already."

"Oh . . . no, I haven't heard a thing. Honestly I haven't."

"It's too early yet to be able to say whether they're going to go through with it, but I have heard that they're quite set on the idea. Well, to cut a long story short, some finance capitalists are planning to take over certain industries. They're taking their cue from American financiers who have got control of industry."

Wu Sun-fu half closed his eyes and gently shook his head.

"You don't think they can do it?" pursued Li Yu-ting. "Don't forget the Shanghai bankers made a total profit of two hundred million dollars last year, and now, of course, they're looking for something to invest all this surplus capital in."

"The obvious thing to do with it," retorted Wu Sun-fu contemptuously, "is to put it into the government stock market, or else real estate or building. They wouldn't dream of looking beyond investments like that."

His face was flushed with drinking, and his self-confidence was probably inspired by the fact that he was becoming slightly tipsy. His companion, who had also been imbibing freely, was waxing eloquent, and was not to be gainsaid.

"I'm afraid you're underestimating them, Sun-fu. They're really set on this scheme, even though they haven't got the foundations solidly laid so far. You can't afford to ignore them, though, even at this early stage — especially when a number of American financiers are backing their scheme. I hear the first thing they're planning to do is to get the government to issue a vast number of industrial bonds, so that they can buy them up and gradually gain control over industry on the pretence of aiding it. But this'll be only the beginning of the control of industrial capital by financial capital: the possibilities of a further —"

"But the government won't issue enough bonds to meet their military expenses, let alone start financing industrial construction!"

"That's true at the moment, but then the war's still on. What these people are hoping is that the war will end with a government victory and that the whole country will become united. And of course their American friends hope so, too. So far as I can see, their wishes look like coming true; and I bet when that happens you won't be saying that their scheme is just a lot of wishful thinking! How can you possibly say that they can't put it through, considering all the American experience and dollars they'll have behind them? Listen, Sun-fu, you know the way it goes in Western countries: financial capital's swallowing industrial capital all the time. Well, just think how much worse it will be in China, where industry's still in its infancy — and not a very flourishing one at that — and where the American dollar is always looking for a chance to get a foothold —"

"But that'd be throwing our national industry to the wolves!" Wu Sun-fu suddenly interrupted through clenched teeth. His tipsiness had worn off and left his face pale and his eyes bloodshot. He could no longer even muster up his usual cool, contemptuous smile. His sudden indignation came as a surprise to Li Yu-ting, who promptly fell silent for a while, then, as if to ease the tense atmosphere, muttered to himself:

"On the other hand, the scheme may fizzle out. After all, America still doesn't have all her own way in the world, especially in the East, where she has two serious rivals."

"England and Japan, do you mean?" asked Wu Sun-fu, gazing blankly out of the window. Then, without conviction: "Yes, well, perhaps when the war's over things may not pan out just as the financiers are hoping they will."

His brain was in a whirl just at the moment. His righteous indignation at the fate of China's national industries was beginning to cool down and make way for apprehension about his own personal interests; and this apprehension became more and more insistent, until he could think of nothing else. Li Yu-ting was right, of course, when he said China's industry was based on a very shaky foundation. As for the weakest going to the wall, well, that's just what was happening among the Chinese industrialists themselves. Wasn't he himself scheming to swallow up Chu Yin-chiu, who was weaker than he was? And now he himself was in danger of being swallowed up — just when he was already in the middle of three decisive battles, too. The more he thought about it all, the worse he felt.

His despondent reverie was suddenly interrupted by someone calling his name. He looked up to see Han Meng-hsiang, looking very pleased with himself, raise his hand to bid him goodbye, then hurry out with his three companions in tow, the one with the moustache unhurriedly bringing up the rear.

"Off to the Exchange, I suppose," said Li Yu-ting in low, rather mournful tones as he gazed at their retreating figures and then glanced back at his companion. "The Exchange today is just like a battlefield."

The waiter served their coffee. Wu Sun-fu took a sip at his, then put down his cup and asked Li Yu-ting, "It seems, then, that the people behind this scheme are American financiers; but who have they got helping them here? Whoever they are, they're letting the wolf into the fold!"

"They say Shang Chung-li and Chao Po-tao are among them," said Li Yu-ting off-handedly, engrossed in his coffee. Wu Sun-fu's expression changed in a flash to one of dismay: So it was Chao Po-tao again, eh? I've been taken in properly this time, he thought, and this "bull company" idea is just a trap. He snorted, but made no comment. His mortification, however, quickly evaporated and gave way to anger and thoughts of revenge; now that he had accepted defeat as inevitable, he became strangely calm and his courage began to return. All he wanted now was to ascertain the full extent of his losses, so that he could begin to salvage what he could from the wreckage and plan a counter-attack at the first opportunity.

After he had taken his leave of Li Yu-ting, Wu Sun-fu drove straight home. As he sat in the car, the thoughts raced through his head like the wheels beneath him as once again he carefully turned over in his mind all that he had just learnt from Li Yu-ting. He tried to comfort himself with the thought that perhaps, after all, the scheme might not prove practicable — it might not exist, even. It was probably just a wild idea of Chao Po-tao's, reinforced by American bourgeois megalomania. Hadn't some European scholar once said that after the World War this megalomania of the American bourgeoisie had developed out of all proportion? And hadn't the world depression also struck the United States? . . . But then they'd had Dawes and Young. Yes, the United States might be preparing a second Dawes Plan for China. As soon as the war was over and the country had a unified government, it would fall pat into the hands of the Yankee, and a second Dawes Plan would come into operation. Ah, but what about the other two Powers in the East? — If

His righteous indignation at the fate of China's industries was beginning to cool down and make way for apprehension about his own personal interests....

this happened, their interests would be threatened and the three of them might come to blows! The thought brought a sardonic smile to Wu Sun-fu's lips. It was at this point in his musings that the car turned in at his front gate and swished up the drive.

Another shower greeted him as he got out of the car. The overcast sky shrouded the garden in a twilight gloom, and indoors all the lights were on. In the big drawing-room he found his wife, his sister Huei-fang and Tu Hsin-to. He stopped for a few words with them, then hurried off to his study. He did not relish the idea of having people see him when he was upset; and besides, he had a pile of correspondence to deal with.

He got a number of routine business letters out of the way first, then turned his attention to a long letter from a friend in Wusih who owned a cotton mill and was anxious that Wu Sun-fu should take up some of the new shares he was issuing to enable him to increase the number of spindles in his factory. The request had come just at the wrong moment, and as he scribbled a reply, his ill-humour seemed to find expression in his wording, so that when he went through it afterwards he was amazed that he could have written such a peevishly worded letter. He tore it up and, hardly feeling in a mood to rewrite it, went back into the drawing-room.

When he walked in, Lin Pei-shan was playing a dismal tune on the piano, while the yellow lamp-light, as dismal as the music, fell on her slender figure, which was sheathed in deep-blue silk. Wu Sun-fu frowned and was just going to say something, when he heard a sigh. His frown deepened as he looked round to see his wife sitting there, her eyes red with weeping and her cheeks still wet. Her sigh was echoed by a lugubrious utterance from Tu Hsin-to.

"Life is like the morning dew! And that's just the mood that this tune expresses. It's just the right tune to play on such a dark, rainy day as this, in this dreamy lamp-light."

Wu Sun-fu's face darkened at these ominous words, and an overpowering sense of foreboding clutched at his heart like a steel claw. He was about to give vent to his fury, when the butler, Kao Sheng, came in with a message that made his heart miss a beat.

"You're wanted on the phone, sir. It's the factory." Wu Sun-fu spun round and hurried out. So they'd rung through at last! But which was it to be — success or disaster? His hand trembled in spite of himself as he picked up the receiver. A brief pause, then his face lit up with relief as he answered in a clear, cheerful voice:

"Well done! . . . All right, if you insist: two weeks' double pay for Kuei Chang-lin. See you at nine in the morning."

The trouble at the factory was ended, and victory was his. There was no need for him to worry about the "home front" any longer.

He replaced the receiver with a smile. By now the shower had passed, and a shaft of golden sunlight streamed in through the window from the west. Outside the window, the trees in the garden were a vivid green and seemed to be dripping rhythmically. Light of heart and step, Wu Sun-fu went along a veranda and out into the rain-washed garden. Strolling along the drive, he felt that the air had never been so fresh before. As he approached the front door, he heard the furious blare of a horn, and a car raced up the drive. It had hardly stopped before the house, when Tu Chu-chai scrambled out. It was not like him to be in such a tearing hurry!

"What's happened, Chu-chai?" asked Wu Sun-fu as he hurried across to the car in a torment of suspense. But he did not need to wait for a reply to know that they had won, for Tu Chu-chai's goat-like face, care-worn as it was, beamed with undisguised satisfaction. As they went up the steps together, Tu Chu-chai told him in a triumphant whisper:

"All the bears made a last-minute rush to cover in the afternoon session; the rise was terrific and almost reached the limit and caused trading to close. If we'd bought in two or three million more, we could easily have got rid of them today. Pity we were too cautious! Our present position —"

"Skip it," smiled Wu Sun-fu, "we've done well enough for a start pulling this little lot off. There's always time to go into it in a big way later on."

The setting sun shone full on his face, lighting it up with a rosy glow. The dismal look which had been lurking in his eyes all day had quite vanished. The siege was broken, and two of his three big battles were won. As for the great scheme — the great plot, if you will — which Li Yu-ting had told him about, it held no terrors for him now as he basked in the glow of his victories.

VIII

THE last-minute rise in government-issue quotations had taken many indiscriminate speculators by surprise, and they had crashed badly. Among their number were the three men Wu Sun-fu had seen that day when he dined at the Bankers' Club; the worst hit of the three was Feng Yun-ching, the fiftyish man with the long face and the drooping moustache.

Until six months ago, this Feng Yun-ching had enjoyed an idle, comfortable life down in the country. Back in the time of the Ching dynasty he had passed the preliminary official examinations, but had got no further and so had not qualified to take his place among the "gentry," who had charge of local affairs. Failing in this ambition, he had diverted his energies into other channels — exploitation of the peasantry as a usurious money-lender. As it turned out, this second course proved equally rewarding, for it yielded him a fair amount of property. When he made his "countryside loans" to local peasants, he did not insist on cash repayments, nor did he press for prompt cash settlements of his loans, which at the end of six months had earned him interest equal to the original loan. No, what he was interested in was to let a loan grow until he could foreclose the peasant of his mortgaged land. He had a genius for making a five- or ten-dollar loan and letting it bring him in an acre or two of land at the end of two years. This was, of course, quite a common method among the landlords up country, but Feng Yun-ching, "the Smiling Tiger," distinguished himself by his skill in giving his debtors just enough rope to hang themselves with. Like the spider that spins its web and waits patiently for its prey, he cast his nets with care, and when his victim found himself with a debt he could not repay — it might be as little as a dollar — he would invariably end up by forfeiting his land to Feng Yun-ching. Then, when his land was gone, he would be forced to become a mere tenant working on his land, and as such he would be no more than a slave, a beast of burden. Five years ago, he had already amassed about four hundred acres by this means, using every shift of deceit and guile, just half an acre or an acre at a time; and every acre wet with the sweat and tears of the dispossessed peasant. And so it was that, from the wrecked lives of hundreds of peasants, Feng Yun-ching had been able to win himself a life of luxury and dissipation. Before long, he contrived to worm his way into local political circles, where his extended influence enabled him to cast his net of usury wider and exert greater pressure on his peasant victims, so that, within the short space of two years, he managed to add two hundred acres or so to his holdings. By this time, however, his newly acquired concubine, Chiu, on whom he doted, began to spend his money for him with remarkable liberality. Nor was this all. The possession of a vivacious young concubine was a drain on his energy. The effect of all this made itself felt when rioting broke out among the peasantry and swarms of bandits made their appearance. Feng Yun-ching's accustomed boldness and imperturbability deserted him, and he collected up all his ready cash and removed himself and his family to Shanghai — partly for fear of the peasants and bandits, and partly because his concubine Chiu wished it.

Now, though a respectable citizen of Shanghai, he did not like the idea of living on his uninvested capital. He had well over five hundred acres of land, it is true, and a certain amount of rent was forthcoming, but in these troubled times there was no guarantee that he would be able to collect his usual sixty per cent of his tenants' farm produce as he had in days past. He had brought some eighty thousand dollars in cash with him, but this was not enough to qualify him as a money-lender in a city like Shanghai. If he put the money in a bank, the rate of interest was too low to meet his current household expenses, which came to nearly a thousand dollars a month if one included his concubine's opium money. It was a problem requiring very careful thought. Fortunately, the government had issued large quantities of different kinds of bonds, and the armed clashes between the warlords, which dragged on from year to year, had kept the stock market in a state of flux and provided a constant excellent opportunity for speculation. Feng Yun-ching, with his eighty thousand dollars, had therefore plunged into the stock market. His luck had held for six months running, his monthly profit being a good two and a half per cent. He had almost begun to call himself a "stock expert." And now he had suffered this shattering blow. He could hardly believe it.

When he came to reckon up his losses, he found he had really come to grief. His deposit of fifty thousand dollars in the Exchange was all gone, and he owed thirty thousand more, which he would have to pay within three days — his broker, Han Meng-hsiang, had been in once already to press for payment. Ever since he had got up at half past eleven that morning, Feng Yun-ching had been hard at work with an abacus. It was now two o'clock in the afternoon and he had not had a bite of food; and still he could not find a way to make ends meet. What grieved him most was that he could see no way of winning back his money.

Sunlight was streaming through the bamboo blinds and throwing a criss-cross pattern of light and shade over part of the room. At the slightest breeze the blinds gently swayed, and this filigree of shadows rippled over the chairs and tables in a black and white fantasy. Sitting at a square mahogany table under the window, Feng Yun-ching was turning the pages of an account-book with his right hand and holding a cigarette in his left. As the shadows danced across the pages of his book, the columns of figures seemed to dance with them, much to his annoyance. Bringing his palm down on the book with an impatient thwack, he left his seat and paced through into the rear part of the house, where he lay down on a mahogany couch and closed his eyes with a sigh. Until yesterday he had been a rich man; today he was not only penniless, but tens of thousands of dollars in debt! Was it his own fault? No; that was something he would never admit! "It's just my bad luck," he told himself with another sigh. Yet why should his luck, which had stood him in good stead these twenty years and more, suddenly desert him now?

He was knitting his brows in search of an answer, when suddenly something fell with a heavy thud on the floor above him, and he sat up with a nervous start. Then the electric bell in the servants' quarters began ringing, and continued to ring for fully three minutes. It was his concubine ringing for the maid after waking up — the night before, she had not come home until dawn. This was now her usual custom, and Feng Yun-ching had long resigned himself to it; but today when he had just found himself bankrupt, it annoyed him, and it suddenly occurred to him that there must be some connection between his bad luck and her bad behaviour. Who had ever heard of a betrayed husband being lucky?

Feng Yun-ching stood up and started towards the door, but changed his mind and turned round again, his straggly moustache twitching agitatedly. He had half a mind to go up and tell her to her face to behave herself, but he thought better of it and stayed where he was; he remembered in time that concubines of her category could be dangerous when roused. He swallowed his anger and turned his eyes vacantly on the *Maxims for Keeping Order in a Family* inscribed on a scroll hanging on the wall above the couch. He stared at it glumly, and soon became lost in thought.

Presently there came the click of high-heeled shoes as footsteps approached and suddenly stopped outside the door. The door was flung open, and a girl of about eighteen fluttered into the room. Her face was a shade too long and narrow, but this shortcoming was amply compensated by an attractive mouth, a shapely chin — neither too pointed nor too round — and long, wavy hair hanging loosely over her shoulders. Her dress was of light-blue patterned silk with a lining of deep yellow and long side-slits which flared open as she walked, to give a glimpse of her smooth, shapely thighs — a striking contrast to the high, stiff collar which hid her neck. When she saw Feng Yun-ching staring abstractedly at the scroll she paused uncertainly in the doorway a moment, then giggled and went over to him, her hips swaying as she walked.

"Daddy," she cooed, "I'm going out shopping —"

Feng Yun-ching turned round and looked at her wide-eyed.

"Just a few little things," she said, twisting her hips and looking down at the floor. "A hundred dollars should be enough, I think. I must go straight away."

Suddenly she flitted across the room, leant over the square table, and switched on the electric fan. She turned her back to the wind, and wheedled, "Why don't you use the electric fan, Daddy? Look how you're perspiring! Come on, it's nice and cool here. . . . Just a hundred dollars, Daddy!"

Feng Yun-ching shook his head regretfully, walked slowly across to her, looked at her silently for a while, then said with a note of determination in his voice:

"Mei-ching, you don't know what a setback I've just had in the stock market. I'm over thirty thousand dollars in debt, and I can't pay up. I can't even settle the small accounts due at the Dragon-boat Festival. For instance, I've got a bill for five hundred dollars from your dress-maker —"

"But I only had a few dresses made, Daddy."

"Hm — but now you're asking for another hundred dollars. What do you need this time? Mei-ching, you spend more money than I do!"

"Even so, I spend much less than Chiu does!" Mei-ching retorted, pouting out her lips. With a twist of her waist she swung herself on to a sofa and looked up into her father's face, which was creased with embarrassment and worry. Reading his mind, she pursued deliberately, "If she can spend as much as she likes, why shouldn't everybody else? I don't see why I should have to give in to her!"

"Don't worry, Mei-ching!" Feng Yun-ching urged, forcing a placating smile to his lips. "Just give me a day or two, and then I can let you have it. How's that?"

His daughter did not reply, but sat twisting her handkerchief and looking round at the pictures on the walls. On one wall was a combined display of Chinese and Western art: Chang Ta-chien's tiger in the centre, supported on each side by two Western landscape etchings in colour representing the four seasons, their gilt frames glinting in the sunlight which flickered on them through the bamboo blinds. As Feng Yun-ching followed his daughter's eyes to the pictures, he began turning over in his mind how he could get rid of her. Suddenly he remembered something in connection with these etchings, which he had received as a house-warming present from one of his concubine's "sworn sisters." She had quite a few "sworn sisters," but this one, the sender of the present, was no ordinary girl. She was concubine to a man with considerable influence in the underworld, the man on whom Feng Yun-ching depended for his personal safety while he was in Shanghai. In three days' time the Dragon-boat Festival would be upon them, and he had quite forgotten until now that he would have to send his protector an expensive present to show his gratitude.

As he suddenly remembered that he had this important duty to perform, Feng Yun-ching decided that he had no money at all to spare for his daughter.

"Mei-ching, my dear, just wait until the festival's over to do your shopping. You see, I still have to send presents to several important people. Your poor father's really hard up just now. . . . Just my luck to go and lose a packet in the stock market. Mei-ching, you're my only daughter. Do you think I'd refuse you anything if I could help it?"

Feng Yun-ching could not go on, for a lump was rising in his throat. He looked up at the ceiling, and nervously stroked his straggly moustache.

For a few moments neither of them spoke, and the silence was broken only by the sound of the concubine clearing her throat in the room above. Feng Yun-ching was worrying about his debts, while the despondent Mei-ching was despairing of ever getting her hundred dollars. It looked as if the pleasant programme she had worked out for the festival would have to be cancelled, so how was she going to spend the three days' holiday? She could not just stay at home and read "eternal triangle" stories. Besides, she had already made a date with a friend, so how could she back out now? In her mind's-eye she could already see her boy friend's disappointed and suspicious looks if she called off the holiday programme.

Three successive rings on the bell at the gate startled Feng Yun-ching from his reverie. He looked out of the window and saw his rickshaw boy Ah-shun opening the gate and ushering in a round-faced middle-aged man in a round, black alpaca cap. "Oh, here's Ho Shen-an!" he gasped, and rose to go out to meet him; but his visitor was too quick for him, and almost immediately appeared in the doorway and called his name, at the same time shaking his clasped hands together, with his walking-stick dangling between them. Doing her best to keep a straight face, Mei-ching made an especially low bow in order to hide her amusement, for every time she saw him in his little round cap, bobbing up and down with his stick held in front of him, she just couldn't help laughing.

"Mei-ching, run and tell the maid to serve tea," said Feng Yun-ching, then offered Ho Shen-an a seat on the couch. As Mei-ching tripped lightly out of the room, Ho Shen-an gazed after her. With a thoughtful twitch of his eyebrows, he turned seriously to Feng Yun-ching:

"I'm not trying to flatter you, Yun-ching, but you've got a wonderful daughter there. You're a lucky man."

Feng Yun-ching took it as an ordinary compliment and smiled woodenly, wondering how his friend who had also been hit by the recent stock exchange fluctuations could be so cheerful. Glancing at his own reflection in the long mirror standing in the corner of the room, he was surprised to find that he had aged overnight by at least ten years. A sigh broke from his lips, and he said in a low voice:

"Han Meng-hsiang came yesterday for the money I owe the Exchange, but I just hadn't got it to give him. Though I must say this for Han Meng-hsiang: he always treats his friends decently. Don't you remember how he advised us to cover without delay the other day when we were lunching at the club? If we'd taken any notice of him, we wouldn't have come a cropper like this. Ah! You made a bit of a blunder this time, Shen-an: your friends in the North — the Peiyang clique — have been leading you up the garden path —"

"And serves us right, too!" interrupted Ho Shen-an, with a rueful grin. "They set the trap for us, and we walked right into it. And as for Han Meng-hsiang being a good friend to us — hah! He's only Chao Po-tao's mouthpiece. They set out to trap us right from the start. It was just a big conspiracy. And now I've found out all about it."

He threw the stub of his cigarette viciously into a spittoon, then picked up a cup of tea from the table and took a sip at it.

"What do you mean, conspiracy? You're not trying to tell me they rigged a victory at the front as part of their trap?"

"Why not? So it wasn't our bad luck that did it for us; it was our honesty!"

Feng Yun-ching's eyes rolled in amazement, while his straggly moustache twitched, and he broke out into a cold sweat all over. There was no reason to disbelieve what he had just been told. He had become so used to setting traps for peasants all these years that it came as rather a shock to him to find he had walked into a snare himself. He stroked his moustache agitatedly as he slowly pulled himself together, then grumbled miserably:

"It means . . . it means I've been slaving all these years just to put money in *their* pockets! Shen-an, you don't know how hard it's been for me to make what little money I had. You'd be surprised how much breath you have to waste over a mere half acre of land. They're a woolly-minded lot, these country people. They want loans, but they don't want to give up their farms! Usually, I had to go to a lot of trouble with them — invite them to a tea-house, and reason patiently with them, until I could finally make them realize that I was not robbing them of their farms, but merely trying to get back the interest on my loans. You know yourself, Shen-an, how reasonable I am. For example, whenever I went down to the village to collect my rents, I never took any strong-arm men with me to beat up my tenants. I always used the method of gentle persuasion — though, of course, I never came away with a halfpenny less than I went for! And that's how I managed to get together a few hundred acres of land. I can tell you, it wasn't so easy for me to make money as it was for you when you were a county magistrate. Yours was a soft job — you just cooked the land-tax accounts and reserved yourself a percentage of the opium pool, so that what you made in a month would have taken me a year to scrape together. . . ."

Feng Yun-ching paused and drew violently at his cigarette. He was about to go on when Ho Shen-an stopped him:

"Come now, that's all past history. What's the point in going over it all again? But tell me, though: Are you going to have another go at the stock business?"

"Another go? Well, to tell you the truth, I'm a bit scared now. I was going over the ups and downs of the stock market this morning, and I decided the stock business is a bit too tricky. Now that you've told me about the crafty dodges they get up to, I'm finished with it for good. Besides, after a crash like that, I've got nothing left to start with — but what about you, Shen-an?"

"Every penny of ten years' savings down the drain! Yesterday I sold a few curios at a tea-house gathering just to get a thousand dollars or so to tide me over the festival. But I'm sure you're better off. You've got plenty of land, and the rent alone must be quite a —"

Ho Shen-an broke off as Feng Yun-ching sprang to his feet and threw himself down on the couch again. All the colour had drained from his face, his eyes were bloodshot and staring, and the corners of his mouth twitched uncontrollably. Ho Shen-an gaped at him in surprise and scratched his head. After a moment, Feng Yun-ching raised his hand tensely and slammed it down on a low table beside him.

"Rent?" he spat out between clenched teeth. "Who dares go down into the villages for rent these days? If I could collect my rents, d'you think I'd have left a perfectly good country house of that size to come and live in this hole in Shanghai and stay here worrying myself to death about robbery and kidnapping day in, day out?"

He slumped down on the couch and closed his eyes, panting hard.

"No, it's none too peaceful down in the country, I know," Ho Shen-an said slowly after a moment's pause. "But, Yun-ching, why should you let those damned tenants of yours get away with it? What's to stop you taking a few strong-arm men down to persuade them?"

As he spoke, he toyed with his alpaca cap, gazing at it, and blowing at it between phrases. Finally, he fished out a handkerchief and flicked at specks of dust on it, a shadow of a smile on his smooth, oily round face.

Sprawled on his back, Feng Yun-ching could only sigh in answer to this question. He was, of course, well acquainted with the method of collecting rents with an armed escort, but he was also quite aware that the peasants were not like they used to be. If you went with a mere handful of men, they were no use at all; if you took a lot, they ate their heads off, and even if they did manage to get you something, it was never enough to pay their wages and expenses. No, the game was not worth the candle. That was a lesson Feng Yun-ching had already learned once to his cost. "The Smiling Tiger," shrewd old rogue that he was, had since preferred to let his rents fall in arrears for a year, and count on the chance that the coming year would be peaceful enough for him to go down to the village and use his usual old tricks to make his tenants fork out every cent of the compound interest.

Ho Shen-an lit another cigarette, puffed at it, and started on a new topic:

"Well, Yun-ching, let's consider how we're going to recover our losses."

"Recover what losses?" Feng Yun-ching asked nervously, sitting up with a start. He was still thinking about his property in the country and his tenants. He seemed to see the grievances of his tenants issuing like vapours from the murky depths of their huddled, straw-thatched huts — grievances which dated back thousands of years, grievances against oppression and exploitation, now crying out for revenge and redress, grievances which were about to erupt like a volcano and burn and destroy their fetters and shackles. Yet Ho Shen-an knew nothing of this, and answered with a smile:

" 'He who has broken his arm three times makes a good surgeon.' Go back to where you lost and recoup your losses!"

"Oh, I see, you're still talking about the stock business."

"Of course I am. Don't tell me you've lost heart."

"I haven't exactly lost heart, I've just got cold feet," Feng Yun-ching answered with another sigh, trying hard to keep back his tears. "The way they set that trap and let us walk right into it!"

Ho Shen-an burst out laughing. He picked up his walking-stick, pointed it at Feng Yun-ching, described an arc in the air with it, then thumped it against the floor as he boomed:

"Come, come, old man! I can quite understand that you're a bit shaken up after the crash, but don't you see? — The mere fact that people can set traps and get away with it shows that success is not a matter of luck: it depends on your *method* of doing business. And that's why I say we've got a fair chance of recouping our losses —"

"Shen-an —"

"Don't interrupt. Now, listen! It was Chao Po-tao and his friends who set this trap. They're experts at that sort of game and we obviously don't stand a chance against them. Now if only we can do a little snooping and get hold of their secret, we can recover our losses easily!"

As Ho Shen-an made this pronouncement, he beamed complacently and wagged his head. He suddenly slapped his thighs and stood up, then planted himself before Feng Yun-ching with narrowed eyes, and was about to come out with something important, when Feng Yun-ching knit his brows and said:

"I don't see how you think you're going to go about the snooping, though. Chao Po-tao's a wily old fox —"

"But he's like Prince Huei of Liang: 'I have one weakness: I like a pretty face.' With a woman as a decoy we can catch Chao Po-tao just like that!"

He said this in an undertone, bending forward with his lips to Feng Yun-ching's ear, then exploded with laughter.

Feng Yun-ching stared at him wide-eyed. He himself still wore a frown, but a faint blush suffused his pale face. He suspected that his friend was pulling his leg, for even he must have heard about the way Feng Yun-ching's concubine did not get home from her nightly jaunts until the next morning. To cover his embarrassment, he pretended not to notice the suspected insinuation, and half-heartedly tried to steer the conversation away.

"An excellent idea!" he said, clucking his tongue in admira-

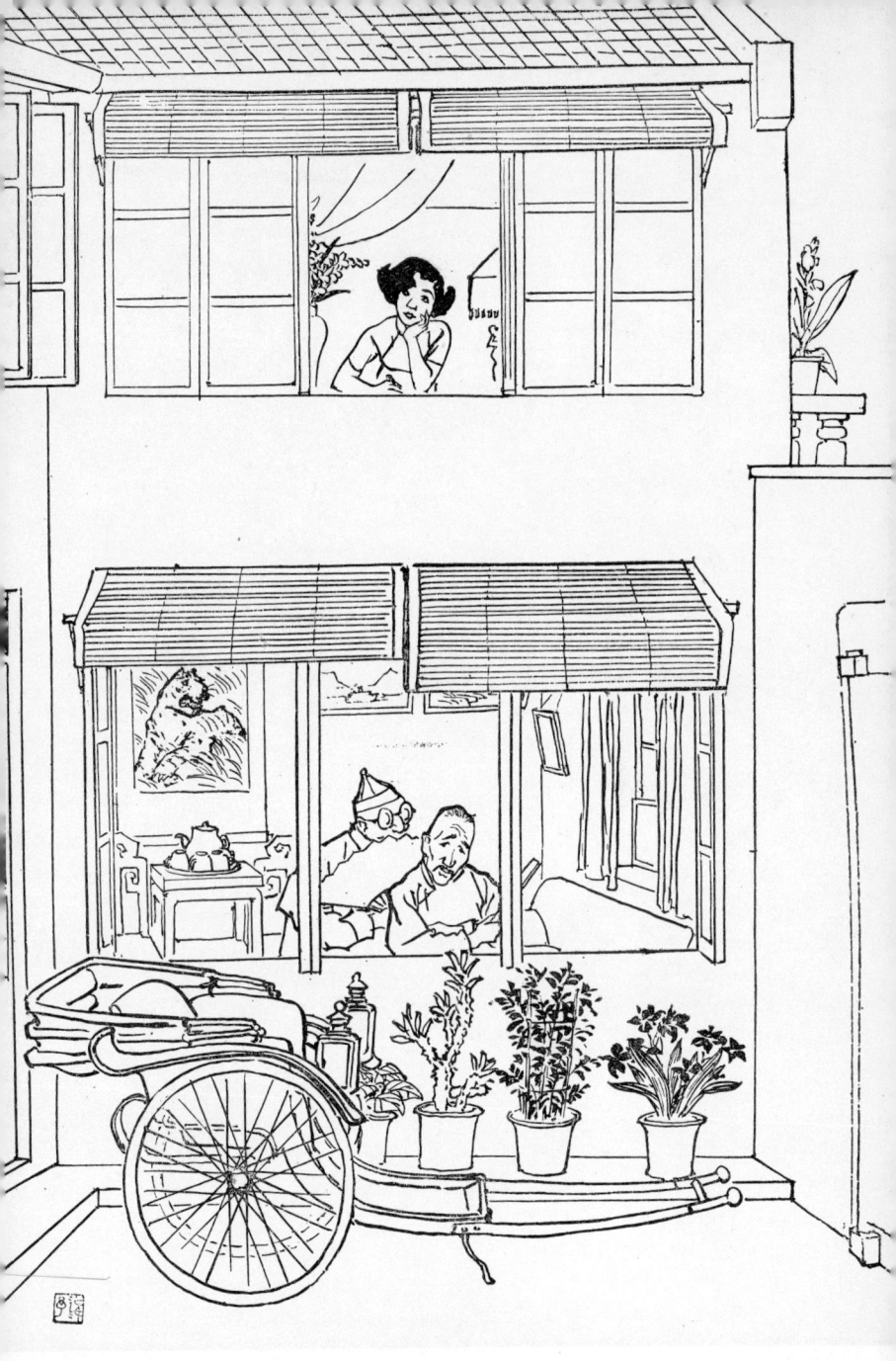

"With a woman as a decoy we can catch Chao Po-tao just like that!"

tion. "That's what ten years' experience on the stormy seas of officialdom does for you! I hope when you've pulled it off you'll let me have a finger in the pie, Shen-an."

"I'm afraid you've missed a point," replied Ho Shen-an, looking serious. "This is a job for you. I can only advise you how to go about it."

His voice had fallen to an almost inaudible whisper, yet it thundered in Feng Yun-ching's ears. His face fell, and his heart beat wildly, though whether from delight or anger — or was it perhaps fear? — he could not tell. Being quite at a loss how to reply, he could only stare blankly at Ho Shen-an's oily, smiling round face. Ho Shen-an shook his head, then opened his mouth and let the tip of his yellow-furred tongue flicker out and in again.

"People admire Chao Po-tao for his shrewdness," he resumed quietly. "They say he can tell a genuine gem from a fake at a glance, and that he can tell a virgin straight away. He likes his women brand-new, and so long as he's the first, he doesn't worry particularly what they're like: they're all grist to his mill. He's got a room in a hotel which he keeps specially for this purpose, and he's always prowling around a certain roof-garden in search of fresh talent. So, you see, it'll be quite easy to hook him if only we can —"

"If only we can what?" Feng Yun-ching asked eagerly as he rose from the couch, his eyes gleaming with interest.

"If only we can find a clever, pretty and reliable girl . . . like your daughter, say," replied Ho Shen-an calmly and unhurriedly, a smile on his lips. He still spoke in an undertone, but enunciated each word clearly and carefully.

Feng Yun-ching gulped uncomfortably, and his face blanched as he sat dazedly down on the couch again and stared up into his friend's plump face. The latter, however, betrayed no sign of emotion, but moved closer and went on furtively:

"It's our only way! You're afraid it won't work? You needn't be afraid of that. I give you my word it'll work! Yun-ching, you don't know how lucky you are to have a daughter like that. . . ."

"But, Shen-an!"

"Once you've hooked him, you can do what you like with him afterwards. You can go ahead with your business in the smooth way or the rough way; the old-fashioned way or the modern way — take your pick. Don't worry. You can trust me. I'm a most reliable adviser. To be frank, Yun-ching, you beat me hollow when it comes to fleecing peasants, but I'm better than you at snooping around, and setting a pretty sprat to catch a fat mackerel!"

Ho Shen-an chuckled and took a sip at his tea, then clasped his hands behind his back and turned to look up at a photograph hanging on the wall — a family group with Feng Yun-ching's daughter Mei-ching gracefully occupying the centre of the picture. He stood gazing a long time at the photograph, so as to give Feng Yun-ching plenty of time to turn his suggestion over in his mind. As he stood there, the sun went behind the clouds, leaving the room gloomy. From upstairs came the sound of girlish laughter and somewhere a tap was running, while the lane outside echoed with the cries of pedlars hawking meat-pies, dumplings and noodles.

But not a sound came from Feng Yun-ching.

Ho Shen-an turned to look in the long mirror as it stood like a transparent door in the corner of the room. In it was reflected Feng Yun-ching's face, wary and undecided. Suddenly, the corners of his mouth twitched and wrinkled up and his beady eyes shifted from side to side — he seemed to be making up his mind at last. Ho Shen-an could not help turning round to look at him. Just at that moment, Feng Yun-ching muttered to himself:

"Set a trap for *him* to walk into, eh?"

"That's right, Yun-ching!" Ho Shen-an hurriedly assured him, then sat down opposite him. Feng Yun-ching twisted his lips into an uneasy smile and tried another tack:

"Joking apart, Shen-an, you say it's the battles at the front that affect the stock market, but that's not the whole of it. I think the big speculators' manipulations are also an important factor. They've got the money to manoeuvre with. This fellow Chao Po-tao's one of them, but how can we get his secrets out of him? You're a crafty old fox if you can do that, Shen-an!"

Ho Shen-an did not seem to be in any hurry to enlighten him. He just raised his eyebrows and burst out laughing. He saw through Feng Yun-ching, who was already becoming interested in his proposition, though he did not dare admit it to his face.

Realizing his embarrassment, Ho Shen-an smiled to himself, then stood up and patted Feng Yun-ching on the shoulder.

"Don't be so modest, old man," he said. "I'm no cleverer than you are. Just do as you think fit! But now I must be off."

*

Feng Yun-ching saw his friend to the gate, then turned back and lingered a moment in the little yard, staring absently at the pots of red azaleas and the goldfish tank. Suddenly, he burst out laughing to himself, but hardly had he stopped laughing, when a couple of tears rolled down his cheeks. He raised two fingers and felt his eyes, as if he could not believe they were actually tears. As he looked at the azaleas through his blurred eyes, they seemed to be transformed into his daughter's dimples. He looked at the goldfish tank: the fish had turned into gold bars. He heaved a sigh and came to, then hurried back indoors and slumped on to a sofa.

He puckered his forehead in an effort to sort out in his mind the various urgent matters requiring his attention, but the same three things kept going round and round in his head: that his daughter was pretty; that money was so precious; and that Chao Po-tao could easily be hooked. All of a sudden, he flared up, slapped himself on the face, and began reviling himself through clenched teeth!

"You old cuckold! You're making yourself ridiculous! Ho Shen-an's just making a fool of you! Anyone who's meddled with officialdom for long must be lower than a snake's belly, and Ho Shen-an's just that sort. You're a respectable landlord, and you come from a good family. How could you ever listen to Ho Shen-an's nonsense? Are you so weak that you'd sink to that? No! You must try to do something with your property in the country!"

After this he felt a bit better and squared his shoulders again, but another problem kept nagging at his mind: the peasants were rioting and most probably he was no longer able to call all those hundreds of acres of good land his own — yet he still had to pay land-tax on them just the same. He shook his head ruefully as he stood up and looked round to make sure that he was still in his own comfortable room. He seemed to be hearing the distant rumble of explosions coming nearer and nearer, louder and louder!

He was jolted out of his day-dream by a loud knocking at the gate. Startled, he shambled out and peeped through the crack of the door at the caller outside. When he saw that it was not Han Meng-hsiang coming again for the money, or anybody else from the Exchange, the colour returned to his face.

The visitor was Li Chuang-fei, a middle-aged man who distinguished himself by wearing an up-to-date toothbrush moustache. He was one of Feng Yun-ching's fellow-speculators in government bonds and a recently-made acquaintance of his.

Feng Yun-ching bowed his friend into the room, glancing at him as he did so to see how he looked after the disaster in the stock market, and was surprised to find a rather elated smile on his face, a smile reminiscent of Ho Shen-an's when he came in. Feng Yun-ching immediately felt ill at ease. He was afraid this "revolutionary" ex-magistrate also had some worrying, fantastic plan up his sleeve, something to throw him into another dilemma. Aged by the events of the past few days, Feng Yun-ching felt that his tormented nerves could stand no more worry.

It came as a surprise to him, then, when Li Chuang-fei began getting his own tale of woe off his chest the moment he sat down:

"I just can't help being a bit superstitious, Yun-ching: I'm fated to be unlucky this year. Every single plan I've made since New Year's Day has fallen through. In March I managed to secure a position as a county magistrate, but less than a month later the Communists came and bang went my job. And what could I do in a month? However hard I'd been on the peasants, I could never have made enough to cover the money I'd laid out when I bought the post. How could I? Never mind, at least I got a glimpse of what the job was like. The next thing I did was even more disastrous. I paid out every penny of eighteen thousand dollars for a post as an inspector of taxes. They assured me it was a cushy job with plenty of pickings, and my superiors sent about a dozen relatives of theirs to be clerks in my office. I hurried down to my new post in the highest spirits, but I'd only been settled in two days when the war — damn it! — had to break out right in my area of all places. The enemy took over my district and sent one of their own officials to replace me. If I hadn't made my escape there and then, there's no telling what would have happened to me! So you see, Yun-ching, it's no fun at all being any sort of official these days —"

"But I know you never say die! You've still got a whole army of secretaries and clerks around you, and your rooms in the hotel are more like a yamen than anything else."

Feng Yun-ching forced a smile as he said this, because he had heard that Li Chuang-fei, the famous "revolutionary magistrate," used his "revolutionary" methods not only in public affairs but also in his financial dealings with friends. Though he had never benefited from Li Chuang-fei's kind attentions, Feng Yun-ching had long been aware of his reputation, and as he now listened to his outpourings of woe, he was naturally rather wary.

Li Chuang-fei smiled, looked round furtively, and said in a low voice:

"To tell you the truth, those secretaries and clerks of mine are all 'log-rollers' for me, and I couldn't very well get rid of them. On the other hand, I have to spend a lot on their upkeep, and that keeps me short. On top of that, I lost quite a lot on the stock market the other day, as you probably know. And now it's nearly quarter-day and I've got a lot of accounts to settle — just guess how much I'm short of still!"

So it was just as Feng Yun-ching had feared! His heart missed a beat and his face fell. He could not think what to say for a moment. Li Chuang-fei seemed to read his thoughts, for he looked glum and said in a more sober tone of voice:

"Don't misunderstand me, Yun-ching! I know you've lost quite heavily this time, but surely you're not going to wash your hands of it? I have discovered a way of recouping our losses, and I came specially to discuss it with you. If only we can get it financed properly, this plan will give great results."

Far from being inspired by Li Chuang-fei's optimism, Feng Yun-ching became all the more uneasy, and the expression on his face became more troubled than ever. He just stood there without a word, gazing wide-eyed into space. For a few moments Li Chuang-fei stood looking at him with a sardonic smile.

"Call yourself 'the Smiling Tiger' when you're floored by a little bit of trouble like this?" he jeered. "— Though I'm not surprised, really. You've been used to a nice, comfortable life as a wealthy landlord, just collecting your rents and interest. But if you're going to gamble on the Stock Exchange these days, you'll find you're half a million up today and broke tomorrow, and you don't like that sort of game, apparently. Well, Yun-ching, I'll give you a word of advice which will help you to like it. There's only one thing you've got to be if you're going to speculate: ruthless! Now, suppose you're a bull and you buy a hundred thousand Disbandment and the settlement leaves you nothing at all. All right! You go ahead and buy two hundred thousand more, and so you keep on, snowball-fashion. You'll notice that's exactly how the government issues bonds: in the first half of the year they issue two lots of seventy million, and in the second half, sure as eggs is eggs, they'll issue four lots — otherwise, how could they carry on financially?"

"But what's that got to do with us coming a cropper on the Exchange?" objected Feng Yun-ching. "Other people —"

He broke off with a sigh, and Li Chuang-fei quickly stepped in again:

"Ah, but don't you see, that's where *we* come in! Since the market's bound to be flooded with more and more money, it's going to fluctuate more and more from day to day. The smallest change in the political situation will immediately affect the prices, and give the stock-jobber an excellent opportunity of fishing in troubled waters. Go and ask any old hand at the game, and he'll tell you he's never happier than when the war-lords start making trouble again. On the other hand, if the political situation remains stable, and you lose, then you lose for good, and there's no chance of going in again tomorrow and recouping your losses. As it is, you've got every opportunity — any day — of recovering what you've lost."

"Do you mean to tell me you *like* wars?"

"Not always. When I was an inspector of taxes, I was anything but pleased about it. Now that I'm a stock-jobber, naturally my likes and dislikes have changed. And I'll tell you another thing: now, you know we all go in for Disbandment and Disarmament? Well, the government makes these two issues under the pretence of trying to end the civil war once and for all, whereas, in actual fact, these bonds are only adding fuel to the flames. It's like this: as soon as a war breaks out, the peasants down in the country turn bandits and the Communists become twice as active, with the result that the rich landlords pack their bags and flock into Shanghai with their money to get away from them; then, as ready cash accumulates in Shanghai, so the government issues bonds to absorb it — tens of millions of dollars' worth at a time. But the money they raise in this way goes to finance the fighting, and as the fighting gets worse, so does the unrest among the peasants. Result: more and more rich landlords flock into Shanghai from the country with their money, and the government seizes the opportunity to issue more bonds. And so you get a vicious circle of bonds and bombs. Do you get the hang of it now, Yun-ching? Civil war may mean disaster for other businessmen, but stock-jobbers thrive on it. If the civil war went on for a thousand years, you can bet your bottom dollar there'd be a thousand years of prosperity for the stock-jobbing business!"

When he paused, Feng Yun-ching used the spittoon and asked in a worried voice, "Do you think there's going to be trouble in the country for a long time yet, then, Chuang-fei?"

"Oh, come now, old man, you're not still dreaming that you can go back to being a happy-go-lucky landlord, are you? I tell you: in a year or two's time, you wouldn't be able to *give* your land-deeds away, let alone sell them!"

This reply came as a cold douche to Feng Yun-ching, who could only gape in consternation at Li Chuang-fei's plump, impudent face, waiting for him to go on. When he saw that he had no more to say, and that he was in dead earnest, Feng Yun-ching suddenly felt a buzzing in his ears, and his head swam. For several days he had been racking his brains what to do about his landed property, and now he had his answer — though it broke his heart to hear it. With an effort he pulled himself together and fumed through clenched teeth:

"If that's the case, then the government is definitely failing to do its duty by us landowners!"

"I wouldn't say that. After all, the government's always issuing large quantities of bonds and giving you landowners who come to the city a chance to get rich! The opportunity to make a hundred thousand or two hundred thousand dollars at one stroke is not to be sneezed at!"

Whether naturally or deliberately it was hard to say, Li Chuang-fei's voice was the acme of calmness and his face wore a cheerful grin as he gave this reply. Feng Yun-ching was heart-broken and on the verge of tears. Nevertheless, he had at last made up his mind about the dilemma in which he had found himself since Ho Shen-an's visit: he had decided that he had no alternative but to throw everything he had into a do-or-die effort to regain his fortunes on the Exchange. His voice trembled as he raised his head and said:

"But I'm ruined! How can you sit there and talk about me making a fortune? Though — Chuang-fei, just what *is* this plan of yours?"

Instead of replying immediately, Li Chuang-fei drew deeply at his cigarette, then calmly began blowing smoke-rings into the air. He knew that once he had caught the sly fox he need not worry about him escaping. He let a good three minutes pass before he proposed abruptly, "Yun-ching, I think your landholdings down in the country could be mortgaged for cash before it's too late. Why not dispose of them while you can?"

It was now Feng Yun-ching's turn to be reticent. He merely rolled his eyes uneasily and nodded slightly.

"Now, don't misunderstand me. I'm only advising you for your own good to dispose of your property. — To get back to the question of speculating in government bonds, what I suggest is briefly as follows. You and I will go into partnership, and the decision on what to buy or sell will rest entirely with me.

If we lose, we'll go fifty-fifty; if we make a profit, we'll also go fifty-fifty, but you'll give up thirty per cent of your share of the profits as a special bonus for me. There's one other thing I must make clear: When we pay the deposit, you'll pay sixty per cent, and I'll pay forty — call this my advantage, if you like. I've got a draft for thirty thousand dollars on a local bank on me, but I don't want to discount it before it falls due, because I won't get very much for it if I do, what with the crippling charges. And it doesn't fall due until the sixteenth of next month —"

"When it comes to cash I'm even worse off than you are," Feng Yun-ching assured him hurriedly, which was quite true; and besides, Li Chuang-fei's methods were so unorthodox that Feng Yun-ching decided he could not be too cautious. Not to be outdone, the versatile Li Chuang-fei immediately found a chink in the other's armour and plunged in:

"Come off it! If you're short of cash, all you've got to do is to mortgage your estate in the country. Matter of fact, I know a certain major-general who comes from your part of the country. I can easily persuade him to invest in a bit of property in his own district. You can safely leave the whole business in my hands. If you need a few thousand to tide you over the festival, just let me know and I'll let you have what you want — and without security, too. There's just one thing, though: the Exchange opens again the day after tomorrow, and you'll have to look sharp about it if you're thinking of going in again. Whether you're buying or selling, remember the early bird gets the worm!"

"What would you advise me to do, precisely?"

"Ah! I can give you it in a nutshell. Everybody knows that the one man who's made a packet this time is Chao Po-tao, but the brain behind him is Wu Sun-fu. Wu Sun-fu has a good friend in the army fighting at the front, and this friend of his sends him red-hot information about the latest developments. Now, I know a stockbroker who's a relative of Wu Sun-fu's, and who handles most of Wu Sun-fu's business on the Exchange — a man by the name of Lu Kuang-shih. The thing is, I've come to an agreement with this fellow: he'll tip me off from time to time about what Wu Sun-fu's doing in the Exchange, so that we can follow his line; then, if we make anything out of it, he'll get a cut of the takings. How does that strike you? Remember, Yun-ching: he who hesitates is lost!"

With this Li Chuang-fei rose to go, smoothing his moustache with one hand and reaching for his Panama hat with the other.

Just at that moment, the sound of two women quarrelling came from upstairs. As soon as he heard it, Feng Yun-ching knew that it was his concubine and his daughter and he became more distraught than ever. He stood up mechanically, bowed to Li Chuang-fei with clasped hands, and said hurriedly:

"It was very good of you to call, and I'm most grateful for all you've told me. To tell you the truth, I could do with a few thousand to see me through, so I think I'll take you up on your offer of a loan — I'll drop in to see you at the hotel tomorrow."

Li Chuang-fei assented effusively, told Feng Yun-ching the best time to call, and departed well pleased with himself. As soon as he had gone, Feng Yun-ching dashed upstairs in a flurry, intending to make peace between the quarrelling women. As he reached the door of his room, he heard a crash, followed by a sneering laugh from his concubine. White as a sheet, he stopped dead in his tracks. He stood for a moment with his head on one side, scratching his ear, but almost immediately plucked up courage, lifted the door-curtain gently aside, and slipped into the room, where he found his concubine sitting on the opium-couch, looking as black as thunder, and her maid kneeling on the floor picking up the fragments of a broken porcelain bowl. There was a pool of bird's-nest porridge on the blue and white carpet in front of the couch. Chin Mah, the hairdresser maid, stood behind the concubine, smiling to herself and toying with a comb.

Seeing that his daughter was not there, Feng Yun-ching felt slightly relieved. It looked as though his daughter had made a lightning attack and retired immediately from the battlefield, leaving her enemy to vent her rage on the maid.

"So here you are at last!" the concubine sneered. "Are you sure you haven't come into the wrong room? You ought to have gone and seen your darling little daughter first — she got the worst of it!"

She turned her head sulkily away as she spoke, but at the same time watched Feng Yun-ching out of the corner of her eye. He doubled up with laughter, but it had a hollow ring; then he started taking it out on the maid:

"Huh! You get worse and worse! Can't you even carry a bowl of porridge without dropping it? Go on, hurry up and fetch another — don't just squat there!"

"Don't pretend to be telling her off when it's me you're having a dig at!" snapped the concubine, jerking her head sharply round and glaring at Feng Yun-ching, her beady eyes ablaze with fury. When she saw that he was smiling tenderly at her, she gave a bitter laugh and went on:

"Even this little bitch is taking liberties with me — giving me scalding hot porridge to eat! — Though she'd never have dared to do it if somebody else hadn't put her up to it. Now tell me straight —"

"There, there, my dear. Don't get so upset about it. Have a smoke to calm your nerves. I'll roast you a few beads of opium myself. Chin Mah, hurry up and do your mistress's hair. There's a special contest at the Ming Gardens at nine o'clock tonight. Oh, and, Chiu: Mr. Pai's concubine Woo rang through and suggested a dozen games of mahjong with you first before you all go off to the Ming Gardens. Look, the sun's going down so you'd better hurry up. And don't get so upset over a silly little thing like that."

As he tried to soothe her, he tipped Chin Mah a wink to do up her hair. Then, with a hearty laugh, he settled himself on the couch and picked up the needle, put a bead of opium on it, and began roasting it over the flame. Despite his outward cheerfulness, he felt thoroughly miserable.

"Yes," began Chin Mah, trying to cheer her mistress up as she deftly combed the concubine's hair into shape, "our Miss Mei-ching may look like a grown-up, but she's still only a child, really, and she doesn't realize what she's saying. Later on, when you feel better, you should explain to her that she must behave herself, and not upset you like this. — Now, what about doing you a horizontal S, madam?"

The concubine made no reply, for she was thinking about

Mr. Pai's concubine Woo, a "sworn sister" of hers. The reason why Chiu had such a hold over Feng Yun-ching was that she had a certain amount of influence with Mr. Pai through his concubine. When Feng Yun-ching had first arrived in Shanghai, he had received threatening letters from kidnappers demanding protection-money. His concubine did a little string-pulling through Mr. Pai's concubine, and was so successful that nothing more was heard from the kidnappers. It was only then that Feng Yun-ching realized that a rich man from the country who had come to find himself a comfortable niche in Shanghai was not half so powerful as a concubine with her wide social connections. And this was why he had long ceased to question his concubine about her night life.

When the maid had picked up the broken pieces and cleaned up the spilled porridge, she brought in a fresh bowl of bird's-nest porridge — this time neither too hot nor too cool. Chin Mah had finished doing the concubine's hair and had gone into the next room to lay out her clothes. Feng Yun-ching had put a bead of opium in the bowl of the opium-pipe and laid it ready on the plate, and had now closed his eyes to consider once more Ho Shen-an's and Li Chuang-fei's suggestions. He thought that if he could believe what Li had told him, then Li's plan was much better than Ho's idea of "snooping." Of course, the chances of succeeding would be twice as good if both their plans were put into execution together. . . . But how could he do what Ho had suggested? After all, he had the high family traditions to consider! And another thing: his concubine had already got the upper hand of him for "special reasons" — what if his daughter should now get a hold over him in the same way? With two of them exerting pressure on him, he'd be between the devil and the deep blue sea! If only he could believe everything Li Chuang-fei told him! And yet —

At this point his train of thought was interrupted by his concubine's voice as she sipped the bird's-nest porridge and clinked the silver spoon against the bowl:

"It's the Dragon-boat Festival the day after tomorrow. I suppose you've done everything?"

"Eh? What did you say?" asked Feng Yun-ching nervously, looking up quickly.

"Don't tell me you don't know what you ought to have done! I mean about the presents, of course! Mr. Pai's Woo and the others have been very good to you. You can't very well let the festival go by without giving them anything!"

"Oh, er — no. I hadn't forgotten it for a moment. But, my dear Chiu, you know I've lost every penny I had on the Exchange, and I'm nearly six thousand dollars in debt as well. I was wondering if you could think of a way of helping me out —"

"If you want me to get you a loan of ten thousand dollars, or eight, or whatever you want, that's easy enough, but what about securities? You don't think anybody would take your old land-deeds as security!"

"That's just it. That's why I was hoping you'd be able to help me out. There's a friend of mine named Li who's promised me a loan, but I don't think I can depend on him. I've only got a couple of days, anyway. I'd be in a bit of a mess if I couldn't pay up!"

When he had had his say, the concubine returned to her porridge. When she had finished it, she put her head on one side and tittered, but said nothing. She knew all about his coming to grief over the government bonds, but she refused to believe he was as badly off as all that. If he wanted her to get him a loan, she had no objection. The money would pass through her hands, and she could take her commission to meet her own expenses over the festival.

She began to pick her teeth, and after a while she smiled and said:

"Of course, I could quite easily borrow a few thousand even without any security. If I ask my friend Woo for it, she wouldn't like to make me lose face by refusing it. But I think we should try and save face a bit by offering her some security. Don't you agree? Now, your land-deeds wouldn't be any good, but I seem to remember you've got a deposit account of ten thousand dollars in the Yuan Feng Local Bank. . . ."

"Er — oh, no! No, we can't touch that!" Feng Yun-ching answered hastily, springing up and all but overturning the opium-lamp as he did so. His concubine pursed her lips in annoyance and snorted scornfully, then lay down on the couch, picked up the pipe, and began drawing noisily at it.

"No, we mustn't use that money, Chiu," Feng Yun-ching gasped in horror, creasing his brow. "It belongs to Mei-ching. When her mother died, her uncles got together to discuss what to do with the money she'd left, and they decided to set aside this ten thousand dollars and put it in the bank, and it wasn't to be touched until Mei-ching marries and takes it along with her as her dowry."

From the dowry his thoughts travelled back to just after his wife's death, when he had acquired this concubine despite the protests of Mei-ching's uncles. His brother-in-law had not liked the concubine from the moment he had clapped eyes on her, and had told Feng Yun-ching, "This woman with her flat round face is sure to bring you bad luck and ruin you: I can tell it from her features." As if in fulfilment of the prophecy, his luck had become worse from year to year, until he had found himself in his present straits. He sighed involuntarily, then glanced quickly at his concubine to see if she was reading his thoughts, and was rather disconcerted to find her sharp eyes on him. As he caught her eye, he looked uncomfortably away and stared at the sizzling bowl of the opium-pipe, an uneasy smile on his face.

Fortunately for him, it seemed she had not noticed his changes of expression, for she merely moved her pipe an inch or two away from her mouth, breathed out two plumes of grey smoke from her nostrils, and said in an unusually gentle voice:

"Very eager to be a father-in-law, eh? Yes, everything's ready for the wedding, dowry and all — all you want now is for your future son-in-law to come and kowtow to you. But don't kid yourself — it won't work out like that at all! You seem to think you're still — pah! You're dreaming! Wake up, do!"

"What d'you mean?"

"Don't you really know or are you only pretending not to?" She tittered. She seemed more exultant than angry.

"I don't understand."

"No, and I don't understand either why a girl of good family should not prefer to have a big, stylish wedding and why she should even turn her nose up at a nice, fat dowry of ten thousand dollars or so —"

"Chiu! —" cried Feng Yun-ching goaded beyond endurance. She sounded to him as if she was revelling in his discomfiture, but with two pipefuls of opium inside her there was no stopping her, and he did not have a chance of getting a word in edgeways.

"Don't you shout at me! I'm only a poor ignorant girl and I don't understand these new ways — not like your daughter! She's a student, a modern girl; she speaks English, and has her own way of doing things: once she's taken a fancy to a man, she'd just sneak away with him. These modern girls have got their own way of showing respect for their parents — they just marry themselves off, and their parents just have to lump it!"

She laid down the pipe and shook her head disapprovingly. Her face was serious now.

"I don't believe it!" Feng Yun-ching burst out, his face quite pale now. His straggly moustache twitched nervously, and his eyes glazed. He stared at his concubine with a mingled look of suspicion and alarm. One question kept preying on his mind: Was it inevitable that she would take advantage of her freedom to elope with some man or other? But the concubine had further shocks in store for him:

"You don't believe it? All right, so I'm making it up, then! But just you wait and see! He looks like a good-for-nothing student; comes from away somewhere; funny-looking chap — probably one of these Communists that you hear about. Anyway, I don't expect you'd be very keen on him as a son-in-law. But even if you're not, it won't make any difference. These new-fangled girls are as slippery as eels!"

Feng Yun-ching felt like a criminal who has just heard his sentence pronounced: his fate was sealed. He gulped and looked wildly about him, his fingertips trembling. When he closed his eyes, he could see Ho Shen-an's flabby round face with its leering smile — a smile which he now realized to be one of mockery. . . . The so-and-so must have known all along about the shameful way Mei-ching was carrying on, and he probably only came to make fun of me! As this thought suddenly flashed through his mind, he felt a strange sensation, for he was not sure whether to be furious with his daughter for her bad behaviour and her disregard for him, or whether to be piqued that such an affair, with a man of her own choice might stand in the way of the plan which Ho Shen-an had suggested. Whichever it was, he felt that all was now lost.

Just then he felt a soft hand stroking the pit of his stomach and heard an even softer voice murmuring tenderly in his ear:

"There, there! You mustn't upset yourself like that. Perhaps I shouldn't have told you."

Feng Yun-ching shook his head dismally and squeezed her stroking hand. After a short pause he moaned:

"This house is disgraced! It's all come as such a shock! But I've never known Mei-ching to stay out all night. She's always in by eleven or twelve at the very latest. And during the day she's at school, so she — she — but I just don't see how she can ever have had the time to be enticed away by anybody —"

As he said the last few words, a note of incredulity crept into his voice, which his concubine was not slow to notice. A flush of anger sprang to her cheeks as she snatched her hand from his chest and spat in his face.

"Pah! You doddering old fool!" she blazed. "Keep your insinuations to yourself! Yes, I know I don't come home till morning every day. Well, what of it? If you think I've got a lover, just you try and prove it!"

He stared back at her in silence, while a smarting bitterness welled up inside him and his momentary flush of embarrassment gave way to an angry lividness. He could scarcely contain himself any longer, and was just going to give vent to his rage, when a second blow fell:

"Well, I do have other men, so there! Mr. Pai's Woo and I team up together and go out hunting. You just go and ask her if you don't believe it!"

She rounded this declaration off with a cynical laugh and slumped back on to the couch, where she busied herself with the roasting of another bead of opium. The mere mention "Mr. Pai's Woo" had struck terror into his heart. He was like a dog on a lead, and his concubine needed only to mention Mr. Pai's concubine casually to bring him to heel — in this case, to make him realize that, even though she picked up with men outside, she had Woo's backing, and that he would have to like it or lump it. There was nothing Feng Yun-ching could do about it now but smile submissively and beg her pardon.

Fortunately for him, she was in a hurry to get to her mahjong party, and seemed willing to let it go at that. He fussed around her until she had changed and driven off, without so much as a glance over her shoulder, in the car that had been ordered for her. Once she was gone, he breathed freely once more and turned to the problem of what to do about his daughter. He paced up and down, his face ashen and his lips quivering. He was not only angry with her for bringing disgrace upon his "family traditions," but was also rather irked that she had not had the sense to make better use of her physical charms. One thought kept running round in his head: Now that she's cheapened herself and surrendered her innocence in this senseless and indiscreet manner, why shouldn't I draw her into Ho Shen-an's scheme? Even though I am her father, there wouldn't really be anything wrong in it. A self-satisfied smile began to spread across his face, but gave way in a flash to a frown as a sudden misgiving assailed his ranging mind: What if his daughter should decide in favour of her lover and refuse to have anything to do with this brilliant scheme? Chao Po-tao was well into his forties and, although he had a stalwart frame, there was not the least thing attractive about him.

The sudden raucous cry of a crow on the roof just outside the window made him start up in surprise. "If she *does* refuse," he muttered through clenched teeth, "she's got no consideration at all for her father — none at all!"

He agitatedly paced round the room several times, then looked up at the electric clock: ten past six. Another day as good as gone. It was late, and he had no time to waste. He made up his mind and cleared his throat as if to reassure himself: he was going to have a talk with his daughter.

*

Feng Mei-ching was in her room writing a letter to her friend, explaining why she would have to cancel their plans for a gay time over the holiday. She could not very well say that her father would not give her the money, and she was hard put to it to find a suitable pretext. She tried at first to write in Chinese, but she found it did not read very smoothly, so she stopped in the middle, and tore it up. She changed to English, but found to her annoyance that the words she wanted now were not the ones her teacher had taught her, nor could she find them in her reader; in fact, she was stuck halfway through the first sentence. She rested her chin on her left palm and racked her brains for a while, then shifted it to her right hand, her Parker pen still between her fingers. Her cheeks were delicately flushed and her eyes clear and sparkling, though slightly tired. Finally, unable to concentrate any longer, she fell to doodling on the writing-pad. Suddenly, she heard the knob turn in the door, and her father came into the room.

She had not expected that it would be her father, and with a little "oh!" of surprise she bent her head over the desk and tried to cover up the untidy pad with her arms, at the same time giggling nervously. Silent and suspicious, Feng Yun-ching peered round the room as if looking for something, but he saw nothing unusual, just the usual litter of sheet-music, handkerchiefs, powder-puffs, scent-bottles and lip-sticks lying all over the place. Having completed his survey, he came and stood before his daughter, wondering just how he should begin.

Mei-ching had stopped giggling, and now looked up into her father's face. He seemed to sense a certain resentment in her clear gaze, and dropped his eyes, only to find himself favoured with a generous side-view of her firm, jutting breasts. He was immediately conscious of a strange sensation, as if he had only just realized that she was already a woman. At the same time he felt resentful of the blow she had delivered at his paternal authority by carrying on as she pleased behind his back. His anger rose, and he began in an unexpectedly stern voice:

"Mei-ching, you . . . you're no longer a child!"

She giggled again, and her father, finding it hard to maintain his stern manner, paused a moment, then went on in a pleasanter voice:

"You're already seventeen, Mei-ching, and there are a lot of bad men about in Shanghai. You must be very careful who you make friends with, and not let them take advantage of you —"

"Take advantage of me?" she protested, standing up. "Who's taken advantage of me now?" She had frowned a little, but at the same time some of the colour had left her cheeks. He quickly forced a smile and decided to modify what he had been going to say.

"I mean they might be imposing on your generosity," he explained, and his voice was milder still. "Just think: how much do you spend a month? About a hundred and fifty dollars, don't you? You could never spend that much on your own! I was thinking somebody might be sponging on you, eh?"

"You want me to account for my pocket money, Daddy? All right: I can tell you my expenses from memory now, if you like."

"Oh, there's no need to do that. But I would like to tell you something: I crashed completely on the Stock Exchange this time. Now, that means somebody else has made quite a lot. And do you know who it is that's made a pile this time, Mei-ching? — A man named Chao. He's got a room in a hotel, and strolls round a certain roof-garden every evening — a big, imposing sort of man in his forties. A great collector of gems and diamonds — you ought to see his fingers. . . ."

Feng Yun-ching suddenly stopped and just stood there humming and hawing, his faltering gaze wandering distractedly over her face. He had now come to the crucial point, and could not make up his mind whether to come straight out with it or whether to go at it in a roundabout way by first offering her an inducement. Suddenly a third idea struck him, adding to his mental confusion; it was nothing clear-cut, just a vague uneasiness stirring at the back of his mind. He suddenly wished the skies would fall and the earth open up and swallow him, and with him his daughter, Chao Po-tao, the Exchange — everything. As he looked at his daughter's sparkling eyes and her gently heaving breasts, he suddenly imagined a most improper scene, which in turn was followed by another highly improper scene with himself as the chief actor. And then he seemed to hear someone whispering in his ear, "Your concubine isn't your first wife, so you can let her do as she likes; but your daughter's your own flesh and blood." He shivered. His heart was pounding and he was on the verge of tears. All this passed through his mind in a flash — so quickly that he had no chance to weigh the alternatives and decide what to do.

It was at this juncture that Mei-ching gave him a dazzling smile and blurted out:

"Oh, I know who you mean, Daddy — Chao Po-tao!"

"You — well!" Feng Yun-ching gasped in astonishment. The mental turmoil instantly ceased, leaving only two impressions in his mind: amazement and delight. His immediate reaction was to fire a question at her, though his voice trembled slightly as he spoke:

"Do you know him? How did you get to know him?"

"I've a friend — a girl friend, who knows him."

"You're sure it's Chao Po-tao? Chao Po-tao the stock-king, the famous big bull, a big, imposing-looking man?"

"Yes, that's right," Mei-ching answered rather impatiently. "That's him all right!" She picked up a handkerchief and dabbed at the corner of her mouth, giggling softly. She could not understand why her father should be so agitated and surprised, though she had noticed a slight look of disappointment when she had told him that it was one of her girl friends who knew Chao Po-tao. But he had not finished with her yet:

"This friend of yours, Mei-ching — is she older than you, or younger?"

"Oh, I suppose she's about three or four years older."

"Ah, that means she's twenty-one or twenty-two. Where's she from? Is she married?"

"Er — was: her husband died last year."

"She's a widow, then. Strange! Wait a minute, what does she look like? Has she ever been here?"

"But, Daddy! Why do you want to know all this?"

"Ah, I have my reasons, Mei-ching, I have my reasons. You just tell me what I want to know, and later on I'll tell you all about it. Now, has she ever been here?"

Mei-ching did not answer at once. She sat down, smiled at her father, and began twisting her handkerchief round her finger.

Suddenly she gave a musical little laugh and said, "No, she hasn't but you must have seen her — you may even *know* her."

"Eh?"

"She often goes to the Exchange. She's a bit taller than me, and she has a little, oval face with a few faint pockmarks beside her nose — though you wouldn't notice them unless you looked. She has a slender waist, pretty lips, and a well-developed figure, and she walks like a European. Can't you think now who she is, Daddy? She's always down at the Exchange. Her name's Liu Yu-ying, and her father-in-law's Lu Kuang-shih, the stockbroker."

"Ah! Lu Kuang-shih, eh?" Feng Yun-ching cried excitedly. "Yes, that's the Lu Kuang-shih Li Chuang-fei was telling me about this afternoon!"

He nodded his head repeatedly as if he had managed to solve some knotty problem. After a moment he turned and peered closely at his daughter's face, as if comparing her features with Liu Yu-ying's. Then, taking a deep breath, he inquired anxiously:

"But this friend of yours is related to Chao Po-tao, isn't she?"

Instead of replying, Mei-ching gave a strange little laugh and, tilting her head on one side, she shook her long wavy hair, her eyes fixed on the floor. Then, with a sudden titter, she raised her head and looked at her father.

"What does it matter whether she's related to him or not?" she exclaimed. "Anyway, she's — oh, Daddy! What do you want to know all these things about her for?"

Feng Yun-ching could not help laughing, for now he understood everything. So she was not so innocent, after all. Everything was predestined, and the best thing he could do was to resign himself to the inevitable. As this general idea had quite taken possession of him, he got down to the point straight away, weighing his words carefully:

"I've got a very good reason for asking all these questions, Mei-ching. It's like this. This man Chao Po-tao seems to have the devil at his elbow — every time he speculates in government bonds, he pulls off a victory. This last time he netted well over a million dollars. We bears were all expecting a nice slump, seeing that the Central Army was getting the worst of it against the North, so you can guess how surprised everybody was when the situation suddenly changed in favour of the bulls. Your father went flat broke overnight, Mei-ching! But don't you worry. I've still got a good chance of winning back the money. The only trouble is that they're in the know and I'm still in the dark. That's where I'm sunk. There's only one thing to do, and that's to ferret out Chao Po-tao's secrets. This man Chao Po-tao may be clever, but he's got one great weakness — he's too fond of the ladies. A woman can twist him round her little finger and find out just what she wants! Now, this girl friend of yours is on good terms with him, isn't she, Mei-ching? That's a godsend: I'm saved! And now I'm entrusting you with an important mission. You're clever, you're pretty . . . oh, you know what I mean, of course."

Feng Yun-ching heaved a deep sigh of relief and grinned sheepishly at his daughter. Suddenly he was assailed by an overwhelming inner conflict: on the one hand, he was afraid his daughter would shake her head; on the other, he was afraid to see her nod in acquiescence. But Mei-ching looked quite natural and showed no signs of embarrassment as she smiled and nodded her head. She had not quite taken her father's meaning, and thought that he wanted Liu Yu-ying to ferret out Chao Po-tao's secrets for him.

When he saw her nod her head, Feng Yun-ching's heart missed a beat, but almost immediately he felt curiously peaceful. He drew a little sigh of relief — the die was cast! There was nothing for it now but to sit tight and see it through. An inevitable situation had forced him upon an inevitable course.

"What if Liu Yu-ying's not willing?" Mei-ching suddenly asked in a low voice. Her cheeks had crimsoned and her eyes were fixed on the floor as she spoke. She moved restlessly in her seat, and kept twisting her handkerchief round and round between her fingers. Feng Yun-ching was stumped for a moment. This time it was he who misunderstood his daughter. He could only assume she was not experienced enough after all, child that she was. She looked up at him with twinkling eyes, as if waiting for a clear-cut answer. He put as bold a face as he could on it:

"You silly girl! Surely you don't need me to tell you that? You'll just have to sail with the wind. As she's a friend of yours, you must know just how jealous she's likely to be. If you think it better not to try and hide it from her, then don't. On the other hand, you can go ahead on your own if you think it better to give her a wide berth —"

"Oh!" cried Mei-ching faintly, leaning back against the back of the chair. Holding her face in her hands, she began giggling uncontrollably. Feng Yun-ching quickly made his escape before she could ask any more of these questions which he as a father would find it embarrassing to answer.

Scarcely had he sat down in his room downstairs when she appeared carrying a crocodile handbag, as if she was just going out.

"Give me some money, Daddy," she said, pausing in the doorway and kicking her high-heels against the doorsill, as if anxious to be away without more ado. "I can't very well go visiting friends without a penny in my pocket."

After a moment's hesitation Feng Yun-ching handed over a hundred dollars. He felt he ought to say something more to her, but when he had seen her to the gate and watched her spring lightly into a rickshaw, he had still said nothing. He stood absently for a while at the gate, half satisfied and half sorry. As he turned to go back in, a charcoal drawing on the whitewashed wall beside the gate caught his eye. It was a hastily-scrawled tortoise, representing a time-honoured Chinese insult. Nearby, a couple of slogans, boldly daubed in thick black printer's ink: "Join in the Thirtieth of May Demonstration" and "Support the Soviet." He caught his breath and went suddenly pale, then shivered and walked dazedly back to his room, where he sank down on the couch, feeling sick at heart — how he hated those peasants and Communists! It was all their fault, with their rebellions and disturbances, that he had to come and seek refuge in Shanghai, and once in Shanghai, he had been obliged to turn a blind eye to his concubine's dissolute night life, to speculate in government bonds, and finally even to employ his own daughter's charms to get information and save himself. So far as he could see, this whole series of misfortunes was locked in a logical sequence, and it was all due to the fact that the peasants had taken to rioting and abandoned the temperate ways of their forefathers. He sighed bitterly and said to himself:

"So now it's come to this: I've given both my concubine and my daughter away to be communized! To think that I of all people should be making a contribution to the 'communal wife' system! And that it should happen here in Shanghai of all places! It doesn't make sense — it just doesn't make sense!"

IX

THE next day was the anniversary of the famous "May Thirtieth Massacre," and the Dragon-boat Festival was only two days away. While some of the citizens of Shanghai, like Feng Yun-ching for example, were bustling around trying to raise enough money to tide them over quarter-day by employing every trick from using women as decoys to blackmail, a number of other citizens were busily engaged in something of a totally different nature: organizing a demonstration to mark the anniversary. Within the past few days, the telegraph poles in the main streets and the walls of the big houses in the side-streets had been scrawled and plastered all over with slogans of every description. It had already been made public that the demonstration would be held in Nanking Road — the scene of the original incident.

The police authorities of the Chinese section, the French Concession and the International Settlement had already met to discuss how they should co-ordinate their various measures to prevent the demonstration. On the day itself, at about nine o'clock in the morning, the Settlement police set up a five-mile-long cordon from the west end of Nanking Road to the Bund and then down to the north end of North Szechuan Road. The whole route was being continually patrolled by armed police on foot and motorcycle combinations mounted with light machine-guns. At strategic points, armoured cars had been parked across the roads with their machine-guns trained on the busier street intersections.

At the west end of Nanking Road mounted police patrols galloped through the traffic and the crowds in a flurry of flying hooves and foam-flecked bits.

About this time, two young men and a girl, all in their early twenties, were strolling past the race course in Tibet Road, heading northwards towards Nanking Road. As they walked along, they looked expectantly about them and chatted among themselves. The two young men were dressed in European style. One was respectably dressed in light grey, with knife-edge creases in his carefully-pressed trousers, while the other wore a shabby, dark-blue suit with baggy, untidy trousers. The girl wore a long dress of peacock-green gauze lined with white silk. Needless to say, the sight of this incongruously attired trio walking at such a time and in such a place attracted a certain amount of attention.

When they reached the New World Restaurant, they stopped to gaze at a mounted patrol of three policemen trotting past, the barrels of the rifles slung on their backs gleaming in the morning sun. They stood watching until the patrol was out of sight, then the girl said with an air of impatience:

"Where are we going? We've drifted up and down this road three times already. I'm just . . . fed up! Hadn't we better stop and wait in one place? — Though I suppose you're going to disagree again, Pai Ching? Besides, it's nearly half past nine, and still nothing's happened. I can't see the demonstration coming off at all today with all these policemen about."

"Don't shout so, Su-su. There's a sergeant coming!"

"H'm! If you're so chicken-hearted, Chih-sheng, you shouldn't have come out with us in the first place. Are you sure you didn't get the time and place wrong, Mr. Pai?"

"No mistake about it," answered the young man in the baggy trousers. "Tsai Chen told me quite clearly that they were going to start from Muddy Bridge, go straight down Nanking Road to the Bund, then turn into North Szechuan Road, and break up at the range near the park. And it starts at ten, so there's no hurry, Miss Chang; there's half an hour to go yet."

The speaker, Pai Ching, was a fellow-student of Wu Chih-sheng's. They had been standing there more than five minutes when they noticed a couple of hefty-looking fellows — apparently plain-clothes men — coming towards them with a menacing air. Su-su was the first to notice them, and when she did so she tugged at Pai Ching's coat and started moving away. When she reached the side-entrance of the race course, she turned round to the young men following her and said:

"Did you see those two men in black gowns? They looked for all the world like twin brothers of that bodyguard of Wu Sun-fu's!"

As she spoke, she gave a little giggle of delight, for today's little adventure had come as a welcome break in the dull monotony of her life, and the appearance of the detectives had cheered her up just when she was getting tired of walking up and down without running into anything exciting. When Wu Chih-sheng had told her the day before that a fellow-student of his by the name of Pai Ching was taking him along to join in the demonstration, she had promised herself plenty of excitement and fun. She had hardly been able to sleep during the night, and early in the morning she had dashed round to the college to fetch Wu Chih-sheng and his friend. In the matter of enthusiasm, she left them far behind.

When Wu Chih-sheng and Pai Ching turned round to look, the two men in black had disappeared. A red police van drew up and stopped nearby, but it soon drove off again, its horn blaring hideously.

"That's the van they take them away in," Pai Ching told Chang Su-su, and his face took on a more serious expression. She smiled, but said nothing, for she was absorbed in watching the crowds milling round at the corner of Nanking Road and Tibet Road. She felt sure that there must be quite a lot of people among the crowd who were only waiting for the signal to begin the demonstration, and her face became flushed as she felt a wave of excitement rising inside her.

Wu Chih-sheng was also gazing all round him, puzzled that he did not see any of his fellow-students or acquaintances in the crowd. He looked up at the clock above the grandstand and saw that it was still only twenty minutes to ten. Feeling suddenly hungry, he turned to Pai Ching and was going to suggest that they go for a snack first, but he thought better of it and said instead, "I wonder what's happening at the front. Have you heard from your family lately?"

"So far as I can see, it's a case of 'when Greek meets Greek.' My home town's been bombed flat and my people have gone to Pengpu. These blasted warlords —"

The rest of what he said was lost as a No. 1 bus pulled up in front of them. Half a dozen passengers got off and a handful of people waiting at the stop got on. When the bus moved off, the three of them were left standing alone there. Just then a Sikh policeman came up to them, tapped Wu Chih-sheng on the shoulder with his truncheon and told them to "Move along there!" They moved along. Back past the New World Restaurant they went, then turned down along Tibet Road.

This time the road looked quite different. Four mounted policemen were strung out across the road, holding on to their saddles with one hand while they turned this way and that, watching for signs of trouble, as if they were prepared to dash forward at the first suggestion of a disturbance. Along the road, three mounted patrols with two riders apiece were strung out at forty-yard intervals, and were engaged in breaking up knots of bystanders along the sides of the road. A motorcycle carrying two European sergeants raced past at a frantic speed, followed by an armoured car which advanced majestically, hooting like a soul in torment all the way along the road. The crowds along Tibet Road were now denser than ever and at the corners of the five side-streets which formed right angles with Tibet Road the crowds were surging this way and that like the tailrace of a millstream. Chinese, European and Indian patrols wheeled round and round, brandishing their truncheons and revolvers in a desperate effort to keep back the crowds, which were already breaking through the cordon here and there.

Wu Chih-sheng, Pai Ching, and Chang Su-su now found it impossible to stand still at any one spot without being moved on by the police, so they decided to move farther down the road. As they were passing a leather-goods shop, a man of about thirty in European clothes dashed up and grasped Wu Chih-sheng by the shoulder.

"Hey! Chih-sheng!" he shouted. "Don't go that way! It's dangerous!"

This was Ko Chung-mou, a friend of Chiu Chun, the lawyer.

He was a newspaper reporter and also a frequent visitor to Wu Sun-fu's house.

Before Wu Chih-sheng could reply, Chang Su-su broke in, "What's happening down there? Has anyone been arrested?"

"Ah, Miss Chang! So you're here too, eh? Joining in the demonstration or just out to see the fun? If it's fun you're after, Miss Chang, I should advise you to get back home as quick as you can!"

"What do you mean?"

"I think you know what I mean. You get people coming to a demonstration like this for one of two reasons: either they're against it, or else they're ardent supporters. People who just come to watch the fun would be well advised to keep out of it. Frankly, Miss Chang, I don't think you're a whole-hearted supporter, even though you're not against it —"

"Well, what are *you* doing here, then, Mr. Ko?" Chang Su-su retorted hastily, looking slightly belligerent. She resented Ko Chung-mou's scornful tone, and his implication that she was a frail, timid creature. The reporter, however, held up his camera and waved it under her nose.

"What am I doing here?" he smiled. "I'm a journalist. Mine's a free profession, and I'm here as an independent observer!"

With a brief nod he was off across the road, swinging his camera as he went.

Chang Su-su gave a contemptuous laugh and glanced at Wu Chih-sheng and Pai Ching as much as to say: "I suppose *you* look down on me because I'm a girl, too! Well, just you wait. I'll show you what I'm made of!" Just then, a disturbance broke out among a crowd across the road, and police-whistles shrilled around them. Chang Su-su trembled all over with excitement, and, without a word to her two companions, she flew across the road towards the scene of the disturbance. But before she could get there, the crowd dispersed before a couple of policemen, who had appeared among them brandishing their truncheons. This made Chang Su-su pause, and she stood there hesitantly, craning her neck to watch. Suddenly, a firecracker went off nearby — the signal to start the demonstration. It was followed immediately by a chorus of shouting from the crowd, which, though fairly small at first, was quickly joined by demonstrators rushing up from all sides. Chang Su-su felt a tingle of excitement, and her heart began thumping wildly. She started forward mechanically, though in her agitation she did not know quite what to do. Hearing a sudden clatter of hooves bearing down on her from behind, she ran quickly to the side of the road in the general stampede. She looked round to see the patrol charging a knot of demonstrators not far away from her. They scattered, but quickly formed up again and pressed on up the road, chanting slogans at the top of their voices and scattering leaflets as they went. They were mostly students and working people. Chang Su-su, her heart pounding with excitement and her cheeks flushed, just stood and laughed. Suddenly a voice behind her bawled:

"Stop the warlords making civil war! Down with —"

Chang Su-su turned round to look and saw that it was Pai Ching. He glanced at her quickly, but did not speak, then darted out to join the ranks of the demonstrators, who were just passing by where Chang Su-su was standing. They were being harried from behind by a large detachment of police on foot, and a short distance behind these followed mounted patrols and armoured cars. Chang Su-su was swept along up the road by the crowds of spectators, only to meet another detachment of police bearing down on them from the other direction and wielding their truncheons. The crowd scattered in all directions, and in the stampede somebody caught Chang Su-su by the hand and led her out of harm's reach. It was Wu Chih-sheng. He was looking rather distraught, but managed to smile at her. When they reached the Hsin Hsin Department Store, they saw that the main body of the demonstrators had forced their way past the junction of Nanking Road and Chekiang Road and had split up into small groups. Chang Su-su heaved a sigh of relief, but her exhilaration had given way to depression. She was in no mood for laughing now, and she felt cold down to the tips of her fingers. The demonstrators, now in groups of seven or eight, were still circling around the blocks dominated by the three big department stores of Nanking Road, shouting slogans. As Chang Su-su and Wu Chih-sheng stood in the crowd milling round in

...in the stampede somebody caught Chang Su-su by the hand and led her out of harm's reach.

front of the Hsin Hsin Department Store, a red police van suddenly hurtled round the corner from Yunnan Road and stopped right in front of them. Half a dozen policemen jumped out and began rounding up the demonstrators there. Panic-stricken, Chang Su-su turned and tried to run into the store, but was stopped by a group of salesmen shouting "Keep out!" and closing the iron gates. Wu Chih-sheng had already made a dash for the other side of the road, and Chang Su-su now took the plunge and ran after him. When they reached the pavement on the opposite side of the road, she grasped his hand again, and found that both their hands were trembling and clammy.

The ground here was strewn with leaflets, and Wu Chih-sheng and Chang Su-su trampled on them in their flight. The police-whistles continued to shrill, and the noise made it impossible to hear what the demonstrators were shouting. Wu Chih-sheng and Chang Su-su both looked pale and shaken. Seeing the Ta San Yuan Restaurant just ahead of them, with its doors still open, they dived in, just as another wave of shouting rose behind them in the street. Without even a glance over her shoulder, Chang Su-su ran straight up the stairs to the first floor.

*

The restaurant was filled to overflowing, and they despaired of ever finding a seat. They had only come in to hide for a while, but once in, their appetites were sharpened by the aroma of food. They had to stand in a corner waiting for a vacant table, disappointed and frowning, until a helpful waiter suggested that they should share a table with a gentleman who had already been there half an hour, not so much eating as reading newspapers. At first, the customer was apparently unwilling to share his table, but when Chang Su-su peeped over into his cubicle he saw her, threw aside his newspaper, and stood up, shaking with laughter. It was Fan Po-wen.

Chang Su-su gave a little cry of surprise when she saw who it was, then burst out laughing with him.

"So it's you, is it?" she cried. "And on your own, too! What are you hiding in here for?"

"Let me guess," put in Wu Chih-sheng, sitting down on Fan

Po-wen's left. "You're not waiting for anybody, and you don't seem to be here for the benefit of your stomach, so you must be collecting material for your poems — in other words, to see the demonstration!"

As he spoke, he picked up the newspapers and found they consisted of a complete set of that morning's tabloids.

With an indignant glance at Wu Chih-sheng, Fan Po-wen turned to Chang Su-su:

"It's a good subject, but this time they bungled it. I've seen practically all of it from beginning to end. By the way, what do you think of my grandstand view from here? You can see everything from Muddy Bridge at one end to the Sunrise Tea-House at the other. Though as a poet I must say again that they bungled the demonstration this time, and I couldn't very well leave them out and only describe the policemen prancing around like a lot of monkeys and the armoured cars crawling along like great tortoises. No, I'm not a cringing poetaster licking the hand of authority. I think one should also paint the other side of the picture. In that immortal epic, the *Iliad,* Homer may sing the praises of the heroes on the Greek side, but he doesn't forget a word of praise for the brave Hector. The only trouble with today's performance was that the demonstrators just weren't up to scratch. To tell the truth, Su-su, it wasn't that that I came here for today, but for something else — though I was disappointed in that, as well!"

"Also connected with getting inspiration for your poetry?" asked Chang Su-su rather absently, at the same time running her little finger down the menu and indicating to the waiter what she wanted. Fan Po-wen blushed, sighed, and nodded reluctantly, but said nothing. He wanted to have his secret dragged out of him, rather than tell it voluntarily, but this was too subtle for Chang Su-su, who always abandoned an unanswered question, as the rules of social etiquette demanded. Besides, she was eager to talk about the demonstration, in which she had, in a way, taken part in person. But Wu Chih-sheng, who knew Fan Po-wen inside out, threw aside his newspaper and clapped him on the shoulder.

"Come on, out with it, poet!" he growled with mock severity. "What are you skulking in here for on your own?"

Fan Po-wen, looking ill at ease, shrugged his shoulders and gave a hollow laugh. Chang Su-su also laughed, though rather out of sympathy for the cornered poet than anything. She was just going to change the subject in an effort to save his face, when she heard a tap on the partition, followed by the sound of a woman giggling in the next cubicle. Then a voice asked:

"Is that you, Su-su?"

There was no mistaking Lin Pei-shan's voice. Fan Po-wen blushed more furiously than ever and Wu Chih-sheng roared with laughter.

Chang Su-su seemed to realize what it was all about, for she glanced quickly at Fan Po-wen, and slipped out of the cubicle. In a moment or two she came back hand in hand with Lin Pei-shan, followed by Tu Hsin-to, a stick hanging from his arm and a straw hat in his hand.

No sooner had they come in than Lin Pei-shan rested her head languidly on Chang Su-su's shoulder and, looking at Fan Po-wen out of the corner of her eye from behind Chang Su-su's loose, bobbed hair, she began teasing him.

"Po-wen, I'd like to give you a present: a packet of visiting cards printed like this: 'Fan Po-wen. Pastoral poet and detective-story writer.' How would that be?"

She giggled, and they all burst out laughing. Fan Po-wen joined in the laugh, and immediately seemed more cheerful. He bowed slightly to Lin Pei-shan, at the same time placing his right hand flat on his chest in a Buddhist monk's salute. He then shook hands with Tu Hsin-to and asked with a smile:

"And what about you, Hsin-to? What are you going to give me?"

"Me? Oh, I'll give you a copy of Shakespeare's masterpiece, *Love's Labour's Lost*," Tu Hsin-to answered calmly, with a superior smile. He had changed back into Chinese dress today, and his lean frame was draped in a long, navy-blue flannel gown, giving him the air of a worthy descendant of some famous scholar. Fan Po-wen winced at this sly dig, but he covered up his annoyance with a smile, as if he were grateful for the offer, and said:

"Well, let's hope I don't get hold of the wrong partner in our masquerade."

"Good for you! but I don't mind telling you that as a new-comer I can't yet imagine myself taking part in your masquerade!"

At this, the two of them shared a knowing laugh. By now, Lin Pei-shan and Chang Su-su were engaged in an animated conversation, while Wu Chih-sheng sat opposite them and nodded his confirmation from time to time. Chang Su-su was telling Lin Pei-shan how she had taken part in the demonstration and of the narrow escapes she had had. She had by now forgotten all about her trembling, clammy hands and her panic at the time, and when she looked back on it all, all she could remember was how the main body of the demonstrators had withstood the attempts of the mounted police patrols to disperse them, and how they had eventually broken through the police cordon and marched straight up Nanking Road. She told Lin Pei-shan how her enthusiasm had been fired so that she jeered at the charging patrols, regardless of her personal safety, as they swept down upon her. As she spoke, her face became flushed again, her eyes gleamed with excitement, and the more she went on, the more fluent and unrestrained she became. Lin Pei-shan listened wide-eyed, her hand gripping Chang Su-su's. Suddenly she interrupted, her voice shrill with excitement:

"Oh, Su-su! How awful! To think of all those Sikhs on those huge horses of theirs charging up behind you! Ugh! Chih-sheng, did you see that horse brush past Su-su's head, and almost knock her over and trample on her? Oh, my dear!"

Wu Chih-sheng nodded and laughed excitedly.

But Chang Su-su did not share his amusement. Her expression was grave now as she borrowed the tiny lace handkerchief which Lin Pei-shan was wearing for ornament in her lapel, and dabbed at her forehead with it. She was about to go on when Lin Pei-shan grasped both her hands and exclaimed:

"And your friend actually shouted a slogan, Su-su! Well! And was it then that the policemen chased you up to the Hsin

Hsin Department Store? And did they arrest your friend then?"

As she said this, Lin Pei-shan turned to Wu Chih-sheng, who, not having heard properly what it was all about, nodded mechanically. Chang Su-su did not know what had happened to Pai Ching, but when she saw Wu Chih-sheng nod in agreement with the suggestion that he had been arrested, she jumped up with a sudden cry, flung her arms round Lin Pei-shan's neck and shook her unceremoniously.

"So that's one young man sacrificed for the cause!" she exulted. "But he's only one — one that we saw with our own eyes, and one that we knew! Oh, what a man — what a hero! To have broken through a cordon of policemen and mounted patrols and armoured cars! Oh, I shall never, never be able to forget this day!"

"I saw two or three men arrested, too," Fan Po-wen told Tu Hsin-to with an inexplicable sigh, "and I'm perfectly certain that one of them was only an innocent passer-by."

The latter nodded without emotion and made no comment. Fan Po-wen glanced over his shoulder at Chang Su-su, and when he saw what a state of excitement she had worked herself up into, he could not restrain another sigh. He said loudly:

"Everything's going downhill! Even the mass movement has degenerated to an unbelievable extent! Five years ago I took part in the famous Thirtieth of May demonstration, and on that day — well, 'the world is world, and man is man!' — on that day, I tell you, masses occupied Nanking Road all day long! Now that was something like a demonstration! But today, all they did was to break through the cordon! Small beer for anyone who's been through the real thing! Frankly, I thought today's affair rather a bore."

Chang Su-su and Lin Pei-shan turned to stare at Fan Po-wen in astonishment. Coming into the world later than Fan Po-wen, they had not witnessed the actual incident themselves, and they could only gape tongue-tied at Fan Po-wen's blasé judgement, not knowing whether to believe him or not. Their astonishment only served to make Fan Po-wen feel all the more pleased with himself. He sat staring out of the window at the sky, apparently engrossed in intoxicating memories of the stirring deeds of five years ago, until a sudden splutter of cynical laughter behind him brought him back to earth. Wu Chih-sheng had been listening to him in silence, but could now contain himself no longer.

"I thoroughly agree with you when you say that everything's degenerated, Po-wen — just look at yourself, for instance! Five years ago, you took part in the demonstration, but what are you doing today? You sit up here in a restaurant looking on with a jaundiced eye like Nero fiddling while Rome burned!"

Fan Po-wen turned slowly and smiled wanly at Wu Chih-sheng with apparent unconcern, then cast a hopeful glance at Chang Su-su and Lin Pei-shan as much as to say: At least you two believe me, don't you? But they said nothing: they just smiled knowingly at each other. He was beginning to feel rather embarrassed, when Tu Hsin-to came to his rescue.

"What's so wonderful about occupying Nanking Road for a whole day, anyway? That sort of thing's always happening abroad. Townspeople are very restless and they're always making trouble —"

"You call it making trouble, do you?" Chang Su-su protested indignantly, at the same time shaking Lin Pei-shan's shoulder vigorously. Unabashed, Tu Hsin-to answered in a cool, firm voice:

"Yes, that's just what I do call it: making trouble. Just go through all the history books — Chinese and foreign, ancient and modern — and you won't find a single country making herself wealthy and strong by such methods as agitation and demonstration. They're nothing but the acts of ignorant people guided by impulses — destructive, not constructive, acts."

"Then perhaps you'll be good enough to tell us what acts *are* constructive, and not destructive," Wu Chih-sheng hastened to ask before Chang Su-su could say anything, tugging at her wrist as he spoke. Instead of replying, Tu Hsin-to smiled and began quietly whistling the *Marseillaise*. Fan Po-wen blinked in surprise, and Lin Pei-shan tittered. Chang Su-su puffed out her cheeks and turned to Wu Chih-sheng:

"There's no need to ask him that. He'll tell you the government should pursue the so-called 'iron-hand policy,' the same as his uncle Tu Hsueh-shih is always telling us!"

"That's just where you're wrong, Miss Chang," said Tu Hsin-to, the smile never leaving his lips. "My contention is that there's no ruling a country like this with *any* sort of policy."

This proposition was greeted with an immediate outcry of protest from Chang Su-su and Wu Chih-sheng. Fan Po-wen, on the other hand, reached out and patted Tu Hsin-to on the back, then gave the "thumbs up" sign, flourishing his hand under Tu Hsin-to's nose as he did so. Just at that moment the waiter came in with their order, and as Fan Po-wen's arm swung out it almost knocked the food out of his hands. This was too much for Lin Pei-shan, whose stifled amusement now gave way to shrieks of laughter as she supported herself on her chair with one hand and held her side with the other.

"Po-wen, you —" Chang Su-su began, intending to scold Fan Po-wen, but her scowl changed to a smile as she went on:

"Hsin-to, you and your uncle Hsueh-shih make a perfect pair. You're too cold and he's too hot, so that your family are the proud possessors of one of each kind: one hot and one cold!"

"Thanks for the compliment," said Tu Hsin-to. "Since it's summer at the moment, it's much better to keep cool. — Well, let's have some dumplings — that's one thing I *do* like hot!"

He gave a dry laugh, then sat down and started on the dumplings. As if transferring her exasperation to the food, Chang Su-su took a dumpling and bit viciously into it, then turned angrily to Fan Po-wen:

"And what about you? I suppose you're just lukewarm?"

"He'll make poetry out of anything," put in Wu Chih-sheng, seeing an opportunity of making fun of Fan Po-wen. "Warmth, coldness, arrests, bloodshed — all's grist to his mill!"

Actually, he was even more annoyed with Tu Hsin-to than with Fan Po-wen, but he intended this sally against Fan as an indirect attack on Tu. Anyway, he thought, they were both tarred with the same brush, and differed only in degree. He could not remember when he had come to this conclusion, but the conviction had steadily grown as their competition for Lin Pei-shan had become increasingly obvious. Having delivered his dig at Fan Po-wen, he glanced at Tu Hsin-to and then Lin Pei-shan. Tu Hsin-to, still impassive and undisturbed, chewed silently and meditatively; Lin Pei-shan, leaning against the back of Chang Su-su's chair, was absorbed in her own thoughts.

Ignoring Wu Chih-sheng's taunt, Fan Po-wen went and sat beside Chang Su-su. Suddenly he took a deep breath and muttered, "I become hot at the touch of something hot, but I don't necessarily become cold at the touch of something cold. I'm not averse to a bit of leg-pulling, but deep down inside me I'm actually quite serious. I've always wanted to do something really serious — something to shake me out of the rut. By the way, why didn't you call for me this morning? Don't tell me you'd decided I wouldn't go with you! Oh, and that friend of yours that was probably arrested — I'd like to get to know him."

Chang Su-su smiled and took another dumpling as she answered.

"You should have told me beforehand that you wanted to come along. How was I to know you'd want to? As a matter of fact —"

She paused and looked quickly round at Lin Pei-shan who was still slumped sideways against the back of her chair gazing blankly into space. Chang Su-su laughed mischievously and was going to make a further sarcastic remark, when she noticed that Lin Pei-shan was blushing furiously. This made Chang Su-su laugh all the louder. At this juncture, Tu Hsin-to picked up a chopstick and began tapping it on the table. A faint, cynical smile lingered round his lips as he burst into an ancient poem:

> *Our youth like lightning flashes by,*
>   *Like wind time passes soon;*
> *On grass yet green the frost is white;*
>   *With sunset comes the moon.*
> *Black hair fades with the fading year,*
>   *And soon turn grey it must;*
> *The noble change to storks and apes,*
>   *The mean to fleas and dust.*

Chang Su-su frowned at this and snorted. As she did so, the door of the cubicle swung open, and there appeared in the doorway a peering pair of spectacles perched on a large, prominent nose. The spectacles were as thick as the bottoms of tumblers, and the quaintly questing head belonged to Li Yu-ting. He was apparently still trying to make out how many people were there and who they were. His sudden appearance took Chang Su-su unawares, and she fidgeted uneasily. When Tu Hsin-to saw him he put down the chopstick and rose to greet him, at the same time casting a meaningful glance at Chang Su-su.

"What brings you here, Professor Li?" he asked. "Have you been here long? Perhaps you're taking lessons in detective-story writing from Fan Po-wen?"

"You're asking for it, Hsin-to!" said Fan Po-wen, shooting Tu Hsin-to a reproachful look. He noticed that Chang Su-su was looking rather ill at ease now that Li Yu-ting had appeared. Unconscious of all this, the short-sighted professor groped his way across to the table and beamed at the others.

"Ah, so there are five of you! All taking refuge in here, eh? The streets are just packed — and the police are being rather rough. And what with my bad eyesight, I had rather a job making my way through the crowds. In fact, I had a narrowish escape a moment ago —"

"Eh? D'you mean to say the demonstration is still on?" asked Wu Chih-sheng hastily through a mouthful of dumpling.

"Yes, it is, indeed. I was going along Tung Hsin Bridge Street in a rickshaw, when I ran into a procession of several hundred people, armed with bottles and stones, fighting with the police. While I was there somebody must have thrown some leaflets into my rickshaw — I was too busy telling the rickshaw boy to get a move on to notice at the time. Just as we were coming into Ta Hsin Street, we ran into another lot of policemen rounding up demonstrators. They happened to see the leaflets on me, and stopped me on the spot. I showed them my card, but they still wouldn't let me go. I appealed to a sergeant, but that wasn't any use, either. In the end they took me off to the police station — rickshaw and rickshaw boy as well. They treated me very well at the station, and after some explanation they soon let me go again. Even now, the atmosphere in Nanking Road's still very tense — big crowds everywhere, milling round and round. And all the big shops are bolted and barred —"

Li Yu-ting suddenly broke off, whereupon Fan Po-wen threw back his head and roared with laughter, pointing at Wu Chih-sheng with one hand and at Chang Su-su with the other. He was just going to regale Li Yu-ting with an account of their "adventures" in the demonstration, enlivening it with a few brilliant shafts of wit which he had just thought up, when a sudden uproar was heard in the street just under their window, and there was a rush of feet as people in the restaurant stampeded to the head of the stairs. Fan Po-wen, pale and speechless with fright, ducked his head as if he was going to dive under the table, while Chang Su-su and Wu Chih-sheng rushed to the window to see what was happening. Li Yu-ting stood there wringing his hands in agitation, and Lin Pei-shan cowered in the corner, her eyes and mouth wide with fear.

Only Tu Hsin-to seemed unperturbed; though the colour had left his cheeks, he still managed to force a smile to his lips.

"Huh! Not worth going to look — it's all over now," said Chang Su-su disappointedly as she came back from the window. When she looked round and saw the agitated expression on Lin Pei-shan's face, she could not help laughing at her. Lin Pei-shan peered apprehensively around and asked:

"What happened? Oh, Su-su! Weren't you afraid of being hit by a stray bullet?"

Chang Su-su shook her head, but it was not clear whether this meant she was not afraid of stray bullets, or whether it meant she did not know what all the noise in the street had been about. Still in need of reassurance, Lin Pei-shan glanced at Tu Hsin-to inquiringly. She had noticed just now that he seemed perfectly calm as if he had known all along that everything would be all right.

"Who cares what happened, anyway?" exclaimed Tu Hsin-to with an air of utter nonchalance and a sidelong glance at the two girls. "In any case, it couldn't be serious. I've every confidence in the ability of the foreigners to keep order! As a matter of fact, I don't see why the authorities in the Settlement should get in such a stew and take such strict precautions — they only cause a panic doing that."

Li Yu-ting shook his head as he listened to Tu Hsin-to. He was more certain than ever now that Tu Hsin-to was nothing more than a frivolous young hedonist. Unable to restrain himself any longer, he took a step forward and rasped, "Don't be too optimistic! At this moment Shanghai's heading for a crisis, too. Just look at the way rice has gone up to twenty dollars a picul and the way prices in general are shooting up. Since March there's been one strike after another — the trams, the buses, the cotton mills. They say the Communists are planning a general strike for some time in May —"

"Well, have they done it? Today is May the thirtieth, isn't it?"

"Yes, I suppose May is practically over — but that doesn't mean to say that the danger of a crisis has passed! Along the Lunghai and Peking-Hankow lines, the war is getting bloodier and bloodier, and the combined forces of Chang Fa-kuei and Pai Chung-hsi are marching on Hunan Province; the whole country will soon be drawn into the maelstrom of civil war. Everywhere the peasants are rioting, and there's no telling how many groups of bandits are taking advantage of the situation to give themselves out as Communists and hoist the red flag. Only a few days ago something happened in your part of the country: out of one battalion of the local garrison two companies mutinied and went over to the Communists. The Communists will expand their activities every day that the civil war drags on. June and July will be worse still, so the worst is yet to come —"

"But Shanghai —"

"Even in Shanghai the situation is getting worse day by day. Only these last few days they discovered that Communists had infiltrated into units stationed around Shanghai, and they even found Communist leaflets and groups in the city garrison itself. They say that quite a large proportion of the troops are unreliable now. Even the workers at the arsenal have got a secret organization. And this morning, despite all the precautions of the Settlement police, the workers and students held the demonstration just the same and even broke through the police cordon. How can you blame the Settlement authorities for 'getting in a stew' about it?"

Li Yu-ting's voice gradually dropped lower and lower as he spoke, but his words were like thunder in the ears of his listeners. Tu Hsin-to's frown deepened, but he said nothing. Chang Su-su's face was flushed and her eyes alight with excitement. Wu Chih-sheng tugged at Fan Po-wen's jacket and said half in jest and half in earnest:

"Just wait, Po-wen! It won't be long now before you have something to write about!"

Fan Po-wen nodded quite seriously, then turned to Li Yu-ting; he was just going to say something, when Lin Pei-shan cut him short, "Anyway, Shanghai should be safe enough. We can always pop across into the International Settlement or the French Concession!"

Before Li Yu-ting had time to reply, Tu Hsin-to put in, "Oh, yes, Shanghai is safe for one or two days at least yet, perhaps for another week, another month, or two months, even. Apart from Shanghai, a few other large ports like Tientsin, Hankow, Canton, Macao and so on are also safe for a few months yet. And after that we have Japan, France and America that are even safer. Yes, there are still plenty of places in the world safe for our leisure and pleasure. Why should we worry about it?"

Relieved by his assurances, Lin Pei-shan giggled. She was a gay, lively girl, and did not see why she should allow the prospect of unknown dangers looming ahead stop her from enjoying herself while she could. Yet the others apparently felt quite differently about it: Li Yu-ting gazed in amazement at Tu Hsin-to for a while, then looked at Wu Chih-sheng, then at Fan Po-wen. He seemed to be looking for someone to join him in a serious conversation. At length, he went on with a sigh:

"If the war goes on and on like this, and if the politicians, the businessmen and the students here at home all split up into quarrelling groups and factions, like the people fighting at the front, I can see the total collapse of the nation just round the corner. When the Tsarists were removed from power, they could flee the country and live abroad, but when our turn comes, we shan't be so lucky, I fear, because by that time revolutions will be breaking out all over the world, and the propertied classes in every country —"

He broke off and bent his head in thought, heart-broken because the government, the party leaders, and the heads of society could not sink their differences and stop squabbling among themselves. This thing he had on hand now, for instance: Wu

Sun-fu had entrusted him with the job of going along and negotiating with Chao Po-tao on his behalf — patching up a quarrel between them, actually. Ever since he had run into the demonstration in Tung Hsin Bridge Street, he had been turning a proverb over in his mind: "A powerful enemy is not so much to be feared as dissension in one's own camp." What grieved him now was to see the enemy's inroads widening and deepening the split in his own camp.

He was startled abruptly out of his gloomy musings by a laugh. It was Tu Hsin-to, leaning against the doorpost, a cynical smile on his lips. When Li Yu-ting looked round, he began reciting a poem quietly as if to himself:

> *Make merry, and take no heed for the morrow:*
> *With women and wine forget your sorrow;*
> *Drown your cares in sparkling wine,*
> *And in soft arms yourself entwine.*

Then he suddenly raised his voice: "I say, everybody, why do we have to bury ourselves in this god-forsaken hole on such a glorious day? I know of a wonderful new pleasure-garden run by a White Russian émigré — Rio Rita's. They've got good wine and good music, and there are White Russian princesses, princes' daughters, imperial concubines and ladies-in-waiting to dance attendance on you. Green, shady trees and lawns as smooth as velvet. And then there's a little lake for boating . . . ah, it reminds me of the happy hours I spent on the banks of the Seine . . . lily-white bosoms and thighs . . . and the burning passions of the French girls!"

As he said this, he turned and took his hat and stick from a hook on the partition. He seemed surprised that his suggestion brought no response from the others. Nevertheless he smiled calmly as he went across to Lin Pei-shan, held out his hand to her, and said with a slight bow:

"Miss Lin, if you were going home, perhaps Miss Chang would go with you for company —"

With a puzzled smile, Lin Pei-shan darted a glance at Chang Su-su and the others, then, as if she had made up her mind, she nodded and departed arm in arm with Tu Hsin-to.

At this Wu Chih-sheng gave Fan Po-wen a meaningful look, but the poet passed it off with a careless laugh and proceeded to take it out on Li Yu-ting:

"You may be a professor, Yu-ting, but you do talk a lot of rot! All your preaching and theorizing runs off Tu Hsin-to like water off a duck's back — it just makes him all the more determined to enjoy himself while he can. 'Tonight we have wine, so tonight we get drunk!' He doesn't give two hoots for all your weeping and wailing and gnashing of teeth!"

"Oh, give it a rest!" exclaimed Chang Su-su. "Let's go up to North Szechuan Road. Chih-sheng, didn't Pai Ching say the procession would break up somewhere around there?"

So saying, she threw a note on the table and turned to go, followed by Wu Chih-sheng. Fan Po-wen hesitated a second, then shouted "Just a minute," and, with a fleeting smile at Li Yu-ting, ran down the stairs after them.

Left alone in the cubicle, Li Yu-ting leaned out of the window and strained his eyes to see what was happening in the street. The crowds had begun to melt away and he could see the three of them walking abreast with Chang Su-su in the middle, chatting and gesticulating gaily. A doubt assailed his mind as he watched them out of sight: What were they going to North Szechuan Road for? Although he had not quite caught Chang Su-su's last few words, he had a shrewd idea of her intentions from her expression; in any case, he was well enough acquainted with her temperament and ideas to be able to guess. And isn't this just another indication of the inevitable disintegration of the present time? With this pessimistic thought, and a growing sense of despondency, he shook his head, and, with one last look down into the street, he made his way out of the restaurant.

*

Once out in the street, he walked westward. Arriving at the Hua An Building, he glanced at his wrist watch: half past ten. He went in and took the lift to the fourth floor. In the corridor he scribbled a few words on his card and gave it to a page. After a considerable wait, the white-liveried page returned and showed him to a luxurious suite — two rooms and a bathroom — looking out over the race course. The bathroom door stood ajar, and the other two rooms were filled with scent-laden steam. Since his glasses had immediately misted over, Li Yu-ting saw everything through a white haze. Suddenly, he seemed to see the blurred outline of a white figure flash past him and disappear into the bedroom, leaving behind a trail of heady perfume and the echo of a woman's silvery laughter. Li Yu-ting quickly wiped his glasses with his finger and peered round again. He saw Chao Po-tao curled up on his side on a sofa, wearing a cream-coloured flannel bathrobe, his hairy legs propped up on one arm of the sofa. He was, of course, resting after a bath.

Chao Po-tao did not get up; he just nodded casually, vaguely waved a hand at Li Yu-ting, and then turned his head and called towards the bedroom:

"Yu-ying! Come on out! Come and meet Mr. Li here. He's near-sighted, and I don't think he saw you when you went past him just now. No, you needn't dress up: come out just as you are."

Li Yu-ting gaped in wonder, wondering what the purpose of this move was. Almost immediately, the woman appeared in a haze of perfume, giggling and swaying her hips. A large, snowy bath-towel was draped round her like a monk's robe, and as she tripped across the room with her shoulders thrown back, her unusually prominent breasts could be seen bobbing up and down beneath the towel. Her face was small and oval, and her vivid lips were curved in a persistent smile. Glancing sharply at Li Yu-ting with a faint grin, Chao Po-tao reached out and pinched the woman's plump seat.

"Ouch!" she yelped coquettishly. Chao Po-tao laughed boisterously and touched her thigh so that she spun round to avoid him. He made her twirl round once again, then shoved her roughly away and grunted:

"That's enough! Now go back and get dressed — and shut the door behind you!"

It was as if he had displayed his treasure for a moment and then quickly locked it away in its casket again. When she had gone, he turned to Li Yu-ting:

"Why! What's the matter with you, Yu-ting? You're blushing! Look at yourself in the mirror! Ha! Ha! You're a proper greenhorn, aren't you! They say I'm fond of the women: yes, I certainly am, and I make no secret of it. If I do anything, I do it straight out. I don't like having people guessing about me as if I were not an ordinary human being but a fiend. — You yourself, for instance: the moment you came in just now, you saw I had a woman here, but because of your bad eyesight you couldn't quite see her properly. That set you guessing — I could see it. But now you've had a good look at her, and you may even have recognized her. Not bad, eh? She has the figure and skin of a European!"

With this, Chao Po-tao suddenly swung his feet to the floor and stood up. He took a cigar from the case on the table and stuck it between his teeth, then slid the cigar-case towards Li Yu-ting with a gesture of invitation to help himself. He settled himself on the sofa again, propped up his legs, slowly struck a match, and began lighting his cigar. He looked as if he had not a care in the world and was now settling down for a good loaf. Instead of taking a cigar, Li Yu-ting ran his fingers lightly and absently along the edge of the cigar-case: he was wrestling with the problem of how to carry out the task entrusted to him by Wu Sun-fu without bungling and at the same time without offending Chao Po-tao. He was waiting for Chao Po-tao to broach the subject first, for he wanted to avoid giving the impression that he had been specially sent as a negotiator, and he did not want to appear to be one of the "Wu clique." But Chao Po-tao smoked on without a word and hardly glanced at Li Yu-ting. After five minutes like this, Li Yu-ting could hold out no longer, and decided to put out a feeler.

"Did you see Sun-fu yesterday, Mr. Chao?"

Chao Po-tao shook his head and took the cigar out of his mouth as if he was going to speak at last. But, after flicking off the ash, he put it back into his mouth.

"Sun-fu's home town's been plundered by the bandits," Li Yu-ting went on, "and he's lost quite a bit there, so of course he's not in a very good mood — in fact, he gets quite short-tempered sometimes. For example, there are a couple of things he can't agree with you about: the Exchange settlement and the loan to Chu Yin-chiu. As a matter of fact. . . ."

Li Yu-ting held on to the "fact" while he watched Chao Po-tao's expression closely. He had intended to say "As a matter of fact, this is a mere trifle" but thought better of it. He decided to change it to "As a matter of fact, we can easily find a solution," but before he could get the words out of his mouth, Chao Po-tao broke in.

"Oh, it's that that's upsetting him, is it? Ah, well, we can easily find a way round that. But tell me, Yu-ting, have you come here to talk terms with me on behalf of Wu Sun-fu, or just to pump me?"

This sudden blow, straight from the shoulder, caught Li Yu-ting off his guard. True, he had Wu Sun-fu's terms with him and also the intention of sounding Chao Po-tao; but now that Chao Po-tao had called his bluff, he was in a quandary how to proceed. Not wishing to be caught between two fires, he decided it would be in his best interests to tread warily and try to please both of them. He accordingly smiled and hastened to assure Chao Po-tao.

"Oh, no! Far from it! You and Wu Sun-fu are old friends; if you had anything to discuss you could do it yourselves without going through me —"

"Of course!" interrupted Chao Po-tao, fixing Li Yu-ting with a sharp look. "From which we may assume that you're here to pump me! All right, then, I'll be quite frank with you. I like to do things the straightforward way!"

"I quite agree, Mr. Chao; the straightforward way's always the best," replied Li Yu-ting. Cornered as he was, there was not much else he could say. Much as he resented Chao Po-tao's merciless directness, he realized it would be the height of folly for him to attempt any sort of double-dealing with a man like this. He would have to change his tactics. But Chao Po-tao, as if he had read Li Yu-ting's thoughts, threw back his head and laughed. He stood up and clapped Li Yu-ting on the shoulder.

"You and I are old friends, too, Yu-ting, so there's no need for us to beat about the bush. I don't believe in having secrets, myself. In the matter of women, for instance: if Wu Sun-fu had a mistress, can you see *him* parading her in public? — Like to have another look at her, Yu-ting? See what she's like when she's dressed up? Damn it all, she's a widow you know! I don't usually go in for second-hand stuff, as you know, but this one's an exception: she's not like all the rest — she's a real houri!"

"Ah, but then you're a well-known collector and connoisseur," said Li Yu-ting, feeling that he had to say something, "so of course you have to have a specimen of every species!"

He was getting rather worried for he feared Chao Po-tao was deliberately digressing, but his anxiety was unnecessary, for Chao Po-tao chuckled his acknowledgement, then returned to the sofa and began of his own accord to explain his attitude towards his disagreement with Wu Sun-fu.

"We can skip all the developments to date, as you're well enough acquainted with them. Well, to put it in a nutshell, Wu Sun-fu needn't worry about the Exchange settlement — I'm willing to accept Tu Chu-chai's original proposals and let it go at that. But in the matter of the loan to Chu Yin-chiu, I've already given him my promise, so I can't go back on it — unless, of course, Chu Yin-chiu should want to call it off himself."

As Chao Po-tao spoke, Li Yu-ting scanned his face carefully and weighed his every word. He was beginning to fear that he was running his mission on the rocks, for the one thing Chao Po-tao was insisting on was the very thing Wu Sun-fu was not prepared to give way on. Wu Sun-fu was determined to compensate himself for his losses in his home town not only by swallowing Chu Yin-chiu's factory but also by acquiring the latter's large stock of cocoons at the cheapest possible price, then rush them through his filatures to fill his orders in time. If he succeeded in pulling off this scheme quickly, he could make something out of it even while the price of silk was dropping. Li Yu-ting knew all this only too well, but Chao Po-tao's shrewd eyes told him that he had seen through the scheme as well, and now intended to nip Wu Sun-fu where it hurt most. He would rather lose twenty or thirty thousand dollars to Wu Sun-fu over the government bonds transaction than let him get his hands on Chu Yin-chiu's factory and cocoons. After a moment's hesitation, Li Yu-ting sighed lightly and said:

"But it's just this question of the loan to Chu Yin-chiu that

Wu Sun-fu's so concerned about. If you'd like my own opinion as an independent observer —"

"Ah, I know why he's so interested in the loan," interrupted Chao Po-tao, slapping his thigh and laughing triumphantly. "It's because there are some clauses about Chu Yin-chiu's cocoons in the agreement!"

Shaken by this unexpected thrust, Li Yu-ting broke out into a cold sweat. He was anxious for Wu Sun-fu and miserable at his own failure. Nevertheless, his anxiety made him abandon his humming and hawing. He smiled wryly and said in a different tone of voice, "You're a sharp one, and no mistake! What stumps me, though, is what use the cocoons are to you. After all, you and Sun-fu are old friends, so why do you have to tease him like this? If he doesn't get Chu Yin-chiu's cocoons, he'll be in a bit of a jam —"

Li Yu-ting broke off helplessly here, for Chao Po-tao suddenly gave a derisive laugh; he tilted back his head and blew a cloud of cigar smoke, his flabby face wrinkling with amusement. Li Yu-ting's scalp prickled at Chao Po-tao's steely voice when he next spoke, "You don't understand? Come now, you're joking! — Now, I like to keep everything I do above-board, and if a man's perfectly frank with me, then I'll be perfectly frank with him. Now, Yu-ting, since you're here as Wu Sun-fu's deputy, I may as well put forward a proposal for him to consider: I recommend Shang Chung-li as manager of Wu Sun-fu's Yi Chung Trust Company."

"Oh, but — er — well, I've heard that they've already decided to have Mr. Tang for manager."

"Yes, so I hear — but I also hear that he belongs to the Wang Ching-wei clique."

At this reply Li Yu-ting's heart missed a beat; he saw it all now: the tussle between Chao Po-tao and Wu Sun-fu was not of a purely commercial nature. The realization of this fact made him despair of ever effecting a rapprochement between the two sides. Staring at Chao Po-tao with eyes wide with anxiety, he asked imploringly, "Haven't you any other ideas, Mr. Chao? What about — what about having Tu Chu-chai for manager? He's above politics, you see."

Chao Po-tao smiled. "So's Shang Chung-li!" came his swift reply.

Li Yu-ting smiled uncomfortably, realizing suddenly that he had gone a little too far for an allegedly neutral observer, and decided to put on the brake. He glanced at Chao Po-tao, and was about to declare that his position was that of loyal friend to both sides, when the former stretched and said in a more casual voice:

"So far as Wu Sun-fu's ability and initiative are concerned, I take my hat off to him; but I must say that he's too confident of his own capabilities, and that, I'm afraid, is where he'll come unstuck. That idea of his about forming the Yi Chung Company was quite a good one, but he didn't talk it over with me first, whereas if I've got a good plan up my sleeve I always give him a chance of coming in on it — like our recent venture on the Exchange, for instance. And if I now suggest Shang Chung-li as manager of his company, it's just because I'd like to co-operate with him. Now, I'm a plain-spoken man, Yu-ting, and I don't mind telling you if Wu Sun-fu's going to be so obstinate and refuses to come to his senses, that's quite all right with me. I only hope he'll be able to weather all the storms he's going to run into. If he can make a go of it, I'll be the first to congratulate him!"

Chao Po-tao rounded off his ultimatum with a hearty laugh as he swung himself to his feet. He flexed his arms and stretched, then went across to open the bedroom door. Realizing that he was going to let out his precious nymph once more, Li Yu-ting hurriedly stood up and made a last appeal:

"Mr. Chao —"

Chao Po-tao turned and looked impatiently at Li Yu-ting, who started forward and invited with an ingratiating smile:

"Come and have dinner with me tonight. Sun-fu and Chu-chai'll be there, so if you'd care to come along, you can talk it over with Sun-fu himself."

Chao Po-tao let his gaze wander thoughtfully over Li Yu-ting's face for a moment, then replied with a ghost of a smile:

"But if Sun-fu refuses to see sense, I'm afraid your hospitality would be wasted."

"Not at all: I'm sure there's every possibility that he'll soon realize that it's better to play a part in a big show than try to run a one-man show."

Li Yu-ting spoke with great assurance, though in his heart of hearts he feared the result would be exactly the opposite: the odds were that Wu Sun-fu would refuse to give way to Chao Po-tao.

Chao Po-tao's reaction was a guffaw of amusement. He clapped Li Yu-ting heavily on the shoulder, muttered something in Cantonese, then roared in common Chinese, "What? Did you say he will *soon* realize it? Oh no, Yu-ting, don't think you can fool me — Chao Po-tao! Unless, of course, by 'soon' you mean a good six months. I happen to know a thing or two about Sun-fu's tactics. I say six months because I know that if he's set on promoting this company of his it'll give him a clear six months' grace. For the first three months he'll have a fairly free hand, but after that he'll begin to feel the strain — he'll find that lack of money is cramping his style. And then, if his bankers draw in the rope a little, he'll really start feeling the pinch! Just now, he's sitting pretty, so he expects the other fellow to come round to his point of view. As for him coming round to the other fellow's — well, another three months and we'll see! Perhaps sooner!"

"Ah, but you're taking a long-term view of things, Mr. Chao, whereas I'm looking at the more immediate problems. Say, for instance, this problem of getting Chu Yin-chiu's cocoons as a pledge can't be resolved the way Wu Sun-fu wants it, then he's going to be in a fix: if he hasn't got the cocoons, he can't keep his factory running; and if he has to close down —"

Chao Po-tao shrugged and smiled grimly, but Li Yu-ting went on doggedly:

"Then there'll be more unemployed. Mr. Chao, you know as well as I do that since January labour troubles in Shanghai have been getting worse and worse, so that they're a serious menace to public order and safety. In the interest of all concerned, Sun-fu should, of course, make some concessions. But it would make things a lot easier if you, for your part, would be good enough to forget about Chu Yin-chiu's cocoons just this once."

Having delivered himself of this final appeal, Li Yu-ting felt easier in his mind. He had done his level best as a mediator, and had taken care not to pour oil on the flames. He looked closely at Chao Po-tao's triangular face, hoping to find there some sign of assent, but found none. Chao Po-tao shook his head contemptuously and returned to the sofa. He propped his legs, and said briefly and without a trace of emotion:

"You're overdoing it."

This was worse than a slap in the face for Li Yu-ting, and he flushed hotly. He felt hurt that Chao Po-tao should reject his good offices so scornfully, and he sat in morose silence for a while. Nevertheless he decided to brave the storm once more. He squared his shoulders and was just going to put everything he knew and all the skill at his command into one last effort at persuading Chao Po-tao, when suddenly the bedroom door opened an inch or so, and through the crack a pair of little red lips chirped:

"Did you want me? I thought you called."

The lips were replaced by a gleaming black eye. Chao Po-tao smiled and beckoned. The door swung open and in floated the woman as daintily as lotus-blossom on the water. She smiled first at Chao Po-tao, her head on one side, then turned her head and nodded to Li Yu-ting. Chao Po-tao stretched out his hand to give her snow-white arm a playful pinch, then burst out:

"Yu-ying, Mr. Li here says the Communists are coming to Shanghai soon! Are you afraid?"

"What, those little demons who're always chalking up slogans everywhere? Oh, I saw one the other night as I was going along Chang Pang Road in a rickshaw. When he saw someone coming, he scuttled away, just like a rat."

"But when you're off your guard," Li Yu-ting put in quickly, "a Communist can change himself from a rat into a tiger. You'll find some of these tigers in Hunan, Hupeh, Kiangsi, and also in Kiangsu and Chekiang!"

He said this hoping that he would be able to steer the conversation back to Wu Sun-fu, but, to his disappointment, the woman's lips parted in a smile and she twittered ostentatiously:

"Dear, dear! Tigers, are they? You're kidding! — Well, if they are tigers, there are always tiger-killers like Wu Sung!"

Chao Po-tao glanced at Li Yu-ting and wound up grimly, "Well, Yu-ting, you'd better go back and tell Sun-fu what I think about it. I hope he'll think it over carefully and let me know what he intends to do. If there are tigers running amok, I'll take precautions, but that's no reason why I should give in to Wu Sun-fu completely. Are you free tomorrow evening? Come to the Great China and we'll have dinner together and watch the dancing."

As he spoke, he stood up and they shook hands, then he saw Li Yu-ting out into the corridor with a great show of politeness.

Out in the street once more, Li Yu-ting straightened up and heaved a sigh of relief, then started back the way he had come. He began turning over in his mind what Chao Po-tao had said, then suddenly remembered he still had to go to the police station to bail out the rickshaw boy and his rickshaw. In the Nanking Road area the police were still taking strict precautions, and the pavements were still littered with leaflets. A car sped past, making a wind which sent the leaflets whirling in all directions. One of them blew against Li Yu-ting's chest; he grabbed at it and ran his eye over it. The few sentences that he read appalled him:

> . . . Under the direction of the imperialists, a concerted attack is being launched by the warlords, bureaucrats, landlords and compradore-capitalists upon the Chinese revolutionary forces in an attempt to put an end to the revolution once and for all. But the imperialists and the Chinese ruling classes are divided among themselves and the divisions are daily widening. The present mêlée between the Southern and Northern warlords is an indication that their disagreements are coming to a head. At such a time as this, revolutionary Chinese people must intensify —

Li Yu-ting quickly threw the piece of paper away and fled in a panic as if he had the devil at his heels. A veil of darkness seemed to fall before his eyes, and a macabre scene took shape: Wu Sun-fu was strangling Chu Yin-chiu while Chao Po-tao was clutching at Wu Sun-fu's hair from behind. The three of them were struggling frantically together, heedless of the man who stood beside them, sword in hand, waiting to strike them down.

"We're doomed, doomed!" his tortured mind cried. His very bones seemed to turn to water, and his heart was a dead weight within him.

X

AT length, the Dragon-boat Festival came and went in an atmosphere of unrest. Merchants found they had to break the old rule and leave the settlement of their first quarter's accounts until the end of the next quarter — the Mid-Autumn Festival. The war was changing the normal pattern of their life.

"Eat your moon-cakes in Peking!" So said the government's military authorities, meaning that they expected to bring the war to an end by the Mid-Autumn Festival at the very latest.

Nevertheless, at the present moment, there were still no signs of the war being brought to an end. Along the Lunghai line the situation was fluid and both sides were said to be in more or less the same positions as at the outbreak of the war, while around Hankow, up the Yangtse, events were moving more rapidly day by day. It came as a surprise when the combined forces of Chang Fa-kuei and Pai Chung-hsi suddenly captured Changsha! That was on June the 4th, two days after the Dragon-boat Festival. The news threw the Shanghai stock market into an immediate turmoil of excitement. All sorts of rumours were rife, and the speculators attached to the Shanghai Stock and Bond Exchange swallowed these rumours eagerly, while at the same time they themselves manufactured and circulated new rumours.

Then came a bombshell: Yochow, a city not far from Hankow, had been taken by the Red Army commanded by Peng Teh-huai.

Li Yu-ting had been to a Japanese friend to confirm the news and had come home in an ague of anxiety. For a while he was so stunned that he could only keep polishing his tumbler-bottom spectacles with a handkerchief over and over again; then he decided to go and see Wu Sun-fu and offer him some more advice. Ever since his visit to Chao Po-tao on the day of the demonstration he had been very careful not to involve himself in their controversy, but he was always ready to play the peacemaker should a suitable opportunity present itself. He had already made a private attempt to persuade Tu Chu-chai to exert some pressure on his brother-in-law Wu Sun-fu "in the public interest," so that there would be at least some possibility of a rapprochement between the latter and Chao Po-tao. He had told Tu Chu-chai that Wu Sun-fu's obstinacy and over-confidence would be his downfall.

So Li Yu-ting hurried off to Wu Sun-fu's house and arrived to find he had visitors — in the drawing-room were several people hovering about, seemingly waiting with bated breath to see whether Wu Sun-fu would smile or frown. They were strangers to Li Yu-ting, though he seemed to remember seeing one of them before — a man of about fifty with a little wisp of a beard.

Wu Sun-fu was standing with his back to them, an unusually tense expression on his face. As he caught sight of Li Yu-ting coming in, he waved a hand in greeting and called out, "I'm sorry, Yu-ting, but I wonder if you'd mind waiting a moment in the small drawing-room?"

He found someone ahead of him in the small drawing-room — Chiu Chun, the lawyer. He was sitting there with a large portfolio open on his lap, fiddling with the corner of a sheaf of documents with one hand and stroking his chin with the other. He seemed deep in thought, so Li Yu-ting sat down quietly without disturbing him and began wondering what was afoot: what with the strangers in the other room, he thought, and a legal adviser in here, Sun-fu must have something important on his hands. . . .

In the large drawing-room Wu Sun-fu was pacing up and down like a caged lion, glancing fiercely every now and then at the man with the straggly beard and then at the other three men standing there in awed silence. He suddenly stopped with a snort and asked the bearded one in an incredulous voice, "Hsiao-sheng, did you say the provincial government advised us to keep the Hung Chang Pawnshop open for business?"

"Yes, I did," replied Fei Little Beard, his eyes fixed on the floor. "And they said that the local bank, the oil mill, the power-house and the rice-mill must also carry on. The man from the county council said that the prosperity of the town depended on your shops and factories and that it would be a terrible blow to the town if you decided to close them down altogether."

He himself secretly hoped that the shops and so on would remain open, but this hope was not motivated by any concern for the welfare of the town, but rather for the welfare of Fei Little Beard. Although he was quite sure of being offered another job in the event of Wu Sun-fu's closing down all his shops in the town — a job in the Shanghai factory, say — he much preferred to remain as Wu Sun-fu's agent in the town, a position which afforded him a comfortable living and a certain amount of prestige. Besides, he had boasted confidently to the county official that he could easily persuade Wu Sun-fu to change his mind.

"Huh!" Wu Sun-fu snorted, and grimaced. "It's all very well for them to talk about the prosperity of the town, but what protection can they give us?"

Despite his cynical tone, he was inwardly rather pleased to hear that the people at home looked up to him as the leader of the business circles in the town. Shrewdly guessing what was going on in his mind, Fei Little Beard pursued:

"Just now, everything's quiet in the town — very quiet indeed. The new garrison that's recently taken over is in a different class altogether to Colonel Ho's lot that we had before."

"I wouldn't be too sure about that!" one of the three men suddenly interrupted. "You don't need to go half a mile outside the town to find yourself in Communist territory. They hold all the villages round about, and they send their patrols right in as far as West End Market. Oh yes, it's quiet enough in the town itself, but the town's surrounded! The most our one battalion can manage is to keep the road to the county town open. And I've heard that when they're sent out on patrol they very often desert and take their guns with them. The Communists have got twice as many men and weapons as they had before!"

The speaker was Wu Wei-cheng, a man in his thirties and a

distant nephew of Wu Sun-fu's who had come in from their home town with Fei Little Beard.

"And they say they've set up some of these Soviets in the villages!" added a youngster of about twenty who was standing next to Wu Wei-cheng. He was Ma Ching-shan, a brother-in-law of Tseng Chia-chu — who had already been staying with Wu Sun-fu for two weeks — and he had also just arrived with Fei Little Beard. Standing shoulder-to-shoulder with him was Tseng Chia-chu, gaping wide-eyed.

Wu Sun-fu scowled as he glanced at Wu Wei-cheng and nodded curtly. At this brief nod Fei Little Beard's heart missed a beat, for it hurt him more than a good dressing down would have done. He hastily tried to explain it all away. "Yes, yes, that's as may be, but the provincial government's sending troops down to surround the Communists and finish them off, so there won't be any more trouble in the town."

Wu Wei-cheng gave a cynical laugh and was just going to contradict Fei Little Beard again, when they heard the blare of a motorcar horn outside the main gate. Wu Sun-fu dismissed them with an impatient wave of the hand and strode out on to the front steps to meet the visitor. The slanting rays of the setting sun threw the shadows of trees on the stone steps, and as the trees swayed in the breeze, a pattern of light and shade danced over the five steps. Wu Sun-fu glanced down at the shadows, then stamped on them in his vexation.

The car drew up in front of the house and Kao Sheng, the butler, dashed across to open the car door. Tu Chu-chai hurriedly squeezed out, and when he looked up and saw Wu Sun-fu standing on the steps, he made a grimace and shook his head. Wu Sun-fu's face darkened when he saw that his visitor was the bearer of ill tidings, but he managed to force a smile of greeting.

"It's fantastic!" gasped Tu Chu-chai as he came up the steps, mopping his face with a snowy cambric handkerchief. "Terrific rise — trading nearly closed!"

Wu Sun-fu said nothing, but just knit his brows in a puzzled frown. With no more than a glance at Tu Chu-chai, he turned and went back into the drawing-room. The scowl immediately returned to his face as he said to Fei Little Beard:

"Now look here! I couldn't care less whether everything's peaceful in the town or not. I opened my shops in the first place, and if I choose to close them down, then closed down they will be! I'm not a charitable institution, and it's no concern of mine whether trade's slack in the town or not. I don't care who asks me, county council or provincial government or whoever they are, that's my answer, and it's final!"

"Yes, of course, Mr. Wu. That's just what I told them, but they —"

But Wu Sun-fu's patience was exhausted. His lips twisted in a sneer as he cut Fei Little Beard short. "Yes, I know all about their bluff and nonsense! You still haven't told me how much you've collected on the loans that fell due at the Dragon-boat Festival. You told me last time you could count on sixty per cent, though I expected more than that, of course. Well, how much did you collect after all? I suppose you've brought the money with you?"

"Er — no, I haven't. You see, the people in the town are leaving last quarter's accounts over to next quarter-day, the same as here."

"What!" roared Wu Sun-fu angrily. This setback was the last thing he had expected. Although it was only a matter of seventy or eighty thousand dollars, he was very short of ready cash just at the moment, and even seventy or eighty thousand would have come in very handy. He set his face in a scowl and paced up and down, then paused to look at Tu Chu-chai, who was sitting on a sofa taking snuff. The sight of Tu Chu-chai reminded him painfully of the sudden steep rise in government bonds.

His nostrils full of snuff, his eyes closed and his mouth wide open, Tu Chu-chai was waiting for a sneeze to come.

"If you do close down all your shops, including the local bank," murmured Fei Little Beard, coming closer, "it'll mean that we won't be able to get back the loans even at the Mid-Autumn Festival."

Wu Sun-fu shrugged his shoulders; after a moment's pause he laughed and spat out, "Hah! The Mid-Autumn Festival, eh? Well, perhaps by that time I shan't need to call in my money from that quarter!"

"Is it just that you're afraid the town's still in danger, then, Mr. Wu?" said Fei Little Beard, seeing an opportunity of delivering a little speech he had prepared. His eyes shifted uncomfortably from side to side as he went on.

"Well, of course, Wei-cheng was exaggerating a bit just now. And the provincial government really is sending down a strong detachment of troops to surround the Communists and finish them off. As I said before, both the provincial and county authorities are hoping that you will agree to play your part in maintaining the prosperity of the town. After all, it is your home town. And besides, if you close down your businesses you'll never be able to collect your loans. Under the circumstances, I think you'd best give in to them just for the time being. If you'll just wait till the Mid-Autumn Festival you'll see that everything will turn out all right in the end. Of course, the pawnshop is another matter altogether, since it was gutted in the fire."

Wu Sun-fu smiled non-committally, then turned and sat down on a chair. He now had the whole picture: the bandit trouble had not only lost him fifty or sixty thousand dollars outright, but it had also pinned down his loans for twice that amount, and he had no way of touching the money. He began to feel that it was impossible to make everything under the sun go just the way one wished. On the other hand, he consoled himself, the reason things had gone wrong was that it was all happening miles away down in the country, where he had very little say in the doings of the troops. Well, just look at the enterprises he was managing personally: there, everything was running as smoothly as you like. For instance, the Yi Chung Trust Company was proceeding according to plan, and Chen Chun-yi's silk goods manufactory and a number of smaller factories were about to fall into his hands.

Thus encouraged, he rapped out his orders to Fei Little Beard in a brisk, decisive voice:

"I think you're right, Hsiao-sheng: I ought to do my duty by the old town. Apart from the pawnshop, which is out of commission, I shall do my best to keep all my factories and shops going until the Mid-Autumn Festival. But you must get on to the battalion commander and make sure he's going to keep a close watch on the Communists in the surrounding villages."

Fei Little Beard, his eyes still on the floor, replied with a string of deferential yeses. Suddenly, he said, "The local bank still has more than ten thousand dollars in cash left. I was wondering whether we should leave it where it is —"

"I'll leave it there for use in an emergency," said Wu Sun-fu quickly, " — for my own shops only. Mind you don't let anybody else touch it!"

He dismissed him with a wave of the hand, then stood up and went over to attend to Tu Chu-chai. Fei Little Beard said "Very good" and, realizing that that was all, was just going to take himself off when he saw the wild-looking Tseng Chia-chu still standing stiffly between Wu Wei-cheng and Ma Ching-shan near the window, and he suddenly remembered there was something else to discuss. He hurried across to Wu Sun-fu again before the latter had begun talking with Tu Chu-chai and hastily called him from behind:

"Mr. Wu! There's just one other thing —"

Wu Sun-fu turned round and glowered impatiently at him.

"It's about Wei-cheng and Ching-shan," he said timidly. "They'd both like to come and work for you in Shanghai. They're putting up in the hotel with me today, but I'll be going back home tomorrow, so I wonder if you could tell me what to do with them?"

As he spoke he contrived to tip the young men a wink to come across but they did not budge. Just then, Tu Chu-chai startled them all with a sudden deafening sneeze. When he had recovered, he rubbed his nose and muttered as he did so: "Everybody's coming to Shanghai to find work, but they don't realize that the people who've already got jobs in Shanghai are losing them! The banks, the factories, the big firms — they're all laying off staff and cutting down wages. There are tens of thousands of unemployed walking the streets with no hope of finding a job. When the post office advertised for only sixty clerks, more than a thousand applicants sat for the examinations. People down in the country just don't realize what conditions are like here, and so they keep flocking into Shanghai. I've got seven or eight people down for a job when I can find them one, myself."

Wu Sun-fu made no comment. He frowned and narrowed his eyes to scan the two new arrivals. As they stood there beside Tseng Chia-chu, they struck him as rather more promising than this young man. Wu Wei-cheng's square features promised intelligence and ability, and Ma Ching-shan was no fool, he judged. Yes, they both looked quite a bit brighter than Tseng Chia-chu. It occurred to him that he might be able to make something of them yet.

Wu Sun-fu beckoned the two young men over and asked them a few questions about their schooling and past experience.

Meanwhile, Fei Little Beard was hovering around Tu Chu-chai and regaling him with a few well-chosen honeyed words. When he saw Tseng Chia-chu still standing there with a vacant expression on his face, he drew him outside and whispered, "Your wife asked me to give you a message: she wants you to go back home as soon as possible."

"I know. Ma Ching-shan just told me. But I'm not going. I'm getting cousin Sun-fu to find me a job in Shanghai."

"Has he found you one? What sort of work are you going to do? I'd like to know, so that I can tell your wife when I get back."

"It's not settled yet. But with my party card I can easily find a job in a government office."

Fei Little Beard could not help laughing at this. It struck him that this self-important young greenhorn must have been rather a headache for Wu Sun-fu all this time.

*

Meanwhile, the silence had been broken in the small drawing-room. Chiu Chun, the lawyer, put the sheaf of documents back into the portfolio, stretched his limbs, and lit a cigarette before he replied to Li Yu-ting's last remark.

"Now look," he argued, "it's the way of the world — you always get the big fish swallowing the little fish. Even if what you say is true about certain Chinese bankers joining forces with the Americans with a view to bringing Chinese industry under their control and making the manufacturers their managers, even so, factory-owners like Wu Sun-fu are still swallowing up their smaller competitors. As a matter of fact, the fate of seven or eight such victims has just been sealed, and the papers are in my case here. In a day or two I'll be going along to see them as representative of the Yi Chung Trust Company and they'll be signing contracts handing over the management of their factories to the trust company — actually, it amounts to making them into the Wu Sun-fu Company, the Sun Chi-jen Company, or the Wang Ho-fu Company! . . . No, Yu-ting, I don't believe all this talk about an American-financed trust in Shanghai. In fact, I rather suspect it's a rumour put about by Wu Sun-fu and the rest of them to pull the wool over people's eyes. I think the Americans are making enough out of selling their products here; they're hardly likely to want to run factories in this country as well, especially when the country's in such a bad way."

"Oh, no, I'm sure Wu Sun-fu isn't up to anything like that!" Li Yu-ting assured him confidently. "No. I know all about the trouble he's having with Chao Po-tao."

Chiu Chun laughed and drew hard at his cigarette, then tilted back his head to look up at the fine workmanship of the grape-vine-patterned plaster mouldings on the ceiling. Li Yu-ting followed the direction of his eyes, then glanced down again at Chiu Chun and said quietly, "Seven or eight factories at one fell swoop, eh? Well, you can't say Wu Sun-fu's letting the grass grow under his feet! What sort of factories are they?"

"Oh, all sorts: there's an electric light bulb factory, a thermos flask factory, a glass factory, a rubber goods factory, a sunshade factory, a soap factory, a celluloid factory — none of any size, though."

"All bought on the cheap, I suppose?" asked Li Yu-ting quickly; but Chiu Chun was not to be drawn. Although Li Yu-ting was a close friend of the family, Chiu Chun felt it would be a breach of professional honour to give away a client's business secrets. He chuckled and changed the subject.

"There'll have to be peace in the country before factories can prosper."

So saying, he tucked his portfolio under his arm and walked out of the room, closing the door behind him.

The slam of the door made Li Yu-ting jump. He glanced at his watch and saw that it was just on five o'clock. He had only been waiting here for ten minutes, but it seemed much longer than that. Now that he was alone, he felt like someone kicking his heels waiting to be called to an interview. He was beginning to feel thoroughly bored and restless. He stood up and went across to look at a silk-embroidered picture on the wall — *The Imperial Concubine Chao-chun Leaving the Frontier.* Then he wandered over to the window and stared out at the trees in the garden. Recognizing Tu Chu-chai's car parked out in the drive, he suddenly became more restless than ever. There were strangers in the other room, then there was Wu Sun-fu's legal adviser, who had just left the room, and now there was Tu Chu-chai's car parked outside. Yes, it all pointed to something big in the air. And when Li Yu-ting comes along, it's not convenient to see him, so they leave him here to cool his heels alone — apparently Wu Sun-fu did not trust him any longer! After all, he thought, he was the same old Li Yu-ting that he always had been — he had not changed in any way. There was just that little matter of the dinner he had been invited to by Chao Po-tao the other night — just the two of them, alone. They had, it's true, talked about Wu Sun-fu, but what of it?

A cold shiver ran down Li Yu-ting's spine. He was under suspicion — wrongly — and it made him feel frightened and hurt. He felt he had only himself to blame: he had been too enthusiastic about helping his friends, whose interests he had at heart and whose reconciliation was his one aim. If the truth were known, Tu Chu-chai had probably let on to Wu Sun-fu that he, Li Yu-ting, had suggested (though with the best will in the world) that Tu Chu-chai should try to curb Wu Sun-fu's insistency on paddling his own canoe. They probably thought he was a petty creature trying to make bad blood between them! Perhaps they were keeping things from him like this because they regarded him as a sneaking spy in the service of Chao Po-tao!

There was a side-door leading out into the garden; he was tempted to slip out quietly that way and have done with Wu Sun-fu, but on second thoughts he decided that he could not very well leave without saying goodbye. Suddenly, he heard a roar of laughter from the people in the other room. He interpreted the laughter as meaning "He's a spy — and he's shut away in there!" His heart pounded, and his finger-tips felt suddenly cold. On an impulse, he gritted his teeth and muttered: "Since they suspect me of being a spy, I may as well be one for once!" He tiptoed to the door and had just bent down to put his ear to the keyhole to listen, when he thought better of it. "What's the use!" he thought. "Even if I play the spy for Chao Po-tao, he won't necessarily want me for one!" He straightened up, took a deep breath, and sank back into a chair. Just at that moment the door opened, and in came Wu Sun-fu, a smile on his lips. Behind him came Tu Chu-chai, carrying his snuff-box in one hand and rubbing his nose with the other.

"Sorry to have kept you waiting, Yu-ting!" smiled Wu Sun-fu. "Just had some people up from home — some slight business I had to attend to."

Tu Chu-chai vaguely waved a hand in greeting and was immediately convulsed by one of his sneezes.

"Oh . . . I see . . ." Li Yu-ting muttered, forcing a smile. He felt more like crying, for Wu Sun-fu's smile cut him to the quick. He stole another glance at Tu Chu-chai, and saw that he was fiddling with his snuff-box and looking extremely worried.

The three men sat down facing each other and began casually chatting. Seeing that Wu Sun-fu looked his usual self, Li Yu-ting felt slightly relieved. He slowly began to feel himself once more, and decided he would continue his role as the impartial mediator with everyone's interests at heart. Accordingly, when Tu Chu-chai mentioned the increased activity of bandits in the countryside, Li Yu-ting turned to Wu Sun-fu and said earnestly:

"The news that Yochow has fallen is not a rumour, after all: it's true!"

"So it's true, is it?" smiled Wu Sun-fu casually. "Well, it's no more than we expected. Chang Fa-kuei and Pai Chung-hsi must have Yochow in order to protect Changsha, which is otherwise isolated and difficult to hold."

Tu Chu-chai nodded his agreement. Li Yu-ting was puzzled for a second, then burst out:

"No, it's not Chang and Pai that have captured Yochow — it's Peng Teh-huai's Red Army! Surely you must have heard the news, Sun-fu?"

"It's just a rumour!" said Wu Sun-fu calmly. "Trying to lay all the blame on the Communists!"

He looked up at the parrot, which was shelling a peanut, and Li Yu-ting followed his eyes to the bird. Li Yu-ting was rather nonplussed for the moment, but, his faith in reports from Japanese sources being as unshakable as it was, he decided that Wu Sun-fu had been misled by propaganda from some other source. Turning to Tu Chu-chai, he repeated obstinately:

"But it *is* the Red Army! I'm afraid Sun-fu's version comes from someone with an axe to grind. The fact is, while Chang Fa-kuei and Pai Chung-hsi were attacking Changsha the Red Army was already storming Yochow. The two cities fell almost simultaneously. Frankly, Sun-fu, I think all this fighting in Hunan is giving the Communists a rare opportunity. Really, Chu-chai, I don't see why they can't be satisfied with a final showdown along the Lunghai line, instead of carrying the war into Hunan as well, when they know quite well that the whole province is just riddled with Communists."

Tu Chu-chai nodded again, but made no comment. Wu Sun-fu was still smiling, but a slight frown was beginning to appear on his face. Seeing that he had an audience, Li Yu-ting went on excitedly, "Just now the situation's going from bad to worse. There's fighting everywhere on both sides of the Yangtse, and there's trouble brewing from the Communists in Kiangsi. The Hankow area is very badly garrisoned, and there are Communist guerrilla bands operating within twenty miles of Hankow itself. In Shasi and Ichang, the local troops and the Reds get on famously together — like cats and mice living in the same hole!"

"That's right enough!" interrupted Wu Sun-fu. "Only the other day one of Sun Chi-jen's down-river boats was commandeered near Shasi, and he still hasn't found out whether the troops who took it were some of the local riff-raff or whether they were the Reds!"

He stood up restlessly, but sat down again without doing more than stretch his legs.

"Yes, Sun Chi-jen's certainly had a run of bad luck this month!" put in Tu Chu-chai, stroking his chin. "First they requisition his buses, and now one of his steam-launches has vanished. They tell me it was new last year — hasn't been in service six months. It cost him three hundred thousand taels of silver, too!"

Although he seemed to be taking part in the conversation, his mind was elsewhere. He was worried by the unaccountable movement of the stock market — the whole country was in chaos, yet government bonds were going up instead of down! He could make neither head nor tail of it.

Meanwhile, Wu Sun-fu had stood up again and was pacing round the table, now and then glancing casually or deliberately at Li Yu-ting, but the latter did not notice his glances at all, for he was still wondering how he could make Wu Sun-fu realize that in the present crisis it was his duty to co-operate with Chao Po-tao. But he was not to have an opportunity to bring the subject up again, for just then the butler came in to tell Wu Sun-fu that Chu Yin-chiu was on the telephone. Wu Sun-fu's eyebrows shot up and he and Tu Chu-chai exchanged a glance of surprise. Seeing that he could not very well stay on now, Li Yu-ting took his leave and departed miserable and frustrated.

A cigar in his mouth, Tu Chu-chai wandered aimlessly upstairs. He was trying to puzzle out why Chu Yin-chiu should have rung. He found the ladies playing mahjong under an awning on the small roof-garden. Mrs. Wu, her sister Lin Pei-shan and Wu Sun-fu's sisters, Fu-fang and Huei-fang, made up a foursome, while Ah-hsuan and Tu Hsin-to looked on, and the tiles clicked and rattled drowsily. Seeing her husband approaching, Fu-fang called out:

"Come and take my place for a game, Chu-chai!"

Tu Chu-chai smiled and shook his head, then slowly took the

cigar out of his mouth and wandered over to the table to have a look.

"Tired?" he asked. "Why not let Hsin-to take over? Anyway, how much a game are you playing for?"

"I don't think you could be bothered to play for half-pennies, Dad!" Tu Hsin-to challenged his father good-humouredly, winking at Lin Pei-shan.

"Come and join us if you want to, Chu-chai," invited Mrs. Wu. "I know you don't look at mahjong the way Sun-fu does — he says it's a slow-moving and tedious game and that if he gambles at all he prefers fast dice games!"

She gave a pleasant little laugh, but it struck one as rather vague and absent-minded. But then she was always vague and absent-minded these days — in fact, while speaking to Tu Chu-chai just now, she had missed making a pair of "blank tiles." They had only played six rounds, and she had already lost her stake twice. No one seemed to notice her inattention except Tu Hsin-to. He had noticed it quite casually, but had no idea what the reason for it was.

His mother had now left her seat, and he sat down in her place, opposite Lin Pei-shan. Mrs. Wu had also stood up and was making Ah-hsuan take her place.

"Now," she laughed, "let's see you and Huei-fang, the two amateurs, beat the two experts!" The laugh died away and the worried look returned to her face. She glanced absent-mindedly up at the sky and slipped away.

Tu Chu-chai and his wife, Fu-fang, strolled away to the other end of the roof, away from the mahjong table, and leaned on the parapet, looking out over the garden. Behind them the game was now in full swing, and they could hear Ah-hsuan and Lin Pei-shan above the voices of the other two. Fu-fang turned to watch them a moment, then said in a low voice, "There's something you ought to know: Pei-yao whispered to me just now that our Hsin-to and her sister Pei-shan seem to be very keen on each other. He's always coming round to take her out!"

"Well, what's wrong with that? Everybody does it these days."

"Oh, dear! You are slow! Don't you realize they belong to

two different generations in the family? Pei-shan is a generation senior to Hsin-to!"

Tu Chu-chai frowned and stretched his hand out over the parapet to flick the ash off his cigar. He took a deep breath, but remained silent. With another backward glance at the mahjong table, his wife went on:

"Pei-yao's also rather worried about it all. Someone else is asking for Pei-shan's hand, and she thinks he'd make a good match for her."

"Who is it? Fan Po-wen, I suppose?"

"No, it's Colonel Lei."

"Oho, Colonel Lei, is it? But he's away fighting at the front. There's no telling whether he'll come out of it alive or not."

"But he's coming back soon, so Pei-yao tells me."

Looking rather embarrassed, Tu Chu-chai glanced over his shoulder at Hsin-to and Pei-shan. After a while, he mumbled, "After all, they are related, so there's no harm in their going around together. The only snag is that morals are so slack these days, and young people take to the new ways so easily — anyway, Hsin-to isn't a child any longer, and you can't very well keep him in check. There's not really very much you can do about it, my dear."

"Fiddlesticks! If anything should happen, both families would lose face!"

"Well, what do *you* think we should do, then?"

"Don't you ever listen to what I say? I wanted all along to make a match between your brother Hsueh-shih and Pei-shan, but you wouldn't hear of it because you said the Lins had no money —"

"All right, all right, my dear! There's no need to go bringing up old scores! I'll speak to Hsin-to later on. Though of course it all depends on the girl. If she's really made up her mind and knows where she stands, I don't think you need be afraid of anything going wrong."

"But her sister says she's still only a child and doesn't know what's —"

"Humph!"

Tu Chu-chai shook his head as if he did not believe it, but

said nothing more. Just then Mrs. Wu came up to the roof-garden again, and when she saw Tu Chu-chai and his wife talking together, she guessed what it was about and shot them a knowing smile. She went over to the mahjong table to see how the game was going, then turned and moved daintily towards Tu Chu-chai and his wife. She was just going to speak, when suddenly Kao Sheng, the butler, called up from the garden, "Mr. Tu! Mr. Wu wants to speak to you!"

Tu Chu-chai escaped, and Mrs. Wu, looking hard at her sister-in-law, asked her, "Did you mention it to him, Fu-fang?"

For answer, Mrs. Tu smiled; then the two women stood with their heads together and conversed in an undertone for a while. Only a few words had passed between them when Mrs. Wu burst out laughing. Afterwards they turned and walked back to the table to watch the game.

*

When Tu Chu-chai hurried into the study, he found Wu Sun-fu on the telephone, and the voice at the other end sounded like Tang Yun-shan's. They were talking about "the news leaking out after the *Hamburg* had loaded and sailed" or some such thing, but it did not mean anything to him. Finally, Wu Sun-fu said, "Anyway, come round straight away," and rang off.

His face tense and excited, Wu Sun-fu sat down opposite Tu Chu-chai and picked up the list of the day's opening and closing prices on the Stock Exchange, which his broker Lu Kuang-shih sent him every day. He glanced at it, then tossed it aside and said, "Chu-chai, can you raise five hundred thousand dollars tomorrow?"

Tu Chu-chai looked at Wu Sun-fu in amazement, but before he could reply the latter went on:

"The price went up one dollar yesterday, and today it almost reached the limit. It's just incredible! I suspected all along that Chao Po-tao was behind it, and now Tang Yun-shan's just told me it's true. He says Wang Ho-fu has discovered that Chao Po-tao and some of his Cantonese colleagues are bulling again; they buy in whenever a low price appears, but not a large quantity — they just buy enough to peg the price and hold it at what it was before the fourth of this month —"

"In that case we're sunk!" broke in Tu Chu-chai agitatedly, throwing away his cigar stub. "We should have covered yesterday!" Tiny beads of sweat began to appear on his forehead.

"Even if we had covered yesterday, we should still have made a loss. The situation's quite clear: what with the Hankow area being threatened and the fighting along the Lunghai line dragging on, prices are bound to drop sooner or later. If only we can stop the rise and keep the price down, we've got nothing to fear. It's now a battle of wits between Chao Po-tao and us! If they're really set on buying in whenever the quotation goes down and if they keep it up till the end of the month, then they'll win. If, on the other hand, we have sufficient reserves —"

"If we've sufficient reserves, and if we sell every time there's a rise, and keep it up till the end of this month, then *we'll* win — is that what you mean?" As he said this, Tu Chu-chai looked hard at Wu Sun-fu, and there was a note of incredulity in his voice.

Wu Sun-fu smiled and nodded.

"But that's gambling, pure and simple! Now, Sun-fu! We're in the stock-jobbing game to make a profit, and it's too risky to do things like that!"

Though he felt he had to turn the idea down bluntly like this, Tu Chu-chai preserved his customary calm. Wu Sun-fu was silent for a while, his eyes fixed upwards as if he was engaged in some calculation or other. Suddenly he smacked the flat of his hand on the corner of the table and said in an earnest voice:

"There's no risk attached to it, Chu-chai; you can rest assured of that. If you can let me have five hundred thousand dollars, I'll put the pressure on tomorrow, then prices will come down again, and there'll be a panic among the small investors. This, coupled with the fresh advances that Chang Fa-kuei and Pai Chung-hsi are bound to make on the Changsha front within the next few days, will act as a sort of pincer movement, so to speak, with the result that there'll be a rush to sell government issues, and however hard he tries, Chao Po-tao won't be able to stop the rot! I tell you, Chu-chai, we wouldn't be running any risk, we'd be winning by means of a surprise attack!"

Tu Chu-chai closed his eyes and shook his head, but said nothing. He remembered what Li Yu-ting had said about Wu Sun-fu's pig-headed independence, and decided he would have to part company with him. He saw clearly that there was no talking him round. After a while he opened his eyes and answered unhurriedly:

"Whether there's any risk or not remains to be seen, but I still can't manage five hundred thousand. If you're so set on it, and you're sure of pulling it off, you can always draw on the four or five hundred thousand in the Yi Chung Trust Company. I don't see why you shouldn't take the whole lot for stock-jobbing."

"Nothing doing there, I'm afraid. All the money was allocated to various uses at the board meeting the day before yesterday. Chiu Chun has just brought me the contracts and I've already signed them. We decided to take over the small factories, and I'm afraid the company couldn't spare what little money is left — there's hardly enough left to put the factories on their feet again!"

As Wu Sun-fu spoke, his eyes gleamed with elation at the thought that he had succeeded in buying out the factories on extremely favourable terms. It was his first victory since his trust company had come into being a short while ago — a highly gratifying coup, in his opinion. Tu Chu-chai, on the other hand, was none too happy about it. When he recalled how they argued at the board meeting, he was exasperated and retorted bitterly:

"What did you expect? The company's only just been launched, and it's crying out for capital already! If you must go in for stock-jobbing, you'll have to drop the factories. And anyway, to go throwing our capital into factories which have already gone broke once, and where you've no guarantee of success — no, honestly, I just don't see how it adds up —"

"Now, Chu-chai —" cried Wu Sun-fu, trying to interrupt Tu Chu-chai's tale of woe; but Tu Chu-chai brushed the interruption firmly aside:

"Just let me finish! I haven't forgotten what you and the

"There's no risk attached to it, Chu-chai; you can rest assured of that."

others said at the time. You all said that the factories had failed because they were short of capital or because they had been badly managed. You also said that they owed the company more than a hundred thousand dollars before we took it over, and that the old Yi Chung Company was being dragged down by this bad debt. Then we went and bought over this bad debt from the old Yi Chung Company for a mere forty per cent of its estimated value — we got the best of the bargain there — so in actual fact we bought out eight factories, valued at three hundred thousand dollars, for a mere fifty or sixty thousand. Oh, yes, it looks a bargain to get control of eight factories for an outlay of a mere fifty thousand or so — at present — but then —"

Tu Chu-chai paused, and Wu Sun-fu burst out laughing. Still laughing, he broke in, "so you think we'd lose by putting in another five hundred thousand dollars, eh, Chu-chai? Well, if we don't, the first fifty thousand will have been thrown away. If a horse has lost flesh, you have to feed it well before it'll be any use to you; in the same way, these factories have got to be supplied with new capital if they're going to bring in profits. Besides, if we hadn't spent that fifty thousand on taking over these factories, the forty per cent that we paid for the bad debt would have been thrown away as well!"

"So in order to retrieve the bad debt you propose to throw in ten times as much again, eh? Seems to me you're putting too much spice into your bean-curd and making it cost as much as meat."

"Not on your life!" Wu Sun-fu retorted emphatically and somewhat irritably. He rose abruptly from his seat and paced up and down, smiling grimly to himself. He had never expected that, far from winning Tu Chu-chai round and persuading him to finance his stock-jobbing, he would make matters worse by annoying him with his transactions through the Yi Chung Trust Company. As a matter of fact, ever since they had disagreed at the company meeting over the purchase of the factories, he had noticed that Tu Chu-chai seemed to be losing interest in the future of the company, and he was beginning to fear that Tu Chu-chai might decide to drop out or refuse to pay up when the second instalment on the shares fell due. If that should happen, it would be a serious blow to the company. It was no use trying to interest Tu Chu-chai in anything which involved long-term plans: all he was interested in was "get-rich-quick" schemes which brought him profits tomorrow on today's investments — and even then he needed a lot of coaxing. The other day, when the purchase of the factories was being discussed at the company meeting, Tu Chu-chai had hotly contested it until Wang Ho-fu had said jokingly that buying these factories was like buying second-hand goods cheap, an idea which appealed to Tu Chu-chai. Wu Sun-fu now realized that if he was to hold Tu Chu-chai, he must exploit this weakness of his. Once he had Tu Chu-chai's support he could at least negotiate loans with the banks more easily. But first he must make sure of this man. He continued to pace up and down, trying to think up something which would appeal to Tu Chu-chai. Presently, he smiled and turned to his glum companion.

"Now, look, Chu-chai," he said quietly, "there are two things we've got to consider: the financing of the eight factories that the company's bought, and the one million bonds we sold out on the third. It's a case of 'in for a penny, in for a pound,' and the best thing we can do is to put a bold face on it and do what we can. It's rather like pushing a wheelbarrow up a steep hill — you can't turn round, so you have to keep on. And that's why I must have five hundred thousand dollars more — to enable me to go on bearing in the stock market, and to finance the company's eight factories."

"No, it's too risky for me," Tu Chu-chai answered shortly, shaking his head sadly.

So, for all his stirring speeches, Wu Sun-fu had failed to strike even a spark of enthusiasm from Tu Chu-chai. Knitting his brows, Wu Sun-fu pressed him further:

"If that's your attitude, we may as well say goodbye to the money we've put into the company!"

"No, we can still cut our losses and salvage something from the wreck. Sorry, but my mind's made up!"

An unusual note had crept into Tu Chu-chai's voice, and his face was set.

Wu Sun-fu's heart sank. Nevertheless, he managed a careless laugh as he took a step forward and patted Tu Chu-chai on the shoulder.

"Come, now, Chu-chai!" he cried heartily. "Never say die! Nobody wants you to speculate recklessly. We can always find another way out. Now, you know there are certain fly individuals in Shanghai who take a tumble-down house, redecorate it and patch it up, and then let it for a nice fat sum of key-money. If the worst comes to the worst, we can always follow their example and do the same with the factories — though of course in our case we do need to be more patient."

"Don't forget you've got to find a customer who's willing to take your reconditioned house!"

"Oh, there'll be plenty of customers!" laughed Wu Sun-fu. "If we make a good job of redecorating it and patching it up, there's one man at least who'd be willing to offer us a good price: the great Chao Po-tao himself!"

He squared his shoulders and began pacing up and down the study with confident strides.

Half-convinced, Tu Chu-chai sat watching Wu Sun-fu as he paced to and fro. He said nothing, but his face betrayed a hint of animation. He remembered Wu Sun-fu saying something about Chao Po-tao forming a trust company, and was inclined to believe that Chao Po-tao might actually have something like that up his sleeve; the fact that Chao Po-tao would not give way over Chu Yin-chiu's loan seemed to confirm the rumour. He suddenly remembered that Chu Yin-chiu had just rung Wu Sun-fu up — perhaps it was about the loan. He was just going to ask Wu Sun-fu about it when the latter paced back, planted himself in front of Tu Chu-chai, and began enthusiastically:

"Now about our speculation in government bonds: we may have lost twenty thousand dollars or so to date, but there's twenty days and more to go before settlement day, and we've plenty of time to turn our defeat into a victory. If we work it the way I suggested just now we can't go far wrong. If there were any money left in the Yi Chung Trust Company, we could do it through the company; I'm sure Wang Ho-fu and Sun Chi-jen wouldn't object to it. But as the company's money's already tied up, it seems we'll have to do it on our own. Though of course, our personal interests are closely bound up with those of the company. The trouble is, what with one thing and another, I haven't much left to play with. Even Fei Little Beard's let me down, blast him! Tell you what, Chu-chai, let's go halves on raising this five hundred thousand! We can't just sit back and watch while Chao Po-tao rigs the market as he pleases!"

Again Tu Chu-chai closed his eyes and shook his head, but said nothing. The more enthusiastic Wu Sun-fu became, the less he felt like having a hand in it. He feared that the news that changes were imminent in the Hankow area was simply a piece of bluff on the part of Tang Yun-shan, and, what was more to the point, he had not the courage to cross swords with Chao Po-tao — he realized that Chao Po-tao knew too many tricks and was much more ruthless than he was.

Well as he was acquainted with Tu Chu-chai's character, Wu Sun-fu was groping in the dark this time and had failed completely to see the working of his brother-in-law's mind. He had tried everything from persuasion to goading, but Tu Chu-chai was adamant. The only response he could get was closed eyes and a shake of the head — not even a word of refusal. Wu Sun-fu's patience was running out. Finally, however, Tu Chu-chai said in a voice which implied that he was making a great concession:

"Look, why not wait a day or two so that we can get a clearer picture of the market before we do anything: we can't rush these things."

"There's no time to be lost!" Wu Sun-fu burst out impatiently, and the pimples on his face turned an angry red. "Speculation's like fighting a battle — you must seize the bull by the horns, and move fast! Especially when you're up against an unpredictable devil like Chao Po-tao!"

Tu Chu-chai's face was paling, and he felt as though his blood was rushing to his heart and chewing it to a stop. As a matter of fact, he was lending only half an ear to what Wu Sun-fu was saying, for he was busy considering ways and means of protecting his own interests. His ideas were no more than a vague outline at first, but gradually they became stronger and clearer, until they converged into one single thought: he had two hundred thousand dollars tied up in the Yi Chung Trust Company. He had put this money into the company under the impression that he was supplying some "floating capital" which was to be used for investment in government bonds and for providing loans against securities. He now realized that he was wrong, and that he had been tricked into parting with his money. He had better withdraw his capital while he could, before the company went broke. Whatever the prospects of the eight factories, he was determined to go while the going was good. It would probably upset the others, but then you can't please everybody! — And then there's Wu Sun-fu here still nattering on about government bonds and the rest of it. Well, yes, admittedly, so far as today's closing prices went they had lost some twenty thousand on government bonds, but, since the transaction had been in the name of the Yi Chung Company, the loss would be stood by the four of them — a mere five thousand dollars each; why, he might easily have lost that much on eight rounds of mahjong at the stakes he usually played for! . . . Tu Chu-chai smiled unconsciously to himself as he decided that it was far better to say goodbye to his five thousand than to worry himself to death day in day out over the fate of another hundred and ninety-five thousand. Nevertheless, he could not find it in his heart to spring this decision of his on Wu Sun-fu without warning; he ought to break it gently to him, really. Slowly stroking his chin, he gazed thoughtfully at the excited face of Wu Sun-fu.

Wu Sun-fu's expression was rather frightening just now, and he seemed torn by some inner conflict. He would probably have looked worse if he had known what was going on in Tu Chu-chai's mind. As a matter of fact, far from suspecting the truth, he was wondering how he could approach his sister — Tu Chu-chai's wife — and get her to instil a little courage into her husband. What more could he do single-handed with a man who sat there with his eyes closed, shaking his head and never saying a word?

Suddenly, the man in question stood up, stretched, and broke the silence of his own accord. "Sun-fu! If you're quite set on trying to outwit Chao Po-tao, just be careful you don't come a cropper in the process! I've known a lot of people trip up at that game!"

Wu Sun-fu's eyebrows shot up and he laughed. He imagined that Tu Chu-chai was coming round to his point of view. After a pause, the latter went on, "Another thing: when Li Yu-ting was reporting back about his conversation with Chao Po-tao the other day, he said something rather significant —"

"What was that?" Wu Sun-fu asked hastily, rising from his seat and going across to Tu Chu-chai.

"Then he said that Tang Yun-shan had political connections! It's true that Chao Po-tao has political connections himself, but, Sun-fu, what's the use of dragging ourselves into politics? Chao Po-tao doesn't want to let you have Chu Yin-chiu's cocoons, and it's more than likely that he'll use this as an excuse to make trouble for you —"

Tu Chu-chai paused again to fish out a handkerchief and mop his forehead triumphantly. He thought the moment was now ripe to break the news gently that he was finished with the Yi Chung Trust Company, but before he could begin Wu Sun-fu suddenly stamped his foot and laughed grimly.

"Don't worry about that! — Oh, yes, Chu-chai, I forgot to tell you: Chu Yin-chiu rang me up just now to tell me that he's going to sell me his cocoons and his factory as well!"

"Well I'm damned! But why?"

"I suppose Chao Po-tao's heard that I've managed to get hold of some cocoons, and realizes there's no point in keeping Chu Yin-chiu's from me any longer, so he's changed his tactics. He knows I'm short of cash and he knows I've already got enough cocoons, so he's deliberately trying to push Chu Yin-chiu's cocoons on to me so as to leave me with no cash and more cocoons than I need. In short, he's doing everything he can possibly think of to get me in a tight corner. But I don't think he bargained for Chu Yin-chiu selling me his factory as well!"

Wu Sun-fu's voice was calm as he said this, and he showed no sign of vexation, for, though he was short of cash for the moment, his mind was still seething with ambitious plans for expanding his business, and this served to soften the blow of all his other misfortunes. Tu Chu-chai, on the other hand, looked worried, for he was rather concerned on Wu Sun-fu's account and was more convinced than ever that Wu Sun-fu was playing with fire pitting his wits against Chao Po-tao. His voice was anxious as he asked, "Have you made up your mind to buy Chu Yin-chiu's factory, then?"

"I'll see tomorrow when I've had a talk with him —"

He broke off as the door opened and the butler, Kao Sheng, showed in a visitor. It was Tang Yun-shan, and he looked distraught: clearly, something serious had happened. Wu Sun-fu and Tu Chu-chai were rather startled.

"Chang Fa-kuei and Pai Chung-hsi are retreating from Changsha!"

Having delivered himself of this announcement, Tang Yun-shan dropped on to a sofa and sat open-mouthed, scratching his head.

There was a deathly silence in the room. Wu Sun-fu narrowed his eyes and glanced from Tang Yun-shan to the day's list of opening and closing prices which lay on the table. Could the military situation really be turning against him like this? It was too fantastic! Tu Chu-chai let out a faint sigh: he was totalling up his probable losses — no longer five thousand dollars, but ten, fifteen, even twenty thousand. He had just resigned himself to losing five thousand, which he could do without too much mental anguish, but now it looked as if he might have to lose anything up to twenty thousand, which was quite another matter!

After a moment or two, Wu Sun-fu grated through clenched teeth, "Is this just a rumour, Yun-shan, or is it inside information? Didn't you tell me this morning that Chang Fa-kuei's Ironsides were marching east towards the Kiangsi border?"

"Yes, but it now turns out that they're actually retreating. They kept away from the Wuchang-Changsha Railway so as to avoid any unnecessary losses. Just after I phoned you this morning, Huang Fen rang me up and told me about it — he'd only just heard about it himself. I suppose he'd had a telegram in code from his intelligence agent in Hankow. Ten to one the information's reliable."

"Then if nobody else besides us knows about it, we can still save the situation," Wu Sun-fu muttered as if to himself, and the wrinkles on his forehead relaxed slightly. Tu Chu-chai heaved another sigh and resigned himself to a clear loss of twenty thousand dollars. He swallowed and mechanically fished out his snuff-box. Wu Sun-fu was rubbing his hands and staring thoughtfully at the floor. Suddenly, he looked up and turned to Tu Chu-chai:

"We must do what we can. Do you think there's still a way out, Chu-chai? Yun-shan's news is a secret, and it's real inside information. In all probability Changsha's still in the hands of the Kwangsi Army, and the movement of Chang Fa-kuei's Ironsides towards Kiangsi is sure to be taken by the public to be a drive on Nanchang. We must strike while the iron's hot and get to work this very evening. You, Chu-chai, can put it round among your banker friends that you're going to demand additional collaterals for all loans made on government bonds as the only security. That'll depress the market tomorrow morning, and then we'll begin covering in separate lots —"

"I guarantee Changsha will still be in our hands the day after tomorrow!" interrupted Tang Yun-shan with great assurance, laughing boisterously for no particular reason.

Tu Chu-chai nodded his head in silence. For the sake of his twenty thousand dollars, he was warming once more to the affairs of the Yi Chung Trust Company — he even forgot his snuff-box. He glanced at his watch: it was ten to six. He could not afford to lose a minute, so, pausing only to tell Wu Sun-fu to make the necessary arrangements with the brokers, he hurried off. Left alone, Wu Sun-fu and Tang Yun-shan turned to some other business. Wu Sun-fu was the first to speak:

"Since the secret about the shipment has leaked out, I'm afraid we can't land it at Chefoo as the navy might intercept it off the Shantung coast. I've just been thinking about it, and so far as I can see the only way out is to nip down to Hongkong and try to make arrangements on the spot to have the stuff shipped somewhere else."

"Just what I was thinking. I'd better leave tomorrow. I hope you can take over from me as general manager of the company while I'm away."

"Out of the question. You'd better ask Wang Ho-fu to do it."

"Suppose I'll have to. But — oh, I don't know, the last fortnight's been just one setback after another. We've just fixed everything up nicely with the local troops along the upper Yangtse, and then at the last minute they go and change their mind and let us down — they just stand by and watch. Result: the armies under Chang Fa-kuei and Pai Chung-hsi are forced to retreat when they're within an ace of beating the Central Army. Well, that wasn't so serious: what's worse is that the Shansi Army hasn't been putting everything they've got into it, while the Northwestern Army has been really hard pushed for the last month, with heavy casualties and ammunition running short. And now even this little business of the arms shipment that we'd got so well planned suddenly leaks out!"

Tang Yun-shan seemed to be in despair as he scratched his head and looked first at Wu Sun-fu and then out of the window. Behind the pavilion overlooking the pond the evening sky glowed a deep red, and the trees around were splashed with gold.

Wu Sun-fu sat with bent head, his left hand on his hip and his right describing circles on the desk. His expression gradually changed from one of contemptuous hauteur to one of gloomy indecision. Presently, the gloom gave way to a flush of excitement and he looked up abruptly.

"So the outlook is still a bit hazy, eh, Yun-shan? You don't think there'll be any change in Shantung before the end of the month, do you?"

"As things are now I daren't say anything for certain," replied Tang Yun-shan miserably. "We'll just have to wait and see. Oh, it's enough to make one give up!"

Wu Sun-fu broke into a sudden, bitter laugh, then slumped back in his revolving chair and closed his eyes. His face was ashen now, and beads of sweat broke out on his temples. For the first time in his life he felt utterly incapable and insignificant. His business would run into heavy seas before long, and he would be floundering helplessly — there was absolutely nothing he could do about it!

After he had seen Tang Yun-shan off, he took a turn in the garden. The last gleam had faded in the west, and night was creeping out from among the shadowy trees. Lights blazed from every window in the front of the house. As if repelled by the glare, Wu Sun-fu made for the edge of the pond, where he sat down in a cane-chair which happened to be left there, and heaved a deep sigh.

He tried once more to take stock of his business. This was not the first time he had faced wave upon wave of crises, and he had always managed to weather the storm and afterwards hoist his sails again and carry on, so that today he was all set for such large-scale enterprise as he had never before attempted. He, Sun Chi-jen and Wang Ho-fu shared the right to control eight factories, all manufacturing household commodities. They had also advanced new capital — over four hundred thousand dollars — to develop these factories and increase the production of electric light bulbs, thermos flasks, parasols, soap and galoshes, making these things available even to the most out-of-the-way village in the country, and so dealing a fatal blow to the Japanese factories which had recently been transplanted in Shanghai! Apart from all this, he was going to take over and run on his own account both Chen Chun-yi's silk goods manufactory and Chu Yin-chiu's filature. He had achieved all this only after a bitter struggle, and the struggle he would have to face to keep and increase his gains would be no less bitter. Heavy seas were only to be expected. "While the priest climbs a foot, the devil climbs ten!" was the way it went, but he and his partners were battle-scarred veterans. So what had he to fear?

When he reached this point in his mental stock-taking, he could not help smiling to himself. A cool evening breeze ruffled his gown and he raised his head and looked about him, feeling insignificant no longer and far from being helpless and alone. He had noticed that among the old managers of the eight factories they had taken over were several who would make useful assistants; with training, they would make quite an efficient team of executives. The only trouble was that there was a shortage of clerical staff. He remembered his two relatives,

Wu Wei-cheng and Ma Ching-shan, who had been to him for a job that day. He could probably find a use for them. Even though they would not be a patch on Tu Wei-yueh, they would probably be miles better than that old dodderer Mo Kan-cheng.

Suddenly he realized that someone was approaching, and a breath of perfume came to his nostrils. He quickly turned his head and recognized the tall, graceful figure that emerged from the gloom as that of his wife.

"We've just had a telegram from Colonel Lei," she said softly, leaning on the back of his chair. There was a very slight shake in her voice as she said this. "The funny thing is, it was sent from Tientsin."

"From Tientsin, eh? What does it say?"

"It says he'll soon be finished up there and then he'll be coming back to Shanghai," she replied in a strange voice, as if she was happy and afraid at the same time; but her husband noticed nothing. At the mention of Tientsin a swarm of doubts had assailed his over-wrought mind. What could Colonel Lei be doing in Tientsin? He was commanding a brigade on active service — surely they couldn't have fought their way right up to Tientsin? If they had, then think of the effect the news would have on the stock market tomorrow! His momentary optimism and elation had deserted him now. He felt hot all over, and his wife's perfume made him feel sick. He stood up and snapped at her:

"That's some queer scent you've got on, Pei-yao! Come on, let's go back in. Fu-fang still here?"

Without waiting for her answer, he walked off. All the way back to the house his mind was seething with questions and answers. Should he switch over to bulling? No, he couldn't do that if Tu Chu-chai wouldn't fork out and help him. Should he write off his eighty thousand dollars as a dead loss and give up speculating in government bonds for good? No, he could not very well do that: eighty thousand dollars was enough to start a decent rubber goods factory. And besides, if he failed to get the better of Chao Po-tao in the matter of government bonds, his rival would be in a position to throw a spanner into the works of the Yi Chung Company. . . .

He found his sister Fu-fang — Tu Chu-chai's wife — chatting with Wu Wei-cheng in the drawing-room. He went straight up to her and said with a smile, "Can I have a word with you, Fu-fang?"

Fu-fang seemed taken aback for a moment. She glanced at her son Hsin-to and Lin Pei-shan who were sitting side by side at the piano and leafing through some scores, then nodded and smiled. As he held open the door of the small drawing-room for her, he turned to Wu Wei-cheng:

"You and Ma Ching-shan had better come down to the factory tomorrow and when I see how you get on the first few days I'll be able to decide what to do with you."

"Oh, Sun-fu, there's the young man from the Tsengs as well," hurriedly added Mrs. Wu, who had just that moment come into the room. "He's been waiting here a fortnight, you know. Couldn't you give him a try-out at the same time?" Wu Sun-fu winced at the mention of Tseng Chia-chu, but nodded his head all the same. He beckoned his wife aside and whispered in her ear, "I want to get Fu-fang to talk Chu-chai into plucking up courage and having another go at government bonds with me. I want you to tell her that Colonel Lei's been taken prisoner and sent to Tientsin after losing a battle and getting wounded — Now, make it sound as convincing as you can, and be careful you don't let the cat out of the bag!"

She was bewildered and could not make out what he meant. For some reason she felt a pang of grief as the picture of a wounded, captured Colonel Lei appeared before her. Wu Sun-fu smiled and followed her into the next room, where his sister was waiting. Just as he was about to close the door, he suddenly remembered something and put his head back round the door to call out to the butler:

"Kao Sheng, ring up Mr. Lu Kuang-shih and ask him to pop round before nine o'clock."

XI

IT was nine o'clock in the morning, and half a gale was howling along the Bund. At high tide during the night the level of the Whangpoo had topped the landing-stages, and although the river was beginning to drop now, the water was still rough and choppy, and several black cones had been hoisted above the towering meteorological observatory in Edward VII Road.

This was the opening attack of the season by one of the storms with which Shanghai was favoured each summer.

A No. 1 tram running eastward towards the Bund to the end of Nanking Road was battling with the powerful head-wind, and its windows rattled noisily as if trembling with fear. It finally came to a halt at the stop in front of the Cathay Hotel, and a fashionably-dressed young woman got off. She ran straight across the road as if driven forward by the wind and flew up the stone steps in front of the hotel. At this moment a young man in smart European dress, with a walking-stick hanging from the crook of his arm, dashed out through the hotel entrance. The skirt of the woman's dress, which had very long side-slits, flapped in the high wind, and as they passed it became entangled with the young man's walking-stick and the thin silk tore with a pfft!

"Blast you!" the woman swore under her breath as she turned to see who it was. A smile immediately appeared on her lips, for the man was an acquaintance of hers: it was Han Meng-hsiang, a stockbroker. The young woman herself, a beauty *a l'européenne*, was Liu Yu-ying, the widowed daughter-in-law of Han Meng-hsiang's colleague, Lu Kuang-shih.

"Hullo, you're out early!" he said, smiling and giving her a wink. "Not much fun for you leaving your warm bed and running into a gale like this!"

He stepped back to the side of the semi-circular steps and she followed him, glaring at him with pretended indignation. Suddenly she smiled and said softly, "Now stop ragging, Meng-hsiang, and tell me the number of Chao Po-tao's room — I can't remember it for the moment."

A gust of wind raised the front flap of her dress so that it wrapped itself round his leg and blew her long hair over her eyes.

Han Meng-hsiang grunted and put up a hand to stop his Panama hat being blown away. After a moment he sighed and said, "What a wind! It's rising like government bonds! I suppose you've bought ten or twenty thousand this time, haven't you, Yu-ying?"

"I haven't the money. Now come on, do tell me the number of his room."

"If you really want to see him, it's room number four —"

Just then a more violent gust still caught him full in the face, and he quickly turned his back to the wind without finishing what he was saying. Liu Yu-ying muttered a brief "Thank you," pushed her hair back and, hips a-sway, disappeared into the hotel. He turned and watched her retreating figure with a smile, then went slowly down the steps and across the road to look at the *North-China Daily News* placard on the corner. "Reds Threaten Hankow, Reported!" screamed the headlines, but Han Meng-hsiang shrugged unconcernedly at the news. Glancing back at the hotel entrance, he caught sight of Liu Yu-ying coming out again with a look of mortification on her face. Pausing at the top of the steps, she looked all round and seemed to have spotted Han Meng-hsiang across the road, when suddenly a tram pulled up at the stop, blotting them out from each other's view. When it moved off again, she ran across to him and, stamping her foot, she exclaimed:

"You're a fine one, Han Meng-hsiang!"

"Well, if you must dash off in such a hurry before I can finish what I'm saying . . ." he replied with a sly grin, then turned away down the street, swinging his stick, though he was careful not to walk too fast. When she had recovered her temper, she straggled behind him for a while, then caught up with him and walked along beside him, though she did not speak. She was sure that he knew where Chao Po-tao had gone, and she was thinking of some way of worming the truth out of this sly young fellow. The wind was blowing with a vengeance, damp and cold, and Liu Yu-ying's dress was of the flimsiest; she gradually edged closer to him, until her long, perfumed hair was blowing against his face and tickling his ear.

"But surely he went to the Great China Hotel," he said, as they were approaching the Customs House Building. He turned towards her as he spoke, and his leg brushed against hers.

"I waited there till daybreak but he didn't turn up —" she began with a shake of her head, but just then a gust of wind took her breath away and she broke off in the middle of what she was saying. She turned her back to the wind and the flap of her dress flew up to reveal a bare white thigh. She bit her lip and shot the young man a coquettish smile, then exclaimed peevishly:

"Oh, what a beast of a wind!"

"But I tell you it's a 'rising' wind, so it's a good omen for bulls like Chao Po-tao!"

"Is that so? Well, perhaps you can tell me where he spent the night. I never forget a good turn, you know!"

"Oho! Let's arrange it like this, then, Yu-ying! I'll go and find out all about it, and then we'll meet again somewhere —"

"Shut up. . . ."

"Oh, I'm sorry if I've said more than I needed. I was forgetting you're an old hand at the game. You naturally prefer to give me your tacit consent. Am I right?"

"Oh, all right, then: now tell me!"

She rolled her eyes at him and smiled seductively. He hesitated a moment and looked up at the patches of white cloud scudding across the sky, then squared his shoulders as if he had made up his mind and bent over to whisper something in Liu Yu-ying's ear. She immediately frowned and her eyes blazed angrily. As she parted her lips in a mirthless smile, her even white teeth were bared as if ready to bite. He shuddered in spite of himself, for he had never imagined that a woman with such a soft, creamy skin could look so ghastly when she was angry! Almost immediately, however, her expression returned to normal, and she pursed her lips into a smile. Just then another fierce gust of wind threatened to sweep her off her feet, and she grasped his arm for support.

"Thanks!" she exclaimed. "But I think I'll go and see him all the same."

"Now don't go upsetting yourself over it," he urged her candidly as he armed her along. "You'd best wait until he wants you and asks for you, rather than go rushing in. I can tell, he can be really nasty sometimes. When he doesn't want you, he cuts you dead. The only exception is Hsu Man-li, and he can't afford to ignore her!"

The wind was fiercer than ever now, and its howling completely drowned the roar of the city. Grey and white clouds raced helter-skelter across the sky, and the wind blew damper and chillier still. Yet Liu Yu-ying felt it was still not bracing enough, and her thoughts raced faster than the clouds overhead. As they reached Hankow Road she stopped dead and pulled her arm out of his, then stepped back with a disarming smile, blew him a kiss, and jumped into a rickshaw. Han Meng-hsiang stood rooted to the ground, gaping after her receding figure.

The words "Ring you later!" and a tinkling laugh came back to him on the wind.

*

Half an hour later, Liu Yu-ying found herself embarking on a little adventure in a five-storeyed building in Avenue Joffre. She wrote the name "Hsu Man-li" on a slip of paper and gave it to a page. As she followed him up to the room, she went over once more in her mind the three sets of tactics she had worked out for her coming encounter with Chao Po-tao.

The door opened, and she slipped in, smiling, but was taken aback when she found that Chao Po-tao's companion was not a woman at all: it was his crony Shang Chung-li! She immediately decided that none of her carefully-planned tactics would be of any use now. His face dark with anger, Chao Po-tao leapt to his feet and barked:

"So it's you! Who sent you here?"

"Hsu Man-li," she said, on the spur of the moment. She was beginning to fear that she was going to fail in her adventure this time. But, not forgetting she still had her "woman's armoury," she put on her brightest smile, greeted Shang Chung-li and sat down with her back to the window. She was sitting in a strong draught, but she was too busy to notice it — closely watching Chao Po-tao's face, calming her own mind, and working out a new plan of attack.

"Nonsense!" snorted Chao Po-tao, shrugging his shoulders and smiling sardonically. "Hsu Man-li doesn't know I'm here — unless she's got second sight! You must have wheedled it out of young Han Meng-hsiang!"

So her bluff was called, just like that. Her heart was pounding, but suddenly she guessed that he had not seen Hsu Man-li during the last few days. It was worth the risk to tell another lie to cover up the first one — and she was a skilful liar, too. In no time at all she had concocted her story — based on what Han Meng-hsiang had told her about Chao Po-tao's relations with Hsu Man-li and on other scraps of hearsay she had picked up about her. Her smile vanished, and she assumed a look of injured innocence.

"Now that's hardly fair: you've got it all wrong! As a matter of fact, I came here of my own accord but it was from Hsu Man-li that I found out where you were. I waited for you last night in the Great China Hotel, but you didn't come and I was feeling fed up, so I went into the ballroom to have a look round, and there she was; but she didn't recognize me. She was muttering away to some man, and I happened to overhear what she was saying — nobody else would have guessed who it was she was talking about, but I knew straight away it was you she meant. She — she —"

She stopped, not knowing quite how to go on. As luck would have it, a gust of wind blew her hair over her eyes; seizing her opportunity, she stood up and closed the window, and so was able to disguise her hesitation.

"Did she tell him I was staying here?" Chao Po-tao asked impatiently.

"Yes, she told him that you were staying here and that you had some new dodge up your sleeve —"

"Eh! Do you know who the man was?" Chao Po-tao interrupted, wide-eyed. "What does he look like?"

Something in his look told her that he was not only anxious to know who the man was, but also that he had made a confident guess about his identity already. She had hardly expected this, and her heart began pounding again. She frowned and put her head on one side, then suddenly smiled and said, "Oh, I think he must be a friend of yours! He's not all that tall, and not particularly good-looking . . . I think I've met him somewhere before."

Chao Po-tao winced and looked significantly at Shang Chung-li, who pulled at his beard and smiled.

Liu Yu-ying felt suddenly hot. She stood up and opened the window again, then remained standing there, looking out. A gust of wind struck her in the face, carrying with it a tiny leaf. The trees lining the street were swaying drunkenly, and the wind seemed to be blowing as hard as ever.

"It *must* be Wu Sun-fu!" Chao Po-tao muttered to Shang Chung-li, bringing the flat of his hand down with an agitated thwack on the arm of the sofa. "Damn it, she's gone and hooked him too!"

"Wu Sun-fu?" Yes, she knew who that was. So she really had met him, after all. She remembered her father-in-law, Lu Kuang-shih, mentioning Wu Sun-fu just recently in connection with some political party or other. She also remembered Han Meng-hsiang dropping a remark about Wu Sun-fu and Chao Po-tao falling out over something. She was so overjoyed that she nearly burst out laughing. Her makeshift lie had done the trick, and she now felt perfectly at ease. She decided she would embroider her masterpiece of deception still further. She was ready to lie the devil out of countenance today!

"I expected something like this all along," replied Shang Chung-li in an undertone, slowly stroking his beard and shooting Liu Yu-ying an appraising glance. "That's why I advised you to keep a firm grip on Hsu Man-li."

Chao Po-tao turned to Liu Yu-ying again and asked icily, "What else were they talking about?"

"Well, I didn't understand a lot of it, so I can't really remember, but it seemed to be something about the stock market and that sort of thing. And then I heard the word 'gun' — I suppose they meant that somebody ought to be shot — and then the man pulled a face and made a gesture as if —"

She had got as far as this with her fairy-tale, and was feeling quite pleased with herself, when Chao Po-tao suddenly threw back his head and roared with laughter, while Shang Chung-li narrowed his eyes at her and shook his head. Didn't they believe her, then? Her heart began pounding again. Chao Po-tao's laughter subsided, and his face became quite stern. Suddenly he sprang to his feet, clapped her sharply on the shoulder, and cried:

"Yu-ying, your heart's in the right place! You've told us quite enough! Now, there's somebody in the other room, an acquaintance of yours. You can go and keep her company for a while!"

As he spoke, he waved towards the door on the left, then grasped her by the arm, shoved her into the room, and closed the door behind her.

She found herself in a luxuriously-furnished bedroom with French windows opening on to a balcony. A double bed occupied the centre of the room, with one end against the wall and the other towards the windows. On the bed lay a woman in a white silk night-dress, her face to the other side of the room. Liu Yu-ying just stood there in a trance, wondering what it had all meant: why had Chao Po-tao suddenly burst out laughing like that, and then shoved her into this room? She could not make up her mind for the moment whether it was a good sign or a bad one. She strained her ears to hear what was going on in the next room: not a sound! She peeped through the keyhole and saw that Chao Po-tao was smoking a cigar, while Shang Chung-li was stroking his beard.

One of the French windows was open, and the wind was

blowing in in intermittent gusts. Now and then the woman's silk night-dress puffed up like a soft, translucent shell, and her newly-waved hair fluttered on the pillow. Yet the woman slept on. Feeling calmer now, Liu Yu-ying tiptoed across to the bed; when she saw who it was she all but shrieked with surprise. Who should it be but her bosom friend Feng Mei-ching! So it was this little girl of sixteen or seventeen who had been the cause of her waiting all night in vain for Chao Po-tao at the Great China Hotel! Although Liu Yu-ying had often told herself that, so long as she could tap him for money from time to time, she could not care less how many girls Chao Po-tao picked up to sleep with, nevertheless, just at this moment, she was consumed with jealousy, and had half a mind to wake Feng Mei-ching up and ask her what the devil she thought she was doing. It was at that moment that the girl woke up of her own accord. She rubbed her eyes, turned on to her back, and languidly raised her legs, so that her night-dress slipped down to her waist, leaving her thighs unashamedly bare.

Liu Yu-ying smiled to herself and slipped out on to the balcony. She was thinking of playing a joke on Feng Mei-ching, just to get her own back, but she suddenly caught a snatch of conversation, and the voice was Chao Po-tao's:

"You're quite right: the 'guns' they were talking about must mean the shipment of arms. Oh, hell! It was just my bad luck that Hsu Man-li should still have been hanging about at my place the day that German came to see me; I forgot for the moment that she knew a few words of English. . . ."

"*Cherchez la femme*," came Shang Chung-li's voice. "Your trouble is, you're too fond of 'em — you've got two here this very minute!"

When Liu Yu-ying heard this, she swore under her breath: "Oh, go to hell, you old —!" Then she heard a roar of laughter from Chao Po-tao.

"It doesn't look as if we can trust that German. He's probably buttering his bread on both sides. He gets fifty thousand dollars from us and then goes and blabs to Wu Sun-fu!"

"Blast him! The bribe is a small matter — we could get it back if it came to that. The point is, our reputation's at stake!

If we let our people down this time, they'll never trust us again. We must stop the shipment falling into their hands at all costs!"

"Well, what about taking the matter up with the broker? . . ."

Suddenly a plane-tree in front of the balcony rustled in the wind, so that it was impossible to hear any more of the conversation. The wind, which slackened off some time since, now suddenly rose again. Liu Yu-ying was standing with her face to the east, and was forced to close her eyes, so strong was the wind. A sudden bang startled her as the window blew to and immediately swung open again. She looked round to find that Feng Mei-ching had raised her head and was staring in wide-eyed amazement. The two women's eyes met for a second, then looked away again. Feng Mei-ching blushed but Liu Yu-ying bit her lip and smiled.

"What are you doing here, Yu-ying?" asked the embarrassed Feng Mei-ching, clambering off the bed and shaking down her night-dress. She joined Liu Yu-ying on the balcony, where the wind first made her full-bottomed night-dress belly out, then whisked it up to reveal her plump white buttocks. Liu Yu-ying tittered and exclaimed:

"Mei-ching! Somebody down in the street is looking up at you!"

"Where's Fatty? Oh, bother the wind! Looks like rain. Have you been to my place, Yu-ying? And what are you doing here?"

While she rambled on like this, she held down her night-dress with her hand, and her eyes never left Liu Yu-ying's face. The look in her eyes was a mixture of apprehension, disgust, shame and jealousy. But Liu Yu-ying paid no attention whatsoever to all this, for she was too busy eavesdropping on the conversation going on in the next room. A moment ago she had happened to catch a phrase or two which had aroused her curiosity, and which made her realize suddenly why Chao Po-tao could not afford to slight Hsu Man-li.

"Oh, bother the wind!" she muttered as if to herself, instead of answering Feng Mei-ching's string of questions. She frowned and strained her ears, but she could only catch a few blurred, disjointed words of which she could make neither head nor tail.

Nothing could be heard clearly above the noise of the wind, and she imagined that the wind was blowing all sound of the conversation next door away in the opposite direction. She heaved a sigh of disappointment.

"Who are you so angry with, Yu-ying? I haven't done anything to you —"

Feng Mei-ching seemed unable to contain herself any longer. Her face was pale and she was looking daggers at Liu Yu-ying. Liu Yu-ying had not expected this; it made her blood boil, and she flushed to the tips of her ears. She was on the verge of flaring up, but thought better of it and beat her anger back, then took Feng Mei-ching's hand gently in hers and said with a smile:

"Well, well! It's only a few days since I saw you last, but you've changed completely! You're more sure of yourself — no one could help noticing the difference. I came today to offer you my congratulations, so how could I possibly be angry with you?"

At this Feng Mei-ching crimsoned and jerked her hand out of Liu Yu-ying's grip. Without a word, she ran back into the room and flung herself on the bed. Liu Yu-ying smiled with satisfaction, and was just going to go back into the room again, when suddenly Chao Po-tao's voice could be heard once more; this time it was loud and excited, ringing with optimism and confidence.

"Just you wait and see! Wu Sun-fu is overreaching himself this time, and he'll soon find himself in hot water! Any Chinese who runs industrial enterprises without foreign capital behind him is doomed to failure. And then look at the way he speculates in government bonds: huh! This month he started off as a bear; then, when he saw that the situation in Changsha was quite peaceful, he changed over to bulling, and at the moment he's probably holding six or seven million. If my guess is correct, he's got a tidy lot of futures booked for delivery next month. What he's banking on is that the Shansi Army won't start any large-scale operations, and that there won't be any major battles on the Tientsin-Pukow line, until about the tenth of next month, ha ha! Wu Sun-fu's very shrewd in his calculations, but, unfortunately for him, Chao Po-tao is going to have a bit of fun at his expense! I'll wait until he's got halfway up the hill, and then I'll pull him down by his leg!"

After a moment's silence there was a rapid exchange of questions and answers, and the two men's voices were so jumbled together that Liu Yu-ying could make nothing of it. She stood lost in thought, wondering just how Chao Po-tao proposed to "pull Wu Sun-fu down by his leg"; anyway, she wasn't really interested when they just talked shop: she was just listening in case there should be any more interesting bits about Hsu Man-li. Meanwhile, Feng Mei-ching was giving Liu Yu-ying venomous looks and working off her feelings by biting the corner of her handkerchief. Liu Yu-ying smiled and deliberately turned her back on her as if she were put out. Just then she heard Shang Chung-li's voice again:

"So you've decided to fight it out with them, eh? . . . How much are you going to get rid of?"

"It all depends. As the prices go up, I'll unload, and I'll continue unloading until Wu Sun-fu collapses and the Yi Chung Trust Company folds up! And what's more, Chung-li, I had the tip-off some time ago that a strategic withdrawal has been planned from the northern section of the Tientsin-Pukow line — it'll only be a matter of time. Today's the seventeenth, and there's still ten days to go before the settlement. If our plan hasn't been successful by then, and Wu Sun-fu looks like getting the better of us, we can always resort to the old method which proved so effective last month, can't we?"

Then came roars of laughter which seemed to come nearer and nearer, until Chao Po-tao's head suddenly popped out of the window of the next room. Fortunately for Liu Yu-ying, he looked straight down at the street. She started with surprise and slipped back hastily into the room. She bounded across the room and sat down on the bed beside Feng Mei-ching with her hand pressed against her chest.

Feng Mei-ching angrily straightened her legs and rolled over so that she put a foot or so between Liu Yu-ying and herself, as if her friend were covered with prickles.

"Oh, don't be so childish, Mei-ching!" smiled Liu Yu-ying,

who had now recovered her composure. "What's it all about, eh? Like good sisters, we should bare our hearts to each other."

She sat staring at Feng Mei-ching's back as she spoke, but her attention was otherwise engaged. She was turning over and over in her mind the scraps of conversation which she had just overheard. Of course, she was perfectly well aware what Feng Mei-ching was cross about, but she had not the time to bother herself with her petty jealousies. Encouraged by the unexpected progress she had made in the course of her "adventure," she was now busy planning how best she might become a second Hsu Man-li and then get Chao Po-tao under her thumb even more skilfully than Hsu Man-li herself had done. As she racked her brains, she reached out and rolled Feng Mei-ching over again.

"Now listen, Mei-ching, you must believe what I say," she urged. "I didn't come here to pick a quarrel with you, and I didn't come to talk to Chao Po-tao. I happened to be passing by and I just popped in to see you. You must know by now what I'm really like: ever since my husband died, I've had no heart for anything, and I just go on from day to day enjoying myself when I can. I don't want to fight anybody. We're good friends, and all I want to do is to help you. You don't imagine I came to spoil your little game?"

"All right, then, tell me the truth: did Fatty ask you to come here?"

"No, I came here for something else," Liu Yu-ying answered offhandedly, and smiled. She was trying to make up her mind whether to leave without more ado, or whether to wait until she had a chance to tell Chao Po-tao some more lies.

"Fatty in the next room?" asked Feng Mei-ching. She smiled and gazed into Liu Yu-ying's face, waiting for an answer, her eyes betraying a childish naivety that was quite ludicrous.

"He's out there with a visitor — surely you knew?" Liu Yu-ying replied quietly, resting her chin on Feng Mei-ching's shoulder. She was still trying to make up her mind what to do. Feng Mei-ching shook her head without a word and smiled languidly. Now that she had got over her jealousy, her head was beginning to feel heavy and her limbs weak. She had rather overdone it during the night.

For a while there was silence in the room, broken only by the whistling and moaning of the wind outside the windows.

"Well, I must be off now, Mei-ching. Fatty's still busy with his visitor. Come to the pictures with me tomorrow."

As she said this, Liu Yu-ying opened the door and slipped into the other room. Her plans were laid. To her surprise, she found Shang Chung-li sitting there alone with a cigar in his mouth, lost in thought. Their eyes met, but the old man just stroked his beard and smiled vaguely as if only half aware of her. Liu Yu-ying decided she would have to abandon her plan. Glancing at Shang Chung-li and pointing towards the door of the bedroom, she tittered and went out.

When she reached the street, she went into a shop to ring for a taxi. She was going to see Han Meng-hsiang and make sure she had him under her thumb before she did anything else. In a few moments she was sitting in the car, which battled forward against the howling gale, and as she sat there the thoughts raced through her head faster than the wind outside. She bit her lip and smiled as she thought: "Chao Po-tao, my lad, if you don't agree to my terms, all right: then we part company for good. Wu Sun-fu would be only too glad to pay me a good price for that little secret of yours! Well, whoever pays me a fair price can have it!"

Liu Yu-ying was a clever girl. She had been to school for several years until she was seventeen, and she knew more Chinese than her friend Feng Mei-ching. She had had a thorough grounding in all the intricacies of stock exchange business and was quite at home in it. About ten years before, her father had gone bankrupt and committed suicide after a great upheaval on the Exchange. Her brother had made a living on the merry-go-round of get-rich-quick gambles and moonlight flits until last year, when he had lost heavily on his speculations in gold bars and had then received a prison sentence for embezzlement; he was still in prison at that time. Her father-in-law, Lu Kuang-shih, and her late husband had talked of nothing else but gold bars and government bonds every time they opened their mouths.

She herself had lately come to use the floor of the Exchange as her "home" during the day, and there, guided by some sixth sense, she would buy or sell anything up to ten thousand at a time, though she always took great care not to involve herself too deeply. She had learned a lesson from the failures of her father, her brother, her father-in-law and her husband, and preferred to play safe and be satisfied with making fifty or sixty dollars on ten thousand government bonds.

Being a woman, she realized that men and women had different ways of making money: men used money as capital, whereas women used themselves as capital. This was why, although she played safe where government bonds were concerned, she was prepared to gamble recklessly in her relations with Chao Po-tao. When, a month or so ago, she had first got to know him through Han Meng-hsiang, she had decided at once that he was just another kind of "speculation." And out of this speculation she was expecting to make quite a packet!

And now her "harvest" was ready for reaping. Every nerve in her body was tensed, and her brain piled up one plan after another, one cunning move after another. When she reached the Exchange, she thought to herself: "It might be a good idea to sell my secret retail. For the last month everybody here has been snooping around trying to find out the secret of Chao Po-tao's success!" She had employed her wits to analyse and sift everything she had overheard and had come to the conclusion that the "shipment of munitions" and "the German" would be of interest only to Wu Sun-fu. So far as speculation in government bonds was concerned, she concluded that Chao Po-tao was not only intending to turn bear, but also had up his sleeve what he called "the old method," which guaranteed him success every time. She was not very clear what this "old method" was, but she firmly believed that Chao Po-tao had a whole bag of tricks at his disposal and could do what he said.

The floor of the Stock Exchange was even more crowded and noisy than a busy market-place. The air was suffocating and reeked of sweat. Unable to squeeze through the crowd to the front, Liu Yu-ying craned her neck above the sea of heads until she caught sight of Han Meng-hsiang's glossy black head of hair, but he was too far away for her to be able to attract his attention. Up on the platform the announcer and the telephonists were all red in the face as they gesticulated and shouted, but it was impossible to hear a word they were saying. Seventy or eighty brokers, together with their hundred-odd assistants and innumerable speculators, produced between them such a deafening pandemonium of shouting and bidding that no ordinary ear could have made anything of it.

When "Reorganization and Disbandment for This Month" was posted on the board above the platform, an even louder and longer roar of figures thundered through the Exchange, and the sea of excited faces surged right and left as they fought to get to the front. Unable to keep even the place she had got, Liu Yu-ying was forced back to the door. After a pause for breath, she returned to the attack and eventually managed to fight her way through the crowd and get a seat on the benches between the entrance and the exit, against the wall where the Exchange notices and lists of brokers' names and numbers were posted up. This was a sort of "rear hospital" where those who had been put *hors de combat* at the front came to sit and pant. Here it was impossible to see even the head of the announcer on the platform, though one could just see his hand held up in the distance.

When Liu Yu-ying looked down and saw that her dress of pale blue gauze was soaked with sweat and that her nipples showed through as two round, rosy blurs, she could not help smiling. How comical it all was, she thought: here in the Exchange was the "madding crowd," while somewhere outside away from it all Chao Po-tao and Wu Sun-fu were lounging on their sofas with their cigars and pulling the strings that made these puppets dance! As for herself, she now held the secrets of the two string-pullers in the palm of her hand. All these men here were fighting in the dark, and she alone knew what was going on. What an immense joke it all was!

She wriggled her hips and twisted her lips into a smile. How little did the men sitting around her realize what a fabulous secret she had! Red-faced, their bloodshot eyes staring, they sat there jabbering and arguing, while the veins stood out like cords on their temples. The odd one or two sat alone, their heads bent in silence; you knew at once that they had fought and lost. Their lack-lustre eyes stared hopelessly into a wretched future as they contemplated selling their property, or absconding, leaving their debts unpaid.

On a bench opposite Liu Yu-ying two men, one with a drooping moustache and the other with a toothbrush moustache, were conversing in conspiratorial whispers. She recognized the first as Feng Mei-ching's father, Feng Yun-ching. The old man's blotchy face wore a hang-dog look as he listened in silence to his companion whispering on and on. Suddenly, a round-faced man in his forties squeezed his way out of the crowd and staggered into the "rear hospital" area. He rushed up to Feng Yun-ching and yelled:

"Yun-ching, Yun-ching! They're going up now! Ten cents, fifteen cents, twenty cents! A steady rise! How about it? Shall we buy in ten thousand?"

"Ha ha ha!" Feng Yun-ching's companion chimed in. " 'Buy,' he says! I'm for selling out twenty or thirty thousand, myself!"

He stood up with the intention of squeezing his way through to the "front" again. He was in his thirties and had a fashionable toothbrush moustache, and his face seemed familiar to Liu Yu-ying. While Feng Yun-ching was hesitating what to do, the round-faced man squeezed back into the crowd and craned his neck to see the quotations flashing out one after another on the board in the distance. The man with a toothbrush moustache urged Feng Yun-ching:

"Well, now, what about selling out twenty thousand? The prices have been rising steadily for three days now — they must turn and come down again soon!"

"Oh dear! You say they're going to drop, and Shen-an says they're going to keep rising. I think I'll give them another day and see what happens then."

Feng Yun-ching's face was flushed as he hastily made this reply. Now the round-faced man was squeezing his way back again, his mouth awry.

"They're falling again!" he shouted. "They're back to the opening price again!"

Immediately, the man with the toothbrush moustache snorted with exasperation, sprang to his feet and fought his way frantically into the crowd. Feng Yun-ching sat speechless, his eyes staring. The round-faced man edged up to him and panted, "It's a queer go, Yun-ching! It looks as if two strong groups of bulls and bears are fighting tooth and nail!"

"You're telling me! That's why I prefer to wait and see for a while. But you know, Shen-an, Chuang-fei's been complaining that I didn't have the courage to sell short on the fourth. Now he's even more annoyed that I won't unload a few. He says I'm making a big mistake. . . . As a matter of fact, since we three are in it together, I'm ready to do what the majority want. If you and Chuang-fei are agreed, there's nothing I can say!"

"Oh, no, it's not like that at all!" protested the man they called Shen-an, knitting his brows and sitting down in the empty space beside Feng Yun-ching. "Since the prices keep fluctuating like this, I agree with you that it would be better to wait and see."

Having heard and understood all that passed between them, Liu Yu-ying could not help smiling again. She looked down at the hollow of her palm, in which she seemed to be holding the fate of three men with three different hearts but bound together in a common endeavour. But no, they were not the only three! She held in the palm of her hand the fates of every one of these men who were sweating and fighting over "Reorganization and Disbandment" in a seething mass before her! She stood up impulsively, moved unselfconsciously across to Feng Yun-ching, and greeted him in a crystal-clear voice:

"Good morning, Mr. Feng! How's your luck today?"

"Ah! Miss Liu! Ah, I knew there was something I wanted to ask you: have you seen Mei-ching about? The day before yesterday she —"

"Ah, I'll tell you all about it later on," replied Liu Yu-ying with a winning smile, casually flashing a sideway glance at Ho Shen-an. "The market's gone mad today, hasn't it? I hope you're not going to miss this chance of making a fortune, Mr. Feng!"

All of a sudden, an uproar arose in the centre of the scrimmage — not an ordinary one following a new quotation, but a deafening roar that rose above the usual hubbub. Immediately, those at the "front" surged backwards like a tidal wave, while many in the tightly crowded "rear hospital" sprang to their feet and tried to make their way forward and some stood on the benches to see what was happening. Feng Yun-ching and Ho Shen-an were scared to death.

"The barrier's given way!" shouted someone up in the gallery above the platform, cupping his hands around his mouth and leaning out over the balustrade. "Keep calm, there's nothing to worry about! It's only the barrier collapsed!"

"Oh, they're off their heads — it's worse than a battlefield!" sighed Liu Yu-ying. She laid her hand on her chest, and found that her gauze dress, which had half dried out while she had been sitting there, had suddenly become wet through with perspiration again. The panic soon passed and the Exchange resumed its normal round of struggle and turmoil, with every man fighting desperately to snatch a victory before the close of the session. Ho Shen-an turned to Liu Yu-ying and said with a smile:

"I'm sure I've met you before, Miss Liu. Do you come here often? Are you expecting a rise or a drop? I think it's going to be a rise."

"And some people are expecting a slump! But tell me, Mr. Feng, how much are you in for? All going well, I hope?"

"Oh, nothing big, nothing big. There's three of us in it — just two hundred thousand dollars or so between us. At the moment we're neither gaining nor losing anything. We're waiting to see which way things go in the next ten days."

"Are you buying?"

"Surely. Mr. Feng thinks that for the last six months the bears have been out of luck, and I must say I agree with him. When we had that big drop around the middle of last month, everybody thought that government issues were heading for a slump, so it came as a great surprise when the prices shot up again at the end of the month. — I say, Miss Liu, have you

"Good morning, Mr. Feng! How's your luck today?"

heard about that fellow Chao Po-tao? He's never made a mistake yet, and they say he's buying again this time!"

Ho Shen-an lowered his voice to a whisper as he said this, and stretched out his neck and put his mouth to Liu Yu-ying's ear — perhaps because he thought it was a secret, or perhaps because she was so attractive and he could not resist doing it. All this left her quite unmoved, but she glanced sideways at him and acknowledged the tip with a smile. She suddenly remembered her plan for "selling her secret retail." Here was an opportunity, so why shouldn't she try it out? After all, Feng Yun-ching was not a stranger. She decided to drop a hint straight away.

"Yes, that's quite right. But I've heard something else —"

"Er, Miss Liu, what about Mei-ching?" interrupted Feng Yun-ching just at the crucial moment. His dark face flushed slightly, and Liu Yu-ying noticed it at once. An idea suddenly struck her. She tugged at his sleeve and whispered in his ear:

"Didn't you know? She's busy with some little scheme or other! I met her at Chao Po-tao's place only a short while ago. It looks as if he's making a pot of money again this month — several hundred thousand dollars, I expect! I know him, he — oh, Mr. Feng, you didn't say you were *buying*, did you? oh dear —"

She suddenly stopped and turned to smile at him. She had said as much as she dared, and the hint was as plain as a hint could be, but Feng Yun-ching just sat there, flushed and silent, with not a glimmer of response in his eyes. When he heard that his daughter was actually at Chao Po-tao's, his mind had been plunged into an absolute turmoil: his hopes of her success, his sense of shame, which had not yet been completely crushed, and his fear that the prize might slip from his grasp — all these emotions made a simultaneous impact on his mind at that moment, and he had just not taken in the rest of what Liu Yu-ying had said.

"Now I want you to get this straight, Mr. Feng," she said, still in a whisper. She had decided to stop beating about the bush, and to come directly to the point. "Liu Yu-ying has never yet been known to double-cross anybody, and I don't ask much: a very small reward will do the trick!"

This time he heard every word, but, having lost the thread of what she was saying, he had no idea what she meant and just sat staring at her blankly. Just then, their conversation was interrupted.

A sudden change had taken place on the floor of the Exchange. The hubbub of business transactions, a deafening roar of voices consisting almost wholly of shouted figures — such as five thousand, ten thousand, fifty thousand, a hundred thousand, or it might be ten cents, fifteen cents, one dollar — had given way to the sort of babel of voices, interspersed with roars of laughter and sighs, that one hears in a theatre. Those at the "front" drifted away, and some left the floor altogether. Trading in "Reorganization and Disbandment" had closed with a rise of half a dollar.

"The Seventh-Year Long Term" appeared on the board above the platform. This old government loan was followed by others issued by the former régime in Peking, none of them attracting much interest from speculators or forming the main line of business of the Exchange. The warlike "thunder of figures" had abated and quite a number of people had left. Li Chuang-fei, the man with a toothbrush moustache, now hurried elatedly back, his face bathed in sweat. He glanced at Ho Shen-an, slapped Feng Yun-ching on the back, and bellowed:

"The closing price was half a dollar up! Whatever you say about it, I've got rid of ten thousand!"

"Good heavens, man! What on earth possessed you to do that?" shrieked Ho Shen-an, leaping to his feet. One would have thought Li Chuang-fei had just sliced a hunk of flesh off him. Feng Yun-ching said nothing but just sat staring blankly.

"What's the matter with that? You know me: all straight and above-board! If it goes up again, I'll stand the loss. If it drops, will you pay the difference?"

"That's all right by me, but what are we going by: tomorrow's closing price or the last price before the settlement?"

Ho Shen-an and Li Chuang-fei threw themselves into a heated argument. Feng Yun-ching was still engrossed in his own worries. He had decided on his plan of campaign; once he had questioned his daughter and discovered Chao Po-tao's secret, he would know just how to proceed. When that time came, apart from the joint buying out of the pool of two hundred thousand dollars, he was going to launch out on his own without letting on to his two partners.

Liu Yu-ying had been listening in to Ho Shen-an and Li Chuang-fei with a deal of amusement.

"Now, Chuang-fei! Surely you don't believe all these so-called stop-press reports? They're rumours pure and simple! All these clerks and assistants that you keep in your hotel, now *they're* the sort of people who write these reports! You just show me any one of their telegrams that they didn't cook up out of their own heads! How can you be so certain that the market's going bearish?"

"It's no good arguing with you. Time will tell who's right."

Li Chuang-fei's voice betrayed a slight uncertainty. Ho Shen-an was about to press home his argument when someone squeezed through the crowd and broke in:

"Holding a court debate between a new and old magistrate?"

It was Han Meng-hsiang, the very man Liu Yu-ying had come to see. He must have just caught sight of her in the distance and come across.

The announcer on the platform banged with his gavel to open "September the Sixth Loan," which had long been worth hardly more than the paper it was printed on. Some business was done on it, nevertheless. The floor was quieter now than it had been for a long time.

"Ah! Yu-ying!" Han Meng-hsiang exclaimed, catching sight of her and manoeuvring his way through to her. "So here you are! Have you found Fatty yet? What a girl!"

Liu Yu-ying immediately tipped him a wink and motioned towards the others. Han Meng-hsiang smiled, and Liu Yu-ying languidly moved forward.

"Have you any idea how much changed hands altogether this session?" Li Chuang-fei inquired of Han Meng-hsiang in a low voice, and shifted closer to him. The pair of them then drifted away from the others and began conferring together in whispers, while Feng Yun-ching and Ho Shen-an also settled down to a private conversation. Suddenly Li Chuang-fei burst out laughing, scurried past Han Meng-hsiang, and went across to talk with someone by the platform.

The morning session was now over, only a dozen or so brokers and customers remained, chatting in twos and threes. The cleaners were sprinkling water on the floor and sweeping up the cigarette-ends. From time to time a telephone would ring in the brokers' offices. One man stood with notebook and pencil, peering up at the quotation boards and jotting down the price-changes. These blackboards, chalked with figures, hung in a neat row all along the latticed balustrade of the gallery. All was peaceful and calm — except the minds of the speculators, which were still as tense as ever. During this short lull in the fighting they were preparing for another fierce battle in the afternoon.

"I say!" whispered Li Chuang-fei to his two partners when he returned from his conversation with the man by the platform. "Lu Kuang-shih says that Wu Sun-fu's buying! I don't understand it at all! What do you make of it?"

His face, which had been glowing with elation before, was now pale with chagrin.

Feng Yun-ching and Ho Shen-an exchanged glances but made no comment. After a moment a whispered dispute broke out between the three of them. It was short and sharp, and ended with Li Chuang-fei stalking out in high dudgeon. After he had gone, first Feng Yun-ching and then Ho Shen-an left the Exchange. As he passed through the main entrance Feng Yun-ching saw Liu Yu-ying and Han Meng-hsiang standing there in conversation, and he had a sudden vision of his daughter Mei-ching, his "ray of hope" and the one "beacon" in the dark sea of his bewilderment.

Liu Yu-ying watched his retreating figure, her lips compressed into a contemptuous line.

*

Feng Yun-ching took a rickshaw home. He rode with closed eyes, for the wind, which was now fiercer than ever, was blowing straight into his face. The trees lining the streets added their strident voices to the noise of the wind, and it seemed to Feng Yun-ching as he bowled along in the rickshaw that he could still hear the pandemonium on the floor of the Exchange. As he neared home he experienced an overwhelming anxiety. He began to ask himself what he should do if Mei-ching had failed in her mission, or if she had misunderstood. It had become a matter of life or death for him.

Once he was home, however, his anxiety passed. He had faith in his daughter, and faith also in the aid and protection for which he had prayed so earnestly to the spirits of his ancestors the night before last.

The first thing he asked the servant when he got in was: "Has Mei-ching come home yet?" He had already decided that if the answer was yes, it would be a good omen and the odds were that his luck had held. After all, Heaven helps those who help themselves! As it turned out, his daughter had just returned and was now asleep in her room. When he heard this, his pale, haggard face lit up with delight. Forgetting that he was tired and hungry, he immediately dashed upstairs.

Finding the door of her room closed, he pulled up abruptly and hesitated. He could not decide whether to knock and go in or wait a while until she was ready. He was naturally agog to hear the precious news as soon as possible so that he would be free to get things going; but then she had only just got back and her door was shut, so perhaps she wanted a little privacy — she might be changing or having a wash. If he butted in at this inopportune moment he would most probably offend the God of Good Luck, and then his good luck would be changed to bad!

While he was standing there hesitating, his concubine suddenly appeared with a bulging handbag in her hand, evidently just off out.

"Ah! Just the man I want!" she shrilled. "I've got a bone to pick with you!"

So saying, she grabbed him by the ear and hauled him into her room.

A sheaf of bills was thrust into his hand: fortnight-old bills from the rice-shop, the coal merchant, the car-hire people, the greengrocer, the tailor, and the confectioner. There were a couple of receipts among them — one from the Electricity Company and one for last month's rent. His eyes opened wide as he went through them one by one, and when he came to tot them up in his head he found they came to about four hundred dollars.

"But, Chiu, didn't you tell the rice-shop, the coal merchant and the car-hire people that we'll settle up in full next quarter-day?"

"Bah! It's all very well you standing there and saying that, but do you expect me to have the cheek to go and say it to them, too? Let me tell you this: I've paid all the bills — every one of them! Four hundred and thirty-one dollars odd — and I want it back today! I had to borrow the money of one of my friends!"

"Oh, dear! Look, Chiu, give me a few days and I can let you have it. I'm hanged if I've got even a hundred dollars on me today!"

He smiled placatingly and tucked the bills away in his pocket.

"All right, then: if you can't pay me in cash you can give me the passbook for that ten thousand dollars in the Yuan Feng Bank and we'll leave it at that. — Just as a pledge."

"Oh no, Chiu! I couldn't do that! It wouldn't be right! In any case, it's only a matter of four hundred dollars or so. You can't expect a passbook for ten thousand dollars as a pledge for that amount —"

"What do you mean 'only four hundred dollars!' You're off your head! What about the five thousand dollars I borrowed for you from Woo? Four hundred indeed! She lent us that money out of the kindness of her heart. She trusted us and didn't even ask for a security. The month will soon be up. I hope you're not thinking of letting us down!"

As she spoke, the concubine arched her pencilled eyebrows, and with every word she became angrier and more fearsome.

Feng Yun-ching was doing his best to hold his apologetic smile. So far as the five-thousand-dollar loan was concerned, he had a shrewd idea that all this talk about having borrowed the money from Mr. Pai's concubine Woo was just not true. He strongly suspected that it had come out of Chiu's own savings, though it was more than he dared do to let on that he knew.

She gave him a few more lashes with the end of her tongue, then, realizing that it was getting late, she took herself off.

When she had gone, Feng Yun-ching jumped up and stretched as if he had just been granted an amnesty. He thought for a moment, then strode back to the door of his daughter's room. It was now standing ajar. He gave a warning cough, then pushed the door open and walked in. Feng Mei-ching was sitting at her dressing-table by the window, gazing into the mirror with a faraway look in her eyes. She turned and when she saw it was her father she giggled and quickly buried her face in her arms on the dressing-table.

Outside the window, the wind was whistling and blowing against the bamboo screen, so that it tapped against the glass. As he stood beside his daughter, Feng Yun-ching's eyes moved from her head of black hair and her snowy neck down over to her slender, half-turned waist to her shapely legs, which were stretched out sideways outside the leg of the dressing-table. Presently, he heaved a satisfied-sounding sigh and asked quietly:

"Well, Mei-ching, have you found out all about it?"

"About what?" Mei-ching asked, lifting her head abruptly and starting as if with surprise — no, not "as if": her surprise was genuine, for she had clean forgotten about all her father's careful instructions about finding an opportunity to get the required information from Chao Po-tao. It was not until her father asked her about it that she suddenly remembered it.

"Oh, Mei-ching, about government bonds, of course! Is he a bull after all, or is he a bear? —"

"Oh . . . that!" Mei-ching answered hesitantly, looking into her father's face. "But Daddy, I don't quite understand what you mean." Her mind was in a turmoil. Should she tell her father straight out that she had not yet tried to find out, or should she just beat about the bush and hope she could muddle through? Or should she simply make something up to put him off? She decided to try and muddle through.

"You don't understand what I mean? What don't you understand?"

"Well, all this about 'bulls' and 'bears.' I've heard people talking about them, but I'm not quite sure what they mean."

"Ha ha! You must have found out about it, then! You silly girl! A 'bull' is a man who buys government bonds, and a 'bear' is a man who sells government bonds."

"Oh, then he must be a bull!" she said without hesitation, then giggled. She was not consciously telling a lie. After all, wasn't Chao Po-tao a rich man? Only a rich man could afford to buy things, and anyone who had to sell things must be poor! Being still but a child at heart, she reasoned that if Chao Po-tao were reduced to selling things, he would cease to be Chao Po-tao — at least, he would cease to be the Chao Po-tao that the women were fond of!

"Er — are you quite sure? You're sure he's a bull?" Feng Yun-ching insisted, fearing that he might have misheard. Even as he spoke his leathery old face was beaming with delight and his heart was pounding violently.

"Yes, I'm certain of it!" she replied after a moment's thought, then burst out giggling again and buried her face in her arms on the dressing-table as if to hide her embarrassment.

Just then a sudden gust of wind lifted the bamboo screen outside the window and banged it against the eaves. Then came a fiercer gust still, which made the window rattle loudly.

Feng Yun-ching was startled for the moment, but immediately decided this was a good omen; he remembered there was a proverb which went something like this: "When a bamboo screen flies up on to the roof, the master of the house is going to make a fortune." Thereupon he decided to stake his all on one throw of the dice: he was going in as a bull! He would even appropriate that sacred ten-thousand-dollar deposit which was set aside as his daughter's dowry. He hurried out of her room and went straight out into the street.

XII

WU Sun-fu's careless smile was fading and giving way to a brooding expression; his purplish, pimpled face twitched slightly, and tiny beads of sweat gradually appeared on his temples. Avoiding Liu Yu-ying's eye, he sat looking sideways out of the window and drawing crosses on the table-top with the middle finger of his right hand.

A passer-by had apparently stopped just outside, for the shadow of the top of a head had appeared on the patterned window-pane. The shadow moved away, and another one appeared. Suddenly, there came the voice of a newsboy running past the window: " 'Stop-press News!' Read all about it! Yen Hsi-shan orders his troops to the front! Big battle at Tehchow! Tsinan threatened! Read all about it! Circular telegram from the other side of the Great Wall!" Then came the voice of another newsboy selling the "Stop-press News," bawling as he ran past.

Wu Sun-fu's eyebrows jerked up, and he suddenly sprang to his feet and began pacing round the room. He stopped in front of Liu Yu-ying and stood quite close to her, his piercing eyes searching her made-up face and boring into her eyes, which had a suspicion of dark rings under them, as if he hoped to see through into the recesses of her mind.

She submitted to this scrutiny in unsmiling silence, patiently waiting for his next move.

"Yu-ying, you must do as I tell you —" he said slowly and quite firmly, without withdrawing his piercing gaze. Then he paused as if to arrange his ideas in proper order before telling her just what it was she was to do. Liu Yu-ying's lips twisted into a smile as she realized she was "getting results." Her heart pulsed with excitement and she could not help breaking in:

"But Uncle, I hope you realize the difficulties of my position."

"Yes, I fully realize your position. You want to be sure you've got something to fall back on in case Chao Po-tao should find you out, don't you? Well, you can leave that to me to take care of. After all, we're relations, and we ought to stand by one another. Now, listen, Yu-ying: first of all you must make sure of Han Meng-hsiang. I'm sure you'll be able to manage that all right. And don't —"

Liu Yu-ying smiled again and blushed.

"And don't go ringing round everywhere trying to find me in future, and don't come to see me at the Yi Chung Trust Company! If you do, Chao Po-tao will soon find out that you're in touch with me and then he'll be on his guard against you —"

"Oh, I quite realize that. I was trying to get in touch with you for the first time today, and the only way I could do it was to ring up the different places. I'll be very careful in future."

"Ah, I can see you've got your wits about you! Right, now the other thing is this: I want you to take a room in a nice quiet hotel so that we'll have somewhere to meet and talk things over. I'll come round to see you every evening about six o'clock, so you be there waiting for me — can you manage it all right?"

"I'm afraid I can't make it every evening. I can never tell when I'm going to be busy."

"Oh, that's all right. So long as you just give me a ring at the Yi Chung Company if you find you can't get away."

"And what if you're not there?"

"I'm always there from four to five. If by any chance I'm not there, ask for Mr. Wang — Wang Ho-fu, H-o-f-u. You can always give him a message. You can't mistake him: he's a northerner and he always shouts."

Liu Yu-ying nodded and smiled understandingly. Suddenly the shadow of a head flashed across the patterned window-panes again, and then there was a thud as the head bumped against the window, almost knocking it open. Wu Sun-fu turned his head sharply towards the window and looked slightly annoyed. By now, the shadows of two heads were visible, one higher than the other, jerking to and fro. Suddenly suspicious, Wu Sun-fu moved quickly over to the window and snatched it open to reveal two angry faces glaring at each other with a fierce determination to fight it out if necessary. A couple of tramps quarrelling. Wu Sun-fu shrugged and closed the window, then returned to his seat at the table and wrote out a cheque. As he handed it to Liu Yu-ying he said quietly:

"And mind you don't take a room like this: it's too noisy! You want one upstairs and without a passage under the window."

"Don't worry, I'll arrange everything just right. Is that all, Uncle? There's just one thing I'd like to mention —"

"What's that?" asked Wu Sun-fu, tilting his head and raising his eyebrows slightly.

"You'll have to get round Hsu Man-li and stick close to her so that Chao Po-tao will go on suspecting her and giving her the cold shoulder. That's the only way we can make sure that she doesn't give me the lie and ruin my chances of seeing him frequently and finding out anything more. If you don't know her very well, you'll have to hurry up and get to know her."

Wu Sun-fu puckered up his brows, but nodded all the same.

Outside the window, the two tramps suddenly burst into streams of abuse. They were apparently quarrelling about money. "Think you can double-cross me, eh? I'll show you a thing or two!" The voice rose clear and loud, and when Wu Sun-fu heard it his frown deepened. Glancing at Liu Yu-ying, he shook himself and stood up, but she was already making a second request.

"One thing more, Uncle. I think I can manage Han Meng-hsiang all right, but not if I have to rely on just talking him round — we'll have to make it worth his while. Chao Po-tao's very fond of 'dollar diplomacy,' you know! If you're prepared to give Han Meng-hsiang some encouragement, you must give me some idea of how far you can go so that I can get to work on him at the first opportunity."

"Er — well, I can't say for certain straight away — I'll let you know in a day or two."

"Oh, and one other thing —" she began, then stopped and giggled. She blushed and flashed a glance at him.

"Well, come on, let's hear what it is," he said hesitantly, noticing something peculiar about her smile and the look she gave him. He could not help feeling that this woman detective was proving rather too much of a stickler for detail for his liking; and, with things going the way they were, he was beginning to have his doubts about her — at least, he was not so sure he could handle her easily.

"Well, it's this: What shall I call you when you come to see me in our private room?" she said softly. She made an apparent effort to stop giggling, and her dark eyes gleamed seductively.

When he heard what it was she wanted to know, he smiled briefly, but failed to notice her blatantly suggestive look. He drew a sigh of relief, then stood up and said indifferently, "We're relations, so I shall still be 'Uncle.' "

So saying, he waved her a perfunctory good-bye and hurried off. As he drove away from the hotel, he became suddenly conscious of the suggestion implicit in her smile, her blushes and the look she had given him a moment ago, and his heart leapt wildly; but the emotional disturbance was purely momentary, and his thoughts returned immediately to Chao Po-tao and the subject of government bonds. When the chauffeur turned his head inquiringly, he just snapped:

"The Stock Exchange — and fast!"

*

It was getting on for three o'clock, and a scorching sun had softened the asphalted roadways, so that each passing car left its pattern of tyre-marks imprinted on the surface. In the streets, grimy, perspiring tramps and urchins were hawking the various "Stop-press editions," bawling a bewildering variety of mutually contradictory headlines in an equal variety of voices.

Wu Sun-fu had flashed in and out of the Exchange and was driving to the Yi Chung Company offices. His mind was totally absorbed in plans for his various businesses, when suddenly he realized that he was full of serious contradictions himself. As an industrialist whose one great ambition was to help develop

China's own industry, he had all along objected on principle to the way financiers like Tu Chu-chai employed their large capital solely in speculation in real estate, gold bars, and government bonds; yet he himself was now head over ears in government bonds! He had been hoping that a truly democratic régime would soon materialize in China, and so he had also hoped for a speedy and successful conclusion of the military campaign being waged by the Enlarged Conference of the North; but, now that he had heard from Liu Yu-ying that his rival Chao Po-tao was turning bear and was preparing to resort to his "old methods" to snatch a victory, his main fear was that the campaign might be developing too rapidly for his present purposes! The last thing he wanted was to see any changes in the military situation in Shantung during the present month — that is to say, within the next five or six days. On top of this contradiction he had another: he had to use the limited capital in the Yi Chung Trust Company both for speculation in government bonds and for developing the eight recently-purchased factories. A month ago he had spared no effort to lay his hands on Chu Yin-chiu's cocoons and up-to-date filatures, but now that he had succeeded, and had taken one more factory into his "iron hand," he found it was something of a white elephant without the capital to run it, and was more trouble than it was worth.

All these contradictions had come upon him all at once and so quickly that he had become deeply involved without realizing what was happening. Although he was now fully aware of their existence, it was already too late to pull out. He knit his brows in a tight frown and smiled wryly to himself.

But he was not a man to be easily daunted, for he had enough confidence in himself to see him through. Difficulties, he reassured himself, were only stepping-stones to success, only hurdles to be jumped. Was it not for the sake of foiling Chao Po-tao's conspiracy to establish a "finance trust" that he, Wu Sun-fu, was determined to wrestle with him on the Exchange floor and defeat him there? This was the chief cause of all the trouble. Such was the "rational" interpretation Wu Sun-fu put on his contradictions. There was just one problem that still worried him — that of the Yi Chung Trust Company: he still had to find a practical solution to the problem of how to speculate in government bonds and expand the eight factories at the same time. To make things worse, there was not the slightest hope of dissuading Tu Chu-chai from backing out of the company, and the loss of his support would prejudice the company's chances of getting the help they had hoped to get from the banks. This presented the biggest difficulty of all at the moment. Until he had cleared this obstacle, there was no point in considering his next step!

The car stopped and his train of thought stopped with it for the time being. As he hurried into the company building he was worried, though not to the extent of despairing.

As he passed the counter, he noticed someone withdrawing a deposit and arguing heatedly with the cashier. What was the matter? he wondered. Was there anything wrong with the seal? Or was the figure incorrect? Whatever it was, it could not warrant such a red-faced display of anger! Wu Sun-fu glanced at the customer with a frown, then dashed straight up the stairs and burst into the general manager's office. Although it was called an office, it was furnished like a conference room, and the general manager's actual office was a "private den" next door to it. At that moment Wang Ho-fu and Sun Chi-jen were engaged in a tête-à-tête in the conference room; when Wu Sun-fu dashed in looking rather distraught, they sprang to their feet in wide-eyed surprise. Wu Sun-fu smiled reassuringly, but was in for a shock himself, for Wang Ho-fu immediately burst out:

"So you've come, Sun-fu! We've run into a bit of trouble! We've been on the phone hunting for you high and low but couldn't find you anywhere!"

"He had a job chasing me up, too," added Sun Chi-jen. His voice was as calm and unhurried as usual, but his face betrayed a certain anxiety. "We were just discussing what to do about it. It's not as serious as all that, but it's come just at a time when we're pressed for money, so it's a bit of a nuisance! The point is, you know that loan of a hundred thousand dollars that the Yuan Ta Native Bank promised us last week? Well, now they've changed their minds — though they were very nice about it, of course! Well, that's the score."

Wu Sun-fu was calmer now. Although the blow had fallen rather earlier than he had counted on, it was not altogether unexpected. Since the loan had been arranged through the good offices of Tu Chu-chai, it was only natural that it would fall through now that Tu Chu-chai had dropped out of the company. Calming himself with an effort and temporarily dismissing from his mind the question of government bonds, Wu Sun-fu concentrated his attention on the problem of bridging this sudden gap.

The loan had been intended to defray the payment of the wages of the two thousand six hundred workers in the eight factories and to buy new stocks of raw materials.

Wang Ho-fu brought out a pile of books and papers for Wu Sun-fu and Sun Chi-jen to look over, and gave them a brief summing-up:

"The wages total a little over fifty thousand dollars. They're paid at the end of the month, which gives us five or six days' grace, so it's not all that urgent. What really does matter is that we've taken delivery of certain raw materials — rubber, umbrella-frames, electrical goods, turps and sulphuric acid — which come to over seventy thousand dollars altogether; and all the goods must be paid for within two or three days."

Wu Sun-fu, who had been deep in thought, stroking his chin absent-mindedly, glanced up at Sun Chi-jen. With the end of the month only a few days away, he himself had to find the money to pay the workers in his own silk factory and also the one recently taken over from Chu Yin-chiu. This meant he would have to do some fast thinking on his own account. His enterprises, it was true, had multiplied, but never before had he found himself so short of ready money. The total value of his assets had gone up by leaps and bounds — at a conservative estimate, he put the increase at two hundred thousand dollars — but a hundred thousand of this was locked up in the cocoons stowed away in a warehouse. On top of that, there had recently been a sharp drop in silk prices, so that he just could not afford to sell off his stock of silk, which meant another one hundred thousand tied up. To crown it all, more than a hundred thousand was frozen down in the country as a result of the peasant rising.

Consequently, the company's present deficit, though it amounted to no more than a hundred thousand, was proving an insurmountable difficulty however hard he racked his brains.

"So we must have seventy thousand dollars within two or three days, eh? Well, just you leave it to me! —" This cheerful offer to find the money came from Sun Chi-jen. As he said this, he glanced at Wu Sun-fu, for he was well aware of the latter's financial straits. He paused a moment to flick through the books and papers, then went on:

"Though of course all this robbing Peter to pay Paul won't provide a permanent solution to the problem, even though it'll tide us over. Apart from the eight factories, we've got Chen Chun-yi's silk goods manufactory on our hands on a one-year contract, so that although you can't say we're going in for things in a really big way, we've still got our hands full. This means we *must* have an over-all plan. We started with a paid-up capital of eight hundred thousand dollars, which we laid out on buying the old Yi Chung Trust Company together with the eight factories. Now that Tu Chu-chai's withdrawn his share of the capital, we've only got about four hundred thousand left, and this has gradually become locked up in government bonds. I was thinking, this small amount of capital is just not enough to run the factories and speculate on the stock market, both at the same time. We'll just have to drop one or the other of them. The trouble is, we're in both things right up to the neck, and we can't easily give up either one of them."

"If it's just a question of keeping the eight factories running as they are now," said Wang Ho-fu, "I think we might be able to scrape through on four hundred thousand dollars; but I thought we'd decided to expand them? Besides, we've still got Chen Chun-yi's silk goods manufactory to think about. No, I don't think four hundred thousand *would* be enough! And what with the war disrupting communications, there's no way of shipping our products anywhere. We haven't even been able to cover our overheads this month. Yes, I agree with Chi-jen that we must have an over-all plan!"

The factories were Wang Ho-fu's special responsibility, so it was the factories that he emphasized.

While listening to his partners, Wu Sun-fu had been thinking things over, and now his face suddenly took on a look of determination. He glanced up at them, his eyes alight with courage and optimism. The look in his eyes was the one which could always inspire his colleagues with enthusiasm, fire their imagination and steel their will; it was that look of compelling intensity which came into his eyes whenever he was drawing up some great plan or making an important decision, a look that made lesser mortals quake.

Just as he was going to speak, however, there was suddenly a tap on the door.

"Who's that? Come in!" called Wang Ho-fu, turning towards the door and then rising from his seat with an air of impatience.

The head of the business department downstairs appeared. Hunched forward, he tiptoed lightly and swiftly across to Wang Ho-fu, and said in a low voice:

"There's someone else here who wants to withdraw his deposit before the time's up. We showed him our new regulations, but he wouldn't take any notice. He said he was quite willing to forfeit his four months' interest. We suggested that he might discount it, but he wouldn't hear of it. He's making a great deal of noise at the counter. What should I do about it, sir?"

Wang Ho-fu snorted, and instead of replying he glanced round at his two partners. Wu Sun-fu frowned, while Sun Chi-jen rubbed his chin and smiled wryly. Wang Ho-fu turned to the head of the business department again and asked, "How much is it?"

"Ten thousand dollars."

"Oh, ten thousand, eh? Oh, all right, let him have it. And don't insist on discounting it, either. Oh, damn!"

The man nodded with a respectful smile and quickly tiptoed out again. The door, which was fitted with a Yale automatic closing device, closed slowly and lightly behind him; there was a slight thud, after which a deathly hush suddenly filled the room.

"What a nuisance! It happens almost every day!" muttered Wang Ho-fu to himself as he sat down again. Lighting a Garrick and blowing out a cloud of smoke, he went on, "All these odds and ends of deposits were passed over to us by our predecessors. Now about sixty per cent of the total amount has been withdrawn."

"Oh! — What about the deposits we've taken in ourselves?" asked Sun Chi-jen.

"Oh, there's enough to see us through," Wang Ho-fu replied, leafing through the books. "Tang Yun-shan has roped in over a hundred thousand dollars in deposits, some fixed and some current. I think we have quite good prospects of absorbing more."

Wu Sun-fu smiled, then suddenly his eyes smouldered. He looked from Wang Ho-fu to Sun Chi-jen, then said firmly:

"Let's send round a circular tomorrow informing the old depositors that we'll accommodate them by permitting them to withdraw their deposits prior to maturity within the next fortnight with interest calculated on a daily basis. What do you say to that, Chi-jen? We're just wasting our time messing about with these odds and ends. There must be a reason for all these old depositors rushing to withdraw their money, and it's my conviction that they've heard rumours that our credit isn't good. And you know who our champion rumour-monger is — Chao Po-tao! Just now he's doing everything he can to put a spoke in our wheel. He said once that if the banks tightened their credit a little, we'd be done for. That was no idle threat: he's up to his tricks already!"

"You're quite right!" Wang Ho-fu hurriedly put in. "The way the Yuan Ta Native Bank let us down today must have been Chao Po-tao's work, too. I detected it in the way the manager spoke this morning."

"And then again, look at this business of Tu Chu-chai. It appeared on the face of it that the reason why he backed out of the company was that he couldn't agree to the purchase of the eight factories. If the truth were known, it was because Chao Po-tao had put the wind up him with his rumours. Tu Chu-chai wouldn't admit that to me, but it stood out a mile. When he found that Tang Yun-shan had left for Hongkong, he kept on at me to bring Shang Chung-li into the company, but I absolutely refused, and the next day he decides to withdraw!"

"Ha ha! He's rather timid, Tu Chu-chai is rather timid," said Wang Ho-fu. "But, in all justice to him, he's never shown any great interest in running factories."

He glanced at Sun Chi-jen, who nodded abstractedly. At this moment, a dark cloud was gradually settling on Sun Chi-jen's mind: he was no more keen on stock speculation than Tu Chu-chai was on factories. Not that he was averse to speculation on principle, but he already had quite enough to cope with, and felt he was not equal to speculation on top of his industrial enterprises. As it was, the company was deeply involved in both things, and at every turn new dangers were looming up: it was becoming more and more evident that Chao Po-tao's projected "financial blockade" against the company had already been put into operation. Things were so disheartening that he had come to the conclusion that there was not much chance of their succeeding in running the blockade. Still, they had no alternative but to press on.

In spite of everything, Sun Chi-jen remained calm. Realizing that Wu Sun-fu was waiting for him to express his opinion and that Wang Ho-fu had no definite views of his own, he looked calmly into Wu Sun-fu's purplish face, which now looked alert and excited, and said in his usual unhurried way:

"If we put our own house in order, we've got nothing to be afraid of. Credit is credit, and rumours are only rumours: we mustn't let ourselves get flustered. I quite agree with Sun-fu that we shouldn't waste our time on trifles, and that since the old depositors have been swallowing rumours we ought to send out the circular and make them sit up with a jerk. But the first thing we must do is to put ourselves in a strong position by reorganizing the factories and putting them on a firm footing. Now, let's get it clear in our minds which of the factories can be overhauled so as to cut down costs, and which of them should be expanded and the minimum amount of extra capital that would take. Ho-fu's just said that four or five hundred thousand dollars won't be enough, so even if we withdraw the capital now invested in government bonds we'll still be short and we'll have to find some way of making it up. But just how much is needed for expansion? How much can be saved on overheads? And how much must we be prepared to lose during the next two or three months due to a possible dull market? We must work out realistic figures to cover all these things."

"The cost of expansion has already been worked out in detail," replied Wang Ho-fu, for the factories were principally his responsibility. "It comes to a total of three hundred thousand dollars for the eight factories together. And that's an absolute minimum!"

As he said this he was wondering to himself how their government bonds were faring, since all the company's ready money of three hundred thousand dollars was invested in bonds. He turned to Wu Sun-fu and was just going to ask about the state of the stock market, when Wu Sun-fu forestalled him:

"As for the whole of the company's capital going into government bonds, we just had no choice in the matter. On the third we just bought a million, in the hope of making a bit while the going was good, but when the situation changed after that, we had to hold out in spite of ourselves until we actually turned bulls. At the moment we're holding ten million in bonds. At this morning's closing price we ought to be able to net around three hundred thousand dollars, which isn't *too* bad. Before I came round here I told our broker to sell five million first thing this afternoon."

The light of victory shone in Wu Sun-fu's eyes, and he rubbed his hands with glee.

"But Sun-fu," Wang Ho-fu chimed in hastily, looking as gleeful as Wu Sun-fu, "don't you think the rise will probably continue? Ever since the fifteenth prices have been rising steadily, even though it's only been a matter of twenty or thirty cents a day."

"I wouldn't be too sure about that!" Wu Sun-fu replied. He was smiling, but his voice was perfectly serious. He turned and looked at Sun Chi-jen with such a look of determination and confidence in his eyes as would have made the most hesitant of men decide there and then to follow him. He now spoke rapidly and clearly, and every word went home:

"Yes, the first thing we must do is to make sure our feet are on firm ground! We're fighting a battle, a battle against two enemies, one in front and one behind. Our enemy to the front is competition from the Japanese factories in Shanghai; the enemy to our rear is Chao Po-tao; and before we can get our feet on firm ground, we'll have to beat both of them! As soon as we possibly can we must put the eight new factories into decent shape by tightening up on the management, putting really efficient men in key positions, drastically cutting down waste of materials, getting rid of redundant office staff and sacking any undesirable elements among the workers! I don't doubt for one moment that the budget for every one of these factories could be cut by twenty per cent!"

"Right-o, then," said Sun Chi-jen calmly, apparently ignoring the first and more important part of Wu Sun-fu's remarks, "let's cut their budgets by twenty per cent as from next month! So far as the present office staff is concerned, I've thought all along that they're practically useless, but it's so difficult to get hold of competent people just now that we've had to keep them on; but now we must come down on them hard. Ho-fu, you're down inspecting the factories practically every day, so you must have some idea who should be the first to go."

The gleam in Wu Sun-fu's eyes — the gleam of optimism and determination to fight it out with Chao Po-tao — was now reflected in Sun Chi-jen's eyes. This was not lost on Wu Sun-fu, who seized the opportunity to press his argument home:

"I was telling you just now that we had got rid of half of our ten-million holding of bonds. Even so, it's going to be a close thing, because Chao Po-tao's all set to 'kill the bulls.' Fortunately for us, his secret leaked out today — someone who's well in with him sold me the information for a mere two thousand dollars and promised to keep us informed of his activities into the bargain! Chao Po-tao's plan is to knock the bottom out of the market just before the settlement at the end of the month. But he little thought that we should unload half of our holdings today! Tomorrow we'll get rid of the rest, and Chao Po-tao's little scheme will be knocked for six!"

As he was speaking, Wu Sun-fu sprang to his feet. He looked for all the world like some great general telling the story of a decisive battle he had won, and he was almost watering at the eyes with excitement. He smiled at his two partners and added, "We've got a better chance of beating Chao Po-tao now than we've ever had!"

The question of reorganizing the factories was then temporarily shelved, and their discussion concentrated on Chao Po-tao and government bonds. Wu Sun-fu had won his victory. He first put his own defence line in order: he made Sun Chi-jen and Wang Ho-fu realize that to speculate in government bonds and expand the factories at the same time, far from being a contradiction, was in fact a necessary step towards success; he explained to them that it would be suicidal to adopt a passive policy of "self-sufficiency" — in other words, to try to manage without financial assistance from the bankers; and he showed them that they must defeat Chao Po-tao and run the "blockade" he had engineered before they could really be sure of being able to stand their ground. In the end, Wu Sun-fu had succeeded in increasing his partners' knowledge of Chao Po-tao and ensuring their animosity towards him, thus transforming the Yi Chung Trust Company into the headquarters of the "anti-Chao camp."

Finally, they returned to the subject of reorganizing the factories. In view of what had just been said, their efforts in this direction were naturally redoubled. The reduction of staff, a wage-cut, the increasing of working hours, besides a new set of draconian regulations for putting the factories under the strictest control, were all proposed and decided on in principle in little more than ten minutes.

"Between three and five hundred workers to be discharged, then," began Wang Ho-fu, summing up, "Sunday overtime to be abolished; working day to be extended by one hour without additional pay; workers to be searched at the gate, both when coming in and going out; ten per cent of the monthly wage to be deducted by the management and retained as a deposit up to a maximum of sixty-five dollars for each worker, to be refunded in the event of discharge.... I think all these regulations can come into force immediately. Now, the last item — a ten-per-cent wage-cut — well, I'm afraid they'll kick up rough about that! The stopping of Sunday overtime is already as good as a ten-per-cent wage-cut. If we knock off another ten per cent on top of that, it's going to be the last straw, and it's quite likely they'll come out on strike, which will put us in a tight spot. I propose we shelve this suggestion for the time being — what do you say?"

Wang Ho-fu scratched his head and looked hesitantly at Wu Sun-fu, whose face was tense.

Wu Sun-fu smiled, but before he could answer Sun Chi-jen butted in, his voice betraying an unwonted excitement:

"No, no, I can't agree with you, Ho-fu! I think we're strict where we must be, and more liberal than other people wherever we can afford to be. Have you forgotten that we're going to grant a special bonus to those workers who exceed the norm which we set? Take the electric light bulb factory, for instance: the present daily quota for each worker is two hundred bulbs, which is really a very considerate norm; but a skilful, conscientious man can easily make two hundred and fifty a day. If he does, we'll give him a bonus of fifteen cents, which will mean that over a month he'll earn more than he ever did in the past."

"Yes, Chi-jen, I must agree with you that we do very well by our workers," said Wang Ho-fu, who was not to be silenced so easily. "But you must remember they're a very unreasonable lot: if you cut their wages, they notice it; if you offer them a bonus, they don't! Now, don't think I'm afraid of trouble, Sun-fu, but I really do think we should give the matter our careful consideration."

Being in charge of the eight factories, Wang Ho-fu was aware of signs of unrest that had existed among the two thousand-odd workers in them for some time.

Wu Sun-fu and Sun Chi-jen said nothing for the moment, and the room was again plunged into a silence broken only by the intermittent rumbling of trams passing under the windows, through which the rays of the setting sun picked out the snowy tablecloth and the sofa covers in a blaze of golden light.

A look of intense absorption and concentration had appeared on Wu Sun-fu's face. He was not worrying about a possible strike, for he was always having one sort of trouble or another in his own factory, and every time he had settled it without much difficulty. There was one thing he had learned from these experiences, however: that one must have loyal and competent executives in one's factory if one is to come out on top. At present, he had not any such "good" staff for any of the company's eight factories, and the problem was made all the more difficult by the fact that there was no co-ordination between the eight factories. No, Wang Ho-fu's fears could not be dismissed just like that!

It so happened that what Sun Chi-jen next said showed that he and Wu Sun-fu had been thinking along exactly the same lines.

"Yes, I think it would be all right to leave the question of a wage-cut open for a month or so; but there's no getting away from the fact that the executive staffs of the factories must be reshuffled at once! Young hotheads and old stick-in-the-muds must all go to make way for new blood! I was wondering if you could spare a few men from your own factory, Sun-fu? We must set ourselves a time-limit of one month to complete the staff changes, and then during the following month we can announce the wage-cut. But the bonus system should be introduced without delay, so that the workers realize that we're playing fair with them and that those who are more highly skilled and who work hard can earn a nice fat pay-packet!"

As he listened, Wu Sun-fu nodded his approval. Then, all of a sudden, there came the sound of heavy, hurried footsteps pounding right up to the office door, and the agitated voice of the office boy: "Who do you want to see? You can't go rushing in just like that!" The three men in the room looked up in surprise just as the door flew open and their visitor burst in; he had a bulging briefcase under his arm, and his face was bathed in perspiration. He kicked the door to behind him, and as he marched across the room he rapped out, "Yen Hsi-shan's army's on the march! Tehchow's in a state of chaos! How's Tang Yun-shan getting on in Hongkong? Have you heard from him yet?"

The intruder was Huang Fen, the famous blusterer.

Wu Sun-fu's face fell, but Wang Ho-fu laughed as he jumped up and asked quickly, "Is that true? When did you hear about it?"

"Only half an hour ago — 'course it's true!" Huang Fen

gasped, thumping the briefcase under his arm as much as to say that he had the important news stowed safely away in it, so there could be no mistake about it. "Had a wire from Yun-shan yet?"

"How about Tsinan?" Wu Sun-fu asked hastily, his bushy eyebrows now quivering with agitation. "Surely they'll have a big battle on their hands when they get to Tsinan?"

"They'll take Tsinan in a matter of four or five days. No question of a big battle there; the heaviest fighting will be along the southern part of the Tientsin-Pukow Railway!"

"A matter of four or five days, eh?" Wu Sun-fu muttered to himself. "And no heavy fighting!"

He laughed hysterically, then stepped back and flopped on to a sofa; his face had suddenly become quite ashen and a look of ferocity had come into his eyes. The military situation along the northern part of the Tientsin-Pukow line was changing much too rapidly! So rapidly, in fact, that even he could not keep pace with it, for all his alertness and agility!

The significance of the news had also struck Sun Chi-jen; he heaved a deep sigh, then glanced from Wu Sun-fu to the clock on the wall: just on four o'clock. His thoughts immediately went to the Exchange: perhaps at this very minute prices were plunging down to the limit amid the frantic yelling of the crowd! His heart pounded wildly, and he dared not think about it any more.

"Can't understand you not hearing from Yun-shan!" said Huang Fen, turning to go as abruptly as he had come. "Let me know the moment you hear anything, Ho-fu!"

Wu Sun-fu sprang to his feet again, his teeth clenched tightly together and his eyes glaring. He paced savagely round the room, then suddenly wheeled round, stopped in front of an apprehensive Wang Ho-fu and a mournful, brooding Sun Chi-jen, and said in an excited, agitated voice, "So far as I can see there's only one thing we can do — bribe the brokers to bring the settlement forward two days! Didn't Huang Fen say that they wouldn't be in Tsinan for four or five days yet? Let's say four days; that means that if we can bring the settlement forward two days we can just get it in before Tsinan falls, so that for all the rumours there won't be too rapid a slump. If the settlement's advanced by two days, that'll mean that the account will be closed in three days' time. The bears won't be able to do much tomorrow, and tomorrow we'll get rid of our remaining five million. If we can work it like this, we should be able to break even. Hm-m, I wonder what they're up to now, suddenly putting in a whole army like that?"

"Still, we're lucky to have heard about it in time," said Sun Chi-jen. "It was the same last month: we heard in good time about Chang Fa-kuei and the Kwangsi armies evacuating Changsha, and so we were able to save ourselves before the rot set in."

He said this partly to express his agreement with Wu Sun-fu's suggestion, and partly to give himself what consolation he could.

"Sun-fu, I think you're right! Let's get cracking straight away!"

Now that he had caught on to the idea, Wang Ho-fu was his usual cheerful self again; he had faith in Wu Sun-fu's resourcefulness in a crisis.

"All right," replied Wu Sun-fu, "I'll ring up Lu Kuang-shih and ask him to come round straight away. 'Man proposes, God disposes.' I think ten thousand dollars would probably do the trick."

His voice was calmer now, and as he spoke he looked up at the clock with puckered brows. Never, he thought, was the proverb "An inch of time is an inch of gold" more true than now. He smiled grimly and hurried into the "private den" next door to ring up the broker.

Wang Ho-fu and Sun Chi-jen sat silent. The latter gazed at a vase on the table in front of him, and then up at the chart on the wall: "Plans for Industrial Development." He was still fairly calm, except that he kept stroking his chin. Wang Ho-fu, however, was fidgety. He went across to the window and stood looking out for a moment, then suddenly came back and pressed the bell. After a moment a young clerk poked his head round the door and looked inquiringly at Wang Ho-fu, who beckoned him in and indicated that he should sit down at a Chinese typewriter under the window. When the typist had sat down, Wang Ho-fu said:

"Now, type as I dictate. 'New Bonus System. As an experiment... in scientific management... with a view to increasing production....' — Come on, slow-coach! Can't you go quicker than that? '— with a view to increasing production... and in order to encourage good workers... we have decided... to adopt... the following new system....' Come on, don't dawdle! ... 'the following new system' — got it? Now, new paragraph. ..."

"What's the news, Sun-fu?" Sun Chi-jen suddenly demanded. Wang Ho-fu abandoned his typist and whirled round to find Wu Sun-fu standing by the table, his hands clasped in front of his chest and a look of exasperation on his face. Wang Ho-fu grunted, then turned and snapped at the typist's back:

"That's all! You can go now!"

When the three of them were alone again, Wu Sun-fu muttered through clenched teeth, "Half a dollar down already!"

Wang Ho-fu felt the blood freeze in his veins, and Sun Chi-jen heaved a sigh. Wu Sun-fu took a couple of steps forward, his head on his chest. When he looked up again, his eyes were fierce.

"The session closed with a drop of half a dollar," he muttered. "Our five million was unloaded first thing, when the quotation was even five cents higher than the closing quotation of the morning session. After that, the rot set in. We'll probably make a profit of about a hundred and twenty or thirty thousand dollars on the first five million, but it's a job to say whether we'll make anything on the other five million. 'Man proposes, God disposes.'"

"Don't you believe it!" said Sun Chi-jen. He forced a smile, but his voice trembled slightly. "There's still tomorrow! Let's push ahead with our original plan. It's man that does the disposing!"

"That's quite right!" echoed Wang Ho-fu, though without Sun Chi-jen's smile. "It's man who does the disposing, and we've still got tomorrow!"

Suddenly he turned, pulled the unfinished notice about the "bonus system" out of the typewriter and flourished it at his partners.

"As for the factories," he cried, "we'll get cracking on them tomorrow: discharge of three to five hundred workers, no working overtime on Sundays, working day to be increased by one hour without extra pay, a deposit to be stopped out of wages, and last but not least... a ten-per-cent wage-cut! I'll put up the notice tomorrow morning. And if the workers cut up rough? Huh! We'll bloody well close down the factories for a couple of weeks and see how they like that! And, of course, all this will apply to the silk goods factory on loan from Chen Chun-yi!"

"That's the stuff! 'Man disposes!' Go ahead, Ho-fu!" Wu Sun-fu and Sun Chi-jen simultaneously voiced their approval. Three pairs of eyes now gleamed with an iron determination to squeeze out of the nine factories, by every means in their power, compensation for their possible loss on the Stock Exchange: it was their only way out!

*

It was nine o'clock when Wu Sun-fu arrived home. He was dead-beat. It was a muggy evening, with a sky full of stars, and a slender, almost invisible crescent moon. Only in the shade of the trees was there any suggestion of a breeze. His wife and several others had come out into the garden for a breath of fresh air, leaving the house in darkness except for two lighted windows on the second floor, so that the building looked like some great monster crouching in the gloom, while the two windows were its gleaming, ravening eyes.

Mrs. Wu and her three companions were sitting under the trees fringing the pond. Only one or two of the lights fixed on the trees were on, and their clothes showed white against the dark background of the trees. They were silent except for an occasional faint sigh.

Suddenly Lin Pei-shan broke into a dreamy rendering of the melancholy popular song *Ramona*; then suddenly she stopped again.

Ah-hsuan gave a low, despairing laugh.

A carp splashed in the pond.

Huei-fang was quite taken by the tune Lin Pei-shan had begun singing, for it echoed her mood exactly. She thought how lucky people were who could sing. Singing was another way of speak-

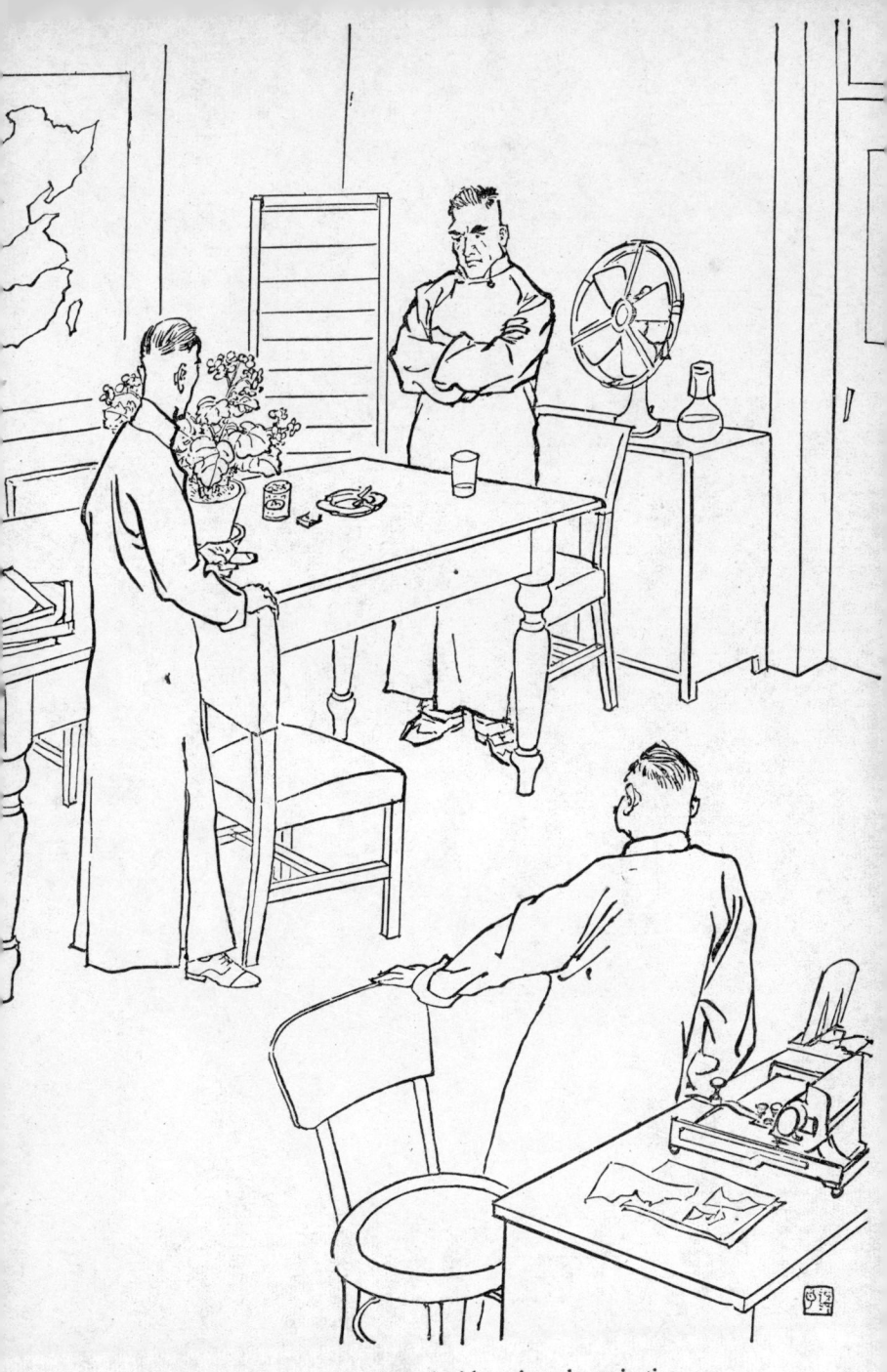

Three pairs of eyes now gleamed with an iron determination to squeeze out of the nine factories, by every means in their power, compensation for their possible loss on the Stock Exchange....

ing. When you had something you wanted to say, and no way of saying it, and you sang, it was as if you were telling a dear friend your inmost thoughts. She thought of what Fan Po-wen had said to her that day, and in her pounding heart she felt happy and afraid.

A pall of silence hung over the pond and over the four people on the bank, each of whom was savouring the silence according to his or her own individual mood. Suddenly, the silence was shattered by an uproar which flooded outwards from some distant storm-centre and swept over the group at the edge of the pond. It was the angry voice of Wu Sun-fu raging and storming in the house.

"Let's have some lights on here! It's enough to give you the creeps!"

When the lights went on, his pyjama-clad figure was suddenly visible in the blaze of light. He was standing on the veranda in front of the drawing-room windows, looking angrily all round as if seeking something to vent his rage on. The bath had washed away his tiredness, but inside him there still seethed a volcano of anger. He caught sight of the four white figures by the pond: "Creeping about there like four ghosts!" he thought, and a sudden fury welled up inside him. Just then the maid Wang Mah happened to walk past him carrying a tray of tea-things and heading for the pond. Immediately seizing this opportunity to let himself go, he roared at her:

"Wang Mah! What are you going out there for?"

"Madame and the others are sitting out there by the pond —"

Without waiting for her to finish, he waved her impatiently away, then turned and stalked back into the drawing-room. He suddenly realized how ridiculous he had just made himself by his display of bad temper. It was not at all like him to behave like this, he thought. The glare of the lights in the drawing-room, however, only served to make him more bad-tempered than ever, and every bulb seemed to be a little furnace scorching and blistering his skin. To make things worse, there was not a single servant in attendance there. "Where have they all sneaked off to?" he muttered. "Lazy good-for-nothings!" Furious, he bounded out on to the front steps and roared:

"Come here, somebody! Blast you!"

"Here we are, sir!" came two voices simultaneously from the bottom of the steps. As a matter of fact, the butler, Kao Sheng, and Li Kuei, one of the footmen, had been waiting round the corner all the time. Wu Sun-fu was taken aback by their sudden appearance, and just fixed them with a stony stare while he tried to think of something to say to them. After a moment he hit on something.

"Kao Sheng! Did you ring up Mr. Tu Wei-yueh and ask him to come round as I told you? Why hasn't he turned up yet?"

"Yes, I rang him, sir; but didn't you say you wanted him over at ten, sir? Mr. Tu said he was busy but that he could get here by half past — "

"Nonsense!" Wu Sun-fu interrupted with a sudden fury. "What do you mean, 'half past'! Don't tell me you agreed to half past ten?"

From the direction of the pond came the dreamy strains of Lin Pei-shan's melancholy *Ramona*. The effect on Wu Sun-fu's anger was to pour oil on the flames. He stamped his foot, ground his teeth and raved at Kao Sheng, "You blasted idiot! Go and ring him up again and tell him to come round at once!"

He threw the last few words over his shoulder as he stalked off fuming towards the pond, leaving Kao Sheng and Li Kuei gazing open-mouthed at each other.

The romantic, melancholy atmosphere among the group by the pond suddenly became still and tense: every one of them could sense the approach of the "storm-centre," and they prepared themselves for an outburst of gratuitous invective. The nimble-witted Lin Pei-shan darted away and hid in the trees, where she put her hand over her mouth to stifle a laugh and peeped out, straining her ears and eyes. Ah-hsuan, who was not over-bright on occasions like this, just stood there going through the motions of throwing a recently-acquired and highly-prized throwing-knife. His sister Huei-fang had become suddenly absorbed in watching the carp which kept rising to the surface of the pond and sending up bubbles. Mrs. Wu, who knew what was coming, lolled lazily against the back of her chair with a smile on her lips.

Wu Sun-fu, however, did not flare up at once. He frowned

and narrowed his eyes and looked around as if selecting a victim to get his teeth into. Actually, he really did feel like biting! He felt that only by "getting his teeth into" someone could he work off the rage that had consumed him ever since his return home. Such a "bite" would not, of course, be a real one, but it would afford him the same relief as a physical bite. He glared round for a moment until his eyes fell on the thing in Ah-hsuan's hand. Like the mousing cat that stalks in silence and keeps her sharp teeth and claws hidden, he asked in a quiet voice:

"Ah-hsuan, what's that you've got in your hand?"

Ah-hsuan was so flustered that, instead of answering, he just held out his precious throwing-knife for his elder brother's inspection.

"What the devil's this! Who teaches you to play about with this sort of thing?"

Wu Sun-fu was fierce both in look and voice, but Ah-hsuan's manner was so laugh-provoking that the former precariously parted his lips for a second.

"Er — Old Kuan is teaching me to use it," Ah-hsuan stammered, withdrawing his throwing-knife and turning to slip away; but Wu Sun-fu peremptorily called him to a halt.

"Stop! Where do you think you're going? 'Throwing-knife' indeed! Get rid of it! Throw it in the pond! A young fellow turned seventeen and still wasting your time on such nonsense as this! The trouble is, you've been spoiled down in the country! The summer holidays are nearly over and you ought to be thinking about getting ready to go back to school! Go on, throw it in the pond!"

There was a heavy splash, and Ah-hsuan gazed miserably at the ripples spreading out above his precious knife.

Wu Sun-fu's irascibility appeared to have abated somewhat, for his frown disappeared. His hard eyes turned next to his sister Huei-fang. He was well aware that she had been getting much more friendly with Fan Po-wen lately — quite the reverse of what he wished! As he remembered this, another wave of anger swept over him. Nevertheless, he turned away from her and looked at his wife again. She was leaning back in the chair and gazing up bemusedly at the stars in the sky. Just lately she had seemed to be pining away, and even her eyes, once so sparkling and eloquent, had now acquired a vacant stare; when, occasionally, they recaptured their old vividness it was only to blaze with anger. Something seemed to be continually gnawing at her heart. And this change had come over her so slowly that Wu Sun-fu had never noticed it. Once or twice he had had a vague feeling that all was not well with her, but he had dismissed it and immediately forgotten it. Now he seemed to be realizing it for the first time, and the sudden discovery only intensified his exasperation. He immediately abandoned Huei-fang and turned his attention to his wife.

"Pei-yao," he said sharply, "you don't have to stand on ceremony with my own brother and sister! If they do anything wrong you shouldn't try to shield them! I don't like all this hole-and-corner business!"

His wife stared absently at him, smiling but silent, which only made him all the more incensed. He snorted savagely and went on grimly, "Take Huei-fang for instance. I'm not an old-fashioned diehard, and when it comes to a question of marriage I'm all for taking account of the views of the people concerned. But I, too, have a right to be consulted, to see whether it's a good match on both sides or not. It's no use trying to go behind my back! As a matter of fact, I've been giving a lot of thought to this matter, and somebody has actually approached me about arranging a match for her; but you people have to go behind my back and make a mess of it — you're going to make us look a pack of fools!"

"Well, this sounds a bit strange to me," said his wife, feeling she ought to make some protest. "I don't understand what you mean about making a mess! If you've a suitable man in mind, you might at least let us know who it is!"

He made no answer, but turned abruptly to his sister and said sternly.

"Huei-fang, if you've got anything to say on the subject, let's hear it. We must get things straight so that I know what to do."

Huei-fang hung her head till her chin rested on her chest; there was not a single word from her in reply. Her heart was pounding wildly. She was afraid of her brother, and she hated him.

"All right, then: if you've no ideas of your own, I'll arrange everything for you!"

Wu Sun-fu felt the satisfaction of an archer in ambush whose arrow has struck down an enemy. With a triumphant laugh he turned and walked away. By the time he reached his study, this crumb of satisfaction had evaporated, and he again felt the need to "bite" someone — not just to relieve his pent-up rage, as he had done a moment ago — but to "bite" at his real enemy in any way he could to compensate himself for his loss. His angry mood had passed, and it was in a cool, stubborn, relentless frame of mind that he now set himself to the problem of making a desperate attempt to fight his way out of the net which was closing around him; but almost immediately he was gripped by a dismal feeling of frustration and despair. His heart now leapt with excitement, now sank into a torpor of despondency. His spinning brain seemed no longer to obey his will: he was just recalling the momentous decisions he and his partners had made in the managing director's office of the Yi Chung Trust Company, when suddenly he was assailed by a vision of Liu Yu-ying's seductive smile, her blush as she flashed her eyes at him, and the echo of the murmured temptation: "What shall I call you when you come to see me . . . ?" And just as he was cheerfully deciding how to dispose his forces for a resounding attack on the eight factories, he suddenly found himself faced with the prospect of the two thousand-odd workers rising up in a desperate counter-attack. . . .

No matter how he tried, he just could not concentrate; especially when the memory of Liu Yu-ying's inviting smile, her lovely voice and her limpid eyes kept hammering away at his brain and distracting him as he tried to wrestle with his business problems. This was madness! It was just not like him to lose his head over a pretty face!

"Bah!" he roared, suddenly leaping to his feet and crashing his fist on the table. "You Jezebel!"

" — bel!" echoed the walls of the study. The trees outside the window rustled as if they were laughing at his vexation and confusion. He collapsed into his chair again and gritted his teeth in an effort to pull himself together and shake off this shameful weakness and decadence that had taken possession of him and rid himself of this feeling of pessimism and despair.

At this juncture the door opened softly and Tu Wei-yueh appeared; he stood drawn up to his full height for a moment, then bowed gravely. He turned to close the door behind him, then walked calmly up to Wu Sun-fu's desk and looked at him with eyes that were placid yet alert.

For fully two or three minutes neither of them spoke.

Wu Sun-fu reached out and extracted a document from a pile on the desk. He bent over as if he were perusing it, then picked up a pen and twirled it in his fingers, so as to give himself time to compose his features and recover his self-possession. After a moment he looked up and indicated that Tu Wei-yueh should sit down. His tone was casual and there was a smile on his lips as he began, "I understand you said you were going to be very busy the first time I rang. Are you free now?"

"Quite free," came his laconic answer; but his twinkling eyes spoke volumes. They seemed to intimate that he was quite aware that Wu Sun-fu had been just having a fit of temper and depression, and that his present air of studied nonchalance was nothing more than a pose — it was the slow circling of a hawk before it swoops to the kill.

Wu Sun-fu lowered his eyes so that the young man should not be able to read his thoughts. Still twirling the pen between his fingers, he said, "I hear they're having trouble with the workers in some of the factories in Hongkew. Do you think anything will come of it? And if anything does happen, do you think it might affect our factories in Chapei?"

"Hard to say."

This answer was one word longer than the first one, and Tu Wei-yueh smiled guardedly as he made it. Wu Sun-fu looked swiftly up and roared with what looked like feigned surprise, "What! You sit there and say 'Hard to say'! I should have thought you would have stuck out your chest and said 'No fear of that in *our* factories!' I don't want to hear you say 'Hard to say.' What I want to hear is 'I'm sure of it!' All right!"

"I could have said that in the first place, but the moment I came in I smelt a rat — I guessed that you had orders for a wage-cut to give me, so I changed my mind and said 'Hard to say.' Since you now want me to say 'I'm sure of it,' well, all right, I am!"

Wu Sun-fu listened attentively, while his eyes scanned Tu Wei-yueh's imperturbable face. After a short pause he asked, "Have you made all necessary arrangements?"

"Still one or two things to see to — nothing much, though. Of course, sir, when the axe falls, there's bound to be a certain amount of resistance; but within a day or two — three days at the most — everything will be under control. Though it may be —"

"What!" interrupted Wu Sun-fu. "You mean they might go on strike? And for three days at that? No, I won't have it! If they dare start any trouble, I must have it settled the same day! D'you hear? The same day! And what were you saying about 'It may be'? It may be that the strike will last more than three days, I suppose!"

His voice was harsh as he said this, though his expression remained calm and unruffled.

"It may be," replied Tu Wei-yueh with a mocking smile, "that a single spark of trouble in our factory would set off a general strike involving every silk filature in Shanghai!"

This was the fateful ladle of oil, so to speak, and the smouldering fires of Wu Sun-fu's anger, which he had been managing to control all this time, suddenly burst into flame. He flung down his pen and with blazing eyes raved at Tu Wei-yueh:

"I don't give a damn whether it means a general strike or not! If there's the slightest hint of trouble in *my* factory, I'll have it settled the same day without any ifs or buts!"

"In that case you'll have to resort to force —"

"Quite! That's just what I will do!"

"All right, in that case, sir, I must ask permission to resign!"

As he said this, Tu Wei-yueh stood up and fixed Wu Sun-fu with a hard, fearless stare. A brief silence. Wu Sun-fu's expression changed gradually from amazement to cool indifference. Finally, he asked impatiently, "So you don't like the idea of using force, eh? Afraid?"

"Not a bit of it! Now, honestly, Mr. Wu: have I ever shown any signs of being afraid? I don't mind telling you, I think I've put more than my share of hard work into the factory in the past month, and I refuse to be a party to undoing all that I've achieved through a solid month's planning and effort! Still, you're the boss, and it's up to you to do what you think best. All I ask is that you accept my immediate resignation! And may I repeat that I'm not in the least afraid!"

He squared his shoulders proudly and riveted his keen eyes on Wu Sun-fu's face.

"I'm well aware that you've been making all these plans and arrangements. I now intend to put them to the test and see if they work!"

"All right, Mr. Wu; since you know all about it, let me tell you one thing more. You say I must use force and settle any trouble the same day. Nothing simpler: police, detectives, security guards — they're all ready and at our disposal. But if we settle the trouble today, and it breaks out again in ten days or a couple of weeks' time, I don't think you'd be at all happy about it. Besides, I just couldn't bring myself to betray your trust in me by doing as you say — in fact, my present position of trust means a great deal to me."

For a while Wu Sun-fu could think of nothing to say. He picked up his pen again, twirled it between his fingers, and sat staring at Tu Wei-yueh's face for quite a while. Tu Wei-yueh, his face betraying not the faintest trace of emotion, was quite content to let him look, though he was secretly rather surprised at Wu Sun-fu's unaccustomed hesitation.

After some deliberation, Wu Sun-fu asked at length, "Well, what do *you* think we should do?"

"Well, I'm in favour of using a little force myself — but not till the very end! Our workers aren't all cast in the same mould. Some of them are a bad influence — Communists, most likely — and some of the more stupid of the workers just tag along with them; but the majority are timid and don't want to get into trouble. The reason I ask for three days to finish the job is because three days of unrest will give me an excellent opportunity of finding out for sure just who these suspected Communists are, and then netting them all at one fell swoop! That's where the use of a little force comes in! After that, I think we can be sure of peace and quiet for six months at least. This is what I've been working so hard for for the last month!"

Tu Wei-yueh had spoken calmly and self-confidently, a smile on his lips; Wu Sun-fu had listened with concentrated attention, but now he suddenly rolled his eyes upwards and laughed grimly, then jumped up and roared excitedly:

"You may be very clever, Wei-yueh, but there are still certain things that you don't understand. You can't make a clean sweep of them just like that! They're like moths in a fur in the rainy season — they just keep appearing one after the other! You catch them all today, but tomorrow there's another lot there! All you can do is to wait until the rainy season is over. Unfortunately, we're just coming into a 'rainy season' now, and it's going to be a long, long time — nobody knows just how long — before it's over! Well, that's that: your little plan will have to keep for the time being. We just can't afford that kind of patience as things are at present!"

Tu Wei-yueh bowed but said nothing. He was thinking that with this reverse his fate was surely sealed. If he did not resign, his "régime" in the factory was doomed, and Chien Pao-sheng and his clique would step into his shoes. Suddenly, Wu Sun-fu flew into a rage again. His face dark with anger, he barked out his orders:

"I don't care whether there's a strike or not, or whether there's a general strike for that matter. My mind's made up! Starting next month, there's going to be a twenty-per-cent wage-cut! If the price of silk goes up to over nine hundred taels a picul again, I may consider a wage-increase. Very well, you can go now! And I won't allow you to resign!"

"In that case, Mr. Wu, you must give me three days to do the job!"

"Out of the question!" Wu Sun-fu bellowed. "I can't even give you one day!"

Tu Wei-yueh's face twitched and his eyes glinted dangerously. Quite unexpectedly, Wu Sun-fu's manner suddenly changed again; he gestured impatiently and said, "Idiot! Thinking you can tie me down! Wait until they're gone on strike first, and then we'll see about it."

Tu Wei-yueh smiled and bowed again, but said nothing. He could see quite clearly that Wu Sun-fu was not his usual self — he seemed slightly abnormal, slightly flustered. And then he remembered that he himself was probably heading for disaster. But he was tough, and there was plenty of fight left in him yet.

XIII

THERE had been no lightning yet, only an occasional rumble of thunder like the sound of a heavily-laden lorry passing by. Overhead hung a canopy of grey, unbroken but for a rift in the western sky, where a minute patch of purple cloud showed through. Behind this purple cloud a disconcerted sun was dropping down towards the horizon.

In the workshop of the Yu Hua Silk Filature all the lights were already on. Spindles and fingers moved so quickly that the workshop seemed to be one great nervously-pulsating machine. The electric lights showed sallow-faced through the dense clouds of steam, as if on the verge of fainting away. The women, their ears dulled by the eternal noise of the machines, could not hear the rumbles of thunder from the sky outside, but they could still hear the babble of their own excited voices; here, too, was an ominous growl of thunder, but of a different kind. Their faces were flushed, and their tongues were as busy as their hands. The foremen and forewomen seemed to be pretending to be deaf — though not pretending to be dumb — and when they occasionally muttered something a chorus of jeers burst from the women.

All of a sudden the hooter blared through the factory, and there was a commotion in the workshop. As the sound of the filatures gradually died down the voices seemed to get louder. The women jostled out of the workshop with their empty lunch-baskets on their arms, milled around at the gate waiting to be searched, and then swarmed out into the roadway. It was only then that they realized that it was thundering and that an overcast sky awaited them with its promise of a storm.

All was silent now in the factory, and the lights in the workshop were off, which made those that streamed from the windows of the offices seem all the brighter. Tu Wei-yueh was sitting in his office with bent head. The 32-watt bulb above him threw a pale light on his face, which was as expressionless as that of a statue. Suddenly the door opened, and Mo Kan-cheng's flustered face appeared round the edge of the door. He came in and said in a low voice:

"Look here, Wei-yueh, Mr. Wu's just rung up to ask whether the notice about the wage-cut's been put up yet. I told him you were going to do it tomorrow, and he didn't sound at all pleased about it! What are you going to do about it? The women were kicking up a row when they knocked off just now; they must have got wind of it the same as they did last time —"

"So what?" said Tu Wei-yueh with a smile. "They've got to know sooner or later!" He glanced at Mo Kan-cheng, then looked out of the window.

"If Mr. Wu cuts up rough about it tomorrow, don't blame me!"

"Of course not!"

Tu Wei-yueh was becoming impatient. Mo Kan-cheng fixed his beady eyes on Tu Wei-yueh's face for a moment, then hunched up his shoulders; pulling a face as much as to say, "I should worry!" he turned on his heel and went out, slamming the door behind him.

Tu Wei-yueh smiled unconcernedly, but he could not go on sitting there as motionless as a statue; he fished out his watch and glanced at it, looked out of the window once more, then opened the door and went out. He was just walking away when his sharp eyes caught sight of two figures hurrying through the gloom. They went straight into his office, and he retraced his steps. Just as he reached the doorway someone came up behind him, tapped him on the shoulder, and giggled.

"Now, Ah Chen!" he whispered over his shoulder. "No skylarking. We're on our best behaviour tonight!"

He went into his office, and she followed behind him.

The two men waiting in the room were Kuei Chang-lin and Pockmarked Li. The moment they saw Tu Wei-yueh, they both uttered an excited "Ah!" and tried to get a word in first; but Tu

Wei-yueh checked them with a look and waved the two of them and Ah Chen to a bench in the corner of the room, while he himself went and stood with his back to the window. The electric light seemed suddenly dimmer, and the atmosphere in the room was tense. Outside, thunder rolled slowly across the sky. A little colour had returned to Tu Wei-yueh's pale face. He glanced at his three companions.

"Hm! Where's Yao Chin-feng got to?"

"We didn't bring her along in case we attracted too much attention," Ah Chen put in hastily. "If you've got a job for her, I can easily pass it on to her later." As she spoke, she threw Tu Wei-yueh a coquettish glance. He nodded briefly, but said nothing; nor did he return her amorous glance. His expression suddenly became grim and he raised his voice slightly.

"From now on we must all put our backs into it and work together! There's to be no more chasing after girls, no more petty jealousies, and no more squabbling among ourselves!"

Ah Chen pulled a face and hemmed. Pretending not to have noticed this, Tu Wei-yueh went on:

"Wang Chin-chen is unable to come, because I've sent her off on something else; so there will be just the four of us in on this discussion. Well, a short while ago, Mr. Wu rang up to see why I hadn't put the notice up yet. He's getting pretty het-up about it and he didn't sound at all pleased. I promised I'd announce the wage-cut tomorrow for sure. Mr. Wu understands, of course, that we need a little time to finish making all our arrangements before the cut is announced. We shouldn't have any trouble coming to terms with *him* all right, but I can see our rivals trying to get round him and cutting the ground from under our feet; so I think we must use seventy per cent of our strength against them and thirty per cent of it against the women! Chang-lin, do you think we'll have trouble when the notice goes up tomorrow?"

"No doubt about it! Chien Pao-sheng and his lot are just spoiling for a fight and they'll make the most of this to try and put paid to us! Dirty rats!"

"Mr. Tu!" put in Pockmarked Li quickly when he saw that Kuei Chang-lin had no suggestions for definite action. "We've only got to get my lads in, and then if there's any trouble tomorrow we won't stand any nonsense — we'll just run 'em down to the police station and see how they like that! If we're nippy about it we can get it over before Chien Pao-sheng and them have a chance to do the dirty on us!"

Highly pleased with himself, he held out his great paws, spat into them, rubbed them together, clenched them into fists, placed them on his knees, and adopted an aggressive attitude. Tu Wei-yueh paid no attention to all this; he just smiled faintly and turned again to Ah Chen.

"Ah Chen! Why don't you say something? What were things like in the workshop when you were there just now? How did the women react to the rumour we put out about the wage-cut? What did Hsueh Pao-chu and that girl Chou Erh-chieh have to say about it? Well, let's hear it! Don't keep us waiting!"

"I don't know!" Ah Chen snapped, pursing her lips and turning her face away to look at the wall. "You'd better have Yao Chin-feng in and ask her about it!"

Tu Wei-yueh's face suddenly darkened. Kuei Chang-lin and Pockmarked Li were amused and began making faces at Ah Chen to tease her. His eyes blazing, Tu Wei-yueh stamped his foot and was just going to let himself go, when Ah Chen gave in and said crossly:

"What did they say? They said, 'Down with Chamber-pot Tu!' — meaning you! What did Hsueh Pao-chu and Chou Erh-chieh say? They said, 'Chamber-pot Tu is playing a dirty trick on us!' and a lot of other nice things, but I can't remember them all now — you've got nothing to laugh about, Chang-lin! They want to get rid of you, too!"

Outside the windows the first flash of lightning lit up the sky. A few seconds later a rumble of thunder was heard in the distance. Suddenly, a violent gust of wind swept into the room, and the four of them gave a shiver.

A roar of indignation leapt to Pockmarked Li's lips, but Tu Wei-yueh silenced him with a wave of the hand and said imperturbably:

"We've got solid proof that Chien Pao-sheng and his lot are trying to put a spoke in our wheel. What are we going to do about it? Last night I told Mr. Wu that I wanted to resign, but he wouldn't hear of it for a moment. So all I can do is carry on. Strictly speaking, disputes between different groups in the trade union are none of my business; but I believe in seeing fair play! Frankly, I think Kuei Chang-lin and his supporters are being treated really badly and that Chien Pao-sheng's being too high-handed. Don't you agree with me, Li?"

"You're dead right! Down with Chien Pao-sheng!" chorused Pockmarked Li and Kuei Chang-lin, while Ah Chen giggled with her hand over her mouth. Tu Wei-yueh squared his shoulders, took a deep breath, and went on:

"It's not that we want to make things difficult for Mr. Wu, but the fact remains that Chien Pao-sheng and his crew are working for their own ends under the pretence of helping the workers, and making use of them to establish their own power. We shan't have a day's peace all the time they remain here. We're all suffering merely to serve their selfish ends, which is grossly unfair! Tomorrow they'll be trying to set the women against us. Very well, we'll take them on! Once we've got Chien Pao-sheng and his gang out of the factory, we can then deal with the strike, if there is one. In three days it'll all be over — three days at the outside!"

"Ah, but in the workshop today they got round the women so well that a lot of them are on their side now," said Ah Chen, pursing her lips. Kuei Chang-lin immediately knit his brows in a worried frown. He had never had much influence with the workwomen, and the little footing he had recently acquired among them was due entirely to Tu Wei-yueh's efforts. Tu Wei-yueh's shrewd eyes saw through him at a glance; he snorted contemptuously and despised him for being such a broken reed. He returned his gaze to the uncouth Pockmarked Li, with his glaring eyes and his tightly-clenched fists, the undisguised and distinctive badges of his kind, indicating that he was ready to fight for whoever would pay him. Tu Wei-yueh was satisfied with this man. He took a step forward, so that he was standing right under the light, and said to Ah Chen:

"So the women believe what Chien Pao-sheng tells them, eh? Now, Ah Chen! Don't tell me that you with your smooth tongue can't beat Hsueh Pao-chu! And can't Yao Chin-feng go one better than Chou Erh-chieh? If those two can pull the wool over the women's eyes, why can't you two do it as well? If the workwomen don't yet realize that Chou Erh-chieh is one of Chien Pao-sheng's cat's-paws, why should you imagine that they know you're on our side? It's not as if you've got the word 'spy' branded on your forehead! Surely you can easily unmask Chou Erh-chieh and let them see her for what she is? Now off you go, Ah Chen, and tell Yao Chin-feng what's got to be done. Get around among the women and stir them up against Chien Pao-sheng, Hsueh Pao-chu, and Chou Erh-chieh. Don't worry about them going on strike tomorrow! Now look snappy! Later on I'll get some others to back you up. You'll get a first-class 'merit' for it!"

"Who do you think cares a straw for your 'merits'? I'm doing my job and I'll be satisfied if everybody plays fair!"

Ah Chen stood up, and as she went out she threw Tu Wei-yueh a deliberately disdainful look. Tu Wei-yueh stood with his head on one side for a moment, thinking; then he stepped up to Pockmarked Li, clapped him on the back, and asked in an undertone, "Look here, old man! Can you round up twenty of your lads for tonight?"

"You bet!" said Pockmarked Li, leaping to his feet, his face glowing with joy and his saliva generously splashing Tu Wei-yueh's face. "Twenty, you say? Easy get you fifty if you like!" Tu Wei-yueh smiled.

"Excellent! Though twenty'll do for tonight. I want them to walk around the women's huts — get it? Just walk around and not get involved in any quarrels. There are just two girls I want shadowed — Ho Hsiu-mei and Chang Ah-hsin. Chang Ah-hsin's the girl with a flat face and big breasts; know the one I mean? And I'll want your twenty chaps back here at the factory tomorrow morning. What's the work? Let you know in the morning. And now go round to Mr. Mo and take a hundred dollars. All right, that's all."

Only Tu Wei-yueh and Kuei Chang-lin were left in the room now, and for a while neither of them spoke. The thunder reverberating across the sky was louder now, but more leisurely, like the subdued rumble of a night-soil cart on its early-morning rounds. There was a flash of lightning every two or three minutes, but it was no more than a brief flicker. The wind was rising now, and the lights hanging from the ceiling were swinging in the breeze. Outside the windows it was pitch dark. Tu Wei-yueh glanced at his watch: it was just on half past seven.

"Mr. Tu, if we have a strike and it drags on a long time, I think we'll probably be the losers," Kuei Chang-lin said slowly and quietly, and with a tone of ill-concealed pessimism in his voice. "Those three new men in the general office — Tseng, Ma, and that distant nephew of Mr. Wu's — they're all running you down behind your back. Seems to me they're well in with Chien Pao-sheng."

Tu Wei-yueh shrugged and smiled. He was afraid of nothing. Narrowing one of his beady eyes, Kuei Chang-lin went on in a dismal voice, "You forgot to warn Pockmarked Li not to let on in front of Ah Hsiang. That was a mistake. I've always suspected that this fellow Ah Hsiang is spying on us for Chien Pao-sheng. Though Pockmarked Li is very thick with him."

"Chang-lin, you're too timid ever to make a go of anything big! We're hard pressed for helpers just now, and so we'll just have to take certain chances. Don't worry about Ah Hsiang: I can take care of him all right! The real difficulty lies with the women. I've given the Old Man my word that I'll end the strike within three days if it comes, and that I'll make a clean sweep of all the trouble-makers at the same time, so that there won't be any more strikes for the next six months. So we'll let them go on strike tomorrow — anyway, we couldn't stop them even if we wanted to — but I've decided that we shouldn't use force tomorrow. We'll give them their heads for a couple of days, so that they'll have plenty of time to finish off Chien Pao-sheng and his lot, and then we'll settle *their* hash in no uncertain manner! So you see, Chang-lin, you have to put your best foot forward and work the majority of the women round on to your side."

"Shall I tell my people to pretend they're against the wage-cut, then?"

"Yes, of course. We'll settle Ho Hsiu-mei and her lot first, and then we'll be able to kid the women into going back to work; after that we can talk terms with them. I'm perfectly certain Ho Hsiu-mei and Chang Ah-hsin are the trouble-makers, but there must be others besides, and it's up to us to find out who they are. I'm giving you the job of finding out, Chang-lin, and I want you to report back to me tomorrow."

As he said this, Tu Wei-yueh glanced at his watch again, then dismissed Kuei Chang-lin and left the office himself.

Flashes of lightning lit up the dark, cloudy sky, whose uniform leaden gloom had by now broken up into patches of black and grey. Great, solid banks of cloud, anvil-topped, towered up like a range of mountains, black at the bases and grey at the summits. The thunder was now even louder than before. Tu Wei-yueh cut across an open space piled high with wooden boxes and came to a small building. This was the office where Wu Sun-fu interviewed his office staff when visiting the factory. It was normally unoccupied, but just now glimmers of light showed through the cracks of the tightly-closed slatted shutters. When Tu Wei-yueh pushed the door open and went in, the two people in the room stood up. He smiled and signed to them to sit down again and asked one of them, who was Wang Chin-chen, forewoman No. 2:

"Have you told her yet?"

"No, we've only just this minute arrived, and I thought you'd like to speak to her yourself, Mr. Tu," replied Wang Chin-chen mysteriously. She winked at Tu Wei-yueh and stood up as if to go, but Tu Wei-yueh waved her back to her seat, at the same time turning to look at the young factory girl who sat there very ill at ease. She was a girl of about twenty with bobbed hair and of middling height. Her skin was dark, but she had a lovely complexion and lively, sparkling eyes. She blushed hotly under Tu Wei-yueh's compelling gaze.

When he had stared at her for a while he smiled and said gently, "Chu Kuei-ying, you've been here for almost two years. You're very good at your work and you're well-behaved. I've mentioned your name to the proprietor, and we're thinking of making you a forewoman. This will be a special promotion in your case, as I expect you'll appreciate."

Chu Kuei-ying did not reply, but sat with crimson cheeks and downcast eyes. Her heart was pounding and her mind was in a whirl, for when Wang Chin-chen had gone to fetch her she had only told her that she was wanted in the office, and she had supposed that she was going to be on the carpet for expressing her opposition to the wage-cut before she knocked off work, and that some informer must have reported her. Now it turned out that they wanted to promote her, and she did not know what to think. Besides, this man in charge of the factory, Tu Wei-yueh, had once been in the habit of pestering her with his attentions at every opportunity, so perhaps he was just trying to get round her by doing this. When this thought struck her, she felt more tongue-tied than ever. Now Wang Chin-chen put in a word to help persuade her.

"Mr. Wu is really being very fair and Mr. Tu is trying to help you, too, but they wouldn't do it if it wasn't that you deserve it, Kuei-ying!"

"Wang Chin-chen's right, you know," said Tu Wei-yueh in the same gentle voice, while his keen eyes looked her up and down. "Mr. Wu's a fair man and he's very considerate. He often says that if it had not been for the drop in silk prices, which meant that he would make a loss, he would gladly have agreed to a cost-of-living allowance last time. And if it were not for the fact that prices have recently dropped even lower, the idea of a wage-cut would never have entered his head! Although he's making a loss, Mr. Wu still sees to it that those who work hard and behave themselves are fairly treated. That's why you're getting special promotion!"

Although Chu Kuei-ying still hung her head, she was conscious of his eye on her. When she had finally made up her mind, she looked up, her face now white, and said quietly but firmly:

"Thank you very much, Mr. Tu, but this sort of thing is not for me!"

Just then there was a flash of lightning and a sudden crash of thunder right overhead which seemed to shake the room.

Tu Wei-yueh winced, but whether because of the sudden noise, or whether because of her reply, it was not clear. Knitting his brows, he tipped Wang Chin-chen a wink. She nodded and pulled a face, then slipped quietly out. Chu Kuei-ying immediately stood up, but Tu Wei-yueh stopped her.

"Mr. Tu! What do you want me for now?"

"What's the hurry? I've got something more to tell you yet —"

Chu Kuei-ying blushed furiously. She was now quite certain that he was out for a spot of philandering. She had not disliked him before when he had been a junior clerk in the factory, but ever since his promotion to his present position as the most powerful man in the office she had felt as if a high mountain had sprung up between them, and had been very ill at ease at having to talk with him more than she could help. And now he had tricked her into coming here, and was refusing to let her go!

"I don't want to hear it!" she said, fixing him with a stare and standing her ground. "You can have me into the office tomorrow and tell me then!"

"You needn't be afraid," he said with a sardonic smile. "I always behave myself with women: I don't flirt with them and I don't take advantage of them! All I wanted was to find out why you don't want to be promoted to forewoman. We're not expecting a lot of you — all we want you to do is to help us with something. All you've got to do is to tell me which of the girls have anything to do with those dubious characters, the Communists. Don't worry, I won't let on that you told me. Why, I've even sent Wang Chin-chen away!"

He said this in the same gentle undertone, but it came as a great shock to Chu Kuei-ying, and the colour drained from her cheeks. This was something even worse than the philandering which she had expected. She simply loathed him now.

"I don't know what you're talking about!" she said, dashing past him and straight out through the door. She heard Wang Chin-chen's voice calling after her, and then a shout from Tu Wei-yueh as if he was telling Wang Chin-chen to be quiet. With never a look behind her, Chu Kuei-ying raced round the workshop and made for the main gate.

About fifteen yards from the gate was the gloomy row of sheds where the cocoons were stored. Just as Chu Kuei-ying was running past this place, a flash of lightning suddenly lit up everywhere as bright as day. There was a crash of thunder overhead, and as the thunder broke someone sprang out on her and threw his arms round her in a tight embrace. It all happened so suddenly that the strength went out of her limbs. Her heart pounded wildly and she was too stunned to cry out until the man had already dragged her several paces away with him.

"Help! You —" she shouted as she began to struggle with him, thinking it was Tu Wei-yueh. But the noise of the thunder as it rumbled across the sky drowned her voice. Suddenly, another flash of lightning flooded the scene with a glare of white light, and she was able to see that it was not Tu Wei-yueh at all! At this juncture, someone else, a hurricane-lamp in his hand, came running towards them, shouting:

"What do you think you're on?"

It was Tu Wei-yueh's voice. Chu Kuei-ying's attacker now let go of her and turned to slip away, but Tu Wei-yueh grabbed him with one hand and lifted the light to his face with the other: it was Tseng Chia-chu. Tu Wei-yueh scowled and fixed him with a contemptuous stare. A long peal of thunder came echoing across the sky. Tu Wei-yueh released Tseng Chia-chu and turned to look at Chu Kuei-ying, a cynical smile on his lips.

"If you don't want to help me that's all right by me," he said, his tone as polite as ever. "There's no need to go running away like this. How do you imagine you can get past the watchman at the main gate if you're on your own? You'd better go out with Wang Chin-chen."

He then called Wang Chin-chen over to escort her, and went back the way he had come.

*

When Chu Kuei-ying reached her "home," it had already started raining, and heavy, scattered drops were pattering against the bamboo door. The little thatched hut was in darkness except for a glimmer of light from a neighbour's lamp filtering through a crack in the clay-plastered party-wall. When she had recovered her breath, she became aware that groans were coming from the rickety bamboo bed — her mother.

"What's the matter, Mum? Are you ill or something?"

Chu Kuei-ying went across to her mother and laid her hand on the old lady's much-wrinkled forehead. For a moment the old lady seemed glad to see her daughter, then suddenly she burst into tears. Chu Kuei-ying took no notice, for her mother often cried like this. She heaved a sigh and her thoughts returned to the nightmarish events of that evening and the rumour of an impending twenty-per-cent wage-cut. Her heart was ablaze with anxiety and hatred. After a moment her mother cried out in a voice choked with sobs:

"Kuei-ying, these days . . . there's only one way out for poor people like us . . . and that's to die!"

Chu Kuei-ying stared dazedly at her mother for a moment, but said nothing. The only way out is to die? Chu Kuei-ying realized full well that they were on the verge of destitution, but she was a young girl of nineteen, toughened by a life of poverty and hardship, and she had no intention of just giving up like that and dying — as a matter of fact, she believed that she had a right to a decent life, like anyone else. She patted her mother's chest and asked in a soothing voice, "What's the matter, Mum? Business bad today?"

"Business bad? Ah! You know very well it's always the same, Kuei-ying. Every day business is so bad it makes me cry. But today . . . just look at my basket over there!"

The old lady suddenly boiled over: she hauled herself painfully up and sat there, her lips pressed together, fuming with indignation.

Chu Kuei-ying picked up out of the corner the wicker basket from which her mother peddled peanuts. She found that the rim had been torn away, so that it was now useless, and that it was quite empty. She tossed it aside and puffed out her cheeks with annoyance.

"I suppose you've been quarrelling with somebody, eh, Mum?"

"Quarrelling? As if I would! It was some bullying devil — blast him! — came and set on me for no reason at all! He snatched my basket, took my peanuts and threatened to run me in!"

"But what should anybody want to do a thing like that for?"

"He said I was — oh, I can't remember what it was now! Have a look at them papers there! He said I'm breaking the law having them!"

She had stopped crying now, and the more she spoke the more excited she became. She groped on the table for a match and lit an oil lamp. Chu Kuei-ying looked in the bottom of the basket and saw a few small sheets of paper with something printed on them in red. It was the paper her mother used for wrapping up her peanuts. She remembered that Sze Hsi-tse, the rag-and-bone boy from next door, had picked up a thick wad of these sheets of paper somewhere in the streets a couple of weeks before, and that her mother had given him some peanuts in exchange for some of it for wrapping-paper. How could she be breaking the law by using it? She picked up a sheet and looked at it closely; three of the signs on it looked rather familiar. She thought for a moment and then she remembered: they stood for "Communist Party." She had often seen these words scrawled on the walls beside the factory gate and on telegraph poles by the roadside, and her brother Little San-tse had told her what they stood for. And then this was what Tu Wei-yueh had asked her about when he had sent for her a short while ago.

"And I'm not the only one who uses that sort of paper," the old lady complained indignantly, her lips trembling as she spoke. "Old Pah the cooked-beef man uses it, too. And then —"

Chu Kuei-ying was shrewd enough to guess that it was a case of some tramp roving the streets looking for a free meal and finding a pretext to do himself a good turn. She tossed the sheets of paper aside and fell silent for a moment, then picked up the basket again to see whether it could be mended and used again. Suddenly she looked worried; she let the basket fall to the mud floor and put her head on one side to listen.

A hubbub of argument and angry words was coming from the neighbours in the next hut — girls working in the same factory as Chu Kuei-ying. The hiss of the rain on the bamboo doors was louder and more insistent than ever and overhead the rumble of thunder still rolled across the sky, but the sound of voices which rose from the huts was even fiercer than the angry roar of the storm. Doors groaned on their hinges as people went in and out of the huts, and the whole settlement of workers from the silk factory was a hive of activity. While one storm raged overhead, another kind of storm was about to break in this little shanty-town!

Chu Kuei-ying was becoming restless, and she had just sprung to her feet to go out when the bamboo door of her own hut creaked open and in burst a skinny youngster in a blue jacket, swearing at the top of his voice:

"That perishing old swine of a boss we've got! He's got plenty of money to throw around on whores and gambling and building posh houses! But when it comes to paying out wages and keeping his factory going, he makes out he's broke! Rotten old bastard!"

This was Chu Kuei-ying's brother Little San-tse, who worked in a match factory. Too excited to pay any attention to his mother and sister asking him what it was all about, he raved angrily on:

"We used to get sixty cents a day; in the spring it was cut down to fifty cents; and now today, if you please, that old perisher Chou Chung-wei sticks up a notice about 'high costs' or some such nonsense, and saying he's losing a lot of money so he's got to cut us down to forty cents!"

As he spoke, Little San-tse picked up the box of matches on the table and slapped his hand against it.

"Two coppers a box he gets for these, and he tells us he's losing money! Give me eight coppers, Kuei-ying: I want to get some scones for my supper. The blokes in the factory are having a meeting tonight, and I'm going along with Chin Ho-shang from next door. If that old swine Chou's going to cut our wages down, we're bloody well going on strike!"

When the old lady realized that they were going to have another wage-cut at the factory where her son worked, she felt disaster had finally overtaken them. By the time the full realization of it had come home to her, Little San-tse had gone. After a moment Chu Kuei-ying followed him out. The pelting rain felt cool and pleasant to her face. She was seething with rage and indignation and her face was so hot that it seemed as if the raindrops would dry as soon as they touched it.

Outside the bamboo door the ground was strewn with rubbish washed down by the heavy rain. A flash of lightning lit up the huddle of huts, and in the brilliant white glare she could see a number of people hurrying through the downpour. When the flash had passed the darkness seemed blacker than ever. Chu Kuei-ying's destination was the east end of the slum, about fifteen yards away. She was going to the "home" of Chang Ah-hsin, one of the girls she worked with, to tell her how Tu Wei-yueh had sent for her and tried to pump her about the people who were mixed up with the Communists. At this moment her thoughts were moving faster than her feet. She had almost reached Chang Ah-hsin's hut, when in the darkness she suddenly felt somebody's arms round her.

"Kuei-ying!" cried a voice in her ear, and as she recognized it Chu Kuei-ying's heart began to beat less violently. It was Chin Hsiao-mei, one of the girls who worked in the same factory. She was only thirteen, but was much older in the head. She was the younger sister of Chin Ho-shang, one of Chu Kuei-ying's neighbours. Gripping Chu Kuei-ying's arm, she asked, "Where are you going?"

"To Chang Ah-hsin's place."

"It's no good going there: they've all gone over to Yao Chin-feng's. Come on, let's go over together."

The two girls retraced their steps and turned left. As they walked along, Chin Hsiao-mei poured out all the latest news, and as she listened Chu Kuei-ying glowed with excitement, so that she forgot that it was raining and that her clothes were wet through. So Yao Chin-feng is out to lead us again! Then Hsueh Pao-chu must have been wrong when she accused her of being a spy for the boss. Who else? Chou Erh-chieh and Chien Chiao-lin? Well! But Chien Chiao-lin is Chien Pao-sheng's sister, isn't she? And now even she's having a go! Fancy that! So the workers are ready to help their mates after all!

Soon they were approaching Yao Chin-feng's home. This was also a straw-and-mud affair but cleaner than most and boasting a wooden door. While they were still some distance away they could hear a babel of voices from inside. Chu Kuei-ying's heart leapt for joy. The last meeting — when they had decided to "go slow" — had been nowhere near as noisy and daring as this: it had been held in secret, and very quietly.

Chin Hsiao-mei dashed forward to open the door, and as Chu Kuei-ying squeezed in she was met by a breath of hot, close air and the reek of sweat. The room was packed and everyone seemed to be shouting at once. An oil lamp shed a pool of light no more than a few feet square, and in this pool of light was a plump white face with drooping eyelids — Chien Chiao-lin, of all people!

"It's all the fault of Kuei Chang-lin and Chamber-pot Tu!" she was shouting, while a teardrop oozed out from under one of her drooping eyelids. "They're always crawling round the boss! We must strike! We must strike tomorrow! We've got to beat these two crawlers!"

"Strike! That's right: strike! There's several factories in Hongkew already out!"

"Shouldn't we send somebody to get in touch with them —?"

"When they come round and burst into the factory tomorrow, we'll down tools and march out!"

From this medley of voices Chu Kuei-ying could only identify that of the last speaker — Hsu Ah-yi, a woman in her thirties who was ordinarily timid and quiet.

"Sling Chamber-pot Tu out of the factory! — And Kuei Chang-lin with him!" bawled dumpy little Chou Erh-chieh, poking her head out from behind Chien Chiao-lin, but immediately another voice shouted:

"Sling Chien Pao-sheng out, as well! We don't want a trade union that's out to swindle us! We want a trade union of our own!"

A deathly hush suddenly descended on the room, and sweat-beaded faces peered this way and that to see who had spoken. It was Ho Hsiu-mei, her face flushed and her staring eyes fixed on Chien Chiao-lin. Almost at once the tense silence was broken, and Yao Chin-feng's little oval face with its faint white pockmarks flashed in the dim pool of light from the oil lamp.

"That's right!" she shrilled. "Sling Chien Pao-sheng out and

"Strike! That's right: strike! There's several factories in Hongkew already out!"

sling his stooge out with him! Chou Erh-chieh's his stooge!"

"You bitch! You're Chamber-pot Tu's stooge yourself!" screamed Chou Erh-chieh. She sprang up and flew at Yao Chin-feng, and for a moment the two of them struggled together. The girls came to Yao Chin-feng's rescue and parted them. As they hustled Chou Erh-chieh away into a corner, they all shouted at her:

"The one who starts a fight is always in the wrong!"

"Listen, girls!" panted Yao Chin-feng. "When I say that Chou Erh-chieh is Chien Pao-sheng's stooge, I know what I'm talking about! He's sent her here to spy on us!"

She ran her eyes over the circle of faces to see what effect her accusation would have. All at once pandemonium broke out again and it was impossible to hear what anybody was saying. One thing, however, was clear to everybody: Chou Erh-chieh was up to no good at this meeting! Chang Ah-hsin's voice alone could be heard shrilling above the din.

"Chien Chiao-lin's here to spy on us, as well! She can't be any good if she's Chien Pao-sheng's sister! Throw her out!"

"She's always flirting with that new fellow Tseng!" cried another voice. "And he's the boss's cousin or something!"

All was confusion now, and if at this moment Chou Erh-chieh or Chien Chiao-lin had shown the slightest sign of protest, they would have been beaten up. Taken completely unawares by this sudden attack, they did not know quite what to do for a moment. One thing was clear to both of them: it would be unhealthy to stay just now. At the first opportunity they slipped out. This gave Chu Kuei-ying a chance to edge further into the room, and she almost managed to get through to Chang Ah-hsin.

"They've got away!" shouted the timid Hsu Ah-yi at the top of her voice, trying to push her way through the crowd. "They're sure to go and report us! We'll have to break up straight away!"

They all heard what she said, but no one agreed.

"No, no, don't break up yet! Don't be scared! We haven't decided anything yet!"

"First thing tomorrow morning, we should elect our representatives and then walk out on strike!"

"And then we'll break into Wu Sun-fu's new factories and make the girls down tools and join us! We'll go round all the factories in Chapei and make them all come out on strike with us!"

"I think we'd better send somebody round to see the strikers in Hongkew first. If they'll come and break into our factory, we'll shut down the machines and join them!"

This proposal to "wait and see" was made in an anxious voice and came from a girl standing right beside Chu Kuei-ying. She recognized her as Lu Hsiao-pao.

"Pah! Only a crawler would wait for a walk-in from outside!" snapped Ho Hsiu-mei, and spat at Lu Hsiao-pao. Lu Hsiao-pao stood her ground, and the two of them indulged in a brief slanging-match.

The question was now whether they should wait for a walk-in from outside or whether they should walk out themselves and then break into the other factories, and on this point the eight or so girls were divided into two groups; Ho Hsiu-mei, Chang Ah-hsin, and one or two others, including Chu Kuei-ying, were for walking out of their own accord, and in this Yao Chin-feng also agreed with them. Each of the girls represented two or three rows of girls in their workshops, so any resolution made this evening could be carried out the next day. Hsu Ah-yi now urged them once more:

"Come on, hurry up! They must have gone and reported us by now. Somebody's sure to come round!"

It was at this moment that Chin Hsiao-mei squeezed hurriedly in through the crowd to say that she had just seen several "toughs" walking up and down in the vicinity as if they were looking for somebody. Everybody looked alarmed except Yao Chin-feng, who knew what it meant as she had been told all about it by Ah Chen. Nevertheless, she seized this opportunity to suggest that they should close the meeting now and make the final decision in the workshop next morning. Her "mission" was accomplished, and she was anxious to dash off and report to Ah Chen how she had got on at the meeting.

It was not raining so hard now, but it was chilly outside and the girls shivered as they came out of the hut. Chu Kuei-ying,

Chang Ah-hsin, and another girl, Chen Yueh-ngo, went off arm in arm and huddled close together. Chen Yueh-ngo whispered in Chang Ah-hsin's ear:

"Looks as if there's really going to be a strike tomorrow! Ma Chin's still waiting for us to report back."

"Let's go there straight away," replied Chang Ah-hsin, also in a whisper. "Though it's very cold, and we'll get wet through again."

Chu Kuei-ying overheard what they were saying, and it reminded her that Tu Wei-yueh had not long ago been offering to promote her to forewoman to buy her over. She was just going to tell her friends about it, when she suddenly caught sight of an individual in a black gown slip out from a side-turning and tag along behind them. She immediately nudged Chang Ah-hsin and pointed over her shoulder with her lips. Chen Yueh-ngo spotted him at the same time; she dug Chang Ah-hsin in the ribs with her elbow and deliberately raised her voice:

"Br-r-r! Isn't it cold tonight! Well, Ah-hsin, we'll have to say good-night now. See you tomorrow!"

The three of them unlinked their arms and went off in three different directions.

When she had gone a few steps, Chen Yueh-ngo turned her head and stared hard over her shoulder: the black-gowned individual was following hard on Chang Ah-hsin's heels. Her heart missed a beat, for she knew that Chang Ah-hsin did not always keep her wits about her. She immediately stopped and shouted, "Ah-hsin! You've left your handkerchief in my hand!"

Chang Ah-hsin looked round and then she, too, saw the fellow in the black gown behind her. She shouted back, "Keep it till tomorrow," and headed straight for home. He of the black gown again emerged from the shadows and paced stolidly on behind her.

When she had made sure that she herself was not being tailed, Chen Yueh-ngo quickened her steps. Leaving the slum behind her, she turned into a squalid alleyway. When she reached the other end she tapped three times on the back door of a house and slipped quickly inside.

The front-room upstairs was furnished with three rickety beds and one square table. Two girls with their hair cut short were sitting hunched over the table, writing something by the dim light of a solitary bulb hanging from the ceiling. Chen Yueh-ngo crept in very quietly, but the two girls heard her coming. One of them raised a vivid pair of eyes and greeted her with a stare, then lowered her head and went on with her writing. As she wrote she said to the other girl:

"You'd better hurry up and finish, Tsai Chen. Yueh-ngo's here, and it's getting late, so we'd better start the discussion straight away."

"All right, let's get started," said the girl addressed as Tsai Chen, stretching and putting down her pen. "We can finish the writing off afterwards."

She stood up and stretched again. She was taller than Chen Yueh-ngo, and, like her, she wore a short white calico jacket and a pair of baggy black slacks. She was dressed like one of the girls from the silk factory, but her sophisticated expression and manner proclaimed her to be an intellectual. Her eyes were heavy for lack of sleep and her face was pale.

The other girl also stopped writing. Her sharp, vivacious eyes flashed a glance at Chen Yueh-ngo as she asked quickly, "Well, Yueh-ngo, how are things going in the factory? If you can get things moving tomorrow, we've got a good chance of bringing off a general strike involving all the silk factories in the Chapei area."

After a struggle, Chen Yueh-ngo managed to give some account of what had happened in the factory during the day and at the meeting a short while ago in Yao Chin-feng's hut. Her diction was of the simplest, but she larded it freely with some of the jargon she had lately picked up — the women's "spirit of struggle" was running high; given "leadership," there was no question of their not being "mobilized" immediately. She was very excited, and every now and then she interrupted her report to recover her breath. Beads of perspiration glistened on her forehead.

"Same situation as in Hongkew," commented Tsai Chen; then, making a clean sweep of the questions left unanswered by Chen Yueh-ngo's report, she concluded briskly, "Your people must walk out tomorrow without fail, and after that they must go round bringing out the other factories until we've got a general strike of all the silk factories in Chapei!"

Her keen-eyed companion, Ma Chin, had made no comment, but still watched Chen Yueh-ngo with an intense stare, as if trying to detect any exaggerations the latter might be making in her "report." She had the feeling that there were some complicated problems involved in the "report," yet, not being a swift thinker, she could not for the moment make an accurate analysis of what these problems were — she just had a vague sense of uneasiness.

Outside the window the rain was hissing down and the lightning was flashing again. A tense silence hung over the room.

"Come on, Ma Chin, let's hear your decision!" Tsai Chen urged impatiently, drumming her pen on the table. "We've got other things to do yet."

As Tsai Chen looked at it, the question was simple enough: "the workers' spirit of struggle was running high" because the "high tide of revolution" was at this moment sweeping the country! Since March, there had been strikes by the bus- and tram-drivers in the International Settlement and by the workers in the power-house in the French Concession. The "spontaneous struggle" of the workers had been kept up without a break in factories all over Shanghai, and every "economic struggle" had a way of turning instantly into a "political struggle," with the result that "the revolution has now reached high tide." Tsai Chen had heard all this time and again from Ke Tso-fu and had adopted it as her own formula for thinking.

This "formula" sounded simple, clear and "reasonable," and, along with a lot of other jargon, had been firmly memorized by Chen Yueh-ngo and through her instilled into the minds of Chang Ah-hsin and Ho Hsiu-mei, whose simple minds and warm hearts were just the right sort of fertile soil for "formulas" of this kind.

Ma Chin, however, thought differently; she felt that there were flaws in Tsai Chen's "formula," but, with her scanty knowledge and experience, she was unable to explain just where — she just felt it was so. Besides, it was not in her nature to make hasty statements; she preferred to go over all the facts first. This was the reason for her present hesitation about Chen Yueh-ngo's report. Now that Tsai Chen was hurrying her up, she just had to express what she felt as best she could.

"There's no point in rushing things. We must study the situation carefully. Yueh-ngo says Yao Chin-feng's putting up a better show this time, but don't forget she wasn't all that reliable last time. Besides, she may be Kuei Chang-lin's tool in the war between the yellow trade union factions. Maybe she's wormed her way in to win over the masses and lead a strike herself for her own ends. I think we must take all this into consideration before we can make a decision."

"You're wrong!" Tsai Chen immediately expostulated. "The fact is, the revolutionary spirit of the masses has put an end to Yao Chin-feng's wavering. What's more, you're disregarding the fighting spirit of the masses at a time when the tide of revolution is in full flood, you're underestimating the power of the masses to discipline wavering elements, and you think that the tools of a yellow trade union can lead the masses! You're taking a rightist view of things!"

As she reeled off her formulas and scraps of jargon one after the other, her pasty face became flushed. Chen Yueh-ngo sat listening, and although she did not understand much of what Tsai Chen was saying, she was quite impressed by it.

Ma Chin also flushed and at once demanded, "What do you mean, 'rightist view'!"

"I mean that you doubt the great revolutionary power of the masses and that you fail to see the upsurge of the fighting spirit of the masses!" said Tsai Chen, glibly quoting another formula. Ma Chin's face suddenly paled. She sprang to her feet and said harshly:

"I'm *not* taking a rightist view! I'm only trying to analyse a complicated fact. I suspect Yao Chin-feng of covering something up with her leftist exhibition!"

"Well, have we got to stop rousing the masses to action just because we're afraid that Yao Chin-feng might take over the leadership from us, then? If that isn't a rightist point of view, what is it?"

"I didn't say we'd got to stop activating the masses! All I'm proposing is that we should decide our tactics before we begin launching the masses into action."

"What do you mean by 'tactics'? So you're thinking of deciding our tactics, eh? You're forgetting our general line! That's rightist deviation!"

"I'm not going to start arguing with you about rightism and leftism, Tsai Chen. All I'm concerned with is whether or not we're going to find ways and means of dealing with the two yellow trade union factions and their stooges in the Yu Hua Silk Factory."

"Pooh! 'Ways and means'? You're not suggesting we should play one clique off against the other? Why, that's opportunism! The one correct way is to go all out to raise the revolutionary spirit of the masses to the utmost and provide correct leadership for their great revolutionary power!"

"Yes, yes, I know all about that, but these theoretical problems can be discussed later at a group meeting. What we've got to discuss now is the practical side. Yueh-ngo's waited long enough for our decision. I propose that when we get the strike going tomorrow we should ask Yao Chin-feng to make up her mind where she stands —"

"I think we can quite safely leave it to the masses to keep an eye on her," said Tsai Chen with casual confidence and a mocking smile. In the ordinary way she had great respect for Ma Chin, who was hard-working, unafraid of hardships, and correct in her views; but at this particular moment she was beginning to have her doubts about her — at least, she suspected Ma Chin of shrinking in the face of the "high tide of revolution."

"We needn't be afraid of Yao Chin-feng playing tricks," Chen Yueh-ngo chimed in. "The girls will make short work of anybody they find ratting! Yao Chin-feng wouldn't dare risk it."

Her patience was rapidly being exhausted, though mainly because she did not understand all these formulas and scraps of jargon which Tsai Chen and Ma Chin were using. Nevertheless, she was a factory worker with an ardent revolutionary spirit and was very eager to learn all she could, so she continued to listen patiently.

"I suspect that Yao Chin-feng has already ratted! — Oh, come on, let's stop arguing and decide what we're going to do once we've got the strike started."

With this call for a truce in the interminable controversy of formula versus formula, Ma Chin sorted through the papers she had just been working on, picked up one of them and began reading out the programme she had jotted down. The discussion now centred on purely practical issues: the formation of a strike committee and the nomination of committee members, terms for the resumption of work, liaison with other factories on strike in Chapei, contact with factories in Hongkew. . . . Now that they were coming down to brass tacks, Chen Yueh-ngo joined in the discussion instead of just listening to the other two. Each of them had plenty to say and their faces were flushed with enthusiasm.

Meanwhile the crash of thunder, the lightning and the torrential rain raged through the night with ever-increasing fury, until the house rocked precariously; but the three girls were oblivious of all this, for they were completely engrossed in the other storm that was coming.

XIV

WHEN the night of storm had passed, daybreak brought a gentle breeze and scattered, rose-tinted patches of cloud, and the rising sun was a blood-red disc.

The several hundred spinning-machines in the Yu Hua Filature that had been running at full pressure suddenly stopped. The thunder of the oppressed was being unleashed! The girls surged out of the workshop like a tidal wave, swept across to the notice-board in front of the office like an angry squall, scattered the handful of clerks who had come out to see what it was all about, and tore down the notice which had just been put up announcing the wage-cut.

"Down with the blacklegs! Down with the crawlers!"

"Death to Chien Pao-sheng and Hsueh Pao-chu!"

"No wage-cut! We want Sunday overtime! We want a cost-of-living allowance!"

Thundering their demands, the crowd of angry women spread out in line and closed in on the office, which represented their shackles — the shackles they were going to break asunder!

"Down with Chamber-pot Tu!"

"Sling out Kuei Chang-lin and Wang Chin-chen!"

The crowd was shouting raggedly now, instead of in chorus as at first. The main body of the women had now surged forward to the veranda in front of the row of office buildings, which they had by now surrounded; but their progress was blocked by Pockmarked Li and his twenty bullies, who were swearing at them and threatening them with lead-weighted lengths of hose. Among them was Ah Hsiang, who kept glancing at Pockmarked Li to see what he would do. The latter, however, had not received his orders to go into action, so they could only stand guard and hold themselves in readiness.

Suddenly, Tu Wei-yueh's slim figure made its appearance before the door of the office. He held himself erect, and his face wore its customary sardonic smile.

The crowd was taken aback: he was certainly a game 'un, this "Chamber-pot"! But their hesitation was momentary, and the next instant they were surging forward with redoubled boldness, until they were almost on top of Li's strong-arm men. Their shouting had risen to a deafening roar. They were angry, and they were ready for a deliberate, all-out attack on their enemy, a hand-to-hand encounter! Their smouldering anger had been fanned into flame at last! One detachment of the crowd had already poured on to the other end of the veranda. There was a crash and tinkle of breaking glass. The first blow had been struck! The crowd fanned out and moved in to the attack. Any moment now the storm would break.

Pockmarked Li could wait no longer, and he and his twenty men struck out wildly at the section of the crowd which was closing in on them, though they retreated step by step as they fought.

Tu Wei-yueh also stepped back. Suddenly, someone sprang out from behind him. It was Wu Wei-cheng.

"Go on, Li, give 'em what for!" he yelled. "Give the bitches a good hiding! Run 'em in!"

"Pitch into 'em! . . . Call the police! Open fire!" yelled two other voices: Ma Ching-shan and Tseng Chia-chu were hanging out of a window to shout encouragement.

Pockmarked Li and his men were still retreating, fighting as they went. In the mêlée several of the women had become caught up in the middle of the bullies and were now trying hard to fight their way out. The main body of the crowd had by now got on to the veranda, and the office was on the point of "falling" at any moment. At this juncture, however, their rear was thrown into confusion by the arrival of a dozen or so policemen, who charged into the crowd, using their bayonets to clear a way. Pockmarked Li and his men immediately took the offensive, and the five or six women who had been cornered were now seized by the bullies. The main body of the crowd drew back slightly, and the policemen took up positions on the porch.

Far from retreating, the women stood their ground, shouting angrily and rallying for a second attack.

Wu Wei-cheng, Ma Ching-shan, and Tseng Chia-chu came dashing out together and stamped their feet as they yelled at the top of their voices:

"Open fire! Finish the bitches off!"

The crowd's reaction was immediate: their ranks stirred and they began moving forward with a deafening roar. The policemen automatically raised their rifles. Suddenly, Tu Wei-yueh stepped out again and stopped them with a wave of the hand, at the same time shouting at the top of his voice:

"Don't open fire! . . . Girls, listen to me! We're not going to shoot at you! Just listen to me for a moment!"

"We don't want to listen to your bluff! Clear off!" roared a small group of women in the crowd, still moving resolutely forward. But the majority stopped and stood still.

Tu Wei-yueh smiled calmly and walked out on to the steps in front of the veranda.

"Now, be sensible," he bellowed. "You don't imagine your bare fists are going to be any good against guns and bayonets? You swear at me and want to kick me out, but we're all in this together — you *and* me. We all depend on the factory for a living, and if you smash up the factory, you'll be taking the food out of your own mouths! If you've got any demands, go back and send a representative to discuss them with me. Now, go on back! I'm the only one here still in favour of a peaceful settlement! If you go on making trouble like this, you'll be the losers by it!"

Suddenly, Kuei Chang-lin slipped out and went across to the main body of the women, who were standing still and seemed to have calmed down.

"Mr. Tu's quite right!" he shouted. "Everybody go on back now and leave it to the union to take the matter up with the management! We won't let you down!"

"We don't want anything to do with your lousy union!"

shrilled a voice from the crowd. "We'll have a union of our own!"

By now even the small group of women had stopped, and a confused jabber of voices rose from the main body of the crowd. It was clear that they were no longer shouting for an attack, but were busy arguing among themselves about what their next step should be. All at once, one of the girls left the crowd to address them. It was Yao Chin-feng.

"Listen, girls!" she shouted. "They're holding half-a-dozen of us! If they don't let them go, we'll carry on to the bitter end!"

The crowd's response was a deafening roar. There was something else they wanted now! Yao Chin-feng took a step forward and looked Tu Wei-yueh straight in the eyes:

"Let the girls go!"

"You can't do that!" yelled Wu Wei-cheng as he and the other two squeezed out to the front. Pockmarked Li looked at Tu Wei-yueh, and saw that he was smiling his usual cold smile. Quite firmly, Tu Wei-yueh gave Pockmarked Li his orders:

"Let them go!"

"They've let them go!" yelled Kuei Chang-lin at the top of his voice, running round the main body of the crowd. "They've let them go! Everybody can go back now! If you've got any demands you can send up a representative to discuss them!"

The crowd cheered and the human tide began to move again, but this time it had changed direction and was moving towards the main gate. As she went along, Ho Hsiu-mei shouted, "Down with Chamber-pot Tu! Down with Kuei Chang-lin!" but only a hundred or so voices took up her slogan. Then: "Down with Chien Pao-sheng!" shouted Yao Chin-feng, and this time the whole crowd took up the cry. Chen Yueh-ngo and Chang Ah-hsin walked along together, their jaws set firm. Chen Yueh-ngo now recalled the argument between Ma Chin and Tsai Chen the night before. She was afraid that the plan to march into the other factories might now fall through.

Nevertheless, when the crowd had surged up to the gate-way,

and Chang Ah-hsin shouted, "March into the other factories!" the crowd's response was as deafening as ever:

"March into the other factories! Let's break into the 'new factory' first!"

"General strike! We want a trade union of our own!"

They thundered their way across the street and stormed into Wu Sun-fu's "new factory." The workers of two factories joined forces and marched into a third factory, then into a fourth, swelling their ranks to two thousand, three thousand, four thousand, five thousand, so that in less than an hour every silk filature in Chapei, large or small, was out on strike. The whole area was in a state of tension, and police patrols were doubled.

*

The workshop of the Yu Hua Filature was as silent as the grave. Four policemen had been posted at the main gate. Inside the office, on the other hand, the atmosphere was unusually tense. Wu Wei-cheng, Ma Ching-shan, and Tseng Chia-chu were badgering Tu Wei-yueh and accusing him of being a weakling. Tu Wei-yueh made no attempt to argue with them, but just smiled his usual cool, unruffled smile.

A motorcar horn blared furiously from the main gate. Tu Wei-yueh strolled calmly out of the office to find that Wu Sun-fu had already got out of his car. His face was livid with fury and his eyes blazed. He did not give anybody so much as a look.

Mo Kan-cheng stood to one side, his head drooping and his face deathly pale.

Tu Wei-yueh squared his shoulders and walked across to Wu Sun-fu with a cool, open smile.

Wu Sun-fu threw him a glance, then, without a word, beckoned the two of them to follow him. He went first to look at the broken office window, then made a tour of inspection through the deserted workshop and every other part of the factory. When he saw that no other damage had been done, his expression gradually relaxed.

Finally, he went into his office and settled himself down to hear Tu Wei-yueh's report.

Golden sunlight was streaming in through the window, and a golden-coloured electric fan was turning from side to side behind Wu Sun-fu's back. Dark shadows moved across the window as some eavesdroppers strolled to and fro outside. Tu Wei-yueh noticed them quite clearly as he made his report, and smiled sardonically to himself.

Wu Sun-fu listened with his brows drawn together in a frown. His lips were pressed tightly together and his keen glance darted all round. Suddenly, he broke in with impatience, "Do you think they'd dare smash the machines? Or set fire to the premises? Or start a riot?"

"They're like a lot of raving lunatics at the moment, and I wouldn't put anything past them. Though it can't last long: once the crowds dispersed they'll quieten down again."

"In other words, you think we're very lucky to have come through it with nothing worse than a broken window, eh? That's what you'd call a victory for us, I suppose?"

There was an edge to Wu Sun-fu's voice as he said this, and his eyes glinted coldly. Tu Wei-yueh drew himself up and smiled.

"I hear we've caught several of the rioters red-handed," Wu Sun-fu went on icily. "You've turned them over to the police, I suppose?"

Tu Wei-yueh saw straight away what was behind this question: he guessed that someone had already reported the girls' release to Wu Sun-fu — and had done a lot more back-biting at the same time, no doubt. He kept a straight face and said, "I've already let them go."

"What! Just let them go like that? And I suppose you did that to save my factory, eh? Huh!"

"No, not at all! As you said yourself only the other day, 'You can't net them all.' Besides, there's no point at all in detaining half-a-dozen sheep who just follow the crowd."

Sensing the second piece of sarcasm, Tu Wei-yueh paid Wu Sun-fu back in his own coin. He threw out his chest and put on a look as much as to say, "You can kill a gentleman but you cannot insult him." He knew that this was a good way of bringing the violent, refractory Wu Sun-fu to heel.

For a while neither of them spoke. A shadow flitted across the window again. This time Wu Sun-fu also saw it. He frowned. He realized quite well what was going on, and he had never liked this kind of sneaking, creeping monkey-business. He laughed grimly and said in an intentionally loud voice:

"All right, Wei-yueh, I give you a free hand! But we're starting work tomorrow! Got it? Tomorrow!"

"I'll do my best to carry out your instructions, sir," replied Tu Wei-yueh in an equally loud voice. He realized that his own "régime" was safe again for the time being. Wu Sun-fu smiled and waved him away, but as Tu Wei-yueh rose to go, Wu Sun-fu suddenly said:

"I hear certain people in the factory don't hit it off with you. Is that right?"

"Who exactly are you referring to, sir?"

"People in the office, your colleagues."

"Well, I don't know anything about it. I can hardly imagine anybody being like that. We all are working for you, Mr. Wu, and you treat us all the same. Whatever authority you give me is only so that I can carry out your instructions."

Though he spoke calmly and unhurriedly, Tu Wei-yueh had a sinking feeling in the pit of his stomach. He made a slight but grave bow and left the room.

Mo Kan-cheng was summoned in next. As the old fellow came into the room he was trembling at the knees. The moment he clapped eyes on him, Wu Sun-fu felt a twinge of annoyance. He deliberately avoided looking at the pitiful-looking old creature, and sat silent, his eyes fixed on the flickering patterns of light and shade on the window. His mind was occupied with the problem of Tu Wei-yueh. Surely the fellow couldn't really be ignorant of the fact that certain people in the office were not satisfied with the way he had handled things today? No! He must know! But why wouldn't he admit it? Was he afraid of losing face? Pride, that was it! This young man did have plenty of pride, too. Well, let's wait and see how he acquits himself today! ... Suddenly, Wu Sun-fu was assailed by a doubt. He shook his head vigorously, then turned to Mo Kan-cheng and said in a harsh voice:

"Kan-cheng, you're a senior member of the staff. When you find these youngsters quarrelling, it's up to you to sort things out and make peace between them!"

"But sir —"

"Hold your tongue! You know very well I don't like people coming and whispering to me against this one and that. I'm capable of making up my own mind, so I don't need to listen to gossip! I can see quite clearly who's any good and who's not, and anybody who comes and blows his own trumpet to me is wasting his breath! Understand? Go and tell them, then!"

"Very good, sir!"

"I also hear that Tseng Chia-chu and Tu Wei-yueh are fighting for the same girl, and that there was a little to-do here last night. That true?"

"I . . . I don't know much about it."

Mo Kan-cheng was flustered, and his miserable expression was almost laughable. As a matter of fact, he knew all about it, but he was afraid to say anything with the echoes of Wu Sun-fu's harangue still ringing in his ears. Realizing what was worrying him, Wu Sun-fu laughed despite himself and went on, "What do you mean, you don't know much about it! Can't you even answer a straightforward question when I ask you? I know just what you people in the office are like. You've got no ears for anything decent; all you're ever interested in is bits of scandal. The minute there's some rivalry over a girl, your ears start flapping. I hear Tu Wei-yueh's to blame in this case. He sets a bad example, doesn't he?"

Mo Kan-cheng just stood and gaped wide-eyed. For a moment he could not make up his mind what to do. Should he confirm what Wu Sun-fu had said? Or should he tell the truth? In the end, he decided to tell the truth. After all, Tu Wei-yueh still enjoyed Wu Sun-fu's confidence.

"Mr. Wu, the fact of the matter is, young Mr. Tseng's really gone too far —"

Wu Sun-fu nodded and smiled, and Mo Kan-cheng felt encouraged to go on. "Wang Chin-chen, forewoman No. 2, saw it all with her own eyes. All I know is what she's told me. Mr. Tu hasn't mentioned a single word to me about it yet. Last night, Mr. Tu sent Wang Chin-chen to fetch one of the girls — Chu Kuei-ying — up to the office to ask her which of the girls had anything to do with the Communists — as a matter of fact, they were in this very room, and Wang Chin-chen was here, too. Afterwards, when Chu Kuei-ying was leaving the factory, she had just got to the cocoon-store, when young Mr. Tseng stopped her and started annoying her. We didn't hear her shouting or anything, because it was in the middle of a thunderstorm, but Mr. Tu and Wang Chin-chen happened to run into them and saw what was happening. Well, that's the long and the short of it."

Wu Sun-fu knit his brows in silence. He could see it all now. He realized that the account his nephew Wu Wei-cheng had given him of things was a completely distorted one. It suddenly struck him that it had been a mistake to put three of his relatives — Tseng Chia-chu, Ma Ching-shan and Wu Wei-cheng — in the same factory: there would be no end of trouble from them!

"I see! Now, Kan-cheng, go and tell everybody in the office that there's to be no more gossiping about it!"

With this, Wu Sun-fu waved Mo Kan-cheng away. He tilted his head on one side and thought for a moment, then picked up a pen with the intention of writing a memorandum about transferring his three relatives to three of the factories run by the Yi Chung Trust Company. You can't run a factory properly when it's chock-full of relations and old friends! With this thought, he set to work on the memorandum, but he had hardly begun when he was interrupted by an uninvited visitor — his nephew Wu Wei-cheng.

"Who sent you here?" he snapped irritably, throwing the pen back on the table. "Mo Kan-cheng?"

He glared sharply at Wu Wei-cheng's rather intelligent-looking face. Closing the door behind him, Wu Wei-cheng remained on the other side of the room away from the desk. His manner was calm and self-possessed as he spoke:

"I've got something to tell you, Uncle."

Wu Sun-fu frowned, but let him go on.

"Chien Pao-sheng's just told me that the girls had a meeting last night in one of the girls' homes — Yao Chin-feng's. When the girls rioted today, she was one of those who wanted to smash up the office. She was also the one who shouted to the crowd to fight it out if we refused to release the six girls that we'd arrested. It was this same girl, Yao Chin-feng, who was the backstage ringleader when we had that trouble in the factory a month ago. They say that Tu Wei-yueh managed to buy her over after that, but the meeting last night was actually held in her hut! She's very radical and I'm sure she's still a secret ringleader."

Wu Sun-fu was watching his nephew's face intently. He smiled faintly, but said nothing. He had already heard from Tu Wei-yueh that Yao Chin-feng had been present at the girls' meeting the night before, so he had learned nothing new from what Wu Wei-cheng had told him. Nevertheless, the mention of Yao Chin-feng's name aroused some association in his mind. He remembered that she was a woman of about thirty, tall and slim, with a small oval face faintly marked by smallpox. He also remembered that after Tu Wei-yueh had bought her over there had been a slight hitch: one of the forewomen, Hsueh Pao-chu, had given the game away — though the trouble had been smoothed out afterwards.

"So far as I can see, Uncle, this present trouble is the result of Tu Wei-yueh's connivance. He could easily have done something to prevent it yesterday, but he didn't. And then this morning, all he did was to play the kind good-hearted mediator! He's in league with that trade union fellow Kuei Chang-lin to win the girls over between them!"

Wu Sun-fu's expression changed abruptly: he was hearing something "new" after all! However, after a moment's thought he quickly pulled himself together and put on a serious expression, then banged his fist on the desk and shouted (though without conviction):

"I'm surprised at you, Wei-cheng! I've given Tu Wei-yueh full authority to manage the factory for me, and I don't need any advice from you!... What you've just told me is private, so don't breathe a word of it outside! Understand? All right, you can go now."

Having waved Wu Wei-cheng away, Wu Sun-fu picked up the memorandum he had been writing, glanced at it, then slowly crumpled it into a ball, hesitation and indecision written all over his face. All of a sudden, he leapt abruptly to his feet, smoothed out the crumpled sheet of paper, and read it through once more; then, with a shake of the head and a snort, he tore it up and threw it into the spittoon. He had finally reversed his decision not to have his relatives in his own factory. He snatched up his pen again and began making out a notice:

> The present reduction of wages has been dictated by the pressure of circumstances, and as soon as the price of silk begins to return to normal the original wage-scale will, of course, come into force again. All employees are strongly advised to return to work without delay, and not allow themselves to be led astray by undesirable elements and so get into trouble. For some time now, the management has borne with patience the continued feud between trade union factions. Let it be clearly understood that, in the event of further attempts to sow dissension and foment unrest among the workers, the management will have no alternative but to take drastic action.

Having given the notice to Mo Kan-cheng to put up, he left the office. Just as he was getting into his car, he turned round to give Tu Wei-yueh his final warning:

"I don't care how you do it, I want the women back at work *tomorrow*!"

*

At one o'clock in the afternoon, Tu Wei-yueh was pacing to and fro in his office, now smiling grimly, now drawing his brows together in a frown. The reason for this nervous anxiety was that he was now on the borderline of success and failure. That morning, when the strike had begun, he had been confident that he would win, for all the shouts of "Down with Chamber-pot Tu!" With the arrival of Wu Sun-fu on the scene, however, his confidence had given way to doubt. Even though Wu Sun-fu had repeatedly assured him that he was giving him an absolutely free hand, he had not been slow to grasp the implication that the "free hand" would only be his until "tomorrow."

If he couldn't bring the strike to an end the following morning, there would be no question of his fate — the sack!

It had been obvious to Tu Wei-yueh for some time that Wu Sun-fu had not been able to make up his mind from the very beginning. He was also fully aware of the difficulties involved in working for a man like Wu Sun-fu who was normally obstinate and ruthless, but who had given way to doubt and indecision.

Suddenly, a shadow flitted across the window. Tu Wei-yueh at once stopped and went to see who it was, then hurried out. It was Kuei Chang-lin. The two men exchanged glances, but said nothing, then walked together into Mo Kan-cheng's office, where they found several people, including Mo Kan-cheng, sitting and waiting quietly.

With a rueful smile on his lips, Tu Wei-yueh glanced round the room and began:

"Mr. Wu's orders are that the women should go back to work tomorrow without fail, which only leaves us this afternoon and this evening to arrange things. This morning we tried to get the women to send a representative to talk things over, but we didn't have any luck. They refuse to recognize the existing trade union, and they've now set up a strike committee. I sent Kuei Chang-lin to negotiate with the strike committee, but they say they're waiting for orders from the silk filature's general strike committee. They're just being bloody-minded about it! I don't think we should concern ourselves with this so-called 'general' strike committee, but get on with stopping the strike in this factory alone. The most important thing at the moment is to get them back to work tomorrow by hook or by crook! Even if we only get them working at half-pressure, it'll be something to show to Mr. Wu. Chang-lin, do you think we'll be able to get them back to work tomorrow? What actually is it that they're demanding?"

Kuei Chang-lin did not reply at once. He glanced from Tu Wei-yueh to Mo Kan-cheng, then shook his head and sighed.

"I give up! I've been run off my feet since yesterday evening trying to bring about a peaceful settlement and save people's face all round, then somebody goes running to the boss behind my back and turning him against me! You ask me to come along and give my opinion, Mr. Tu. If I don't say what I think, people will say I'm being paid for doing nothing; if I do say what I think, people will say that I've got an axe to grind or that I'm having a go at somebody. Mr. Mo, don't you see what an awkward position I am in?"

Silence fell upon the room. Tu Wei-yueh was frowning unhappily and gnawing his lips. Mo Kan-cheng looked flustered. Ah Chen, sitting in the corner, was smiling surreptitiously behind her hand. She nudged Wang Chin-chen, who was sitting beside her, and then threw Tu Wei-yueh a sidelong glance. They both knew only too well what was upsetting Kuei Chang-lin. Pockmarked Li, however, was becoming impatient.

"You've only got to give us the word, Mr. Tu, and we'll go straight in and finish the job!"

"That's right!" put in Wang Chin-chen. "You've only got to tell us what you want done, Mr. Tu! But, Chang-lin, let's hear what it is you've got to say, so that we can decide what to do about it."

As she said this she kept her eye on Mo Kan-cheng, who somehow knew what was coming. Tu Wei-yueh nodded slowly, looking first at Pockmarked Li and then towards Kuei Chang-lin.

"All right, then," the latter began hesitantly, "I'll say what I think's right. The girls know very well the boss is losing money. They also understand perfectly well what he said on the notice — he's had to cut their wages because he's not getting enough for his silk, and he's going to reconsider later on. Now this strike's about two things: it's half because of that wage-cut and half because of certain people they don't like. Hsueh Pao-chu's too domineering, and the girls hate her like poison. And then there's Chien Chiao-lin and Chou Erh-chieh;

they're another thorn in everybody's side. If you want to make sure of getting the girls back to work tomorrow, you'll have to keep these three out of the way for a few days."

As he spoke, Kuei Chang-lin looked steadily at Mo Kan-cheng's startled face. Every now and then Tu Wei-yueh also ran his eye over Mo Kan-cheng's face, and by the time Kuei Chang-lin stopped, all eyes were turned to the old man. Mo Kan-cheng felt flustered, but did not lose his sense of proportion. He was always careful to steer a course between the two sides. He could not afford to risk being suspected of supporting the other side, so he hastened to ingratiate himself with this side.

"Yes, you're quite right! Provided they do go back to work tomorrow!"

Tu Wei-yueh smiled sardonically, for he knew that this exchange had paved the way nicely for him and that he could now proceed, without any further delay, to give them the instructions he had already worked out in advance. His face became suddenly grave as he raised his hand and motioned them to pay attention.

"We can't afford to worry about how certain people are going to take it," he began grimly. "If we've found a way to get the girls back to work tomorrow, then it's up to us all to do what's right and get on with it! Ah Chen, did you get in touch with Yao Chin-feng? Have you found out who's on this strike committee, or whatever it is, besides her? Which of the committee members get on well with her?"

"There's no need to ask who the others are! Ho Hsiu-mei, Chang Ah-hsin and that crowd, of course! There's two that I know of who're on good terms with Yao Chin-feng: Hsu Ah-yi and Lu Hsiao-pao."

As she spoke, Ah Chen pouted out her lips and gave Tu Wei-yueh a sidelong glance. The eternal flirt. Tu Wei-yueh suddenly lost his temper.

"You're always bungling, Ah Chen! We *must know* exactly who these people on the strike committee are! Wang Chin-chen can help you. First you can tell Yao Chin-feng to work on Hsu Ah-yi and Lu Hsiao-pao, and tell them they'd better watch their step, because Ho Hsiu-mei and all that bunch are Communists and the police are going to arrest them! If the girls don't turn up at work tomorrow, Mr. Wu will be anything but gentle to them! If they've got any demands to make, they can do it after they've gone back to work. Then you can get all the forewomen together and go round the huts in ones and twos and tell the girls to call off the strike and not to be taken in by the agitators!"

"But we can't do that!" Wang Chin-chen and Ah Chen protested in unison. "Anybody who goes round the huts at a time like this is just asking for a good hiding!"

"What are you afraid of?" Tu Wei-yueh snapped impatiently. "You can always hit back, can't you? I suppose you'll be wanting bodyguards next! All right, then: Li, you'd better call up your men to keep an eye on them."

Ah Chen crimsoned and was going to argue, but Wang Chin-chen tugged at her sleeve and stopped her. Ignoring the two girls, Tu Wei-yueh turned to Kuei Chang-lin:

"What's this so-called general strike committee they've got? And who's behind it pulling the strings?"

"The Communists, of course! Just making the most of a chance to stir up trouble! There's over a hundred factories, big ones and small ones, out on strike now in Hongkew and Chapei. They've got a general headquarters — in some hotel or other, so they say — though I can find out all about it this evening."

"It'll be too late by then! We must have the information this afternoon! Though I've got another urgent job for you in the meantime, Chang-lin. The girls are so sure of themselves only because there are so many of them out on strike, and if the strikers in the other factories around don't go back to work tomorrow, we're going to have a job to persuade our girls here to go back. What I want you to do, Chang-lin, is to go round the local factories and talk the managements into making tomorrow the deadline for the end of the strike. Tell them to use force to make them go back, and get more policemen in! If there's any picketing at the gates, the pickets must be arrested!"

"That's the stuff!" broke in Pockmarked Li quickly, hearing that force was to be used. "That's just what we ought to do at this place, Mr. Tu! I've just been waiting for a chance to stop their little game once and for all!"

He slapped his thighs with his huge paws. He was a rough, simple-minded fellow, and he had been trying to puzzle out all the morning why Tu Wei-yueh would not use force. But for his "loyalty" to Tu Wei-yueh, he too would have joined in the back-biting. Unable to contain himself any longer, he had stated his own view of the situation and now looked up as obediently as ever into Tu Wei-yueh's face.

Tu Wei-yueh gazed back at Pockmarked Li with a faint smile — it may have been a smile of sympathy, or it may have been one of approbation. Then he said to Pockmarked Li in a tone of voice that was a mixture of coaxing and peremptoriness:

"Don't worry, Li, old chap. Sooner or later there'll be plenty of work for your fists, but don't forget: a good fighter doesn't have to get the first blow in! Besides, our factory's different from the rest. There are so many difficulties involved that if we just plunge in without getting a clear picture of the situation first, we'll quite likely end up by making things worse than they are now. Mr. Wu's always given us plenty of rope, so it's up to us to do things as he wants them done. See what I mean, Chang-lin? Let our neighbour kill a chicken as a warning to our monkey!"

"Just you leave it to me, and I'll make a good job of it."

"Good! . . . Now, Mr. Mo," said Tu Wei-yueh grimly, turning abruptly to Mo Kan-cheng, "I'd like you to put up a notice straight away dismissing Chien Chiao-lin, Hsueh Pao-chu, and Chou Erh-chieh."

Pockmarked Li and the two women were rather surprised at this. They had hardly expected, when it had been suggested that these people should be "kept out of the way for a few days," that they would be dismissed just like that. When they looked at Tu Wei-yueh and saw the glint of firmness in his eyes, they realized that his decision was irrevocable. So that was the end of Chien Pao-sheng and his bunch!

It had come as something of a shock to Mo Kan-cheng, as well. He looked at Tu Wei-yueh's forbidding expression and said nothing for a moment. After a while he scratched uneasily at his cheek and said hesitantly, "Couldn't you save Hsueh Pao-chu's face a bit by asking Mr. Wu to transfer her to one of his 'new' factories?"

"That's a matter for Mr. Wu's kind-heartedness," replied Tu Wei-yueh coldly. "It's no concern of ours. All we're concerned with here is putting up the dismissal notice!"

He turned from Mo Kan-cheng to the other four and went on grimly, "You all know that Hsueh Pao-chu and the other two were the first to stir up the girls against the wage-cut in the workshop yesterday afternoon. They've never tried to work conscientiously in this factory, and they seek every opportunity to settle their personal grievances by playing off the women against Kuei Chang-lin! But they're such nasty pieces of work at the best of times that, however much they try to get round the girls, the girls will still hate the three of them like poison. If we're now giving them the sack, it's not because we want to gain any personal advantage; it's because one, they're trouble-makers, and two, it'll give the girls a chance to let off steam — once they've got rid of these three they'll go back to work! Mr. Wu Sun-fu won't let me resign, so I'll have to carry on — though it'll mean I'm going to upset some people. I hope I can rely on you people to give me your full support, so that we can get everything properly arranged tonight to ensure that the girls go back to work tomorrow without any fuss or trouble. — Though once they're back I'm going to hand in my resignation once more!"

Mo Kan-cheng and the others exchanged surreptitious glances, but no one said anything.

"We haven't a moment to lose," said Tu Wei-yueh, then sternly gave his final order: "Right! All of you go and put your backs into it and report back to me by five o'clock! ... Li, I've got another job for you." He signed to Pockmarked Li to follow him and left the room. The latter made a grimace at the two women and gleefully hurried out behind Tu Wei-yueh.

Tu Wei-yueh stopped when he got to the end of the veranda which ran along the front of the office buildings. Pockmarked Li hurried up and stood in front of him, his lips parted in an elated grin to reveal his large teeth. Part of Tu Wei-yueh's face was in the sun and showed smooth and shiny while the rest of it was in shadow and had a rather pallid appearance. He tilted his head in thought for a moment, then turned his keen eyes on Pockmarked Li and asked in a whisper:

"Haven't you found anything out yet, tailing them all this time?"

"No, not yet. The only people those two have had any contact with are other girls from the factory. We've kept tabs on both of them, but they never went outside the slum."

"You don't mean to say they know they're being shadowed?"

"No fear of that! All my blokes are old hands at the game: you wouldn't find *them* giving themselves away!"

"Any strangers been seen?"

"No. The only people that Ho Hsiu-mei and Chang Ah-hsin ever see are girls from the factory."

Tu Wei-yueh cast another sharp glance at Pockmarked Li, then tilted his head on one side and closed one eye. He was fairly certain in his own mind that Pockmarked Li's men were too stupid and clumsy not to have given themselves away. He had long been aware that Ho Hsiu-mei and Chang Ah-hsin had something up their sleeves. He slewed his eyes round to Pockmarked Li again and went on:

"Who was with them when they left Yao Chin-feng's hut last night?"

"Er — last night? Well, Ho Hsiu-mei and Lu Hsiao-pao were walking along together quarrelling. Chang Ah-hsin went off with two other girls and before they'd gone very far they split up and went three different ways."

"And what about the other two — were they from the factory? Do you know their names?"

"They were factory girls all right. They'd just been to the meeting at Yao Chin-feng's place. I didn't see them myself, but some of my men did. One of them was of middling height, round face, bright eyes, darkish skin. The other one was a bit taller, but they didn't remember exactly what she looked like."

A cold smile suddenly appeared on Tu Wei-yueh's lips. Round face, bright eyes, darkish skin, of medium height: he knew who that was.

"Did they talk on the way?"

"Didn't I just say: they split up before they'd gone very far. The three of them were walking along arm in arm like the best of friends."

Pockmarked Li seemed to be getting impatient. He wiped his mouth with the back of his hand and looked at Tu Wei-yueh with staring eyes.

A shadow flitted across the corner of the wall. Tu Wei-yueh's sharp eyes had not missed it, and he at once stepped forward to see who it was. It was Ah Hsiang, a new "recruit" to whom Tu Wei-yueh had not yet entrusted any important mission. When he saw Tu Wei-yueh, he stopped. Tu Wei-yueh frowned briefly, then called out to him:

"Ah Hsiang! All the forewomen have gone down to the huts to persuade the girls to go back to work tomorrow, because Mr. Wu's put up a notice promising to talk things over with them once they've gone back. I want you to go and keep your eye on them and see that all of the forewomen have gone down. If you find that any of them haven't gone, come back and report *them* to me."

"If there's any trouble, let them have it," added Pockmarked Li. "Just shout if you want any help! We've got the whole place surrounded!" He opened his mouth wide and laughed. Tu Wei-yueh smiled briefly, but his expression immediately became serious again as he turned back to Pockmarked Li:

"We're going down there, too — to look for somebody. I want half a dozen of your chaps to go with us."

Now that he was quite sure that the dark-skinned, good-looking Chu Kuei-ying was mixed up in the plot, Tu Wei-yueh had decided to go and investigate in person.

As they made their way down to the slum, they found the whole area alive with policemen and militiamen patrolling in pairs, while small knots of factory girls buzzed excitedly by the roadside. Their faces shiny with perspiration in the broiling sun, they swarmed noisily up and down, fearless and excited. As they neared the slum, they felt a growing tension in the air. The girls were swarming and humming like mosquitoes at dusk. They were discussing the dismissal of the three girls from the factory. A voice rang out clear above the din: "No mention of the twenty-per-cent wage-cut? They're trying to diddle us!"

With Pockmarked Li and his bullies in tow, Tu Wei-yueh now entered the slum. His lips were set in his usual sardonic smile, but his face was pale and he could feel countless hostile eyes watching him from all sides. "Look, the Chamber-pot!" "Let's get him!" The voices were subdued and sporadic at first, but they became louder and louder as more girls took up the cry. Tu Wei-yueh cast a furtive glance at Pockmarked Li and saw that his face was dark and his jaw set firm.

The bullies were now moving about in twos and threes among the knots of girls, looking for all the world like so many black beetles in their black gowns or black silk jackets. These henchmen of Pockmarked Li's were deliberately barging into the cat-calling groups of girls and clawing at their breasts through their tight, sweat-soaked jackets. Every now and then there would be a little skirmish and shouts would be exchanged, but in a few seconds it would be over. The girls were trying not to be involved in a full-blooded fight with the bullies, and the latter were holding their fire until they received the order to lash out in earnest.

Tu Wei-yueh kept his head down and hurried on, while Pockmarked Li led him to Chu Kuei-ying's hut.

"Look out! Chamber-pot Tu's coming to get us!"

The sudden shout came from the doorway of a hut. The next moment a little girl darted out. It was Chin Hsiao-mei, the little factory-hand who lived in the next hut to Chu Kuei-ying. Pockmarked Li snorted angrily and rushed forward to grab her with his rough, grimy paw, but she was too nimble for him: she ducked and dodged out of the way, then ran for dear life. Tu Wei-yueh signed to Pockmarked Li not to pursue her, and the two of them turned and charged into Chu Kuei-ying's hut, leaving the bullies outside to keep watch.

When Tu Wei-yueh's eyes had got accustomed to the gloom inside the hut, he saw Chu Kuei-ying standing in front of him, her blazing eyes riveted on his. Her oval, olive-skinned face was suffused with anger and her little lips were bloodless. There were only the three of them in the hut: Chu Kuei-ying, Pockmarked Li and Tu Wei-yueh. For a moment there was a tense silence, while outside the hut a babel of voices was gradually rising like a tide, louder and louder.

Forcing a smile, Tu Wei-yueh broke the silence. "Chu Kuei-ying, it's been reported to me that you're a Communist. There are two ways open to you, and it's up to you to choose: either you tell me about the other Communists you go with, in which case you'll be promoted forewoman, or else you don't tell me, in which case you'll go to jail."

"I'm not a Communist and I don't know any Communists!"

"Ah, but I know all about it, you see! Besides you there's Ho Hsiu-mei and Chang Ah-hsin...."

Chu Kuei-ying's heart missed a beat, and a slight change came over her face. Tu Wei-yueh saw it quite clearly. He smiled and pressed her further. "And now *you're* going to tell *me* who else there is besides those two!"

"I tell you I don't know any Communists. You can take me to the police station if you like, but I'll still say the same thing!"

Chu Kuei-ying's expression was a little calmer now, though her lips were paler still and her bright eyes were ablaze. Tu Wei-yueh gave a derisive snort, then suddenly swung round to Pockmarked Li and rasped:

"Search the house!"

By now the sound of angry voices outside had become louder still. A din of shouting and cursing suddenly broke out, then stopped abruptly, only to be replaced by the swish and thud of bamboo and wood on human flesh, voices snarling through clenched teeth, blood-curdling howls, and a sudden rush of feet. Then, unexpectedly, a roar of triumph as a crowd of angry women burst into the hut and hurled themselves straight at Tu Wei-yueh and Pockmarked Li. In the ensuing silent scuffle in the darkness of the hut the plank table and the rickety bamboo bedstead were both overturned.

Tu Wei-yueh wielded a bench as he fought his way out through the tangle of bodies, but just as he got to the door a second wave burst into the hut and cut off his retreat. The din from the crowd outside was deafening. Tu Wei-yueh was now wrestling frantically with two of the girls. In the confusion he caught a clear glimpse of one of them: it was Chang Ah-hsin. All of a sudden Pockmarked Li grabbed hold of a girl in both hands and used her as a battering-ram to clear a way through to Tu Wei-yueh. The girls surrounding Tu Wei-yueh abandoned him and turned their attention to Pockmarked Li. Tu Wei-yueh saw his chance to escape and dashed out of the hut only to be caught up in another crowd. Fortunately for him, these were not infuriated girls, but a dozen or so of Pockmarked Li's bullies fleeing before a veritable deluge of women close on their heels. When they reached the narrow street running alongside the slum, the girls caught up with the bullies and another rough-and-tumble broke out. The shrill screech of police-whistles suddenly pierced through the din and the white of police cap-bands mingled with the girls' flying hair.

Bang! Bang! Warning shots passed over the heads of the crowd.

Pockmarked Li had also escaped from the hut, and still had hold of the same girl. He smirked at Tu Wei-yueh.

*

Ten minutes later all was quiet again in the vicinity of Chu Kuei-ying's hut. The muddy ground was littered with splinters of bamboo, and in the middle lay a night-stool brush which had been used as a weapon. The bamboo door of the hut had been damaged and now hung askew like the broken wing of a bird. Down at the east end of the slum, however, a noisy crowd had gathered on a rubbish dump: the girls were holding a meeting. What few policemen there were, were watching from a safe distance. Half a dozen or more of Pockmarked Li's henchmen stood scattered around the policemen.

The meeting had been called on the spur of the moment and was over in no time at all. It had been called just in time to catch the women's will to fight at its zenith. Tu Wei-yueh's swoop on the slum soon had its effect on the struggle among the women themselves.

"Chamber-pot Tu's a twister!" shrilled Chang Ah-hsin. She was addressing the meeting from the top of a rubbish-heap and gesticulating wildly. "He only gave Hsueh Pao-chu and the other two the sack so that he can trick us into going back to work! Hsueh Pao-chu and the other two girls have been going against him, so he has to find an excuse to get rid of them! And then he comes down here with Pockmarked Li to round us up! Down with Chamber-pot Tu, I say! No going back tomorrow! Anybody who goes back's a rat!"

A thunderous roar broke from the crowd at this:

"Anybody who goes back's a rat!"

"Anybody who tries to get us to go back is a rat, too!"

"Give Yao Chin-feng a good hiding! She's a rat!"

"If they cut down our wages, we'd rather die than go back!" continued Chang Ah-hsin. "We demand that Chamber-pot Tu be slung out! And Kuei Chang-lin with him! Get rid of Wang Chin-chen, Pockmarked Li, Ah Chen, and Yao Chin-feng, and bring back Ho Hsiu-mei! We want...."

She stopped, too hoarse to shout any more. Suddenly, she clapped her hands to her stomach and doubled up, then sank on to her haunches. Immediately, another girl sprang up to take her place. It was Chen Yueh-ngo. She had two bloody weals across her face from when she had fought with Tu Wei-yueh. In a voice which was even louder than Chang Ah-hsin's had been, she shouted:

"We must reorganize the strike committee! We must throw out Yao Chin-feng, Hsu Ah-yi, and Lu Hsiao-pao from the committee! They want us to go back tomorrow, so we should throw them out neck and crop!"

"Chuck 'em out!" was the ear-splitting reply from the crowd. Suddenly, Chang Ah-hsin leapt to her feet, her face suffused with a dark flush, and shrilled at the top of her voice:

"We mustn't go back until the general strike committee tells us to! Now listen, girls! A representative of the general strike committee has got something to say to you!"

A sudden silence fell upon the crowd. A representative of the general strike committee? Who was it? Where was she? The women's faces, bathed in sweat and flushed with excitement, turned from side to side as they craned and peered to see who it was, and a hum of conversation rose from the crowd. After a moment, a young woman dressed like a factory girl, with large eloquent eyes, scrambled up on to the rubbish-heap and stood between Chang Ah-hsin and Chen Yueh-ngo. It was Ma Chin.

"Sisters! A hundred and two silk factories in Shanghai are out on strike together! It was *you* who were brave enough to give the lead! The rats and blacklegs in your factory may fight among themselves, but they're still united when it comes to oppressing you and swindling you! The only way you can achieve victory is to rely on your own strength alone! Throw out the rats and blacklegs, and organize your own trade union! And don't go back till the general strike committee tells you!"

"No going back till we're told!" shouted Chang Ah-hsin and Chen Yueh-ngo, giving the crowd a slogan.

"No going back till we're told!" echoed the closely-packed ranks of the crowd. It was almost literally an echo, in fact. Although Ma Chin had done her best to "purge" her speech of formulas and jargon, it was still an "intellectual's" speech and so it had not made an immediate appeal to the girls' hearts.

"Don't forget, girls!" shouted Chen Yueh-ngo. "We've got to stick together! No going back! No going back! . . . Meeting closed!"

So saying, she jumped down from the rubbish-heap, followed by Chang Ah-hsin and Ma Chin. The crowd broke up and drifted away, shouting slogans as they went. Before long, a squad of armed policemen on motorcycles arrived from the police station, followed by a large force of foot police, but the girls had already dispersed and all they found was an empty rubbish dump. All the police could do was to post a guard over it to stop the girls holding another meeting there. The Chinese section of Shanghai had been under martial law for the last month, and meetings were absolutely prohibited.

*

Yao Chin-feng and Ah Chen had already scurried back to the factory to give Tu Wei-yueh a detailed report of the meeting. They ended by clamouring for protection.

Tu Wei-yueh frowned, but said nothing. He had never expected that, after all the trouble he had taken to cultivate these contacts among the women, they would now prove useless. He had once thought that he would not have to devote more than a third of his energies to dealing with the girls, but he realized now that he would have to devote his last ounce of energy to dealing with them.

"Miserable, scatter-brained creatures!" he muttered viciously to himself through clenched teeth. "Seems a good hiding's all they'll understand! I'll give them 'Chamber-pot Tu'!"

With this he left the two girls and went through into the front office. He was met by an agitated Mo Kan-cheng, who button-holed him and stammered excitedly:

"I...I say, Wei-yueh! I was j — just looking for you! Mr. Wu's been on the phone and he's in a — a terrible rage! Will they...will they go back to work tomorrow, after all? D'you think they will?"

"I'm sure they will!"

Tu Wei-yueh was as resolute and confident as ever, and a cool smile played around his lips. Mo Kan-cheng half closed one eye and gave him a puzzled look.

"Mr. Wu's coming over straight away."

"What for?" asked Tu Wei-yueh in a low voice, shrugging his shoulders, then quickly put on a grim look and roared:

"What the hell's happened to Wang Chin-chen and the rest of the useless crew? You can never find them when you want them! Send somebody out to look for them, Mr. Mo. When they come, tell them to wait for me in your office. And please be quick about it!"

So saying, Tu Wei-yueh stalked quickly away before Mo Kan-cheng could get another word in. He went first to the main gate to see how things were there. The iron gate was closed fast and four policemen stood on guard. Pockmarked Li and his bullies were roving about the place. Some of them were squatting on the steps in front of the cocoon-store, looking like defeated game-cocks. When he saw Tu Wei-yueh, Pockmarked Li hurried across to him and said quietly, "Chien Pao-sheng's lot were in that fight just now. Did you know?"

"How do you know?"

"Ah Hsiang told me."

Tu Wei-yueh gave a derisive snort, narrowed his eyes at the sky for a moment, then looked back at Pockmarked Li again. "Now I'll need fifty men. Go and round them up straight away, Li, and have them wait here till I tell you what to do."

Leaving the main gate, Tu Wei-yueh walked off to inspect the side gates and the rear gate. By this time he had made up his mind what he was going to do, and now headed back towards the office. When he got there, he found Wu Wei-cheng, Ma Ching-shan and Tseng Chia-chu whispering together on the veranda. He gave them a casual glance, then suddenly changed direction, slipped round the back of the office buildings, and made his way to a waste-store next to the boiler-house. He went in.

Squatting on the floor, her hands tied behind her back, was Ho Hsiu-mei. When she saw that it was Tu Wei-yueh, she quickly averted her face and jerked herself furiously round away from him.

He smiled sardonically and began looking her carefully up and down. For a while he remained perfectly quiet and said nothing. Suddenly, Ho Hsiu-mei cast a furtive glance over her shoulder as if to see whether he was still there or not. As it happened, her eyes immediately met his, still cold and hard. Unable to restrain himself, Tu Wei-yueh burst out laughing.

"Ho Hsiu-mei," he said. "Just wait patiently a little longer. After six o'clock, when we've finished discussing terms with your representatives, we'll let you go."

Ho Hsiu-mei stared at him in silence. This time she did not turn her head away.

"The representatives are Lu Hsiao-pao, Yao Chin-feng, and somebody else... a friend of yours... Chang Ah-hsin!"

Ho Hsiu-mei gave a start and a look of surprise came into her face. She continued to stare at Tu Wei-yueh, as if waiting for him to go on.

"Now Chang Ah-hsin knows which side her bread is buttered. I've had a sincere, heart-to-heart talk with her, and now she's come to see sense. She was quite frank with me, and she's told me everything. You've got a good, loyal friend there. She gave me her word that you're a good girl, really, but she says you're young and don't know any better, so that you've played into the Communists' hands. That's right, isn't it?"

Ho Hsiu-mei gave a frightened yelp and her face turned deathly pale. Her terrified eyes were riveted on Tu Wei-yueh's.

"And then there are the other girls in your little group. They're all good friends of yours, your 'comrades,' aren't they? Yes, Chang Ah-hsin told me all about it! But don't worry, I'm not going to have them arrested. I've always got on very well with you girls! I'll tell you what, though: if the police ever find out you're in with the Communists, you'll be arrested and shot. Now just think, Ho Hsiu-mei: some of your friends must be sensible girls that we can talk round. If you can think of any, I'll be only too willing to help them out."

"Oh, Ah-hsin! Ah-hsin!"

Ho Hsiu-mei shuddered as she moaned these words, then let her head slump forward, heart-broken. Tu Wei-yueh gnawed at his lip and smiled, then stepped forward, bent over her, and began in what sounded like a thoroughly sincere tone of voice:

"You shouldn't blame Ah-hsin! Don't blame her! If you just stop and think about it for a moment, you'll understand what it's all about. Look at the many strikes in Shanghai: they were all started by Communists. But who goes to prison in the end? You workers, of course. Meanwhile, the Communists themselves are sitting pretty and taking things easy in their big, modern houses. Every time you go on strike, they put in a nice big claim for expenses and go and have a good time on the proceeds. Take that girl student, for instance — the one that's been leading you and Chang Ah-hsin on. Now *you* never knew where she lived, did you? I'll tell you: she lives in a big luxurious modern house! Though when she comes to a meeting, she has to change into shabby old clothes. And every time she comes over here for a meeting she gets ten or twenty dollars for her fare, whereas you girls have to go on your two feet! She lives in this big, modern house and even her maids are better off than you girls will ever be! Chang Ah-hsin ran into her one day and found out what she was really like. So what did she do? Slipped Ah-hsin a five-dollar note and told her to keep her mouth shut! Though hasn't Ah-hsin told you all about this herself? She's not being quite honest with you if she hasn't. However, she's been a very good friend to you, and she swears you're all right!"

Ho Hsiu-mei hung her head in silence. Suddenly, she burst out crying. It was like a little child crying. Then, abruptly, she forced herself to stop and raised her tear-stained face to look at Tu Wei-yueh. She stared and stared, and all the time the corners of her mouth twitched, as if she was torn by some inner conflict which she could not resolve. Noticing the twitching of her lips, and realizing what it meant, Tu Wei-yueh put on as sympathetic an expression as he could, and pressed home his advantage.

"Don't worry, Ho Hsiu-mei! It won't be long now before we let you go home. Now that we've dismissed Hsueh Pao-chu, we need another girl to take her place. I'm thinking of recommending you to Mr. Wu for promotion to forewoman. Then we'll all get on very well together, with no more quarrels, and everything'll be all right!"

Ho Hsiu-mei's face crimsoned, and tears suddenly started from her eyes, though her sobbing had stopped.

"But Hsiu-mei, can't you think of any of your friends who would listen to good advice? Now think hard, and we'll go and talk them round."

Ho Hsiu-mei suddenly went into a trance. Her head bent in thought, she mechanically twisted the tail of her jacket between her fingers. After a moment she sighed and murmured, "You'll have to ask Chang Ah-hsin. She knows more about it than I do."

It was all she could find to say. She hung her head again and trembled slightly. When he saw that he would not get anything out of her, Tu Wei-yueh shrugged his shoulders, inwardly despising this useless Communist. With a contemptuous glance at her, he turned on his heel and stalked out. His spirits were buoyant as he walked back to the office. He found Ah Hsiang standing idle in front of the veranda and gave him a job:

"Ah Hsiang, go down to the huts and persuade Chang Ah-hsin to come up here with you. If you can't coax her, bring her by force. And be as quick as you can about it."

Just then, a car drove into the factory. Wu Sun-fu's bodyguard Kuan jumped out and held the door open, and Wu Sun-fu himself clambered out. Seeing Tu Wei-yueh coming across to meet him, he said:

"Things are getting worse and worse! I just don't see how you can ever get them back to work tomorrow."

"Mr. Wu," said Tu Wei-yueh with a bow, "the night is sometimes darkest just before daybreak — no stars, no moon." His voice was perfectly calm and confident. Wu Sun-fu forced a brief smile and began pacing along the cinder path on which his car was parked. After he had gone a few steps he swung round to Tu Wei-yueh, who was following him.

"So you're sure about it, eh? All right, then perhaps you'll just tell me how you're going to go about it?"

His voice was just a little too genial, and Tu Wei-yueh suddenly felt uneasy. He was afraid this might be the prelude to an unpleasant scene. After a moment's hesitation, he ran briefly through the principal developments to date; as he spoke, he scanned Wu Sun-fu's face carefully. The light of the low, westering sun lit up one side of Wu Sun-fu's face, so that it appeared shiny and colourful by contrast with the other side, which was in shadow. The antithesis of light and shade might have been symbolic of the two sides of his character. Tu Wei-yueh relaxed a little now and gazed up at the eastern sky, where vast heaps of flaming cloud hung over the horizon.

"So the girl you've caught, this Ho — er — Ho Hsiu-mei, is going to be released, then, eh?"

"Not till it gets dark, and when she is released she'll be shadowed. I think we'll be able to net the whole bunch of them this time." The shadow of a smile flickered round his lips as he said this.

"All right, do it your way and we'll see what happens. In the meantime, Wei-yueh, make an announcement that tomorrow's the deadline for the end of the strike! Those who don't go back tomorrow will be sacked!"

Suddenly, Wu Sun-fu was seized with a fit of exasperation.

Without waiting for Tu Wei-yueh's reply, he scrambled back into the car. His bodyguard settled himself in beside the chauffeur, and the car moved slowly off. The big iron gates were swung right back to let it through, while Pockmarked Li supervised the operation in stentorian tones. The car had only got half way through the gates, when a great roar went up outside, and a crowd of girls surged forward and blocked its path. Immediately, the whole area of the main gate was thrown into confusion. The policemen, followed by Pockmarked Li and his bullies, came rushing up to clear the way, but all the time more and more girls came flocking in until the crowd was twice, three times, four times, five times its original size. The road outside the gate was now completely blocked and there was no hope of ever getting the car through. Inside the car, Wu Sun-fu's heart was pounding violently.

"Let Ho Hsiu-mei go, and we'll let you go!" shouted the girls, as they burst through the cordon of policemen and bullies and made straight for the car. They were quite unarmed, but their determined onslaught made them more terrifying than if they had been armed to the teeth.

The bodyguard, Kuan, leapt out on to the running-board of the car with a murderous expression on his face and pulled out his gun. The girls did not budge. Then, from the back of the crowd, stones and clods began sailing over, though they went wide of the mark. The girls were providing themselves with weapons now, but apparently they had no serious intention of starting a full-scale battle. Sitting in his car, his face livid, Wu Sun-fu shouted repeatedly at the chauffeur:

"Drive on! Straight through 'em at full speed!"

The chauffeur was hard put to it. He tried sounding the horn. This had a slight effect, for it made the girls immediately in front of the car step back instinctively. The car began to move, but the girls would not retreat another step. Angry shouts went up and a hail of stones and clods came flying over from the back of the crowd, this time hitting the car. Kuan gave a roar of fury, raised his gun, and aimed into the middle of the crowd. Just then, someone burst through from behind him. An arm flashed out and the bodyguard's arm was knocked

"Let Ho Hsiu-mei go, and we'll let you go!"

up in the air. At the same moment the gun went off and the shot went skywards.

It was Tu Wei-yueh. Turning away from the bodyguard, he bellowed at the chauffeur:

"You idiot! Back out and turn the car round!"

The car backed in through the gates again, this time without a warning blare from the horn. Wu Sun-fu sprawled back in his seat and showed his teeth in a derisive grin. The chauffeur quickly turned the car round, then drove back along the cinder path and out through the back gate. Meanwhile, part of the crowd had poured in through the gateway, but the greater part of the crowd had been held back outside. Inside and out all was confusion and turmoil, but the girls had no definite aim now. The main body of the crowd was soon dispersed by the police, while the few dozen girls inside were forcibly ejected by Pockmarked Li and his bullies.

As darkness gradually fell the wind rose again. Everywhere was quiet again around the factory, but the atmosphere was still tense and everyone was on edge. Extra sentries had been put on the main gate. The general office was packed; all the forewomen were there, including Wang Chin-chen and Ah Chen, noisily discussing the incident at the gate. The fifty-odd men brought along by Pockmarked Li were waiting for orders on or near the veranda. With the day gone, and only one night left, everyone had given up hope of getting the girls back to work the next day. Yet when they saw that Tu Wei-yueh was as confident as ever, and heard his firm, calm voice, their doubts quickly vanished.

"Right, we've got to get cracking!" he said, addressing the forewomen. "You've got a night's work ahead of you yet! Now get down to the huts and get a grip of the girls! Tell them that anybody who doesn't go back tomorrow will be sacked! If none of them comes back, Mr. Wu will close down the factory! And if they come kicking up a row at the gate again, the whole lot of them will be run inside! If they go back tomorrow without any fuss, we're prepared to discuss things with them afterwards. Now, get cracking and put your backs into it! There'll be somebody down there to make sure you do the job properly!"

None of the forewomen dared to utter a word; they just looked furtively at each other and pulled long faces.

Tu Wei-yueh now called Pockmarked Li in and gave him his orders:

"Got all your men here, Li? They've got a hard night's work in front of them, though it's only for one night. Tell them to split up into twos and threes and patrol all round the huts. If they see any girls getting together, tell them to charge straight in and do what they like with them. If fists are needed, don't hesitate to use them! If they find the girls holding a meeting in any of the huts, tell them to force their way in and round up as many as they can of them. If they see any girls walking about outside, they're to shadow them, whoever they are. Got it? Right, here's two hundred dollars. Share it out among your men."

Tu Wei-yueh threw a roll of notes on the table in front of Pockmarked Li, then looked all round and bellowed, "Where's Ah Hsiang? I suppose you've brought Chang Ah-hsin along?"

Ah Hsiang squeezed through from behind the forewomen, looking very down in the mouth. Tu Wei-yueh's face immediately darkened.

"I've hunted everywhere but I still can't find her," said Ah Hsiang, reddening. "I can't think where she can be hiding. Bitch! I'll go and have another look for her."

As he spoke he stole a glance at Pockmarked Li, as if he hoped that he would put in a good word for him. Tu Wei-yueh turned away from him with a snort and addressed the room at large:

"Did you all hear that? One of the perishers has already gone into hiding! — Now, look here, Ah Hsiang! You've made a muck-up of it and let one of the ringleaders escape! There's no point in going down to have another look for her. Hang on here a minute; I've got another job for you."

Tu Wei-yueh stood up as he said this, and waved to the forewomen and Pockmarked Li to leave the room. Only Ah Hsiang remained behind, looking very uncomfortable as he waited for his orders.

It was already quite dark outside, and the cawing of crows came from the roof of the workshop opposite. Tu Wei-yueh stared intently at Ah Hsiang, as if to make sure whether this young man was capable of assuming a heavy responsibility. At length, he made up his mind and fixed his gimlet eyes on Ah Hsiang's.

"When we let Ho Hsiu-mei go, I want you to shadow her. And make sure you don't slip up this time!"

Having now disposed his forces, he rang up the local police station and asked them to send up extra policemen to guard the factory.

*

Around nine o'clock that evening, Wu Sun-fu was entertaining a number of friends and relatives who had come to see how he was after his unpleasant experience at the factory gate. The house and garden were ablaze with lights, and the whir of electric fans was everywhere. It was the same old "bright and happy" world as ever.

Mrs. Wu and her sister Pei-shan and Mrs. Tu and her sister Huei-fang were playing mahjong in the dining-room, while Wu Sun-fu was entertaining his guests (including Colonel Lei, who had just returned to Shanghai from the front) in the large drawing-room, and chatting about the wave of strikes which had been sweeping Shanghai for the past two months. It was an informal conversation, but their laughter sounded rather forced. Wu Sun-fu felt as if his mind was being tugged outwards in half a dozen directions at once, and try as he might, he just could not concentrate for two moments together. His unruly state of mind showed in his face, which was now dark, now flushed, now pale.

Presently, an awkward silence fell over the room, broken only by the drowsy whir of the electric fan, like some monotonous lullaby. From the dining-room came the clatter of mahjong-tiles and the sound of Ah-hsuan's laughter. After a moment, two men came into the room, arguing as they went: Tu Hsueh-shih and his nephew, Tu Hsin-to.

"What do you mean my theory is mere fantasy which won't work in practice?" Tu Hsueh-shih was protesting. "What about yours? Have you ever run a factory? All you can do is lie in bed and dream about doing things!"

He was furious, and his cat-like eyes now stared like those of a startled hare. Though he was actually three or four years younger than his nephew, and though he was not, like him, a "Doctor of God-knows-what" just back from the universities of France, he was still very fond of playing the venerable uncle when he was with Tu Hsin-to, and indulging his fondness for lecturing people. Tu Hsin-to, wearing his usual air of blasé superiority, draped himself nonchalantly against the doorpost and smiled faintly.

"The trouble with you is that your experience has been rather limited. My theory isn't something I've dreamed up in bed; it's something that's been tried out and has produced results in England, or it may have been America, I don't remember exactly which — anyway, it was one of the two. And it's also mentioned in some elementary book on economics, where it says that this shoe factory where all the workers have shares in the business has made great strides and has never had any labour trouble whatsoever. If that isn't practical proof I'd like to know what is!"

"All right, then: *my* theory's also being put into practice," retorted Tu Hsueh-shih. "And producing good results, too. Just look at Italy!" He smiled triumphantly.

"Ah, but it'll never work in this country. Go and ask any factory-owner, and he'll soon tell you whether it'll work or not."

"And I suppose you're going to tell me that your theory *will* work in China? What about you asking a factory-owner yourself? Sun-fu, for instance!"

Tu Hsueh-shih looked annoyed, but his annoyance was tinged with satisfaction at having found a qualified arbitrator in Wu Sun-fu. Without waiting for Tu Hsin-to's reply or asking his opinion of his choice of arbitrator, he took a step forward and called out loudly to Wu Sun-fu:

"Sun-fu! If you tried to get all the girls in your factory to buy shares in the business, so that they could be shareholders of Yu Hua Silk Filature like yourself, would it work?"

This sudden query startled Wu Sun-fu out of his reverie. He looked round and frowned. Li Yu-ting, who was sitting opposite Wu Sun-fu, also looked round in surprise at the grim expression on Tu Hsueh-shih's face. However, being a professor of economics and having heard a snatch or two of their conversation in the doorway, Li Yu-ting sized up the situation readily. He instinctively raised his hand to scratch his head, as he invariably did when about to deliver himself of his opinion on anything, but Tu Hsueh-shih beat him to it, and hastened to explain in a ponderous but agitated voice. He was evidently taking the matter very seriously.

"We're discussing how to prevent labour trouble. Hsin-to says there'll be no labour trouble if the workers are all shareholders, and he mentions a shoe factory in England as an example. But I say his theory won't work: if a worker's rich enough to be a shareholder, he ceases to be a worker, and if a factory has only shareholders and no workers it's going to be a queer sort of factory!"

Tu Hsueh-shih paused for breath, and immediately a gale of laughter swept the room. Even Tu Hsin-to joined in. The only exception was Wu Sun-fu, who just parted his lips in a barely perceptible smile.

The sound of laughter brought Wu Chih-sheng and Fan Po-wen in from the dining-room, where they had been watching the game of mahjong. They immediately joined in the merriment as if they knew what was going on.

"You've got it all wrong, Uncle Hsueh-shih," declared Tu Hsin-to quietly amid the laughter. "My theory isn't as simple as all that."

Tu Hsueh-shih immediately scowled and turned angrily on Tu Hsin-to. "Perhaps you'll explain your theory yourself, then?"

Tu Hsin-to smiled and shook his head, then pursed his lips and began quietly whistling a popular French tune. Tu Hsueh-shih took this attitude of his nephew as a downright insult and crimsoned violently. Fortunately, Fan Po-wen came to the rescue.

"I think I know what Tu Hsin-to means. He's suggesting that in a factory the shareholders should be workers and the workers shareholders. That is to say, the share capital is contributed and controlled by the workers themselves instead of being concentrated in the hands of a few big shareholders. This may be a good solution to the problem. The only trouble is that the women employed in Sun-fu's factory are so poor that they've nothing left to call their own except their ever-hungry mouths!"

This time even Wu Sun-fu had to laugh. But he still made no comment. He had never had any time for all this empty theorizing that these youngsters were so fond of.

Colonel Lei sat with one leg crossed over the other, drawing on a cigarette and slowly shaking his head. He had been back in Shanghai for three days now, but his terrible experiences under fire at the front and his worries and grievances as a prisoner of war — the result of misjudging enemy positions — were still fresh in his mind. He had become pessimistic about the war and about his own career as well. Hence the worried way in which he was shaking his head.

"There you are then!" resumed Tu Hsueh-shih. "Hsin-to's theory just wouldn't work! Now, I've got a better one. I'm dead against factory-owners closing down, or even cutting down production, just because they're suffering some temporary setback. If Chinese industry is to be developed, our industrialists must be prepared to suffer certain initial losses. Both sides must do their level best to help the country: the workers should be forbidden to strike, and factory-owners should be forbidden to suspend operations!"

Having, in his opinion, finally disposed of his nephew's argument, Tu Hsueh-shih fully expected that when he brought out his own theory he would have an attentive audience; but to his mortification no one paid the least attention to what he was saying. Tu Hsin-to had joined Fan Po-wen and Wu Chihsheng and gone out on to the front steps to discuss something else. Wu Sun-fu, Li Yu-ting and Colonel Lei chatted for a moment about the idea of having "worker-shareholders," but the conversation gradually veered back to the continual ebb and flow of the front line. A scowl contorted Tu Hsueh-shih's cat-like face, and he stalked off in high dudgeon to watch the mahjong game in the dining-room again.

The discussion of the latest events in the war was now in full swing, and Wu Sun-fu's face was flushed with excitement once more. Although the recent changes in the military situation along the northern section of the Tientsin-Pukow line had involved the Yi Chung Trust Company in certain losses over their government bond investments, Wu Sun-fu had great hopes of an early improvement in the situation, and so he was in fairly high spirits. He turned to Colonel Lei:

"It looks as if the war's fast coming to an end, don't you think? The bankers had definite confirmation today that Tsinan's been evacuated."

"Hm! I don't think it's going to be as easy as all that," countered Colonel Lei, the "optimist" again now that his opinion was wanted. "After Tsinan, there's still Hsuchow! War's a mysterious affair, unpredictable. Sometimes a battered line or surrounded city can hold out for as long as six months. No, I think the war's going to drag on for some time yet!"

Wu Sun-fu smiled faintly to himself. Although he did not know all the ins and outs of why the colonel had gone to Tientsin from the front line and then come back to Shanghai, he could make a very shrewd guess at the reason, so it was only natural that he should smile to himself at what Colonel Lei was now saying. The last thing Wu Sun-fu wanted was another long-drawn-out struggle at Hsuchow after the one at Tsinan — that would be too great a blow to his speculations! He now turned to Li Yu-ting, who, to his surprise, suddenly leapt to his feet in great agitation.

"What! The war drags on for another six months? But, Colonel Lei, that would be terrible! Just think of the present situation: there's Ho Lung in and out of Shasi and Tayeh, Peng Teh-huai in Liuyang, Fang Chih-min holding Chingtehchen, and Mao Tsetung and Chu Teh prodding at Chian. If the war drags on for another six months, there's no telling how far these Communists will go! We'll all be done for in no time!"

"You're surely not worrying about those bandits?" exclaimed the colonel. "They'll just fold up before a proper army. No, we don't take them seriously. Though of course the Japanese newspapers exaggerate the danger from that direction — but then they've got an axe to grind. The reason the Japanese are spreading these rumours is to damage the prestige of the Central Government."

Colonel Lei's "optimism" was getting the better of him now, and the light of battle gleamed in his eyes. Li Yu-ting shook his head as if in disbelief, then turned to Wu Sun-fu and gave him a solemn warning:

"You know, Sun-fu, it's a great pity that you're having this trouble in your factory at a time like this! You must settle it at once — by force, if necessary! This general strike of the silk-workers is just one part of the Communists' plan for nation-wide riots during July, and the present trouble is the starting-signal! When your girls stoned your car this afternoon, they were actually rioting! If you don't crush them first, they may quite easily go and do something like setting fire to the factory! You couldn't recover your losses then, even if you killed the lot of them!"

Wu Sun-fu winced as the memory of the afternoon's frightening episode at the factory gate came back to him. The hum of the electric fan reminded him of the angry roar of the crowd. To make things worse, something else now occurred to prod at his troubled mind: Kao Sheng suddenly appeared with two men from the factory — Wu Wei-cheng and Ma Ching-shan, both looking rather agitated.

Wu Sun-fu sprang to his feet and asked in a stern voice, though with a hint of trepidation, "Have you just come from the factory? How are things down there? No trouble, I hope?"

"Not up to the time we left," they replied, both speaking at the same time. "But we've got some important news for you."

As they spoke, they stared at Wu Sun-fu in a peculiar manner.

Wu Sun-fu felt slightly relieved and did not immediately demand to know what this important news was that had brought them hurrying over at this time of night. He paced to and fro for a moment, a forced smile on his lips, then shot Wu Wei-cheng and Ma Ching-shan a sharp look, as much as to say, "So you're here to inform against Tu Wei-yueh again, eh?" The two of them just stood there rather stiffly and said nothing.

When Colonel Lei saw that Wu Sun-fu was going to be busy, he took his leave. Li Yu-ting strolled out into the garden to join Tu Hsin-to and Fan Po-wen. Left alone in the room, Wu Wei-cheng and Ma Ching-shan exchanged glances and wondered whether they were to succeed or fail in their task. The clatter of mahjong-tiles came from the dining-room next door.

"Now, what's this important business of yours?" demanded Wu Sun-fu crossly as he came back from seeing the colonel off. "Tu Wei-yueh in the wrong again, I suppose?"

He indicated with a wave of his hand that they should sit down.

But this time the two young men had not very much to say against Tu Wei-yueh. They had come to offer Wu Sun-fu a solution to the strike problem. Actually, they had been sent by Chien Pao-sheng, the author of the plan.

"Uncle Sun-fu," began Wu Wei-cheng. "Chien Pao-sheng has a lot of influence in the trade union. He knows practically everything there is to know about the girls. For two days now Tu Wei-yueh's been hunting around, but he still hasn't been able to find out which of the girls are Communists, whereas Chien Pao-sheng has known all the time. What Chien Pao-sheng suggests is that we should arrest the Communists and at the same time get rid of a whole batch of trouble-makers among the girls. His idea is that once we've done that the union should be responsible for bringing in new girls and guaranteeing for their good conduct. If the management wants to cut wages or stop the payment of overtime for Sunday work or anything like that, he thinks the union should be consulted first, so that they can take the matter up with the women. Chien Pao-sheng says he can guarantee to prevent any further trouble of this kind even if you decide to cut wages by forty or fifty per cent. . . . Uncle Sun-fu, if you'll only try what Chien Pao-sheng suggests, you'll find you won't have to spend all your time worrying about labour trouble, which will be quite a load off your mind. Don't you think it's a wonderful idea? Chien Pao-sheng would have liked to tell you about it himself long ago, but he was afraid you wouldn't listen to him, so he put it off till today, when he told me and Ching-shan about it. He's the sort of man that if he says he'll do a thing, he'll do it!"

"As for getting the girls back to work tomorrow as he says he will," added Ma Ching-shan, "why, Tu Wei-yueh will never manage it! The girls hate him like poison! This afternoon he went down to their huts to arrest somebody, which only made things worse! He's just asking for trouble, doing a thing like that! The girls all realize that you're losing money, and they say they're quite willing to discuss the matter of a wage-cut with you; but they say they'd rather die than go back to work while this fellow Tu is still in charge! The situation now is that all the girls in the factory are lined up against one man — Tu Wei-yueh! They absolutely hate him! And all the forewomen hate him as well!"

As he spoke, Ma Ching-shan's shifty eyes darted uneasily from Wu Sun-fu to Wu Wei-cheng and back again. Wu Wei-cheng sat there in a respectful attitude, nodding his head and looking anxious, though listening with half an ear to the clicking of mahjong-tiles in the next room and silvery laughter of Lin Pei-shan.

Wu Sun-fu smiled darkly as if to remind them that "to hear is not to believe," but his eyes betrayed his growing indecision. He raised his hand to finger his chin and raised his eyebrows as if he was going to say something, but changed his mind and jerked his hand up from his chin to his forehead; he wiped it down the whole length of his face, then let it fall on to the arm of his chair. Still he said nothing. To all the other worries which were tugging his mind in different directions there was now added another worry. He felt he no longer had the energy to continue the struggle to preserve his mental balance. The smouldering fires of his resentment blazed into life once more, and Wu Wei-cheng chose this moment to pour oil on the flames.

"Uncle Sun-fu! It's not that I like running people down, but I'm just fed up with Tu Wei-yueh and I feel I must tell you about him. He just relies on bluff and putting on a show with his bright ideas and his swank! His specialty's bribery, but he's just throwing your money away by the handful! And now he's promised the forewomen and supervisors a dollar for every girl they get to go back to work — don't you think that's a cheek?"

Wu Sun-fu's face suddenly darkened; his confidence in Tu Wei-yueh was now completely shaken. He crashed his fist down on the arm of the chair and roared, "Is that true? You're not lying to me, are you?"

"As if I'd dare! Ching-shan knows about it, too."

"Humph! How is it that Mo Kan-cheng hasn't told me anything about it? The old scoundrel, he hasn't said a word to me about it!"

"Perhaps even Mr. Mo doesn't know about it yet," Ma Ching-shan put in hurriedly. "Tu Wei-yueh's a real dictator — he keeps everybody in the dark about what he's up to."

He tipped Wu Wei-cheng a furtive wink, though Wu Sun-fu was so overcome with rage that he did not notice it. He suddenly sprang to his feet and bellowed through the door, "Kao Sheng! Ring up Mr. Mo and ask him to come round at once — no, wait a minute, ring up the factory and get Tu Wei-yueh to come to the phone. I want to speak to him!"

"But, Uncle, you don't have to be so hasty about it," hurriedly intervened Wu Wei-cheng. "It's only hearsay, so far. We haven't any definite proof yet, and Tu Wei-yueh may deny it."

He tipped Ma Ching-shan a wink, but the latter was too agitated to speak and just sat and gaped, wide-eyed.

Wu Sun-fu inclined his head in thought for a moment, then snorted and returned to his chair. After a moment he flapped a hand at Kao Sheng, who was waiting just outside the door for his orders, and said peevishly, "You can go. There's no need to ring anybody now."

"I think it would be best, Uncle, if you were to send for Chien Pao-sheng tomorrow and ask him about it," suggested Wu Wei-cheng, trying to beat a hasty retreat before Wu Sun-fu saw through them. "If Tu Wei-yueh fails in his attempt to get the girls back to work tomorrow, there's no reason why you shouldn't give Chien Pao-sheng's plan a trial." As he spoke, he gave Ma Ching-shan another sly wink.

For a moment there was silence in the room. Outside in the garden the trees could be heard rustling in the wind, and from time to time there came roars of laughter from Li Yu-ting and the others. From the dining-room came the sound of mahjong-tiles being shuffled round on the surface of the table and the shrill voices of the ladies as they commented on the extraordinary luck of the banker in the game they had just finished.

All these noises irritated Wu Sun-fu, but he just could not shut his ears to them as they hammered away at his mind. His head was in such a whirl that it was beyond him to make up his mind. At one moment he felt that Tu Wei-yueh was hard to handle, too obstinate, too cunning, too confident; at the next he began to have his doubts about the truth of what he had just heard, and decided he must believe his eyes rather than his ears. He shook his head wearily and turned to the two young men, who were beginning to show signs of nervousness.

"All right, I've heard what you've got to say. You can go now, but mind you don't gossip about it to anyone else."

Having disposed of Wu Wei-cheng and Ma Ching-shan in the patronizing tone of a family elder, Wu Sun-fu got up and walked out. His growing irascibility was now accompanied by a strange, unaccountable feeling of despair.

He shut himself up in his study and began reviewing in minute detail all that Tu Wei-yueh had said and done during the past two days, and comparing it with the criticisms of Wu Wei-cheng and Ma Ching-shan; but the more he thought about everything, the sharper became his conflicting moods of anger and despair. He was surprised at himself, and at the way his customary ruthlessness and strength of purpose had deserted him. Even his never-failing energy seemed to have run out of him. As he sat there, his jumbled thoughts creeping sluggishly through his head, he became aware of the sound of the wind in the trees outside his window. It reminded him of the noise of the crowd which had hemmed him in at the factory gate that afternoon, and he felt again the same thrill of fear. As he looked at the glow of light which lit up the yellow silk shade of the lamp on his desk, he could imagine the glow from a blazing factory —

his own factory, fired by the girls! No, he just wasn't his usual self any more!

Yet still these sick fancies kept hammering at his mind, and his thoughts drifted from the factory to the Yi Chung Trust Company — to his loss of eighty thousand dollars in government bond speculation, to Chao Po-tao's financial blockade, to the eight dried-up factories crying out for large sums of money, to the costly "white elephant" of a silk factory which he had taken over from Chu Yin-chiu. . . . All these problems rose up before him and whirled in a frantic merry-go-round through his head, until, no longer able to think clearly, he just sat and groaned under the pitiless excesses of his imagination.

Suddenly, the door-handle turned with a creak, and Wu Sun-fu woke from his nightmare with a start to see Wang Ho-fu's round face, wearing a worried frown and a wry smile. He rubbed his eyes and looked again — it really was Wang Ho-fu, and he had sat down. Without quite realizing what he was doing, Wu Sun-fu blurted out:

"Why, Ho-fu! Is something wrong at the eight factories?"

"Well, yes, but it's nothing much. — You don't mean to say you already know about it, Sun-fu?"

Wu Sun-fu shook his head, still sure that he was dreaming. He fixed his eyes on Wang Ho-fu's moustache in a vacant stare.

"It's nothing very serious at the moment," said Wang Ho-fu. "It's just that everywhere's being affected by the war and a depression's setting in. Every consignment we sent out last week has simply been returned intact. What are we going to do from now on? We work our fingers to the bone to raise the necessary capital, sink it in these eight factories, and then, just when production is getting under way, there's no market for the goods, so we have to put them in the warehouse and pay for storage. We just can't carry on indefinitely like this."

He heaved a sigh and fixed his eyes on Wu Sun-fu.

So it was not that the factories had gone on strike, as Wu Sun-fu had at first feared. He felt slightly relieved at that, but in a flash this sense of relief vanished, to be replaced by an even fiercer feeling of anger and despair. At this moment, every one of his worries seemed to be tearing at his mind at once. His spirit was shattered and he found it absolutely impossible to bear the strain. His will was gone, and there remained only a sullen fury and despair.

When no reply was forthcoming, Wang Ho-fu frowned slightly and went on slowly:

"There's something else. I hear the Central Army has not been appreciably weakened, even though they've lost Tsinan. On top of that, a really strong defence-line has been built up in front of every single key point south of Tsinan. It's going to be a long-drawn-out tussle — several months, I should say. Some people even predict that it'll see the year out. Oh, what a mess! As things are, we'll have to make a swift, realistic decision about what we're going to do about these eight factories of ours. If we don't, we're going to go under the way the others have done!"

"The fighting last the year out? Impossible! . . . Though you can never tell!"

Wu Sun-fu had said something at last, but he might just as well have said nothing. It was not like him to contradict himself in the same sentence like that, and Wang Ho-fu was rather surprised himself. He supposed Wu Sun-fu had been overdoing it in his own factory the past few days, so that his mind was now a little blurred. He looked at Wu Sun-fu's face and decided he did look out of sorts. He heaved a sigh of disappointment.

"I can see you're tired, Sun-fu, so I won't disturb you any longer. We can talk about it tomorrow."

"No, no, don't go yet! I insist that we thrash the matter out now!"

"All right, then . . . Sun Chi-jen and I have talked it over, and we suggest that, starting next month, the eight factories should go on half time — that is, in addition to the wage-cut and the reduction of staff that we've already agreed upon. After a month like that, we can see how things are going, and decide what to do."

"Eh? Go on half time?" exclaimed Wu Sun-fu, springing to his feet. His dark face was flushed and his expression was strange and rather frightening. "Why, that'd be asking for trouble! Workers nowadays are liable to smash up the factory or set it on fire just as soon as they look at you!"

Wang Ho-fu was taken aback for a moment, but he quickly put on a smile and said, "Oh, no, no fear of anything like that happening. You're forgetting that these are all small factories ranging from a hundred to three hundred workers apiece at the most. There's not enough of them to riot. You look really worn out, Sun-fu. You don't want to overdo it, you know. Why not take a few days' holiday?"

"Oh, it's nothing, really; I'll be all right. Well, you'd better put them on half time, then."

"Except for the silk goods factory, which will have to stay on full time until we've filled our orders for the autumn," Wang Ho-fu added. He was quite sure now that there was something wrong with Wu Sun-fu, and after a few casual words, he took his departure.

The sky was now a pall of black cloud. Li Yu-ting and the others had left, and the garden was deserted. The lights among the thick foliage of the trees had been switched off, and a heavy gloom had descended on the garden. From the windows of the dining-room there still came the blaze of lights, the clatter of mahjong-tiles, and the excited voices of the players, while in the large drawing-room the wireless was twanging out the last item of the day's programme — a popular Shanghai ballad. Having seen his visitors off, Wu Sun-fu wandered back to the study. Now, bit by bit, his conversation with Wang Ho-fu began to come back to him like the memory of a dream, and he realized how agitated he had been and how feeble he must have appeared.

As this realization came home to him, he was seized once more by a consuming rage — and not just rage alone, but by hatred of himself. This hate and anger he now transferred to everything around him. He paced up and down the study in a frenzy, his eyes bloodshot and his teeth clenched. All he wanted now was someone to vent his rage upon. He wanted to destroy something. All the reverses he had suffered over his own factory and over the Yi Chung Trust Company now fused into a single savage impulse, the impulse to destroy something!

He lowered himself on to the swivel chair behind his desk and sat there like some wild beast lying in wait for its prey, his eyes darting from side to side in search of something whose destruction would give him the satisfaction he needed and provide an outlet for his savage desire to destroy!

The maid, Wang Mah, came in with a bowl of bird's-nest gruel for him. Wu Sun-fu did not notice her until she placed the bowl on the desk in front of him, when his burning gaze suddenly fell upon her hands, white, plump and dimpled. The fierce flames of his mad desire to destroy suddenly rose to white heat. He jerked up his head and fixed his bloodshot eyes on her face. To him Wang Mah was no longer Wang Mah, the maid, but an object, an object to be violated, an object whose violation would best afford him satisfaction!

He sprang up and swooped on her, on this object that he would violate. Wang Mah seemed taken aback for a fleeting moment, but then she smiled invitingly as if she understood and stepped daintily back, watching him with amorous eyes which nevertheless betrayed a hint of apprehension and shyness. Before he had time to realize what she was doing, she moved quickly back into the corner and stood there leaning against the wall. Then the plump, dimpled hand moved upwards to the light-switch. The ceiling-light went out, leaving only the pool of yellow light beneath the lamp on the desk. Then even this light was extinguished, and the room was plunged in darkness, except for the faint glow of a distant light which flecked the net curtains over the window with leaf-shadows.

When the light came on again, Wu Sun-fu was lying alone on the sofa, his brows knit in a frown and his eyes staring vacantly. His strange fury had passed, but his mind was now occupied by a puzzled feeling of not knowing exactly what he had been doing. He felt as if it had all been a monstrous dream. Gradually, the same old merry-go-round began again — would the girls go back tomorrow? How could he dispose of the goods produced by the eight factories? What should he do about Tu Wei-yueh and Chien Pao-sheng? All these problems had soon taken possession of his mind again.

He smiled wryly, then closed his eyes and gnawed his lips.

The clock in the study showed the first hour of the new day, but the dining-room still rang with talk and laughter and the clatter of mahjong-tiles.

XV

NEXT morning, the sky was hidden by a white mist. While the night-soil carts still rumbled through the streets, the hooter sounded in the Yu Hua Silk Filature. Outside the factory gate stood a line of policemen, armed with rifles and Mausers, to ensure that the return to work should go off without a hitch. Pockmarked Li, Wang Chin-chen and all the other supervisors and forewomen were patrolling up and down around the workshop. Their faces were pale after a sleepless night, their eyes were bloodshot, and they were tense with excitement.

This was the decisive moment of a decisive battle! These well-tried, highly-honoured "heroes and heroines" were preparing to "quaff the cup of victory" — though not, of course, without some qualms about the possible outcome.

On the veranda in front of the office building, Tu Wei-yueh was pacing up and down like some great general awaiting news of victory from the front. His air was resolute and confident. He was well aware that Wu Wei-cheng and Ma Ching-shan had been to see Wu Sun-fu the night before, but that did not worry him in the least. He had made all his arrangements down to the last detail, and he was well satisfied with the results achieved by the forewomen and supervisors in a hard night's work. There was only one little thing that worried him — Ah Hsiang had not yet reported back to him, the bastard!

The hooter went a second time, this time longer and louder than the first. After it had stopped, Tu Wei-yueh's ears still rang for a few seconds. Now, all the lights in the workshop went on together, though through the thick mist they showed as blurs like will-o'-the-wisps.

Just then, Kuei Chang-lin came running up. His little beady

eyes, set slightly askew in his long, square-jawed face, were fixed steadily on Tu Wei-yueh as he ran.

"Well? How are things going, Chang-lin?"

"The girls are coming back! In twos and threes, and in dozens, too!"

The two men smiled together. The worst was over! Tu Wei-yueh turned and ran into the office, picked up the telephone and gave the operator Wu Sun-fu's home number. He was anxious to pass on the news of their first victory. Wu Wei-cheng, Ma Ching-shan and Tseng Chia-chu were in the room, grimacing and giving each other significant glances. Just as Tu Wei-yueh eventually got through, a sudden sound of shouting came from outside. Wu Wei-cheng and the other two immediately rushed out. Tu Wei-yueh turned his head to look out of the window and smiled sardonically. He knew what the noise meant — evidently some of the more recalcitrant girls were trying to picket the gate. This was no more than he had expected — in fact, he had already given orders that anyone attempting to picket the factory should be arrested without more ado. He had nothing to worry about. When he turned back to the telephone, he found that he had been cut off. He was just going to ring through again, when an even louder roar was heard outside. The next moment someone burst into the office shouting at the top of her voice: it was Ah Chen, her hair hanging loose over her face.

"They're fighting! They're fighting!" she shouted, flinging herself almost into Tu Wei-yueh's arms. He dropped the receiver with a cry of rage, then thrust Ah Chen aside and flew out of the door. Just as he came out on to the veranda he collided with Wang Chin-chen, who was also racing up like one possessed, her face a deathly white.

"Picketing, eh? Run them straight in!" shouted Tu Wei-yueh as he ran towards the gate. He was pale with rage at Kuei Chang-lin and Pockmarked Li for being so utterly useless. But when he reached the cocoon-stores he stopped. A woe-begone Kuei Chang-lin was running towards him with a bleeding face. Down at the gate a scuffle was going on, with the police trying to part the combatants in a half-hearted, face-saving sort of way. There did not appear to be any girls among them, though outside the gate several dozen girls were standing in clusters some distance away, shouting and gesticulating excitedly. Kuei Chang-lin tried to hold Tu Wei-yueh back.

"Don't go down there!" he gasped. "Our people are getting beaten up! Don't go!"

"Nonsense! Haven't any of you got any guts? What's happened to Pockmarked Li?"

"He's down there in the middle of the crowd!"

"The useless idiot! He hasn't got a clue!"

Swearing angrily, Tu Wei-yueh brushed Kuei Chang-lin aside and ran on. Kuei Chang-lin turned and ran after him, still shouting "Don't go!" Near the gate Tu Wei-yueh found Tseng Chia-chu standing on a bench with Wu Wei-cheng and Ma Ching-shan standing in front of him; the three of them looked highly elated and were shouting encouragement to the tussling crowd. On one side of the gateway stood Chien Pao-sheng, talking with someone who looked like a police sergeant. Tu Wei-yueh took it all in at a glance and began to realize what was happening. He saw red. Dashing up to Tseng Chia-chu and the other two, he bellowed furiously:

"What are you lot doing here? Directing the fight? Just you wait, I'll report this to Mr. Wu!"

The three young men were taken aback for the moment, then Tseng Chia-chu hurled himself at Tu Wei-yueh with a snarl, but Kuei Chang-lin quickly tripped him up from behind and he went sprawling. Tu Wei-yueh now dashed across to the gate, thrust Chien Pao-sheng unceremoniously aside, and addressed the police sergeant:

"I'm the manager, name of Tu! Please tell your men to round up these hooligans who are attacking my people from the factory!"

"Ah, but we can't tell which are which!"

"Then round up the whole lot of them!" bawled Tu Wei-yueh. "We can sort them out later on!"

He turned to look for Chien Pao-sheng, but he had already made himself scarce. The sergeant now began blowing his whistle and running towards the crowd. The crowd broke up and a dozen or so of them took to their heels, while at the

"They're fighting! They're fighting!"

same time three or four policemen came running up to the gate in answer to the whistle. Tu Wei-yueh caught sight of Ah Hsiang among those who were running away, and now he understood everything. He pointed Ah Hsiang out to the policemen. "Stop that man! We want him! Bring him round to the accounts office!"

Ah Hsiang gaped dumbstruck at his captors, then tried to explain, but Tu Wei-yueh was already racing back in through the gate.

The whole disturbance had lasted only six or seven minutes, but it seemed like a hundred years to Ah Chen, who was still hiding in the office, trembling with fear. As Tu Wei-yueh came back into the room, Ah Chen sprang up, her hair still tousled, and caught hold of his arm. He gave her a contemptuous glance, then shook her off and snarled, "You made sure you didn't get your precious hide damaged, then! If everybody was like you, I might as well give up straight away!"

"You didn't see how fierce those devils were! They —"

"Shut up!" he snapped. "It's all over now. Go and fetch Kuei Chang-lin and Pockmarked Li!"

He went quickly across to the telephone and picked up the receiver, which was still off the hook from last time. He began calling the operator, but suddenly changed his mind, hung it up again, and ran out of the office. For one fleeting moment he had had an idea, but now it had gone clean out of his head. He stamped his foot with annoyance and began pacing up and down, fuming with vexation. Just at that moment he saw Mo Kan-cheng shambling hurriedly towards him, a pair of ancient, down-at-heel shoes on his feet and a long gown draped round his shoulders.

"I say, Wei-yueh, what are you holding Ah Hsiang for?" he demanded abruptly.

Tu Wei-yueh's face hardened and he gave no answer. His lips suddenly twisted in a mirthless smile and he roared in Mo Kan-cheng's face, "Mr. Mo! Will you please tell them from me that I, Tu Wei-yueh, am quite willing to talk things over quietly, but I just won't stand being pushed around! What the hell do they think they're doing setting a gang of hooligans on us just when we're getting the factory going again! Ah Hsiang's an overseer, and if he has a hand in making trouble, of course he must be punished! In any case, until Mr. Wu comes in, I alone am responsible for everything that goes on in this factory!"

"Can't the two of you come to some peaceable arrangement, if only to save an old man's old face? After all, you're really old friends —"

"No! When Mr. Wu comes, I'll hand in my resignation and clear out of here, bag and baggage. It's no good asking me to make peace with those hooligans. I just can't! — Now, Mr. Mo, will you watch the phone and make sure that *nobody* uses it! If anything happens through your negligence, you'll be held responsible!"

Tu Wei-yueh's face was dark now, and his gimlet eyes bored into Mo Kan-cheng's. He knew the old man was as soft as wax. Mo Kan-cheng narrowed his rat-like eyes and was just going to speak, when Kuei Chang-lin and Pockmarked Li came round the corner, followed by Wang Chin-chen and Ah Chen. One side of Pockmarked Li's face was bruised and swollen.

"And don't go ringing up Mr. Wu!" said Tu Wei-yueh to Mo Kan-cheng in a severe voice. "I'll ask him to come round myself later on, and then everybody concerned can have it all out in front of him!"

With this he went across to meet Kuei Chang-lin and the others to hear what they had to say.

They all went across and stood by the notice-board in front of the veranda. The morning mist was lifting now, and the sunlight filtered through and fell on their faces. While Tu Wei-yueh was listening to Kuei Chang-lin, the idea which had escaped him a short while before suddenly struck him again. His face immediately lit up; he motioned to Kuei Chang-lin to stop and turned to Ah Chen:

"Go and tell them to give another blast on the hooter, and make it really long and loud this time!"

"It's no good blowing the hooter!" Ah Chen protested. "You don't think they're going to come in after all that fighting, do you?"

Tu Wei-yueh's face immediately darkened with anger, and

Ah Chen quickly made off. He snorted and glanced round at the others. Suddenly, his features set firm and he rapped out in a voice as hard as iron, "You needn't tell me any more: I know all about it! It was half the fault of some of the girls trying to picket the gate, and half the fault of that perisher Chien Pao-sheng throwing a spanner in the works! Those bastards don't care a damn about the welfare of the factory! One thing, though: we've got hold of Ah Hsiang, and once we've interrogated him we'll have definite proof! I'll teach him to play tricks on me, the low-down thing! He'll go straight down to the police station! And as for Chien Pao-sheng, we'll have him up for inciting the women to strike and preventing them from returning to work by using violence! I've been patient with them long enough, and I can't let them get away with it any longer!"

"I think you're wronging Ah Hsiang. He was only trying to stop the fight!" said Pockmarked Li anxiously, sticking up for his friend. Deep down inside, he was longing to put an end to all this quarrelling with Chien Pao-sheng, though he did not like to say so openly. Tu Wei-yueh saw his dilemma at a glance and burst out laughing. Being rather slow in the uptake, Kuei Chang-lin turned on Pockmarked Li and protested indignantly:

"We're not wronging Ah Hsiang at all! I saw him with my own eyes. He was telling them to stop and at the same time he was helping Chien Pao-sheng with his fists!"

"Ah, but it's always better to lose an enemy than to make one, Chang-lin! There's no point in being too hard on them. The way I see it, we should get Chien Pao-sheng over here and talk things over properly. If he still refuses to come round, all right, then he'll only get rough treatment from Pockmarked Li! Don't you agree, Mr. Tu? Let's make a friendly gesture to him and see how he takes it!"

Just then the factory hooter went again, this time for a good three minutes, howling away like an injured animal in pain.

"How many of the girls have come back so far?" asked Tu Wei-yueh, changing the subject with a calm smile — though his calmness was forced, quite different from his usual manner.

"Before the fight started, I'd counted over forty," replied Wang Chin-chen, drawing a muffled sigh and shooting a glance at Kuei Chang-lin. The latter was staring up at the ceiling, his jaw set firm and the veins standing out blue on his forehead. Tu Wei-yueh smiled grimly, feeling that his "régime" really was tottering this time. For all his manoeuvring and for all his skill in winning over Pockmarked Li, now that the crisis had come the long-established ties of friendship between Pockmarked Li and Chien Pao-sheng had proved stronger than his own influence. He thought for a moment, and then tried another tack.

"All right, Li; since you say so, I'll let it pass this time! I'm quite willing to have Chien Pao-sheng over and listen to anything he's got to say. But it's imperative that the girls should call off the strike today! We've just tried the hooter again. I expect you'll find Chien Pao-sheng in the little tea-house over the way. Tell him that since we're all good friends we can talk things over quite amicably — though if he tries any more of his old tricks, I'll have to take him in hand to keep order!"

"If you want me to go, Mr. Tu, I'll go, but wouldn't it be better if Kuei Chang-lin came with me?"

"No! I'd rather you went on your own this time," said Tu Wei-yueh quickly, getting in first before Kuei Chang-lin could say anything. "I've got another job for Chang-lin." He shot Pockmarked Li a last shrewd glance, then turned to Wang Chin-chen and told her to take the other forewomen down to keep an eye on the workshop. He then set off back towards the office, taking Kuei Chang-lin with him. When he got there he found Mo Kan-cheng in whispered conversation with Ma Ching-shan and the other two of the trio. When they saw Tu Wei-yueh, they all fell silent. Pretending not to notice, he went straight across to the three young men and said with a smile:

"You three gentlemen have had quite a busy time! I've got to the bottom of the matter and I now know what it was all about. There's no harm in a couple of fellows having a little dust-up: they can shake hands afterwards, and that's that. Only one little thing went wrong: the girls were frightened away. But never mind, they'll be back any minute now."

The three of them just gaped at him, speechless. Tu Wei-yueh smiled calmly at these three enemies of his and walked out. Kuei Chang-lin was walking to and fro on the veranda waiting. When he saw Tu Wei-yueh coming out, he looked round to make sure there was no one within earshot, then shifted closer to him and asked in an undertone, "You're not going to surrender to Chien Pao-sheng like this, are you, Mr. Tu?"

Tu Wei-yueh smiled but did not reply — he just kept walking. Kuei Chang-lin followed him in silence. After they had gone some little distance Tu Wei-yueh said quietly and calmly, "Who's Chien Pao-sheng that you think I'm surrendering to him?"

"But you've sent Pockmarked Li to fetch him!"

"Don't be so dense! We've got to soft-soap him for the time being, until the girls have all come back to work; once they're back we can easily settle his hash! I've got Ah Hsiang locked up in an empty room round the back, which means that we've still got means of proving that they started the trouble. If Pockmarked Li won't toe the line, we'll just have to find somebody else, though that'll probably take us some time!"

"Chien Pao-sheng's a wily old bird, you know. He'll very likely see through your little game."

"Of course he will! But he can't afford to make Pockmarked Li lose too much face. We've given Pockmarked Li a chance to save his face, and if Chien Pao-sheng doesn't do the same for him, he'll come right round on to our side."

Both men laughed and stopped on the open space in front of the workshop to wait for Pockmarked Li to come back from his errand.

By now the fog had lifted completely, and the sky was blue with a few blobs of white cloud. The two men began to feel a pleasant warmth as they stood bathed in sunlight. It was about half past eight now. Tu Wei-yueh had gone to bed very late the night before, and ever since five o'clock he had been run off his feet with not a moment's rest. He was tired, it was true, but he would not admit it. When he had been standing there waiting for a while, and was beginning to get impatient, he suddenly remembered something and swung round to his companion.

"There! They've worried me into such a state that I nearly forgot! Chang-lin, I've got an important job for you! Go down to the police station and tell them we want two of the girls arrested: Ho Hsiu-mei and Chang Ah-hsin! You'll have to show them the way. Damn Ah Hsiang! I told him last night to shadow those two, but you can bet your life he didn't — he went straight round to Chien Pao-sheng and his gang and then came round with them this morning to stab us in the back! And Chang-lin, if you find anybody else in Ho Hsiu-mei's hut or in Chang Ah-hsin's, arrest the whole bunch and don't let any of them get away!"

Tu Wei-yueh waved Kuei Chang-lin away and turned and went into the workshop. Work had not yet begun properly, and the filatures were running idly. More than a hundred girls had come back, but they were sitting silent and sullen beside their machines. The forewomen were posted all round the workshop like sentries. Putting on his most agreeable smile Tu Wei-yueh signed to Ah Chen, who had come up, to have the machines switched off. Immediately, a dead silence descended on the workshop, except for the faint gurgling of boiling water in the cauldrons and pans. Tu Wei-yueh took up a position in the centre of the workshop where the aisles crossed, with Wang Chin-chen on his left and Ah Chen on his right. He squared his shoulders and shot a keen glance all round, then, in the most solemn and sincere voice he could muster, he launched out into a "pep-talk" to the hundred-odd girls:

"I wish to say a few words. I've been here for over two years now, and I've always got on very well with everybody. It's more than a month since Mr. Wu made me general manager, and I think I can say I've never given myself airs. I know you are all very hard up: I'm no better off myself. If it's humanly possible to help you out, I'll do it like a shot! The trouble is, the price of silk keeps falling, and every factory-owner is losing money. All they get is about four hundred taels a bale! Get it? Four hundred taels of silver! That means about six hundred dollars! No factory-owner can lay golden eggs, so the only solution would be to close down the factory. And if the factory's closed down, we all go hungry! As you all know, more than twenty silk factories in Shanghai have already been closed down. But Mr. Wu has done everything in his power to keep our factory going. He's run into debt and he's mortgaged his house. The only reason why he hasn't closed down the factory is that he doesn't want us all to starve! And the only reason why he's cutting down wages is that he's in a very difficult position and has no alternative. If you'll just think about it for a minute, I think you'll agree that it's no joke being a factory-owner! The only way we can tide over the crisis is for everybody, employer and employees, to work together and help one another! You girls here have been very sensible about it and come back to work today. What you should do when you go home is to tell the other girls that if they don't return to work they're taking the bread out of their own mouths! It's costing Mr. Wu a lot to keep the factory open, and if people don't appreciate what he's doing for them, he's going to be very upset. If he should close down the factory, you wouldn't even get the new reduced rate of pay — not anywhere! If the trouble is that you can't get on with me, that can easily be settled. There's no need for you to go on strike — I can! As a matter of fact, I've already sent in my resignation once, but Mr. Wu hasn't agreed to let me go yet, so for the time being I'll just have to carry on as I am now. If you've got anything to say, please don't hesitate to speak up and let me know!"

There was not a sound but the grumbling of the boiling water in the cauldrons and pans. The girls' faces, flushed by the hot, steamy atmosphere, were as expressionless as the faces of statues. Inwardly, they were boiling with indignation and hatred, but their feelings did not show on their faces: they stuck in their throats.

Tu Wei-yueh felt strangely alone and deserted. Although the temperature in the workshop must have been about ninety degrees, he felt an icy shiver running down his spine and gradually spreading all over his body. He wandered miserably up and down for a moment, then looked at Wang Chin-chen and shrugged his shoulders as much as to say, "That's all — better get the machines started," then made his escape.

In front of the veranda of the office building stood Pockmarked Li and another man, looking all round expectantly. Seeing Tu Wei-yueh in the distance, coming across with his hands clasped behind him, Pockmarked Li called to him gleefully, "Mr. Tu! We've been looking for you for a long time! Chien Pao-sheng's here with me!"

Tu Wei-yueh stopped at once and looked across at them with a calm smile, then straightened himself up and walked slowly over. The lassitude which had followed his harangue in the workshop suddenly evaporated, and his head immediately began buzzing with ideas and schemes. He was now dealing with Chien Pao-sheng, which was quite a different matter from dealing with the girls. He felt quite at home dealing with a fellow like Chien. Here at least was someone who could never give him that cold shiver down the spine!

Chien Pao-sheng greeted him with a faint smile, but said nothing. It was a smile of triumph. Tu Wei-yueh pretended not to notice it, though under his mask of urbanity he resented it bitterly.

The three men walked in silence round to the other side of the office building, each thinking his own thoughts, except that Pockmarked Li was making irrelevant remarks and laughing excitedly. They went into Wu Sun-fu's office, where they were not likely to be disturbed, and got down to their discussion. Since he was the victor, Chien Pao-sheng put all his cards on the table straight away: he demanded that Hsueh Pao-chu, Chien Chiao-lin and Chou Erh-chieh be reinstated; that Kuei Chang-lin be transferred to some other factory; that Tu Wei-yueh should in future get his consent before taking on or dismissing any employees; and, finally, that the control and disposal of all "secret expenses" be entrusted solely to him. In conclusion, he solemnly announced that he was offering these terms on behalf of the trade union.

"But Kuei Chang-lin's also a committee member of the trade union, isn't he?" Tu Wei-yueh asked with a sarcastic smile, making no comment on the demands. The policy he had decided on was to prolong the negotiations as much as possible to give himself more time for his own preparations and arrangements. Chien Pao-sheng's swarthy face creased angrily.

"Committee member my foot!" he exploded, crashing his fist on the table. "Well, all right, he *is* a committee member, but nobody takes any notice of him! He's bloody useless! He's only one of half a dozen committee members, and anyway he's just a windbag! Me, I represent the majority!"

"Don't fly off the handle, Pao-sheng!" put in Pockmarked Li, holding down the fist with which Chien Pao-sheng had been pounding the table. "Let's be peaceable about it and talk things over properly!"

Tu Wei-yueh smiled calmly and changed the subject. "Let's leave it at that then! It's up to the union to settle its own affairs. All we're concerned with at this moment is the factory. Mr. Wu has made today the deadline for the end of the strike. Now we're all in this together, and it's up to every one of us to pull together. Before we do anything else, we must talk the girls round and get the factory going again without delay. Besides, with this general strike of all the silk factories in Shanghai, it's a very tricky situation, and one more day's delay might be disastrous. I can't imagine you trade union people wanting to see us involved in really serious trouble! If there *is* any really serious trouble, you would have to take some of the responsibility for it. So let's discuss first how we're going to ensure a full-scale return to work."

"That's right!" said Pockmarked Li to keep the conversation going, when he saw that Chien Pao-sheng had no reply ready. "Let's get the strike over and done with first of all!"

Tu Wei-yueh's eyes moved swiftly from one side to the other, and again he quickly changed the subject.

"Pao-sheng," he said calmly, "I find your terms quite reasonable and I think we could easily reach agreement on them. That little performance of yours this morning, though, was a bit hard to swallow, and you've succeeded in putting everybody's back up with it. If Mr. Wu got to hear of it, there'd be hell to pay. I've warned them not to let on to him about it, because I think we can settle it between ourselves. Let's agree once and for all that there won't be a repeat performance of this morning's unpleasant business. It doesn't look at all well when we start fighting among ourselves, and it wrecks our chances of calling off the strike!"

"What do you mean! That's slander!" exclaimed Chien Pao-sheng. His expression was indignant and he made as if to thump the table again; but, behind this façade of righteous indignation, it was obvious that he was a little cowed and alarmed. Seeing through him immediately, and realizing that his own diplomacy was winning him the upper hand, Tu Wei-yueh calmly pressed his advantage.

"How can you say I'm slandering you? Quite a few of our people were knocked about. Look at Li's nose! Isn't that proof enough?"

"That's because you got so many people in from outside without notifying me in advance. When you get so many people together like that without letting me know what you're doing, a few of them are bound to get hurt in the confusion."

"The reason why we got people in was to prevent the girls picketing —"

"And my chaps were also there to prevent picketing! They were only there to help out!"

"It's no use hedging! We've got Ah Hsiang as a witness that it was your people that started it! While our men were dealing with the pickets, yours came along and went for them and started a fight!"

"Ah Hsiang's talking a lot of rot!" Chien Pao-sheng roared through clenched teeth; beads of sweat stood out on his forehead. He paused a moment, then suddenly changed his tone.

"What's done can't be undone. Why keep harping on it? Now let me put it to you straight out: do you agree to my terms or don't you? Let's have it straight, with no more beating about the bush! The union's waiting for me to give them a definite answer!"

"But first we must have your word for it that we won't have a repeat performance of the nonsense we had this morning! It's not that I'm afraid of anything myself, but all this fighting among ourselves makes us look ridiculous outside. Besides, it's just playing into the hands of the trouble-makers!"

"All right then, but only if you'll agree not to call in people from outside any more?"

"We have to call people in to prevent the women picketing and stirring up trouble! We can't do anything else! Am I right, Li?"

"Yes, that's quite right. You've got nothing to worry about, Pao-sheng. All these chaps were called in by me, so there's no danger of their going against you!"

"Of course there isn't! What Li says is clear enough! That's settled, then: no more nonsense like we had this morning! All right, Pao-sheng, you'd better go and tell your men about it now. Once you've sent them away, and Mr. Wu's here, I'll tell him your terms, and then they can be discussed properly."

By seizing this opportunity to clinch the matter, Tu Wei-yueh had now managed to put off the discussion of Chien Pao-sheng's terms. He was helped out by a word from Pockmarked Li.

"That's right, Pao-sheng, you go and tell your chaps now that there's to be no more trouble, so that Mr. Tu can set his mind at rest."

"There's no need to tell them. They won't lift a finger till I give them the word!" Chien Pao-sheng assured him, tapping his chest confidently. No sooner were the words out of his mouth than a sudden uproar was heard in the distance. Tu Wei-yueh looked alarmed and sprang to his feet. There was a patter of footsteps outside the window, and Mo Kan-cheng burst into the room.

"They — they're at it again!" he stuttered.

Tu Wei-yueh gave Chien Pao-sheng a withering look as much as to say, "So you're stirring up trouble again!" Kicking his chair aside, he dashed out of the room. His face flushed, Pockmarked Li also sprang up and grabbed Chien Pao-sheng by the arm.

"Pao-sheng!" he protested angrily, his lips flecked with saliva. "This is a bit *too* thick! It's the limit!"

Chien Pao-sheng was speechless with rage. He also grasped

421

Pockmarked Li's arm, and the two of them, still holding on to each other, hurried out of the room. As they ran, Chien Pao-sheng at last managed to say something, "Let's go and see! Let's see what's happening!... The bloody idiots!"

They ran for all they were worth and soon caught up with Tu Wei-yueh. In the distance they could see a vast crowd outside the gate, milling round and roaring their heads off. When the three of them got to the gate and saw what was going on, they yelped with alarm and their faces paled. They were confronted by a crowd of girls like so many enraged tigresses! The three of them immediately wheeled round and started to run, but it was too late. They were swept off their feet by an angry flood that swept up to the gate, and swallowed up in the crowd. Another wave of women came screaming up the street and hurled itself on the one in front, so that the thin line of defenders in front of the gate began to give under the pressure. And as these shock-troops pressed forward, their shrill slogans rent the air:

"Join the general strike! Join the general strike!"

"Only blacklegs go back!"

"Shut down your machines and come and join us!"

The thin defence line now fell back, and the girls swept forward like a prairie-fire. They surged in through the narrow side gate and also burst open the main gate. It all happened with the speed of lightning and with cataclysmic violence. But just as suddenly, a crowd of men charged in upon the women from one side and cut their ranks in two like a pair of shears cutting through a piece of cloth. It was Kuei Chang-lin arriving in the nick of time with a squad of policemen. Their whistles shrilled above the roar of the crowd. There was a volley of warning shots over the heads of the crowd, then another volley, this time in real earnest! The defenders inside the gate now began a counter-attack. There was nothing the women inside could do now but make a retreat. They surged out through the gate on to the street again, sweeping aside Kuei Chang-lin and the policemen as they went.

"After 'em!" roared Kuei Chang-lin. "Don't let 'em get away!"

Just then, whistles began to shrill from every direction as more policemen arrived on the scene from the various police stations in the neighbourhood and began to round up the women. Kuei Chang-lin and his squad of police made straight for the workers' slum. They swept through it from end to end, leaving the claw-marks of terrorism behind each rickety bamboo door. They caught a couple of dozen girls and drove over two hundred from the slum to the factory, where they herded them into the workshop.

Tu Wei-yueh and Chien Pao-sheng had both been injured in the fray. A couple of stray bullets had hit Chien Pao-sheng in the leg and deprived him of a chunk of his greasy hide. Yet he was grateful to Kuei Chang-lin for coming in the nick of time and saving his life.

In Tu Wei-yueh's bedroom, an elated Kuei Chang-lin said, "More than three hundred girls back at work! Just listen to those machines! And we've caught Ho Hsiu-mei and Chang Ah-hsin, too. We roped in a dozen or so more while we were at it. It won't hurt them to cool their heels in jail for a few days, even if some of them are not in the wrong! Those bitches who rushed the gate — they didn't give a damn what happened to them, anyway! Besides, most of them weren't our girls at all: they came in from other factories! . . . By the way, Mr. Tu, how did you get on with Chien Pao-sheng?"

"We've come out on top!" said Tu Wei-yueh with a smile of satisfaction. "Chang-lin, you can go and ring up Mr. Wu and tell him!"

A thought suddenly struck him: there was still someone whose whereabouts he wanted to check on, but before he could ask he felt a sudden twinge of pain where he had been wounded. His face turned pale and a cold sweat broke out on his forehead. He gritted his teeth in silence.

*

So one of the strongest links in the chain of the general strike of silk filatures was broken! It was around seven o'clock in the evening, and the gathering darkness brought with it the prospect of the general strike collapsing. The slum where the factory girls lived was under close surveillance and was now as silent as the grave. A glimpse of a girl's pale face in the gloom or the sound of a low moan breaking the stillness of the breathless evening air was enough to alert the watching policemen, and then shouts and the noise of running feet would shatter the sepulchral silence for a moment.

From a dark corner of the slum a shadow was creeping silently out, like a thieving little dog nosing around, trying to find an unguarded break in the police cordon. Overhead, stars were twinkling in the deep blue of the sky. A faint breeze stirred and wafted the frightened crying of a child from somewhere in the slum. A blast on a police-whistle! . . . With slow but purposeful movements the shadow stole forward until it was finally outside the police cordon. Now its movements became swifter, and the twinkling stars watched it dart from one patch of cover to another and finally turn into a squalid alleyway. It gave three taps on the back door of the end house. The door opened a few inches, and the shadow slipped inside.

In the front room upstairs were three rickety beds with no mosquito nets and a single square table. The fifteen-watt light shone on a girl lying on a bed under the window and another girl sitting beside her. They were talking in an undertone. The girl on the chair suddenly jerked her head round and exclaimed:

"Ah, Yueh-ngo! . . . Nobody with you?"

"Ho Hsiu-mei and Chang Ah-hsin have been arrested. Didn't you know?"

"Yes, but I mean where's Chu — what's her name, Chu Kuei-ying, isn't it? The one who's just joined. Why didn't she come with you?"

"I just couldn't get to her. It was as much as I could do to get here myself. They've got people watching all round the huts."

Chen Yueh-ngo shook her head and spat, then sat down at the table, poured herself out a cup of tea, and sat there sipping at it. The girl on the bed patted her companion on the shoulder. "Just what happened in Hongkew! You know, Ma Chin, I'm afraid this general strike's fizzling out again!"

Ma Chin snorted angrily but made no reply. She fixed her

vivid black eyes on Chen Yueh-ngo's face and saw that she looked listless, or rather, dazed and frustrated by this latest setback. Feeling Ma Chin's eye on her, she put down her cup and asked anxiously, "What are we going to do about it, then? Hurry up and tell me, do!"

"Wait until Ke Tso-fu comes, and then we'll have a discussion. Tsai Chen, what's the time? What's keeping Ke Tso-fu, I wonder? No sign of Su Lun, either."

"Twenty past seven," replied Tsai Chen, rolling over cumbrously on the bed and sitting up. "I can't wait much longer. I've got a meeting in Hongkew at half past eight! Oh bother!" She suddenly threw her arms round Ma Chin and began gently worrying her neck with her teeth. Ma Chin freed herself impatiently and reproved Tsai Chen good-humouredly:

"What d'you think you're doing? Nymphomaniac! — By the way, Yueh-ngo, what's the 'fighting spirit' of the girls in your factory like? All right? Most of the girls here in Chapei are firm enough. This morning, as soon as they heard that some of the girls in your factory had gone back to work, they set out at once of their own accord to break into your factory. So long as the girls in your factory can remain firm, the general strike can still go on. It makes things very awkward to have you girls going back unconditionally just now! If we should fail completely this time, there wouldn't be much point in trying again!"

"We're not finished yet by any means!" Tsai Chen put in quickly. "Now listen, Ma Chin! I suggest we go out tonight and make a great effort to mobilize as many girls as possible to break into the factories again tomorrow! Backs to the wall this time! Even if we fail, it'll be a glorious failure! . . . Yes, on second thought, Ma Chin, I think we should go back to what I suggested in the first place: we should consider no sacrifice too great, and we should be prepared for a glorious failure!"

So saying, Tsai Chen ran across to Chen Yueh-ngo, threw her arms round her, and pressed her cheek against hers. Chen Yueh-ngo blushed furiously and twisted away from her in embarrassment. Tsai Chen went off into peals of hysterical laughter and threw herself back on the bed, where she tossed up and down until the bedstead creaked in protest.

"Be quiet, Tsai Chen!" said Ma Chin, gently reproachful. "Glorious failure, eh? Hm!"

She sat down at the table and began questioning Chen Yueh-ngo closely about the events in the factory, but they had not got very far when two men came into the room, one after the other. The one in front sat himself down with a bump on the edge of the table; he fished out a pocket-watch, glanced at it, then began rapping out orders:

"It's half past seven already! Come on, look alive! Ma Chin, stop your conversation! Tsai Chen, get up! You all look half asleep!"

"You're late yourself, Tso-fu!" protested Tsai Chen, springing off the bed. "Come on, don't waste time! Ma Chin! Yueh ngo! I'll have to leave here for a meeting in Hongkew at half past eight!"

She sat down beside Ke Tso-fu. He was young — still in his twenties — slightly taller than Tsai Chen, and with a thin, pale face which was remarkable only for the thin, tightly-compressed lips suggestive of his strength of will. The other young man was rather on the plump side; his eyes were alert, though edged with wrinkles of tiredness. He grinned at Ma Chin and sat down beside her.

The atmosphere in the room at once became tense as they sat down together beneath the dim light of the fifteen-watt bulb. Ke Tso-fu spoke first to the other young man:

"Your work's nowhere near up to scratch, Su Lun! The way you conducted that meeting of activists from the silk factories this afternoon was all wrong! You don't seem able to seize on the revolutionary spirit of the masses and lead them on from one struggle to another and to develop the struggle further and further! Your leadership is tinged with rightism. You're just marking time and even tailing along *behind* the masses! Now that the general strike of the silk factories has reached a critical stage, the first thing we must do is to overcome this sort of tailism! Ma Chin, let's hear your report on the work in Chapei!"

"Oh, hurry up!" urged Tsai Chen, drumming her pencil on

the table. "Make it as short as you can, because I'm off to the meeting at half past eight!"

Ma Chin spoke for about five minutes. Her manner was calm, and she made one main point: as a result of harsher measures from the employers, they had suffered drastic losses of progressive elements among the workers, so that their footing among the masses was now weaker. Ke Tso-fu listened to her with an air of impatience, glancing now and then at his watch; his thin lips were pressed together tighter than ever.

"I disagree with Ma Chin's conclusion!" broke in Tsai Chen, glancing quickly across at Su Lun. "The longer the struggle, the more new progressive elements will be produced, and the stronger our footing among the masses will be! Ma Chin's timid attitude is a sign of tailism!"

She was now fully determined to push the first suggestion that she had made that evening. Just because this ordinary-looking young man Ke Tso-fu always began by accusing people of rightism or tailism, she felt that he must be right in whatever he said.

Ke Tso-fu was silent, and his lips were closed tighter than ever. As usual, he was waiting to the last before drawing his conclusions and giving his orders.

Su Lun, who had had the glance shot at him by Tsai Chen, nevertheless supported Ma Chin's view. He naturally did not admit his "tailism," but adopted an easy-going manner.

"While Tsai Chen deals in theories," he said, "Ma Chin bases herself on facts. And facts are one thing we shouldn't overlook. Tso-fu says I made mistakes at the activists' meeting this afternoon. All right, I admit that I did make mistakes. But the fact remains that today's activists' meeting was a flop right from the start! Only half the expected number of delegates turned up, and the progress reports were unrealistic and largely irrelevant. — And those who spoke in the discussion that followed were rambling and incoherent. This meeting's clearly exposed the incompetence of our junior cadres in leading the masses! If I've been guilty of tailism, our present junior cadres as a whole are tailists as well! And Tsai Chen and Ma Chin, who are actually organizing the strikes, are just tailing along behind the junior cadres!"

"What right have you to say I'm tailing along behind! —"

"Don't talk nonsense!" snapped Ma Chin. "Let's get a move on and decide on a course of action! I expect Chen Yueh-ngo's got something to say!"

By saying this she had warded off a dispute between Tsai Chen and Su Lun and at the same time brought Chen Yueh-ngo to Ke Tso-fu's notice. Ke Tso-fu turned his head slightly and looked expectantly at Chen Yueh-ngo.

"I wish you'd hurry up and tell me what to do," said Chen Yueh-ngo. "The other two comrades in my factory have been arrested, and there's only me left now! The girls — the girls only went back today because they were forced to by the police! If only we can think of a good way, we can get them out on strike again tomorrow! I'm just waiting for you to tell me what to do!"

Chen Yueh-ngo looked agitated and also very excited. It was obvious that she was perplexed by all the "technical terms" used by Ke Tso-fu and Su Lun, and that she had plenty of ideas but could not find the right words. She only felt that Ma Chin was right, for hadn't their position been weakened by the arrest of Ho Hsiu-mei and Chang Ah-hsin? On the other hand, she dared not disagree with what Tsai Chen had said, for she had a vague feeling that Tsai Chen's words were quotations from revolutionary classics. Now that she had said as much as she could find words for — though even that had been difficult — she remained gazing at Ke Tso-fu with anxious eyes.

Ke Tso-fu's lean, ordinary-looking face suddenly took on a severe expression. He glanced once more at his watch, then said firmly:

"Tonight, you all go out and work harder than ever to heighten the fighting spirit of the masses and ensure that they don't return to work tomorrow! This applies especially to the Yu Hua Factory. The girls there must come out on strike again tomorrow! Whatever happens, you must overcome all difficulties and have them out again tomorrow! Give the masses these slogans: 'Oppose Capitalists Using Hooligans!' and 'Oppose Capitalists Arresting Workers!'"

For a moment there was silence. From the alleyway outside came the "tock-tock!" of a dumpling-pedlar striking his bamboo tube. In a neighbouring house a baby was crying. The dim yellow light of the fifteen-watt bulb flickered overhead. Ma Chin's calm voice broke the silence.

"We've almost completely lost our foothold among the girls of the Yu Hua Factory, and the masses are under close surveillance by the police. Until we've made some readjustment, we shouldn't take chances!"

"What do you mean, 'readjustment'? At a time like this, when the fate of the general strike is in the balance, there's no time for any leisurely readjustments! The only time we've got left for readjustments is tonight, and tonight we've got to mobilize new fighting elements so that we can launch a new offensive!"

"But we can never do it in one night!" contended Ma Chin firmly, her dark eyes flashing round the circle of faces. "Our organization among the workers has been completely wrecked, and the enemy has the workers under strict surveillance — no, we shouldn't risk it! If we insist on going forward with a new offensive under the present circumstances, it'll be suppressed immediately, and then what little foothold we still have left will be completely destroyed!"

Ke Tso-fu sat tight-lipped and silent, adamant as ever. It began to look as if a deadlock had been reached. Tsai Chen suddenly made a sound in her throat as if she were going to speak, but said nothing. Her "second proposal," which had been pushed to the back of her mind, was now forcing its way to the front again and struggling with her "first proposal," on which she had set her mind. She was biting her lips, which were drawn back with tension. Chen Yueh-ngo was waiting, her eyes wide with worry. Su Lun now intervened in an effort to break the deadlock.

"Ma Chin, tell us what *you* think we ought to do!"

"I don't see any reason why we shouldn't make a slight modification in the alignment of the general strike. In the factories where it is possible to keep the workers out on strike, we should fight as hard as we can. That's only natural. But in the factories where we have suffered serious losses we shouldn't run any more risks; we should give the girls a rest to recuperate. We should then go all out to make a readjustment and get them properly organized. In other words, we should conserve our strength until a suitable opportunity presents itself, and then we can —"

Before Ma Chin had a chance to finish, Ke Tso-fu interrupted her with a stern reproof. "Your proposal is tantamount to calling off the general strike! It's beating a cowardly retreat at a critical stage in the high tide of the revolution! It's rightism!"

"Yes, Ma Chin," Tsai Chen quickly chimed in as her "first proposal" got the upper hand again. "You want to break the ranks of the general strike on the one hand, but on the other you're expecting the girls in the other factories to hold out! The two things are contradictory!"

Ma Chin's face flushed crimson, and she went on resolutely, "What do you mean, 'contradictory'? It'll work out in practice all right! To take a risk like this would be suicidal!"

"If only we can find a good way," put in Chen Yueh-ngo with a glance at Ma Chin, "we can get our factory out on strike again tomorrow. The only thing is, there are not many of our people left now, and the masses are afraid of further oppression. If the same old method is used again, we'll never get anywhere! So I think the most important thing is to find a good new method!"

It had cost Chen Yueh-ngo a great deal of effort to find words to express what she wanted to say, but neither Ke Tso-fu nor Tsai Chen paid the slightest attention to her. Su Lun, who agreed with Ma Chin and also understood what Chen Yueh-ngo was trying to say, made another attempt to resolve the deadlock.

"What Yueh-ngo says is based on actual facts! By a good new method she means a change in our tactics — isn't that so, Yueh-ngo? Let me make a proposal: since the organization of the girls in the Yu Hua Factory has been so badly damaged that it requires a readjustment which will take longer than one night to carry out, we should allow one more day for this, so that we can bring them out again the day after tomorrow. This would mean that the over-all alignment of the general strike would remain intact."

"No, no!" protested Tsai Chen vehemently. "If we don't go on fighting tomorrow with still greater forces, the general strike will fizzle out! If the workers at the Yu Hua remain at work tomorrow, the workers at all the other factories will begin to waver!"

Unable to contain herself any longer, Ma Chin burst out acrimoniously, "If this general strike can fizzle out as easily as all that, then it's obvious that it's premature! It's putschism! Adventurism!"

At this, Ke Tso-fu scowled. He brought both his hands down with a thump on the table and snapped Ma Chin's head off:

"Ma Chin! You're criticizing the Party line! This rightist deviation of yours is very serious! The Party is determined to do away with all such rightist views! If the girls at the Yu Hua Factory don't come out on strike again tomorrow, it will be a case of undermining the general strike and disobeying the Party line! The Party would have to apply strict disciplinary measures!"

"But in actual practice," countered Ma Chin, "it just amounts to giving more comrades into the enemy's hands. What do you say to that?"

She was still adamant; her face was flushed, but her lips were bloodless. Ke Tso-fu snarled and pounded the table. "Now I'm warning you, Ma Chin! The Party has iron discipline! No Party member is permitted to disobey orders! You will go at once with Chen Yueh-ngo and mobilize the women for tomorrow's struggle! Whatever the costs, it must be done! That's an order!"

Ma Chin hung her head in silence. Ke Tso-fu gave her a withering look and turned to Tsai Chen and Su Lun. "You'll have to put the pressure on in Hongkew, Tsai Chen! You must carry out all orders with firmness and purge all rightist views! Su Lun, I want you now to tell the girls what important resolutions on the general strike were passed by the general strike committee!"

With this, Ke Tso-fu glanced at his watch once more, then stood up and took his departure.

For a moment, none of the people left in the little room spoke. Tsai Chen stretched, then turned and threw herself heavily on the bed again, making it creak noisily. Su Lun sat gazing up at the light bulb with a faint smile on his lips. Chen Yueh-ngo was staring anxiously at Ma Chin. Out in the lane two men were quarrelling, and a dog was barking.

Ma Chin lifted her head and smiled at Chen Yueh-ngo, then turned to the recumbent Tsai Chen. "Come on, Tsai Chen! We've got our orders — 'at all costs it must be done!' Now, let's share out the work between us. Come on, buck up your ideas! It's getting late!"

"Oh dear!" exclaimed Tsai Chen, springing off the bed. "I've got my meeting in Hongkew at half past eight! It's nearly eight already!" She rushed across the room, hit Su Lun, who seemed to be dozing off, on the head in passing, and flung herself on Ma Chin.

"Oh, Ma Chin!" she gasped in her ear. "There's a lump in my heart, as if it's going to explode, something that's going to burst out and burn all our enemies! I'd just like to get my hands on an enemy and shoot him dead! Feel my face, feel how it's burning! . . . Never mind, though, let's divide up the work, Ma Chin!"

Ignoring Tsai Chen, Ma Chin turned away and addressed Chen Yueh-ngo in a stern voice:

"You go back now, Yueh-ngo, and go and see Chu Kuei-ying and any other close friends that you have and tell them that the girls in all the other factories in Hongkew and Chapei are determined not to go back to work, and that if the girls at the Yu Hua Factory go in to work again tomorrow, the girls from all the other factories will come and break in. When all the other factories are out on strike to back up your factory, it wouldn't be playing the game if you girls went back now! If only you can hold out for a day or two longer, your boss will have to give in! Now go and do your best to stir up the girls, Yueh-ngo, and don't even think about failing! I'll come and see you in half an hour. It's now — er — eight o'clock. I'll make it half past eight at the latest. You be waiting for me at your place. And mind you don't make a hash of it! Afterwards, we'll go to the general strike representatives' meeting together."

"That's right!" Tsai Chen put in hurriedly. "Both of you be at the inn at half past nine. There's no need to get there earlier. I won't get there with the representatives from Hongkew until then, anyway."

She skipped away from them, gaily humming a tune.

"Right, then! Everything's settled! Though there are still the representatives from the other Chapei factories that Ah Ying's going to contact; they may get there a few minutes early. Still, they can wait there. Now, come on, Yueh-ngo, you should be gone! You too, Tsai Chen, you'd better not hang about any longer! Remember — half past nine, general strike representatives' meeting! I'll still be here for a while yet. If Ah Ying doesn't turn up in the next quarter of an hour, she won't be here at all. Still, we can always see her at the meeting."

"Hang on a minute, Tsai Chen!" Su Lun said hurriedly, fishing out a piece of paper from his pocket. "Here are the resolutions of the general strike committee for you to pass on to the representatives' meeting."

But Tsai Chen was in a great hurry to be off. She snatched the piece of paper from Su Lun, glanced at it, then tossed it back to Su Lun. She grabbed Chen Yueh-ngo's hand and threw over her shoulder, "I can't read your spidery scrawl! You'll have to tell Ma Chin what it's about! Come on, Yueh-ngo, let's go! Mm, I do love you!"

Only Ma Chin and Su Lun were now left in the room. It took them five minutes to go through the resolutions of the general strike committee, and then they relapsed into silence. Ma Chin was pacing slowly up and down, her face wrinkled with concentration. Suddenly she began muttering to herself and slowly nodding her head.

"Yes, we must certainly take the offensive, but we must definitely look after our rear as well. I *must* think of a way to keep what little footing we still have in the Yu Hua!"

Su Lun turned and watched her face for a moment, then grinned and said quietly in an imitation of Ke Tso-fu's voice,

"I'm warning you, Ma Chin!... Whatever the cost, it must be done! That's an order!"

"Oh, shut up, you clown!" she muttered, coming to a halt. "You needn't be funny about it!" She smiled, but Su Lun suddenly became serious, he heaved a sharp sigh and said grimly:

"Frankly, I feel the same as you do about all this rushing blindly ahead and ignoring the risk. Doesn't seem right. But what can you do about it? The moment you come out with a different opinion, you're called a right opportunist, a liquidationist! And then some little tin god swats you with his 'orders'! Commandism, that's what it is!"

Ma Chin glanced at Su Lun with her lively but gentle eyes, as if she sympathized with him. Su Lun was something of a "theorist," and had "the gift of the gab." She had always looked up to him in a way, but at this moment she suddenly felt that he was somehow even more imposing than ever — clear-minded, able to speak without relying on "formulas," always smiling that intelligent smile of his, and always calm and sensible. Apart from the respect she had always had for him, she now felt her heart warming to him as well.

"I wonder what's keeping Ah Ying away," she said, changing the subject. "It looks as if she won't be coming tonight."

She went across and lay down on the bed under the window. Her face was still turned towards Su Lun, and her thoughtful, tender eyes were still on him.

Su Lun followed her across, his eyes never leaving her for a moment. Suddenly he laughed. "I'm perfectly certain Ah Ying won't be coming here tonight. She's too busy with the dual task lately!"

"What do you mean, 'dual task'?"

Su Lun sat down on the edge of the bed, his lips parted in a grin. Ma Chin smiled and asked, "What are you laughing at?"

"Because you don't understand what I mean by 'dual task.'"

Ma Chin jerked round on the bed and gave Su Lun a strange look, then said quite casually, "Don't start a rumour!"

"But I'm not! Haven't you noticed how thin she's getting just lately? And haven't you noticed that Tsai Chen's losing weight, too? It's the same reason in both cases: the demands of sex and the demands of the revolution both taking their toll at the same time!"

Ma Chin laughed and shook her head disbelievingly. Su Lun edged closer and said, "Li Pa's been looking for you all over the place again today!"

"The man's a nuisance!"

"He says he's going to arrange for you to work at his place and 'live in on the job.' He's trying to persuade Tso-fu to transfer you!"

"Humph! The man's more of a nuisance than I thought!"

"Why don't you love him?"

Ma Chin gave another laugh but did not answer him. After a moment, Su Lun heaved a sigh and said, "Since Little Wang left Shanghai she's deserted me!"

Ma Chin laughed and squirmed round on the bed, then looked up into Su Lun's plump face and said teasingly, "I suppose you've been feeling pretty low just lately, then?"

"Well, it's only natural that I should feel rather put out —"

Ma Chin laughed herself into a fit of coughing. She undid her top button, still laughing and coughing at the same time.

"I can't help feeling rather put out about it, Ma Chin, now can I? I know we shouldn't take these love affairs too seriously, but I can't help feeling rather put out, all the same. It's the same with all these comrades we've lost lately: I know they were martyrs for the cause, yet it always makes me feel rather miserable to think about it!"

Su Lun's head drooped as he spoke; Ma Chin was still laughing.

"Ha! Ha! You're not a revolutionary, Su Lun. You've turned into a little girl!"

"You know, Ma Chin, sometimes I really do feel like a little girl! Ma Chin, I need someone to comfort me, someone to encourage me. Would you, Ma Chin? I need —"

Su Lun's head drooped as he spoke; Ma Chin was still and at the same time pressed his face to hers. Ma Chin did not move, but gave a suppressed giggle. Su Lun now pressed his cheek against hers. She just giggled, without resisting.

"What nice, firm little breasts you have, Ma Chin!"

Ma Chin giggled even more excitedly, then suddenly rolled over, pushed Su Lun away and sprang off the bed.

"It's getting late! I must be off to see Yueh-ngo!"

Su Lun had stealthily put his arms round her again, and again she pushed him away. She ran across the room to one of the other beds and picked up her "working girl's clothes," but before she could put them on, Su Lun suddenly threw himself on her and grasped her so violently that they both fell on the bed. Ma Chin laughed and shouted:

"No, no, you barbarian! I've got work to do!"

"Work? Yes, the devil's work! Commandism! Putchism! I can see through it all!"

"What can you see through?"

"I can see well enough that our work is a waste of time! That the Party line is a suicidal policy, that our Soviet is a tourist Soviet, that our Red Army is a robber-band brought up to date! — Now come on, Ma Chin, you needn't be so feudalistic. . . ."

Ma Chin suddenly snarled and thrust him savagely away, then sprang to her feet, her eyes blazing with anger, and snapped:

"How dare you say such a thing! You're giving yourself away — you're tarred with the same brush as the liquidationists!"

With that she flew downstairs and out of the house to the alleyway.

Above her head shimmered a star-studded sky. As she walked along, Ma Chin remembered her dispute with Ke Tso-fu and Su Lun's beastly behaviour. She felt angry and resentful, but she tried to forget these unpleasant things and concentrate her mind on one thing: her work, her mission. She was now approaching the workers' slum. Very cautiously she slipped through the police cordon and made her way stealthily towards Chen Yueh-ngo's hut. A dim figure appeared just ahead of her. She stopped and slipped aside into the shadows, every sense alert and taut. The figure moved across to Chen Yueh-ngo's hut and stopped. The bamboo door gave a muffled creak. Ma Chin realized what it meant and went swiftly and softly across to the door. With a glance over her shoulder, she slipped inside.

Chen Yueh-ngo and Chu Kuei-ying were both there. A tiny

flame burnt in the oil lamp on the table. Stentorian snores came from the shadows — Chen Yueh-ngo's elder brother, a stevedore. Ma Chin asked them in a whisper, "Have you been round to them all?"

"Yes; fairly good results, too. They said that so long as the others come and break in they'll all shut down their machines and join them."

Ma Chin frowned. She seemed to hear a noise outside the door. The three girls cocked their heads on one side and listened intently, but the noise was not repeated. Ma Chin then went on in an undertone, "Right, then, we'd better be off to the representatives' meeting! Though I'd like to go and have a chat with some of the girls first. You know which of them are reliable, so you can take me round!"

"Not a chance!" whispered Chen Yueh-ngo in a scarcely audible voice. "We're being too closely watched. The moment you move, they're down on you like a shot!"

But Ma Chin was adamant and insisted that she should be taken round. Then Chu Kuei-ying tugged at Chen Yueh-ngo's sleeve. "I'll take her round," she offered. "I'm not being shadowed."

"You don't realize it but you are! Chamber-pot Tu's a sly one — too sly to overlook you! I think we'd better let Hsiao-mei go with Ma Chin."

As she said this, Chen Yueh-ngo nudged Ma Chin to call her attention to a little figure in the corner by the bamboo door. It was Chin Hsiao-mei, and when she heard that they wanted her to take Ma Chin round, her eyes sparkled with delight. Ma Chin glanced at her and nodded her consent.

"Hsiao-mei won't do, either," objected Chu Kuei-ying. "She's a little chatterbox, and anyway she's being watched by the police as well!"

Ma Chin was getting impatient. "No more arguing! We'll all go together! Kuei-ying, you go in front; I'll follow on three or four yards behind you; and Chen Yueh-ngo can follow on the same distance behind me. Whoever finds herself being shadowed warns the rest of us!"

There were no more objections, and they set out. Not far

away from Chen Yueh-ngo's hut there lived a girl who they thought was "progressive." Chu Kuei-ying went in first, leaving the bamboo door ajar. Just as Ma Chin was going to follow her in, a shout suddenly rang out in the darkness:

"What are you up to?"

Startled, Chen Yueh-ngo turned and ran, but she was caught and held almost at once. Then a police-whistle shrilled, and Pockmarked Li and Kuei Chang-lin came on the scene with their men. They burst into the hut and seized everyone they could lay hands on. A commotion arose in the slum, but within about ten minutes all was quiet again. Then a bevy of smiling forewomen came on the scene and went round the huts reassuring the startled girls:

"There's nothing to be afraid of! They're only rounding up a few Communists! Just come in to work in the morning and everything will be all right! Mr. Wu will soon make things right with everybody!"

XVI

IT was almost daylight before Chu Kuei-ying's mother eventually began to calm down. She lay on her rickety bamboo cot after a night of weeping and cursing and frenziedly trailing up and down the slum in search of her daughter. She had tried several times to force her way into the factory to see Tu Wei-yueh and risk her life if necessary. By now the old lady was so exhausted that she could not stir an inch, yet she could not get to sleep. She just lay there staring into space with her bloodshot eyes. Her rage had now passed, and the icy fingers of fear were clutching at her heart.

The oil lamp on the table had burnt down to the last drop of oil, and the flame sank lower and lower until it finally died. Outside the bamboo door, a dull white gleam was gradually spreading across the sky. It seemed to the old lady that a ghostly hand was pressing down on her chest and tearing at her heart. She heard the bamboo door creak and looked round — her daughter's head, all bloody, was rolling across the floor towards her bed! She sprang up at once, but instead of her daughter's head she now saw two figures standing before her. She peered through the gloom and when she saw that it was her son Little San-tse and their next-door neighbour Chin Ho-shang, she seemed suddenly relieved.

"Have you found where they've locked her up?" she asked quickly. "Wasn't that her head that rolled in just now?"

"Her head? Of course not! Some say she's been sent down to the police station and some say she's shut up in the factory — everybody says something different! Blast 'em!"

Chin Ho-shang ground his teeth. There was a sudden clatter as Little San-tse kicked a rickety stool out of the way and grunted savagely. His mother gaped for a moment, then went off into another fit of weeping and cursing, beating her chest and stamping her feet.

The slum now began to stir into life, and the factory hooter sounded its imperious summons. Hurried footsteps began pattering past the door, mingled with shouts, laughter and curses, as well as the smutty banter of the rowdies as they teased the passing girls.

Suddenly a tall, thin, rather attractive woman came into the hut. When he saw that it was Yao Chin-feng, Little San-tse suddenly rounded his eyes and was just going to swear at her, but just then another girl came in behind her. It was Lu Hsiao-pao. She pulled him aside to the doorway and whispered, "I've found out about Kuei-ying for you. She's in the factory. You might be able to get round Mr. Tu to let her go."

Before Little San-tse could make a reply, he heard Yao Chin-feng laughing and commenting loudly:

"She only has herself to blame! Mr. Tu had his eye on her once, but she threw her chance away! Don't worry, though: I'll put in a word for her! Mr. Tu's a good chap at heart! Though I'm afraid Kuei-ying will have to change her ideas —"

Before Yao Chin-feng could finish what she was saying, Little San-tse rushed across and grabbed hold of her, his eyes glaring with rage.

"I'll teach you to come smarming round us, you saucy bitch!"

The next moment the two of them were wrestling together. Then Chin Ho-shang pulled Little San-tse off, while Lu Hsiao-pao dragged Yao Chin-feng away. As they went out the old lady shouted after them.

"It was you two that got her into this mess! You're trying to crawl round Chamber-pot Tu and be his concubines! You dirty bitches, you! Makes me feel sick to look at you!"

She slammed the bamboo door to. Suddenly she pulled herself together and stopped crying as an overpowering feeling of hatred came over her. She hated Chamber-pot Tu and Yao Chin-feng; she hated all the girls who were going back to work. Then out of this burning hatred there grew a vague kind of pride in her mind: her daughter was not a blackleg!

Chin Ho-shang and Little San-tse seemed to be infused with similar feelings, though they were discussing something else now. Chin Ho-shang spoke first.

"It's getting late! You know we decided yesterday to all go down together and give that bastard Chou Chung-wei a shaking-up, well, are you coming?"

"Yes, 'course I am! If that bloody 'Red-tipped Match' is going to shut down the factory, we'll go and burn him into a 'black-tipped match'! We'll smash up his kennel!"

"Ah, but he might have bolted by now! Or he might have the police outside on guard!"

"Bah!" Little San-tse roared, pounding the flimsy table with his fist. "Didn't we all agree yesterday that if he bolts we'll wait down at his kennel till he comes back?"

Realizing what it was all about, his mother suddenly stamped her foot and shouted at the top of her voice. "I'm coming along too! I'm not going to stay here and see you all run in by the police one after the other! I'm coming with you!"

As she shouted, she seized hold of her son's arm and clung desperately to him, though whether she did it because she wanted to go with him or whether to hold back, she did not really know. Whatever the reason she clung to him, crying and shouting. Chin Ho-shang did not know quite what to do, while Little San-tse, his face flushed, stamped his feet and shouted at her:

"Don't be a fool, Mum! We don't want old women like you in on this sort of thing! It's no picnic we're going on!"

With a great effort he shook off his mother and ran out taking Chin Ho-shang with him.

*

The sun was high in the sky by the time Chin Ho-shang, Little San-tse and fifty or sixty other workers from the match factory arrived at the street where their employer Chou Chung-wei lived. His house lay back from the street at the end of a narrow lane, the entrance of which was guarded by a policeman, who would only admit eight delegates out of the sixty of them, so that the rest had to wait outside in the street, where they squatted on the pavement and used the corners of their jackets to wipe their perspiring foreheads and fan themselves with.

Little San-tse was one of the eight delegates. They found the front door of the house shut tight, and though they bawled at the top of their voices for a considerable time, the house might have been empty for all the answer they got. Little San-tse lost his temper and began pounding loudly on the door with his fist and raving at the top of his voice, "You won't get rid of us by hiding in there! If you don't show yourself, we'll bloody well set light to your house and see if that doesn't fetch you out!"

"We're setting fire to it now!" the other seven delegates shouted in chorus. "We're going to burn you out!" One of them was actually taking a box of matches out of his pocket, when a sudden roar of laughter came from the balcony above their heads. They recognized the laugh and quickly looked up to see Chou Chung-wei himself standing up there, barefoot and wearing a silk jacket, smiling down at them. The delegates responded to this provocation by dancing with rage and cursing and shouting at him, but Chou Chung-wei just smiled. Suddenly, he shook his head, stood on tiptoe, and leant his short, fat body over the balustrade.

"So you're going to set fire to the place, are you?" he shouted. "You're welcome! My belongings are covered by a thirty-thousand-dollar fire-policy, and I'd be extremely grateful to you for helping me to the money! The house doesn't belong to me, so set fire to it by all means! There's just one thing though — my wife's ill in bed and you'll have to take her out on a stretcher before you start!"

At this he went off into another fit of laughter and laughed until he was quite red in the face. The delegates did not know what to do with him, so they just kept hurling abuse at him. He took it broad-mindedly — the harder they swore, the louder he laughed. Suddenly he stopped laughing and addressed them in a serious voice:

"Now listen to me, dear friends! I've got a brilliant idea! Go and burn down the factory as well! It's insured for eighty

"If you don't show yourself, we'll bloody well set light to your house and see if that doesn't fetch you out!"

thousand dollars and the policy expires in a couple of weeks! So you'd better hurry up if you're going to burn it down! The insurance company's owned by a foreigner, and we'd all like to make a packet at the foreigners' expense! If only you'll help me get my hands on a nice little windfall like that, I shall never know how to thank you! Tell you what: I'll stand you all a slap-up feed at the Good Luck Restaurant! That's a promise!"

The delegates were ready to burst with rage. They had cursed themselves hoarse, but still they had made not the slightest impression on the imperturbable Chou Chung-wei. In any case, there were only eight of them and even if they did find some way of dealing with him, there was not much they could do on their own, so after a brief consultation they retired to see the others about it.

Chou Chung-wei remained on the balcony to see the delegates off. When they had disappeared round the corner, he stepped back into the room, still shaking with laughter. Chou Chung-wei's "residence" was the usual type of thing: three storeys of three rooms each. Since his match factory had folded up, he had vacated one wing in case he had to sub-let part of the house, and dismissed one cook and two maids. An atmosphere of gloom had descended on the house, the more so now that his wife was in the third stage of consumption, so that she was completely bed-ridden; yet Chou Chung-wei could still often wear a smile. He had started out in life without a penny to his name and had made his way as a compradore. He had never been really well off, though he had been able to keep up appearances. He had a genius for "getting rich quick" — and for losing his money even faster. And however bad his luck, he could always raise a smile.

Having repulsed the eight delegates, he now hurried back downstairs to the side-room where he had been playing with his "models." Two tables had been placed end to end, and on them was set out a complete set of toys representing a birthday party. The fortieth anniversary of his coming into the world was due in August next year, and he was already rehearsing in miniature the magnificent birthday party in the old-fashioned style that he had promised himself. He had started his rehearsal early in the morning, and was just beginning to enjoy himself when the eight delegates had arrived and made such an infernal din outside that he had had to dash up to the balcony and keep them amused. Now he had come back to his "little display." It suddenly struck him that his wife's death might occur before his own great event, so he cancelled the birthday party and began rearranging his toys to represent an old-fashioned funeral service. He set up a three-inch-high funeral curtain and laid white satin covers over the miniature ebony chairs, arranging every detail with greater care and enthusiasm than he would ever have expended on his match factory.

He had just arranged a pair of lanterns the size of oranges, and was about to set up the eastern and western archways for funeral procession, when two visitors burst into the room and he had to abandon his great project.

The two intruders were Chu Yin-chiu and Chen Chun-yi. When they caught sight of the paraphernalia on the two tables, they both burst out laughing. Chou Chung-wei himself rubbed his hands with glee and joined in their laughter. Chu Yin-chiu clapped him on the shoulder and said, "Chung-wei, I take my hat off to you: you've got the patience of a saint! And all the time your employees are asking for you outside — blocking the entrance to the lane and quarrelling with the policeman!"

"Eh? Are you serious? I haven't heard a sound myself! Well, you'll have to excuse me, then. I'd better go and see what it's all about!"

He put on a look of great surprise as he said this, and let the smile fade from his lips. He began buttoning up his jacket, as if preparing to go out, but Chen Chun-yi grasped him by the arm and held him back.

"You mustn't go out there! Let them shout as much as they like. Remember, Chung-wei: 'Discretion is the better part of valour!' It wouldn't be wise for you to show yourself just now!"

"Chun-yi's right," said Chu Yin-chiu. "Only two days ago Wu Sun-fu nearly had his car smashed with him inside it! The way the workers are getting out of hand just lately is simply preposterous! Though you know, Chung-wei, I never expected to see you losing money in the match business and being driven to closing down your factory! You ought to be much better off than we are, when you think that matches are indispensable in every home — as indispensable as food and fuel. Even the tramps in the street, who can go for hours without food, still have to pick up dog-ends for a smoke. And they can't smoke them without matches! So even the tramps are bringing you trade!"

He picked up one of the miniature lanterns and toyed with it, an amused smile on his lips.

Chou Chung-wei did not reply, but suddenly roared with laughter and skipped into the back room like a toad lolloping along. He rummaged among a pile of old letters on a desk and presently came back with a duplicated circular clutched between his pudgy fingers. He handed it to his two visitors.

"If you two gentlemen will cast your eye over this, you'll see just how prosperous the match business is!"

It was a circular from the All-China Association of Match Manufacturers to all its members. Attached to it was a copy of a petition sent to the Ministry of Commerce and Industry by the Kwangtung branch of the association. The circular itself read as follows:

> Dear Member — We have received a letter from our Kwangtung branch informing us that, according to reports appearing in newspapers in Kwangtung Province and Hongkong, the Swedish China Match Company, an enterprise conducted by Swedish merchants in this country, has made the government a loan in return for a monopoly of the match business in China for a number of years.
>
> Greatly alarmed by these reports, our Kwangtung branch has asked us to make investigations and give them a reply which will dispel the uncertainty which surrounds the whole affair. They enclosed with their letter a copy of the petition they are sending to the Ministry of Commerce and Industry.
>
> We are also in receipt of a letter to the same effect from

our Northeastern Provinces branch, who heard the news from certain Japanese match manufacturers in China, who in turn heard it from their Consul-General in Shanghai. Again, the Northeastern Provinces branch asks us to make inquiries and confirm or deny the rumour of a Swedish monopoly.

In view of the currency of these reports, we should like to point out that we began to investigate the matter as far back as June, and that repeated inquiries show that the proposed loan from the Swedish company has not yet materialized; nevertheless, realizing that, in default of a clear declaration by the government, the fact that the rumour is still gaining ground must necessarily cause our members considerable anxiety, we ourselves have addressed an inquiry to the Ministry of Commerce and Industry, requesting that they give us a definite reply. As soon as the reply is received, we shall transmit it to you without delay.

We enclose for your information a copy of the petition sent by the Kwangtung branch to the Ministry of Commerce and Industry and a copy of our own petition to the ministry.

Standing on tiptoe behind Chu Yin-chiu's seat, Chou Chung-wei read the letter aloud from beginning to end. After pausing a moment for breath, he went on to read at the top of his voice part of the petition from the Kwangtung branch:

... As the civil war drags on from year to year, it brings slump and depression in its train and has reduced trade and industry to their lowest ebb. In order to offset its financial deficits, the government has repeatedly raised the import duty on the raw materials used by the match industry, increased taxation and issued government bonds, with the result that business and industry have been saddled with a crippling burden which has depressed them beyond recovery.

The Swedish Match Trust is taking advantage of this situation to squeeze out Chinese match manufacturers by flooding the Chinese market with their own products, which enjoy a light import duty, and undercutting Chinese manufacturers, who are burdened with heavy production-costs.

The result is that our own products are piling up in mountains, and that we are having to sell them at a loss in order to keep the industry alive.

It is impossible for Chinese manufacturers, with their limited capital, to compete with the Swedish Match Trust, whose immense capital and great influence have enabled it to extend its ruthless dominion to every corner of the globe; as a result, over fifty per cent of Chinese match factories have been forced to close down one after the other.

Shaking his head, Chou Chung-wei suddenly burst out laughing again:

"Well, there you are, gentlemen! You can see for yourselves what a good business my trade is! — It must be. Otherwise, the Swedish Match Trust wouldn't be so keen to get their hands on it!"

Chen Chun-yi and Chu Yin-chiu looked at one another and frowned. To them, Chou Chung-wei's laughter sounded like the laughter of despair, but so far as Chou Chung-wei himself was concerned, it was the real thing. He could always raise a boisterous laugh. Otherwise, how could he be as fat as he was?

Just then, Chou Chung-wei's rickshaw boy dashed in in a state of great agitation to report that the workers had chosen ten delegates, who were now trying to get into the lane. With a tug at Chen Chun-yi's sleeve, Chu Yin-chiu rose to go, but Chou Chung-wei barred the way and would not let him pass.

"Don't go yet!" he urged. "I've got something important I want to discuss with you! Surely you're not afraid of these ten delegates?"

"No, no, it isn't that, Chung-wei! Since you'll have to have it out with them, there's no point in our staying — we'll only be in the way! If you've got something important to discuss, we can leave it until this afternoon. All right?"

"Afraid not! Look here, old man, I'm very sorry, but since you're here, I'm going to ask you to stay a little longer so that you two can be my bodyguards in this emergency! Don't worry, my employees are very civilized people, and I treat them in a civilized manner! If they should happen to upset you, I'd offer you my apologies!"

Chou Chung-wei's face was quite flushed now, and as he spoke he bowed to his visitors with clasped hands. Then he spread out his arms to keep them in their seats and prevent them from leaving. The two visitors were mystified by his antics and wondered what the "Red-tipped Match" was up to now, but they could not help laughing.

But the laughter died on their lips as there suddenly came a thunderous pounding on the front door, and they began to look uncomfortable rather than amused. The angry shouts of the delegates could be heard with painful clarity: "Chou, you old swine! Come out, you old thief!" The two visitors were beginning to feel embarrassed and their faces crimsoned to the tips of their ears, but Chou Chung-wei himself was still grinning. He patted himself on the chest and looked straight at his two friends.

"Didn't I tell you they were civilized people?" he said. "As civilized as they make 'em! Still, it'll take more than rude names to spoil my appetite! Y'know, Chun-yi, back in the old compradore days, our foreign boss often got out of bed on the wrong side and raved and swore at us, and it was a lot worse than this, I can tell you! In this case, the workers are Chinese, and we are also Chinese, so that by cursing us they're as good as cursing themselves!"

"I can't help admiring your great self-control, Chung-wei!" teased Chen Chun-yi, straight-faced. "I bet you wouldn't turn a hair even if they slapped you in the face, would you?"

Chu Yin-chiu frowned at this, but Chou Chung-wei at once shook his head and said in a serious voice:

"Of course not! I remember the boss of a certain foreign firm — he might have been an American or he might have been a German, I don't remember which; anyway, he was a foreigner. He said to me one day, 'You Chinese are wonderful. When somebody knocks you over on to the ground, you just lie there and say you're more comfortable than when you were standing. When you can no longer walk on your legs, you just roll along on the ground!' Don't you agree, Chun-yi? There was a man who understood the Chinese temperament! Yes, we Chinese certainly know how to enjoy ourselves come what may!"

By now the uproar outside was more furious than ever. Suddenly two heads appeared outside the barred window overlooking the lane and peeped into the room. Chu Yin-chiu was the first to see them, and he could not suppress a start. The heads sank out of sight again, and immediately the sound of shouting and cursing rose in a crescendo, so that the three men inside could no longer hear their own conversation. Chu Yin-chiu sighed and turned to Chou Chung-wei.

"You can't afford to ignore them, Chung-wei! You'd best ring up the police station and ask them to send some men round to drive them away!"

"Yes, Chung-wei, I think you ought to do that. Your wife's seriously ill and it's not right that she should be disturbed like this!"

"Oh, that doesn't matter! She's stone deaf. Now don't take me seriously, but her life insurance policy expires on the day after tomorrow, so if anything does happen to her today, it would be a case of pennies from heaven for a very deserving case! Ha! Ha! — Though they've been shouting so long now that they've shouted themselves hoarse. I feel really sorry for them and I think I ought to send them home now. It'd be a help if you two gentlemen could give me a little moral support while I speak to them. I'm sure you don't mind helping me out once in a while for old times' sake!"

"Tell us first what you're up to, Chung-wei," said Chen Chun-yi nervously, getting to his feet. "You're running a great risk if you're thinking of pulling their legs!"

Seeing him get up, Chu Yin-chiu followed suit. The shouting outside suddenly began to die down.

"I can assure you that not a hair of your heads will be touched! I just ask you to do one thing: whatever I say to them, you vouch for my sincerity, and I'll be extremely grateful."

Chou Chung-wei accompanied his cryptic request with a roar of laughter, then went and opened the front door and shouted at the delegates:

"Now shut up, all of you! Don't you know the old proverb — 'Save your breath to cool your porridge'? And I'm seeing to it that you all get your porridge, too!"

The crowd outside had by now increased by one more — an armed policeman trying to restore order. When they saw Chou Chung-wei coming out, the ten delegates immediately swarmed up and surrounded him, everyone shouting at once. Although Chou Chung-wei was an old stager who had been through the mill, he now felt suddenly nervous. The blood had rushed to his cheeks and his forehead was bathed in sweat. He could not think how to begin. He thought of escape, but that was now impossible.

"Now stop your noise!" bawled the policeman, forcing his way through the ring of delegates. "Wait and hear what Mr. Chou's got to say before you start opening your mouths! Where's your manners?"

Chou Chung-wei raised his hand to wipe his perspiring forehead, then swallowed and shouted at the top of his voice:

"Now listen to me! You're Chinese, and I'm Chinese — Chinese should help Chinese! Now what is it you want? You want me to open up the factory again, don't you? Well and good! If the factory remains closed any longer, you'll starve to death — and so shall I! So you see, I'd have opened the factory again even if you hadn't come here and kicked up a row! Though you ought to thank your lucky stars that I've just had two Gods of Wealth come to see me — look, there they are in my room! They've promised me a loan, so tomorrow we all go back to work again!"

Chou Chung-wei broke into an exultant laugh, but by now he was out of breath and so excited that his laughter quickly petered out and left him standing there open-mouthed and panting for breath, his eyes wide and staring. Some of the delegates began to look threateningly at him again — though they made no sound — while others ran through the front door to see if there really were any Gods of Wealth there. Chou Chung-wei quickly ran in after them, and shouted into the side-room in spite of his panting:

"Mr. Chen the banker and Mr. Chu the director! Would you

be so good as to step this way and meet my employees' representatives?"

Chu Yin-chiu did his best to keep a straight face as he walked slowly into the drawing-room, and stood looking out at the delegates, a frown on his face. Behind him came Chen Chun-yi, though he was still smiling.

The delegates suddenly fell silent, then began to look inquiringly at one another as if unable to decide whether or not these two "Gods of Wealth" were the genuine article.

"There you are, then!" bawled the policeman. "Mr. Chou's promised to open the factory again, so there's nothing for you to wait about here for! Now come on, it's against the regulations to kick up a row like this! Any more trouble, and you'll go straight down to the station!"

He began to move them on, but Chou Chung-wei stopped him and addressed the delegates again, this time smiling and shaking his clasped hands respectfully up and down.

"I should like to thank you all from the bottom of my heart! If you hadn't made such a noise just now, my two friends, the banker and the director here, wouldn't have lent me the money! All's well that ends well, and tomorrow we'll be back at work. And when I say a thing I mean it!"

"And don't think you can run away, either!" shouted Little San-tse as he moved off behind the other delegates, then spat in the direction of the front door.

As the three proprietors came back into the room, they all burst out laughing at once. Chou Chung-wei began walking up and down, his fleshy head wagging with elation, as if he had actually obtained a loan. He had always kept at the back of his mind two ways of getting financial assistance, and in his present mood of elation they suddenly came back to him and he began toying with them in a make-believe sort of way; he glanced at Chu Yin-chiu and thought to himself: "Let's pretend he's the head of that Japanese firm!" The idea so amused him that he could not help laughing again. He was still laughing when Chen Chun-yi suddenly said in a solemn voice:

"Chung-wei, you really must think of a way out. You got rid of them today by pulling their legs, but you're going to find yourself in a bit of a mess when they come back tomorrow and start kicking up a row again!"

"Chun-yi's right," put in Chu Yin-chiu. "When they come back tomorrow, you'll find they won't be so civilized as they were just now. You'll have to forestall them!"

He frowned, and Chou Chung-wei thought how much more he resembled the head of the Japanese firm when he frowned. The thought made him smile as he replied:

"A way out? Ah, but I've got one! And you are the people who can help me out!"

The two visitors were taken aback for a moment, especially as Chou Chung-wei did not look as if he was joking. Putting on his gravest expression, he went on:

"I've got it all worked out. I'm fed up with my business and whoever wants what's left of my factory can have it. It's a pity the Swedish Match Trust isn't going to run factories in this country, otherwise I might co-operate with them. Now a short while ago I told you I'd got something important that I wanted to consult you about. Well, here it is. So far as I can see, there are two ways open to me: either I go to see the head of a Japanese firm I know quite well and who's willing to help me out, or else I approach the Yi Chung Trust Company. Being a Chinese, I naturally prefer to give one of my own kind the first chance. Besides, Wang Ho-fu, Sun Chi-jen and Wu Sun-fu are old friends of mine and it's only natural that I should approach someone I know very well first. Well, that's the way I look at it, though of course, I don't know what their reaction would be. Now the thing is, both of you have very close dealings with the Yi Chung Company, so I was hoping you'd be able to tell me whether they'd help me out or not."

"I see . . . you're thinking of trying that way, eh?" said Chen Chun-yi hesitantly, with a glance at Chu Yin-chiu. "Are you thinking of leasing your factory or selling out? They don't make loans on pledges, you know!"

Chou Chung-wei's reference to the Yi Chung Trust Company had touched one of Chu Yin-chiu's tender spots, and, being suspicious by nature, he assumed that Chou Chung-wei was purposely taunting him. He frowned and sighed, but said nothing.

"Doesn't matter which! Either way will do!" replied Chou Chung-wei quickly. "In any case, we're all friends, so we can easily come to an agreement on that!"

One would have assumed from his eagerness that Chen Chun-yi was a representative from the Yi Chung Company and that their informal exchanges were serious negotiations for a contract! Chen Chun-yi smiled. Although he felt that Chou Chung-wei was being rather too precipitate, he fully sympathized with him, and his voice was earnest as he went on:

"As you probably know, Chung-wei, Wu Sun-fu is the real power behind the Yi Chung Trust Company. He's very sharp, is Sun-fu, and fastidious, too! Offer him something, and he'll pick holes in it; but let him once take a fancy to your factory, and it's a different story altogether: he'll badger you and harry you until you're in an impossible position, and you'll end up by going and begging him to take it! Our friend Yin-chiu here, for instance, had suffered at his hands in exactly that way —"

"Your best bet's your Japanese friend!" interrupted Chu Yin-chiu, and heaved a sigh of resentment. "You might as well try to take a piece of meat out of a tiger's mouth as have dealings with Wu Sun-fu!"

So it was good-bye to Chou Chung-wei's castles in the air. His face was flushed and his eyes were wide and staring. As a matter of fact, he had already made overtures to his Japanese friend, but the latter's terms had been so harsh that he had been driven to consider trying the Yi Chung Trust Company. Now that he had heard what his two friends had to say about Wu Sun-fu, he was beginning to feel desperate. For the first time in his life, he could not even raise a laugh! Nevertheless, he had not yet entirely given up hope, for he did not mind being badly treated, so long as the ill-treatment was accompanied by a cash profit, however small. He wiped his hand across his perspiring forehead, then, a lugubrious expression on his face, he asked in an agitated voice:

"Now tell me, Chun-yi, how does one go about leasing out a factory? I suppose both of you leased yours?"

"Yes, both of us. Yin-chiu's turned over his factory to Wu

Sun-fu, lock, stock and barrel. He doesn't have anything to do with it now, except to collect the rent for it — five hundred taels of silver a month. As for me, I'm in charge of my factory the same as before, with the empty title of general manager, and they pay me a monthly salary. People outside think I'm still the proprietor, but as a matter of fact I can't do a thing without asking Wang Ho-fu first — still, I can't grumble: Wang Ho-fu's a decent chap and we get on well enough together! Instead of me collecting rent for the factory buildings and machinery, we have a special arrangement whereby I get one per cent of the price of every piece of goods produced as compensation for the depreciation of the buildings and machinery. Well, that's the way they work. You see how sharp they are!"

"Well, I'm perfectly agreeable to an arrangement such as yours! Perfectly agreeable!" exclaimed Chou Chung-wei, leaping to his feet. His hopes had revived and he could smile once again. But Chu Yin-chiu threw cold water on his rising spirits when he said gloomily:

"I'm afraid you're going to change your tune when you hear what sort of a monthly salary Chun-yi gets! Two hundred and fifty dollars! A mere two hundred and fifty dollars for managing a silk goods factory employing over three hundred workers! Wu Sun-fu has the cheek to offer it, and Chun-yi has the goodness to take it. I wouldn't!"

"I've got no choice in the matter!" said Chen Chun-yi. "It's better than closing down the factory and letting the machinery go rusty! My machinery is good, and I couldn't bear to see it go rusty. That's where the shoe pinches: they've got the better of me whatever I do! Still, so long as I can still have the run of my factory and keep an eye on things, I don't mind so much. Don't you agree, Chung-wei?"

Chou Chung-wei nodded but did not speak. An unusually grim expression clouded his plump face: he was thinking hard. He was rather taken by the idea of leasing out his factory under the same arrangement as Chen Chun-yi. It appealed to him mainly because by staying on as manager he would still be the proprietor so far as people outside were concerned. For Chou

Chung-wei, this was not merely a matter of vanity, but also something which meant a lot to him financially. For years now he struggled to keep up appearances, and this he had managed to do almost entirely on the strength of his impressive but worthless title of "proprietor of a match factory." If ever he should lose this title, he would be unmasked and hard put to it to deal with the swarm of creditors who would descend upon him. And that would be an end to his easy laughter.

So Chou Chung-wei decided to try his luck with Wu Sun-fu. His ambition now was to become "Chen Chun-yi the Second."

He suddenly sprang to his feet, clapped his hands together, and turned to Chen Chun-yi:

"You're perfectly right when you say that one shouldn't let one's machinery lie idle and go rusty! And as you saw, that petition from the Kwangtung branch association stated quite clearly that over fifty per cent of the Chinese match factories have closed down! Being a Chinese, I'm under an obligation to protect Chinese factories! My Japanese friend has offered me a high price for my factory, and although he's a Japanese, China and Japan have always been friendly neighbours and have the same linguistic and racial origins, so it's not the same thing as selling out to a beaky-nosed European like a Swedish match king; nevertheless, for all that, I won't let him have it! I'd much rather let the Yi Chung Company have the benefit of my factory. It's up to us Chinese to help one another! That's that, then! I'm off to see Wu Sun-fu about it this very minute!"

"You're wasting your time, Chung-wei!" said Chu Yin-chiu gloomily, dousing Chou Chung-wei's hopes once more. "I don't need a crystal ball to tell you that you won't cut any ice with Wu Sun-fu, and that you'll come away with a flea in your ear!"

Chou Chung-wei sprang up in alarm, his face flushed. Chen Chun-yi quickly intervened:

"There's no harm in trying, Chung-wei. Not so long ago the Yi Chung Company bought out eight factories all at once, so it would seem that your proposition is in their line of business. Though I shouldn't advise you to see Wu Sun-fu, you'd much better approach Wang Ho-fu. He's easier to deal with, and anyway, he's the company's general manager."

Chou Chung-wei looked slightly relieved and nodded his head. He was so eager to become "Chen Chun-yi the Second" that everything Chen Chun-yi said was music in his ears. It gave him the creeps to listen to that bird of ill omen, the pessimistic Chu Yin-chiu. He cast a sidelong glance at Chu Yin-chiu, and had to laugh despite himself. He was thinking: "The more I look at you, the more you look like that Japanese fellow! A bad lot, that Jap!"

*

At one o'clock that afternoon, Chou Chung-wei was sitting in the manager's office of the Yi Chung Trust Company, talking with Wang Ho-fu and cherishing great hopes. At a desk under the window sat a young typist tapping steadily away at a Chinese typewriter. Wang Ho-fu sat there with a worried expression on his face, listening absently to what Chou Chung-wei was saying and glancing every now and then at the typist, as if he was not satisfied with his speed. Suddenly, the muffled jangle of a telephone came from the private office next door, and a clerk came into the room and drew Wang Ho-fu's attention to it:

"Phone for you, sir."

"Excuse me, Mr. Chou. I won't be a moment."

So saying, Wang Ho-fu hurried off, despite the fact that Chou Chung-wei was just coming to the crucial point, and the door of the private office slammed shut behind him.

Chou Chung-wei drew a deep breath, mopped his perspiring brow, and gulped down a mouthful of tea. The room seemed like an oven to him. His corpulent frame was bathed in sweat and he was finding it difficult to breathe. The breeze from the electric fan seemed hot and stifling and only served to add to his discomfort. He stood up and walked up and down for a moment, then stopped behind the typist and glanced casually at what he was typing. He was half-way through a notice, and Chou Chung-wei would have given it no more than a passing glance if one particular sentence had not leapt up at him and held his attention. As he stared at it, his hopes gradually began to ebb away until they had almost vanished. This is what had caught his eye: "In order to cut down production, the eight factories will operate on half time for the time being."

When Chou Chung-wei sat down again, he was perspiring more profusely than ever, yet the icy fingers of despair were closing round his ever-cheerful heart and sapping his vitality. He sat there mechanically wiping his forehead with his hand and staring anxiously at the door of the private office, wishing that Wang Ho-fu would hurry up and come out again.

Five minutes passed, then ten, but still there was no sign of Wang Ho-fu. Although Chou Chung-wei was normally quite patient, he was beginning to feel he had been left to cool his heels too long. Meanwhile, the typist had finished what he was doing, stretched, and was now leaning out of the window and watching the fashionably-dressed girls and round-bellied businessmen in the street below.

Unable to wait any longer — especially in this stifling heat — Chou Chung-wei decided to go and fetch Wang Ho-fu back, but he was in such a flurry that he went the wrong way — over to the door leading to the corridor. He did not realize his mistake until he had his hand on the door. He laughed at his mistake; the door at once swung open as if he had laughed it open, and a gust of perfume struck him. He found himself face to face with a man and a woman, both acquaintances of his, who stood there smiling at him. The woman was Hsu Man-li and the man was Colonel Lei, and they were arm in arm.

"Well! If it isn't Colonel Lei!" Chou Chung-wei exclaimed, beaming at him. "How long have you been back? This is a pleasant surprise!"

His low spirits had suddenly vanished. Before the colonel could reply, he turned quickly to Hsu Man-li and greeted her as warmly. His numbed mind had revived again — he had a brain-wave. Here under his very nose was the opportunity he had been looking for. From Hsu Man-li his thoughts had flashed to Chao Po-tao, from Chao Po-tao to the news of Chao Po-tao's latest success in stock-jobbing, and then, what was most important, from Chao Po-tao's success to the widely-circulated rumour that Chao Po-tao was organizing some kind of trust to buy up factories! His smouldering hopes had burst into flame once more, and he began reproaching himself for being so stupid as not to have thought of the idea before, for Chao Po-tao was a real "God of Wealth" if anyone was!

Wang Ho-fu now emerged from his private office, and after the usual exchange of courtesies he drew Colonel Lei to one side and they had a whispered conversation together. His mind now buzzing with ideas, Chou Chung-wei seized on this opportunity to ingratiate himself with Hsu Man-li and soon the room was ringing with his boisterous laughter. Hsu Man-li pursed her lips in a smile and cooed:

"It's very nice of you, Mr. Chou, to play the host and entertain me like this! No wonder they call you the 'Red-tipped Match'!"

At this he laughed louder than ever. Suddenly, he stopped and the smile vanished from his face.

"Miss Hsu," he said in a serious voice. "I wonder if you'd do me a little favour? It's nothing much, but you're the only person who can help me!"

"Er — what is it, then?"

"It's — it's just a trifle, really. You see, as a result of the war, my factory's been running into difficulties —"

"Ah, yes, I know! Everyone who owns a factory feels the pinch in wartime. But you have nothing to worry about, Mr. Chou! You're the famous 'Red-tipped Match' and you strike up friendships wherever you go!"

"Ah, but this is an unusually black year for me. Very unusual. All the ready money which should be in circulation is locked up in stocks and bonds, and if you ask anybody for a loan of a few thousand dollars, he just shakes his head. Fact is, I'm in a bit of a jam at the moment. I don't need much — matter of fifty thousand dollars; though even twenty or thirty thousand would probably tide me over. I'm sure you'll help me out, Miss Hsu?"

"What! Me help you? You're pulling my leg!"

"Not at all! I'm quite serious about it! I know Chao Po-tao gives loans right and left, but I haven't lived up to my name 'Red-tipped Match' by striking up acquaintance with that God of Wealth. I don't know what I've done to deserve this stroke of good luck, running into you like this today, Miss Hsu — I must have had very virtuous ancestors! What I want you to do is to be so good as to put a word in for me. One word from you would be better than an imperial edict; one nod from Chao Po-tao and I'm saved!"

Before Chou Chung-wei had finished what he was saying, Hsu Man-li's pretty face suddenly clouded over. She shot him one indignant glance as much as to say, "Stop trying to take the rise out of me!" then turned her head away and shook her shoulders peevishly. Realizing that something had gone wrong, Chou Chung-wei suddenly felt at a loss. He licked his lips and dared not say anything more. After a while, Hsu Man-li looked round again and said with a wry smile:

"I'm having nothing more to do with Chao Po-tao, the scoundrel! If you want an introduction to him, you'll have to get somebody else to do it for you!"

Chou Chung-wei's heart sank completely at this. One more ray of hope had been quenched. His mind was numb. Hsu Man-li now rose lightly to her feet with a sway of her hips and threw Chou Chung-wei a glance which held a hint of mockery. He sprang up in great agitation to make a final appeal, but Hsu Man-li had already turned and glided away. Wang Ho-fu now came across and patted Chou Chung-wei on the shoulder.

"We didn't finish our conversation just now, Chung-wei, but think I know well enough what it was you came about. When we first set up this company — you remember how we first discussed the idea at Old Mr. Wu's funeral — we originally intended to make it the foundation for an industrial bank to finance our colleagues in industry. Unfortunately, conditions have changed since then, and as a result we've been able to manage very little in the way of industrial loans, and we're unable to meet all requests we get from our friends. We've taken over eight factories, it's true, but the war has dulled our markets along the Yangtse, and we've run up against keen competition from the local Japanese factories, so that we're now reduced to cutting down production, putting the factories on half time. There's nothing we'd like better than to help you, but we just can't manage it. Sorry to have to disappoint you."

"Yes, Chinese industry's been going to the dogs for the past six months!" put in Colonel Lei, who had just walked across to join them. "The flour mills in Tientsin have always done a roaring trade and been the pride of the Chinese flour industry; but look at them now: seven of the eight big mills are closed down, and the remaining one only works one day in three!"

Chou Chung-wei was bathed in sweat, and found it hard to speak, even. When he finally managed to get a few words out, it was in a voice which he hardly recognized as his own. All he could do was to repeat over and over again that his requirements were very modest, that his products were selling steadily, and that his business had not suffered as a result of the war.

"We all run factories, Chung-wei, so we all know what the position is, and we can well appreciate each other's difficulties. The fact of the matter is that in this company we launched out on a large scale without the necessary capital behind us. As a result, we just haven't got the money to make any more loans."

"Even so, Mr. Wang, surely you can at least take over my factory on lease, the same as you did with Chen Chun-yi's factory?"

"If you'd come to us with this proposition a month ago, Chung-wei, we could have accommodated you. As it is, I'm afraid you'll have to forgive us."

As he made this flat refusal, Wang Ho-fu looked into Chou Chung-wei's perspiring face with a grim smile.

Now that all his hopes were dashed to the ground, Chou Chung-wei suddenly burst out laughing. He pointed at Colonel Lei with one hand and at Wang Ho-fu with the other, and shouted hysterically:

"I say! Do you remember? The day of Old Mr. Wu's funeral! Miss Hsu Man-li was there, too! Remember how she danced on the billiard-table? And lost one of her shoes? Ha ha! Wonderful time we had — seems like a dream now! But you mustn't apologize for not being able to help me, Ho-fu. We're old friends and we don't have to be so formal about it! But let me tell you something: every Chinese factory will sooner or later be as dead as a door-nail, unless they get a transfusion of foreign blood! Don't you agree, Colonel Lei? Just you wait and see! Ha ha! Come on, Miss Hsu, give us another dance! This table here's nice and smooth! Let's enjoy ourselves while we can!"

Colonel Lei and Miss Hsu both laughed, but Wang Ho-fu frowned and his face darkened as he remembered all that had happened since the day of Old Mr. Wu's funeral. Yes, "dream" was the right word. They had dreamed of giving industry a new lease of life, but now — now it looked as if they would soon be brought back to earth with a jolt!

"It's getting late," Hsu Man-li reminded Colonel Lei and Wang Ho-fu with a slight frown. "We'll have to hurry up if we're going to keep our appointment with Sun-fu at two o'clock!"

She gave Chou Chung-wei what could have been a significant glance, but he seemed to be quite unaware that the three of them had some private business of their own to attend to. Nevertheless the words "two o'clock" seemed to have a magical effect on him, for he suddenly leapt to his feet with a "Cheerio!" and raced out. As he went down the stairs he laughed to himself and before he was out of the building he had made up his mind to go straight round to his Japanese friend and ask him for "a transfusion of Japanese blood." Now he was his cheerful self once again. As he sat in his private rickshaw, he reasoned with himself in this fashion: China and Japan are old friends with common linguistic and racial origins, which means that a Japanese must be better than a beaky-nosed European. When you try to be patriotic and they won't let you, what else is there you can do? In any case, he wouldn't be the first by any means to throw in his lot with the foreigners!

A motorcar roared up behind him and flashed past.

He caught a glimpse of the people in the car — Hsu Man-li and Wang Ho-fu, with Colonel Lei between them. They struck him as an incongruous trio. "Up to no good, I'll bet," he thought. This suspicion flashed across his mind, but the next instant the thought of his coming interview with the Japanese returned and engaged his full attention. He smiled to himself and nodded as he made up his mind to fall back on the only way left open to him — to make every concession demanded of him so long as he could keep the title of "proprietor." Once he lost this title, his creditors would descend on him in a swarm, and he would be worse off than ever.

On the following day the doors of Chou Chung-wei's match factory opened again. Overnight he had copied out a new set of regulations which had proved even more exacting than the old ones. Two Japanese who could hardly speak Shanghai dialect followed him into the factory, one as a technician and the other as a supervisor.

Chou Chung-wei was beaming as he bounced to and fro and showed the two new arrivals over the factory. Finally, he called all his fifty or sixty employees together and made a speech:

"I promised you yesterday that I'd open the factory again, and here we are! You can see I'm a man of my word! Although the factory's losing money, I've got to carry on. Why? First, because if I closed down the factory you'd soon starve. But you're Chinese, and I'm also Chinese. As a Chinese employer it's up to me to stand by my Chinese employees! The second reason is that all the time the market's being flooded with imported matches, Chinese dollars are being drained out of the country into the foreigners' pockets — hundreds of millions a year! Now this is a Chinese factory, and you're Chinese workers making Chinese matches, so it's up to you as Chinese workers to help your Chinese employer! Production-costs are heavy, which makes Chinese goods hard to sell. The best way you can help me is to accept slightly lower wages. Then, once the factory starts making money, we all shall be in clover. Now I, as a Chinese employer, refuse to close down my factory, even though I'm losing money, because it's my duty to help my Chinese employees. In the same way, it's up to you as Chinese workers to help your Chinese employer by working your hardest and keeping down costs! That's all. Long live Chinese factories!"

It was as much as the corpulent Chou Chung-wei could do to get this last sentence out, for he was quite out of breath by now. As he gasped out the final phrase, the word "factories" trailed away into something like a sob. The veins stood out on his round, flushed face despite its plumpness, and beads of sweat rolled down his forehead.

The workers were as silent and expressionless as statues. As he panted for breath, Chou Chung-wei tried to smile, and dismissed his audience with a flap of his hand. Before long, the machines started rumbling and the matches began to come out in bundles on the conveyor belts, which ran on and on like never-ending cartridge-belts. As the belts ran on and on, so did Chou Chung-wei's thoughts: he was reviewing his life, episode by episode, stage by stage. He had begun as a compradore; later, he had become a factory-owner — his own master; now he was a compradore again — though a compradore of a different kind, a mere figure-head! It had indeed been a dream, and now the wheel had come full circle!

He suddenly laughed. Whatever happened, he could always laugh.

XVII

THERE was no wind. Scattered white clouds hung motionless against the pale blue curtain of the sky, and a smiling moon peeped down between the clouds at the secrets of the world below. The Whangpoo was a glistening ribbon of drab yellow; it flowed with a quiet contentment. A steam-launch pushed its leisurely way through the smooth waters of the river with an occasional majestic hoot. Its deck was ablaze with a galaxy of red and green lights which vied in the cool stillness of the night with the stars shimmering overhead. It was evidently a pleasure-boat.

The boat was now passing Kaochiaosha, where the river was wide, and moving solemnly northwards, while the busy industrial and commercial heart of Shanghai faded into the distance behind it. The tall chimney of the power station, the last outpost of industrial Shanghai, swept past in the twinkling of an eye. The fields on either bank seemed veiled in a thin grey haze as they slept in the moonlight.

The revellers on deck were mildly drunk. More than twenty minutes of uninterrupted laughter and joking had tired their tongues and they were now gazing out in silence at the mysterious moonlit world around them, their wine-flushed faces gradually taking on a look of frustrated boredom. Now that they were temporarily removed from the vortex of business competition, now that their eyes were suddenly opened to the quiet calm of the moonlit countryside, it was only natural that they should feel dejected as they licked the wounds they had received in the daily battles of the business world. In addition to the feeling of frustrated boredom, they now began to feel pessimistic about the vicissitudes of life and to itch with the desire for something fresh to give them the excitement they needed.

One member of the party was suffering worse than the others — Wu Sun-fu. Tonight's celebration had been at his suggestion and his guests were his old friends Sun Chi-jen, Wang Ho-fu, and Han Meng-hsiang, as well as one woman, Hsu Man-li. It was in her honour that this special party was being held, for, according to her, it was at this hour of the rising of the moon just twenty-four years before that she had first seen the light in this weary world. The bunting and the coloured lights, the wine and the expensive food, then, were all to celebrate her birthday. In addition, Sun Chi-jen had wired his agent to send down his new steam-launch for this special occasion.

The boat was going even slower now, and the engine chugged monotonously beneath them as if it were singing a lullaby. The skipper, sensing the mood of the party on deck, had cut down the speed to please them, and the boat was now so steady that one could have balanced an egg on one end on the deck. Suddenly, Wu Sun-fu turned to Sun Chi-jen:

"How many knots can this boat do at full speed?"

"Oh, thirteen, I should think. She might even get up to fifteen or sixteen when she's drawing as little water as she is now — though she'd roll like the very devil. Why — do you want to go fast?"

Wu Sun-fu smiled and nodded. Sun Chi-jen had read his thoughts and realized that his jaded spirits craved some violent stimulus — speed, power, anything. But Wang Ho-fu disagreed and offered a more practical suggestion:

"We're the only boat for miles; there'd be no fun in racing her here. Let's go back along the Bund where there's plenty of life and bustle, and then give her her head. That'd be more to the point!"

"There's no need to go back so soon!" said Hsu Man-li in her clear, tinkling voice. "Let's run down to Woosung where the river meets the sea before we turn back — and at full speed, too!"

Everyone clapped their approval, for just before, when they had been laughing and joking, they had agreed that the slightest whim of the "guest of honour" should be their command. Accordingly, the order for full speed ahead was immediately given, and the engine revved up and the boat began trembling as if in the throes of malaria; white foam churned up a foot high around the cutwater, and the bow-wave trailed out far across the river in a long white V. The waters of the Whangpoo splashed and gurgled around the laughing, wine-flushed party on deck.

"We must do something to keep alive the memory of this gala night!" shouted Han Meng-hsiang, holding his glass aloft. "I suggest that Sun Chi-jen should rename this boat the *Man-li*. All agreed?"

Just then the boat suddenly swerved and Han Meng-hsiang lost his balance and fell against Wang Ho-fu, while the glass of champagne splashed on Hsu Man-li's head and drenched her long, wavy hair. Exclamations of dismay came from Wu Sun-fu and others, then everyone burst out laughing. As she laughed, Hsu Man-li tried to shake the wine out of her hair and protested in a coquettish voice:

"You are a clumsy oaf, Meng-hsiang! My hair's soaked! Now you'll have to suck it dry!"

She was only joking, but Wang Ho-fu pretended to take it seriously and clapped his hands for silence.

"Did you hear that, everybody? Her Highness commands Han Meng-hsiang to lap up the wine in her hair! It's a great honour to be entrusted with such a task, Meng-hsiang! You must carry it out without delay —"

"Don't be silly!" interrupted Hsu Man-li, kicking at Wang Ho-fu's shin under the table to stop him. "I was only joking! I didn't mean it!"

Wang Ho-fu pretended not to hear and urged Han Meng-hsiang all the harder to "Obey Her Highness at once!" Wu Sun-fu and Sun Chi-jen clapped and cheered him on. Now that something new had come along to stimulate their jaded spirits, they were unwilling to let it go, especially in their present state of tipsiness. Han Meng-hsiang was smiling darkly and seemed to have no objection. The only difficulty was that Hsu Man-li, for all her rich experience of men, had become strangely shy.

She smiled woodenly and flashed a glance round the men's faces: three pairs of eyes, bloodshot with drinking, watched her closely, as if she were a monkey about to perform. She had a fleeting sensation, a feeling that she was being used as a plaything, but this feeling was too short-lived to annoy her. She pursed her lips in a smile and giggled. She found it rather embarrassing to be forced into a game of this sort and to be watched over while she played it.

Nevertheless, Wang Ho-fu had already gone into action. He held Han Meng-hsiang's head between his hands and pushed it close to Hsu Man-li's face. She giggled and leant away, only to find herself pushing against Wu Sun-fu's shoulder. Laughing noisily, Wu Sun-fu caught hold of her head and held it to Han Meng-hsiang's lips. Sun Chi-jen now assumed the role of master of ceremonies and shouted above the noise of their laughter:

"Suck one! Suck two! Suck — three! Ceremony completed!"

"Thank you very much, the lot of you! Now my hair's dirtier than ever! First champagne and then this!" she protested coyly as she tidied her hair, then began giggling again. As if hoping to carry the joke further, Wang Ho-fu quickly put in:

"All right, then, we'll have another try, but this time you mustn't pretend to be so shy!"

"That'll do!" said Wu Sun-fu, who felt the joke had gone far enough and wanted a change. "Man-li has broken the rules herself, so I suggest we think up a punishment for her."

Han Meng-hsiang, who was fond of dancing, suggested that she should be made to dance a foxtrot, but Sun Chi-jen was afraid there might be an accident on his boat and hurriedly objected.

"No, you can't do that! The boat's rolling terribly, and it's no joke to fall into the Whangpoo! Let's let her off for now — we can always think of something later on."

The steam-launch had now reached the Woosung delta. Three or four foreign warships were moored in the river, the lights on top of their mainmasts gleaming against the sky like unusually bright stars. The clear notes of a bugle-call came to their ears from one of the ships. Then there was a sudden silence. As far as the eye could see there was nothing but water and cold moonlight. The launch slowed down as it swept round in a wide circle at the river's mouth, then headed back up the river towards Shanghai. Suddenly Wang Ho-fu said in a serious voice:

"This afternoon two American gun-boats and three Japanese torpedo-boats left for Hankow under urgent orders, though I don't know what for. Chi-jen, has your company had any news from Changsha? I hear they're in a tight spot there again."

"I've had a wire, but it doesn't say anything much."

"Perhaps they couldn't give any details because of the censorship. So far as I can make out, the Reds are getting ready to attack Changsha. Hem!"

"That's just another Japanese rumour," said Han Meng-hsiang. "The Japanese news agency's always harping on the 'Red menace in Kiangsi and Hunan,' and telling us that Changsha is threatened — and Chian, too. The rumour was going round the Exchange today, but it doesn't seem to be affecting the market at all. In fact, the market's quite steady today!"

He yawned, and the yawn proved infectious: Hsu Man-li was the first to go down, and Sun Chi-jen came precariously near it, but managed to suppress it. He turned to Wu Sun-fu:

"Everything the Japanese say isn't necessarily a rumour, though. As a matter of fact, both those two provinces are in a bad way. With the war between the North and the South dragging on and on, they keep sending troops from the two provinces to the front, and never send any back to replace them. As the garrisons become depleted, they find it more and more difficult to cope with the Reds, who're just overrunning the whole place. There's no telling how it's all going to end!"

"Yes, it's a job to say what's going to come of it all," Wu Sun-fu agreed. "When the war first broke out, everybody expected that it would be over in two months at the latest, but here we are in the third month and still the end's not in sight. Though the casualties at the front are really frightful! They even make an old campaigner like Colonel Lei shake his head when you mention them. These army people have estimated that the total number of men called up by both sides is three million, and that the number of casualties to date is at least three hundred thousand! It must be the biggest war we've ever had!"

As Wu Sun-fu said this, he looked thoroughly dispirited; his eyes were closed, and he was stroking his chin. Hsu Man-li, who had not spoken for some time, suddenly joined in the conversation.

"Oh, they're a terrible sight, all these wounded soldiers! They just don't look like human beings! Ship after ship and train after train of them, every day they're coming in! Just look at all the military hospitals along the railways to Nanking and Hangchow — every city and town is full of them. When the temples are full they put them in the guildhalls, and when the guildhalls are full they put them in the schools. Sometimes there's nowhere to put them, so they just have to stay on station platforms for days on end in the wind and rain! Soochow and Hangchow were always called paradises on earth, but just at the moment these two cities are more like hell with all the wounded soldiers they've got!"

"I should think the war will be over by the end of July, though," Wu Sun-fu said optimistically, forcing a smile. "They can't go on much longer with casualties as heavy as that!"

Wang Ho-fu shook his head in disagreement.

"Not necessarily, I'm afraid! I've heard that they're digging the most up-to-date kind of defence-works all round Hsuchow under the supervision of a foreign military adviser. He guarantees that the Central Army can hold this defence-line for at least a year! Just think, another year! They say that this defence-line alone will cost three million dollars — some say five million! So it looks as if the war will still be on when New Year's Day comes round. What a mess!"

"However heavy the casualties are, there are plenty of new recruits to replace them!" said Han Meng-hsiang. "There are recruiting stations at Chinkiang, Soochow, Hangchow and Ningpo, and each station pulls in from three hundred to a thousand men every day and sends them up to Shanghai and then on to Nanking for training. They've also got a recruiting banner up in Shanghai North Railway Station; they enrol a matter of two or three hundred recruits every day there!"

Whether he realized it or not, Han Meng-hsiang had dealt a mortal blow to Wu Sun-fu's optimism with this.

A silence fell over the party. Was the civil war going to drag on indefinitely? This was the question which lay behind the glances that passed between the five of them. The chugging of the engine had now changed to a higher, softer key, and every beat jabbed at their frayed nerves and added to their depression. With Hsu Man-li and Han Meng-hsiang this depression was nothing more than a passing mood which quickly evaporated; but it had come to stay with the other three — Wu Sun-fu, Sun Chi-jen and Wang Ho-fu — and became worse as time went on. If the war should drag on for a long time yet, their businesses would be ruined!

A thin mist now hung over the river, and in the distance lightning flashed and thunder began to rumble. The wind was rising, a violent southeaster which met them head-on. The steam-launch forged angrily ahead in the teeth of the wind, and battled against the noisy onslaught of the waves. Presently, the gay, twinkling lights of Shanghai could be seen coming nearer and nearer through the thin mist.

"What a miserable lot we are!" came Hsu Man-li's tinkling voice, breaking the tense, gloomy atmosphere with its cheerfulness. "What's the matter with you all? Have you been struck dumb?"

It annoyed her to think that their evening of gaiety had been marred by the mention of wounded soldiers and defence-lines, and she was now determined to use all her charm to dispel the awkward silence that hung over them. Han Meng-hsiang was, as usual, quick to respond.

"Let's have one drink all round," he suggested, "and then each of us in turn drinks a toast to our guest of honour. How's that?"

No one disagreed with this suggestion. Though Wu Sun-fu and his companions realized that it would take more than a few drinks to dispel their low spirits, they were agreeable to having a drink if only to take their minds off their troubles for one brief moment and replace their depression with a temporary gaiety. When the toasts had been drunk, Wang Ho-fu was ready with another suggestion.

"So much for the drinks; now for a bit of fun! Chi-jen, you tell the skipper to order full speed ahead — as fast as she'll go! Man-li, you stand on the table on one leg and keep the other leg up. — You needn't be afraid of falling off, because we'll stand one on each side of the table. If you fall, the one who catches you will have good luck all the year and make his fortune this month!"

"No, I can't do a thing like that!" she protested coyly. "We're just coming into the busy part of the river, and I don't want to make a fool of myself!"

She turned to slip away, but the four men just laughed and applauded her insistently. Still laughing, Wu Sun-fu grasped her unexpectedly round the waist and planted her on the table with a thud. He held her there to stop her getting down and called to the others:

"Every man to his post! And remember, Man-li, no favouritism! Come on, everybody!"

There was no escape for her now, and she did not want to escape, but she was laughing so much that she felt weak at the knees and could not even stand up. The four men took up their positions, roaring with laughter and urging her on. The boat was now racing madly like a runaway horse. Hsu Man-li had only just stood up and raised one leg, when a gust of wind caught her dress and blew it up over her face. She gave a lurch and toppled towards one corner, where she was caught by Sun Chi-jen and Han Meng-hsiang together.

"That's the first prize gone!" laughed Wang Ho-fu, clapping his hands. "Half each! Up you go again and we'll see who gets the second prize!"

Just then, a sudden blast from the boat's siren startled the merry-makers and the next moment the boat jarred violently against something and seemed to rear up in the water. The sudden jolt sent the glasses and dishes on the table crashing to the deck. Everyone was thrown off balance, and Han Meng-hsiang, who was near the side, nearly went overboard. They were all pale with fright. The boat had stopped, and members of the crew were running along the sides with long bamboo poles in their hands. A muffled shout came from the river:

"Help! Help!"

The launch had hit a sampan and overturned it. Now Hsu Man-li could not give the "second prize." Wu Sun-fu frowned and smiled grimly to himself.

One of the crew managed to hook the sampan with his bamboo pole. In the water, clinging to the stern of the sampan was a man with only his head showing above the water. He was the sampan man, the only one who had fallen into the water. Ten minutes later, the launch was speeding on its way again and heading for the Customs Jetty. The five people on deck were laughing noisily once again. They dared not stop, for if they did they would immediately find themselves in the grip of a terrible despondency and the frightening uncertainties of the military situation and the crisis in business and industry would again be gnawing at their minds.

*

It was midnight. Most of the inhabitants of the industrial and financial world of Shanghai were already asleep and groaning through nightmares of cut-throat competition, but the bar of the night club still echoed with the clinking of knives and forks and the popping of corks. Wu Sun-fu was gazing absently at the people passing by him in the bar, his left hand supporting his chin, and his right over the top of a wineglass. He and Wang Ho-fu had got through half a bottle of port between them, but their faces were not flushed in the least. The port might have been so much pure water for all the effect it had on their jaded spirits. To make things worse, they had no idea why they should feel so depressed.

After landing at the Customs Jetty, they had all gone off to Hsu Man-li's place and spent a hilarious half-hour there. After that they had paid a visit to the famous house of romance known as No. 94, where they had set Madame a very difficult task. Finally they had come to this night club, where they had spent the last half-hour. They had played cards and dice, but none of these amusements had been of the slightest use in reviv-

"If you fall, the one who catches you will have good luck all the year and make his fortune this month!"

ing their spirits. They sat there as depressed as ever, feeling as if their chests were congested and making their breathing difficult. They felt prickly all over and it was an effort to move. What irked them most was that their usually alert minds seemed clogged and numb. Only the strongest stimulus could rouse them to mental activity, and then only for a moment.

"Whew! I feel whacked!" Wu Sun-fu muttered to himself and took a sip at his glass. He was still staring dazedly at the blurred shapes passing in and out of the bar.

"I feel washed out, too," yawned Wang Ho-fu. "Felt washed out for the last five or six days."

Their eyes met and parted at once, and each resumed his absent-minded staring. They might just as well have not spoken, for neither of them was really conscious of what they were saying or hearing. In fact, their conscious minds were a complete blank.

Suddenly, a tall, sturdy figure appeared in the doorway with three or four people clustered round him. They brushed past Wu Sun-fu's table, talking and laughing, and vanished into the room at the back of the bar. This sudden irruption seemed to jar the numbed nerves of Wu Sun-fu and Wang Ho-fu back to life, for they exchanged glances and smiled dismally at each other. Wu Sun-fu muttered as if to himself:

"Wonder if it was. Looked like Chao Po-tao."

"Chao Po-tao?" echoed Wang Ho-fu, instinctively glancing towards the door of the backroom, then asked:

"Who were the others?"

"I didn't notice. Anyway, I didn't see the old chap among them — Shang Chung-li."

"I saw somebody wearing glasses. What's his name, now — that's it, Li Yu-ting, the one who's always at your place."

"Are you sure it's him?" said Wu Sun-fu, then chuckled and picked up his glass for another sip. Just then the man in glasses came out of the backroom and came straight across to their table. It was Li Yu-ting, after all. He had come back specially to pay his respects to the two men of property. Wang Ho-fu laughed.

"Talk of the devil! Fancy meeting a university professor in a night club! I'll have it put in the papers tomorrow!"

"Don't worry! Our lawyer friend Chiu Chun dragged me here. Have you seen him?"

"No, but we saw Chao Po-tao when you came with him a minute ago."

At this chance remark of Wu Sun-fu's Li Yu-ting unexpectedly blushed to the tips of his ears. He felt as guilty and embarrassed as a woman whose husband has caught her with a lover. He forced a smile and hurriedly changed the subject:

"I hear the government's moving to Hangchow. It may only be a rumour, but everybody's talking about it. Haven't you heard about it?"

Wu Sun-fu and Wang Ho-fu shook their heads. They received the news with a curious mixture of delight and despondency. Li Yu-ting went on:

"The fact that the North's going to set up their own government, and that the Central Government's moving to Hangchow, means that neither side's willing to make peace and that they're both determined to fight it out. I tell you, Sun-fu, the war's going to drag on — perhaps even six months or a year! It's going to be the worst stretch of fighting since the republic was set up. There's never been such a vast number of men called up before, and the front line is so long that all the central provinces have been caught in the maelstrom. And then there are the Reds making havoc everywhere. In fact, the outlook couldn't be blacker!"

"We'll carry on as long as we can!" Wang Ho-fu said with a sigh. He was more disheartened now than he had ever been. Li Yu-ting felt sorry for him. He turned to look at Wu Sun-fu and saw a face as worried as Wang Ho-fu's. Li Yu-ting had never seen Wu Sun-fu looking as miserable as this before. He sighed despite himself and tried to think of something to say to dispel the unpleasant atmosphere that hung over them. Presently he spoke again:

"For all that the stock market's still firm: no sign of a slump yet. That shows that the general public are still quite optimistic about the future!"

"Ha ha! You're right they are!" Wu Sun-fu laughed with a sudden bitterness. He gave Wang Ho-fu a knowing look. Wang Ho-fu missed it, but Li Yu-ting noticed it and realized at once that he had inadvertently touched Wu Sun-fu's tender spot. He quickly tried to pass it off with a forced laugh and changed the subject again, this time to Chiu Chun, the lawyer:

"A native bank down in Nantao went broke, over four hundred thousand dollars in debt. Four-fifths of the money belongs to the depositors, who are getting Chiu Chun to sue the bank for them. As a matter of fact, Sun-fu, your relative Fan Po-wen happens to be one of the claimants. I hear he's reading up civil law now, instead of writing poetry. They say the bank lost a lot in the stock market."

Wu Sun-fu nodded and smiled. He was amused to hear that it had taken the loss of his bank deposits to make Fan Po-wen take up law. Wang Ho-fu said cynically, "If nobody ever went broke, nobody would ever make a fortune! It's hard luck on the small depositors, though!"

"Yes, it is," agreed Li Yu-ting. "My own feeling is that for the last few years the money business in Shanghai has been developing in the wrong direction. I think the development of industry is the only use of money which will benefit the nation's economy. As it is, industry in this city is going from bad to worse. A case in point is the cigarette industry — during the last two or three years quite a large number of new cigarette factories have sprung up in Shanghai, but they soon find they haven't a chance against foreign competition. And now, on top of that, they're being hit by the war. Even the China Tobacco Company, with the best-known brands and the biggest capital, is shutting down its Shanghai factory for the time being. Such is the fate of the luxury industries."

Having finished his impassioned harangue, Li Yu-ting stood up to go, then suddenly bent down and whispered in Wu Sun-fu's ear:

"Chao Po-tao's got something big up his sleeve. He wants to talk it over with you. I wonder if you mind coming into the backroom? It's quieter in there than it is here."

Wu Sun-fu was rather taken aback for the moment, and did

not reply at once. Li Yu-ting chuckled as much as to say, "Think it over" and walked off.

For a moment Wu Sun-fu just sat there gazing at Li Yu-ting's receding back. He was puzzled. Why should Chao Po-tao want to see him all of a sudden? And why should Li Yu-ting be so furtive about it, as if he did not want Wang Ho-fu to hear? He glanced round at Wang Ho-fu and decided he had better go and see what Chao Po-tao's game was.

"Ho-fu, Li Yu-ting's just told me that Chao Po-tao's got something to discuss with us. Let's go through and see him."

"Oh, I don't think you'll need me. I'm going to have a look at the roulette table. So Chao Po-tao's playing the Napoleon, eh? He's won his battle and now he's going to dictate his terms!"

The two men glanced at each other and laughed as if they felt some slight relief from their depression.

So Wu Sun-fu went alone. He found Chao Po-tao at a small table tucked away in a corner and sat down with him, trying his best to smile calmly. Since their joint speculation in government bonds a month before the two of them had met from time to time at social functions, but had never exchanged more than a few casual words. Now they had met once again for a serious private discussion. Chao Po-tao was his usual cheerful, straightforward self. He did not beat about the bush, and made no attempt to disguise the fact that he knew he had finally won.

"I'll be quite frank with you, Sun-fu. It's time we wrote off all our old scores! Though there are one or two things I must clear up before we start. In the first place, I admit I've had a hand in organizing a banking consortium — a sort of a trust, if you like. It's a fairly comprehensive sort of thing, but we're not barring anybody who wants to go in with us and we don't necessarily intend to swallow anybody who prefers to go ahead on his own. We've never at any time tried to bring pressure to bear on you, Sun-fu, and we've never had any real interest in the silk industry. If you've been imagining that we've got designs on you, Sun-fu, then you've got a suspicious mind! —"

Wu Sun-fu smiled and shrugged his shoulders. Chao Po-tao did not return his smile, and his keen eyes searched Wu Sun-fu's face. He drew hard at his cigar and went on:

"You don't believe me, Sun-fu? Just as you like. Though I'll tell you this: I was only pulling your leg with all that business about Chu Yin-chiu's loan. The last thing I want is to make things awkward for you! If you imagined that I had some ulterior motive, well, that's quite understandable — I'd probably react in the same way if I were in your place. And now let's pass on to the other thing. You people suspect that I'm leaving no stone unturned to wreck the Yi Chung Company. Ha ha! Yes, I admit I've done some underhand things, but only on a very small scale, never anything serious. You think I'm enforcing an 'economic blockade' against you behind the scenes. Yes, Sun-fu, I expect I could if I really wanted to, but as it happens I don't want to! It would be pointless to stab you in the back when you're one of us!"

"Ha ha! I see, Po-tao, it seems we've all been wronging you! All one big misunderstanding, eh?"

Wu Sun-fu raised his eyebrows as he laughed, but Chao Po-tao's expression remained serious.

"Not at all!" he quickly replied. "I don't mean that you've misunderstood every single thing I've done in the past. I only want to make you understand that we're not necessarily inveterate enemies, that we haven't necessarily got to go two entirely different ways, and that there's room for both of us in this world. You see, even if your company prospers, it doesn't mean to say that I'm going to lose by it, so why should I go to the trouble of making every effort to thwart you? As a matter of fact, I've never tried to do anything of the sort!"

Chao Po-tao's gloating tone of voice was more than Wu Sun-fu could bear, and he demanded acidly, "Surely you didn't send for me just to tell me all this, Po-tao?"

"Partly, yes. All right then, Sun-fu, let bygones be bygones. — Actually, there was something else I wanted to talk over at the same time, but as you seem fed up with the sound of my voice I don't think I should bother you with it. You know me, Sun-fu: I like to have things straight out and not beat about the bush. The reason I asked you over was to see whether we couldn't get together and co-operate from now on —"

"Now, Po-tao," interrupted Wu Sun-fu, "if you've got something else to talk over with me, let's hear it."

He put on a smile, trying to be calm, but he felt extremely uneasy. He suddenly remembered Tu Chu-chai's efforts at mediation when he had first clashed with Chao Po-tao. At that time he had insisted on a policy of "winning a victory before negotiating a peace so that Chao Po-tao will never get the upper hand," and so had rejected Tu Chu-chai's good offices, never expecting that their positions would be so quickly reversed and that Chao Po-tao, as the victor, would be offering him a chance to "co-operate" with him. Wu Sun-fu could scarcely believe that fate could be so unkind to him.

With a faint smile, as if he could see what was going on in Wu Sun-fu's mind, Chao Po-tao said quite frankly:

"The third thing actually is a case of misunderstanding. You think I've taken Tu Chu-chai away from you, whereas, in point of fact, I've done nothing of the kind. On the other hand, you've actually hooked Han Meng-hsiang from me! I don't mind telling you, Sun-fu, I couldn't help admiring the skilful way you did it!"

As Wu Sun-fu listened, his heart thumped and a look of apprehension came into his face. He quickly tried to pass it off with a loud laugh. Then he put out a feeler:

"Han Meng-hsiang's not the only one! I've also bought over someone even more important than him!"

"Oh yes, a woman, perhaps, but that doesn't count for much. I'd be extremely grateful if you would take some of them off my hands! I've got more women than I know what to do with!"

It was now Chao Po-tao's turn to laugh to hide his discomfiture, but Wu Sun-fu was not deceived, and it was now his turn to feel triumphant. His self-confidence was gradually returning and he was managing to shake off his defeatist mood. He braced himself up and took the offensive by returning without more ado to the question of "co-operation."

"You're a good guesser! We've been quite successful with our policy of buying people over! You know, Po-tao, I think even you have got your price! Now I'm plain-spoken like you and I don't believe in wasting breath, so let's have your terms for 'co-operation' straight out. If they're reasonable, I'll consider them seriously."

"Well, then, in a nutshell, I'll recommend a certain banking consortium to make the Yi Chung Trust Company a loan of three million dollars, the first instalment being half a million. The condition is that all the assets of the company should be placed with it as a security."

Wu Sun-fu listened attentively, his eyes riveted on Chao Po-tao's face. When the latter had finished, Wu Sun-fu suddenly threw back his head and roared with laughter, then shrugged his shoulders. Chao Po-tao's expression did not change; he puffed calmly at his cigar and waited quietly for an answer. When his laughter had subsided, Wu Sun-fu put on a serious expression and exclaimed:

"You're joking, Po-tao! Our company's policy is one of gradual development — we'll expand our business as we go along. Admittedly we've got big things planned for the future, but just at the moment we don't really need a loan of three million. In fact, we've got surplus capital that we can't find a use for!"

"You've got me wrong, I'm afraid. The total amount of the loan would be three million, but the first instalment will only be a matter of half a million. How the second would be made is left open. You're an old hand at the game, Sun-fu, so you must probably understand that this loan would in actual fact be a loan of half a million. The only thing is that the banking consortium would have priority in making further loans to bring the total up to three million if necessary."

"But the company couldn't even use a loan of half a million!"

"You sure?"

"Quite sure!" said Wu Sun-fu firmly, steeling himself to say it; yet hardly were the words out of his mouth when his heart missed a beat. He realized that Chao Po-tao was trying to trap him in the same way as he himself had trapped Chu Yin-chiu just a short while before! He realized that, if he refused, Chao Po-tao would organize a full-scale financial blockade against the company in real earnest. With the war dragging on and the eight factories suffering from over-production, such a full-scale financial blockade would give the Yi Chung Company a choice between closing down their factories and selling out. Chao Po-tao's offer, then, was the first warning shot as his financial trust went into action!

Chao Po-tao smiled and blew out a cloud of smoke before pressing home the attack. "So we can't co-operate after all! Your company is a promising one, and it seems a pity to drive it on to the rocks! You've put a lot of hard work into your company, Sun-fu. I can't see you letting it all go by the board! Why not think it over carefully before you let me know what your answer is? Now let's be perfectly honest about it, Sun-fu. You know as well as I do that your company is in financial difficulties. There's every prospect of the war dragging on and spreading to other parts of the country, which means that the company's factories won't find a market for their products before the end of the year. So think it over carefully, Sun-fu, and let me know what you decide."

"Mm —" grunted Wu Sun-fu vaguely, as he suddenly succumbed. Something seemed to snap inside him and his strength deserted him. His self-confidence had gone, and with it his will to resist. One thought was going through his mind: What about a conditional surrender?

Suddenly, he stood up, a wry smile on his lips. He had recaptured something of his ebbing will-power and was determined not to let Chao Po-tao see his dejection and his readiness to surrender. He clapped Chao Po-tao on the shoulder and said cheerfully:

"Say what you will, Po-tao, we all have our own ideas about the military situation! It may well be that something will happen which will bring the war to a sudden end! As far as our company's concerned, we don't worry much about it. Still, we don't mind absorbing a little more capital when we can to expand the business. I'll put your suggestion to the board of directors tomorrow and see you again later."

Wu Sun-fu rounded off the conversation with another roar of laughter and slipped away before Chao Po-tao could say another word. He went back to Wang Ho-fu and told him briefly what it was all about, then sat there frowning. For quite a while neither of them spoke. Presently, Wang Ho-fu muttered through clenched teeth:

"I'll be round at your place with Chi-jen tomorrow morning for a conference!"

*

By the time Wu Sun-fu got home it was half past one in the morning. Both stars and moon were hidden by the dark bank of cloud that covered the sky, and in his gloomy garden the wind was soughing mournfully among the trees. His wife and all the others were still out, and the servants of both sexes were gambling in the porter's lodge, huddled together in a circle, and shouting and laughing excitedly. They did not realize Wu Sun-fu was home until the chauffeur had sounded the horn for the second time. They immediately broke up in a panic and scurried back to their various places of work. Wu Sun-fu had guessed what was going on, and when he got out of the car his face was as black as thunder, for he had strictly forbidden his servants to gamble!

When he found that his wife and everybody else were out he became angrier still. "What sort of a home is this to come home to!" he roared as he stalked into the drawing-room and glared at the furniture, the carpet, the tablecloths, the sofa-covers and the curtains, searching for a pretext to vent his rage on the servants. As his angry voice rang through the house, the servants looked apprehensively at one another. With the wind moaning in the rustling trees outside, everything seemed to be conspiring to make this imposing mansion gloomy and depressing.

An apprehensive Kao Sheng came in with an armful of "in memoriam" scrolls which had been received in the course of the day from friends and relatives (the memorial service for Old Mr. Wu's death was approaching) and asked Wu Sun-fu whether he would like to glance at them. He was greeted with such a storm of abuse that he did not know whether to laugh or cry, and the servants now knew for certain that "the Master" was in an uglier mood than usual tonight.

Kao Sheng's rash intrusion, however, had given Wu Sun-fu

the necessary outlet for his rage, and he now sprawled on a sofa, lost in thought. He was not, of course, thinking about his father's memorial service, for it was still five days away, and anyway, he had entrusted all the arrangements to his wife and sister; he was recalling how he and his friends had conceived the idea of setting up the Yi Chung Company on the day of the old man's funeral. Now, even before the memorial service had been held, all their ambitious plans were going up in smoke!

He now went back in his imagination to the corner of the bar in the night club and went over his conversation with Chao Po-tao again. He recalled with a pounding heart every threat Chao Po-tao had made and every word he had said. His opponent had offered him a clear choice: to surrender to him or to see the Yi Chung go bankrupt! These two alternatives chased each other through his head in a merciless merry-go-round, so that he could not tear himself away from them and think of a third way out. His will to fight, to resist, had vanished without a trace. He was no longer the man he had been two months before, at the funeral! His enthusiasm for his business was now quite dead, and if he wanted to save the Yi Chung Company, it only was because he wanted to salvage the capital of two hundred thousand dollars which he had put into the company. And it was only the thought of losing this money that made him now decide that he had no other way out but to surrender to Chao Po-tao!

"So that two months' hard work was just thrown away!" Wu Sun-fu moaned to himself. His voice sounded strange in the silence of the spacious room. It startled him, and he sprang up, unable to believe that this weird sound had been his own voice, but there was nobody else in the room. The strong lights shone full on his face, and outside the windows were the shadowy shapes of a couple of servants standing by in case they were needed. He frowned and smiled grimly at himself. He lay down on the sofa again and suddenly recalled what he had told Tu Chu-chai not long before: "There are certain fly individuals in Shanghai who take a tumble-down house, redecorate it and patch it up, and then let it for a nice fat sum of key money. If the worst comes to the worst, we can always follow their example and do the same with the eight factories. . . . If we make a good job of redecorating the 'tumble-down house' and patching it up, even the great Chao Po-tao himself will offer us a good price for it!" He had said this in jest, just to talk Tu Chu-chai round, little knowing then that it would prove to be an oracle! Wu Sun-fu could not repress a smile as he thought of it. He was beginning to believe that everything was pre-ordained and that human efforts made no difference!

This thought made him feel slightly calmer. He was beginning to realize that Tu Chu-chai, timid though he was, could sometimes be more far-sighted than he was, and so save himself a lot of trouble. He now began working out the total value of the assets of the Yi Chung Company and considering what terms he should hold out for when it came to actual negotiations with Chao Po-tao. Should he sell out for a lump sum and have done with it, or should he mortgage it and have it on his hands for a while? His mind began to revive and his face became flushed again. He was now a different man not only from what he had been two months before, when he had drawn up his gigantic industrial plans, but also from what he had been only three hours before, when he had sat on the deck of the launch craving for excitement! He now had a "way out." Though it meant surrendering, it was much better than having no way out at all!

His reverie was interrupted when his younger sister Huei-fang stole quietly in and stopped in front of him, gazing at him with anxious eyes.

"Hullo, Huei-fang. Thought you'd be out," he said casually when he had made sure it actually was his sister and not his imagination. He looked rather annoyed at the intrusion.

Huei-fang said nothing, but sat down in a chair beside him and heaved a sigh. Wu Sun-fu frowned and was about to speak sharply to her, but changed his mind. He forced a smile, intending to speak gently instead, but she spoke before he could, "Sun-fu, I want to go back home to the country after father's memorial service!"

"What! Go back to the country?" Wu Sun-fu exclaimed in amazement. He was quite at a loss to understand how such a strange idea could suddenly have entered her head, and stared at her in astonishment as she sat there, her face white and drawn. She hung her head and after a while she mumbled:

"After all these years in the country with father I can't settle down in Shanghai —"

"Two months in Shanghai and you can't settle down?" interrupted Wu Sun-fu, then burst out laughing. He thought his sister was being childish, but he was wrong. Huei-fang raised her head and looked sharply at him. Her eyes had the same imperious glint as her brother's had when he was making a decision. She and her brother shared the same stubborn nature, except that she usually held it in check. Now, however, her latent stubbornness was forcing itself to the fore.

"No, I can't settle down! I've been here long enough to be absolutely certain that I don't like the place! It's not that I don't like the house or the food or anything like that, it's something else that I can't explain. Every day's a nightmare — I just feel on edge all the time. There doesn't seem to be anything to do all day and I always feel at a loose end! I've asked Pei-shan and the others, and they said they never feel like that. I suppose I'm not fit for Shanghai because I have always stayed in the country!"

Huei-fang was exceptionally insistent this time. Suddenly her eyes reddened and tears rolled down her cheeks.

"Well, Huei-fang — I —" Wu Sun-fu faltered, then stopped, not knowing how to go on; his expression was strangely tender. Though he usually treated his younger sister and brother in a rather overbearing manner, he was very kind to them at heart and he always strove to make their life a happy one in the way he thought best, so it naturally upset him to hear his sister complain of the dullness of her life, even though as an industrialist he could hardly be expected to understand a young girl's complex psychological processes and emotional conflicts!

Huei-fang was a sensitive girl, and her brother's gentle expression suddenly reminded her of her mother and of the loving care she had lavished on her when she was alive. This was the first time for ten years that she had known such warmth of affection, for it was the one thing she had missed while looking after her father all these years since her mother's death. Her father had never been more to her than a teacher of religion, and there had always existed between him and her an impassable barrier, so it was not surprising that her brother's new-found gentleness should help to loosen her tongue.

"When I first came to Shanghai, Sun-fu, I was afraid of everybody and everything. I was terribly nervous of meeting people and going out. I'm not afraid any longer, but now I always feel so bored and depressed. A little while ago Pei-yao taught me to play mahjong, but I very soon got fed up with it. I feel fidgety all the time, as if I want something, but I don't really know what it is I want. I just don't seem to be able to interest myself in anything. I'm just on edge all the time!"

"Well, if you've no way of passing the time, Huei-fang, why didn't you go out with Pei-yao today for a change?"

Wu Sun-fu's expression was gentler than ever now, almost the look of a loving mother; but then the businessman in him was becoming impatient with every passing minute.

"I just don't like going out —" Huei-fang said softly. She sighed, but did not go on. She could not bring herself to say what she was going to say. After all, a brother was a brother, especially when he was an elder brother who was usually very stern and serious, and she could not very well expect him to understand all the complicated things that were worrying her. She hung her head and her eyes became moist again. Suddenly, she saw in her mind's-eye a young man and a girl — perhaps Tu Hsin-to and Lin Pei-shan — talking and flirting quite naturally with each other. They seemed so happy together, and she was so lonely! She always felt there was a cord round her heart; when or how it had come to be there she did not know, but it was there all the time, binding her inside herself and preventing her from being easy and natural with men and talking and laughing with them. She hated this cord that bound her, but she could not free herself from it. This was the struggle that had been going on in her mind and causing her so much misery. All she wanted was to hide herself away somewhere where she could shut out the world and all the heartache it caused her. But she had no one she could tell about her unhappiness. She bit her lip, then looked up and said firmly:

"Sun-fu! I'm sure in myself that the only way is for me to go back to the country. There may be some other way out, but this is the only one I can think of at the moment. There's nothing for it but to go back to the country! If I carry on like this, I'll go mad! I'll go mad, Sun-fu!"

"Eh? I've never heard of such a thing!"

"I know it sounds odd, but I just can't understand why —"

"There's nothing to worry about, Huei-fang. Just stick it for a while and you'll find you'll get used to it. Look at Ah-hsuan, he's all right!"

Wu Sun-fu's voice was taking on a tone of sternness now. He shook himself impatiently and stood up, intending to put an end to this dreary debate, but Huei-fang was adamant. She looked her brother straight in the eye and said coldly, "If you won't let me go home to the country, you can at least send me to a lunatic asylum! I'll go mad sooner or later if I stay here!"

"Really, Huei-fang, I don't know what to do with you! You're old enough to understand, but you don't seem to be able to! Where do you imagine you're going to live if you do go back?"

"I could live at our old home all right!"

"But won't you be even more miserable living alone there?"

"Well, I could go and live with Auntie at her place!"

Wu Sun-fu shook his head and snorted, then began pacing up and down. He was quite at a loss to deal with this stubborn sister of his, and he was becoming angry again! He had always been accustomed to being in charge of things and having every order promptly obeyed. Besides, he could not imagine why his sister should want to run away from life in Shanghai. He could only put it down to the fact that she had been living with her father too long and had acquired some of his eccentricities, one of which was an aversion to modern culture and city life. As it happened, this particular prejudice of his father's was the one of which Wu Sun-fu had always most strongly disapproved. He suddenly stopped and turned to his sister again:

"Do you propose to hide yourself away in the country for the rest of your life, then?"

"Not necessarily. One's ideas can always change, you know.

But I think that for the moment at least the country's a better place for me than Shanghai."

Wu Sun-fu could not help laughing, for he felt he had at last found a chink in her armour, but before he could begin his counter-attack, the blare of a motorcar horn came from the drive, followed by a shout from Kao Sheng: "Mrs. Wu, Miss Lin and the young master are back!"

Then came a burst of gay laughter and the click of high-heeled shoes. The first one to burst into the drawing-room was Ah-hsuan, brandishing a stage sword and laughing and fencing with his new toy. He was obviously not expecting to find his brother Sun-fu in the room, and when he turned and saw Sun-fu's baleful glare on him his hand dropped to his side but he stood there grinning impudently. Wu Sun-fu frowned as he remembered the episode of the "throwing knife" and decided that this sword was just a larger replacement. So Ah-hsuan was raising the standard of rebellion against him, eh? He had stopped him playing with his silly "throwing knife," so he had had the cheek to provide himself with an even more fearsome-looking weapon! Who did he think he was?

His wife now walked in and realizing at a glance that Sun-fu was about to fly into a rage at Ah-hsuan, she quickly put in a word for him.

"It's all right, Sun-fu, he didn't buy the sword himself — Hsueh-shih gave it to him. You see, Hsueh-shih's been taking an interest in mediaeval knights or some such thing just lately. He's got a whole collection of swords and spears and things!"

"Pei-yao, what about the telegram from Fei Little Beard?" Lin Pei-shan quickly put in to divert Wu Sun-fu's attention. "You've still got it in your handbag."

Ah-hsuan made the most of this diversion to slip away, taking his sword with him.

The telegram said that a dozen or so shops in Wu Sun-fu's home town had gone bankrupt all at the same time and that their owners had gone into hiding, owing the various local banks a total of more than three hundred thousand dollars. The local bank owned by Wu Sun-fu was involved and now faced a crisis. The telegram ended with an appeal for money to save the situation. Wu Sun-fu's face fell and he sighed. Then, without a word, he walked out and went to his study to write out a reply. It read: "No money to spare. Do what you can."

He was walking through a minefield! Wherever he trod there might be an explosion! Such were the thoughts that tortured Wu Sun-fu's feverish brain as he tossed and turned in his bed, unable to sleep. His authority in society and even in his own home was collapsing like a house of cards! The veins on his temples throbbed, and the spring mattress underneath him felt like a bed of nails. His wife was groaning and moaning in her sleep again as she lay beside him.

He heard a muffled whistle somewhere in the distance, then suddenly he saw his younger sister Huei-fang running towards him and shouting that she must go back to the country and enter a nunnery, then cutting off her hair until she was completely bald. His married sister Fu-fang now appeared and began accusing him of ill-treating Huei-fang and Ah-hsuan and demanding that he share out the property he had inherited so that Huei-fang and Ah-hsuan could set up their own homes. Suddenly, he saw Ah-hsuan and a number of other people performing a sword-dance in the drawing-room, while the garden swarmed with grotesque giants. Finally, he found himself in a hotel, in bed with Liu Yu-ying; she was flushed and giggling, and her soft white hand, as hot as fire, was on his chest. . . .

Wu Sun-fu laughed aloud in his sleep and stretched out his arms to embrace a soft, warm body, then heard the sound of soft, alluring laughter. All of a sudden, he opened his eyes. The net curtains over the windows were splashed with morning sunlight and shadows, and his wife was sitting on the edge of the bed in a dressing-gown. She was smiling at him. He coloured guiltily and quickly sat up. On a silver tray on the bedside table a cup of hot milk was waiting for him, and beside it lay two visiting cards — Wang Ho-fu and Sun Chi-jen. A skin had just begun to form on the milk.

*

In the small drawing-room, Wu Sun-fu, Wang Ho-fu and Sun Chi-jen were just beginning their highly important conference. They first discussed Chao Po-tao's offer in great detail. Wu Sun-fu was inclined to accept it; Wang Ho-fu was non-committal; Sun Chi-jen strongly opposed it. Swaying his long neck, Sun Chi-jen said in a cool, firm voice:

"There are two things involved which we should consider separately. One: if we sell the company to Chao Po-tao, can we recover our capital? Two: do we need to sell it at all? I know Sun-fu's probably thinking that this consortium of Chao Po-tao's is the same thing as the finance trust that all the rumours have been about all this time, but so far as I can see it's all a hoax! If there's one thing Chao Po-tao can do, it's to fabricate rumours! He's deliberately put round this rumour of a trust to cause a panic and persuade people that they must either truckle to him or go bankrupt! I suggest we tell him to go to the devil!"

"But, Chi-jen, all this talk of a trust can't be just a hoax. Aren't they already trying to get their hands on our company?"

"Don't you believe it! Even if he can start handing out loans, this finance trust of his is still nothing but a hoax! Every penny Chao Po-tao possesses is tied up in government bonds; he just hasn't got the resources to go into partnership with the Americans! He may possibly be in league with some foreigner or other to make loans on security to Chinese factory-owners, but even if he is he's nothing more than a broker. If we have factories to sell, there's nothing to stop us finding a buyer ourselves! There's no reason why we should do it through a broker!"

"You're quite right!" agreed Wang Ho-fu. "No matter how formidable Chao Po-tao may appear to be, he's only a broker in disguise! In all these joint enterprises with foreigners, the Chinese are partners in name only; in actual fact they're mere brokers!"

Wu Sun-fu did not press his arguments, but he still seemed rather ill at ease when he next spoke, "If we don't find another buyer and have to fall back on Chao Po-tao later on, he'll just play cat-and-mouse with us. If we don't toe the line, he'll really enforce a financial blockade against us and we'll be in a worse jam than ever. Have you got anybody else in mind, Chi-jen?"

"Not at the moment, but we're pretty certain of finding somebody once we start looking. I said a moment ago that the question falls into two parts, so shall we now go on to the second? What it boils down to is this: as things are now, how much longer can our company hold out?"

Hardly were the words out of Sun Chi-jen's mouth when Wang Ho-fu shook his head pessimistically and Wu Sun-fu sighed and began stroking his chin. The answer to this question could not be more obvious: while the war dragged on indefinitely, every day that the eight factories remained open they were losing money; so the question was, in fact, not whether they *could* keep the factories open, but whether they wanted to. The answer to this was that they did not, for they had long lost heart over the whole project.

The three men looked at each other and smiled grimly. With that smile they had thrown overboard the dream they had set their whole hearts on for the past two months and more. Feeling that a mortgage would only prolong their misery, they decided unanimously to sell out completely and have done with it. Sun Chi-jen had two possible buyers in mind: a British firm and a Japanese company.

After a while Wu Sun-fu laughed mirthlessly. " 'He who knows how to fight and to retreat deserves to be called a brave man!' Anyway, it's all the fault of the war, not bad management on our part!"

Wang Ho-fu laughed heartily; he felt as if a heavy burden had been taken from his shoulders, and he was looking forward to more restful nights from now on. Sun Chi-jen, however, looked serious and absorbed, as if he was working something out. Suddenly, he slapped his thigh and looked gleefully at his two partners.

"The eight factories, including buildings, machinery, raw materials and finished goods, should fetch six hundred thousand dollars. That's without taking into account the seventy thousand in cash deposits in the company. Yes, I think we can get our capital back all right. With the factories gone, we shall have the empty shell of the company left, so we'll be able to carry on absorbing deposits and biding our time until we see an opportunity of going in again. Yun-shan said in his last telegram that he could find some share capital in Hongkong. I think we'd better send him another wire and tell him to go ahead and get as much as he can! Another thing, Sun-fu: we failed over the factories because of the war, but the war offers us an excellent opportunity for stock-jobbing! What about shifting our capital from factories to government bonds? It's time we had another tussle with Chao Po-tao!"

As he listened, Wu Sun-fu nodded his agreement. A warm glow of courage spread through him once more until his fingertips quivered. They had been doing fairly well in government bond speculation of late, and now, with a female spy in his service, he should be able to take the enemy by surprise. He decided to take the plunge.

"Let's start right away then, neck or nothing! There's been a slight rise the last few days, but that's because the bulls have been at work. If the war drags on like this, the three government lines — Tariff, Disbandment and Army Reorganization — are bound to drop sooner or later, perhaps as much as thirty per cent. I suggest we sell several hundred thousand today!"

"Agreed!" said Wang Ho-fu, twirling his beard elatedly. "That's just what I was going to suggest!"

In the past they had managed to run factories and do stock-jobbing at the same time, and even so they had weathered two violent storms on the Exchange without coming to grief, so it was quite natural that they should feel supremely confident now that they were going to concentrate all their capital and energy on stock-jobbing alone. There was no reason whatsoever why they should not feel optimistic about their chances. Their conference came to an end in an atmosphere of excitement and hope with a final enthusiastic contribution from Sun Chi-jen.

"Right, then: I'll start looking for a buyer straight away! Whether we get one or several offers, our total price is fixed at five hundred and twenty thousand dollars. They can take it or leave it! The company will remain in existence, but only for commercial credit. Ho-fu, you'd better chase up that prospect of yours and get that hundred-thousand-dollar deposit. We can do 'savings,' too. And you'd better keep in touch with Huang Fen as well, Ho-fu, for any tips he can give us. Last but not least is the job of dealing with the Stock Exchange side. I'm afraid you'll have to undertake that, Sun-fu. Nobody else could manage it!"

When his two partners had left, Wu Sun-fu immediately busied himself with the telephone. He first got on to his broker Lu Kuang-shih and then gave Han Meng-hsiang his instructions. The news from the Exchange was encouraging, and it seemed that his luck was holding, but he decided to wait until he had got a report from his spy Liu Yu-ying before finally deciding how much to sell. As he rang here, there and everywhere trying to find the elusive Liu Yu-ying, he even forgot that he was getting hungry.

At eleven o'clock Wu Sun-fu's car was moving slowly off down the asphalt drive towards the gate. Flushed with excitement, he was off in person to the front line in the Exchange! As they neared the gate the engine stalled. The chauffeur got out and cranked it up, but it just coughed and stopped again. "A bad omen!" thought Wu Sun-fu, though he had always flattered himself that he was not superstitious. Irritably, he got out of the car and was just going back indoors when a horn blared outside the gate and a car came up the drive. The visitors were Tu Chu-chai and his wife.

Mrs. Tu had come specially to see her brother about the memorial service for their late father. She came straight to the point. "The sutra-chanting ceremony is going to be held in the Jade Buddha Temple tomorrow, so we'd better go over today and have a look at the ceremony hall."

"Er, yes, I know, but — look, Fu-fang, I'm afraid you'll have to go without me. I'm just off on some urgent business. If the car hadn't broken down, I'd be gone by now."

Wu Sun-fu frowned as he spoke, then glanced at Tu Chu-chai. He had suddenly had an idea: if only he could draw Tu Chu-chai into an alliance with him on the Exchange, he would then be in a really strong position and Chao Po-tao wouldn't stand a chance! But how could he best go about it? Wu Sun-fu immediately began racking his brains.

"All right," said Fu-fang. "I can go along with Pei-yao. But you'd better be there at nine o'clock tomorrow morning to burn the incense when they start! And Pei-yao, Huei-fang and Ah-hsuan will have to be there, too!"

"Ah! Speaking of Huei-fang," said Wu Sun-fu, "she wants to go back to the country of all places! I just can't make her see sense!" He had missed the first part of what Mrs. Tu had said, but the mention of Huei-fang's name had registered and reminded him of this particular worry of his.

Mrs. Tu did not seem in the least surprised, and said in quite a matter-of-fact tone of voice, "Oh, young people are always like that — they like to be on the move all the time. You get fed up with Shanghai in no time at all and you soon want to go down to the country for a little holiday!"

"It's more than a little holiday that she wants! I thought you might have a word with her, Fu-fang. Perhaps she'll listen to you. It beats me. I can't make out what's got into her. Anyway, you'll find out all about it when you see her. It might be some form of neurosis."

Having got Mrs. Tu out of the way, Wu Sun-fu now turned to Tu Chu-chai and began his negotiations for an alliance. He talked glibly about the war dragging on for a long time yet and pressed the point that, since the money raised on government bonds was all going to military expenses, the bonds were bound to drop — what a wonderful chance for the bears! He did not openly suggest that Tu Chu-chai should join forces with him, but just did his best to impress on him the advantage of selling short. All he wanted was that Tu Chu-chai should do the same as he was doing.

As he listened, Tu Chu-chai calmly took snuff and nodded, a faint smile on his lips.

XVIII

HUEI-FANG had shut herself in her own room for the last two days. She had taken this step as a final protest against Wu Sun-fu's refusal to let her go back home to the country after the memorial service for her late father. No one had been able to persuade her to leave her room, so they left her to her own devices.

The Supreme Scriptures of Rewards and Punishments, which her father had left her, was now her "talisman." She had rummaged out an ancient incense-burner and several bundles of high-quality incense from the luggage the old man had brought with him to Shanghai two months before. Her father had always considered these accessories essential for the ritual reading of *The Supreme Scriptures of Rewards and Punishments.* She had now begun to say her prayers three times a day — morning, afternoon and evening — and each time she burned incense. Having failed to find her father's prayer-cushion, she had no alternative but to make do with sitting on a sofa with her legs tucked under her.

After careful consideration she had decided to embrace her father's religious teachings. This did not mean that she was given to kindness and charity, but she hoped that her religious exercises would enable her to "cleanse her heart" and "subdue desire," and so help to alleviate her mental anguish. Her first day had been quite successful. As she sat there intoning the verses of the book with the blue smoke from the incense curling round her, she could imagine herself back in the study of her old home. Her father's pious face floated before her, and she was so overcome that her eyes filled with tears. Sweet memories came flooding back, vivid to the minutest detail, of the simple, peaceful life she had led when she had looked after her aged father in their old home; and she derived from these memories a peace of mind she had never known before. A contented smile played round her lips and the sacred verses lay unread before her. Lulled by the fragrance of the incense, she sank limply against the back of the sofa and fell into a trance, no longer thinking or conscious of anything. And so she remained until at long last the incense had burnt out; then she sighed as if she had woken up again, and smiled faintly.

It was in this fashion, lost in dreams and memories, that Hueifang passed her first day of prayer and meditation, unconscious even of the pangs of hunger.

But by the afternoon of the second day the scriptures and the incense began to lose their mysterious power. Her memories came back as they had the day before, but today she did not relish them so much, and began to feel about them the way one feels about an old friend whom one meets after a long absence, who is welcome on the first day but whose company begins to pall on the second. Though she dutifully continued to chant the scriptures over and over again and meditate with her eyes fixed on the tip of her nose and her nose pointing at her heart, nevertheless all sorts of noises forced their way into her unwilling ears and distracted her attention: a car hooting in the street outside, a man's heavy footsteps going past her door, the distant tinkling of the piano in the drawing-room downstairs, the sound of men and women talking and laughing happily together. By the time the first stick of incense had burnt down, the sofa began to feel prickly and the air seemed so close that she thought she would suffocate. She struggled with a desire to go out and have a look round, though what it was she wanted to look at she did not know. Eventually she seemed to settle down again. She picked up the book written in her father's pious hand and stared at it with drooping head. She sighed over and over again, and her eyes became moist.

That night, it was a long time before she could get to sleep, and when she finally did drop off she was troubled by dreams, the sort of wild dreams which had often disturbed her rest before, and from which she always woke sobbing and crying. Now they came back again, one after the other, till she tossed and turned in a semi-conscious daze. Several times during that short summer night she started up from her sleep in terror.

When she got up next morning her face was pale and drawn, her finger-tips icy cold, and her heart weak and trembling. The verses of *The Supreme Scriptures of Rewards and Punishments* seemed to mock at her as she read, and several times she closed it and sighed.

The afternoon was hot and close, and Huei-fang felt as uncomfortable as an earthworm on a hot brick. She lit a stick of incense and picked up the book for her afternoon prayers but her ears rang with noises from the house, from the garden, and from the distant street. Her mind seemed to be analysing and interpreting every little sound. Every time footsteps went past the door her ears pricked up and her heart beat faster. She sat with tears in her eyes, hoping desperately that the footsteps would stop at her door, hoping desperately to hear a tap on the door, so that she might run across and open it to her brother, her sister-in-law — or even Pei-shan, coming to persuade her to go out with them!

But every time she was disappointed. Every time the footsteps went straight past the door and never came back again. She had been forgotten, cast aside like an old-fashioned dress! As she sat there with the blue smoke of the incense curling round her and the book in her hands, she began to feel resentful towards her brother, her sister-in-law, even towards Lin Pei-shan, who was always as happy as a lark. She felt that everybody was free and happy except her, and she was forgotten, deprived of her freedom and happiness! She felt that her present seclusion was not of her own free will: they had forced her to it. They were plotting against her and using this subtle method to deprive her of her human rights!

She remembered a tragic story she had heard when she had been living at her old home: a young lady "of good family" like herself had been locked up indoors by her parents for "unseemly behaviour," and the story was put around that she had gone into voluntary seclusion for "meditation"! The girl had eventually hanged herself. "Isn't that exactly what's happening to

She felt that everybody was free and happy except her, and she was forgotten, deprived of her freedom and happiness!

me?" She felt a thrill of horror as she thought of it. Suddenly, she remembered a dream she had had the night before, a dream which she had had several times and which had become so familiar to her by now that she almost accepted it as reality. The dream seemed to refer to one evening about three weeks ago. She was alone with Fan Po-wen in the hexagonal pavilion on the artificial hill on the other side of the pond in the garden. A storm was gathering in the sky. They chatted together for a while and afterwards she lost her virginity in the darkness of the pavilion. Of all the wild dreams that came to haunt her, one always stood out from the rest and seemed quite real to her, and that was the dream which takes place in the pavilion on that stormy night. As the rain roars on the roof of the pavilion she lies languidly back in an easy-chair with Fan Po-wen sitting opposite. As she sits there with her eyes closed, she hears him come across to her. Suddenly, she goes limp all over, intoxicated and unresisting.

She suddenly screamed, and the book fell to the floor. She automatically bent to pick it up and looked nervously all round. There was a strained smile on her lips and two tear-drops glistened on her lashes. She was firmly convinced that this romantic dream had actually happened and that it was for this misbehaviour that they were confining her to her room, while telling the world outside that it was "voluntary seclusion"! It seemed there was only one way out for her as there had been for the other girl — suicide by swallowing a piece of gold or hanging herself!

She even persuaded herself that, even if she herself did not wish to end her life like this, her tyrant of a brother would sooner or later come in and force her to do so. Her heart pounded madly at the thought and her finger-tips felt icy, but her face was burning. She asked herself through clenched teeth, "Why should I have all the bad luck? Why should I be treated differently from everybody else? Why should the other girls be allowed to go out with boys just as they like? Why should they pretend not to notice the way Pei-shan goes on? Why should I give in and let them treat me like this? But what can I do about it? There *must* be another way out!" She stood up abruptly, her whole being ablaze with the fire of rebellion. But the next moment she flopped down on the sofa again. She was alone in the world, with no one to go to for advice, no one to help her!

Suddenly, hurried footsteps pattered along to the door of her room and stopped. There was a sharp rap on the door. She was convinced that it was her brother coming to force her to take her own life. With a despairing sigh she threw herself on the bed and buried her face in the pillow, her blood freezing in her veins.

"Huei-fang! Are you asleep?" came a girl's shrill voice in her ear. Huei-fang jerked round in surprise to find her vivacious cousin Chang Su-su standing by the side of the bed. She must be dreaming again! She rubbed her eyes and looked again, then suddenly sprang up, grasped Chang Su-su's hand, and burst into tears. At a time like this she would have welcomed any visitor at all with open arms — even a cat or a dog!

Chang Su-su was too surprised to do anything but laugh. She sat down on the edge of the bed, shook Huei-fang by the shoulder, and asked impatiently, "Why, what's the matter with you, Huei-fang? Why do you burst into tears the moment you see me? Are you ill or something? Why don't you say something?"

"It's all right, there's nothing the matter with me," said Huei-fang, shaking her head and forcing back her tears. She felt a little better now that she knew she was not dreaming and that it really was Chang Su-su who had come to see her.

"I really can't understand you, Huei-fang! When everybody goes out you stay here indoors all alone! Why don't you go out and have a good time?"

"I can't —"

She stopped short and heaved a sigh, then squeezed Chang Su-su's hand as if to express what she had left unsaid.

Chang Su-su frowned and looked attentively at Huei-fang's face, but said nothing. Whatever they said, she could see no signs of a "neurosis." Why, then, should she shut herself up in her room like this and refuse to come out? And why this unconvincing attempt at being a nun or a Taoist or whatever it was? The whole thing made Chang Su-su feel rather annoyed. She suddenly recalled how, on the day of Old Mr. Wu's death, she, Fan Po-wen, Wu Chih-sheng and the others had made bets about Huei-fang; she said with a trace of sadness in her voice:

"Huei-fang, some time ago we made a bet about you — that's to say Wu Chih-sheng, Fan Po-wen and Pei-shan — oh, yes, and Tu Hsin-to was there, too. The bet was about whether you would change after you'd lived in Shanghai for a while. Though none of us ever expected that you would change like this!"

"Did you expect me to change, then? Well, in what way did you think I'd change, Su-su?"

"I don't remember now, but whatever it was we all thought you would change. But now — I don't know — it seems so odd: you've changed, and yet you haven't, somehow!"

"Yes, I've noticed it myself. I'm not the same girl that I was when I lived in the country!"

"Oh, but you are, Huei-fang! There was a time when you seemed to be changing, but now you're back in the same old rut again!"

Chang Su-su's voice was impatient as she said this. She was now more convinced than ever that Huei-fang was far from being neurotic and that Wu Sun-fu and the others were exaggerating.

"Back in the same old rut, did you say? But when I was with father in the country I wasn't the same as I am now. I don't think anybody can understand why I'm so unhappy, Su-su! And nobody wants to understand, either!"

Huei-fang's voice was steady, and her eyes were suddenly bright with determination. It was the first time Chang Su-su had seen this steely glint in her eyes, and it rather surprised her. But the next instant her eyes became dull and troubled once again. She sat staring into space and muttered:

"So you bet on me, did you? And Fan Po-wen was in it, too. What — what did he say about it? Do tell me, Su-su — oh, what's the point? Forget it. Let's talk about something else."

Chang Su-su suddenly laughed, then jumped up, threw her arm round Huei-fang's neck and said excitedly in her ear:

"Why shouldn't you ask me about Fan Po-wen? Why

shouldn't we talk about him? I know all about it, Huei-fang; I've known all along that you've got your eye on him! But why be so shy and backward about it? Sun-fu interferes, isn't that it? I've known all along about that, too. He's got no right to interfere in your private affairs! You're free to do what you like!"

Huei-fang immediately crimsoned. Chang Su-su's frank words had struck home. She had brought into the open all the things that had been preying on Huei-fang's mind — all the things she had not dared mention. She grasped Su-su's hand and squeezed it and tears of gratitude welled up in her eyes. But Chang Su-su suddenly pulled her hand away and drew herself up, then fixed her keen eyes on Huei-fang and said earnestly:

"I suppose all this shutting yourself in your room and chanting from this *Book of Rewards and Punishments* here is your way of protesting against Sun-fu's dictatorship, then? You're going about it the wrong way! You've got the will to fight, all right, but your method's all wrong! And another thing: I must warn you that Po-wen is a spineless young man who doesn't dare stand up for himself! He was in love with Pei-shan once, and they used to spend all their time together; but the moment Sun-fu objected, he backed out! I tell you, Huei-fang, if you're going to resist Sun-fu's interference and fight for your freedom, it's no good pinning your hopes on a spineless weakling!"

As she said this, Chang Su-su laughed and brought both her hands down sharply on Huei-fang's shoulders. Huei-fang was not expecting this and almost toppled off, but she had to laugh. Then, as her smile faded, her expression became quite serious again and she searched Chang Su-su's face. She was trying to pluck up courage to make further inquiries about the "spineless" Fan Po-wen, but she was afraid her cousin might laugh at her if she pursued the matter any further. She now looked up to Su-su as her champion, and she did not want to appear too silly in her champion's eyes. After a great struggle, she finally decided to try and tell Su-su what was on her mind.

"I think you understand what's the matter with me, Su-su. I've always been so used to hiding my feelings that I can't bring myself to be frank about them when I want to. I've no one to confide in and no one to advise me! I just can't think straight and I don't know what to do. I'm fed up with the miserable life here and all I want to do is to go back home to the country. When they refused to let me go, I made up my mind to shut myself up in my room and have nothing more to do with them! I've been here two days now, but I'm more miserable than ever! I know I'm going about it the wrong way, Su-su, but what is there I can do?"

Chang Su-su's reply was a long, hilarious roar of laughter. With a swing of her hips she moved up close to Huei-fang, held her face between her hands, and looked at it closely. It was a hot, flushed face with pale, trembling lips. After a moment Chang Su-su said sternly, "It's up to you, Huei-fang. You must pluck up courage and have it out with Sun-fu once and for all! Another thing: you ought to go to school. You must insist that Sun-fu sends you to school next term!"

Huei-fang's only reply was an emphatic shake of her head. Chang Su-su's eyes opened wide in astonishment and her forehead wrinkled.

"Don't you want to go to school, then?"

"Yes, but I don't think any school would have me. I've read shelves and shelves of ancient Chinese classics, but I don't know a thing about all these modern subjects."

"That doesn't matter: you can easily catch up on your own. Now Huei-fang, the longer you stay cooped up in here the more depressed you'll get! Come out for a walk with me!"

As she said this, Chang Su-su dragged her off the bed, then told her to hurry up and have a wash and get herself ready to go out. As she stood bathing her face over the wash basin, Huei-fang smiled to herself and shed a few furtive tears. They were tears of joy, and also tears of determination! Although she had not yet any clear idea what exactly she was going to, she was nevertheless determined to do whatever Chang Su-su told her!

*

Chang Su-su had hired a car and was now taking Huei-fang out for a breath of fresh air. It was past three o'clock and the sun was at its hottest. Huei-fang sat back in the car with her eyes closed, feeling slightly dizzy. Her mood of anxiety was gradually returning again. Her future was, after all, still as much a riddle as ever. She hoped this riddle would soon be solved, but at the same time she was afraid. The car had left the city and was now bumping over a none too smooth road on the outskirts, churning up a swirl of hot, choking yellow dust as it sped along. On either side of the road stretched vividly green fields, dotted here and there with grave-mounds. Suddenly, the car jolted violently and Huei-fang opened her eyes with a start. When she saw they were in the country she thought that she was dreaming again. She pulled herself together and nudged Chang Su-su:

"Look! We're going the wrong way, aren't we?"

Chang Su-su smiled but made no reply, for she was at this moment engrossed in her own day-dreaming. She was a sensitive, warm-hearted girl, and it made her happy to think that she had succeeded in luring Huei-fang out of her room. Just now she was busying herself with plans for Huei-fang's future, a beautiful, exciting future as free as the sea and the sky, a future with boundless possibilities.

Huei-fang took Chang Su-su's silence as an assurance that they had not lost their way and that they really were going out into the country. She was glad. As she turned her whole attention to enjoying the green fields which swirled past them she could imagine for a moment that she was back home. In fact, the only difference between this stretch of country place and her own was the presence of the cars which raced past them with their clouds of yellow dust. Suddenly, Huei-fang gasped in amazement and nudged Chang Su-su once more. The car was slowing down and ahead of them was a row of cars of all shapes and colours parked in the shade of a grove of willow-trees. Walking away from the cars were a number of women, their heads on their escorts' shoulders. Their lips were scarlet, their eyebrows pencilled, and their arms white and bare. So they were still in Shanghai!

As Huei-fang followed Chang Su-su out of the car and into a strange-looking garden, her amazement gradually increased until her head span. It was an ordinary country scene, with trees and the churring of cicadas, but it was still obviously Shanghai with its fashionably-dressed men and women behaving as always in a way she was afraid to look at and yet which she envied. Everywhere she turned she saw something which took her breath away and made her blush uncomfortably. In the shade of a nearby tree a man and a woman were lying on the grass, talking and laughing together, while one of the women's bare legs was propped up high across the other, her high-heeled shoe pointing straight at the sky. A little farther away she saw a couple so close together that they seemed to be one person with two backs! Huei-fang quickly shut her eyes. Her heart was thumping so hard that she could hardly bear it.

Then she caught sight of some familiar faces at a table beneath a large sun-shade. There were three of them. She felt like turning and running away, but Chang Su-su held her back.

"Well I'll be — look! The hermit's left her cell! This deserves to be writ large on the pages of history!"

This came from a young man under the sun-shade. As he sprang to his feet he all but overturned the little table cluttered up with beer bottles, lemonade bottles and plates of food. Huei-fang blushed crimson, for the young man was none other than Fan Po-wen. Suddenly her shameless dream came back to her and her face changed from crimson to a deathly white. She wanted to run away but her feet seemed rooted to the ground. With a supreme effort she managed to turn and say hello to Wu Chih-sheng.

"If it's such an historic event, Po-wen, you'd better write a poem to commemorate it! The subject is —"

"But he can't!" chaffed Wu Chih-sheng before Li Yu-ting could set a subject. "Poverty may make other poets more imaginative, but it leaves Po-wen without an idea in his head! How do you imagine he could write poetry in his present state!"

But Fan Po-wen was unperturbed. He just shook his head and said, "Can't be helped! Even the Muse of Poetry has to follow Mammon around! I've no choice in the matter!"

Everybody laughed and even Huei-fang joined in, though Chang Su-su merely parted her lips in a mechanical smile, then inquired with a puzzled frown, "What are you three doing congregating here, anyway?"

"We might well ask you and Huei-fang the same thing!" parried Wu Chih-sheng. He had spent a lot of time with Fan Po-wen just lately, and was acquiring the poet's fondness for repartee.

"Us? We've come out for a breath of fresh air. I'm taking Huei-fang round to see what the modern youth of Shanghai gets up to when it goes out into the country!"

"Well, as a matter of fact, we're here for much the same reason. Professor Li here believes we're in for an Armageddon any moment now, and it's ruined his appetite. He's afraid we'll all be murdered in our beds before we know where we are. So we've brought him along today to see how even these émigré Russian aristocrats and bourgeois can still scrape a living!"

"I say, Chih-sheng!" protested Li Yu-ting hastily, scratching his head without realizing that he was doing it. "You don't have to keep joking about serious matters!" Chang Su-su looked on and listened, amused and annoyed at the same time. She took hold of Huei-fang's hand and was just going to walk away when Fan Po-wen suddenly sprang up and exclaimed grimly:

"Did you hear that? Professor Li always takes everything seriously and he's always preparing for the worst. He's got the right idea! Just look at that White Russian émigré over there — probably a marquis or an earl or something once! All his life he's had servants to bring him his wine and open his bottles for him, but look at him now: it's now his turn to wait on other people! But he's picked up his new trade pretty quickly — look, he can even hold six lemonade bottles in one hand!"

"Ah, but when our turn comes, we probably won't even have the little luck that they've got!" said Li Yu-ting suddenly in such a mournful voice that Wu Chih-sheng and the others burst out laughing again.

"Just listen to the Three Wise Men! They bore me to tears!" jeered Chang Su-su. She turned and left them, taking Huei-fang with her. They went and sat at a little table under the trees by the river and ordered lemonade. It was quiet here, and they had a view of the river. The water sparkled in the blazing sunlight, and there was not a boat in sight. Huei-fang felt more at ease now, but one thing still puzzled her: why should people come all the way here from the city just to drink lemonade and talk and flirt? It wasn't as if it was a beauty spot! Yet at the same time she had to admit that the gaily-dressed people who came here did help to liven the place up and give it a touch of colour.

Chang Su-su appeared to be upset and sat in moody silence. After a while she muttered to herself, "Decadent lot! Still, it's not to be wondered at, really!"

She broke into a hysterical laugh and took a sip at her lemonade, then stretched and patted Huei-fang on the shoulder. "What will you do if Sun-fu absolutely refuses to let you go to school?"

"What would you suggest?"

"Take him to court!"

"What!" gasped Huei-fang, a flush of colour coming to her cheeks. She stared dubiously at Chang Su-su as much as to say, "You're joking!" Chang Su-su flashed her a look, then tilted her head back and smiled. She had managed to instil a little courage into the girl, and now her protégée was wavering again. Huei-fang now went on:

"You're overdoing it, Su-su. It could never come to that! I can always get Fu-fang to put in a word for me with Sun-fu."

"So much the better. I was only suggesting legal action as a last resort."

"But Su-su, I don't want to go back to that house again! I couldn't bear to live there another day!"

"Eh? —"

It was now Chang Su-su's turn to be surprised. She just could not keep pace with the devious workings of Huei-fang's mind. Huei-fang's face was flushed again. She looked nervously all round, then gazed appealingly at Chang Su-su. After a moment her head drooped despairingly and she murmured, "You don't know how lonely I am in that house!"

"What do you mean, 'lonely'?"

"They've all got friends but me! And I always feel so lost. If I live there any longer I'll go mad!"

Chang Su-su burst out laughing. She had finally found out why Huei-fang was so miserable. "Mostly sexual frustration!" she thought to herself. She glanced at Huei-fang and laughed again despite herself. It came as a disappointment to her to realize that she had overestimated Huei-fang's will to fight, yet she could not help feeling sorry for her when she saw her miserable expression. She thought hard for a moment, unable to decide what to do with this poor, inexperienced girl, but before she made up her mind, Huei-fang said quite firmly, "I don't want to live in that house a day longer! Not a single day! I want to live with you, Su-su, and have you teach me what to do!"

Being a warm-hearted girl, Chang Su-su could not find it in her to disregard this desperate cry for help. Although she had a "friend" herself, which would mean that Huei-fang would still be as lonely as ever even if she came to live with her, Chang Su-su had not the courage to explain this to Huei-fang and so dash all her hopes to the ground.

The sun had disappeared behind a cloud and a cool, refreshing breeze had sprung up. Thinking that her main problem had now been solved, Huei-fang began to dream of her free and happy future. She did not really know much about Chang Su-su, except that she was an undergraduate who was spending her summer vacation at a Y.W.C.A. hostel, yet she was prepared to adopt this cousin of hers as a kind of foster-mother.

Suddenly, the sound of someone singing came across the water on the wind. The accent was that of Huei-fang's home town and the voice seemed familiar to her. She smiled absently at Chang Su-su. As the voice came nearer and nearer, Huei-fang began to catch the words:

> Heav'n and earth are a mighty forge
> Where hidden forces flame,
> And all things in the Universe
> From Nature's anvil came.

She recognized this as a verse from the ancient poem *Ode to the Roc* and the voice as Tu Hsin-to's. She could not help laughing. She thought what a pleasant young man he was, and her thoughts went immediately from him to Lin Pei-shan. By now, Chang Su-su had also recognized the singer. She smiled, then suddenly got up and crept down to the bank of the river, where she crouched down under a tree. Huei-fang stopped laughing and followed Chang Su-su's example.

A skiff came slowly round the bend, keeping close under the nearer bank. Tu Hsin-to was rowing, and with him was a girl in a brown straw hat with yellow ribbons that fluttered in the breeze. Huei-fang recognized the hat — it was Lin Pei-shan's. The boat came nearer, and when it was about three or four yards away Chang Su-su picked up a clod of earth and threw it at the boat.

"Oh!"

It was Lin Pei-shan's voice, all right! The hat moved round, and the boat stopped at once. Then Chang Su-su sprang up and laughed. "Having a good time, you selfish creatures? No wonder some people are lonely!"

Tu Hsin-to and Lin Pei-shan turned round together and saw Chang Su-su standing there, but Huei-fang had not yet shown herself. There was more laughter as the oars splashed again and the boat pulled in to the bank. As she crouched behind the tree, Huei-fang heard the silvery voice of Lin Pei-shan:

"Su-su, you little revolutionary! I thought you were too busy with 'things that matter' to come down here! We didn't ask you to join us because we were afraid of being called decadent and corrupt!"

"But that was a beautiful bit of grenade-throwing, Miss Chang! Qualified revolutionary!"

"Now guess who I've got here with me! If you guess wrong, you'll have to give me Pei-shan as a forfeit!"

"Might be any old Tom, Dick or Harry!" taunted Lin Pei-shan. Huei-fang began to feel rather shy of showing her face now. She heard a rustle as the boat scraped up against the undergrowth that overhung the water's edge, then, without warning, Chang Su-su ran laughing round the tree and pulled her out of her hiding-place so that the couple in the boat could see her. She blushed awkwardly and said:

"Hullo, Pei-shan! I suppose you often come here? Though the place doesn't seem all that wonderful, really!"

"Why, Huei-fang! You're the last person I expected to find here! Congratulations, Su-su! The ruthless revolutionary at work! Nobody else can talk her round, but you succeed in getting her out to a place like this!"

The three girls now began talking and laughing all at the same time. Tu Hsin-to anchored the boat by sticking an oar in the mud and sat there in silence, a smile on his lips. So far as he was concerned, all these ups and downs were just part of the natural course of things and did not really interest him. When Huei-fang had been unable to get what she wanted, she had quite naturally taken refuge in her *Supreme Scriptures of Rewards and Punishments*; it seemed to him just as natural that she should now throw the book aside and come down to the gay Rio Rita Pleasure Garden.

Suddenly, there was a rumble of thunder and flying black clouds began gathering overhead until the sky was blotted out.

"It's going to rain!" said Chang Su-su, looking up at the sky. She grasped Huei-fang's arm. "We'd better be getting back, Huei-fang."

"Don't worry! It'll only be a shower. Come on, come for a row with us."

"Not now. Though if you want to get a party together, Fan Po-wen and the others are just over there! I'll run over and fetch them if you like!"

With this parting shot at Lin Pei-shan, Chang Su-su went off into a peal of laughter, then made off with Huei-fang.

Tu Hsin-to gazed after the two girls with his usual blasé smile on his lips, then shoved off by pushing his oar against a tree-root on the bank. As the boat swung slowly round, Lin Pei-shan's dress began flapping in the strong breeze that had sprung up. She sat with bent head, watching the trees reflected in the water and twisting the hem of her dress round her fingers. After a while she looked up into Tu Hsin-to's face with a look in her eyes which seemed to say, "We can't go on like this!" But Tu Hsin-to still smiled.

The boat was now passing through a sort of tunnel formed by overhanging willows and reeds brushed rustling past its sides. Lin Pei-shan sighed, then edged forward and pillowed her head on Tu Hsin-to's knees. He at once shipped his oars and let the boat drift. Lin Pei-shan shifted her legs and laughed.

"The fact remains, you must find a way out!" she murmured hesitantly. ". . . If only we could get Sun-fu to agree, everything would be all right." She fixed her limpid eyes on him for a moment. "Oh, why don't you say something? Didn't you hear what I said? I said all we want is to get Sun-fu to agree! We must think of a way out —"

"I know Sun-fu: he just won't hear of it!"

"What are we going to do, then?"

"Oh, carry on as long as we can!"

"Hm! And how long will that be, pray?"

"Until we can't go on any longer — until you've got a legal husband!"

"Well! Of all the cheek!"

"Now look, Pei-shan, if you'll just think about it for a moment you'll see that I'm right. You may as well ask for the moon as expect Sun-fu to agree. Unless we elope, they'll marry you off sooner or later to somebody else. But you don't want all the hardship that would follow an elopement, and I'm not so keen on the idea myself, either."

"Well, that's a fine thing to say! One would think there had never been anything between us!"

"Oh, yes, we've had our moments! I'm not forgetting that. But what of it? You're still the same girl — you haven't lost anything! Your lips are just as red, your arms are just as soft and smooth, your eyes are just as eloquent as ever they were! Your youth and beauty are intact. You'll make your future husband happy, and you'll be happy yourself. Isn't that right?"

Lin Pei-shan broke into a laugh. She could find nothing wrong with what Tu Hsin-to had said, for she was still at an age where her heart had not yet awoken to the meaning of true love. She was still a child, and life for her was nothing more than one long game. A trailing willow twig brushed against her face, and she stretched out her hand and snapped it off. She put the end in her mouth and bit off a shred, then spat it out and laughed.

"And who's going to be my legal husband?"

"I don't know yet. Fan Po-wen, I shouldn't wonder!"

"But they want to marry me off to your uncle Hsueh-shih!"

"Very poor taste! Hsueh-shih's a first-class dolt. No good to you for a husband! But never mind: life's only a game!"

Lin Pei-shan laughed and scooped up a handful of water and splashed it in Tu Hsin-to's face with a look of pretended annoyance, but made no comment. The boat now came to the end of the tunnel of willows and out into a narrower stretch of the river. Tu Hsin-to laughed carelessly and took up the oars again. With much splashing and gurgling the boat slowly turned round again.

*

It was about five o'clock when the rain came, driving in from the east. In Wu Sun-fu's house the servants rushed to close all the windows on the east side of the house, but they forgot about Huei-fang's room. Driven by the easterly gale, the rain pelted into the room through the open window and drenched her precious *Book of Rewards and Punishments,* which was lying open on a table just inside, so that the vermilion lines between the columns of characters in the text began to run and spread. The incense-burner became full and the water overflowed and flooded the table, reducing the expensive bundle of incense to a thin yellow pulp, which gradually spread on to the book.

The rain sent everyone scurrying back home. Mrs. Wu was the first one back. Feeling chilly in her damp clothes, she went straight upstairs to change. Then Lin Pei-shan came in, alone. Instead of going to change her wet clothes, she ran upstairs and burst into Huei-fang's room.

She stopped in surprise when she saw how the driving rain was playing havoc with the room. She stood gaping for a moment, then turned and ran along to her sister's room. She shot in through the door, then stood there laughing till her sides ached, unable to get a word out.

Being quite accustomed to her sister's foolish antics, Mrs. Wu showed no signs of surprise, but continued to sit there holding a cup of tea, lost in her own thoughts.

The room was gloomy and the rain was pelting noisily against the window. They heard Wu Sun-fu's car pull up outside the front door. When she had recovered from her fit of laughing, Lin Pei-shan went slowly across to Mrs. Wu and said in a low voice, "Have you heard the news, Pei-yao? Do you know where Huei-fang's gone?"

Mrs. Wu Sun-fu seemed startled for a second, but immediately smiled, thinking that her sister was playing a joke on her.

"I've just seen her — at the Rio Rita!"

Amused at the joke, Mrs. Wu burst out laughing. She gave her sister a look and put down the cup.

"I'm not joking! It's quite true! When it came on to rain everyone left, but she's not home yet! And her room's flooded out!"

Lin Pei-shan's voice rose with excitement as she said this, then she doubled up with laughter. Mrs. Wu frowned at her sister's hilarity, which she thought excessive, and was just going to rebuke her when the door swung noisily open and Wu Sun-fu stormed unceremoniously into the room.

"Pei-yao! How did Huei-fang manage to run away, without your knowing?"

His wife realized from his furious voice and expression that her sister had not been joking after all; but she resented his attitude. She rose to her feet and retorted coldly, "She's not a prisoner, and I'm not a wardress. When she was moody the other day, everybody was trying to get her to go out, and you even accused me of not inviting her out often enough; but now that she's gone down to the Rio Rita for the afternoon of her own accord, you come along here shouting your head off and making a terrible fuss about nothing!"

"Well, if you knew she was going out, why couldn't you stop her until I came home?"

"Well, if that isn't the limit! How was I to know she wasn't allowed out? Anyway, I wasn't here when she went out. The first I knew about it was when Pei-shan told me she'd seen her at the Rio Rita. Isn't that right, Pei-shan?"

"Nonsense!" Wu Sun-fu roared. "Nobody's stopping her from going out for a stroll! But this is different: she's run away! Do you hear? She's *run away*! Look at this note!"

He tossed a ball of paper towards his wife. He threw it so hard that it bounced off the table on to the floor. Mrs. Wu touched it with the toe of her shoe but did not bend down and pick it up. She suddenly looked worried as she remembered the strange way Pei-shan had laughed a moment ago: she must have seen Huei-fang with some man or other at the Rio Rita! And now Huei-fang had "run away"! All these thoughts came crowding on her mind so quickly that she had no time to weigh them up properly. Her eyes turned involuntarily to the floor again, seeking the ball of paper, but Pei-shan had already picked it up and smoothed it out. A mere three lines of elegant handwriting, unmistakably Huei-fang's.

"I suppose you'd already gone out when Su-su came, then?" said Wu Sun-fu, his expression a little calmer now. "It strikes me Su-su's got a hand in this!"

Suddenly, his look of exasperation returned as he snatched the note from his wife and read it carefully once more. Mrs. Wu was more at ease now. She went and sat on a sofa and said gently:

"I don't think it's so serious that we need fly into a passion over it. Though Huei-fang does act rather strangely, I admit. One moment she wants to shut herself up like a nun, the next, she wants to go to school; and now she doesn't even want to live at home, but goes off to live in a Y.W.C.A. hostel of all places —"

"Yes, but if she wants to go to school, she's only got to come and tell me. I'd be the last to refuse! There's no need for her to scribble me a note and slip away as if she were eloping! And if she wants to catch up on her studies before going to school, what's wrong with doing it here? If she wants a tutor, I can easily get her one. But no: she wants Su-su to coach her — as if Su-su could!"

"Why not leave her to it?" Mrs. Wu suggested in a persuasive tone of voice now that her husband's rage seemed to have died down. "In a few days she'll have had enough and then she'll come running back!" Lin Pei-shan now put in, "When I saw Su-su and Huei-fang at the Rio Rita, Huei-fang seemed her usual self and didn't say much. And Su-su didn't mention this business, either. I expect they got talking afterwards and decided to do it on the spur of the moment. I always thought Huei-fang was rather stubborn, but I realize now that she's quite easily led!"

Wu Sun-fu nodded and relapsed into silence. He now began pacing up and down with his hands clasped behind his back, as if he was still worried about it all and trying to think of a solution. Though he was beginning to realize what was behind his sister's recalcitrance, it was still a challenge to his authority, and as such he obviously could not afford to ignore it. To make things worse, Pei-shan's suggestion that Huei-fang was "easily led" had provided him with another headache. He was well aware that Chang Su-su was scatter-brained, meddlesome, and not over-particular in her choice of friends, and the prospect of his "easily led" sister going to live with her annoyed him. It was unthinkable that he, her elder brother, should stand aside and not intervene!

He suddenly stopped and turned to look at his wife. His face looked gloomier than ever in the half-light, and his eyes glinted angrily. He took a pace towards his wife as if to pounce on her, and she, not knowing what storm was now to burst about her ears, felt her heart miss a beat and a cold shudder trickle down her spine. Fortunately for her, there was now an interruption — Wang Mah came in to announce a visitor. Wu Sun-fu rolled his eyes, then turned and began to go out. As he got to the door he stopped and turned to his wife again:

"Pei-yao! Go straight down to this Y.W.C.A. hostel and fetch Huei-fang home! Whatever happens, I insist that she comes home!"

"What's the hurry? Huei-fang's stubborn, and you can't expect her to come back home the very same day that she runs away."

Mrs. Wu's reply had been as tactful as she could make it, but it only made her husband all the more infuriated.

"Don't argue!" he roared. "Get down there straight away! Whatever happens, we must get her back here today! If we don't do it today she'll never come back!"

With this order, and without any explanation of what exactly he meant, Wu Sun-fu hurried downstairs to see his visitor.

The visitor was Wang Ho-fu. He had become impatient waiting for Wu Sun-fu, and when he saw him coming at last he grasped him agitatedly by the sleeve and led him into the small drawing-room. He slammed the door behind him and, without even a word of greeting, plunged straight into his business in a furtive whisper:

"Something urgent! Just had a report from Hsu Man-li! She says Chao Po-tao knows we're selling short and that he's going to do his damnedest to put a spoke in our wheel, the rat! He's going to fight it out with us! Though, according to her, Chao Po-tao hasn't got much to play with, himself!"

Not until Wang Ho-fu had finished did Wu Sun-fu breathe again. He was somewhat relieved to learn that there had not been a real disaster as he had for the moment feared. So Chao Po-tao was up to his tricks again, eh? Well, it wouldn't be the first time, and Wu Sun-fu had no particular reason to worry on that score. If Chao Po-tao was now feeling the pinch himself, it was no more than he deserved! That's what comes of trying to put a spoke in the other chap's wheel all the time! . . . As these thoughts went through his head, Wu Sun-fu even began to feel exultant again, and a smile came to his lips.

"It was only to be expected that Chao Po-tao should go all-out to stop us. Just think, Ho-fu, didn't we do our best to put his back up when we sold the eight factories? We pretended to do business with him, even after we had already negotiated a sale with the British firm and the Japanese company! The result was that he lost his broker's commission and in all probability got a rap on the knuckles from his boss! It was really brilliant the way Chi-jen pulled it off! Yes, we made a good job of showing Chao Po-tao up in his true colours to his boss. No wonder he's nettled with us! — Though I don't quite see, Ho-fu, why he should be feeling the pinch."

"Wait a minute. I'll tell you about his latest trick first. He's organizing some sort of 'Committee for the Maintenance of Government Bonds,' and in their name he's going to wire a petition to the government to stop the practice of selling short!

Our lawyer friend Chiu Chun has also found out from another source that they're also going to petition the Ministry of Finance to order the Central Bank, the Bank of China, the Bank of Communications, and some other note-issuing banks to accept all types of government bonds as pledges or discount them, and at the same time to order the Stock Exchange to make it obligatory for sellers to hand in actual bonds as security before making any sale. This would mean the end of all speculative selling by bears —"

"But it's utterly impossible!" interrupted Wu Sun-fu, still smiling calmly. "It would be tantamount to suspending the business of the Stock Exchange! No, Ho-fu, I think this is just another rumour put round by Chao Po-tao to encourage the bulls!"

But Wang Ho-fu was not to be gainsaid. Perhaps because he had talked himself into a state of excitement, perhaps because he was over-anxious — whatever the reason, he was perspiring profusely. He stared round-eyed at Wu Sun-fu as the latter spoke, then said in a loud voice:

"Not a bit of it! — Now, you may think all that's enough to be going on with, but there's more to come! He's also using his influence to get the Board of Directors of the Stock Exchange and the Brokers' Association to issue immediately a new set of regulations which will increase the seller's cash deposit to twice the present amount! And that, Sun-fu, is quite possible!"

"What! You mean that? And what about the buyer's deposit? No increase, I suppose!"

Wu Sun-fu sprang to his feet, the colour draining from his cheeks. He realized he had underestimated his enemy.

"Of course I mean it. I got it from Han Meng-hsiang. And Lu Kuang-shih says it's all been fixed up and that it'll be announced tomorrow!"

"But it's illegal!" protested Wu Sun-fu, shaking his head. "There're two sides to every transaction — you must have a buyer and a seller, and you can't make fish of one and fowl of the other! It would be illegal!"

The veins stood out blue on his temples, but curiously enough there was no sweat on his forehead. Wang Ho-fu slapped his thigh and sighed.

"You can call it illegal if you like, but there it is! I tell you, Sun-fu, Chao Po-tao's making a hullabaloo all round about 'preserving the integrity of government bonds and steadying the market,' and putting it round that the bears are a menace to the money market and a dangerous nuisance in the Stock Exchange. He browbeats the Board of Directors of the Stock Exchange with this impressive blether, and they just have to give in to him!"

"It's a blatant stab in the back for the bears!" muttered Wu Sun-fu through clenched teeth. "It's scandalous!"

He was now even more apprehensive than Wang Ho-fu had been a moment ago. For a while the two men sat silent and frowning, staring at one another. A motorcar horn sounded just outside, then again at the gate. "That must be Pei-yao going out to fetch Huei-fang home," thought Wu Sun-fu. "Though why couldn't she leave a bit sooner?" His thoughts wandered to Tu Chu-chai. This brother-in-law of his was a bit of a coward . . . would he dare sell in the circumstances? Wu Sun-fu was far from sure, and his heart sank. At length, Wang Ho-fu spoke again:

"I've been talking it over with Chi-jen, and he thinks roughly the same as you. He agrees it's impossible to demand that the actual bonds be deposited before selling them, but he's certain that the doubling of the cash deposit for the seller will come off! In which case, every five thousand dollars of Chao Po-tao's money will be equal to ten thousand of ours! This means that he can jump in just before the settlement and turn the table on us just like that! We don't stand a chance!"

"In that case I suppose we'd better cover as fast as we can. When Chao Po-tao has completed his arrangements the prices will be pushed up!"

"But Chi-jen has a different idea. He's afraid that if we cover now, it'll mean that all our work will have been wasted. He's for fighting to the last ditch! The military situation being what it is, the prices can't very well go up all that much. He thinks we should take a chance — nothing venture, nothing gain! He says that if we do go down he'll look at it as if one of his boats had been sunk — he'd pretend his two hundred thousand dollars had gone to the bottom of the river and he'd take it quite calmly! — You know, I think Chi-jen's got something there!"

Wang Ho-fu's voice was quite firm as he said this, and his big, round eyes were fixed intently on Wu Sun-fu. Two months before a vigorous, stubborn statement like this could have come only from Wu Sun-fu, but Wu Sun-fu was no longer the man he had been, and his mind now tended towards caution and compromise. Now, even with Wang Ho-fu goading him on, he was wavering and hesitant. He frowned dubiously.

"But how *can* we fight to the last ditch?" he asked. "The five hundred thousand dollars we got for the factories is all tied up in bonds, and I have about two hundred thousand more locked up in cocoons and unsold silk. We're stumped without ready cash!"

"Ah, I've already discussed that with Chi-jen. This is how we get round it: we three shall find another five hundred thousand dollars between us, and at the same time you do everything you can to get Tu Chu-chai to sell short again. The two things combined should see us safely through the crisis!"

"We can't rely on Tu Chu-chai, though. The other day when he agreed to sell short, he actually sold as many as three million, but I found out the day before yesterday that he's already covered — covered as soon as he could make a paltry profit of twenty dollars for every ten thousand! And he only made that profit because we'd sold two million! Now I ask you, Ho-fu, what's the use of a coward like that to us? When we got him to go in with us it was on the understanding that we sink or swim together, but now it turns out that he was only out to sponge on us! What can you do with a man like that?"

"I still think you ought to have another go at him, Sun-fu. The settlement's so close that, even if Chu-chai won't sell short, it would be a great help to us if he would agree to remain neutral by not turning bull, either!"

As he said this, Wang Ho-fu chuckled and stroked his beard as if he was quite sure that they would win in the end, and Wu Sun-fu could not very well refuse to try Tu Chu-chai again. They now began to discuss how the three of them could raise the five hundred thousand dollars which they would need. Wang Ho-fu spoke unhurriedly, ticking the sums of money off on his fingers:

"The new cash deposits in our company amount to about two hundred thousand dollars, which leaves three hundred thousand to be found. The three of us should be able to manage a hundred thousand each. And if Tang Yun-shan has had any luck finding new shareholders in Hongkong, and if he can wire us two or three hundred thousand in the next five or six days, we'll be sitting pretty! Besides, I got a tip from Huang Fen today that the military situation is turning in favour of the bears. So, all things considered, we now have a better opportunity than we'll ever have and we mustn't let it slip through our fingers! — I don't know what's the matter with you lately, Sun-fu: you seem to have lost all your strength of will!"

Wu Sun-fu sat in silence for a while, then a flush of excitement crept into his face and his eyes gleamed. He brought his hand down with a thump on the arm of his chair and growled, "That's it, then! Since you and Chi-jen are so keen on the idea, I'm with you! But to tell the truth I'm right out of ready cash. What I'll do is to mortgage my own factory! And my house and its grounds are worth well over a hundred thousand. Yes, I think I could raise a couple of hundred thousand on the factory and the house together!"

Wang Ho-fu laughed with elation and gave Wu Sun-fu the "thumbs up" sign. Wu Sun-fu now went on, "There's only one thing, Ho-fu: I think I can mortgage the house all right by myself, but I'll have to have Chi-jen's help to find someone for the factory."

"That'll be all right! I'll tell Chi-jen to come round and see you. That's settled, then; and you'll be doing your best to talk Chu-chai round!"

Wang Ho-fu was in the best of spirits as he stood up and took his leave. Just as he was getting into his car he turned round to Wu Sun-fu again and said, "Oh, and another thing, Sun-fu: I hear this woman Liu Yu-ying isn't very reliable. She's running with the hare and hunting with the hounds!"

"Aha, so she's spying for Chao Po-tao as well, is she? How do you know?"

"Han Meng-hsiang told me. And Hsu Man-li warned me about her, too. Colonel Lei told her."

"I'll be on my guard against her, then. — So she's hooked Colonel Lei as well, has she?"

He nodded thoughtfully. Wang Ho-fu laughed, then got into the car and drove off.

The rain had gone over by now, and the sky was bright again, streaked with yellow clouds like a vast tiger-skin. Wu Sun-fu remained standing on the front steps, lost in thought. He was thinking of the coming "fight to the last ditch" in the Exchange and of the mortgaging of his factory and house. His thoughts came thick and fast, but he felt sluggish and dispirited. He stood there a long time, until he was startled out of his reverie by the arrival of the car with his wife. He remembered he still had to go and see Tu Chu-chai on his "diplomatic mission."

"Huei-fang utterly refuses to come home!" gasped Mrs. Wu as she got out of the car. "But the hostel looked a quiet and respectable enough place to me, so I think we might let her stay on there a few days and see what happens."

She fully expected another outburst from Wu Sun-fu, but to her relief he just nodded. Then he shepherded her back into the car and told the chauffeur:

"Mr. Tu's! — Got it? Mr. Tu's place!"

As she sat beside her husband, Mrs. Wu could not help smiling. She had not the slightest inkling that Sun-fu was going to see Tu Chu-chai on business, but naturally assumed that he was going to pick up his sister Fu-fang and take her with him to help persuade Huei-fang to come home. She could not help thinking that he was making mountains out of molehills. In any case, she was beginning to sympathize with Huei-fang, for even she had often thought what a dreary, depressing place the house was. As these thoughts passed through her mind, her smile vanished and gave way to a look of melancholy resignation. Suddenly, she felt her husband's hand close round hers. She smiled, stiffly.

XIX

AS the clock struck nine and the clear, measured strokes on the vibrating metal coil twanged in the ears of Wu Sun-fu, who was still asleep in the inner room, his eyelids seemed to flutter, but his mind was still submerged in the heavy black waters of a dream. He had heard the clear, vibrant strokes of the clock in his dream, but for him this sound was the urgent voice of the gong on the platform of the Exchange, the signal for the opening of another session and the signal for the beginning of a fight to the death for himself and his partners.

It was these gong-strokes in the dream that had made his eyelids flutter. The settlement was only three days off, and in the last few days Wu Sun-fu and his partners had thrown the last reinforcements they had been able to muster into the front line and waged a fierce offensive along the whole front, but nothing they could do seemed of any avail in dislodging the bulls from their position. Their only hope now was that Tu Chu-chai would rush in to their rescue. The night before, Wu Sun-fu had worked until the small hours trying to persuade Tu Chu-chai to come in with them. And this had been the fourth time he had tried! Tu Chu-chai had not yet refused outright, so they still had a glimmer of hope — though they realized that whatever happened they were still not out of the wood!

A despairing laugh came from the sleeping Wu Sun-fu, then his brows were drawn tightly together and he clenched his teeth and shuddered violently. Suddenly, his eyes opened wide, bloodshot eyes that stared fixedly as if in a trance, and tiny beads of sweat began breaking out on his forehead as he remembered the horror of his dream. A pale yellow sunlight threw shadows on the curtains and a faint breeze brought the hum of traffic from the distant street.

"Thank Heaven it was only a dream!" he thought, as he scrambled quickly out of bed. He had a wash, only to find Chao Po-tao's face grinning at him from the water in the wash-basin — it was the face that had haunted his dreams with its evil, gloating smile! As he was going past his dressing-mirror, he automatically glanced at it and saw his own face — a face stamped deep with the lines of defeat and despair. Down in the drawing-room and the dining-room, the servants were bustling round changing loose covers and taking the carpets up for beating. The moment his eye fell on this scene of activity, he remembered that the house was mortgaged and that if he could not pay back the loan in time his creditors would foreclose, and then there would be all the bustle and commotion of moving out.

It seemed to him that the house was full of leering eyes glorying in his misfortune. He felt that sitting here in the "rear" waiting for news was ten, twenty times more painful than going up to the "front" himself. Little caring that he had made an appointment with Sun Chi-jen for ten o'clock, he hurried straight out to the car and drove off.

Although the car was speeding along a fairly unfrequented road at the record speed for 1930, Wu Sun-fu felt that even the car was trying to thwart him by refusing to go faster. He suddenly discovered that, without his noticing it, even the dismal pale sunlight had disappeared, and that they were driving through a fine drizzle which looked more like a thick mist. There was something strangely familiar about his gloomy surroundings — as well there might be! For it was on just such a morning as this — a morning of misty drizzle when everything became blurred in outline and acquired an air of grandeur — that he had once before sat in his car plunging headlong in just the same way into an unknown, misty future. Suddenly, it all came back to him: two months before, when he had been co-operating with Chao Po-tao as a bull, the morning of their "decisive battle" had been just such a gloomy, wet morning as this! Nevertheless, though the scene was the same, their roles had now been drastically changed: he and Chao Po-tao were now at daggers drawn! To make things worse, an inscrutable Tu Chu-chai held their fates in the balance!

As he sat there in the car, Wu Sun-fu smiled grimly to himself: What point was there in going down to the Exchange at all? The really decisive days had been the last three, and they had gone. Everything humanly possible had been done and their last penny had already been thrown into the struggle. What difference could he or anyone make to the fortunes of battle at this late hour? Yes, today would be the final skirmish, as when a commander-in-chief sends even his own bodyguard to the front line in a last desperate offensive. But surely it would be enough to leave the execution of his orders to his front-line commander without going up to the front himself? Wu Sun-fu frowned and smiled wryly to himself as he decided to go back home and wait for news there; yet he could not bring himself to tell his chauffeur to turn back. He had now lost even the small amount of will-power needed to do this! No matter how anxiously he urged himself to "Keep calm! Even if you lose, you must keep calm!" he still found it impossible to repress his excitement.

He was still in this state of anxiety and doubt when the car drew up outside the Exchange. He threaded his way in through the main entrance as if in a dream and went straight over to the notice-board to find the number of his broker, Lu Kuang-shih. Trading had apparently not yet begun, yet the Exchange rang with the deafening din of voices. But Wu Sun-fu appeared to be blind and deaf to all this: all he saw was a vision of Chao Po-tao's face, which seemed to fill all the space.

Lu Kuang-shih's cubicle, which was not much bigger than a sentry-box, was completely occupied by a corpulent gentleman — it was, as a matter of fact, Wang Ho-fu — who was using the telephone. The broker himself stood outside talking with a floorman. Wu Sun-fu's arrival attracted no attention until he stopped in front of the cubicle, when Lu Kuang-shih suddenly turned round to find him standing there. Just at that moment Wang Ho-fu hung up the receiver.

"Ah! Sun-fu! Here you are! I've just been trying to get you on the phone!"

As Wang Ho-fu sprang up to greet him, he grasped Wu Sun-fu by the sleeve and pulled him into the cubicle, where he wedged him in the corner beside the telephone, as if he was afraid to expose his friend to public view. The latter smiled cheerlessly and would have spoken had he not been too agitated to find something to say. As it was, Wang Ho-fu immediately bent over and asked in a whisper:

"You haven't seen Sun Chi-jen yet, have you? Oh, well, he'll be here in a moment. What about Tu Chu-chai? Has he made up his mind yet?"

"Not quite. Though I don't think he'll put much on the market, in any case. Not more than a million, anyway."

The moment Wu Sun-fu had opened his mouth and said something, his optimism had begun to return and he now felt somewhat calmer. Wang Ho-fu stroked his beard and smiled.

"You think he'd sell a million? That would be splendid! The thing is, Sun-fu, we're left high and dry today! The mortgaging of your factory didn't come off. Chi-jen and I have tried everybody we can think of, but we've had no luck at all. All we can do today is to —"

"Is to what? Don't tell me we haven't even got the hundred thousand dollars left that we agreed on the day before yesterday!"

"No, it's all right! Though it's all we've got in reserve for today."

"Right, then, get rid of the lot the moment they open! Agreed? Have you told Han Meng-hsiang what we're doing yet?"

"Don't let me hear you mention Han Meng-hsiang's name again! I found out only last night that even he isn't reliable! Every time we've sold short we've done it through him for secrecy's sake, and — would you believe it? — he's now gone and given the show away to Chao Po-tao! It's the worst thing that could have happened!"

As Wang Ho-fu said this, he dropped his voice until it was scarcely audible. Wu Sun-fu did not catch every word, but he understood perfectly. His face suddenly paled, his ears buzzed, and black spots danced madly before his eyes. Another of his subordinates had sold the pass! This was the unkindest cut of all! After a moment, Wu Sun-fu finally managed to mutter through clenched teeth, "You can't trust anybody! Well, Ho-fu, I suppose we'll have to go through Lu Kuang-shih today?"

"No! I've found another broker and everything's already fixed up. The moment they open, we sell!"

Hardly were the words out of his mouth when the gong sounded for the opening. Immediately, a thunderous uproar arose as trading began, until the building seemed to shake. Wang Ho-fu ran out, but Wu Sun-fu remained sitting where he was, unable to move. His legs no longer obeyed him, the buzzing in his ears came back again, and the black spots once more danced before his eyes. He had never felt as weak as this before — it was fantastic!

Suddenly, Wang Ho-fu ran back, panting and dejected; he wrung his hands as he gasped, "Opened with a rise! Up fifty cents!"

"What! Sell out quick!" raved Wu Sun-fu, springing to his feet. "Get rid of the whole hundred thousand in reserve!"

Suddenly, Wu Sun-fu's head swam and he had a feeling of nausea in the pit of his stomach. His legs gave way under him and he collapsed, his eyes staring and his face deathly pale. Wang Ho-fu was so startled that he felt suddenly cold, but quickly stepped forward; he pinched Wu Sun-fu's upper lip with one hand and held him by the hair with the other. For a moment there was no one on hand to help; then, as luck would have it, Sun Chi-jen arrived. Cool and resourceful, he snatched up a glass of cold water, took a mouthful of it, and spurted it in Wu Sun-fu's face. The glazed eyes stirred, and Wu Sun-fu brought up a gobbet of phlegm.

"Sell out quick —" he repeated, his eyes staring wildly. Sun Chi-jen and Wang Ho-fu exchanged glances, then Sun Chi-jen patted Wu Sun-fu on the shoulder and said, "Don't worry, Sun-fu! Ho-fu and I are here to take care of everything. You'd better go home and take it easy. It's suffocating in here and you'll only be worse if you stay!"

"It's nothing!" said Wu Sun-fu, springing to his feet. "It

was just a touch of phlegm, and I'm all right now. But tell me, have you sold them yet?"

His face was a better colour now, and life was returning to his eyes, though his forehead was as red as fire. Sun Chi-jen noticed it and recognized it as a serious sign. Between them, Sun Chi-jen and Wang Ho-fu forcibly dragged Wu Sun-fu out of the Exchange in spite of all his protests and bundled him into his car. Meanwhile the Exchange resounded with the fiercest duel between the bulls and the bears that it had ever known. Wu Sun-fu's partners fired their last shot — they threw one and a half million Disbandment on the market, and the quotations began to drop steadily!

If Wu Sun-fu's supposed ally Tu Chu-chai had now come on the scene and thrown himself into the fray with them, victory would have been assured for the bears. As it happened, Tu Chu-chai's car pulled up in front of the Exchange just as Wu Sun-fu's was moving off. The two chauffeurs honked a greeting at each other in passing, but neither's employer noticed what was happening. At the moment when Tu Chu-chai's car grated to a stop, Wu Sun-fu's was already speeding homewards.

*

It may have been the noise and lack of fresh air on the floor of the Exchange that had brought on Wu Sun-fu's attack of giddiness, for he felt much better as soon as the car started up. The hectic flush on his temples was gradually fading, and he could think "soberly" once again, though this "sober" thinking brought some of the pallor back to his cheeks and made his heart seem like a heavy weight in his chest, so that he had difficulty in breathing.

The drizzle had now become a downpour, and the wind had an edge to it. When Wu Sun-fu arrived home and got out of the car, he shivered and went gooseflesh all over. Ah-hsuan and Pei-shan were laughing and shouting noisily in the drawing-room, and just as Wu Sun-fu was going past the door, Ah-hsuan dashed out with a book in his hand, pursued by Pei-shan. Wu Sun-fu frowned, but walked on without another look at them. Just lately he had ceased to bother himself with such minor

"Sell out quick—"

"breaches of the peace." Besides, Huei-fang's recalcitrance seemed to have struck a blow at his authority in his own household, for Ah-hsuan, for one, was becoming rowdier than he had ever been before.

As soon as he was seated in his study, Wu Sun-fu sent for the butler. His first order was "Send for Dr. Ting"; his second was "I'm not at home to visitors"; his third — he broke off as he suddenly caught sight of a telegram on the desk. He waved the butler away and tore open the envelope.

The telegram was from Tang Yun-shan in Hongkong and contained forty or so words in code. By the time he had decoded seven or eight words, he had completely forgotten about the third order that he had been going to give. Suddenly, he remembered there was something else he was going to do. He laid the telegram aside and picked up the telephone. After a moment's hesitation he rang Tu Chu-chai's home number. When he heard where Tu Chu-chai had gone, he smiled. The last dying glimmer of hope in his mind now revived and became stronger and stronger.

What raised his hopes higher than ever was the discovery that Tang Yun-shan's telegram was full of good news: apparently, Tang Yun-shan was getting results in Hongkong, and the current situation was turning in their favour; he had made a number of extremely valuable business contacts in Hongkong, and with their assistance the Yi Chung Company could be put on its feet again; and, finally, he was coming back to Shanghai immediately.

Wu Sun-fu was unable to repress a sudden burst of laughter. Heaven helps them who help themselves, and no mistake about it!

Yet almost immediately his elation began to fade. A faint smile still hovered on his lips, but it was a wry one. What if all this talk about "extremely valuable business contacts in Hongkong" were just another of Tang Yun-shan's castles in the air? It wouldn't be the first time he'd been caught that way! In any case, even if there was anything in what he said, "You won't put out a fire with water a league away!" The outcome of the struggle would be decided by the next day at the very latest, and all Wu Sun-fu and his partners were interested in now was *immediate* help, for only immediate help could save them!

Even if Tang Yun-shan had struck lucky this time, Wu Sun-fu was still displeased with the man's muddle-headedness. Hadn't he sent him telegram after telegram urging him to wire any money back the moment he laid hands on it? And still all he got was promises! And what did he mean by "coming back to Shanghai immediately"? Anyone would think Hongkong was still living in the eighteenth century and using bulky silver ingots which Tang Yun-shan could only bring back to Shanghai in person! Here was he crying out for money which Tang Yun-shan was blithely carrying round in his pocket!

As he thought this, even the faint, wry smile vanished from his face. To meet with disappointment after having one's hopes raised was more painful than never having one's hopes raised at all! At first, when he had just decoded the telegram, he had thought of ringing up Sun Chi-jen and Wang Ho-fu to tell them the good news, but now it was more than he dared do. As he sat there with his head in his hands, he felt as if his head was on fire. He stood up and began pacing to and fro, but he shivered at every step, and he felt as if cold water were trickling down his spine. He sat down again, but immediately stood up once more, only to sit down a second time. One moment he felt as if he was in a furnace; the next, as if he had been plunged into an ice-house!

He was at last forced to admit to himself that he was ill. Yes, ever since the go-slow in the factory he had been troubled by this strange malady, and just lately the attacks had become more frequent. And now it had come to this — being overcome with dizziness in the Exchange! It looked suspiciously like the first stages of congestion of the brain — the illness his father had died of! "What's happened to the doctor? Blast him! Just when I need him urgently, he lets me down!" — He was so eager to get someone to vent his anger on!

Suddenly, the telephone rang, and its jangle seemed to hold a note of urgency.

Wu Sun-fu went suddenly tense all over. He was certain it

was a call from Sun Chi-jen on the Exchange floor. His hand trembled as he picked up the receiver. He gritted his teeth for a weak "Hullo?" then held his breath as he listened to what Sun Chi-jen had to report about their desperate struggle. His eyebrows suddenly shot up and his eyes gleamed excitedly and finally he even smiled.

"Oh! . . . Up and then down again, eh? . . . What! Dropped to thirty-three dollars? . . . Whew! . . . What a pity! . . . Well, it looks as if the bulls are losing their appetite at last! . . . What did you say? 'Reorganization' is opening now? . . . What? . . . Selling another two million? . . . The deposit on credit? . . . By all means! . . . I just got a telegram from Tang Yun-shan — says he's struck lucky in Hongkong. . . . Yes, we may as well go the whole hog! . . . No, he hasn't sent the money yet, but I think it's all right to go ahead just the same! . . . Oh, so Chao Po-tao's risking all he's got, as well! — Makes us quits! . . . It shows what a rat Han Meng-hsiang is! If he hadn't gone over to the other side, Chao Po-tao would have given up yesterday! . . . You bet! We'll teach the little rat a lesson he won't forget in a hurry! . . . Chu-chai? He's already down there at the Exchange! . . . Haven't seen him yet? Well, have a look round. . . . Oh! . . ."

As Wu Sun-fu hung up, his features darkened again. This time he was not so much worried as angry. So Han Meng-hsiang *had* let him down, the scoundrel! And Liu Yu-ying, too! Lining her pockets from both sides, the bitch! It had always been the same: all his great schemes had been wrecked by subordinates with neither conscience nor loyalty! It put one's teeth on edge to think about them! He had always played fair and never let anyone down, but his kindness was always repaid with ungrateful treachery! Apart from those two wretches Han Meng-hsiang and Liu Yu-ying, even his own sister had turned on him, and had now run away from home as if he were a cruel monster!

A wave of anger swept over him, and he trembled from head to foot. His face pale with rage and his teeth clenched, he began pacing swiftly up and down. These last few days his prestige had been trampled in the mud! He must do something about it! As soon as the present crisis on the Exchange was over, he must firmly re-establish his waning authority! Both in public and in his own home he must again set himself up as the incarnation of authority! As he paced to and fro, he began planning all that he would be and do, once he had won this present battle on the Exchange!

Suddenly the telephone rang again with that same note of urgency.

This time he was not so nervous as he had been the time before, for he had already been fortified by the good news so far. As he picked up the receiver his hand was steady and deft. As a voice spoke at the other end of the line, he cried:

"That you, Ho-fu? . . . What is it? . . . Never mind that! Tell me what's happening!"

A sudden blast of wind swept through the garden and howled in the trees. As he listened, Wu Sun-fu's face suddenly paled.

"What!" he gasped. "Up again? . . . Somebody buying in while we're holding the price down? . . . Eh? Not Chao Po-tao? A new bull? Who? Who? . . . What! Chu-chai? . . . Well, I'll be damned! . . . We're sunk, then! Finished! . . ."

Crash! The receiver fell on to the desk as Wu Sun-fu staggered back and collapsed on a sofa, where he sat wide-eyed and panting. Even his own brother-in-law Chu-chai had stabbed him in the back. It was only the night before that he had been perfectly frank with Tu Chu-chai and told him exactly what the situation on the stock market was and what his own plans were — and all the time he had been playing into the hands of a traitor! — "Every man's hand against me and even my own relatives betraying me! What have I done — what have I done to deserve it?" As this one thought hammered at his tortured mind, he suddenly sprang up with a wild laugh and pounced forward; he wrenched open a drawer of his desk, snatched out a revolver, and turned the muzzle towards his heart. His face was purple, and his eyes glared as if they would burst from their sockets.

Outside, the gale howled and drove the rain against the window in a crackling fury. The gun had not been fired. Wu Sun-fu drew a long sigh and collapsed on to the swivel-chair.

The revolver fell to the floor. Just then Li Kuei, one of the servants, came in with Dr. Ting.

Wu Sun-fu leapt to his feet and smiled wryly at the doctor. "Sorry to trouble you. There might have been a little accident just now, but it's all right now. Though now that you've come perhaps you'd like to take a seat."

Dr. Ting shrugged his shoulders in wonder, but before he could say anything, Wu Sun-fu had turned and snatched up the receiver again. This time he was ringing the factory. Having checked that it was Tu Wei-yueh on the other end, he shouted one peremptory sentence into the receiver: "The factory closes down tomorrow!" Disregarding the bewildered twittering from the other end of the line, he hung up and turned a smiling face to Dr. Ting:

"Where do you suggest I go for my summer holiday, Doctor? I feel like a breath of sea air!"

"Tsingtao, without a doubt! Or if you'd like to go farther afield, Chinwangtao is quite pleasant!"

"How about Kuling?"

"Kuling's all right, but you won't find your sea air up there! Besides, I heard a day or so ago that the Red Army is attacking Chian. Changsha is surrounded, and Nanchang and Kiukiang are both threatened!—"

"Ha! Ha! Ha! What does it matter? I've always wanted to have a look at this Red Army that everybody's so afraid of and see if it's all it's made out to be! As likely as not they'll prove to be nothing more than bandits! The only reason they've got away with it so long is that nobody's troubled to do anything about them! Excuse me a moment, Doctor. If you'll just make yourself at home I'll go and see to one or two things. Won't keep you a moment."

Laughing hilariously, Wu Sun-fu left the study and ran straight upstairs. Now that he realized it was all over, he was beginning to feel calm and peaceful once more. He slipped quietly into his room and found his wife curled up on the sofa under the window with a book.

"Pei-yao! Hurry up and tell the servants to pack! We're leaving tonight for our summer holiday!"

His wife leapt to her feet thunderstruck. The book fell off her lap on to the floor and a faded white rose fluttered out from between the pages. This was the third time Wu Sun-fu had seen the book and the rose, but, as on the other two occasions, he was too preoccupied to notice them. Her cheeks flushed, his wife glanced down at them and said absently:

"That's rather short notice, isn't it? Still, anything you say."

ABOUT THE AUTHOR

Shen Yen-ping, who writes under the pen-name Mao Tun, is one of the most outstanding exponents of revolutionary realism to appear in China since the New Literature Movement of 1919. He was born in 1896 in Tunghsiang County, Chekiang Province. Together with Cheng Chen-to, Yeh Sheng-tao and other writers, in November 1920 he founded the Literary Research Society, one of the first organizations to be formed in China to advocate a new outlook in literature. In 1921 he became editor of the *Fiction,* a literary monthly published by the Commercial Press in Shanghai. He completely overhauled this periodical and through it launched a fierce attack on feudal and compradore influences in current Chinese literature.

From 1926 to 1927 he edited the *Minkuo Jihpao,* a revolutionary daily in Hankow. When Chiang Kai-shek betrayed the revolution, and the Kuomintang became firmly anti-Communist, he left Hankow and returned to Shanghai.

From then on he used the pseudonym Mao Tun in his novel-writing, which served to expose the evils of the reactionary Kuomintang régime and to reflect the revolutionary struggle of the people. He wrote the novels *The Canker* — a trilogy in 1927, *Rainbow* in 1930, *Three Companions* in 1931, and *Midnight* in 1933, as well as a number of short stories, essays and articles.

During the War of Resistance Against Japan (1937-45) Mao Tun kept up his literary activities by editing the periodical *The Literary Front* and writing the novels *Corrosion* (1941) and *Frosted Leaves as Red as Flowers in Spring* (1942), the play *Before and After the Chingming Festival* (1944), besides various short stories, essays and articles.

In 1949, after the founding of the People's Republic of China, Mao Tun was made Minister of Culture and continued to hold this portfolio until 1964. In 1954, he was elected a deputy to the First National People's Congress, and later re-elected to the successive National People's Congresses. He is now concurrently Vice-Chairman of the China Federation of Literary and Art Circles, Chairman of the Union of Chinese Writers and Vice-Chairman of the Fifth National Committee of the Chinese People's Political Consultative Conference.